THE REGENCY ABDUCTION CLUB

SONIA BELLHOUSE ~ RENÉE DAHLIA

HEIDI WESSMAN KNEALE

ANNE KNIGHT ~ VIVIAN MURDOCH

ALEXA SANTI ~ EBONY OATEN

TABETHA WAITE

LINDA RAE SANDE

INTRODUCTION

Welcome to *The Regency Abduction Club.* This anthology, and its sister collection, *The Regency Kidnapper's Club*, began with a spark of genius.

In a previous anthology, Catherine Bilson had written a charming novella called *Kidnapping Lord Blaymire*. It sparked a fabulous discussion about creating a whole anthology based on kidnappings - nothing violent or horrid, mind. A 'nice' type of accidental kidnap where nobody was hurt.

We soon realised there would need to be two such anthologies - one sweet and one steamy. This is the steamy one. It features suspected or actual kidnappings and abductions, which soon lead to some steamy situations! Nobody is really hurt in these abductions, but the forced propinquity leads to some hot situations!

As all lovers of Regency know, having someone look at you the wrong way could be fodder for scandal. Spending an hour with the wrong person without a chaperone? The couple will simply *have* to marry to avoid further disaster.

Although there is some heartbreak along the way, all heroes and heroines are mended with the sweetest medicine in the world - Love.

- Ebony Oaten, editor.

THE FIERCEST PIRATE IN SURREY

ANNE KNIGHT

CHAPTER ONE

1810

Hester Fairfax patiently waited for her prey.

The warm spring sun beamed down on her bonnet, and she felt the sun's rays through her pink pelisse.

Sighing, she shifted in the ancient chaise seat as she scanned the bucolic landscape before her. No sign of her quarry yet. *He's taking an awfully long time.* Her gloved hands fidgeted with the reins as she peered down the dirt lane. The copse of oak trees hid the rest of the landscape from her view. *Never mind how long he takes. I shan't fail in this.*

Old Brutus neighed, tossing his head. The tack jingled, making Hester wince at the sound.

"Steady on, old boy," Hester soothed. "Just an hour or so longer and you'll be back in your stall. I promise to give you a bucket of oats for your assistance." The horse was nearing elderly, and Hester couldn't remember the last time her father had taken the chaise and Brutus out.

This wasn't quite the piratical adventure on the high seas she'd imagined as a child—Surrey was landlocked, after all—but it was certainly the most excitement she'd had in at least a year.

A flash of color slipped through the gaps in the trees.

Hester's stomach flipped. *Now.* She took a deep breath and flicked the reins, sending Brutus plodding forward on the road. The wheels wobbled through the half-dried muddy ruts.

Royal blue flitted past the trees, coming round the bend in the path. It was now or never.

And there he was—her prey: Mr. Benjamin George Littleton himself, in a dashing blue ensemble with a white cravat. He walked briskly, holding his hat in one hand and a pink silk shawl in the other, looking as carefree as a lark.

Her determination wavered at the bright look on his face. Was she doing the wrong thing? But no, she had sworn a vow and it must be upheld. She clicked her teeth, wishing Brutus would go faster than a trudge.

Mr. Littleton's face broadened in a smile as he saw her coming toward him. "Hello," he said politely, dipping into a small bow.

Hester pulled Brutus to a halt. "Mr. Littleton," she said evenly. Just a hint of a smile, just enough to make him comfortable. "A good spring morning to you."

He glanced around. "Nice the rain stopped, isn't it, Miss Fairfax?"

Hester nodded and smiled. She pointed to the shawl in his hand. "Going somewhere?"

He glanced down as if surprised to see it. A faint blush crawled up his neck as he met her gaze. "Ah, yes. That. My family has visitors this week and we're off to a picnic."

Hester cocked her head as if that was new information to her. "A lady's shawl. Have you turned into a footman?" She kept her tone too even to be teasing. In the past, he'd always caught on to her mischief because of her voice. She wouldn't let that happen today.

Mr. Littleton's flush deepened, and he looked away from her. "Miss Dunham accidentally left it behind, and I merely volunteered to retrieve it."

Fetching and carrying was a footman's job. If he had volunteered to leave their group instead of sending a servant back to their grand house, then he must've wanted time alone to himself. This fit into her plans perfectly.

Mr. Littleton's eyes flicked behind her, down the lane where the rest of his party was probably already reclining on blankets and eating.

"How is your family?" Hester inquired, desperate to get his attention back before he wandered away and she couldn't put her plan in motion.

He looked back at her but didn't smile. "Doing well, thank you for asking. My eldest brother and his wife just returned from holiday in Brighton, and she won't stop exclaiming about the sea air. My second brother—he's in the church, you knew that, correct?—he recently received an invitation to join the archbishop's diocese in Canterbury."

There was a pause.

"And your parents?" Hester had once known his family as well as her own, had frolicked on the estate and run feral through their fields, but now... they were like strangers.

"My mother is well. She is going to London early this year to see friends."

"And your father?" Hester asked quietly.

A pained expression flickered across his features. "Sir Stanley is quite well, thank you for inquiring." His tone was stiff, formal.

That revelation steadied her nerves. "Well, climb in." She made a show of scooting over and gathering her skirts under her. She wouldn't be able to do this unchaperoned in London or Bath. She probably wouldn't be allowed to drive in the city, either. But this was the country, where rules were far more relaxed.

His gaze flicked over the decrepit vehicle, then at her with confusion. "Pardon me?"

"I'm escorting you to your picnic," she lied. "Your boots will get muddy otherwise."

He gave her a polite smile and shook his head. "I cannot trouble you. If you're going to the village, it's the other direction."

"Mr. Littleton," she began, frowning down at him despite herself.

"It was lovely seeing you again, Miss Fairfax, but I really must hurry back to Miss Dunham." He lifted the shawl as if it was evidence.

"Benjamin."

He paused, already half-turned, then gave her a rueful grin. Exactly the way he'd always done. "I shouldn't."

She arched a brow. "Why? Are you saying I'm a poor driver?"

He barked a laugh. "This vehicle should've been driven one-way to a salvage yard years ago. Why has your father not replaced it?"

"He's always busy with his money schemes. He's probably buried under risk tables and advertisements for new speculations from the Stock Exchange right now," Hester replied. A tinge of sadness must've leaked through, because Benjamin Littleton sighed and climbed up into the tiny vehicle.

Surprise, then delight, flickered through her as he arranged himself, all long arms and legs. He nearly elbowed her in the face twice, but she didn't mind. Not now that the first step in her plan had succeeded.

He settled in beside her, then slipped the pink shawl inside his waistcoat.

Hester turned to hide the scowl that crossed her face, then clucked to Brutus, who was smelling daisies along the side of the path.

He swished his tail, then slowly raised his head and pulled forward.

"I believe my party is back that way." Mr. Littleton turned to point behind him.

"I know," Hester said. "But I cannot turn the vehicle in the mud here. Do you see how bad it is? I need to find a dry spot or the wheels will get stuck."

He settled back in the worn seat, oh so naïve. "How are you, Miss Fairfax?"

Hester bit her lips to hide her smile. She'd missed this. Though it was still odd to hear him call her "Miss Fairfax." Ah, well, men and women could not be intimate friends. "Very well."

"I'm surprised to find you still here in the country." He folded his long-fingered hands together on his knees and looked at her.

Hester, suddenly thankful the wide brim of her bonnet hid most of her expressions, kept her eyes on the road. "My father is old and dislikes traveling, even to London or Bath." Lately, he hadn't even wanted to make his annual visit to the Royal Exchange.

"I thought your sole goal was finding a ship full of pirates and joining the crew, never to see the beloved shores of Mother England again."

Hester snorted. "Yes, well, I think I had a vastly inaccurate view of how many pirates a young woman would come across in the wilds of Surrey."

"If anyone could find pirates in Surrey, you could," Benjamin said gallantly.

"And you?" Hester glanced at him as they passed through the copse of trees. In the distance, Littleton Hall loomed, a smudge of dark stone against the bright blue sky. She shivered.

"I did not find pirates at Harrow or Cambridge, much to my great sorrow." He paused. "Though I did join a rowing team and the captain squawked at us like a hoarse parrot whenever we were too slow in the water. Does that count?"

Hester giggled. "I'm afraid it does not."

"Pity." He quirked a grin at her. "There'll be no pirates at the Dunham Solicitors Firm, either."

Hester affected great nonchalance, though her heart beat wildly. "Oh? Is that what you've chosen to pursue?"

Benjamin sighed, throwing his head back to look at the clouds in the sky. "My father has decided that becoming a barrister and working closely with a well-established London solicitors firm would be an excellent occupation for the third son of a baronet. That's why the Dunhams are visiting." He straightened, glancing around. "I say, it seems we've gone quite a distance. Why don't you turn around here? There's a dry spot." He pointed to a patch of grass.

Hester's breath caught in her chest. "Actually, I think I'll continue on."

"What?" His gaze bored into the side of her face.

Hester smiled brightly at him. "Hold onto your seat, I'm picking up the pace!" And she slapped the reins.

Brutus snorted but began to trot. The chaise bounced and rattled beneath them.

"Hester!" Benjamin grabbed the side and back of the gig to keep from falling off. "What are you doing?"

"I promised!" Hester shouted over the jangling and creaking.

"Promised *what*? Miss Fairfax, I must return to the picnic!" He frowned, glancing over his shoulder at the retreating Littleton Hall.

"Later," Hester said as she somehow coaxed Brutus faster. They veered off the path, Hester bouncing nearly off her seat as Brutus took the chaise over a bump in the open field.

Benjamin threw one long arm around her shoulders, bracketing her against him. "What promise, Miss Fairfax?" he demanded.

Hester's teeth rattled as she grinned at him. "I'm keeping my promise to you." Her bonnet drooped over her eyes, and she could barely see his expression in his silence as Brutus charged ahead.

"Surely you're—" he broke off as one wheel went over a rock. His fingers tightened on her shoulder, hard points of contact that anchored Hester to safety.

"I'm kidnapping you!" Hester shifted the reins to one hand just long enough to fling her bonnet back, then grabbed them up again. Her bonnet dangled down her back, the ribbons in a loose bow at her throat. She fought to keep Brutus and the chaise in check as she glanced up to see Benjamin's reaction.

CHAPTER TWO

Benjamin stared down at his oldest friend in disbelief, even as his backside and lower back pounded against the hard bench, hard enough to leave bruises in the morning.

The picnic, Mother's resigned face, his father's disappointed sigh, Miss Dunham's wan, blank expression all flashed across his mind. Mr. Dunham's florid face filled with expectation. All behind him, nearly by two miles at this point.

He threw back his head and laughed, feeling lighter than he had in years. "Miss Fairfax," he finally got out after catching his breath. "I believe *you* are the fiercest pirate of Surrey."

Hester looked up at him, her smile incandescent. Her honey-brown tresses gleamed in the sunlight as her cupid's bow lips curled with mischievous glee. One dimple peeked out at him, and his heart ached suddenly in nostalgia, for all the days they'd spent together as children. There had once been a time that her dimple was the most familiar sight in the whole world. How had he gone the past years without it?

"I'm a grown man, not a child, you can't kidnap me," he corrected her.

Hester shrugged extravagantly. "Abduct you then. Spirit you away." She shot him a wicked look. "But I distinctly remember vowing to kidnap you, so we'll continue to call this that."

"How long am I to be your hostage?" he asked over the shaking vehicle.

"I'm not sure," she said loftily, gripping the reins tight as Brutus continued his reluctant trot across Littleton fields.

"You haven't decided?" Benjamin tsked with mock disappointment. But his blood thrummed hot in his veins, the taste of freedom in the air.

"At least an hour, perhaps longer." She flashed him an impish grin, one he hadn't realized how badly he'd missed until just now. "We'll sort it on the way."

How long has it been since we've done this? Too long. Once Hester had been his dearest friend, his companion in mischievous enterprises. Then he'd gone to Harrow, and he'd only been able to see her during summers when she could sneak away from her governess. Eventually, he'd gone to Cambridge because that's what the Littleton men did. And he'd assumed she'd... gone to finishing school? Or something? Because her father could certainly afford it, and she wasn't getting much attention or instruction at home.

Hester had been relegated to those sun-drenched, lazy childhood days in his memory as he'd left Cambridge and tried to find his footing as a man in the world of business. Several times over the last three years he thought he'd seen her at a play or soiree in London, and his whole body reacted with nostalgic joy until the women turned their heads and he realized it wasn't Hester Fairfax.

"How long has it been?" Benjamin asked over the noise.

"Since I promised you? Goodness, it was the day before you left for Harrow, so... fourteen years? I was ten."

Benjamin braced as they narrowly avoided a mud puddle with a jerk, wedging himself further into his seat, Hester flush against him. "No, since we've spent time together."

"Three years?" Hester wondered. She grappled with the reins. "Hold fast, Brutus!" They were nearing the edge of the field, where the drystone wall separated the muddy field from the beginnings of the Littleton wood.

The wheel beneath Benjamin wobbled over an errant tree root. He looked down uneasily. "Perhaps I should take the ribbons."

She cast him a scornful look, turning the cart parallel to the wall. "I beg your pardon?"

He knew he tread on dangerous ground. "I've had more experience racing gigs in unfavorable conditions," he hazarded. "If you hand the ribbons over to me I can get us away from these roots and loose stones."

Hester scoffed. "Please. You've been in Cambridge and London for the past six years. You've forgotten all about country riding and driving. I'm the expert now."

Benjamin's temper flared. "I have been working to fulfill family obligations. My father is extremely clear what my path is, and I've been doing my best to uphold the family name. I haven't been drinking, gambling, and whoring my way through London, *Hester*."

Hester stiffened, refusing to look away from Brutus. "I never said you were. I merely said that while you were courting Dunham Solicitors, Esquire, I've grown proficient at driving. This is *my* abduction, anyway. I drive."

His anger faded. What had she been doing in the country? Why wasn't she already married with a babe? She'd had such grand plans for herself when they were adolescents. He'd always halfway believe she'd somehow finagle her way into being captured by pirates on the high seas, so she'd convince a pirate prince to fall in love with her.

The chaise jolted over another root, so hard that both Benjamin and Hester actually bounced in the air before landing hard on the wooden bench again. Brutus was slowing, thankfully, but Benjamin was still unsure of the integrity of the chaise. He took a breath and snapped his long arms forward, grabbing the reins from Hester. "Got it." His left arm crossed in front of his body, his right was still around Hester's shoulders.

She gasped in outrage, glaring up at him. "Excuse me, Mr. Littleton! You will give me back my ribbons at once!"

"Never." He pulled sharply to the right, trying to convince an obstinate Brutus to avoid a messy tangle of roots and mud lying up ahead. "You know, newer models actually have these things called *springs*," he teased, "which lessen the jolting to provide the passengers a more pleasant—"

CRACK!

The world tilted sideways, a blur of blue and green and Hester's bold pink pelisse. Benjamin barely had time to release the reins and grab hold of Hester, pulling her close and tucking his chin over her head before they hit the ground.

All air whooshed out of his lungs upon impact. His vision dimmed, and dull pain throbbed along his back and chest.

Hester's sharp cry cut through the darkness closing in. His chest seized, his arms tightened around the warm weight in his arms. Benjamin blinked, and the world came back into focus.

A gnarled root dug into his side, and the smell of petrichor and leaves filled the air. The spring breeze whipped through the cracks in the drystone wall behind him. "Miss Fairfax," he ground out. "Are you well? Anything broken?"

Hester groaned, stirring in his arms. She lifted her head and the broken brim of her bonnet nearly poked his eye out. "Benji?" she whispered.

"Oh, god I'm so sorry. I'm not a child, I should've known better than to provoke—Hester, where do you hurt?" He plucked the broken bonnet from her head and tossed it beside them, eyes roving over her face for any scrapes or cuts.

She grimaced, pushing off his chest to sit on the ground. "I think I am well." She reached down to swipe mud off her pelisse. Her face went white and she bit her lip.

Benjamin tensed, forcing himself into an upright position, his long legs still splayed awkwardly between the wreckage of the shattered wheel.

"I believe," she said shakily, "I've sprained my wrist." She hugged her left hand to her chest, swallowing hard.

Benjamin surveyed the wreckage around them.

Brutus, unhurt, was attempting to munch on some tall grass, despite the bit in his mouth. Apparently, he was too old to panic. His bridle jangled merrily and one shaft of the chaise dragged on the ground behind him, still attached to the tack. The chaise, however, had splintered into three large pieces. And the left wheel had shattered into four or five pieces. Two spokes had slammed into the soft earth. Benjamin shuddered at the thought of those broken spokes slicing into soft flesh rather than mud.

Old Brutus wandered away, bridle trailing behind him, now free from the broken shafts of the chaise.

"What about you? Any broken bones?" Hester's breathless voice broke his examination.

He took stock of his body, slowly rising into a crouch, and then standing. "I'll be black and blue tomorrow, but no real injuries." The back of his coat and buckskin trousers were covered in mud, based on the oozing wetness he felt, and his hat was somewhere by Brutus. The silk shawl, somehow, had slipped between his coat and waistcoat and had not a speck of mud to be found. Benjamin held out his hand to help Hester rise.

Hester hesitantly stood, hair tumbling around her shoulders, studded with bits of bark, moss, and dirt. Mud covered her pelisse. She wobbled between roots until she found firmer footing.

"I'm sorry," Benjamin repeated, looking again at the broken chaise. "Will your father be very angry?"

So many emotions crossed Hester's face that he couldn't keep track. An odd pang went through him because once upon a time he would've caught and identified each one.

She shrugged, brows knit together as she looked at the damage. "As long as Brutus is unharmed, my father shan't even notice." She looked up at Benjamin and forced a broad grin. "The spiriting has taken a sharp turn, 'tis true. But I still have you in my clutches."

A startled laugh came out of him. He'd grown so used to dour, unhappy Dunhams and his silent, disappointed father that Hester's ability to move past an accident was like a breath of fresh air. Or salve to a festering wound. How did she always have boundless energy and optimism? "You're perfect, never change."

Hester blushed, smiling. She looked down and tried to wipe mud off her pelisse. "What now, hostage?"

Benjamin glanced around. "There's the old gamekeeper's cottage about a ten minutes' walk from here. We should clean up and rest there. Examine ourselves for any other injuries. Then try to get to town. I'll get Brutus and—" he turned for the horse, only to see the animal was already halfway back to the road and heading toward home. "Should... should I get him?"

Hester shook her head. "He'll head straight home. We should head toward that cottage." She held her sprained wrist close and stepped forward.

Benjamin hovered near her. "Do you need me to carry you? I'd hate for you to be hurt further."

Hester laughed up at him, amusement shining in her eyes. "Carry me? Whatever for? I'm not a heroine in a Gothic novel. Goodness. We're just Benji and Hester. Come on, I haven't been to the cottage in ages. You'll have to lead the way. If you can remember."

Benjamin forced a smile at her needling, knowing it was what she expected. "If you feel faint at all, tell me at once and I'll carry you the rest of the way."

She picked up her broken bonnet and gave him a curious look. "Very well. Get your hat and let's be off."

INTERLUDE

1796

Benjamin sucked in a breath as he tiptoed through the house. "Are you sure we can do this?"

Hester glanced over her shoulder and threw him an impish grin. "Of course not. That's why it's so fun." She winked and beckoned him forward. "Mind the floor right there, it creaks."

Benjamin sidestepped one wooden plank. "Maybe we should just keep playing outside. I'd like to visit the cottage again before I leave tomorrow."

Hester whirled. "I told you not to mention leaving!" Her freckled face frowned at him.

Benjamin shrugged, looking down at her, not quite comfortable in his growing body. Until a month ago, Hester and he had been the same height, despite him being two years older. "Beg pardon. It slipped out."

"If we keep mentioning how you're being dragged away to be tortured by evil tutors at Harrow, it will spoil today. Our day. Our last day together." Her frown wobbled and her eyes turned glassy.

Oh, no. He couldn't bear to make her cry. "I shan't do it again," he whispered. "I promise. Please." He gestured down the hallway lined with paintings. "We'll go to your father's study."

Hester pursed her lips.

"And this isn't our last day together, I promise." Benjamin put a hand to his heart. "I'll return, and we'll have all summer together."

"Very well." Her frown disappeared as quickly as it had come. "Hurry, before Mrs. Shaw catches us." She darted away, frizzy curls bobbing behind her.

The housekeeper? She was worried about the *housekeeper*? Benjamin took a deep breath. He'd be far more worried about his father catching them if they were in Littleton Hall right now.

Hester paused at one wooden door, bending over to peer through the keyhole. "No one's there," she whispered. "Come on."

Benjamin dragged his feet forward. How much trouble would they get into if they were caught? This is why he mostly played outside with Hester. But she was fearless, and he didn't want to look like a coward next to her. He was the boy, for goodness' sake. He was supposed to be the brave one.

Hester slowly turned the doorknob and pushed the door open, a mischievous gleam in her eyes. She might be ten years old, but Benjamin sometimes wondered if she really was a fairy imp. "Are you coming?" she hissed.

Benjamin jogged to her side, and they entered the forbidden room together.

"Oh." Hester stood just inside the room, shoulders slumped. "It's *normal*."

Benjamin sidestepped her and shut the door behind him. "What did you think the room would be like?" he laughed. "This looks just like my father's study."

The spacious room had several floor-to-ceiling bookcases. Leather spines of all colors gleamed on the shelves. On the floor was a maroon rug, the white tassels perfectly lined up and stretched out like little soldiers awaiting orders. A desk sat in front of large bay windows, heaps of books and loose papers strewn across it. The curtains were drawn back, and sunlight spilled across the leather chair and the gleaming brass telescope by the windows. It was far less tidy than Benjamin's father's study.

He looked around carefully, just in case Hester's father was lurking somewhere in the room. Ready to jump out with a switch and terrify them. But no one was there.

"Perfect." Hester seemed to have regained her excitement and looked around the room in glee. "See? I'm old enough to be in here. The room shouldn't be off-limits. I'm ten years old, not an infant."

Benjamin wished she'd keep her voice down. "What if the servants hear you?" he whispered. "And tell your father?"

Hester put her hands on her hips and gave him a defiant look. "Let him come in and punish me. I'll laugh in his face."

Benjamin could not conceive of a world where a child would laugh in their father's face. If he did such a thing, his bottom wouldn't be beet red, it would be black and blue. "You're just saying that," he said, laughing shakily. Hester always complained she never saw her father, but Benjamin often secretly envied her freedom.

But Hester was already on to her next goal. "Come on, let's look at the telescope. It shipped all the way from *London*," she exclaimed in dramatic tones. "He only set it up three days ago."

"We're just going to look at it, yes?" Benjamin edged a little closer to the desk and telescope on the other side, while Hester bounded over to it. "We're not going to touch it?"

Hester shot him a scornful look. "Benji. How am I ever supposed to convince a pirate prince to fall in love with me if I cannot navigate properly? I wouldn't be of any use to him on his ship!"

"I think you need an astrolabe. But if I meet any pirates' sons at school I'll show them your direction," Benjamin promised.

Hester paused, hands on the tall wooden tripod holding the fragile instrument. "Are you truly so unhappy to be going?"

Benjamin straightened, pushing his shoulders back. He was going to learn to be a man there, his father said, so he'd best start acting like one. And he was a whole two years older, so. "It'll be a grand opportunity," he said. "I'm very excited to learn and meet other boys and see another piece of England."

Hester's face fell. "I wish I was going," she muttered. "I've never been out of this silly old village, not once, in my *whole life*."

Benjamin sighed. "I'm worried, too," he admitted. He was excited to get out of Littleton Hall, away from his father. But it was his father insisting he attend Harrow. That couldn't do much to recommend the place. "What if I grow up to be just like Father?" he asked. "Reginald comes back every year looking and acting more and more like him," he said, referencing his oldest brother.

"It shan't happen," Hester said stoutly. "You're nothing like him. It would be like a dog turning into a cow. It's impossible."

Benjamin huffed a laugh. "He's my father." He was king, master of the universe, the sole authority to whom all must bow. It never occurred to Benjamin that someone could disobey.

"Benji." Hester came around the desk to squeeze his hands. "I promise you, right now, that I'll never let you turn into some stuffy old lord."

He laughed. "Oh, how's that?"

She shrugged as if it were the simplest thing. "I'll carry you off in my luggage when I meet my pirate. We'll sort it on the way. Perhaps you can stow away onboard and we'll have all sorts of adventures together."

His heart panged, rattling around his ribcage. "Pirates never come to Surrey," he told her.

She set her jaw. "Then I'll go where they are. And if I must, I'll kidnap you."

Benjamin rolled his eyes. "You, kidnap me?"

"Benjamin Littleton, I most certainly can and will." Hester scowled. "You don't want to be kidnapped? It sounds dashing and romantic to me."

"Fine," Benjamin relented, trying to display adolescent insouciance. Even if his pulse quickened at the thought of the idea, just like it always did with her hare-brained ideas. "Kidnap me."

"I will," Hester threatened. "You know I will."

Benjamin grinned then. "If you're so certain, vow it."

Hester raised her eyebrows at him, then dropped one of his hands to cross her heart. "I vow to kidnap you one day so you never turn into a stuffy old lord."

A ball of emotion caught in Benjamin's throat unexpectedly. "Right, then," he said, embarrassed. "Show me that telescope."

CHAPTER THREE

Hester paused at the threshold of the old cottage, breathing hard. Her wrist throbbed, more than she'd admit to Benjamin, and she was glad he was hunting for the key instead of hovering around her. It made her unsettled, the way he hovered. When he was a boy he would've suggested she rub dirt on it and urge her to continue playing.

"It's around here somewhere." He knelt on the ground, picking up rocks and feeling through the rotting leaves.

She waited until her breathing had slowed and the ache in her hand dulled to a low, steady pain. Then she reached up on tiptoes and grabbed the rusty key off the top of the stone lintel, feeling the cold iron through the ripped seams in her glove. "Here." She handed it over, too tired to brandish it like a sword. The way she used to, when it had filled her whole hand.

"Ah." Benjamin rose, once again towering over her, and plucked the key from her hand. His fingertips skimmed her skin and ruffled the torn edges of the glove, sending a jolt through her body. "I suppose it's been a few years." A faint flush spread across his cheeks as he bent over the lock on the door, turning away from her.

Hester cleared her throat, watching him. He'd always been a tall, gangly child. Mostly elbows and knees. The first summer he'd returned from Harrow he'd been thirteen and his Adam's apple had protruded from his skinny neck. Hester had stared at it, surprised to see him turning from boy to adolescent. The next year his voice was breaking, and she'd delighted in mocking him all summer long. And then the next summer he'd spent half of it away with school friends.

Now, although he was still on the slender side, his shoulders had broadened enough for the seams of his coat to have torn during the fall. His long fingers twisted the key in the lock, and she realized with surprise what a fine figure he cut as an adult. His patrician nose came from his father, as did the square jaw. The brown eyes and floppy, mousy brown hair were like his mother's.

"Hester?"

Hester blinked and realized she'd been staring all while he'd cracked open the door and stepped over the threshold. "Oh." She picked up her muddy skirts and stepped inside.

The two-room cottage had a dim, musty smell. Hester hadn't visited in nearly three years. It had once been a refuge against the dull tedium of her life, brimming full of memories and hopes and dreams they'd shared with one another as children. Slowly each of those dreams had turned to ash, and now the cottage taunted her with everything that could not be. That would never be. She shivered under the weight of ghosts of things that had never come to pass.

"Cold?" Benjamin briskly stepped past her to the wide stone hearth. "I'll get a fire going. You sit and rest."

Hester crouched to remove her walking boots, fighting with the tiny buttons coated in mud, and slipped them off with a sigh of relief while Benjamin prepared a packet of old kindling beside the hearth, then struck the flint and striker he'd found along the mantel.

The cottage's front room had bare wooden walls, with a table and cupboard swathed in cobwebs in one corner of the room. Weak light slipped through the gaps in the closed shutters and spilled on the bare stone floor. Another small table with a chair and stool stood against one wall, and beside it an open door led to the small bedroom.

She stripped off her filthy pelisse and gloves and laid them out on the stone hearth, hoping to dry the mud so she could take it home and the housekeeper could brush the pelisse clean. She feared the gloves were destined for the rag bin. Her wrist ached again at the movement, and she gritted her teeth.

Benjamin just barely managed to toe off his close-fitting boots, then unbuttoned his coat beside her, but hissed in pain as tried to slide it from his shoulder.

Alarm shot down Hester's spine. "Benji, did you hurt yourself?"

He clenched his jaw, shaking his head. "Just bruises forming, I believe."

"Let me help." She stepped behind him and took the edge of his stained walking coat and gently peeled it from his shoulders, one-handed.

He stiffened and grunted only once when she had to slide the sleeves off.

"I'm sorry," she whispered, getting the last sleeve off and flinging it on the hearth beside her pelisse. "Better now?"

He sighed, head bowed as he loosened his cravat. "Better," he said gruffly, pulling that dratted pink shawl out and setting it on the hearth. "Thank you." He turned to face her, his cravat unspooling in one hand. "Let's tend your wrist."

The low light from the fire highlighted his hair, revealing a red undertone she'd never seen before. Benjamin's smell filled the air—a bit of leather with sandalwood, now mixed with the earth they'd landed in.

She looked up. He looked down.

Benjamin tenderly took her wrist and wrapped it tight in his cravat, then took the tail and draped it over her shoulder to make a sling. He reached around her, and she inhaled his scent, closing her eyes. His touch was warm and firm, somehow both gentle and confident. She'd never thought a man's touch could be both things. That Benjamin could be that way.

All too soon he finished tying the ends together and lay her wrist back against her bosom in the sling. "Better?" he whispered, letting his hands fall to his sides.

Hester swayed, suddenly lightheaded—and not from the pain.

His chest rose and fell, and she spied the warm pink of his skin when the now-limp collar of his shirt fell open. Something flickered in those brown eyes.

Her body heated, and she had the sudden urge to walk right into that chest, to wrap those long arms around her.

Confused, Hester stepped back. "Hopefully it's just bruising," she laughed, putting a bare hand to her heated cheek. "Do you think we still have those marbles and jacks hidden in one of the cupboards?"

Benjamin looked as confused as she felt. He closed his eyes for a moment, inhaling deeply. "Shall we check?"

An old, grubby deck of cards was found. The top cards stuck together so badly that they tore when Hester pried them apart with her one free hand.

"What *is* this?" she demanded with disgust, holding by the edges.

Benjamin laughed. "Jam? That was your favorite treat for ages." He sprawled on the dusty floor like he used to, leaning against the hearth, watching as she attempted to wipe the cards clean.

Hester finally tossed them aside, on her knees digging in the bottom of the cupboard. "That shan't work." She withdrew a handful of jacks and balls. Grinning, she turned and showed Benjamin. "Care to wager?"

He threw back his head and laughed, the long column of his throat constricting in the dim light. Fascinated, she clenched her fists as she watched, fighting the temptation to reach out and touch him.

"Absolutely not. You cheated as a child. You're certainly no different today."

Hester pretended to be offended as she walked across the floor and settled down across from him. She curled her legs underneath her, arranging her sodden skirt in as ladylike a fashion as she could manage. "You just couldn't bear a girl beating you."

"A stab at my honor?" Benjamin raised his brows and clutched his chest as if wounded. "Miss Fairfax, how dare you."

"A challenge," she replied, arranging the jacks. "Besides," she whispered conspiratorially, "I haven't played in a decade. You'll easily win." Even as she handed the ball to Benjamin, she couldn't help but glance toward the shuttered window. What time was it? Surely it had been over an hour. They should be walking toward Littleton Hall. *Just one game,* she told herself. *It's been ages since we were friends. It's not like there are any pressing social engagements for me for the next... three or four years. It's my one chance for fun.*

Benjamin took the ball from her bare palm, and she wished she felt his fingertips again. But he was too fast. He dropped the ball and moved like lightning.

Hester gawked at the three jacks he suddenly held in his palm along with the ball.

Benjamin grinned at her, half-shy, half-triumphant. "We'll see who wins tonight."

A long time later, surely at least two hours, Hester threw her hand in the air and groaned. "You cheated, I just know it!" The fine linen edge of his cravat rubbed the side of her neck.

Benjamin now lay on his stomach just like he had as a child. He'd cast off his waistcoat an hour ago for a better range of motion, and the shirtsleeves didn't disguise the lean muscle of his arms or chest. He looked up at her and quirked an eyebrow.

Her breath caught. That look wasn't boyish at all. It was masculine and languid and arousing and—she broke off.

Embarrassed and distracted, she grabbed for her little pile of jacks.

Sharp pain pricked under one of her fingernails. "Ouch!" She jerked her hand away, scowling as she brought her middle finger to her lips, unable to keep from sliding it partly into her mouth. "That hurt!"

Benjamin rose to his knees, concern etched across his face. "Was it the sharp edge of one of the jacks?"

She nodded, finger still at her lips.

"Let me see," Benjamin coaxed, holding out his hands.

Hester hesitated, suddenly unsure about the new intimacy between them. *It's just Benji,* she chided herself, and relented.

CHAPTER FOUR

Benjamin took her dainty hand in his massive ones, a tremor passing through him. *Get a hold of yourself,* he ordered. *You've held Miss Dunham's gloveless hand before.* He'd also visited a few Cambridge and London music halls and brothels with his older brothers and friends—which showed quite a lot more of a woman's body than just her hands—but they'd never made him feel so nervous and sweaty.

Blood filled the underside of her index fingernail, trapped between the nail and skin. He held his breath, turning it in the firelight to get a better view. "You poor thing," he murmured. *It's only because it's Hester,* he berated. *I'm nervous because it's like two worlds colliding—my child-hood playmate isn't supposed to have hands like a woman. All I have to do is acknowledge Hester has a lovely hand and then my mind will calm.*

Well, maybe.

After a moment Hester withdrew her hand, heat staining her cheeks. "Clumsy me," she muttered with a small shrug. "Just a scratch though."

"A pirate would pour rum on it and carry on swinging and hacking," Benjamin suggested.

Hester flashed a grin, then glanced toward the window again.

She'd done that a few times in the past couple of hours, and each time Benjamin's stomach felt more and more queasy, like he had an appointment with an executioner rather than his father, future fiancé, and employers.

"Are you feeling peckish?" He slapped his hands together, voice overbright and cheerful.

Hester blinked in surprise. "Peckish?" Her brow furrowed. "Will Miss Dunham be worried? I've kept you far longer than I meant."

Benjamin went to the cupboard and opened it, ignoring her words. "I wonder if there's any food left in here."

Hester walked up behind him. "Benjamin," she began, but he cut her off.

"Miss Fairfax, you are an abominable hostess, you haven't offered your captive food at all." He threw her a grin over his shoulder. "And now you suggest sending me off into the wilderness, in the dark, with no provision? Only an empty belly?" He tsked. "For shame, Miss Fairfax, for shame."

Hester laughed, and the sound went through his body like a lightning bolt. He ached to hear it again. Instead, he reached onto the top shelf and pulled a cream crockery jar off. Dust settled in his eyes, and he coughed, blinking rapidly. He stepped back, only to hit a warm body.

"Oof," Hester got out, toppling backward.

Benjamin whirled, grabbing her shoulder and yanking her close, so she wouldn't fall. Her face barely missed the crockery in his other hand and smooshed against his shirt. His half-buttoned shirt.

Hester mumbled something into his chest. His arm tightened around her shoulders. "Did I hurt you?" he asked.

She reared back. "I said, what are you *doing*?"

Benjamin's face heated and his stomach flipped over in embarrassment. He immediately let her go and stepped backward, this time bumping into the still-open cupboard door. "Pardon me. I thought you were falling and I did not wish you to injure your arm any further." He ignored the sharp pain below his left shoulder blade from the cupboard.

She rolled her eyes. "I'm *fine*, Benji."

Of course she was. Hester was always fine. His eyes drifted down her body before he could help it. More than fine, now. He screwed his eyes shut. *Blast and damn, Benjamin. She's like a sister.*

Hester plucked the jar from his fingers and tried to open it one-handed. "I wonder what's inside."

"Some sort of preserves," he said stupidly.

"I *know*. I meant, what type of preserves? Strawberry? Fig? Apple?" She bent over the jar, twisting. "It's stuck."

Benjamin bit back a smile. "Allow me."

Hester let out an exasperated sigh. "Very well, then." She handed the crockery back over. "Let's see if those bear paws can open it."

Benjamin choked on a laugh as he easily broke the seal. "Bear paws?"

"Well, the rest of you fits those hands now," Hester said absently as she peered inside the jar. "Remember when you were seventeen and your hands were larger than the rest of you?"

He grimaced. "Dreaded growth spurts."

Hester stuck a finger along the rim of the crockery and pulled it out. Red preserves coated it. She held it to her nose. "Strawberry!" she exclaimed. "My favorite."

They ate together on the floor, backs against the hearth, jacks now forgotten, with the fire popping merrily behind them. Benjamin held the jar between them, his knees drawn up, and they took turns scooping strawberry preserves out with their fingers and licking them clean. It was unhygienic, probably disgusting, decadent, and glorious.

"Tell me about Miss Dunham," Hester said suddenly.

Benjamin's gut twisted like it always seemed to do these days. "What do you mean?"

She paused to lick her finger clean. "Goodness, we truly have reverted back to our ten-year-old selves, haven't we?" She went for another fingerful. "The rumor in the neighborhood is that her family is here for you to propose. So tell me how you fell in love."

Benjamin cleared his throat, ignoring how his gut twisted further at her words. "We do not know one another well," he began.

Hester looked at him, eyes sparkling in delight. "So it was love at first sight?"

A frog formed in Benjamin's throat. "Erm," he began a bit desperately. "My father says it's a practical decision for both our families' futures."

The excitement in her eyes dimmed. "So this is one of your father's schemes?" Her tone darkened. "Is it not enough that he has chosen your profession, he must choose your bride also?"

Benjamin squirmed. "It's not like that anymore," he protested weakly. It was exactly like that. It always had been. "I'm a grown man, I've made my own decisions."

"You're right, I apologize. I should not speak so familiarly to you. Many years have passed, and we are children no longer." Hester fell silent.

Somehow her apology made him feel worse. He ground his teeth. "The Dunhams have managed my family's legal matters for nigh a hundred years, but the current Mr. Dunham only has one daughter and no sons. With a great desire to branch into barristery. At Cambridge, I showed an aptitude for numbers and accounting. The solicitors of great families must have a little knowledge of finances, so this seemed the natural step. After I graduated Cambridge my father sent me to one of the Inns of the Courts in London, and I've been there for two years. I only have one year left before I can be called to the Bar, and then we are to marry."

Hester said nothing, just fidgeted with the makeshift sling around her neck.

"Miss Dunham is twenty-two, with a quiet demeanor and pale complexion. My mother says that her solemn nature will be a good balance against my own fretfulness and habit of dashing about, looking for excitement."

Hester mumbled something, but he couldn't catch the words.

"Our families have dined together several times and I've attended a musicale once with her." Benjamin tried not to think about the heavy, weighted silence that had been louder than a scream when in the company of her family. How he'd felt utterly trapped in a carriage with Mr. Dunham, Mrs. Dunham, and Miss Dunham at the end of the night, wishing he was anywhere but with them. Wondering if he'd grow used to the life and find contentment with her.

"Fretfulness?" Hester repeated in an aggrieved tone. "Habit of dashing about? Benji, they make you sound positively frivolous and superficial!"

Benjamin's heart lightened at her words. She always protected his back, always, without fail. "I *can* be a touch anxious at times," he admitted.

"Only because you grew up in that blasted Hall with a disapproving father and distant mother!" Hester clamped her jaw shut. "I apologize, I did it again. I should not speak poorly of your family. I promise I shan't do it again."

He bit back a smile at her words. He'd never felt fretful or without purpose when with Hester. Perhaps that was the magic of an idyllic childhood. "These preserves are so sweet they make my teeth hurt," he admitted.

Hester allowed him the change of subject. "I can't believe we'd eat a whole jar between the two of us in one afternoon."

"And the stomachaches to go along with it," he added.

She groaned and shoved his hand with the jar away. "Enough! Before I get a stomachache this time." She glanced at the fading light slipping in through the window. Resignation crossed her face, and she opened her mouth.

"But what of you?" he blurted. As long as she didn't say, *it's time to return,* then he could pretend that they had the whole evening together. The whole night, even. A feeling like bliss unfurled in his heart at the thought—a whole night away from duty. A whole night remembering the good parts of his life.

"Me?" Hester's brows furrowed. "What of me?"

"Why are you still here?" Benjamin set the jar down on his other side and draped his long arms over his knees, giving her his whole attention. "You're four and twenty if I remember correctly. We've discussed my future. What about yours?"

CHAPTER FIVE

Hester sucked in a breath. She didn't want to tell him. At least he was out in the world, *doing* things, *going* places, *marrying* someone. She was just moldering away, forgotten, in the countryside. And wrecking her father's gig, of course. Mustn't forget that.

"Hester?" he prompted softly.

Drat, he was looking at her, watching her face. She forced a bright smile. "Oh, I've been quite busy. You know my father loves his ledgers, so I've taken to running most of the household." An exaggeration, since the housekeeper was more than capable. Despite several efforts over the years, Hester had been given almost no responsibility as the lady of the house. All Hester did was approve menus and every spring wonder aloud if it was time for the spring cleaning yet. It was as if Mrs. Shaw preferred to be in control of the household and so still considered Hester to be a child. "I attend most of the village assemblies. Oh! Last year I went to London for a few days. Father had engaged a new stock broker and wanted to participate in one of the new state lotteries, so we traveled. It was *glorious*. I walked by a few coffeeshops and heard four different languages being spoken!" She did not mention how her father had purchased two full lottery tickets, a grand total of sixteen pounds, that would've won—if they hadn't been counterfeit.

His brow furrowed.

"And you know how busy things are in the country," she babbled on. "Lambing season, hunting season, church picnics. Two months ago the draper's daughter married the butcher's son, and let me tell you the hullabaloo *that* caused! You'd think it was Romeo and Juliet all over again. But the wedding was lovely, even if it was the dead of winter."

"Why aren't *you* married?" he broke in.

Hester blinked. "I, well, I...."

Two hours ago he would've apologized for overstepping propriety's bounds. But now they were Hester and Benji again, and he never let up on her.

She took a breath. Smiled broadly. "No good offers, I suppose."

Thunder rumbled in the distance, but she ignored it.

The furrow between his eyebrows deepened. "I don't understand."

She shrugged, smoothing the wrinkles in her skirts. "I did have one suitor, but I refused him." Her wrist ached.

"Only *one*?" He sounded affronted. "Surely you're mistaken!"

Hester couldn't help but laugh. "Not many have looked my way. I'm getting too old, I'm no great beauty, and I have little dowry."

He made a sound of protest. Dear Benji, always trying to make her feel better.

"No, 'tis true, I admit it." She flashed him a smile but didn't try to meet his eyes. "My father never set aside money for my dowry, so I have inherited my mother's fifteen hundred pounds. And my forehead is too broad, my eyes too small, and my chin too weak to be a beauty."

"That's rubbish," he growled.

Hester quirked a smile. "Thank you, that's sweet. I think I'm pretty enough to get a dance or two in the assembly hall, but not enough to attract a suitable gentleman who would overlook my scant dowry." At one point in time, her father had saved a dowry for her, an outrageous sum of fifteen thousand pounds. And then it had slowly disappeared each time her father joined a new speculation scheme. The last piece had been a share in a shipload of Chinese silk, except it had sunk to the bottom of the Indian Sea.

"What about your one suitor? Did he jilt you?"

She shook her head. "No. He wasn't in love with me. He offered more out of pity, I think. He is one of Father's friends and is a widower. It was two years ago, and I couldn't bring myself to do it. He was kind enough, but I still had fancies of falling in love at that point, and so refused him." She secretly thought he'd been relieved when she turned him down.

"The men in this county are fools," he stated.

Hester laughed. "Perhaps they are."

"You don't have to stay here if you don't want to, you know." Benji leaned toward her. "You could come to London."

She shook her head ruefully. "And do what, exactly?"

"Well—" he broke off.

"Be your wife's companion? Serve as a governess to your daughters?"

He leaned back, hunched over his knees. "I'm not wed *yet*, don't give me daughters already."

Hester laid an arm on his shoulder. "Thank you for your concern. I have few options, but I am content," she lied. "One day my pirate prince will come."

"It's not right," he insisted. "You deserve a chance to see the world. At the very least, London."

"There is a war on the Peninsula," Hester reminded lightly, far more lightly than she felt. "Most of us are confined to our island anyway. My life isn't much different otherwise."

He set his jaw, mulish as ever, but didn't argue the point.

Rain clattered on the roof, so loud and sudden that Hester jumped. The storm pounded the cottage around them, and the wind blew under the gap in the door. She shivered.

Benjamin jumped up and pulled the curtain back to peer through the grimy window. "Too late to return tonight," he muttered. "I'm not going out in that. I'll fall in a rabbit burrow and break my ankle."

Hester took the worn, ratted rug from the middle of the floor and bunched it against the crack in the door to block the wind awkwardly with one hand. "I'd rather not traipse about in the rain, either."

Benjamin turned to her in indignation, letting the curtain drop. "I wouldn't let you go out!"

Hester bristled. "Pardon me?"

"I mean," he quickly backtracked. "I am a gentleman and no gentleman would allow a lady to walk alone at night, with a wounded wrist, through a thunderstorm."

Hester didn't know whether to laugh or cry. "Benji," she said after a pause. "I'm not truly a lady. I might be a gentleman's daughter, but most people just see me as an eccentric spinster."

He looked her up and down, gaze inscrutable. "You're no spinster."

A flush spread across Hester's body. *Why? He said nothing inappropriate. And it's only Benji.* But something about the low, demanding tone and the way his eyes had lingered made her wonder... made her hope. *Stop this foolishness. He's marrying Miss Dunham.* And since when did that matter to her? She gave him an impish grin. "But I am delightfully eccentric."

"And I would never allow such a lovely and delightfully eccentric maiden out in such dangerous weather." He paused. "I'll beat you to the door if you try."

Hester raised a brow and elaborately turned to look at the door behind her. "I'm closer."

"I have longer legs."

The air seemed charged with tension, as if there was another storm raging in the room between them. This wasn't normal, this was different and strange and...not childlike at all. Desperate to bring this back to familiar corners, Hester threw him a smirk. "We'll see about that." And she flew backward to the door.

Her loose hair tangled around her, and a laugh burst out as she scrambled for the door handle. A heavy body slammed into her back, and then Benjamin somehow lurched forward, those giant arms outstretched, and he slammed both palms flat against the wooden door.

"No, you don't," he said in her ear, amusement leaking through.

Hester, trapped between his chest and the door, relented. She clutched her sprained wrist to her chest and leaned her forehead against the door, right between his palms. "I surrender," she got out through chuckles.

Benjamin shifted behind her, and the heat of his chest burned against her shoulder blades. His breath warmed her neck. "Stay," he whispered.

A shiver went down her spine. She closed her eyes, basking in the warmth of his arms. "I don't think I have much of a choice," she murmured.

He bent his head, and she felt the barest edge of his lips against the shell of her ear. "How the tables have turned, my captor."

A ribbon of heat and desire unspooled in her chest, slipping through her belly like a butterfly and throbbing inside her core. Hester bit her lips to keep back a moan of delight.

His hips slotted against the small of her back, he was so tall compared to her, and he broadened his stance.

Hester opened her eyes and turned her cheek to the cool door. His left hand was mere inches away. His long fingers were flexed against the wood, the large hands warm and capable. What would those hands feel like on her? She shuddered at the thought.

Abruptly, Benjamin withdrew. The blast of cold air that wrapped her back and arms nearly made her cry out. "Forgive me, I forgot myself. We aren't children anymore, are we?" His hands lifted from the door and he took two steps backward. "We should forsake childish games."

Hester bit back a sigh of regret. She took a breath, then another, before turning and forcing an unconcerned smile across her face.

"Well. You've beaten me. How are we spending the night together?" The words caught up to her a heartbeat too late. "I mean... spending the night in the cottage. Not together. It's just you and me. I mean, not you and me." Helpless, she dropped her face in her hand. "I'll stop talking now," she groaned.

Benjamin chuckled. "We're merely old friends."

"I am four and twenty, Benjamin. You are six and twenty. We may be old friends, but no one should know we spent the night together. I mean, not together. I mean—"

He frowned. "Yes, even though you and I understand there's nothing between us—we're too much brother and sister!—the rest of the neighborhood would not see it the same way. In the morning we'll need to get you back to your home immediately so no one pieces together our absence."

Unfortunately, he was correct. If people thought Hester had been ruined, or even slightly soiled, she'd not only give up her slim chance of a good marriage, but she'd be unwelcome at the women's knitting circle, she wouldn't be able to join the church flower rotation, and the few dinner invitations her father received would dwindle away to nothing. The draper's shop might refuse to sell to her or the house-keeper, as long as Mrs. Shaw kept her position with the Fairfaxes. And her father would ignore her even more than he already did.

Benjamin had continued speaking, but she only caught the last part. "But I will, of course, take the floor."

Hester skeptically looked at the hard flagstones. "The floor? You'll wake up with bruises. Even more bruises than you got from the chaise crash!"

He shrugged. "I'll survive."

Hester peered through the doorway to the old mattress. Bits of old chaff peeked out of the ripped seams of the flattened tick mattress. "There's not even any blankets. No, we'll both freeze if you sleep on the floor. I think we'll need to huddle for warmth." She set her chin and looked up, daring him to contradict her.

CHAPTER SIX

Benjamin stared down at her, speechless. His body wasn't speechless, though. His cock had heard "warmth," "bed," and "cuddle" and reacted. It was perking up despite the tight fit of his trousers, and he was absurdly grateful for the deep shadows of the room.

He licked his lips to give himself another heartbeat to think through a response. "Beg pardon?" he rasped.

Hester rolled her eyes. "We need to huddle for warmth. Back to back, and use my pelisse as a blanket."

Huddle, not cuddle. Right. Well, then. That *makes it all better*, he thought sarcastically. "Back to back," Benjamin repeated dumbly.

"Goodness, you look alarmed. Are you worried about Miss Dunham's opinion?"

That name was a splash of cold water across his inappropriate and inexplicable ardor. "Her? What? No." He snorted, attempting a nonchalance he still didn't feel. Truth be told, he hadn't even considered her thoughts and feelings about this. Shouldn't he? If she was to be his fiancé? God, that word still didn't feel real. No, his concern was that he was finding himself knee-deep in danger and desire, with the added potential of embarrassment if Hester realized he was sporting an erection for her, of all people.

His mind cast about for a new topic of conversation, but all he could see was the bed—the rather narrow bed. "It's going to be cold in that room," he said. "I'll move the mattress to the fire."

"Good idea. Do you need any help?"

"No." He hurried into the dark bedroom, eager to escape before she realized he was tenting his trousers. He grabbed one edge of the tick mattress and tugged, nearly ripping one of the side seams further. "No pillows," he called over his shoulder as he disentangled a quilted bedspread from beneath the crumpled mattress. "But there is one quilt."

"We'll sort it," Hester called back, sounding unconcerned.

Benjamin tossed the blanket through the door, rolled the mattress, and was gratified to realize that the brisk action had drawn his blood back to the rest of his body, where it belonged. Holding the mattress vertically, Benjamin walked back to the main room of the cottage. And stopped in his tracks. All air left his lungs.

Hester stood with her back to him, lit by the fire's glow. Her unbound hair rippled down her back, wavy and even frizzy from the storm. She'd taken her muddy dress off while he'd been busy with the mattress. It lay, neatly folded, beside his waistcoat on the hearth.

All she wore now was her stays, chemise, one petticoat, and stockings. She bent her head, revealing the slim nape of her neck, fiddling one-handed with something in front of her.

Benjamin could see the outline of her legs through the sheer muslin petticoat, could practically feel the way the muslin draped across her buttocks as she bent forward, and his body felt as if he'd been struck by lightning.

He must've made some strangled, tortured sound, for she suddenly whirled to face him.

"Oh!" Her face turned bright pink. Her hand stilled on the front lacing of her short stays, half undone. She looked beautiful, like a fairy plucked from a toadstool with her earthy sensuality. Her lips, strawberry bright, were plump and luscious. Benjamin imagined biting into them. His grip on the mattress tightened.

"I... I didn't think you'd be so fast." Her blush heightened, and her fingers twisted together at her waist. "Forgive me."

Benjamin grunted and forced every fantasy he had to the back of his mind. "Don't mind me." *She's your friend,* he told himself again and again. *She's an innocent, she doesn't understand what a temptation she is. Otherwise she'd run from the room screaming–she's an innocent, isolated lady.*

Hester bit her lower lip—that strawberry-sweet lip—and looked at him. "Do you need help with the mattress?" She didn't squeal and turn her back, damn it.

As if he wasn't sporting a cockstand already. His bollocks nearly jumped at those words, in that breathy, Hester-voice. He cleared his throat, forcing his gaze away from the nymph haloed in firelight. "No. You're wounded. I'll roll it out. Finish—" he waved one hand helplessly. "Whatever you're doing, just finish it."

She gave a little snort, one she'd given him a million times. It should've cooled his ardor. But this time it didn't. "Actually..." She took a deep breath, and Benjamin wondered what was on the tip of her tongue. "I'vetriedtounlacethisbutIthinkIneedhelpplease."

Benjamin blinked, certain he'd misunderstood. "What?"

Hester swallowed hard, one hand fidgeting at the loose lacing of her stays, and looked at the ground. "I need help," she mumbled. "My hand. I cannot do it with one hand." Even in the firelight, her cheeks were rosy red.

Benjamin blinked several times, his mind stuck, his mouth unable to form a sentence. His hands gripped the rolled mattress so tightly it began to hurt. "I... I...."

"I'm so terribly sorry," Hester blurted, beginning to look miserable. "I just hadn't expected to be injured, you see. You need not—never mind. I'll find a way to manage."

Benjamin steadied himself with a breath. "I am at fault for your injury," he said, trying to stay on solid ground. "I suppose it makes sense that I help you."

Hester bit her lip and nodded, finally meeting his gaze.

Benjamin realized that she was just as stiff and embarrassed as he. For goodness sake, he shouldn't be aroused by this, not when she merely needed help. "I won't ever tell anyone I've unlaced you," he promised softly, stepping forward. He once again tried to ignore the blood pumping south, the tingling across his skin, and the yearning in his chest ts the intimacy. He flashed her a reassuring smile. *Just friends,* it told her. *Nothing awkward about this.* If only he believed it. He set the mattress on the ground.

Hester stood stock still as Benjamin approached her. Her chemise lay between her stays and her skin, which should've helped create some sort of distance for Benjamin. Yet the neckline was low, skimming all the way down the tops of the stays, so he could see the flush spreading across the tops of her breasts.

Once he stood in front of her, just inches from her body, his cock couldn't help but react. Alarmed, he leaned closer so she wouldn't be able to look down and see what was happening in his trousers. Which only made her sweet scent clearer.

Benjamin held his breath.

Hester's breasts rose and fell as she continued to breathe.

She'd already untied the pretty bow at the top, just where her cleavage began, so he hooked his fingers through the lacing and tugged. He meant to do short, strong tugs—the way he imagined modistes or lady's maids jerked the lacing loose. But instead, he pulled slowly, watching the lacing unspool. The pressure brought Hester even closer to him.

Hester's breath hitched, and the tops of her breasts moved enticingly.

Benjamin froze, wondering if he'd hurt or alarmed her. He flicked his gaze from her bosom up to her face in question.

"Leave it loose, but not all the way unlaced," she whispered. "It'll make tomorrow easier."

He nodded, trying to look unaffected and calm even as his blood thrummed in his veins. He slid his fingers down to the next crossing and pulled gently, firmly, again. The lacing whispered against the cotton body as it slipped through the sewn eyelets. Hester was again pulled nearly flush against him. He could feel her eyes upon him but didn't dare look up in fear she would see the desire burning in his eyes.

Her breasts shifted beneath the chemise, no longer supported by the stays, dipping into a more natural shape. One shoulder tape slipped down, caressing the edge of her shoulder.

Benjamin moved to the next eyelet set, having to pull longer and longer as the lacing loosened. The stays gaped open at the top, revealing the thin chemise. If he strained, he could almost make out the inner edge of one nipple. Or maybe that was a shadow? No, definitely a nipp—what on earth was he doing? Attempting to peek now? He closed his eyes, mentally castigating himself. Hester would be furious and embarrassed if she learned the content of his thoughts.

He tugged the last two crossings loose with fierce precision and speed, determined to end this torment before he gave himself away by doing something foolish, like licking the tops of her breasts. "There," he said, barely holding back a sigh of relief.

"Thank you. I'll be able to tighten the laces by myself in the morning," Hester whispered and moved to pull the loosened garment up over her head. She winced at the movement.

Benjamin wordlessly took the stays from her injured hand and slipped it up for her. She lifted her arms and glided free. This was the most erotic undressing Benjamin had ever seen. He shifted his stance, hoping shadows would hide his arousal. When she was free, standing in only her chemise, he handed her the stays.

Hester folded them in half and set them on top of the rest of her clothes. "Thank you," she said again.

"Of course," he answered lightly. Benjamin ground his teeth in frustration and unrolled the mattress on the floor. He took infinite care in spreading it, then dusted it briskly with his hands. When he was done, he frowned at the worn quilt draped over the mattress, waiting for both of them.

Both of them.

"Finished?" he asked, gruffer than he meant.

"Just stoking the fire," she murmured, and Benjamin heard snaps and pops from behind him.

Then, before he could prepare himself, stockinged feet emerged from the corner of his vision, and she flounced around the edge of the mattress directly in front of him.

Benjamin barely bit back a groan in time.

Her chemise had slipped off one shoulder to reveal a distracting amount of collarbone and smooth expanse of pale skin, dotted with a few freckles.

God, did he love freckles.

Wait. Since when did he love freckles?

Hester, completely unaware of the crisis taking place just beside her, dropped onto the far side of the mattress and shimmied under the threadbare quilt. She hunched her shoulders and brought her knees up as if that could hide the fact she had breasts, and combed her fingers through her hair.

Benjamin's breath caught in his throat.

"It's a good thing we're friends," she remarked, beginning to plait her hair. "Imagine how awkward this would be otherwise." Her profile, with that gentle forehead and pert chin, looked positively wicked in the fire's glow.

Desire burned like a hot coal in his belly, and he was half mad from it already. He crouched still, wondering if he would break if he unbent his limbs.

Wincing at using both her hands, she finished the plait and wrapped the scrap of cloth around the tail, tying it tight. It draped over her shoulder, like a glossy coil of burnished bronze. Benjamin had an image of being lost in the loops of her hair, her captive again, bound by her hair and his desire.

Hester glanced at him, and though she was clearly trying to be modest by hunching and pulling at the quilt, it wasn't working. "Coming to bed?" Her voice came husky, yet innocent.

Benjamin nearly threw himself in the fire.

"Is something wrong?" She looked stricken, her sprained wrist curled against her bosom.

He almost leaned across the mattress to brush the alarm from her face. "No," he said curtly.

Her face cleared. "Worried about your parents?"

No. "Yes."

"You're a good man, Benjamin Littleton. Your father just refuses to see it."

The words cracked him open, and for a moment, sexual desire disappeared to be replaced with an ache soul-deep. He couldn't look at her face. "I never please him."

"And that's his fault," she said firmly. "Benjamin, you have spent your entire life doing whatever he says, all in the family name, and I'm afraid you will cut out your very soul, piece by piece, as an offering to his definition of familial duty, no matter how much it pains you."

A lump formed in his throat, and his vision of the floorboards went blurry. "Gods, Hester." He forced a laugh. "Warn a man before you say things like that."

Suddenly her fingertips touched his chin. "Benjamin," she whispered, offering the barest nudge.

He obeyed, of course, blinking back unshed moisture to look her in the face.

"You are twice the man your father ever was. You are kind, dutiful, honest, caring. His standards are inhuman, and even if you did meet his every standard—if you married Miss Dunham tomorrow, passed the Bar with flying colors, got the best office in the Old Bailey, he would still be unhappy with you. Because that's who he is. It has no reflection upon your character."

He closed his eyes, her fingertips burning into his skin. "I don't know what to say to that."

"Come lie down, your body must be aching after the crash we had." The fingers disappeared as quickly as they'd come.

Benjamin almost grabbed her hand. Instead, he crawled into the flattened mattress and forced himself to roll to his side, facing the fire. It was lumpy. His back pressed against hers. He wore his stockings, trousers, small clothes, and untucked shirt. And by God, he resented every stitch of fabric between them.

Her heat warmed his back, and he imagined he could feel the curve of her spine with just her chemise and his shirt between them.

He gritted his teeth.

The pink shawl, creased and wrinkled on the hearth, lay like an accusation against him.

"It's not so bad," Hester bravely said, even as he felt her curling into a ball, drawing her knees up to her chest on her side.

Benjamin thought he might ignite and set the mattress afire.

"I saw one of my cousins three months ago in London," he blurted suddenly.

"Yes?" Hester didn't seem to mind the sudden change of subject.

He didn't know what he was talking about, not really. He didn't care either. It was just something to keep his mind off the beautiful woman in his bed. "On my mother's side, the ones engaged in trade." *The ones my father refuses to see, even during holidays.*

"Did I ever meet them?" Hester sounded drowsy.

He stared into the flames, the smell of old chaff and straw filling the air. "Perhaps? They did visit one summer, ages ago."

"And how are they?" Hester prompted.

"Peter's quite well. Making a fortune, apparently, in Portugal. In the wine business."

Hester yawned. "How lovely for him."

"His father trades port." Good enough wine for his father to fill their cellars with, but the family wasn't good enough for a baronet to deign to stay in touch on friendly, equal terms. "He's joined the family business. Lives most of the year outside Lisbon. He married a vintner's daughter and he's practically fluent in Portuguese now."

"Mmmm." Hester sounded near sleep. "What a romantic language. I wish I spoke something besides drawing room French. Fat lot of good it does me now, thanks to Boney. But is it safe? I thought Napoleon had invaded again."

"Last year, yes. But the French only had control of Porto for six weeks. Now they're pushed back to Spain. And Lisbon is much further south of there." Benjamin closed his eyes, wishing sleep would come. "He seemed happy. He said I could visit anytime."

"Sounds perfect for a—" she broke off with a yawn— "honeymoon."

A tendril of despair curled around Benjamin's heart. "Yes, it does." He didn't fall asleep for a very, very long time.

CHAPTER SEVEN

Hester sighed in her sleep, then rolled away from the hollowed spot of the mattress where the chaff had left and the tick was bare against the stone floor. Her leg curled around something hard and solid.

Blearily, she blinked her eyes. In the near-darkness, she could just make out a large shape sprawled beside her.

Benjamin.

Her heart fluttered at the realization they were sharing a bed. Cold air slipped in where the ratty quilt had fallen from her shoulders. Shivering, she huddled close to Benjamin for warmth.

He sighed in his sleep, readjusting to her movement. Then his hand fell on her bare shoulder, where not only the quilt had exposed her but also her own chemise. His fingertips traced the slope of her shoulder.

Her breath caught in her throat. She wasn't even sure her heart was beating. Hester didn't dare blink, in case any movement scared him away.

His fingers drifted, first up her neck, then back down to feel her collarbone. Benjamin's wrist accidentally brushed the top of her breast, and she gasped at the exquisite feeling. Instead of frightening him off, the sound emboldened his touch, and his hand slipped beneath the pelisse she was using as a blanket and cupped her breast.

Hester moaned again and curled her legs, bending one over his knee. "Benji," she whispered. "Oh, Benji."

His breathing came harsh and unsteady in the darkness, and his grip tightened on her breast, his thumb searching for her nipple through the fabric. "Hester," he whispered, bringing his mouth to her ear. Just like before, his lips caressed the shell of her ear. "Hester, it's always been you. Just you, my darling."

Hester arched, turning to her side to face him, and gasped in delight as her core began to throb with desire. "Benjamin, please." She broke off, not sure how bold she could be. Not sure if too much fervor would alarm him. But he seemed to understand her plea, for his other arm wrapped around her hips, under the pink pelisse, and tugged her closer until they were flush against one another. His breath heated her cheek, and she couldn't help but smile as she burrowed closer, trying to expose more of her breast to his touch. "Benjamin, you feel so..."

"Hester," he whispered.

Hester purred in response.

"Hester."

The darkness faded around her, leaving Hester dazed and uncertain. "Benji?"

"Hester, wake up."

The delicious heat of his hands and breath faded. A brusque jolt to her shoulder woke her. Her wrist shrieked in response. Hester blinked, and the gray light of dawn filled the room, "Wha—what?" A blurry white shape sat beside her.

"You were talking in your sleep," Benjamin rumbled above her, sounding so different from the passionate, seductive man of her dreams.

Hester froze as everything returned in a blurred, horrifying rush. *Oh, God. Oh dear blessed God.* It had been a dream. Nothing but a dream. And she had been talking aloud. Her face flamed with embarrassment and she cleared her throat to give her an extra second of reprieve. It ended all too soon. Her mouth was dry, but she forced herself half-up, pushing onto her elbows. The pain in her wrist grounded her.

Benjamin sat in his rumpled shirtsleeves and trousers, hair tousled, on the very edge of the mattress. An odd expression lay across his features, something Hester was too mortified to look closer at.

"What, um, what was I saying?" She forced the words past her dry, trembling lips.

He rubbed a hand against the stubble growing on his jaw. "Oh, nothing. I'm not sure, I couldn't make out the words." He stood and turned to the dying fire and used a poker to push some life back into it.

Hester breathed a sigh of relief. *Thank goodness, he hadn't heard.* Because she remembered every detail, every caress, every breath of the dream. The spot between her legs still felt slippery as she sat upright. She stole a glance at Benjamin's back, flushing in a mixture of embarrassment and lingering desire. She couldn't deny it anymore, she wanted him. As both a friend and... well, whatever else that was. She bit her lower lip, refusing to think the word *lover*.

"We should be getting back," Benjamin cut into her thoughts. "The rain stopped."

"Oh. Yes." Hester glanced at his thighs, the fabric taut against his buttocks and legs while he bent over the fireplace. Her fingers itched to slide up his leg. *Oh, no.* Maybe her dream would fade and everything would go back to normal. She clenched her fists under the pelisse. *No, definitely not.* She shook her head to clear her thoughts, and her hair tangled around her shoulders. Not alluring at all. She probably looked like Medusa. "I should dress," she whispered.

"Right." Benjamin stood and looked down at her. He gripped his untucked shirt and spun suddenly. "I'll step outside to let you dress. And see how the weather looks."

Hester blinked in surprise as he nearly fled from the cottage. *Perhaps he misses Miss Dunham,* she thought sourly as she reached for her stays. *I'll need to let him go, even if I just realized what we might've explored.* Her lips twisted. *Goodness, I sound like a character from one of Mrs. Radcliffe's novels. Just because I think we could be wonderful together doesn't mean he agrees.* With that melancholy thought, she began lacing up her stays as best she could one-handed.

Benjamin, control fraying, carefully closed the front door. As soon as he was assured it was shut and Hester could no longer hear or see him, he stumbled to the nearest tree, heedless of the puddles he splashed through along the way. With a desperate, choking sigh he grabbed the trunk with one hand and ripped open the placket of his trousers with the other.

Wet bark pressed against one hand as his other shoved his shirt out of the way and gripped his erection. Benjamin groaned, shutting his eyes, as the heat of his hand stoked his ardor. Water dripped around him, the forest still wet and quiet from the night's storm, but all he could hear or see was Hester in bed beside him.

Hester, with tangled curls burnished bronze from the dying firelight. Hester, with those plump lips open in a soft, sensual moan. Hester, with that flush creeping above the loose neck of her chemise, all fluttering eyelashes and breathy whispers.

Fuck, why did I have to see that? His hand jerked across his shaft so harshly it nearly hurt, and yet he embraced the bite. Even if he was seeking self-pleasure, there should be some punishment for it. Something as penance for thinking these lustful, overwhelming thoughts about his childhood friend.

He had woken to Hester's breathy moans in his ear and realized quickly what sort of dream she was having by the way her legs twisted and her nearly inaudible whispers. Desire had shot through his body just as surely as if Cupid had stood over him with his bow, and suddenly Benjamin's usual morning cockstand was thicker and harder than he'd ever been. He'd nearly rolled atop Hester and sought out her heat for relief. Shame trickled through him, not quite enough to block out the thrumming desire, when he realized he had been about to rut against her like an animal. Not Hester. Even if she was having an amorous dream.

But then she'd whispered his name, and he'd nearly spent himself right there in the lumpy mattress and scratchy quilt. That's when a sliver of sense had cut through the haze of lust and he realized what he'd almost done. Benjamin had jerked upright and then shoved her shoulder to wake her, wanting the temptation to end however possible.

His erect penis, however, didn't care. It stood as hard and ready as ever, even when Hester woke and he had to turn away before she saw the bulge in his trousers. Desperately, he'd untucked his shirt to hide his straining placket and bolted from the room as fast as he could.

Benjamin imagined it was Hester's breath against the nape of his neck instead of the morning chill, Hester's tongue in his ear instead of a dewdrop. He gasped, feeling his bollocks tighten and draw up. What would her lips taste like? What would her nipples taste like? Visions of Hester, naked in a proper bed, hair tangled around her like a pagan goddess, filled his mind. He needed her. He needed her under him, above him, around him, any way he could have her.

His orgasm rocked through him, and he shot all over his hand and the tree roots at his feet. He should be ashamed. He should get her back to her home and never think a wanton thought about her again.

But all he wanted to do was return to the cottage and take her to bed again and again all day long. Forget responsibilities. Forget the Bar and London and the Dunhams.

Yet kissing her would be crossing the Rubicon: no turning back to the easy friendship of childhood.

Benjamin groaned as he wiped his hand on the cuffs of his trousers. *Being abducted by her will be the death of me.* Because now he knew what he'd be missing when he returned to his father and those expectations that made it hard for him to breathe. He'd never have these passions for Miss Dunham. He couldn't imagine Miss Dunham ever abducting him and then laughing when their chaise broke. Or sharing strawberry preserves. If he was someone else, with a different father, a different family, a different occupation, perhaps he could have Hester Fairfax. And now he knew how much it was going to hurt to walk away from the possibilities.

His mind flew to his cousin, the one who seemed so happy as a tradesman married to a Portuguese vintner's daughter. If only he could have a life like that.

Benjamin buttoned himself back up, squared his shoulders, and walked back to the cottage. *I can do this.*

Once inside, he saw that Hester was fully dressed in her dirty clothing. He silently passed her and picked up his waistcoat and jacket. "How's your wrist this morning?" Benjamin asked gruffly.

Hester glanced down at her wrist, which she had rebound in his cravat. "Not as swollen. Still tender, though."

"I'll escort you to the village tavern," Benjamin offered, swiping the disliked shawl off the hearth and tucking it back between his waistcoat and shirt. "We'll find a cart to take you all the way back to your home, and then I'll make my way to the Hall."

Hester nodded, her brow furrowed. "Yes, I suppose that's best."

Stifling a sigh, Benjamin opened the front door for her and left the cottage without a backward look. It would hurt all too much.

INTERLUDE

1807

Hester stifled a yawn behind her punch cup. She had dragged her father all the way here to the assembly hall, so she was going to enjoy herself.

She smiled and nodded to the vicar and his wife, just like she did at each assembly dance every three months. Then she scanned the room and saw all the usual people from the village—the blacksmith's son tuning his violin in the corner, the doctor's wife displaying her newest bonnet to the local landowners' wives. It was all the same as it usually was, right down to the tepid lemonade and the biscuits the Littletons always provided.

Even her dress was the same as the last three times, a faded yellow muslin that her father had promised to replace half a dozen times already.

But no. She was happy to be here. She'd cajoled and pleaded with her father to leave his study for one evening to escort her to the quarterly assembly dance. She'd been counting the days to the event for a week now. It was the highlight of the month, with her chance to host the women's knitting charity circle just after it. Even if she was a half-hearted member and could barely knit a scarf. It was just so nice to remember the outside world existed, beyond the confines of her father's property.

At two minutes past the stroke of nine o'clock, the dancing would begin. It was always meant to be nine on the dot, but the second violinist was always late.

Hester sneaked a glance at her father, who was falling asleep in a chair near a drooping potted fern. His spectacles slid down his nose with every snore. She bit back a smile. He was a devoted financialist, even rarely speaking to her during their evening meals, preferring to read the papers at the table. Nothing excited him more than a new speculation scheme, and their fortune rose and fell depending on the stability of these investments.

Just as the musicians straightened in their seats, a door opened. Normally no one would take notice of it, save for the hushed whispers that followed the brisk autumn air.

Hester craned her neck just like everyone else to see who it was.

A tall, thin man entered the room as if he owned it—because he did. Sir Stanley Littleton's shoes clicked against the floor until he paused at the edge of the dance floor and looked around, stern face unsmiling as usual. Beside him stood his wife, a lovely brunette in a peach gown of silk and lace. She fluttered her fan and smiled graciously at all in attendance. But what had surprised everyone were the figures following behind the baronet and his wife—all three sons.

Hester's heart skipped a beat.

Reginald Littleton trailed after his father, identical in every way save age. On his arm leaned his new wife, a pale slip of a girl with vacuous blue eyes. *Beautiful,* Hester silently corrected herself. *Beautiful eyes. It's unkind to think of them as vacuous.*

William Littleton, the shortest of the brothers, walked by himself in the most blindingly orange waistcoat Hester had ever seen, grinning at all the young ladies like he was God's gift to them.

And then, the very last, came the tall, slender figure of the youngest Littleton: Benjamin.

Hester gripped her cup, wondering if she should run up to him and say hello or pretend they were just any other young lady and gentleman at the village dance. Heavens, it'd been, what, three years since she'd seen him? When he'd come home for a fortnight after graduating from Cambridge. They'd lost touch over the years. Children could exchange letters and plan audacious dreams together. But men and women had no such freedom. *He's got more important things to do in London,* Hester thought with great envy.

The surprise in the crowd came not from a Littleton joining the event, for usually Sir Stanley and his wife or Reginald and his wife would attend. The surprise was that all of them were here, together. It hadn't happened in some time.

Hester held her breath, willing Benjamin to glance over at her, to smile in recognition, to do anything. But his gaze was polite, bland, and trained on some vague middle distance before him.

The musicians started up a country jig, and Hester lost sight of him in the swirl of gowns and laughter.

Mr. Truett, one of her father's neighbors, stepped into Hester's line of vision with a smile. The candlelight gleamed on his balding head. "Would you dance with me?" he inquired.

Hester had never been more relieved to dance with the older man. "Yes," she said with a smile and set her cup down on a nearby table. She spent the next three sets of dances with mostly older gentlemen her father knew. Mr. Truett, a recent widower, seemed to worry over her a bit, asking questions during his second dance with her about how often she and her father socialized and traveled. "My late wife loved visiting Brighton in the summer," he said. "Perhaps we can all arrange a trip sometime."

"Oh!" Hester exclaimed, nearly missing a step of the dance with a rush of excitement. "I've never been to Brighton." She turned, then came back to the man. "But you know how Father is." The elation that had fizzed in her veins now bubbled out. "He prefers the comfort of his home."

Mr. Truett frowned. "A woman your age should be out and about," he began. "Do you have old school friends from finishing school?" But then the dance ended, thank goodness, and he led her back to her corner of the room. Hester breathed a sigh of relief. He was a nice man, but she was determined to be happy tonight. She didn't need reminders of how she'd done nothing, not even finishing school, in her twenty-one years.

Six months ago one of her father's female cousins had invited Hester to spend several weeks in Bath with her. Hester had almost perished with delight at the thought, but her father had decided it was unnecessary and a wasted expense. It was one of the few times she had argued with her father, forcing him to interact with her as a person with her own hopes and desires. But one of his speculations had failed—some gold mine in Argentina—and he hadn't had the money to outfit her for Bath. Hester hadn't bothered asking again, knowing that he'd likely be annoyed and would dismiss her request because of it.

"Pardon, Miss Fairfax, but do you have any room on your dance card left for me?"

Hester whirled to see Benjamin before her, one palm up. "Yes!" She smiled. "I haven't seen you in ages. I'd hoped you would ask me."

His polite smile faltered a little as if he was taken aback by her words. Hester inwardly winced. *Was that too much? But we've known each other forever. We used to be friends. I don't have to pretend to be a Society miss at a London ball, do I?* As she set her gloved hand in his, she resolved to be calm, mature, and not presume upon their old friendship.

They made small talk as they could through the line dance. He inquired after the health of her father. She asked about his life in London. They reminisced over the village church's annual summer picnic, and they agreed that if there was ever an opportunity, they should have tea together.

Benjamin escorted her back to where her father was nodding off.

"It *is* good to see you, Hester." He gave a bashful smile, then hesitated, as if he was parsing through his words.

Hester waited patiently. *He looks busy, but he doesn't look happy.*

"There you are." Sir Stanley burst between them suddenly, voice gruff. He narrowed his eyes at his son. "Benjamin, go dance with your sister." He jerked a thumb over his shoulder at Reginald's wife.

Benjamin's eyes hardened. "Father, I am perfectly capable of choosing my own dance partners."

"The family must be seen dancing together," the baronet insisted, thick brows burrowing further.

Benjamin sighed and glanced away, a muscle ticking in his jaw. "Yes, Father. I'll just return Miss Fairfax to her seat." He strode the last three steps, dismissing his father.

Hester blinked, tugged along in his wake, her hand still in his.

The exchange must've been loud enough to wake her father, for he now blinked at them owlishly, stretching in his chair.

"Father," Hester greeted. "Do you remember Benjamin?"

He looked at Benjamin, then Hester. "Have I met him before?"

Irritation surged through Hester, but she tamped it down. "Benjamin Littleton, Father. Sir Stanley's son. We played together as children. Do you not remember?"

Benjamin released Hester's hand with a little squeeze and bowed. "Pleased to see you again, Mr. Fairfax. I hope you are well."

Her father squinted through his spectacles, then nodded. "I remember Hester getting into all sorts of trouble, such a wayward chit."

Hester pursed her lips. She'd mostly played outside, away from her father and his demands for solitude. She'd gotten into many scrapes as a child, but he'd never noticed most of them.

Benjamin flashed a quick smile at Hester. "I was there with her, urging her onward most of the time."

A sense of camaraderie built between them, and suddenly that friendship didn't feel so old and distant as it had only moments before.

Hester returned the smile. "I imagine you're getting into all sorts of trouble now in London without me."

A shadow crossed over his face, but he nodded. "Sir," he addressed Mr. Fairfax. "A pleasure to see you." He bowed to Hester with an apologetic glance. "Your servant, madam." And he walked away to ask his sister-in-law to dance.

Her father heaved a sigh and stood. "I've had enough. Let's go home."

"But it's not even midnight," Hester protested.

He frowned at her. "I tolerate your whims often enough. We came, you danced, and now it's time to depart. Come, Hester. I'm a busy man and I have to write my broker. The Scottish whiskey investment is reaping a tidy profit and I want to increase my shares."

"At eleven at night?" Hester whispered angrily, though she followed her father to the cloakroom. This was the most stable and long-lasting investment he'd made in years—it paid for all household expenses, so she couldn't argue with him. Before retrieving her pelisse, she glanced back at the flickering candles, laughing guests, and swirling dresses. It was all exactly the same as she saw every three months, probably provincial and quaint to Benjamin's worldly standards now, but she clung to it like floating timber in an ocean.

I'll do something by next year, she promised herself. Perhaps convince her father to travel to Brighton with Mr. Truett. Maybe she could find a husband there—or a rich woman in need of a companion. Perchance she could convince her father to travel to Oxford or London for a famous lecturer. She had options. She wasn't going to molder in Surrey for the rest of her life, no, she'd see some of the world. Or at least some of England, like Benjamin.

But Benjamin hadn't looked that well to her. Possibly he needed help, too. Hester chewed on her lower lip as her father waved down a footman to bring their chaise and horse around. First, she'd get out of the village. Then, if she crossed paths with Benjamin again, she'd find a way to help him.

CHAPTER EIGHT

Hester didn't know what to say as they walked back through the edge of the woods, through the fields, and along the muddy lane. Benjamin had gone silent, withdrawing into himself with each step closer to the village. She worried her bottom lip, wondering what she could say to bring back the simple joy of yesterday.

"I'm glad I kept my promise," she blurted.

Benjamin glanced down at her with a distracted smile. "You certainly surprised me. I'd completely forgotten I'd asked you to do that."

Hester smiled a little as she watched more dried mud flake off her pelisse. The housekeeper was going to despise her after this escapade. "I'm just glad I had the opportunity to follow through! You haven't been home in a few years." *Just in time to realize I'm falling for my dearest friend, right before he marries someone else.* Her stomach churned at the thought. *Hester, you've had no hopes for marriage for a while now. One abduction in less than twenty-four hours shouldn't change that. You're not truly smitten with him. It was just that wonderful dream.*

After a few more moments of silence, it was Benjamin who broke it next. "How's your wrist?"

Truthfully, it still pained her. But as long as Hester stepped carefully and didn't jar her arm, she could ignore the twinges. "Fine," she only half-way lied.

After another mile, they reached the outskirts of the village. Hester glanced around nervously, wondering if she should skulk in the shadows to avoid detection. If anyone caught her, dressed in mud, alone with Benjamin Littleton, also dressed in mud, at just past daybreak... well, her reputation would be ruined despite the great efforts they were going through right now. Thankfully, it appeared most people were still indoors on this gray, overcast morning, still drowsy from the rain during the night. She sneaked a peek up at Benjamin, wondering what was going through his mind. He stared stonily ahead as if heading toward a funeral rather than the public house.

They passed the baker's wife cleaning her front window. Hester pulled her bonnet's brim forward and looked at her feet, holding her breath until they passed her by.

"She didn't see us," Benjamin murmured.

Hester breathed a sigh of relief. When she was a child she never would've cared about such proprieties. In fact, she sought out notoriety to a small extent, as a way to get her father's attention. His nose was always buried in a book or the latest pamphlets from his exchange association. He'd never been an involved father, and since Hester's mother had passed away when she was only five, that left her upbringing to her governess and the housekeeper. Her governess had left when she was fifteen to care for an ill family member, and her father had forgotten to hire a new one. So Hester had run wild, though she hadn't gotten into nearly as much trouble if Benjamin had still been nearby.

Once she realized she was losing her chance of marriage—the best way to get out of the village and see at least *some* of the world—she'd tried to appear proper and demure, a good Englishwoman. But it was useless. Her father's self-imposed isolation meant she rarely met young men. Her own quiet desperation and despair recognized Benjamin's, even if they came from different fates.

Benjamin paused at the door of the house. "They have a back door, don't they?"

Hester nodded. "To reach the stables."

"Why don't you go wait around back, and I'll let you in? That way no one will see us together. You can hide in the private dining room until I arrange for a ride back to your home for you."

Hester wrinkled her nose, not wanting to make the trek around the public house through puddles, but knew it was a good idea. "Very well." She gathered her filthy pelisse around herself and made for the back entrance.

A moment later, when she rounded the last corner, the door was already cracked with Benjamin's head sticking out looking for her. His perpetual frown lessened a fraction when he saw her. "Come in, thank goodness," he muttered.

Hester scurried inside, bringing a puddle of water with her in her slippers. "Did you talk to Mr. Lyon about letting us have the private dining room?"

Benjamin put his hand at the small of her back, ushering her deeper into the public house. The scent of woodsmoke, steaming food, and the rumble of male voices over clinking mugs filled the air. She shivered as heat from the kitchen hit her damp clothing, wishing she could just hide in there by the fire.

"Here we are." Benjamin opened a red-painted door and escorted her in. "I asked Mrs. Lyon to bring you breakfast." The room was small, with just enough space for a table with a few chairs surrounding it. Two faded watercolor paintings hung on the plaster walls.

Hester peeled her pelisse off and sat in the nearest chair. She glanced up at Benjamin. "You don't have to find a cart for me right away."

He stiffened, but she caught the yearning in his eyes. "I really should—"

"Are you not hungry?" She forced a smile, even as her heart ached with the knowledge that this was ending.

He hesitated, then abruptly pulled out the chair opposite her and sat. "I suppose a few moments won't hurt." His bare hand beat an anxious rhythm on the wooden tabletop.

Hester gritted her teeth, not wanting any reminder of his decision to move forward with a life she'd never be a part of. After another moment, she finally laid her bare hand atop his. "Hush," she said gently.

Benjamin froze, hand immediately ceasing. The heat of his hand warmed her palm, and she realized she loved the feel of it, how large and capable it felt beneath hers. But she shouldn't be touching him. Even though they'd spent the night side-by-side, now they were back in reality. Propriety. Biting her lip, she forced herself to shift her hand away from his.

But.

But then.

He caught her hand, twining his fingers through hers in the space of a heartbeat.

Hester's breath caught in her throat, and she could've sworn her heart skipped a beat. Warmth spread across her face, and for a moment she didn't know if she could look away from his hand wrapped around hers. She longed to stroke his fingers, to feel the gentle calluses that came from writing briefs, jotting notes, and preparing arguments. Hester looked up through her eyelashes.

Benjamin sat still, that pensive frown still on his face, staring at their entwined hands. *What is he thinking? Why does he look so miserable?* Hester knew he wasn't excited about his choice of occupation— or his bride, she guessed—but was he truly this unhappy about his father's plans?

"You don't have to follow through," she said quietly.

His eyes flew to hers, that penetrating stare seeking answers. "What do you mean?" he rasped.

The door opened, and a pleasantly plump woman with black curls cascading free of her cap entered, heavily laden tray in hand. She froze in the doorway, staring at Benjamin and Hester.

Flushing, Hester jerked her hand free of Benjamin and clenched her hand into a fist under the table. Her other hand spasmed helplessly in the sling.

"Oh. Oh my goodness." Mrs. Lyon's sharp brown eyes took in the disheveled state of affairs. "You're here. Both of you."

Apprehension prickled along Hester's spine. "What do you mean?"

Mrs. Lyon, the owner's wife, set the wooden tray on the table. The smell of pork, hashed potatoes, and sausage wafted through the air. Hester's stomach rumbled in response.

"I didn't realize when you asked for breakfast that you meant... this." She eyed Benjamin. "Do you realize that your family's servants have spent most of the night looking for you when the storm cleared? They were here near midnight, asking if I'd seen you."

The tips of Benjamin's ears pinked. "We met with some trouble and the storm slowed us down. But we are returning to civilization now. I must beg your discretion, madam. I have no desire to ruin Miss Fairfax's reputation. I only want to send her home safely, as soon as a cart can be arranged."

Mrs. Lyon blinked and turned to Hester. She didn't say anything, but her eyes looked Hester over, a question in them. *Are you well?* It was a question kind women silently asked one another in strange circumstances. *Are you safe? Do you need help?*

Touched by her concern, for Hester and Mrs. Lyon had only had one or two conversations at church in the past, Hester smiled and gave a tiny nod. *Yes, I am well.*

"Well." Mrs. Lyon pursed her lips, frowning at both of them as if they were naughty schoolchildren. Even if she was only a handful of years older than them. "I don't like this. Mr. Littleton, your family's been worried sick over your disappearance!"

"I plan to assure them of my well-being as soon as I see to Miss

Fairfax's safety," he said stiffly. "None of this was intentional, and I deeply regret you being pulled into any of this."

Hester quietly spooned herself a generous portion of sausages, listening to the exchange.

"I'll go see about the cart getting hitched. But best hurry, the mail coach will be passing through in half an hour, and the whole place will be crowded with people. If you want to escape attention, best be gone by then."

Hester's stomach churned at the thought of parting ways from Benjamin forever. She'd go home to a scolding from the housekeeper and a faint nod from her father—they probably hadn't even noticed she was missing yet.

Benjamin took a breath and nodded. "Thank you for your help."

She rolled her eyes affectionately and left, leaving the door cracked.

CHAPTER NINE

Benjamin rubbed his eyes with the heel of his hands, then set about eating breakfast. Even if he wasn't hungry in the slightest. He could feel Hester's eyes on him as he jerkily served himself a ridiculous portion of cold pork, something he wouldn't finish even if he was hungry.

"Are... are you well?" Hester asked.

No, no I'm not. Benjamin ground his teeth, grabbing a fork and shoveling some cold pork into his mouth. *I knew I wasn't happy with the Law or the Dunhams or even a whole, permanent life in London. I knew I was giving up a vague, unknown chance at future happiness. But now I know exactly what I'm losing.* He purposefully hadn't thought much about marriage—either in general or between himself and Miss Dunham specifically. But last night was everything he wanted. Everything he'd purposefully forgotten he wanted. Camaraderie. Laughter. Partnership in hardship. Joy. Companionship. Passion. "Merely thinking," he got out between chewing.

"About?" Hester dragged out the word.

Sodding hell, why can't I just run away with Hester? Leave my family, leave the Law, leave the Dunhams. Just escape on another adventure with her. The thought struck him like a blow. He opened his mouth, still hunting for an answer, when the door out in the main dining area slammed.

"Tobias, don't be slamming my doors!" Mrs. Lyon's voice drifted through the cracked door of the private dining room. "You'll fix my door yourself if you damage it."

The few men in the room grumbled at her words. "Bossy now her husband's off fighting the French," someone muttered. "Thinks she owns the place."

"I certainly run it by myself," Mrs. Lyon responded tartly. "And if you have a problem, you can find another tavern."

Benjamin and Hester both stilled, listening to the noises just outside their door. After a second, Hester broke the silence with a whisper.

"Benji, have you talked to your father about how miserable his plans make you? Couldn't you come up with a different plan together?"

A loud, grumbling voice caught Benjamin's attention. He waved a hand at Hester to shush her, turning his chair closer to the door.

"...It appears Miss Hester Fairfax is missing too," the man finished, annoyed and amused all at once.

"Who?"

"What?"

"Since when?" the voices muddled together, causing the whole tavern to rumble.

Benjamin stood silently and went to the door, eyes fixed on Hester.

Hester paled, her eyes wide, as she put a hand to her open mouth. "I didn't think they'd notice my absence. They never do," she whispered, mostly to herself.

A pang went through Benjamin, and he wished to gather her up in his arms and tell her that her presence mattered, that she deserved a life full of people who would look for her if she went missing, that he'd happily look for her everywhere he went.

"Old Mr. Fairfax's daughter? The hermit?" One older, wavering voice rose above the noise. "I'd forgotten he has a daughter."

Benjamin stared at Hester, their eyes locked together as the horror of the situation slowly washed over them.

"How odd, two people going missing at the same time from our wee village," a reedy, adolescent voice piped up.

A few men guffawed. "Odd's got nothing to do with it," one said.

"How do we know Miss Fairfax is missing, hmm?" Mrs. Lyon's sharp voice cut through the laughter. "Are you making up one of your stories again, Tobias?"

"Am not!" Affront laced his words. "I just came from Woodlea."

"And why would you go there? Paying a social call, were you?" Mrs. Lyon sounded like she was barely holding back laughter.

"Seeing as how Sir Stanley is still looking for his son, I thought I'd drop by. My wife recalls the Fairfax girl and Sir Stanley's son were thick as thieves as children. If he'd run off, I thought maybe she might've known something."

Hester worried her bottom lip, and Benjamin felt a ridiculous urge to soothe it with his thumb. His heart beat a mile a minute, and still, he couldn't look away from her.

"So I finally convinced the housekeeper to talk to me. You know Tilly Shaw? Yes, her. So Tilly listens to me, goes upstairs to check on Miss Fairfax, and lo and behold, the chit isn't there. At all."

Hester swallowed hard, and Benjamin almost left his post as the door to grip her hand.

"Sounds like Sir Stanley is looking in the wrong place for his son," one of the men said with a laugh. "He should be getting his carriage and hieing up to Gretna Green."

The room roared with laughter.

Benjamin's face heated, and Hester dropped her gaze to her lap, her hand wringing her skirts.

"Isn't he supposed to be marrying some Londoner's daughter, though? That's what their kitchen maid told me a few days ago."

"*Gretna Green,*" the first man said with emphasis borne of confidence and two mugs of ale. "Probably halfway there by now. Surely past London."

Knowing laughter filled the tavern again. "She's a pretty thing, so I wouldn't put it past him."

Hester still wouldn't look at him. Benjamin didn't know what to make of that.

"Tobias Cooper!" Mrs. Lyon's voice cracked like a whip. "And just where do you think you're going?"

Footsteps shuffled against the bare wooden floor, much closer than they were a moment ago. "Sir Stanley said the search is going to begin again in the morning, starting here. Just want to settle myself before they arrive."

"In my private dining room?" Mrs. Lyon barked.

Hester's eyes flew to Benjamin's. They couldn't be caught like this —bedraggled, alone, in early morning hours. His cravat wrapped around her neck and arm. Especially now that the whole village seemed to know they'd both been missing all night long.

"We have to get out of here," Hester breathed.

Benjamin agreed, but he pointed to the cracked door. "They're right outside," he mouthed.

"You can sit by the fire like every other customer of mine," Mrs. Lyon said. "I don't want your muddy boots in my one nice room."

"Aw, come on, Franny." Tobias stomped a little closer to the cracked door.

Benjamin held his breath and peered through the crack. He could just make out the burly, middle-aged man in a patched greatcoat and cap.

"That's Mrs. Lyon to you." Beyond the brown figure blocking the short hall, Mrs. Lyon's white mobcap bobbed, and her hands landed on her hips. "You will not be entering my private room until Sir Stanley arrives. Go sit at the tables like everyone else."

Tobias harrumphed but shuffled back toward the main room.

"I certainly hope you're not expecting a reward," Mrs. Lyon continued. "You know Sir Stanley won't part with a shilling any more than he'd part with a guinea."

Tobias grumbled something under his breath.

Benjamin pulled the door open just a hair more. Mrs. Lyon stood in the hall, worry etched across her face. She looked at Benjamin and made a shooing gesture, mouthing, "Go to the stables now!"

Benjamin glanced back at Hester. "Stables now, she says."

Hester bolted from her chair, nearly sending it toppling backward. She grabbed the back just in time, wincing as she silently set it back in place.

Benjamin held out his hand. She took it. Then he pushed the door open and they half ran, half tiptoed to the back door and out into the muddy yard.

Hester tumbled behind him, gasping with surprise or laughter, he wasn't sure which, and the sound lightened his heart. He gripped her hand tighter, pulling her closer, and they sidestepped puddles together as they raced for the stables.

The sun shone through the cloud cover, making dewdrops and rainwater on fence posts and roof eaves sparkle like prisms. The air felt thick with opportunity and rain, and the faint patches of green beyond the yard seemed brighter for the rain. A few daffodils, late for the season, sprang up like a cheerful song against the edge of the stables. For half a heartbeat, Benjamin considered plucking one for Hester. Spring was coming at last.

The yard was small, and they crossed the threshold to the stables in less than a moment. Hester's pelisse fluttered pink and brown behind them, and she burst into laughter the second they entered the stables.

"How utterly ridiculous!" she gasped, eyes sparkling and her cheeks flushed. "I cannot believe this is happening." One wet, tangled curl fell across her forehead.

Benjamin looked at her and wondered for the first time if her sunny disposition was ever her way of coping with loneliness. But he didn't ask her now. Instead, his fingers itched to brush the curl away from her face. He leaned closer to her, aware that she hadn't dropped his hand yet.

Someone cleared their throat, and the spell broke. Benjamin rocked backward and glanced around.

A boy, fifteen or sixteen, stood at the entrance to one of the three stalls. Hay dusted his blond hair, and he glanced between Benjamin and Hester. "You're the one needing the cart and horse?"

Hester cleared her throat, and Benjamin watched as a mask fell across not just her face, but her whole body. Her shoulders bowed inward a bit, her voice softened, her eyes cast downward, and she lost her smile. It was like all the colors of the rainbow had been muted by a cloud. "Yes, I believe that's for me."

Benjamin blinked. This wasn't Hester. *Is this how she survives being forgotten? She makes herself forgettable?*

The boy tossed his head, sending some of his long hair away from his eyes. "Nelly is still finishing her breakfast, you'll need to wait."

Benjamin didn't mind at all. He had a few things he wanted to say to Hester first. "An extra sixpence for you, if you tell no one we were here."

The stableboy's eyes gleamed, and he nodded. "I've got to check the goats anyway, and they're outside. I never saw either of you. I'll just drive an empty cart to Woodlea House for the exercise in half an hour." He picked up a bucket nearby and walked past them.

Benjamin glanced around the small stables, looking for a hiding spot. *There.* In the back, hidden in the shadows, was a corner meant for tack and saddles. Instead, it was mostly bare, save for a carriage rug hung over a rafter. He tangled his fingers in Hester's and tugged her along.

CHAPTER TEN

Hester sucked in a breath as Benjamin led her to a corner of the stables where they could hide and wait. Where he could say goodbye and break her heart.

When the villagers in the tavern had made those jests about Gretna Green, Hester thought she might burst into flames. So many emotions tangled around her heart, casting her adrift in a sea of confusion, longing, embarrassment, hope, despair, and regret. How did this happen? How did she fall in love in less than a day?

Benjamin pulled aside the worn carriage rug, made to keep women's legs warm during long and cold journeys, and tugged her back into the alcove. It was dim, the lighting soft as dust motes drifted through a shaft of sunlight just above his tousled hair.

Hester watched him curiously as he turned and faced her. His hands rested on her shoulders, bracing.

"Hester," he said, jaw firm.

Hester fought to keep her expression calm, pleasant, mildly curious. "Yes?" Her palms itched and she wished her hair wasn't a rat's nest.

His eyes softened, and his thumbs began to stroke her shoulders. She nearly purred under the touch. "Hester," he ground out.

"Yes?" Hester whispered.

And he slowly stepped forward, erasing all distance between them, his large hands sliding up her shoulder, up her neck, to cup her face. His eyes flickered once to hers as he bent his head, questioning. Whatever he saw in her eyes must've spurred him onward, for his lips descended to hers.

Hester nearly gasped in delight and surprise. It was so different than she'd imagined, all those years. His lips were terribly soft as they nudged against her own, but his stubble scraped against her chin in a most intriguing way. Something unfurled in her belly, and a heat blossomed between her legs in response to the intimacy, the realness of the moment.

His hands caressed her face, and she melted at the heat of his body pressed against her. Hester kissed him back, euphoria shooting through her as she memorized the mouth of the man she loved.

Benjamin groaned, and the sound reverberated through both of them. His hands left her face to wrap around her. He splayed his hands across her back, pressing her closer, closer to him. Gently, though, so he didn't crush her injured wrist between them.

Hester gripped the lapel of his coat, her blood running hot through her veins. He slanted his lips against her over and over, until it was a blur of incandescent desire. A whimper escaped her lips as she molded her mouth against his.

"Hester," he whispered, and then a hot flick pressed against the corner of her mouth. He traced her bottom lip with his tongue, then pressed gently against the seam of her lips.

Entranced, Hester opened to him, and delight spiraled, all the way down to her fingers and toes as his tongue entered her mouth. She met him measure for measure, tangling her tongue with his, stroking his lips, and entering his mouth when he gave her a chance. The desire to burrow closer, to press her skin against his grew stronger and stronger.

She wished her blasted wrist wasn't in the way. Her entire body throbbed, and she wished he could soothe its ache.

Abruptly, Benjamin pulled back. He panted a little, eyes wild and feverish, as he stared at her in disbelief.

Hester must look a fright. But she didn't care. Because this was a wonderful kiss and this was her last moment with him and she wasn't going to lose it. Hester had always been the type of person to savor and relish an experience. As a child, she'd eaten her Christmas oranges slice by slow slice, letting the juice trickle down her lips and across her chin and fingers. She'd not rushed it, she'd managed her eagerness, drawing out a gift or an experience to suck the last drop from the bottle. Under usual circumstances, she'd kiss and kiss and kiss all day, reveling in the heady sensations and stoking her desire hotter and hotter, letting it grow into a bonfire before she indulged.

But Benjamin was leaving. Marrying another, returning to London. This was her only chance.

She grabbed his head with one hand and pulled him back down to her, kissing him with a desperation borne of all twenty-four years of her life.

Benjamin, nearly thrown off balance, accidentally pushed her against the wall of the stable, hands on either side of her. It was so similar to their game with the cottage door last night that she grinned and nipped his lip. Had she ever been this enthralled?

He inhaled sharply, then kissed her back with abandon. He sucked and nipped, teased and licked, caressed and whispered, not just her lips, but her cheeks and her ear, his hot breath tickling her there, and he laughed when she laughed at the new feeling. His lips journeyed down her neck, pausing at the hollow of her throat.

Hester panted with desire. "Oh, Benji, yes, oh, right there." She felt so seen in that moment, as if the whole world centered around her for once, and Benjamin would never let her be lost in the dark corners of a room or forgotten along the wayside of life.

And then he took it further. His lips found the edge of her bodice, and his hands came around her sides to cup her breasts through her clothing. So very carefully avoiding her arm and sling.

Hester groaned as every touch drove her to delicious torment. "More, Benji."

His hands danced across what part of her bodice he could touch, then delved nimbly under her neckline to massage the tops of her breasts. Hester wished she hadn't put her stays back on. He would have a hard time reaching her nipples with that pressed against her figure.

"You're so beautiful," Benjamin whispered in her ear.

Hester wasn't sure how true that was, especially considering all that had happened in the last day, but she decided not to argue. "How can this feel so wonderful?" she whispered. "How can you wring such pleasure from my own body?"

"It's you, my love, it's all you," Benjamin exhaled across her skin. His hands, after creating such torture across her bosom, skated downward, molding to the shape of her waist and hips. And then further still. He was so tall he had to lean over a little, and his mouth trailed across the tops of her breasts as one hand stroked her leg, all the way down to her knee. And then he grabbed hold of the hem of her dress and began to pull it up.

Nerves shot through Hester. Was this really happening? Would she wake to discover it had all been a dream? Her hand roved over his hair, burying her fingers in his soft locks, memorizing the feel of him and every groan he made.

He pulled the dress higher until her stockings and knees were exposed to the air. A thrill ran through her at the thought. She leaned back, against a ledge built into the frame of the stable. It wasn't quite enough to sit on, but it did remove some pressure off her feet.

Hester tried so hard to keep quiet, to not pant loudly as his hand slipped up one leg, skimming across bare skin, as it reached her inner thighs.

"So soft," Benjamin whispered, pulling back just far enough to make eye contact while he touched her. Hester felt trapped in his gaze, more vulnerable than if she was spread out on a table stark naked. He saw her, all of her, from the mischievous part who caused this whole fiasco to the lonely, aching part who felt life passing her by. He looked into her eyes and watched everything.

Hester's heart ached with emotion, and one hand went to cup his cheek. How it would hurt when he left. How could she go back to a home where people forgot her after she'd experienced this?

Benjamin gave a little smile, unaware of the thoughts rolling around her head, and his finger slipped past her inner thigh and to the hot, wet center of her.

Hester went rigid at the first brush of his fingertips against her folds. He caught that movement, and for a heartbeat, his hand paused as he raised his brows, gaze never leaving hers. *Good?* his expression asked.

Hester gave a shaky nod. "Good," she whispered.

His little smile grew wicked and his fingers slid along her vulva. His shoulders shook, and the grip of his other hand on her hips tightened almost painfully. "So perfect," he whispered. "Wet and hot and perfect." His fingers played against her skin, sometimes giving soft, soothing touches, sometimes playful. Each stroke made the pleasure build and build inside her. It felt so much better than when she touched herself late at night, wishing for something more in her bed.

One finger slipped inside her, and she pressed her forehead against his for support as sensation after glorious sensation assailed her. "Oh, God, Benjamin, that feels—" she bit her lip and squirmed, unable to keep the rising pressure and desire contained within her body.

His eyes crinkled with delight. "That's right then," he whispered. "Wriggle and gasp and feel all you want. This is yours, for you to do with as you please." Then he pressed his thumb against the nub at the top of her slit, and she mewled.

"Hester," he said, voice ragged. "Please, can I do this? I want—I want so badly to—"

Hester nodded, eyes shut, though she wasn't exactly sure what she was saying yes too. But this was Benjamin, and she knew he'd never steer her wrong.

In one fluid gesture, Benjamin crouched, and the hand that had been between her legs disappeared to push her skirts up even higher at her hips. Before Hester had time to moan a protest, however, she felt his hot breath against her mons.

Startled, Hester looked down. Benjamin had both hands braced at her hips, and his face was alarmingly close to herself.

"Don't scream," he told her, a wicked glint in his eye, and then his mouth fell upon her.

Hester gasped loud enough that it could've been a scream. One hand flew to the stud in the stable wall, and her head flew back and hit the wooden wall. Slick, wicked heat enveloped her, and Hester couldn't believe this was actually happening to her. People did this? People used their mouths in this way? What an ingenious idea! She bit her lips to keep from moaning aloud as Benjamin feasted on her.

He pushed her legs a little wider apart, and she leaned against the ledge as best she could. His stubble prickled against the soft flesh of her inner thighs, which caused mind-dizzying contrast to the slippery, wet tongue that delved between her folds, flickered in her vagina, and then lapped at the wetness of her.

"Sweet as honey," Benjamin pulled back long enough to tell her. "Better than I imagined." Then he went right back, only this time he locked his lips around her nub and gave gentle, rhythmic sucks that made her want to scream.

Hester tried so hard to keep still for him, not wanting anything to distract him from his task. The pleasure grew until she thought her body might tear apart at the seams. And then it rolled over, like a thundering wave. Her body nearly shook at the sensation, as the cataclysm flooded her nerves. Finally, the sensations faded, and she was left sagging against the wall, panting for breath.

Benjamin gave one last gentle swipe of his tongue, sighing in ecstasy. She shivered at the touch, now so sensitive. Then he stood and let her skirts fall back around her. "Hester Fairfax," he whispered and wrapped his arms around her.

Hester fell against his chest, suddenly exhausted and ready to just bask in the glow of her orgasm. "Thank you," she whispered, uncertain what proper social etiquette required at this point.

His arms tightened around her, and he pressed a kiss to the top of her head. "You're more than I ever dreamed," he told her.

Loud voices broke their reverie, like a bucket of cold water. Hester tensed, fear sparking through her at the thought of discovery. She felt Benjamin's body go rigid.

"Quiet," he whispered. "Maybe they won't see us."

CHAPTER ELEVEN

Benjamin held his breath as he backed Hester further into the shadows, trying to shelter her with his body.

The irate voices came closer. Benjamin's body reacted before his mind did. His palms began to sweat, his heart rate picked back up, and he felt the sudden urge to hide even deeper in the shadows. Only after all that, did he pick up on the words and recognize the speaker.

"When I find him I'll thrash him within an inch of his life. He's a Littleton, damn him, and a Littleton always does his duty." His father's voice cut the stillness of the stable. Footsteps plodded, growing louder as the men—two men, Benjamin guessed—stopped to stand in the doorway of the stable. "Third sons," his father sneered. "What good are they?"

"You already have me as the heir, Father, and William as the spare. Benjamin doesn't need—" But Benjamin wouldn't ever know if his brother was about to defend him or malign him as a way to get into their father's good graces, for the baronet cut him off.

"The boy is a hare-brained idiot. I have laid out his future for him, so simple even he should be able to follow it. Cambridge. The Bar. Partnership with Dunham. Even a wife. But no, he had to disappear. Now

Dunham's threatening to hie back to London and his wife has been crying all morning, saying her daughter has been slighted." Something thumped, perhaps his father kicking a stall door in frustration. "Your mother shouldn't have coddled him as a child."

Benjamin glanced down at Hester to make sure she was completely hidden.

Hester glared furiously back up at him. "Is that your *father*?" she demanded silently, jabbing an accusing finger in the general direction.

Benjamin nodded.

Her nostrils flared and righteous anger shined in her eyes. She jerked to attention, shoulders back and eyes blazing. Benjamin didn't believe she'd actually do it until she took a step around him.

Frantic, he grabbed her by her arms and stop her. "No," he whispered. "You do not want to attract his attention."

She fumed, turning her ire up at him. "That man," she hissed, "has no right to talk about you that way. And I'll go tell him myself."

Warmth spread to every corner of his chest, and he couldn't help his lips twitching. *Marvelous girl.* He wrapped his arms around every rigid inch of her and buried his face in her hair. "Thank you," he whispered, but he wasn't sure she heard it. He held her against him, drawing the support that her indignation offered, until she softened against him, putting her arms around him as well. She mumbled something into his shirt, but he didn't care, he just kept on drawing strength from her and trying to listen to her breathing instead of his father's angry words.

"Do you know what he told me?" His father was going full ahead now, knowing he had a captive audience in his eldest son. "He told me his cousin—from the horrid merchant's family—offered him a position! In the wine business! Can you believe it?"

Reginald made a scoffing noise.

Hester made a muffled sound and pulled away to peer up at him in surprise. *You didn't tell me that part!* her face seemed to say.

Benjamin hadn't planned to take the position. He hadn't thought it was offered seriously, and he hadn't thought he had the freedom to take it. He liked his cousin, but they were not close.

"If that boy has tucked tail and run," his father said, "mark me, he will be back on my doorstep in six months, hat in his hand begging for my favor once again. He cannot do anything without me."

"Father," the heir said hesitantly, "A few men in the tavern think he may have traveled to—to Scotland with Miss Fairfax."

"Who?"

"I believe it's his old friend. Remember the girl that used to run around with him, with the tangled hair?"

Benjamin tightened his grip on Hester, wishing they could put an end to this conversation without revealing themselves. He'd borne the brunt of his father's displeasure all his life, he was used to it, but Hester wasn't. He didn't want her to hear whatever his father would say next.

"Scotland," the baronet seethed. "With that snaggle-toothed chit?"

Benjamin had sometimes fantasized about punching his father, just to see what would happen. He'd never gone through with it, but it had been a nice, warming thought when he was an adolescent. But he'd never come so close to marching out and hitting him right now. Only the worry to keep Hester hidden kept him in place.

"He'll definitely ruin the future I've set up for him if he elopes with her." The man barked a laugh. "Benjamin will see just how far outside my grace he has fallen. I'm almost impressed. In one fell swoop, if this is true, he'll have destroyed his life. No connection to the Dunhams, no barrister opportunity, no allowance from me. They'll be destitute and begging for my help within six months. And he won't bloody get it." The last words emerged clipped, heavily emphasized with smug delight.

Someone shifted back and forth in the dirt. "Well, he's not here. Perhaps we should look elsewhere?"

Sir Stanley snorted. "You'll keep looking for your brother. I'm returning home."

There was a pause, as if Reginald was considering protesting, but then decided against it. "Yes, sir." Their footsteps faded.

"Of all the—! Benjamin, he—!" Hester stomped her foot and crossed her arms, stepping back to glare at him. "Your father is an absolute cad. What a horrible man."

Benjamin, strangely, didn't care a whit about any of the things his father had said about him. His mind was focused elsewhere.

"Do you hear me?" Hester demanded. "You *must* take that position with your cousin the wine merchant! You'd be so happy doing that, and I cannot bear the thought of your father quashing you into a London barrister life, smug as could be as you wither away in misery. Defy him and move to Portugal. You have such a way with numbers and your nimble mind will enjoy the challenges of running a business."

A smile spread across Benjamin's face as he envisioned the future Hester described. "Yes. Yes, I think I will." He'd danced to his father's fiddle for far too long. Yes, Sir Stanley was the head of the family, the manager of the purse strings, and yes, Benjamin had some filial duty. But surely not this. Especially when he knew exactly what *would* make him happy and fulfilled. He grinned at Hester. "Yes, I like your plan for us very much."

Hester paused. "Pardon?"

Before Benjamin could answer, a tinny bugle sounded outside the stable, with thundering wheels, jangling tack, and pounding hooves.

"The mail coach!" Hester exclaimed.

Perfect. It was headed straight to London, wasn't it? Benjamin grabbed Hester's hand and tugged her back into the open. "Hurry, we can't miss it."

"What?" Hester halted in her tracks and stared up at him.

The thunderous sound of the coach rolled to a halt, and a loud voice shouted, "Six minutes and we're leaving. Do your business in six minutes or we shall leave without you!"

Benjamin paused, staring back at Hester. "I'm..." He blinked, realizing he hadn't exactly communicated his plan. He'd just assumed she'd go for it like they had when they were children. But they weren't children, and this wasn't a game. "I'm spiriting you away to Gretna Green."

Shock rippled across her face, followed by a slow dawning beam of delight. "Truly?" she whispered. "You and me?"

"Yes." Benjamin rubbed the back of his neck with his free hand. "I mean... if you have no objections?"

"Of *course* I have no objections, Benji." Her eyes shone with joy, and Benjamin didn't think he'd ever seen her smile that large. "Yes, I'll go with you to Gretna Green."

Benjamin's heart fluttered in his chest at the trust she offered him. He wouldn't disappoint her. He'd make something of himself—or they'd do it together, far from his overbearing parents and her negligent one. He tugged her into the yard, where a massive, bright red coach with yellow wheels rested, baggage and mail sacks strapped on top with rope. Six horses snorted and panted at the bit, already tired from their journey.

In a thrice, Benjamin found the coachman, purchased two tickets to London by putting it on his family's tab at the tavern, handed over the pink shawl to Mrs. Lyon with an apology to be passed on to Miss Dunham, and escorted Hester into the coach. "Into the coach, my ravishing captive."

The air inside was stale, the floor muddy. Three other passengers were already taking up most of the room on the cracked leather squabs. But it smelled like freedom and happiness. In fact, the worn leather smelled like what he'd imagined a pirate would—minus the rum and body odor.

Hester grinned up at him as he settled into a seat beside her. "Benjamin," she whispered. "How will we make this work?"

The coach would be in London by that afternoon. He had just enough coins in his pocket to hire a cab to his rooms near the Old Bailey, where he'd pack his belongings, let Hester rest, and find his cousin. And then he'd take what little money he had to purchase a coach ride to Scotland, and then—hopefully—a ship to Lisbon, Portugal. It would make for long, arduous travel days, but with Hester by his side, it would be an adventure. And they could pillage and plunder one another on the way.

A song thrummed in Benjamin's chest as he discreetly settled his hand between their laps and covered her hand with his. "We'll sort it on the way."

EPILOGUE
SIX MONTHS LATER

Benjamin was deep asleep until a fly landed on his nose. Pulled from his slumber, he rubbed his nose with the back of his hand, turning his face into his pillow.

A throaty chuckle sounded above him, and the irritating feeling returned, this time on his cheek.

Benjamin scowled as he scraped the sensation away.

"Benji," whispered a familiar voice. "Benji, wake up."

Benjamin opened his eyes to find the bedroom still bathed in darkness. He could feel more than see his wife hovering beside him in their bed. Her hair spilled over her shoulders and across his pillow—and even his face. "Hester?" he mumbled, voice rough from sleep.

Hester's lips brushed against his, and her sweet smell blossomed around him as her hair fell like a curtain around them, closing them off from the world.

"Mmmm," Benjamin hummed as he kissed her back. His hand freed itself from their bed linens and reached up to cup the back of his wife's head. "In the middle of the night? How shocking, Mrs. Littleton."

Hester ignored that remark, making her kiss deeper. Her tongue darted between his lips, effectively hushing him. She stretched over him, her legs tangling with his, propped on one elbow. Her other hand was quickly sliding under the covers and exploring all parts of him. "I love it when you sleep nude," she whispered and nipped his lower lip.

Portugal is so much hotter than England, he meant to say. But her hand skated down his stomach and grabbed his cock in one daring motion, so he gasped instead.

Hester huffed a pleased laugh at the sound as she stroked him.

It was absolutely insufferable, and he had to do something about it. So Benjamin gripped her hips and flipped, rolling on top of her. The sheets tangled around their legs as he settled his weight over her.

"Oh," Hester said with a breath of surprise.

Benjamin smirked and kissed the corner of her mouth. "Turn about is fair play, I think." And as he propped himself on one forearm so as not to crush her, his other hand drifted across her hip, following the line where it met her thigh, and dipped between her legs.

Hester wiggled under him, widening her legs. "Mmmm."

He fingered her gently, giving soft, feather touches on her outer folds, reveling in the wet heat of her. He'd never grow bored of her. Never grow tired of making love to her or teasing her. Benjamin rained kisses across her face, across the freckles that had emerged under the warm Portuguese sun.

Her own hands ran up and down his shoulders and back as her soft panting filled the cocooned darkness around them. "More, Benjamin. You know I like more."

Benjamin kept his fingers light and quick, playing havoc with her building pleasure. Only gentle pressure against her clitoris. "Yes, my dear," he whispered. "But you know *I* like to tease you." And he knew she responded well to the build-up.

Hester groaned in mock frustration. "You are merciless." But then her breath skipped as he inserted two fingers inside her.

Benjamin groaned then, as overwhelmed by her body as he was the first time. "So good," he murmured against her lips. "Always so good."

He dipped his head to her breasts, capturing one nipple and licking. His blood thrummed in his veins, pulsing and hot. Eager for union and ecstasy with his wife.

She scraped her nails through his hair, down his neck, and his toes curled in response. Fuck, she aroused him with the slightest touches and looks. She'd learned so fast he was nearly afraid he'd expire one day from desiring his own wife. But what a way to go.

His cock ached with the need to enter her, but he held himself back. *Not yet.* His scrotum tightened, but he focused on curling his fingers in her, beckoning her toward her own climax, while his thumb rubbed against the nub at the top of her sex.

Hester embraced him, wrapping her arms so tightly around his back her fingernails raked his skin. The bite, the promise of pleasure and pain, spurred him onward. "Just look at you," he whispered when he released one nipple. "Such a fierce little thing."

She whimpered beneath him, tossing her head from side to side. Benjamin wished they'd lit a candle first, so he could see the glimmer of her hair as it curled in and out of shadows. "Please," she gasped.

Emotion welled inside Benjamin, making his chest tight. He'd give it to her. He'd give her everything her heart desired. Everything. He redoubled his efforts, pinching a nipple just enough to give her the same bite her fingernails had given him, and she made a mewling sound. He stroked her core hard and fast now, whispering all sorts of sweet, naughty things in the darkness.

Suddenly she froze, whole body going rigid in his arms, and her fingernails dug deep into his back. Her legs gripped him, trapping him against her, and her wide, enraptured eyes glinted in the dim light as she locked gazes with him. After an eternity, she relaxed, limbs languorous and skin hot from her climax. "Oh, Benjamin," she breathed. "Come here and kiss me."

His own desire mounting, Benjamin rolled his hips until his cock settled against her entrance. He thrust in one quick movement, nearly melting with the pleasure her tight heat brought him. Benjamin covered her gasp with a kiss. "Take me," he breathed.

Hester wrapped her legs around him, locking her ankles at the small of his back. The bedsheets tangled at his feet. She gripped his face with both her hands and kissed him again and again.

Heart full, Benjamin thrust deep, setting a rhythm that made both of them moan and grab at one another to anchor against the onslaught of sensation. "Take me," he whispered again against her jaw.

"All of you," she promised.

He'd never known such closeness other than with her. First as a friend, now as a lover and wife. The need to be deeper inside her, to touch his soul against hers, drove him forward. He gritted his teeth as his bollocks tightened, then let himself go in the rippling, incandescent pleasure that coursed through him. Hester held him through the earth-shattering climax, held him as he caught his breath, and only released him when he fumbled for the cloths they kept on the nightstand to clean up afterward.

Benjamin parted Hester's legs, pushing her feet flat against the bed so he could reach her. She lay contentedly, watching him through the dawning light that slipped through the curtains. Benjamin loved this part, oddly enough. He'd never given the aftermath much thought before. But he found he loved caring for her, cleaning her gently, soothing her oversensitized flesh and kissing her knees while he did it.

When he finished, he folded the cloth and dropped it over the edge of the bed, ready to snuggle back under the wrecked bed linens for an hour more of rest, his wife tucked under his chin.

Life was good. Hard at times, but good. He'd never been happier, save for their wedding day at the anvil in Scotland. They'd traveled so hard and fast to be wed, then to join his cousin's wine business outside of Lisbon, that he had scarcely time to breathe, let alone trap his wife in bed until they'd found an apartment.

And now here they were, settling into a new life they'd both dreamed of but never imagined was actually possible. Benjamin was learning Portuguese and how to broker agreements with English lords for their port. Hester was learning Portuguese and how to manage a household from their housekeeper. They were slowly developing a set of friends of several nationalities and had not worried about their families at all. Not when they had such full lives to enjoy here.

Napoleon's forces had surged into western Portugal again, but British and Portuguese forces had defeated them at Busaco last month, sending the French back toward Spain just in time for a rainy autumn and winter. Benjamin and Hester had made plans to evacuate if things became worse, but both wanted to stay and support the war effort as best they could in Lisbon. And with hostilities slowing due to seasonal weather, they had a chance to help soldiers recuperate in the port city.

Benjamin sighed and closed his eyes, quite happy in the moment. He reached over to pull Hester against him, but she wriggled out of his grasp.

"Come on, slugabed," she teased and sat up.

Benjamin opened one eye. "What are you doing?"

"I was waking you up."

"You did a marvelous job," Benjamin told her. "Now come back to bed."

"No, see, we have to wake up now. Get dressed, or we'll miss it." The bed shifted, and he heard her bare feet patter across the floor rug.

Benjamin opened his other eye. He'd not miss a chance to see her bare backside in dawnlight. "What are we going to miss?" A shaft of pale light drifted across her lower back, hitting the dimples just above her buttocks. It was a marvelous sight.

She picked up some clothing in the chair by the window and smiled over her shoulder at him. "I'm abducting you. We're going down to the beach. I found a wonderful spot yesterday to watch the sunrise. I've prepared pastries and even some orange juice."

Benjamin wouldn't have minded staying abed. But the sunrise with Hester was tempting. So he rolled out of bed and wrapped her in his arms, pulling her back against his bare chest. "You truly are a pirate."

She sputtered with laughter. "Pardon me?"

"You're abducting me down to the shoreline and tempting me with your wicked ways." He released her to dress. "Fiercest pirate I've ever met."

"The basket is by the door, we'll pick it up on our way out." Hester quickly braided her hair. It looked a wild mess, but he wasn't going to tell her that. He loved her hair, especially when it was wild.

"How do you plan on walking down the rock steps in the dark, if we're to be there before sunrise?" Benjamin hastily tied a simple knot in his cravat and reached for his boots.

Hester laughed. "I hadn't thought about that part. I suppose we'll be careful." She opened their bedroom door and waited in the doorway for him.

"We'll sort it on the way," Benjamin promised, dropping a kiss on her temple. He took her hand in his, and they hurried to their next adventure.

THE END

ABOUT ANNE KNIGHT

Anne Knight has been writing stories since she was three years old. Before she could read or write, she followed her parents and babysitter around, begging them to dictate her words. Eventually she learned the alphabet and began writing herself. She sneaked her first romance novel when she was thirteen, but did not become an avid reader or writer of the genre until after college.

Anne has lived in two countries, studied in three, and traveled through a total of thirty four. Her work history includes ESL teacher, domestic violence advocate, paralegal, and hospital project manager. She lives in Arkansas with her real-life swoony hero, three sons, and two cats. The cats are named Cyrano and Ivanhoe.

Visit anneknightbooks.com for more information about future releases and other fun news!

HIS SULTRY CAPTOR

TABETHA WAITE

For Emmanuelle de Maupassant. Thank you for inviting me to be a part of this fun project, even if we didn't end up getting to work together after all. Some day!

CHAPTER ONE
LONDON, ENGLAND

AUGUST 1814

"**A**re you sure you still want to do this?"

Miss Florentia Parker held the dagger in her grasp and checked the sharpness of the shining blade, before she tucked it securely within the band of her garter and lowered her skirts. She looked at her best friend, Anna Shapley, and said curtly, "Let's go."

Anna sighed heavily but followed Florentia up the steps of the manor house that was blazing with flickering lights.

The shorter, blonde-haired girl with the innocent, blue eyes was the same age as Florentia at two and twenty, but also a young widow. Florentia gritted her teeth, because if things had been different, two months ago she would have been happily married. She had been engaged to a successful ship merchant and held hope of their future together.

But in one night, it all changed, her dreams shattered.

It was all *his* fault, of course, which is why he had to pay for his crimes, and it was obvious the judgement was up to her. She'd learned only a few weeks ago that Archer Grindstone, the Earl of Thanefield, had been responsible for slipping the King's Shilling into Jonathan's mug of ale, causing him to be pressed into service for the Crown in the Royal Navy. He was supposed to sail out to India, and when he returned, they were planning to wed. Instead, he was sent to France, where he boarded a warship and perished at sea.

Florentia's chest ached with the memory of that day, when she was informed that Jonathan was dead. She decided right then that she would have vengeance on the men responsible for it. To her, the Earl of Thanefield might as well have put a gun to Jonathan's temple and pulled the trigger, because he was just as responsible for his death. He'd signed the sentence when he'd dropped that shilling into his drink.

Anna was silent as she walked obediently beside her, but Florentia could tell that she was nervous about attending her first Cyprians' Ball at the Argyll Rooms on Regent Street. It was the first for Florentia as well, but determination pulsed through her veins hotly enough that she would have faced hell and back, if only to drag the earl to his demise.

"Do you still have the powder?" Anna asked, almost reluctantly.

Florentia lifted her reticle, where the vial of belladonna was securely nestled. "Of course. Otherwise, this would be a fruitless endeavor."

Before they could open the front door, Anna grabbed hold of her sleeve and pulled her into a shadowed area behind a large hedge. They were ignored by other guests entering the ball, as they likely thought they were having an impromptu assignation before they joined the rest of the festivities. "This just seems... *wrong*, doesn't it?" Her breathing was heavy, and she looked a bit pale. "I mean, you're seriously considering kidnapping a peer!"

Florentia had been expecting this. But then, Anna's husband had volunteered to join the war against Napoleon. He'd died nobly on a battlefield in service of his country. "You don't have to join me if you feel that strongly about it, Anna. But you know that I can't allow Jonathan's death to go unpunished."

It took a moment for Anna to struggle with her conscience, but then the color returned to her cheeks and she shook her head. She reached out and grabbed Florentia's hand. "I love you, Tia. You know I would do anything for you, even face the threat of being imprisoned in the Tower, because you were there for me when no one else was."

Florentia reached out and gave her friend an impulsive hug. "I love you too, Anna. I wouldn't have made it this far without you either."

Hand in hand, they walked through the front doors.

Archer had been reclining on a settee, an arm behind his head and surveying the scene around him when a dark-haired goddess walked into the parlor. Immediately, his attention was captured by her stunning beauty.

He sat up to get a better look at her, just as his view was abruptly interrupted. *Blast the crowd this evening!* However, he supposed it was a good thing it was a crush, because it reminded him of his true purpose for being there. Unfortunately, he was there for business, and not pleasure.

He frowned darkly, and returned to his earlier, lazy position. It wouldn't do to look too alert. It was only by adopting the insubordinate rake that he had been able to infiltrate the press gangs for so long and try to free the men who were being bullied into service. It had been too late to save his younger brother, but he was hoping he could help others before tragedy struck.

That was the only reason he was here tonight. Most of the members liked to frequent these gatherings. Usually, he was able to distance himself from the salacious proceedings and focus on finding out information that would assist his cause. But that was before the raven-haired goddess walked into the room and he was sorely distracted.

He allowed his gaze to roam at will and saw her again, this time moving slowly throughout the room with a shorter blonde at her side. She was comely as well, but he had always had a weakness for the sultry sort.

Archer couldn't take his eyes off the dark-haired beauty as she glanced about her surroundings. The night was still young, so the usual debauchery was not yet taking place. However, something told him that she wouldn't mind if the entire room was naked. She seemed set on a purpose, as if looking for just the right partner to pair with for the evening.

With that thought, Archer's cock started to stir with interest. He would be more than happy to accommodate her...

No, you wouldn't. He reluctantly started to turn away, but then suddenly, her head turned in his direction. He froze. Even from across the room, he could tell that her eyes were hypnotic, as enchanting and mysterious as the woman herself. Her gown was a shimmering gold satin and reflected the unusual shade of her gaze. He was paralyzed now, helpless to look anywhere—but her. When she started to slide in his direction, he had the urge to glance around him, because surely this wasn't a mutual attraction? His fortune couldn't be that favorable.

Or could it?

She distanced herself from her companion and stopped directly in front of him. With a smile that urged his cock to further interest, she asked in a husky voice, "Are you with anyone this evening, sir?"

Archer didn't have the wherewithal to tell her his title. He was still too stunned to believe she had chosen him. In that regard, could he really turn down the opportunity to entertain such a magnificent creature? "Only with you, madam, if you are willing."

Her smile grew and she reached out a hand to him. "Then perhaps we should move our new acquaintance to somewhere more private?"

Archer had to resist the urge to scramble to his feet. Instead, he calmly reached out and grasped her hand then yanked her forward. Combining her surprise with her momentum, she landed neatly on top of him. Her dark hair fanned around her shoulders. He grasped a section between his thumb and forefinger, and then brought the strands to his nose. He closed his eyes as he inhaled her clean, womanly scent. She was intoxicating.

"Sir, I really must insist—"

"Don't worry," he interrupted smoothly. "I don't intend to share you with anyone else this evening. I merely wanted a sample of your delights first."

He leaned forward and nuzzled the side of her neck. God, he could kiss that smooth skin until the end of his days. But she was right. They really needed to be alone, so he could enjoy her at his leisure.

Tonight's other liaisons would have to be temporarily postponed.

"Are you sure you know what he looks like?" Anna had whispered near Florentia's elbow, as they made their way about the perimeter of the room. She tugged at a section of her bodice. "I swear I feel naked without any stays."

Florentia rolled her eyes at her comment. "It's a Cyprians' Ball. You're not meant to be proper. As for the earl... I saw him once, from a distance," she hedged. She didn't bother to explain that it had been a mere glimpse from a passing carriage. "But I have inquired about him enough that it shouldn't be too difficult."

Anna must have thought more should be forthcoming, because she prodded, "Well, what did you find out?"

Florentia searched her memory. "Tall with a lean build. Brown hair and similarly colored eyes."

There was a pause. "And?"

This was the part she hadn't wanted to offer. "He's supposed to be rather... *handsome*."

"Oh. I see."

Florentia looked at her sharply. "What does that mean?"

In turn, Anna's expression was pure innocence. Florentia wasn't fooled for a moment. "Nothing. I just wondered if perhaps..."

"Yes?"

Anna sighed. "What if he isn't the villain that you believe him to be? You did say that the man who told you his identity was in his cups that night. Perhaps it's not the right man at all."

"I am confident enough that I'm prepared to commit a crime," Florentia pointed out firmly. "I'm sure if there is a misunderstanding, being a gentleman of the peerage, he might be kind enough to offer his assistance."

"After you tie him up and interrogate him, you mean?" Anna retorted dryly.

"Yes, even then." Florentia had suffered enough of this conversation. The "man" in question who had told her about the earl had been Jonathan's loyal first mate. While his eyesight might not have been the most reliable when he was drinking, he would not have intentionally led her astray.

Straightening her shoulders, Florentia decided it was time to get back to work.

Glancing about the crush once again, she paused upon seeing a gentleman reclining on a settee. He was wearing buff trousers, black Hessian boots and a white cambric shirt that was open at the throat. There was no jacket, cravat, or waistcoat in place. He was the epitome of a loathsome libertine who might enslave men.

"It's him."

She spoke to Anna, but her focus was riveted on her target. She wondered if it would be in poor taste to send him an ace of spades with a hole in the middle and watch him squirm, wondering who might despise him so much that they would contemplate murder. She doubted he would believe the warning came from a woman.

His gaze abruptly shifted and clashed with hers. For a moment, all she could do was stare. Although she had fantasized about him lounging on that settee with malicious intent, now her interest suddenly shifted. This man wasn't just handsome, he was *magnificent.* He had a chiseled jawline, aristocratic nose, and dark eyebrows that came together in a coy slash above brown eyes that seduced where she stood. His hair was unruly and begged for her fingers to delve into the fullness.

A decided swirl of heat began in the pit of her stomach, which she quickly squashed before it could take root. She wasn't here to have a tryst. She was here to avenge Jonathan.

She moved forward.

As they conversed, she noted that while his voice was smooth as velvet, he was as dangerous as a viper. She certainly hadn't been prepared for the way he brought her down on top of him, nor her body's traitorous response to his hard, muscular form. Without her usual undergarments, it was even more shocking. It had been eight long weeks without Jonathan's arms around her. Until now, she hadn't realized just how much she'd missed his touch, how much she'd yearned for it. As her target started to nuzzle her neck, she knew it was time to take action.

She rose slowly, ensuring that he got an enticing view of the valley between her breasts. "Come, sir. It's time we start tonight properly."

Archer rose, as if some unseen force were compelling him forward. He had never been led around so effortlessly by any woman, but she was like no one he'd ever beheld before.

His nostrils flared as he watched the tantalizing sway of her hips when she walked up the stairs to the rooms that were set aside for personal entertainment. His cock was fully erect now, anxious to see this evening come to its fruition.

As they passed several closed doors, moans of a sexual nature met his ears. He was nearly panting by the time they reached an open room, but not because of any exertion he'd had thus far. He followed his muse inside the room and shut the door firmly. He started to reach for her when she turned to face him, but she laid a hand on his chest to keep him at a distance.

He frowned. "What's wrong?"

She smiled. "You wouldn't deprive me of a toast to celebrate the occasion, would you?" She gestured to a side table where two glasses and a bottle of wine were sitting. She leaned forward slightly. "I'll meet you on the bed." She slid her hand across his chest, and with a flirtatious glance in those golden eyes, she moved away from him.

Archer was quite sure his body was going to explode long before he even had the chance to worship her properly, but he forced himself to play this game by her rules. However, he didn't intend to savor his wine. When she brought the glass over to him, she sipped slightly, but he downed it all in one gulp.

He reached for her with a husky murmur, "Now, where were we?"

Instead of joining him on the bed, she sat down in a nearby chair and calmly watched him, all while continuing to sip her drink.

At first, he was confused, wondering why her ardor had suddenly cooled. But then, he became aware of his own disorientation. His senses started to dull and he couldn't focus on any one thing in the room, even his tantalizing vixen. She was still oddly collected and—

Damn. He blinked. His head was starting to buzz, but he knew that something wasn't right and she was the cause of it. He put a hand to his forehead. "What... did you... do to... me?" he rasped.

"Nothing that won't be fixed in time." She paused. "Hopefully."

"*Hopefully?*" He choked out. He was starting to fade fast, but he had to know what she'd done. "Did you... poison me?"

"Not particularly. It's only meant to put you to sleep."

"*What...* is?"

She actually had the grace to shift a bit guiltily in her chair. "It was just a bit of nightshade."

Archer coughed in disbelief. "*Night—*" He couldn't even finish the sentence. His mouth was suddenly incapable of working. At least he wouldn't have to worry about his cock finishing before he was ready, because it had died a miserable death long ago.

He steeled his jaw, determined to find out the reasons she would have to attack him when they had just met. He swallowed hard until he forced out a single word. "*Why?*"

As he was starting to lose consciousness, she set aside her half drank glass of wine and strode over to him. She knelt on the bed beside him, where she was at eye level. Now, instead of the sultry female, he might have thought she was a demon, because her eyes glowed with an almost unholy light. "You'll find out my reasons soon enough." She kissed two of her fingers and then pressed them against his mouth. He nearly groaned at the loss of those tantalizing lips, which taunted him even though he was incapacitated. "My vengeance won't rest until you know what you've done."

Archer struggled to stay awake, but the darkness claimed him.

CHAPTER TWO

A wave of guilt washed over Florentia, until she remembered that this was the *enemy*. Whether or not he was an earl, or so devilishly charming that she had wanted to join him on that bed and interrogate him later, she kept her thoughts on Jonathan and did what she'd planned to do.

Walking to the door, she opened it to see Anna lingering apprehensively in the hallway. The blonde rushed inside and together they stared at the prone figure sprawled across the bed. "My God, you actually did it."

"I told you I would," Florentia returned dryly. She crossed her arms and glared at the earl, although now that the deed was done, she was feeling a bit unnerved by it.

"How are we supposed to get him out of here?" Anna asked. "He's quite... large, er... tall."

Florentia snorted. "I suppose we'll just have to make it look as if he's too deep in his cups to walk. Is the carriage ready?"

Anna nodded. "My coachman is waiting patiently, although I'm not sure how pleased he is about this. I didn't dare tell him we were bringing an *earl* home with us."

Another stab of guilt rushed through Florentia. Recently, she'd been forced to rely on the charity of her best friend in London. But sometimes circumstances gave one no other option. With her mouth set grimly, she said softly, "I'm sorry I ever asked you to do this. I should have done it alone."

"Or not at all?" Anna returned. But then she relented and said more gently. "I know you think you're doing what is best for Jonathan, but I feel you could have just invited him alone somewhere and made him tell you the truth. He certainly seemed quite enamored of you." She winced. "Let's just hope he doesn't send the watch after you when you release him."

Florentia straightened her shoulders. "First, we have to get him downstairs."

That turned out to be a bit more trouble than Florentia had anticipated. He was quite cumbersome with all that firm muscle and it took several tries before they were able to roll him off the bed and each get an arm and wrap it around their shoulders. The point had been to make it appear as though he'd been too deep in his cups and couldn't walk without assistance, but when they ended up dragging him down the hallway, it appeared a bit more severe than that.

"Next time... you get an idea like this..." Anna said with a strained breath. "Perhaps I shall just... let you manage without... any assistance." She exhaled heavily. "Bloody hell, he's heavy."

"Just keep moving. We don't need to draw any undue attention to ourselves," Florentia snapped, more upset with herself than the situation at hand.

It had all sounded so simple and the perfect resolution to ease her broken heart with Jonathan's death, but now she was starting to wonder if this had been the correct way to handle things after all. Nevertheless, it was too late to back out now. The earl already knew she was at fault, and when he woke up, he likely wouldn't be very pleased. In truth, he would probably be as mad as a hornet whose nest had been upset.

Her brow was dotted with perspiration by the time they had managed to get the earl to the carriage. When the coachman saw them with their burden, his eyes bulged out of his head, although he did come down from his perch to offer assistance. Without his help, Florentia wasn't sure they would have been able to put him inside the coach. They might have been forced to shove him in the boot at the back.

Before the coachman could say anything, Anna held up a hand and informed him, "Not a word, if you please. Just get us home."

After a side glance at their captive, he reluctantly climbed onto the driver's seat and got the carriage moving.

Only then did the two women collapse onto the velvet squabs. The earl lay stretched out awkwardly on the other side, oblivious to the fact he had just been kidnapped.

"Thank God there wasn't anyone around to question us as we dragged a body out of there," Anna noted with relief. "At least, as far as I could tell."

"Indeed," Florentia returned. She wasn't so naïve to admit that they had been very fortunate. Luckily, most of the attendees there had been heavily... occupied.

The carriage finally came to a halt in Soho Square, where Anna had her residence. As a woman of the gentry, she lived a bit more modestly than those who had the grand townhouses in Mayfair. Florentia was even less well-to-do, her blue blood a bit more watered down. Without any family left to turn to, that had been one of the reasons she had pinned all of her hopes on Jonathan. Now, unsure what to do next, she had prevailed upon Anna to take her in, rather than being forced to turn to more unsavory options.

Then again, she had just drugged an earl and taken him hostage, so there might not be many doors left open for her.

She pushed those thoughts aside to be dissected in the privacy of her chamber. Now was not the time.

The coachman assisted them to the front of the house, where a footman opened the door with a wide-eyed expression. "Don't just stand there," Anna snapped irritably. "Give us a hand."

He took the burden from her and Florentia, and with the coachman's help, began to drag him upstairs. The housekeeper entered a moment later and saw what was going on. She laid a hand against her bosom. "Oh, dear. Was he laid upon by thieves?"

"Something like that," Anna mumbled, as she headed to the second story landing. Florentia was directly on her heels as the earl was carted to the guest room, just as they had planned.

"We can take it from here," Anna ordered.

The footman hesitated. "Don't you think we need to summon a doctor—"

"He's fine," Florentia interrupted. "He just had a bit too much to drink. Once he awakens, I'm sure he'll be fit to go home." Anna slid a sharp glance at Florentia, as if to say, *You had better be right.*

As the two servants left, Anna put a hand to her forehead, while Florentia gathered the rope under the bed and began to fasten it to the four posts.

"You can't seriously think that he needs to be tied up as well?"

Florentia didn't even break stride as she gathered one of the earl's limp wrists and secured it to one of the posts near his head. As she started on the other, she answered her cohort. "Don't you think that he'll be a bit grumpy when he realizes he's not anywhere familiar? We don't need him running off and alerting anyone until I can calm him down and tell him the reasons *why* he is here."

Anna sighed heavily. "Very well. But you need to stay in here with him. I don't need him waking up and bellowing loud enough to summon the entire house in the middle of the night."

Florentia secured his ankles, until he appeared like a starfish upon the sand. "I didn't plan on leaving." She set her hands on her hips and peered at her captive. "What do you think?"

Anna looked at her with a mixture of sadness and disbelief. "I think that grief might have damaged your sensible thinking." She shook her head and said wearily, "I'll see you in the morning." Curling her lip, she lifted a section of her pink dress. "I can't wait to rid myself of this horrid garment."

She was still grumbling when she left.

His head was pounding. That alone told Archer that he wasn't dead, because surely heaven didn't allow such a nuisance beyond the famed, pearly gates. Nevertheless, something definitely wasn't right.

However, when he attempted to move, his arms wouldn't obey the command. He tried again, but to no avail. Confused, and growing a bit irritated, he turned his head. While his vision was blurry, and the light in the room was dim, it wasn't difficult to discern that there was rope around his wrists. "What the devil is this?" he mumbled.

"I fear it was necessary for my protection," a light, feminine voice said. "I wasn't sure how you might react when you woke."

He shifted his gaze to the opposite side of the bed he laid upon and spied the dark-haired goddess from his dreams. Or perhaps it was his nightmares, as his memory came rushing back to him. He set his jaw firmly and tried to speak in an authoritative manner. "Where am I?"

Although she had changed out of the gold gown, she was still dressed informally in a white nightdress and robe. She sat in a nearby chair wearing the same nonchalant expression as she'd worn the moment he had realized she'd drugged him. "Someplace safe."

He snorted. "That's lovely." He lifted a brow. "You have no idea who I am, do you?"

"Archer Grindstone, the Earl of Thanefield," she recited in a bored tone.

He blinked, but his surprise didn't take him aback for long. "Then you know the penalty for..." He gestured to his bindings. "Trying to kill a peer of the realm."

"I'm not trying to kill you," she returned evenly. "I merely kidnapped you."

"Oh, yes. Quite a harmless crime, that," he agreed in a mocking tone. If her face was any indication, she didn't find his humor amusing. He sighed heavily and tugged on his bonds. "I can't feel my limbs. Might you remove these blasted things so I don't feel like a trussed-up pheasant for Yuletide?"

"That depends," she hedged.

He looked at her and waited.

"Do you agree to converse in a sensible manner?"

He barked out a laugh. "You mean in the same *sensible* manner you demonstrated when you absconded with me?"

Instead of appearing ashamed, she rolled her eyes and made to stand. "If you aren't going to take this seriously—"

Fearing that she might actually leave, he gritted his teeth and said, "Fine. You win. Untie me and we'll... *talk.*"

She studied him as if trying to decipher whether or not he was actually telling the truth, but then she walked over to him. She moved aside the lower material of her nightdress to reveal a shapely leg, but it was the dagger she withdrew to neatly slice through the ropes that caused him to raise his brows. "Something tells me you have trust issues."

She shrugged. "I like to be prepared for any situation." She headed for the foot of the bed and freed his leg, and then she moved to his other hand.

With his left hand free and his entire right side undone, he sighed as some of the sensation began to flood back into his neglected body. It wasn't until she returned to her seat that his frown deepened. "I thought you said you were going to free me?" He moved his left leg that was still tied.

She slid the knife back into the delicate sheath and lowered the material of her gown. "That should suffice for now."

He laid his head back against the pillows and muttered a curse, but since it was obvious she wasn't going to offer any further assistance, he moved to his side and propped his head on his elbow. Silhouetted as she was by firelight and a candle next to her on the table, Archer found it rather difficult to remember that he didn't particularly care for this woman after what she'd done.

But then again...

"If you were into something a bit more... brazen when it comes to the bedchamber, you should have just said so. There wasn't a need to go through all this trouble."

She smiled tightly. "That would certainly appease your pride, wouldn't it, my lord?" She shook her head. "I fear you are terribly mistaken about my intentions." Her eyes flashed. "I didn't take you away from that ball for the reasons you might have supposed. You are here out of vengeance."

Florentia hadn't fallen asleep before she heard the bed move and realized that her captive was starting to wake. She steeled herself for an immediate confrontation, but he was calmer than she had expected. And rather witty. And charming.

She clenched her fists. She shouldn't be thinking of the earl in such a way, but even when she'd freed most of his bonds, she'd glanced at him surreptitiously and noted that he was all sinew, bone, and hard muscle. As much as she'd loved Jonathan, for a seaman, even he hadn't had such an impressive build.

Again, she told herself that this man was nothing more than a venomous snake who used the ignorance of others for his own gain.

"Vengeance?" He laughed. "Sweetheart, I've never met you before tonight, so how can you say—"

She narrowed her gaze. "I wasn't the one who was injured. Or in this case, pressed into service by your gang." This seemed to give him pause. "Does that ring a memory, perchance?"

She could tell the moment he shut down. "I don't know what you're talking about."

"I see." She nodded her head thoughtfully. "Then why did my fiancée's first mate tell me that *you* were the one who had dropped the King's Shilling in his mug of ale at The Cooper's Arms pub where he was forced to serve in the Royal Navy, and subsequently perished on a warship two months ago as a result?"

This time, his expression cleared and genuine sympathy touched his features. "I'm sorry about what happened to—"

"His name was Jonathan and he captained the merchant vessel, *Blackadder*. We were due to marry. He was going to have the money when he made one last trip to India, but instead, he was killed, *murdered* in my eyes. By you."

He instantly stilled, a myriad of emotions crossing his face, none of which she could properly identify. She did note, however, that the sympathy he'd shown earlier had vanished. "If you believe the ramblings of some drunken sod, then be my guest. Just know that you have made a grave error in believing that I am the one responsible for this man's impressment. If you release me now, I will not turn this matter over to the authorities and I will ensure that the persons behind these foul deeds are punished."

He looked sincere, and yet, Florentia had long learned not to have faith in the nobility. "How can I trust you?"

"You can't," he returned simply. "Just as I can't trust you to do as you say." Again, he gestured toward the leg still attached to the post. "But believe me when I say I have a personal vendetta of my own involving the press gangs of London. I also lost someone close to me, a younger brother, who didn't live to see nineteen years of age."

For the first time since she'd set out on this quest, doubt began to seep in. Although she had trusted Jonathan's first mate implicitly, when he'd had a bit too much to drink, there were times that he wasn't quite as... accurate as he might have been. If that were true now, then it meant she had committed a crime for no apparent reason.

Anna would be aghast if she knew.

Hopefully, Florentia's nervousness didn't show as she crossed her arms and tried to decide what to do next.

"I can tell that you are deciding what to do with me now," he noted dryly, as if reading her thoughts. It was rather disconcerting. "Again, might I suggest letting me go?"

She put a hand to her brow and massaged her temples. "I'm not sure I can."

He smiled tightly. "Why not?"

Too restless to sit, Florentia got up and began to pace the room. She started talking to herself as if no one else was there with her. "Jonathan always told me that I was too rash for my own good, that my Italian blood always burned too hot. I should have listened to him, or at the very least, Anna when she attempted to dissuade me from this asinine plan to—"

The decided clearing of a throat came from behind her. "I'm still here, in case you were wondering."

She spun on him with a dark glare. "As if I could forget the fact. I did bring you here."

For the first time, curiosity crossed his features. "How did you manage that?" He held up a hand. "No, don't tell me. You had an accomplice."

"Anna is a very dear friend and wanted nothing to do with this from the beginning. It was only with my assistance and her empathy toward a broken heart as a widow herself that she went along with it."

"At least she's loyal."

She couldn't tell if he was being serious or mocking her, but she replied honestly, "She is wonderful, and without her assistance these past few weeks—" She shook her head. "Since Jonathan and I were going to marry, he decided that it would be beneficial if I moved into his apartments in Soho Square. But when he died, I couldn't afford the rent on my own, so I was forced to rely on Anna."

Florentia hadn't meant to divulge so much to her captive, but the words somehow spilled forth. She thought that if he understood her plight, that he might spare her the hangman's noose.

"Where is your ring?"

She blinked. "Pardon?"

He glanced pointedly at her left hand. "Didn't he give you an engagement ring as a sign of his affection?"

Florentia looked down at her bare finger and swallowed, the memory of that poignant day underneath the shaded oak in Hyde Park a special one. "He said that he didn't have the money until he came back from India. He promised me that he would give me one upon his return before we wed."

"So his word was all you had to prove that he wished to marry you?"

She looked at him sharply, her melancholy bubble shattering with the slight accusation. "What are you trying to say?"

"There are people capable of convincing others that their intentions are genuine, when in truth, they are merely pulling the wool over our eyes."

Florentia's mouth dropped open. "Are you actually trying to say that Jonathan was a charlatan?"

He shrugged. "How well did you know him? Had you been together long? What did he do to prove his sincerity?"

Florentia didn't think. She didn't care if she was bound for the Tower or not. Fury was radiating through her entire body as she flew at him. She lifted her arm when she got close and snarled, "How *dare* you!"

Before her palm could make contact with his cheek, the knife had been removed from her stocking and placed at her neck. Just inches from her face, her handsome captive smiled slowly. "How the tables have turned, madam." He lifted a brow, any trace of humor evaporating. "Now untie me."

CHAPTER THREE

Archer wouldn't have harmed a single hair on her head, but neither did he intend to allow her to retain the upper hand. He had some questions of his own that he intended to have answered, but the only way to do that was to do a bit of bluffing. It was how he'd survived so long when he ran with criminals and thieves on a daily basis.

Her nose flared with her anger, and the color rose on her cheeks. Instead of making her less appealing, he would have liked nothing more than to have her soft curves pressed against him. Alas, first he had to assert his authority.

With her golden eyes sparking, she slowly crawled down his length. He had to clench his jaw when her glorious dark hair brushed his aching cock. He lifted a brow. "I know what you're trying to do and it won't work." He sat up and kept the knife pointed at her. "A quick jab is all it would take for me to slit your lovely throat."

She pursed her lips together and started working on the knot holding his ropes in place. When they loosened enough for him to get free, he grabbed the bindings and got up, then gestured to the bed. "Your turn."

Her mouth fell open slightly. "You can't expect me to—"

"Shall I go fetch some belladonna to make you more cooperative?"

She sat down with an irritated sigh, and then laid down as stiffly as a mummy in a coffin. Archer tucked the knife in the back waistband of his trousers and gathered both of her wrists in front of her. He was thankful that he'd had some experience on the sea, thus making sailor's knots a bit easier to achieve. Then again, he'd never imagined, while sailing on his uncle's personal steam yacht, that he would ever use his expertise to reverse kidnap such a comely wench. In truth, he was feeling rather piratical at the moment. He just had to remember not to lead off any sort of interrogation with *Arrgh*.

Once she was secured to one of the posts, he allowed his eyes to travel at will down her delectable, shapely body. Full breasts, a delicious curve of the hips, and well-defined legs made him eager to finish what they'd started at the ball. Unfortunately for his aching cock, he wasn't the sort who took a woman against her will. It was much more entertaining when they were moaning his name with passion.

He removed the knife from behind him and held the weapon in his grasp. The shining silver metal caught the light from the fire and glinted dangerously. He used his thumb to test the blade. "Very nice," he muttered. He turned his attention back to her and sat in the chair she had vacated. Adopting a similar pose, he tucked the blade in the cushion beside him, all while she glared at him with sparks of loathing in her eyes. He paused as he considered what to say. "I suppose I should start this inquisition by asking your name."

She looked as though she wanted to tell him to go to hell instead, but she replied stiffly, "Florentia Parker."

He mulled this over for a moment, searching his memory for any sort of connection. "Were you any relation to the Parkers who lived—"

"I doubt it," she snapped. "My mother was Italian and didn't care for English society. My father was a member of the gentry, although we seldom visited London. It was quite a distance to travel from Biggleswade."

Archer refrained from wincing. "Yes, I don't believe I'm familiar with anyone from there," he murmured.

She continued as if he hadn't even spoken. "This townhouse belongs to Mrs. Anna Shapley, who was my best friend growing up. She was a commoner until she married, but a sight better when it comes to personality among the peerage." She slid a condemning glance at him. "She met her late husband at the local pub and when they wed, I would often visit her here. Jonathan was a mutual friend. When he died and I had nowhere else to go, Anna kindly opened her home to me."

"Do you not have any other family? Siblings?" he prodded.

"No."

"I see." He nodded. "And what was Jonathan the Paragon's surname?"

"Wilden," she snapped.

Again, Archer rolled the name around in his mind, but he shook his head, coming up with nothing. At least, that was what he wanted her to believe.

She snorted. "I can't imagine why you don't remember him. Likely because he was just any number of other men you pressed into service against their will."

He pinned her with a firm look. "I already told you it wasn't my fault, and I won't have my word questioned again. Is that clear?"

She still had daggers shooting out of her gaze, but she relented with a reluctant nod.

"Good." He steepled his hands before him and said, "I suppose now I need to figure out what to do with *you*."

Her eyes widened slightly. "What does that mean?"

"I suppose it doesn't matter if I tell you, because you are now embroiled in my mission."

"Mission?" She blinked. "Are you a *spy*?"

He smiled slowly. "Some might call it that, but I prefer to think of myself as a criminal recovery agent." She didn't appear impressed. He cleared his throat. "Either way, you had no way of knowing this, just as I had no way of knowing that you were going to abscond with my unconscious body this evening. For the past several months, I've been doing my best to infiltrate the press gang that was responsible for taking my brother—and your betrothed. I was doing a fine job of it and was almost finished gathering all the information I needed to take to the Home Office and make my case."

"What does that have to do with me?"

He tilted his head to the side. "Since I haven't yet been completely trusted and brought into their inner circle to meet the leader, and I was likely seen conversing with you before we went upstairs, they will be wondering who you are. Considering your loveliness, there is the very good chance that, as of tonight, Miss Parker, you have just become a new target."

"But that's absurd!" She sputtered. "I'm a *woman*. They can't send me into battle!"

He leaned forward, and keeping his gaze direct, he said, "No, but they can sell you to the highest bidder."

Florentia was quite sure all the blood drained from her face, leaving it colorless. She sagged against the bed. She hadn't once considered the possibility that she would be sold as a slave. "Oh, my."

"Indeed," he concurred. "And since you aren't the common ideal of a British rose, I'm sure you would be a high commodity in certain circles."

She shot him a glare. "Please, don't attempt to ease my concerns."

He shrugged. "I'm merely warning you of the consequences."

Florentia sighed heavily and stared at the ceiling. *Think!* But then, she reminded herself that it had been her idea which had landed her in this current conundrum. Anna had warned her nothing good would come of it. Although she hated the next words that came out of her mouth, she forced herself to ask, "What do you suggest, my lord?"

He didn't even bat an eyelash. "You will need protection, but I am forced to complete my mission—"

"So you will have to hire me a protector." She sighed heavily. "I can't say I like the idea, but the prospect of boarding a ship bound for more treacherous waters holds even less appeal."

He smiled in a tolerant manner. "You didn't allow me to finish, Miss Parker. I was going to say that since you were seen in my company at a rather scandalous affair, the men I have been rubbing elbows with of late will think that you are my current mistress." He grinned broadly, almost dangerously. "I'm afraid that we can't disillusion them. Until my business is concluded, you will have to go along with the assumption."

Her eyes narrowed to slits. "I'm *not* going to be your mistress."

"Fine." He got to his feet and she was surprised that he acquiesced quite so easily. It wasn't until he was headed for the door that he shot over his shoulder. "It's your funeral."

"Wait!" She started to rise and go after him, but her bonds kept her immobile on the bed like a helpless babe.

He paused and faced her slowly, eyebrow raised, as if he knew exactly who held the trump card in this game. Unfortunately, it wasn't her. "Yes?"

She hated him. "What do I have to do?" she grumbled.

He smiled easily. "I'm relieved that you're starting to see sense, Miss Parker. Rest assured, I shall make it as painless on both of us as possible." He sauntered toward her. She eyed him warily when he drew near, but his hands were firmly clasped behind his back. "You played the coquette quite effectively this evening, managing to drug me and truss me up when I have faced more worthy adversaries than even you can imagine. I admit that it takes quite a bit of skill to fool me, but you managed it without much effort at all. I'm quite impressed." He bent down until they were eye level. "All you have to do henceforth is continue to convince my enemies—which are now *your* enemies—that you are madly besotted with me."

She tilted her head to the side. "And how do you know they won't just throw me into a ship's hold regardless of your 'claim' to me?"

"Because, my dear..." His grin broadened. "My notoriety is vastly growing through the ranks. You were fortunate enough to attend a celebration honoring my recent achievements, all of which were staged for my final performance, of course. But all is necessary to provide the *coup de grâce*. Naturally, I will ensure that your friend is also under intense protection from my associates at the Home Office."

Florentia swallowed tightly. He was entirely too close, too... virile for her peace of mind. "In that regard, why can't I just stay here with Anna?"

"Because, my dear..." He leaned forward until their lips nearly brushed. Lowering his voice to a mere whisper, he said, "I intend to prove that we are the perfect match."

She sucked in a breath. "You can do what you wish with me. Jonathan shall always have my heart."

He chuckled. "Again, you mistake me, Miss Parker. I have no designs on your heart. Your body is my ultimate objective."

He brought his mouth down on hers.

The instant Archer kissed her, he knew he was in trouble. His sultry captor was even more passionate than he'd originally hoped she might be when he'd first spied her in that tantalizing golden gown which matched the color of those luminous eyes. Her upper body instantly rose to meet him, the hard tips of her breasts brushing against his chest with urgency.

Rather than tease himself to the point of no return, he pulled back slightly and offered her a crooked grin. "I think that's a good enough start when it comes to proving we are more than compatible." He removed the knife from the chair and held it up to her. "I assume that since we have made a mutual agreement, it's safe to release you now?"

She glared at him mutinously but gave a brief nod of her head. When he sliced through her ropes, she gave a relieved moan and rubbed her wrist.

Just as he hadn't been prepared for the fire of her kiss, he didn't see the slap until her palm connected with his jaw and whipped his head to the side. "I may be allowing this farce for Anna's sake, just don't forget that I'm not anyone's whore, even *yours*," she warned.

He tested his jaw to ensure that it was still in proper working order and then he straightened. "I will take that into consideration," he drawled. "Shall we pay a visit to Mrs. Shapley's chamber and apprise her of the change in circumstances?"

She glanced at the clock on the mantel. "It's not even four in the morning. The servants aren't up at this hour."

"And yet, criminals never sleep," he pointed out. "Until I return with reinforcements to safeguard your friend, I need to ensure that you are both conscious of any impending danger lurking about after I take my leave. I shall be paying a visit to the servant's quarters as well."

She wavered for a moment, but then she gave a reluctant incline of her head. "Very well."

The earl waved a hand so that Florentia could lead the way to Anna's chamber, where he intended to inform the mistress of the house of the change in circumstances.

"Can I have my knife back?"

Archer continued to hold it securely in his grasp. He tossed it in the air, catching it neatly by the hilt. "I'm not sure that's a good idea just yet. Considering the blow you just dealt me, and the entire kidnapping fiasco, I'm not very inclined to grant any favors at this time."

"Fine." She tossed her glorious, dark head. "Have it your way."

As they walked down the hall, Florentia wasn't looking forward to seeing her friend's expression when they appeared. Knowing Anna, she might even faint. With this in mind, Florentia paused before her door and turned to the earl. "Might you give me a moment to tell her what's going on in private before you burst into her chamber?"

He stared at her, and then relented with, "Five minutes."

Her lips twisted mockingly. "You are too kind, my lord."

She walked inside the darkened interior and didn't waste time walking over to Anna's sleeping form. At least, she thought she was in bed lost to dreamland, but instead, the petite blonde rolled over and turned up the lamp on the bedside table. Her voice was anxious, "What's happened?"

Florentia blinked. "You're not asleep?"

Anna rolled her eyes. "Of course, I'm not. As if I could rest knowing what we had just done!" She put a hand on her forehead. "Has he awoken yet? Is he terribly angry? Is he—"

"You can ask me to answer those questions, if you prefer."

Immediately, Anna's face turned ashen as she faced the doorway where the earl stood silhouetted. "You're... here." She turned to Florentia. "But I thought he—"

"Was still tied to the bed? I'm afraid not." He walked inside and shut the door behind him.

Florentia glared at him while Anna was trying not to fall out of bed. Failing in her endeavor, Anna landed on the floor with a loud thud, staring up in disbelief. "Do you not understand the importance of privacy?" Florentia snapped.

"I saw the light shining through the door, so I assumed that was my signal to enter." He crossed his arms, and although Florentia didn't want to admit it, the movement made his shoulders appear wonderfully broader than before.

She snorted, but Anna was the one who replied. "Oh, dear," she whispered. "This is dreadful." Her voice was little more than a whisper when she added, "Are you sending for the watch?"

His gaze flicked to Florentia. "I see my lovely captor hasn't yet informed you of the latest development."

Anna's worried expression lit on her. "What's going on?"

Florentia took a deep breath and told her what the earl had revealed to her. When she was finished, Anna slumped back against the bed pillows and threw an arm over her eyes as dramatic as any actress on the stage preparing to swoon. "This is dreadful, just dreadful," she muttered. And then she abruptly pierced Florentia with an accusing glare. "I told you this was a terrible idea from the beginning! Why do I keep allowing you to talk me into these harebrained schemes of yours?" She looked at the earl. "I daresay this isn't the first time Florentia has made me question my own lack of sense when it comes to trusting her judgement. I can remember, not so long ago, that she and I—"

"Anna, really," Florentia was quick to interject. "The earl doesn't care to hear our entire history growing up as silly, village girls."

"On the contrary." His gaze warmed on her, as if enjoying the fact she was becoming so unnerved. She despised him even more. "I should like to be apprised of a few of these tales someday. Perhaps I shall write a novel in which you are the main protagonist."

Florentia opened her mouth to give him a proper set down, but Anna said, "*That* is a book I should like to read. No doubt it would be very amusing, indeed."

"Anna!" Florentia admonished. "Whose side are you on?"

"At the moment," her friend returned with a mutinous expression in her blue eyes, "I'm not entirely sure. We shall be very fortunate, indeed, if the earl continues to look at this as something of a lark. And if I were you, Tia, I would do my best to act as though you are grateful for his mercy, rather than irritating him any further."

By the time she was finished with her speech, Florentia was quite at a loss for words. As long as she had known Anna, she had never expressed herself quite so forcefully. Instantly, the guilt that wanted to swamp her before, came back with a vengeance. "Anna—"

She broke off because Anna got up with an outstretched hand. "No, Tia. No more excuses or doing your best to placate me. This is the last straw." She snatched her robe from the foot of the bed and shoved her arms inside, but then she paused before the earl. "Lord Thanefield, I'm terribly sorry about all of this. I daresay if you feel the need to turn us over to the press gang, I'm not going to say I would blame you."

CHAPTER FOUR

Archer had to resist the urge to grin. Mrs. Anna Shapley was a force of her own to be reckoned with, but in this instance, as hard as she might try to be convincing, he could see right through her little farce. He supposed the aim was to try and discomfit him, procuring empathy with an equal dose of revenge, whereas she would do her best to console him and leave him ready to walk away feeling as if he'd been the hero, as opposed to the victim in this scenario.

Well played, he silently applauded them, but unfortunately, it wasn't enough.

"Tell me, Mrs. Shapley, were you ever on the stage?" he murmured.

She blinked her big, blue eyes. "What?"

He waved a dismissive hand. "Never mind." He stepped closer to her, as if imparting a secret. "I trust I can rely on your discretion with this matter and you will stay indoors until I can return with the proper... reinforcements?" He paused just long enough to make it sound as though he would be coming back with a dozen of His Majesty's red-coated soldiers instead of the promised protection.

She swallowed hard, but her expression never wavered. "Of course, my lord. You may count upon it."

"Because you realize—" He lifted a pointed brow. "—it is a matter of life and *death*."

She nodded obediently. "Indeed. I am well aware."

He leaned back with a broad grin. "Good. I'm relieved that our concerns are aligned." His gaze slipped past to Florentia. Archer intended to return as quickly as possible, not only to safeguard them when he knew they intended to bolt the moment he was out of sight, but because he couldn't wait until his raven-haired vixen was all his. "Don't miss me too much," he drawled, and then he turned on his heel and walked out of the room.

He roused the housekeeper and spoke briefly to her, and then he walked outside into the incipient rays of dawn. He was grateful that it was still late summer, because he didn't feel any chill in the air without his greatcoat laying across his shoulders. Then again, his blood was running hot just imagining Florentia as his mistress. He fully intended to ensure that it became reality instead of just fantasy. But he was confident enough of his own prowess to tell himself that it would happen. Most women weren't as resistant to his charms, but she still didn't believe him. He knew that, so he would just have to prove his mettle to her by actions rather than words. When she realized he wasn't the cretin she believed him to be, and that her Jonathan Wilden should have never been put on that pedestal she'd built for him, they would all be better off.

Of course, he would have never admitted that the *Blackadder* was a ship he'd been watching for several months, ever since rumors of the merchant vessel carried much more than cotton and coal in its hold. Unfortunately, he'd never actually gotten a close look at the captain, as he was very careful who saw his face. He generally wore a Union Jack handkerchief wrapped around the bottom portion of his face and a tricorn hat on his head.

Until Archer could verify that he was the true leader of the press gang, then more innocent lives would be lost. But now that he knew that Florentia was more than familiar with Jonathan Wilden, he had no doubt she could be the witness he'd been waiting for.

Granted, she could be in true danger from the press gang, but considering Archer was slowly paying off the members to switch their loyalty to him, he had no doubt he would be able to stop any malicious intent toward her with the snap of his fingers and a bit more coin to jangle in their purses. However, since he needed Florentia's keen observation, and her body warming his bed, he might have embellished the danger a bit for her benefit.

Before he rounded the corner of the street, he glanced back behind him to see a light floating through the second story windows. He instantly picked up his pace, because he didn't have long to dally if he wished to make it back before his quarry escaped.

Anna shut the door firmly the moment the earl departed. "Do you think I was convincing enough?" She bit her lip anxiously.

"I couldn't have done any better," Florentia nodded firmly. "For a moment, I was truly convinced that you were upset with me."

"Oh, dearest, never! You have been there for me on so many occasions that there is no way I can ever repay your kindness and generosity." She grabbed the lamp from beside the bed. "Now let's just pray we can get out of here and make it to the docks before he returns and drags us both through the Traitor's Gate." She paused. "We are moving ahead with our original plan to flee to the continent if things ever got too heated here in England, aren't we? Granted, my savings will only get us so far, but I'm confident we can find some sort of modest employment."

Florentia reached out and grabbed her hand. "I haven't forgotten our promise to one another. We're in this together. *Always*."

That was all the confirmation Anna needed before she slowly

opened her bedchamber door, as if she was still expecting the earl to be lingering about.

Florentia rolled her eyes and gave Anna a slight budge. "He's not going to jump out and yell, 'boo,' if he was here."

"Are you sure about that?" Anna snapped in return, although she filed out into the hall. "He seemed like a rather obnoxious man to me. I'm rather glad you proved to him that he wasn't as grand in the instep as he imagined he was."

With a laugh, Florentia said, "Indeed. As am I."

Anna led the way to one of the guest rooms and after looking over her shoulder again, as if one of the servants, or the earl, might come upon them and prevent their escape, she moved a rug on the floor to the side. She handed Florentia the lantern and then crouched down and removed two loose floorboards. Inside was a linen-wrapped bundle that she removed and tossed on the bed. "Stable boy garb, so that we can look innocuous riding across the countryside." She withdrew two tricorn hats which joined the pile, as well as two leather valises. "Hats to tuck our hair into, and small traveling bags that won't weigh us down." She lifted a golden brow. "Do you know what you're taking?"

Florentia thought of the items in her room, but there was only one thing of import that she cared about—other than the knife that the earl had taken. However, all she said was, "Yes."

"Good." Anna inclined her head sharply, and then she took the lantern over to light a single taper candle in a holder. As it took flame, she handed the lantern back to Florentia, she walked over and handed her a bundle of clothes, her hat, and the valise. "Meet me in the foyer when you're finished. No more than ten minutes. We must make haste."

Florentia wasted no time in returning to her chamber. She quickly made short work of her nightdress and robe, leaving it in a crumpled, white heap on the floor. After she donned the trousers, shirt, vest, and boots, she walked over to the looking glass and shoved her dark hair beneath the hat. When she was finished, she took a moment to check her appearance. Moving one way and then the other, she was satisfied, that while she couldn't do anything about the womanly curves she possessed, she looked young enough to pass as a cabin boy dressed as she was. Thankfully, her bosom wasn't as pronounced as Anna's, who had always been a bit fuller in the chest.

Florentia left the empty trunk on the bed and snatched the only thing of value from the dressing table—a miniature of her parents. She paused for a moment to peer into their familiar faces. She wished she would have had more time with them, instead of being forced to mourn their loss from the cholera epidemic that had passed through their village a few years ago. It was the reason she was forced to follow Anna to London, where her life had changed in so many ways.

She snapped out of her reverie. If she didn't wish to repeat the same mistakes, then she needed to ensure she left London this very morning. A handsome face hadn't done her any good before, it had only pressed heartbreak upon her chest. The earl's handsome face would undoubtedly cause more damage. Maybe not to her heart, but certainly to her peace of mind.

She rushed down the steps to find Anna already waiting for her. As Florentia had guessed, her bodice was a bit more fitted, but her friend didn't appear concerned as she frowned at her. "Where are your belongings?"

"I have all I need right here." She tapped the inside pocket of her vest.

Anna shrugged. "Very well. Come on, let's go."

Rather than going out the front door, they rushed toward the back entrance. Anna extinguished the lantern, and then paused and listened for any sound. Putting a finger to her lips, she indicated that they should be silent as they ran across the lawn toward the stables in the back mews. Rather than alert a groom to their actions, they grabbed two bridles and led their mounts out, climbing onto their backs without a saddle. While it might have been rather uncommon to see two society ladies attempt the same, Florentia and Anna had grown up in the country where they rode bareback on numerous occasions.

With the bits secured in their horses' mouths, Florentia was just about to urge her mare into a gallop, when the light from a lantern flared to life, and all movements abruptly halted.

Anna gasped in alarm from her opposite side, but it was the gentleman standing outside a dark, unmarked carriage that held her attention. The earl had donned a black greatcoat, and with the pair of black stallions standing patiently in front to pull their master to his next destination, they blended in quite perfectly to their shadowed surroundings. Unfortunately, neither Florentia nor Anna had noticed them standing innocuously behind an overlarge tree in the alley until he made sure they did.

"Going somewhere, ladies?" he drawled smoothly.

The exasperation on Florentia's face was almost too delicious not to revel in for a brief moment. Mrs. Shapley, on the other hand, looked as though she might take a nasty tumble from her mare. "Might you assist the lovely Anna, Mr. DoGood?"

When a burly, blond man emerged from the dark interior of the carriage, looking more like a Viking eager to plunder ships on the high seas rather than a liveryman, Florentia had to laugh. "*DoGood*? I hardly think that seems an appropriate nickname. He doesn't look as though he's done a good thing in his life."

"I beg to differ." Archer grinned broadly. "Jeremiah is a most loyal associate. And he claims that DoGood is his true, family name."

Florentia saw him reach for Anna just as her friend's eyes rolled back in her head and she slipped off the horse directly into his waiting arms. Without a word, DoGood walked over and set her inside the coach.

Archer turned to her. "Would you care to join her on your own, Miss Parker? Or should you wish to faint into my arms instead?"

Florentia easily dismounted without his assistance. Jeremiah walked to her and held out his hand. She reluctantly put the reins in his grasp and he led both of the horses away. She stood there with hands on her hips and glared at Archer, and for a moment, it was all he could do not to blatantly stare. How she ever imagined that she might have fooled anyone into believing that she was anything other than a luscious, tempting morsel of a lady was beyond him. Her curves were clearly outlined in those trousers and he made a mental note to broach that subject in Parliament the next time they were in session. It was a travesty that women were covered from head to toe in so many layers of clothes when revealing men's clothes suited his tastes much better.

He blinked his lust back into focus and said, "Come for a ride, Miss Parker."

She walked forward and started to brush past him, but just before she disappeared into the coach, she bent close to him and whispered, "You wish."

He laughed richly, because he was quite certain she would have slammed the coach door on that parting comment, had he not been leaning against it at the time.

Florentia glared at Archer when he got inside the coach and sat down beside her. Once he'd settled himself, he knocked on the roof of the carriage so Jeremiah would know they were ready to depart. He glanced in amusement at Anna, who was lounging along the opposite seat, happily unaware of her current surroundings.

"Couldn't you have rode with your DoGood coachman?"

He had to chuckle. "And deprive you of my adoring presence? My dear, Miss Parker, what sort of host might I be to leave two ladies alone when they have fallen under my care?"

"Your *care*?" she countered snidely. "Is that what you would call this? I might choose a different adjective. Perhaps abduction?"

Archer was loving this. The lady had a sharp tongue. It had been some time since he'd been the focus of such a worthy adversary. It was a good test to ensure he was still competent when it came to dealing with new opponents.

He scratched the side of his jaw. "You would know the meaning of the word, considering our little escapade earlier this night." If it were possible, she glared at him even harder. "At least I was considerate enough not to drug either of you." He glanced across at Anna with a wince. "Then again, I didn't have to do much more than send Mr. DoGood in her direction and she was lost to the winds."

"I *despise* you," she snarled.

He merely inclined his head and returned softly, "You wouldn't be the first, and undoubtedly, you won't be the last."

She huffed a sigh and pinched the bridge of her nose. "Where are you taking us?"

"I shouldn't tell you since I didn't get that courtesy, but I suppose it doesn't matter since you'll soon be privy to the location. For now, let's just say it's in something of an... undisclosed location."

She lifted a delicate brow. "You have a secret lair?"

He snorted. "I prefer to consider it as more of a 'personal base of operations,' but I suppose you could call it that. It's not as if I could drag a group of ragtag, press gang criminals to my townhouse, now could I?" He shook his head and muttered. "They might be accepting of the fact I'm an earl, as I figured it wouldn't do any good to withhold the truth when they would uncover it anyway. However, society isn't aware of my double life, and if I take them home, that would be entirely too suspicious should my mother catch wind of it."

Throughout his speech, the only thing she seemed to catch was, "You have a mother?"

He laughed. "I know. Deuced hard to believe, isn't it?"

"No." She waved a dismissive hand, her expression somber. "I just wondered how she was doing after you said your brother—" She broke off quickly, as if perhaps unsure she should bring up a delicate subject.

He was silent, and then he found himself confessing, "She has good and bad days, just as you might imagine. She continues to wear black in honor of Matthias, and he's been gone six months."

A pause. "Do you have any other siblings?"

He tilted his head slightly as he regarded her. If he didn't know better, he thought he might have heard a touch of empathy in her voice. "I regret to say that she only had the heir and the spare."

"And your father? Is he gone as well?"

He nodded. "For several years now." He crossed his arms over his chest. "I think I know where you're going with this, but don't assume that my mother is all alone in the world. She entertains herself with society galas and has one of the most popular gossip salons in London, so don't imagine she is wasting away from her grief."

If Florentia didn't know better, she might have imagined that the earl was a bit sensitive about his family, his mother in particular. But then, that wasn't uncommon. Children born into the aristocracy were seldom coddled. From the time of their birth, they were molded and shaped into what society expected of them. She would almost bet all the money she had in her purse that Lord Thanefield's mother wasn't even aware of his current exploits. Perhaps she never was apprised of what he did in his spare time.

It seemed like quite a lonely existence to Florentia. She had also grown up feeling like an outcast. She never fit in as the quintessential, English beauty. Anna had possessed all the qualities that Florentia had coveted so desperately, and yet, she loved her best friend because she'd never made her feel inferior. She had always treated her as an equal.

As Anna let out a soft groan, Florentia quickly leaned across the expanse and laid a gentle hand on her forehead. "Anna, dearest? Are you well?"

"Tia?" Anna's lids fluttered open and she focused on her. "What... happened?"

Florentia winced slightly. "You fainted."

"I did?" Anna blinked and attempted to sit up. Florentia held her down with a bit of slight pressure on her shoulder. "Take it easy. You know how dizzy you are when you wake from such a spell."

"Oh. Yes." Anna reluctantly laid her head back against the seat cushions. "I'm fortunate that I always have you to watch out for me, Tia."

"And you will always have my friendship. Together forever, remember?"

As the carriage finally came to a halt, the door opened and the large silhouette of Mr. DoGood cast an ominous looking shadow in the interior of the carriage in the early morning dawn. Anna instantly gasped and promptly fainted yet again.

"Oh, dear," Florentia noted with a heavy sigh.

"Don't worry about her. I'll ensure that Jeremiah takes good care of her," the earl noted as he descended from the vehicle. When it was expected of her to do the same, Florentia reluctantly did so, but when she turned back around to the carriage, it was already rolling away, Mr. DoGood sitting in the coachman's seat.

"Wait!" Florentia attempted to step forward and yank the door open, but she was halted by a firm grip on her elbow. She turned her fiery gaze back to Lord Thanefield and snapped, "Where are you taking her? Release me, this instant!"

"I assured you she would be properly taken care of," he returned evenly. "Now, come along like a good little girl."

"Don't you dare condescend to me!" Florentia snapped but considering the carriage that held her best friend had already disappeared, she had no choice but to humor the earl for now.

"I wouldn't dare to dream of it," he murmured mockingly.

She tossed her head slightly in a show of defiance but trod after him.

Although it was light enough outside to see her surroundings, Florentia didn't immediately recognize where she was. Granted, she hadn't always lived in London, but it took her aback to find that they didn't appear to be in some sort of slum neighborhood. In truth, she wondered if they had even crossed over into the East End.

"Where are we?"

"In a little area of London called Fitzrovia." the earl said as he rang the bell at Number 28 Charlotte Street.

Florentia looked at him askance as his summons was answered. Without any sort of password or clue as to his identity, a painted lady that looked entirely too suspicious for Florentia's peace of mind opened the door to allow them entry. "My lord," the buxom brunette purred.

"Ah, Mrs. Berkley. How lovely to see you again." Florentia noticed that he kissed her cheek with quite a bit of familiarity, and she seemed entirely too complacent in allowing it.

The lady's gaze flicked to Florentia and immediately, her gaze brightened with interest. "Have you brought me someone to play with today, my lord?"

The earl wrapped his arm around Florentia's mid-section. "I'm afraid this one is all mine, Theresa," he returned smoothly.

"Pity. I should have liked to flog her properly for wearing those devastating trousers."

Florentia didn't have time to be shocked before the lady turned and took her leave with only a modicum of disappointment in her expression.

She turned to Lord Thanefield with wide eyes. "*What* was she talking about?"

He moved to stand in front of her. "Let's discuss this in my quarters where you'll be more comfortable."

His brown gaze heated by degrees and Florentia wondered if it might have been less dangerous to part with the dominatrix after all.

CHAPTER FIVE

"Why am I not surprised that you should hold a base of operations in a *brothel?*"

Archer shut the door to his rented rooms and smiled broadly. "What gave it away?"

She rolled her eyes, replying with, "We can't be that far from Anna's residence, and yet, you made sure that it took us nearly twice as long to reach our destination."

He shrugged. "I didn't want it to be too easy for you to figure out where you were."

She crossed her arms. "As if I couldn't easily find my way back to her residence on my own."

"You could," he agreed. He turned his head and pinned her with what he hoped was a look filled with sensual promise. "But you won't."

"What makes you so sure?" she countered hotly. "It's not as if I *want* to be here with you in this den of sin."

Instead of being offended, he laughed. "I shall have to tell Theresa that one. No doubt the other ladies will enjoy it as well."

"Other *ladies?*" Florentia drawled. "That's doing it much too brown, isn't it?" She narrowed her eyes. "Don't say there are more establishments in London that cater to these sorts of... sensibilities?"

"Of course," he returned without any hesitation. "There are brothels all over Soho for individuals who wish to explore their special sexual tastes."

Florentia shook her head. "Unbelievable." Without any apparent thought of where she was heading, she walked over to the bed and sank down. "I thought the Cyprians' Ball was dreadful. Little did I know how deprived the aristocracy truly is."

Archer lifted a brow. "I do enjoy where you mind is heading, Miss Parker." He removed his greatcoat and tossed it over the back of a chair. "We can begin any time you like. I'm more than ready to oblige."

She jumped up as if the mattress had suddenly caught fire. "I'll have to pass, thank you." She walked over to the window and looked down at the street beyond.

From this angle, Archer took advantage to admire her loveliness, outlined by the sun's rays where she was standing. She looked like an angel descended from heaven, but instead of salvation, she offered him torment, *everlasting* torment.

She turned around and, faced with that unusual golden stare, he was even more captivated than before. "It's amazing how confident you are—in your position in society and in this place. Don't you believe that at some point, those lines are going to blur?"

He walked over to a side table where his crystal decanter of brandy was ready and waiting. If he said nothing else for Mrs. Berkley, she was assured to take care of his needs. He didn't reply until he'd splashed some of the fine vintage into the tumbler, and then took a seat by the mantel. He took a sip and then let the glass dangle from the tips of his fingers. "I have been in this business a long time, Miss Parker. Perhaps even before you were out of leading strings. I think I know what my limitations are. But I do love how you are concerned for my welfare."

"Oh, I'm not worried in the least," she countered sweetly. "I was just wondering how a seasoned agent, such as yourself, could be manipulated so easily by someone like me, who has no experience whatsoever."

Archer frowned at this, because it had crossed his mind more than once as well. However, careful not to break character, he replied evenly, "You may have surprised me at the ball, Miss Parker, but don't forget that I have leverage to ensure your cooperation where Mrs. Shapley is concerned. In essence, I am back in control of the game."

"Are you?" she purred softly, and then moved across the expanse toward him.

He stiffened his shoulders warily, although his cock responded in an entirely different way. When she was standing directly before him, she removed her hat and allowed her hair to flow freely down her back. Archer's mouth promptly went dry.

"Come now, Lord Thanefield, let's not pretend any longer. We both know I'm in full control of this situation."

She bent down, giving him an enticing view of the valley of her breasts within the open top shirt and waistcoat she was wearing. But when he imagined she might have dared to kiss him to throw him off balance, she reached behind him and snatched the knife.

She danced out of his reach with victory shining out of her gaze and held up her prize.

He inclined his head. "Very well done, Miss Parker, but you seem to have forgotten one very important fact if you intend to use that against me." He downed his drink and carefully set the empty glass on the table next to him.

"Oh? And what is that?"

Her entire stance challenged him, and Archer's muscles were bunching with the anticipation of what would come next. Instead of replying, he shot out of the chair and knocked the knife out of her grasp. It went sailing across the floor with a clatter. She gasped and tried to rush for it, but he grabbed her around the waist then carried her to the bed and tossed her down. She cried out in exasperation and attempted to fly at Archer, but he was prepared. He caught her hand when she tried to connect with his cheek and used his weight to keep her complacent.

"Let me go!" she snarled, her body shifting beneath him.

"In all due time, Miss Parker, but considering that is the second time you've lashed out at me with no provocation other than your own, I'm afraid I'll have to show you that such poor behavior cannot stand."

His mouth swooped downward.

Florentia was afraid this would happen, but not for reasons of distaste. Earlier that night when he'd kissed her in Anna's guest rooms, she had immediately responded. For someone who was supposed to be entirely devoted to Jonathan until the end of her days, she was doing a bad job of pretending indifference to another man. Unfortunately, the earl had a way of persuasion that left her breathless. His experience and skill when it came to bringing something so powerful out of her was shocking. The worst part was that she didn't remember ever feeling this raw passion with Jonathan, and that scared her. Because she had given him everything—her heart, her body, her soul. If that could be wiped away so easily, then it made her wonder if what they'd shared had been as spectacular as she'd always believed.

Neither could she allow the earl to retain the upper hand.

"You're so damned sweet," he whispered as he trailed a path of kisses along her neck.

Although she shivered, she did her best to adopt a bored tone and an expression of revulsion. Rather than strike out at him physically, she would do the most damage by attacking his pride. "I wish I could say the same, but honestly, my lord, if you intend to embark on a seduction, the least you can do is attempt to do so *after* you've used some tooth powder."

He immediately stilled, his dark gaze shifting to her. But rather than appearing upset, he merely laughed. "You will do whatever is necessary to fight this attraction instead of giving in to what could be a wonderful partnership." He rolled onto his back and propped his head on a bent elbow. "Why is it that you insist upon looking at me as a villain so desperately?"

She lifted a brow. "You kidnapped me and absconded with Anna."

"You took me hostage first, and I gave you my word that Mrs. Shapley will be unharmed." He regarded her steadily, his brown eyes assessing. "Could you not simmer down this hostility for a time so that we might work together more harmoniously?"

Florentia knew that he had a point. With a heavy sigh, she said, "Very well. I vow that I won't try to further injure you." She paused. "However, the knife that you have in your possession is somewhat sentimental to me."

"Is it?" He got up and removed the item from the floor. He walked over and extended it to her, hilt first. "A loving gift from dear Jonathan, I assume?"

"Actually, no," Florentia returned. She hated the melancholy in her tone, but she couldn't push it aside. "It belonged to my father." She reached into her vest and looked upon the miniature in her hand. "Other than this, it's all I have left of them." She held it out to the earl as a sort of peace offering.

He took it and gazed upon the image, and then handed it back to her. "They are a handsome couple. No wonder you turned out so comely."

Florentia snorted and tucked the likeness away. She hid the knife away into her vest as well. "I would never aspire to my mother's beauty. She was incomparable."

"As are you, Miss Parker," he returned softly. "You just don't see it yet."

She looked at him, for the first time hearing a touch of sincerity in his voice, something beyond the usual flirtatious aristocrat she had associated with him thus far. She didn't like the devil-may-care earl, because she couldn't decide if he was being truthful about this quest for vengeance or not. If he was genuine about working to avenge his brother and put an end to the press gang's control, then they might find some common ground after all. First, she had to decide who the real Archer Grindstone was.

Restless with the sudden silence, she asked, "So what is our next step?"

He blinked, and then smiled. "We make our first official appearance as master and mistress tonight."

"Here?" she guessed.

"No, actually. We are going to visit another establishment in Soho. It's supposed to be a rather splendid party and a good way to waylay any concerns that my fellow members might have undergone after my untimely disappearance last night." He walked over to the wardrobe and pulled it open. After a few moments of riffling through the items inside, he withdrew a dark purple satin gown that put the gold one she'd worn to the Cyprians' Ball to shame.

When he held it up for her to view, she realized that to call it a dress at all was a stretch of the imagination. There was no way she could comprehend that it was meant to be worn with any sort of undergarments.

"This should work quite nicely."

Florentia crossed her arms firmly. "I'm not wearing that... *thing*."

He sighed tolerantly. "I thought we'd agreed—"

She waved a hand at the offensive item. "I reluctantly agreed to assist you in this endeavor in order to keep Anna safe. I never said that I would compromise my entire moral code to do it."

"Now is not the time to be a prude, Miss Parker."

She gasped. "I am no such thing! I just don't wish to be paraded about as though I'm some oddity to be viewed at the village fair."

He tossed the dress on a nearby chair and walked over to her. She eyed him with distrust, but he grasped her chin lightly and put his face in her line of vision, perhaps silently willing her to see some honesty in his gaze. "I will be with you every step of the way. There is nothing to fear."

Florentia nodded, although she couldn't help but add silently, *Except for you.*

Archer left his lovely mistress-to-be a short time later with the promise that the ladies of the establishment would make sure she was treated with every reverence. She hadn't said much to that, just rolled those adoring, golden eyes as he'd departed with the vow to return for her later that evening.

Once he'd given his instructions over to the madam of the house in her personal parlor, Mrs. Berkley had inclined her head as she pocketed the coins he'd given her with a coy grin. "It's always an honor having you here, Lord Thanefield. I do hope your lady enjoys her stay."

"That will remain to be seen," he murmured. "But if not, I know it won't be due to any negligence on your part."

"And surely not on yours," she added with the incline of a perfect brow. "Any of the girls who have hosted you say you are a very generous lover."

"I like to pride myself as such," he agreed honestly. "But the lady has yet to believe I have any good qualities. She is under the misinterpretation that I whisked off her betrothed with the King's Shilling and pressed him into service where he met his untimely fate."

"Have you not told her your suspicions regarding Mr. Wilden then?"

He doffed his hat as he headed for the door. "If I claimed Jonathan was anything but a saint, she would not believe a word out of my mouth. Miss Parker will have to be shown the truth instead. I just have to uncover it."

"I'm sure you will do your best, my lord." She blew him a soft kiss. "You are always welcome to take out your frustrations here. It is what I thrive on, after all." She reclined on the chaise lounge and allowed one hand to dangle freely at her side. "Punishment doesn't have to be painful. My clients often feel quite liberated after a session. I am anxious for the day you might seek to clear your troubles through me."

"And deprive the rest of London the opportunity to be cleansed thoroughly?" He shook his head. "My conscience would not rest should I allow that to occur." He touched the brim of his hat and strode out the door.

Archer released a heavy breath as he headed down the street. He knew it wouldn't take much for Mrs. Berkley to become his own personal dominatrix. She had long hinted, not so subtly, that she would be willing to take on the role. But Archer had never been interested in anything permanent. None of his relationships had been longer than a few months at a time. No one had ever tempted him beyond that—until he's spied a dark-haired goddess in gold.

Of course, the one woman he might want for all time wanted nothing to do with him. The irony was not lost on him.

After a brief walk, he found himself at the residence of another well-known lady in the same profession as Mrs. Berkely. Mrs. James had rooms at Number 7 Carlisle Street, and most of the press gang members were wont to spend their time between the various establishments for different female companionship. Archer and Jeremiah DoGood were two who preferred to stay in one location, and Mrs. James' establishment was the place Jeremiah had called home for nearly two years. Archer had thought Jeremiah remained because he held a *tendre* for one of the ladies who worked there, but when she'd left the house last week to seek alternate employment, Jeremiah hadn't even batted an eye.

There were times when Archer wondered if he wasn't just tired of playing the same game, and was trying to find a way out, but was too afraid to do so. Many men who became expendable were quickly dealt with in a rather unsavory manner. When this was all over, having finally reached the epic conclusion, Archer vowed that he would do what he could to see that Jeremiah was settled. Out of all the members, he was the one Archer believed could be trusted to start doing good with his life, just as his surname suggested.

After he was admitted to the house, Archer made his way up to Mr. DoGood's rooms. He rapped lightly on the door and it was opened a short time later by Jeremiah, clad only in trousers with his barrel chest bare, and wiping his hands on a strip of linen. The scent of saving soap filled the air. As he admitted Archer, he walked over to the bed and threw a shirt over his head. "Sorry, my lord. I wasn't expecting you this early."

"No need to apologize," Archer murmured. "You know I have long dismissed standing on ceremony where the gang is concerned." He tilted his head to the side. "I don't suppose you heard if the leader will be in attendance this evening at Mrs. Emma Lee's residence?"

"I've only heard that it is yet undetermined," Jeremiah hedged.

"Indeed." Archer sighed. He was growing weary of this game he continued playing with the man he believed might very well be Jonathan Wilden. But with any luck, if he made an appearance tonight, it could be confirmed by the lovely Miss Parker. He was hoping it might even draw him out of hiding should he learn she was there as Archer's new paramour. Changing the subject, he asked, "How is Mrs. Shapley getting along?"

Jeremiah sniffed. "I can't get within ten feet of her before her face turns ashen. I'm starting to think that she has an aversion to men after her husband's death."

Archer chuckled. "No doubt it's just your broad physique. It likely intimidates her. She just has to acclimate herself with the fact that you are a fine specimen."

He shrugged, and Archer decided that it would be in their best interests if he checked in on Anna for himself to see if she truly was frightened of Jeremiah. He prayed that wasn't the case, because he didn't trust anyone else to keep her safe in his absence. And he'd made a promise to Florentia.

He went across the hall and knocked on Mrs. Shapley's door. After a brief pause, it was opened slightly to reveal a blue eye peeking at him from between the door and the frame.

"Might I have a word?"

Her expression cleared slightly, some of her color returning as she opened the door wider for him to enter. Her blond hair was pulled back into a simple chignon, and she was wearing the same boy's garb from before.

"I trust you are being treated well?" he asked, as he made a small inspection of the room. He hadn't spent much time at this establishment, so he was curious how Mrs. James might treat her guests, however unwilling they were.

"As good as can be imagined, considering the circumstances," she returned. "Now I would like some answers. Must I stay here? Why can't I go home? Where's Florentia?"

He smiled tolerantly. "One question at a time. I fear that more than that will cause me a terrible megrim." He glanced at her, but she was merely waiting patiently for him to respond. Had it been Florentia, he knew she would have offered some sort of sarcastic rejoinder on his behalf.

He cleared his throat and said, "Yes, I'm afraid that for now, it is safest if you remain here. I could send Mr. DoGood to watch over you at your personal residence, but there are more people here who would be able to alert him of any sort of questionable behavior. Rest assured, I don't plan for this to be a lengthy event. I plan to expose the leader of the press gang very soon, and then you will be free to go." He paused. "As far as Florentia, I'm sure you can imagine how well she is settling in."

The blonde snorted. "I can't say I envy you for the fight ahead. She has always been very strong willed, but I would do anything for her."

"She does inspire a certain... loyalty, does she not?" Archer agreed with a murmur.

"Only because she offers the same in return."

"Quite. She has certainly given Mr. Wilden her enduring faithfulness."

Anna studied him closely. "Only because he gave her a reason to do so. If you want to earn her trust, then you have to prove you are worthy of it." She lifted a brow. "Are you willing to do that, Lord Thanefield?"

He nodded. "I should like to try." He crossed his arms. "And now I should very much like to know how your relationship with Mr. DoGood is faring."

She shrugged one shoulder and glanced away, a key indication that she was uncomfortable with the subject. "I suppose he's well enough."

"I understand you can't seem to remain upright in his presence. If your aversion of him is that drastic, it could be detrimental to my plans."

Anna hugged herself. "I daresay that's true. And yet, I don't think you fully understand my reticence. It's not because he scares me. If nothing else, he... fascinates me." She shook her head with a touch of amazement. "I loved my late husband. He had a wonderful personality and treated me well, but he was tall and thin. Mr. DoGood is so different that I'm quite overwhelmed whenever he appears. Although I can't say it's in a bad way."

Archer inclined his head, determined to file that information away for further deduction later. "I appreciate your honesty, Mrs. Shapley. I can promise that since you put your faith in me, it will not be in vain. And if you can be patient for a short time, I will make sure you never have to lay eyes on me again."

She laughed. "Lord Thanefield, if you survive Florentia, it may be that you don't want to see either of *us* ever again."

CHAPTER SIX

Florentia was ready and waiting on Lord Thanefield when he returned later that day. She wondered where he might have gone, but since she told herself it didn't matter, she attempted to greet him with a certain nonchalance, even if she might have been pacing the interior of the chamber moments before he'd arrived.

She was surprised when she'd tried the door and found it unlocked the instant he'd taken his leave, but then, where would she possibly go without her dear friend, Anna? And since she didn't know where the cretin had hidden her away, she was currently at Lord Thanefield's mercy, whether she liked it or not.

He walked inside and glanced at her, but immediately did a second take. It was the lingering look he gave her that almost made it worth donning the clinging, purple gown. She'd gritted her teeth the entire time the lady of the house and one of her "girls" had arrived to ensure she looked the part of a well-loved mistress. Florentia's hair had been left to hang down her back in a free-flowing wave that they said gave the appearance of just tumbling out of bed. Naturally, she had been *overjoyed* to hear that.

As the earl crossed his arms and leaned against the wall, allowing his gaze to travel slowly up and down her frame, she felt compelled to lift a haughty brow. "Like what you see?"

He lifted a hand and ran his thumb along his lower lip. For some reason, that simple action caused her stomach to do an odd flip. "Indeed, very much."

"That is unfortunate," she retorted, with a flip of her hair. "Since this farce will never become reality."

He chuckled. "You wouldn't want to reconsider? With so much spirit, I have no doubt you would make an admirable bed companion."

She sniffed. "You'll never know."

He pushed off the wall and walked toward her, but rather than doing his best to try and coerce her, he quite turned the tables when he said huskily, "I would have given you the ride of your life." Florentia clenched her fists when he turned around. He opened the door and looked back at her. "Shall we depart for the evening?"

Rather than reply, she flounced past him.

Again, that horrible laugh followed her down the stairs. When she reached the landing, she scowled at him.

"Oh, that won't do." Mrs. Berkley appeared with a shake of her head. "No one will believe you are swiving with that sort of distaste." She walked forward and took Florentia's hand and drew her closer to the earl. She released her with a wave of her hand. "Now, kiss, and make me believe you want him."

"But, I don't," Florentia returned.

"If you are to succeed in convincing the men this evening that you are not fair game, then you will have to play your part." She shrugged. "Or be prepared to entertain other members of the press gang."

Florentia could feel the blood recede from her face. The last thing she wanted was to be thrown into a pit of venomous snakes who were filled with licentious ideas. She returned her gaze to the earl and decided that if she had to deal with a viper, at least it was one she almost trusted.

She lifted on her tiptoes and wound her arms around his neck.

Pressing her body against him, she fluttered her lashes and cooed, "My darling." She closed her eyes and tried to picture Jonathan in her mind when she kissed Lord Thanefield.

However, the moment she felt the pressure of one hand on her lower back and the other at the nape of her neck, Johnathan's face started to fade. She didn't see his blond hair or blue eyes anymore. They were quickly replaced by another masculine figure with warm, brown eyes and Lord Thanefield's dark hair.

Archer... His given name flowed through her mind like a soft breeze, although the sensations he was causing within her were filled with turmoil. Fire pulsed through her veins as a surge of desire caressed her skin, causing gooseflesh to break out on her arms. His mouth truly was wicked as he coaxed hers to open. When she did, his tongue slid inside and mated with hers, a tantalizing dance of touch and retreat.

Florentia moaned softly when he drew away, reluctant for the moment to end. With heavy eyes, she was still reeling from the encounter when she noted the triumph shining in his gaze.

"I think she'll be just fine, Theresa."

From the look of murder that abruptly entered her gaze, Archer was afraid that he'd pushed his sultry little captor a bit too far, but it was the spark in her golden eyes that told him what he needed to know. And it made him smile.

As he escorted her to the same unmarked, black carriage in which they'd arrived, he was hard pressed not to stare at that curvaceous derriere when Miss Parker climbed inside before him. She made sure to pin him with her best glare when he followed suit, but the height of color on her cheeks couldn't be denied.

He sat down beside her, and her mouth gaped open. "What are you doing?" She pointed across from her. "There's plenty of room over there."

He tapped on the roof to let the driver know they were ready, and then he wasted no time in capturing her lips in a ruthless kiss that soon had her gasping—first in outrage, though it quickly melted into passion. Her hands reached up to clutch the lapels of his jacket, and he took the opportunity to slide his palm up her thigh. When his fingers brushed her core and he found that she was already weeping for him, he nearly fell to his knees and shoved her legs apart to gain better access to that glistening womanhood.

However, since he thought that would be taking it a bit too far at the moment, he started a slow, steady stroke that soon had her breathing heavily. When she moaned, he took advantage of her desire by sweeping a section of her gown away to bare those tempting breasts to his hungry gaze. He licked his lips in delight before he lowered his head and took one taut nipple into his mouth. He laved the pebbled tip until she was arching her back to give him better access.

He teased her mercilessly, until she was almost incoherent. But it didn't take long until she was pulsing around his hand in an orgasm that nearly made those brilliant golden eyes shine like the stars in the heavens.

When she was sated, her entire body relaxed, he removed his hand and lifted his finger to his mouth. She watched him with hooded lids as he put the appendage in his mouth and sucked gently. She inhaled sharply as he said, "Delicious. Someday, I might just have to have a more thorough taste."

He could tell by the sudden change on her face that she wanted to deny his claim, but she hesitated long enough that he lifted a brow and moved to the other side of the carriage.

"I hate you," she whispered, but it lacked any sort of conviction.

He grinned. "Yes. I can tell that you do. Your body tells me how much you *loathe* me."

For an instant, he wondered if she might fly at him with the intent to do bodily harm, but instead, she merely crossed her arms and sat mutinously across from him. He had to withhold the urge to love her into submission once more. She was sweetly erotic when he'd held her in his arms, and he knew that in time, he would wear her down until she gave herself to him completely. It would certainly be in her benefit to do so. He ensured that all of his previous lovers were treated with the utmost respect—and satisfaction. Although his cock was urging him to finish what he'd started and sink into her wet heat, he was not a base scoundrel who heeded his animalistic instincts. He was a gentleman, and so he knew patience was the best option to win her hand—if not her heart.

While he'd never thought about actually settling down and starting a family, as an earl, he was expected to do his duty at some point, and Miss Florentia Parker was currently first on the list when it came to admiring her lovely face for the rest of his days. He nearly chuckled. It was strange how being kidnapped might make him actually contemplate the marital state, as one couldn't become more captive than that.

Florentia pressed her thighs together, but still the ache wouldn't subside. The man across from her had opened a door that she'd thought long closed after she'd received word of Jonathan's demise. She vowed that she wouldn't love again, nor find pleasure with anyone else.

She slid a glance at the earl, who was staring at her with that same look on his face, like he was a jungle cat swishing his tail and waiting for the helpless gazelle to cross in front of its path. The problem was that this particular prey wasn't trying to escape. Instead, she had quite enjoyed his attentions, and she had to admit, much more so than Jonathan's fumbling attempts to please her. She had praised his efforts at the time, of course, but with *Archer*…

No. She mustn't think of him in such an informal manner. To do so would court disaster of the most epic proportions. She *needed* to dislike him because he was holding her best friend hostage. If that wasn't enough motivation, then the fact he had made her forget Jonathan so easily was surely worth a certain amount of hatred.

"We're here, my darling."

She wanted to roll her eyes at the smooth way he spoke, but then she remembered that she had to play her part, lest things come crashing down around them. She'd already caused enough trouble for Anna without adding more. Tonight would be the deciding factor whether they could go their separate ways, or if they would continue to be at the earl's mercy.

She stepped down with a coy glance. "Thank you, my love."

He gave her a wink of approval. "Nicely done," he murmured. "Perhaps it was a bit of incentive that helped to improve your mood?"

She pressed herself against his side as they paused before a house that was lit up from within. The raucous merriment inside was flowing out of the open terrace doors. Florentia might have imagined it, but it appeared that there was a shadowy figure lurking in the corner of the balcony, as if observing the exchange below. She meant to ensure that he received a good show. "And perhaps there might be an encore presentation later?" She fluttered her lashes for effect.

The earl kissed her swiftly, but thoroughly. "I shall count the seconds." He bent down and tossed her over his shoulder as he strode up the steps to the brothel.

She could hear a feminine laugh as the door opened. Light spilled out into the darkness, but that was all Florentia could see. "Lord Thanefield and... guest."

There was another chuckle as he was let inside. "Welcome to you both." A lady's head came into view, lips pursed as she gave a low whistle. "She's a pretty thing, my lord. You might have to keep a sharp eye on her lest she is stolen from beneath your very nose."

He smacked her playfully on the bottom. "I fear this one isn't going anywhere, Mrs. Lee."

Florentia wondered if that statement had a double meaning as he continued walking. They soon reached an area of the house where the noise was loudest. As he entered the room, most of the commotion ceased, and then abruptly erupted in a serious of cheers and shouts of victory.

"Huzzah, my lord!"

"What a fine prize to be had!"

"Can I be the first to use the whip on those rosy cheeks?"

Florentia swallowed after that last comment, and she was grateful when the earl finally set her on her feet. She swiped the hair out of her face and her first glance told her that the earl was the least threatening man present that evening. Most of the occupants in the room had ladies on their lap, some clothed, but most not, and in their hands were various implements of sexual servitude. She actually saw the gleam in one man's eyes as he slid a leather whip across his thigh.

She barely kept herself from cringing, but when she placed a hand on the earl's chest, she had no problem looking into that deep brown gaze and saying, "Sorry, gentleman, but I'm with Lord Thanefield this evening."

She saw his jaw clench, and his eyes darken with passion, and for the first time since she'd learned of Jonathan's death, she wondered if she'd truly been in love with him after all. She certainly hadn't felt this all-consuming ache that came over her whenever she looked into Archer's eyes. It was as if that moment of ecstasy in the carriage had wiped away everything before him.

"We need to find somewhere we can be alone," she murmured softly to him.

His eyes flashed. "Indeed? Are you feeling a bit restless after our earlier interlude, Miss Parker?"

She pressed herself a bit more closely to him. "You could say that."

He groaned lightly, but it appeared that their ploy was working, for a coy voice spoke up from the rest of the crowd that had suddenly gone silent around them. "I daresay I'm surprised to see you here, Florentia. But then, I always thought you were a whore."

Archer's fist clenched at his side as he held Florentia protectively against him. Her head whipped around sharply, as if to give the speaker a piece of her mind. Instead, her face paled and she wavered on her feet. *"Jonathan?"*

At that whisper of disbelief, Archer slowly pivoted until he could pin the newcomer with a more intuitive glare. So this was the lady's long lost love, taken by the press gang and held captive in servitude to the Crown until he perished at sea. Archer thought he looked rather healthy as he slowly sauntered over to them. He wore a smirk on his face that Archer yearned to rid him of, but considering the way the rest of the men in attendance appeared to give him a slight hush of reverence, Archer's suspicions about the captain of the *Blackadder* were abruptly confirmed. No longer did he have any doubt that this was the leader of the press gang.

He despised the fact that Florentia was about to learn the truth too.

"You seem shocked to see me," Jonathan said as he spread his arms and spun in a slow circle, causing a chuckle to come from the rest of the gang.

Florentia's voice was a whisper when she said, "I thought you were *dead* all these months."

"Yes." He nodded his blond head and pierced her with emotionless, blue eyes. "I regret that you had to believe I was killed in action, so that I could continue the good work here in London without any distractions."

Archer could feel her stiffen. "I was a *distraction*? That's all I was to you?" She scoffed with obvious disgust. "We were to be married!"

Jonathan shuddered. "My dear, I would have never gone through with it." He sighed in regret, although there was not a touch of it in his expression. Another good reason for Archer to smash his fist into the cretin's face.

"But why all the pretense?" she demanded.

Jonathan walked over and dared to reach out his hand and brush her hair. Archer's eye twitched. "It was the only way I could get you in my bed." He lifted a brow. "As if you are lamenting *my* cock between your lovely thighs." He glanced at Archer. "You should be glad I broke her in for you. She was a timid virgin until I—"

His words were cut off abruptly as Florentia's dangerous arm flew out and her palm cracked against his cheek. The sound reverberated throughout the assembly as everyone seemed to collectively hold their breath to see how their notorious leader would react to the slight. Archer wanted to crow in triumph until Jonathan laughed, and then jerked her out of his hold.

Archer started to step forward without conscious thought of the danger that would put them both in. That grew even more when the pistol was brought up and pointed directly at his chest. "I'll deal with you later," he snarled to Florentia as he shoved her behind him, where she was caught between two of the gang members.

She struggled, but it was no use. "Don't hurt him!" she shouted at Jonathan's back as he smiled maliciously at Archer.

"You thought you were being clever, didn't you, my lord?" He cocked the hammer back on the pistol, and Archer instantly calmed, became almost detached. There was something about the fact that one's life could end at any moment that changed a man's entire mind-set. "As if I didn't know you were working with the Home Office all this time to ensure I was dealt with." He shook his head. "It was a mistake you won't make again."

The front door abruptly burst open and several armed Bow Street Runners flooded into the room. It was the distraction that Archer had been praying for.

He immediately sprang at Wilden, whose focus had gone to the rest of his gang, who weren't going to be of any assistance to him. Without any warning of the raid, there wasn't enough time to even try to make a run for it. Not a single one managed to escape.

Archer would celebrate his victory later, but first he was determined to see that Wilden met his end, properly this time. His vision clouded with red when he recalled how he'd treated Florentia, and he let his fist lash out and connect with the man's jaw. The blow sent Jonathan's head back enough that Archer was able to wrestle the gun from his grip without much issue.

He didn't immediately go down, but when Florentia suddenly appeared at his side and her delicate fist made contact, it was enough to send him crumpling to the floor.

Without a word, she flew into Archer's arms. Their lips met with a hunger that seemed to surprise them both, but neither did they care.

At the sound of a relieved feminine voice yelling her name, Florentia broke contact with Archer and looked over his shoulder in surprise. "Anna!" She removed herself from the earl and rushed over to embrace her friend. "Thank God you're alive!"

"Of course, I'm alive," the blond returned with a roll of her eyes. "Archer made sure that my every need was met, so long as I stayed where I was."

"He's a scoundrel," Florentia muttered as she sent a glare back over his shoulder to the man who was engaged in conversation with his burly cohort, Jeremiah DoGood.

"Yes, I could see how much you despised him the moment I walked in the door," Anna said with a knowing lift of her brow.

Florentia put a hand to her forehead. "This is all so confusing. I know I shouldn't dare to like someone like him, but I can't seem to stop myself."

"I don't see anything wrong with him at all." Anna shrugged.

Florentia's eyes widened. "He held us against our will!"

"Yes, but it was really for our protection," Anna countered. "And he easily could have turned us over to the authorities when we abducted *him*, but he didn't. Surely that speaks of his good character, now that you know he didn't press Jonathan into service as you believed."

Anna's gaze slid past her and Florentia saw Jonathan's unconscious form being carted away by two Runners. "I hope he faces a firing squad," she muttered. "I can't believe I allowed myself to be deceived so easily."

Her friend reached out and grasped her hand. "I know why. You were lonely and wanted to find the same happiness I'd found with David. I tried to warn you against getting too close to Jonathan because I knew what I'd heard about his reputation, but you were adamant that he loved you because he'd proposed." She offered an empathetic smile. "And yet, he kept finding reasons to postpone the actual ceremony."

"I'm a fool," Florentia whispered. "I certainly don't want to make the same mistake twice."

"I know you may not have the best opinion of the aristocracy, but Lord Thanefield is an honorable man. I believe it with all my heart. And I think, deep down, you do too."

Florentia sighed. She had the feeling that Anna was right, but what could she possibly do about it but be his mistress? She might have some blue blood in her background, but it was terribly diluted. She certainly didn't know how to comport herself in polite society. The first time she was snubbed, she would speak her mind and become even more ostracized.

"But what about us?" Florentia said, squeezing Anna's hand in return. "We promised we would be there for each other."

"And we shall. I might have found... another reason to remain in London." Her cheeks pinkened slightly and Florentia's mouth fell open in shock.

"Not Mr. DoGood!"

"Shh!" Anna waved her hand almost frantically. "I don't want to risk him hearing that we're discussing him."

"I thought you were terrified of him!" Florentia countered a bit softer.

"I might have been at first, because I didn't know what to expect. And even now he frazzles me, but isn't that the point of attraction?"

Since Florentia didn't have a ready reply to that, she kept silent as the earl returned to join them. "Ladies, I fear I shall have to leave you for a time. I need to give a report to the Home Office." He spoke to both of them, but his focus was on Florentia when he added, "And tender my resignation effective immediately."

"You're giving up the life of espionage?"

"I think it's time." His dark eyes warmed on her face. "I need to start thinking of starting a family and carrying on the Thanefield line."

Florentia swallowed. "I see."

He hesitated, as if he wanted to say more, but he bowed lightly to both of them and said, "You are freed from my custody and I'll ensure you are given safe quarter to return to your previous residence."

As he walked away, Florentia looked at him longingly, but she left with Anna.

CHAPTER SEVEN

"I t's only been a day. There's no need to look so forlorn. He'll come back. I *know* it."

Florentia sighed heavily from where she sat in the front parlor of Anna's townhouse. From the moment they had returned, Anna had settled back into her usual routine, but Florentia felt like a wraith, a shell of her former self just going through the motions of eating, sleeping, and waking. "I'm glad you're so confident, because I'm not. I feel just as used now as I was with Jonathan."

Anna stood and set her hands firmly on her hips. "There is no comparison."

"Then where is he?" Florentia countered.

She could tell Anna wanted to continue to dispute the earl's absence, but since she didn't seem to have a proper reason, she just said, "I can't say, but I'm sure there was more work than he'd been prepared for. It was a large press gang that was taken into custody. No doubt there was a lot of paperwork to deal with."

Florentia wanted to roll her eyes, but instead, she refrained as there was a knock at the door. Anna held up a hand. "That could be him right now, and then you'll have to eat your words."

Anna promptly marched out into the foyer, and just because Florentia was too restless to stay still, she wandered there as well, although she kept out of sight from the side of the stairs. She quickly learned that it wasn't Archer's voice that she heard beyond the frame, but rather that of Mr. DoGood.

"Mrs. Shapley?" He cleared his throat almost uncertainly. "Anna. These are for you."

There was a pause and Florentia heard her friend reply, "They're lovely."

"But not so much as you." Again, he cleared his throat and Florentia smiled, because it was almost ironic that such a burly man who had lived a questionable life was now uncertain of his standing with a slip of a woman. "I was wondering if you might like to go for a ride with me today. I know you aren't quite sure of my intentions, but I intend to live right from now on, so I was hoping that in time, you might become more comfortable—"

"I'd love to go with you," Anna cut in. "Let me just grab my cloak and bonnet."

Florentia quickly made her way back to the parlor where she waited for Anna, who appeared moments later. Her face was flooded with color, and Florentia had known her friend long enough to know it meant she was besotted. "It's *Jeremiah*. He's asked me to go riding with him." She paced around the floor and wrung her hands in front of her, obviously distressed.

"Don't you need a wrap?" Florentia prompted.

She stopped. "Oh. Yes, I suppose I do." She looked at Florentia with anxious eyes. "Whatever shall I do? It's been more than a year since I've been intimate in any way with a man. What if he wants to kiss me?"

"Then perhaps... kiss him back?" Florentia suggested, although her friend's uncertainty was melting her heart. "Go," she waved her hands. "Have fun."

"Indeed." Anna's face bloomed into a smile. "Perhaps I shall."

As the front door shut firmly a short time later, Florentia walked over to the window and watched as Mr. DoGood gently assisted Anna into the hired hackney. They left and for a moment, Florentia felt the same wistfulness as before when she used to see Anna and David together. Although she was hoping that the street might hold another gentleman in a carriage hoping to win her hand, it was empty.

Disheartened, she headed to her room. What she needed was a nap to ease this melancholy. When she woke, no doubt she would be feeling much more revived.

She had just entered her chamber and shut the door when an arm slid around her waist and the other covered her mouth with a strong, masculine hand.

"Don't scream. At least, not yet. That's to be saved for later."

As Archer held Florentia's soft body against him, he had to close his eyes. It had been entirely too long since he'd seen her beautiful face or held her in his arms. But he intended to make up for that temporary slight right now.

When she nodded, he slid his arm down the side of her neck until it rested atop her breast. He moved his other arm until it was cradling the second mound and began to knead them both gently. The hitch in her breathing and the way she melted into him told him everything he needed to know. After everything that had happened between them, from their unusual and swift courtship, she still wanted him. And there was no doubt in Archer's mind that he wanted her.

Forever.

"Archer..."

To hear her breathe his name was like the most potent aphrodisiac.

As a reward, he tugged down her bodice so that he could continue teasing her pert breasts without any impediment between them and his hands. He rubbed the taut nipples beneath his palms and she arched her back to give him better access. He loved how responsive she was to him. "Archer, please. I want you. *Now*."

He needed no further encouragement. He spun her around to face him and kissed her with all of the desire that was pounding through his veins. He lowered his head and sucked on her breasts until she was almost panting with need. He paused only long enough to rid her of the irritating garments, until she was laid bare before him. He dropped to his knees and couldn't resist swiping his tongue along her core. He shuddered, for she was so damned sweet. He lifted her leg and set it on his shoulder as he teased and tormented her until she was the one shuddering around his mouth. He greedily drew in all her essence, pleasuring her until she was replete and her legs were shaking in the aftermath.

He lifted her into his arms and carried her to the bed, laying her gently down on top of the counterpane before he shed his clothes and joined her there. He paused to trail a finger along her temple and down her delicate jaw. "I've missed you."

"I missed you too," she whispered.

As he looked into those hypnotic golden eyes, he knew he couldn't hold back any longer. "I wanted to wait until I'd loved you thoroughly, and while I know we haven't been acquainted with each other more than a handful of days, there's no doubt in my mind that you are the one I want to spend the rest of my life with. Say you'll marry me, Miss Florentia Parker. Be my countess and make me the happiest man alive."

Her eyes filled with moisture, but she hesitated, and he knew why.

"Give me a moment." He left her side only long enough to remove the small item from inside the pocket of his vest. He held the ring out to her. "Just so there's not any doubt as to my intentions. This was my mother's ring, and I daresay she was more than happy to part with it when I asked her for it."

"Oh, Archer." She held out her left hand when he slid the perfect ruby onto her ring finger.

"A perfect fit, just like us." He grinned, and then sobered as he laid her back and began to kiss her smooth skin. He spoke softly as he made a trail along her chest and lower torso. "I knew it from the first moment I saw you across that crowded room that you were meant to be mine. Say yes, Florentia."

Florentia had agreed to marry another man, but it hadn't been real. She realized now how thankful she was that he hadn't been. With Archer, she knew that he would follow through on his promise, and he was, without a doubt, the perfect choice. "Yes."

He positioned himself at her entrance, and she spread her legs wider in invitation. He slid into her, and she closed her eyes at the feeling of perfect bliss. When he started to move, she bit her lip, because it was even better than the pleasure he'd given her before. Now, she could feel the connection physically, and not just emotionally. And it was glorious.

Archer was a patient and competent lover, and when the intensity kept building, he ensured she reached her pinnacle before he found his release.

Afterward, he drew her into the circle of his arms as she held the ruby up to the light. "It's beautiful," she said.

"It pales when compared to you," he returned huskily.

She rolled over and laid her hand on his chest and peered at him curiously. "You wouldn't have had anything to do with Jeremiah's appearance earlier, would you?"

He winked at her. "Sometimes all a reticent suitor requires is a push in the right direction."

"Anna seems to like him very much, although she's not sure how to comport herself in his presence."

"Yes," Archer agreed dryly. "I could tell by the way she kept fainting around him."

She smacked him playfully on the arm. "Don't tease her."

"Or what?" He lifted a brow that made her blood stir with heat once again. "You'll kidnap me?"

"Oh, I'm sure I could find some rope somewhere, my lord," she returned in a sultry voice as she started to kiss a path along his chest.

He groaned lightly. "That sounds rather intriguing, Miss Parker. Perhaps you might tell me more?"

"Of course," she said with a smile growing on her face. "First, I would ensure that your hands were bound so that you couldn't escape." She straddled his midsection and then grabbed his hands and held them above his head. In this position, her breasts were at a perfect angle for his mouth, so he locked eyes with her and darted out his tongue to lick her.

She shivered, as he asked, "What next?"

"Then I would take advantage of your helpless position to have my wicked way with you." She reached between them and grabbed his fully erect cock and seated herself upon him. They both moaned at the contact, as it seemed even better when they joined this time.

She moved her hips in a timely rhythm that had them both yearning for that sweet release, but Archer wasn't finished with the fantasy. "When would you release me?" he asked gruffly.

She lifted her arms above her head, mimicking his captured position. His eyes immediately darkened, his gaze riveted on her naked body. "Only when you have been utterly and completely sated."

He lifted his hips, thrusting deeply into her core. It was enough to send them both into the oblivion that they craved. She thrilled at the feel of his cock emptying into her.

When they had stilled, he sat up and wrapped his arms around her, kissing her thoroughly. "You are still my sultry captor, Florentia. Once we are wed, you can keep me captive any time you like."

"Indeed, my lord," she purred. "I think I shall do exactly that."

Less than a week later, Lord Thanefield and Florentia were wed by special license. A handful of people attended the early morning ceremony, including his family and Anna and Jeremiah, who were holding hands and looking quite happy together.

"I think we might have another wedding in the near future," Florentia said for her husband's ears. Archer kept her firmly at his side, even though his mother had wanted a moment alone with her to chat. It was his wedding day, and his mother could talk to Florentia after their honeymoon was concluded, which might take several weeks, if he had anything to say about it. He intended to keep her fully occupied in the bedchamber, and something told him that she wouldn't mind that in the least. She was insatiable, and each day he spent with her, he loved her even more. It was then he realized he hadn't said those precious words to her.

While the rest of the assemblage was distracted, he drew her out of his mother's parlor and into a room across the hall. It was the library.

"I must apologize, Lady Thanefield, as I have been terribly remiss when it comes to you."

"And how is that?" she asked, as she threaded her arms around his neck and pressed her breasts against his chest.

He could tell by the coy look in her gaze that she was expecting him to have his wicked way with her, and that might be a possibility, but first he was determined to have his say.

"I have yet to confess that I love you."

That caused her to still. "What?"

He frowned and adopted a tone of concern. "I didn't realize that you were having difficulty hearing. We should get that inspected at the earliest opportunity..."

She rolled her eyes and said, "I heard you just fine. I'm just... surprised. I wasn't expecting such a declaration."

"I honestly wasn't expecting Cupid's arrow to shoot me so directly either, so we are both at a loss for words, it seems."

She shook her head. "I'm not, because I love you too."

He grinned. "Do you, indeed?"

"I do." She nodded her head firmly, and then that deliciously coy expression entered her gaze once again. "And I think that we should consummate our vows before we return to the assemblage. Just to ensure there's no doubt as to the authenticity of our union."

Archer was already lifting her skirts as he spun her around. She put her hands against the wall as he inserted a finger into her channel, ensuring that she was ready for him, but there was no need to worry. She was always eager for his attentions.

He unfastened the flap of his trousers and then impaled her with a solid thrust of his hips. She wiggled her delectable bottom and tried to get closer to him when he teased her with just the tip of his erection. He held her hips to keep them immobile and then gave her everything that he had, before withdrawing and teasing her weeping core again.

"Archer..."

He knew that when she spoke his name in that breathless quality that she was close to her peak, so he didn't hold back any longer.

When they were both replete, she leaned her head back against his shoulder, and whispered, "Do you think it will always be like this?"

He leaned her head to the side so he could capture her lips. "With us, my dear wife, I think it's a certainty." He smiled against her mouth. "Now about that rope..."

AUTHOR'S NOTE

If you aren't familiar with The Cooper's Arms pub in London where Florentia's fiancée was supposedly pressured into service, then perhaps you will recognize the name Lamb & Flag. The name changed in 1833, although the pub began as early as 1772. It was actually nicknamed "The Bucket of Blood" and had a notorious reputation. It survived for years before finally closing its doors in 2021 due to the COVID pandemic. However, because of its historical significance, there is hope that it will reopen once again.

Being "put on the spot" was an idiom I found rather interesting and decided to use in the story. Pirates used to send the ace of spades with a hole in the middle as a means of letting someone know they were an intended target.

The issue of the press gangs was a very real concern in England starting around the time of Edward I. The King's Shilling one might find in a glass is supposed to be a rumor, but who really knows for sure? Either way, the practice of pressing anyone into military service for the Crown ended in 1815 after the defeat of Napoleon.

ABOUT TABETHA WAITE

Tabetha Waite began her writing journey at a young age. At nine years old, she was crafting stories of all kinds on an old Underwood typewriter. She started reading romance in high school and immediately fell in love with the genre. She gained her first publishing contract with Etopia Press and released her debut novel in July of 2016 - "Why the Earl is After the Girl," the first book in her Ways of Love historical romance series. Since then, she has become a hybrid author of more than forty titles, published with both Soul Mate and Radish Fiction, upcoming works with Wolf Publishing and Dragonblade, as well as transitioning into Indie publishing. She has won several awards for her books.

She is a small town, Missouri girl who continues to make her home in the Midwest with her husband and two wonderful daughters. When she's not writing novels filled with adventure and heart, she is either reading, or searching the local antique mall or flea market for the latest interesting find. You can find her on most any social media site, and she encourages fans of her work to join her mailing list for updates.

https://authortabethawaite.wix.com/romance

THE WRONG TWIN

ALEXA SANTI

Major Lord Philip Avondale had last seen Junia Reynolds as she was leaving the British warship that brought her family from slavery in Maryland to freedom in England. So why was she now working for the villains who abducted him from his brother's doorstep?

When she formed a desperate plan to rescue her beloved father from kidnappers, Junia Reynolds never imagined seeing the man of her girlish dreams as another of their victims, especially when he claimed to be his own twin brother. Can she trust him to help save her father when she cannot trust her own heart?

Content warning: past sexual assault

CHAPTER ONE

Major Lord Philip Avondale had got into many a scrape thanks to his twin brother Peter, but being kidnapped in his sibling's stead was perhaps a step too far, even for a man as tolerant as himself.

A call of, "Oi! Parson!" from the street had distracted him away from a blow directed to his head, disorienting him and giving the villains an opportunity to hustle him into a waiting carriage that smelled distinctly of boiled cabbage and horse manure, with few of the passers-by giving them more than a curious glance. He had been kept pinned to the floor of the carriage for what seemed like hours until they finally arrived at a house, dragged him up the stairs, and dropped him to the floor with a final kick to the ribs.

And here he was. Philip looked around the small and shabby room where they had dumped him, moving his head carefully so as not to cause it to begin pounding again. The surrounding silence told him the house was in the country, not London. The light coming through the one small window was starting to fade. There was a low pallet stuffed with straw in one corner and a chamber pot in the other he hoped was cleaner than the rest of the room.

It was still better quarters than sleeping rough on the Peninsula.

The scrape of a boot outside the door alerted him to stand and face whoever was there, bracing himself against the nausea as he stood too quickly.

The door opened, and two men entered. Complete strangers. The taller of the two sneered at him, while the other seemed to cringe back a little. "Well, parson. I suppose you never expected to find yourself here."

"No, I didn't," Philip said, with perfect truth.

"It won't be for long," the other man piped up. "Just a few days."

"Do you suppose I could get a chair? Perhaps a table?" Philip gestured to the pallet. "I'll be dreadfully uncomfortable if that's the only place for me to sit."

The first man sneered again. Did he even have another expression? "This ain't a dook's palace, you know. You takes what we give you and be grateful for it."

"Now, Dickie," the other man said, "'e's a parson, after all. A man of God ought to get some kind o' consideration, don't you think?"

Dickie contemplated this idea for a moment, and then spat onto the floor, barely missing the toe of Philip's boot. "I known more parsons than you, Jas. Ain't none of them worth a farthing."

As the two men continued to bicker, Philip saw the door open a tiny bit wider so the hunched figure of a woman could creep in. She carried a bucket and a small broom—a maid of all work to clean and lay the fireplace, it seemed.

But something about her was familiar. The way she moved, even while trying not to draw attention to herself. Her figure as she crouched to clean the fireplace, the brown skin of her arms streaked with soot from the work. Her hands, as they briskly swept the hearth.

She was doing her best not to draw attention to herself, but he *knew* her.

She glanced up at him from beneath the brim of a floppy mobcap that barely contained her dark curls. Those same thickly-lashed dark eyes still taunted him from time to time in his dreams, and his breath caught for a moment.

He had not seen her in four years, but Junia Reynolds was unmistakable.

Major Avondale's presence ruined everything.

Junia Reynold racked her brain as she briskly swept the coal dust from the grate. She had expected Dickie and Jasper to stay overnight in London as they usually did, giving her an opportunity to free her father from the room where they were holding him prisoner. A spoonful of valerian in the guards' dinner to make them doze, and she and her father would have had an hours-long head start.

Glancing up from beneath her mobcap, she shot Major Avondale a glare that was only strengthened by the little leap her heart had made when she recognized him. She had not seen him since she and her family left the British warship that had transported them from slavery in Maryland to freedom in England four years ago. Now she realized she had been watching for him around every corner she turned in London, which made her even angrier. Where had he been when she needed him?

Junia ducked her head and concentrated on scrubbing the hearth as she tried to discreetly eavesdrop on Dickie and Jasper, even as her body prickled with awareness of Avondale's presence. The thick London accents were still difficult for her to decipher, but they seemed to disagree about exactly what comforts their prisoner was and was not to be allowed. It was no surprise Dickie was the one arguing for harsher treatment and Jasper for a little softness. She had already seen how they treated her father.

Pappa.

Gripping the scrubbing brush tighter, she pushed away the

thought. She could not come up with a new escape plan if she did not stay calm and keep a clear head.

"Gentlemen, gentlemen," Major Avondale said, and she frowned a little into the flagstones of the hearth as she scrubbed. His voice was different than she remembered. He had been a commanding and self-assured officer on board the ship, not this diffident-seeming man in fashionable civilian clothing.

"Gentlemen, there is no need to argue," he continued when Dickie and Jasper subsided. "If there is no chair or table to be had, then that shall be the lot our Lord has given me."

Dickie grunted, and Jasper smiled tentatively, exposing the several rotting stumps of his teeth. "I thankee, parson. But mebbe the girl can look in the attic for summat for you to sit on."

Junia hunched down under the unexpected attention, scrubbing the hearth vigorously one last time before she laid fresh coals in the grate.

"I would appreciate it," Major Avondale said. She could feel him glance at her, and then away.

With a murmur, she rose back to her half-crouch and scuttled away again, pausing in the hallway just out of sight to see if the conversation continued. To her disappointment, all she heard was the sound of their footsteps towards the door, which sent her hurtling down the narrow steps back to the kitchen.

It wasn't as though there wasn't enough for her to do, even beside her plans to rescue her father. There was a guard at each of the two doors of the house, but she was the only inside servant. She was kept busy all day with the cooking and cleaning for the five—now six—men in the house.

With a sigh, she pushed through the door to the kitchen, where she had left a hearty stew for the evening meal bubbling over the fire. Her skills were meager since she had been trained as a lady's maid, not a cook, but the men didn't seem to have high standards. Plain food and plenty of it seemed to satisfy them and left her enough time to continue to assess the house under the guise of cleaning it, a job which would take a dozen maids a full week to accomplish, at the least.

Her biggest problem was the nighttime guards. Even if she and her father could both get through the tiny window of his room, that window was directly above the door where Robby stood all night, with the other guard, Jem, at the back. Things were a bit looser during the day while the guards slept, but then Dickie and Jasper were constantly underfoot, quarreling and sniping at each other while they walked through the house in their muddy boots and left dishes under the furniture for her to pick up. This was why she had set her plan for when they would be gone overnight... but they had returned unexpectedly, and with Major Avondale in tow.

Once in the kitchen, she set down the coalscuttle, rinsed her hands under the pump in the sink, and floured the table so she could punch down the dough for the week's bread. She had to admit the kneading and punching relieved her feelings at least a little and helped her keep a clearer head as she figured out a way to get around the guards.

The man upstairs must be Major Avondale. He *must* be. She had seen the recognition on his face, as she knew he had seen it on hers. Why Dickie and Jasper thought he was a minister was beyond her, but she hoped she would be able to use their confusion to her advantage.

If she was wrong, and he really was a stranger... well, she had to assume a minister would be interested in her escape plans and willing to help. She could not allow him to stand in the way of her goal.

As she had done every night since the day she had arrived in this house, Junia spooned the evening's dinner into a bowl for Robby, the younger of the two guards, to take upstairs to her father. She tried to be discreet about giving Pappa the best pieces of meat, a secret signal to him that she was still there and still working to free him. Her father was clearly the more valuable of the two prisoners since she was rarely allowed inside his room and, even then, it was under the watchful eye of Dickie or Jasper. So far, they were less watchful with Major Avondale, and she hoped to be able to turn that to her advantage.

When Robby returned with the empty bowl, Junia said, "What about the other, um, guest?"

"T'other?"

"There's a man in the other room. A minister."

Robby frowned. "Dickie didn't tell me about no other pris'ner."

"I saw him today when I cleaned the hearth," she said. "You'd better take him up a bowl, too."

"Yes, Miss Josephine," Robby said meekly, and she dished out more stew. He towered over her and didn't seem very bright, but he would sometimes follow her around like a puppy unless she sent him off to do an errand for her.

"Take it to... the minister for his dinner, and then you may have your own."

Obediently, Robby trotted off and Junia huffed a sigh to brace herself before she went down the hallway to the dining room. It wasn't much—just a table and four chairs—but Dickie insisted he and Jasper should eat there rather than in the kitchen, where she would be much more able to eavesdrop on them.

As usual, Dickie was drinking deep of the cheap gin he brought with him by the case from London, and Jasper wasn't in much better condition. As she cleared their plates, their only discussion was a drunken argument about the latest prizefight they had seen in London. She ignored Dickie's hard pinch on her bottom. He was already too drunk to do anything, and even if he had wanted more, she wedged her bedroom door shut every night to make it not worth his trouble to molest her.

"But why a parson?" Jasper whined, and Junia slowed her movements to listen as she cleaned up.

Dickie took another swig of his tankard of gin and belched. "That's the way it goes sometimes in this business. People stick their noses in where they don't belong and have to get cut out. Best not to worry about it."

"Havin' a parson around makes me feel guilty," Jasper muttered. "Like I shoulda gone to chapel like me mum wanted."

"Don't be stupid," Dickie said, and the conversation turned again until Junia felt she could not dawdle in the room any longer without drawing attention.

Back in the kitchen, she dished out stew for Robby and Jem, the other guard, and cleaned the kitchen up around them as they ate, banking the fire and preparing the ingredients she would need to make porridge in the morning.

Robby pushed his bowl away. "That was right good, Miss Josephine."

"Thank you," Junia said, a thread of nervousness creeping up her spine. Jasper and Jem were indifferent to her, but she was starting to suspect Robby was developing... feelings for her.

She considered for a moment whether it was worth playing on those feelings to help free her father, but filed the idea away for another time. If she could avoid leading a man on, she would, even if he *was* a criminal participating in a kidnapping. Two kidnappings.

Junia turned away to finish her cleaning, ignoring him. Robby hovered for a long moment before Jem punched him lightly on the shoulder and Robby obediently followed the other man out the kitchen door to their posts for the night.

Suppressing a yawn, she lit a candle from the banked fire and made her way to the tiny room behind the kitchen's fireplace. There was barely enough room for her straw pallet and the chest which held an extra work dress and a few chemises, but she preferred the windowless quarters to a more spacious room that would be easier for one of the men to sneak into.

She pushed the wooden wedge under the door, undressed and washed, and lay herself down for the night, head still spinning.

Why did they kidnap Major Avondale? And why did they think he was a clergyman?

As Philip listened carefully that evening, he could hear movement on the other side of the wall. The one to the north, as far as he could tell.

There was a short murmur of voices that quickly faded away. To his surprise, footsteps returned a few minutes later, and the door opened to reveal a large but dull-looking man holding a tray with a bowl and a piece of bread on it.

"She said you was to have it. Miss Josephine."

"Ah. Thank you, then." Philip took the tray and set it on the floor. The other man left as abruptly as he had arrived, locking the door behind him.

At least someone had remembered to feed him. He suspected it was all Junia, and he could have starved for all Dickie and… what was the other name? Jas? They did not strike him as the most diligent of wardens.

As he ate, the pacing began again on the other side of the wall. Up and down. Back and forth. Repetitive, purposeful, as if to fill the time. It was the deliberation of the movement which convinced him the person on the other side of the wall must be a fellow prisoner. Why else would someone pace like that, in repetitive steps which rarely seemed to vary?

Philip waited until the coals in the fire burned low and all sound in the house had died down to tap experimentally on the wall, rapping twice in quick succession, trying to make it loud enough for the sound to reach through the plaster but quiet enough not to be heard by the guards below the window.

There was a long pause. Then a series of soft footfalls to the wall.

Then two raps in response, in the same quick succession.

He had been right. He was not the only one held prisoner in this place.

CHAPTER TWO

As she usually did, Junia rose before dawn and made her way down the short passageway to the kitchen, shivering in the early morning chill. Yawning, she poked at the kitchen fire to bring it back to life, feeding in more wood until she was rewarded with a steady flame. It had been a difficult night's sleep, her fears for her father and her family back in London now joined with fear for Major Avondale. Assuming he really was Major Avondale, and not a minister like Dickie and Jasper seemed to think.

The homely tasks soothed her as she moved around the kitchen, bringing the porridge to a simmer and putting the teakettle over the fire. Those who preferred could slice themselves some bread and cheese from the pantry, assuming the mice had not gotten to it. She wished she had one of her mother's thick knitted shawls to keep her warm, but it was exactly the sort of possession the impoverished maidservant she claimed to be would never have.

She prepared a tray for her father, adding a cup of weak tea in a chipped earthenware mug, and carried it upstairs to where Jem stood outside her father's door. With a nod to her, he unlocked it and stood back so she could carry the tray inside.

Her father was already sitting at the desk, an open account book in front of him, carefully tracing his finger down the row of numbers and consulting the list next to him. All she knew about his task was Dickie and Jasper brought him stacks of accounting books to be altered to written instructions that were then taken away and replaced with more.

She set the tray down on the desk, and he looked up and smiled at her. Junia flashed him a tiny smile before turning away, her heart aching. It had only been two weeks, but he already looked a little ashen to her, drawn and faded by the imprisonment and lack of exercise. She knew he paced the room to pass the time, but it could never replace the long walks through the streets of London her father preferred.

To her surprise, he touched the back of her hand, too swiftly for Jem to see, and she looked back at him. Her father gestured to the far wall with a raise of his eyebrows and then held her gaze. It took her a moment to understand what he was asking before it dawned on her, and she nodded once in confirmation.

Yes, there is another prisoner in that room.

Her father nodded in return and went back to his account book. Junia held back for a moment, checking again that he seemed well, before reluctantly turning back to the door.

She *would* get him out, no matter what it took.

Philip looked up as the door unlocked and opened, trying to keep his expression mild. One of the villains—the one called Jas—stood in the doorway, cap snatched off his greasy hair and twisting in his hands.

"Morning, parson."

"Good morning," Philip said, and smiled. The man seemed to find it reassuring, because he took another step into the room.

"I was thinking... we snatched ye without yer Bible, didn't we?"

"Yes," Philip lied. "I must have dropped it when you pushed me into the carriage."

"It ain't right. A parson without his Bible, I mean. So I brung you one."

The book Jas shoved at him was filthy, the cheap cover torn and folded, but Philip tried to accept it with a believable amount of reverence. "Thank you, my son."

"'Tis nothin', parson."

Philip paged through it, trying to think as he scanned past the familiar verses. At Winchester, he had once won a prize for scripture knowledge, though the headmaster had never known Philip had hidden the answers on the inside of his cuff. The guilt over his cheating had been worth it so he could to lord it over Peter that Philip knew the Bible better than Peter did, even though Peter was the one destined for the Church and Philip for the army.

"Is there... do ye need anywhat else?"

Philip looked up, and fixed the man with his sternest vicar's gaze. "I need my freedom."

The man flinched, but sighed. "Can't do that, parson. I wish I could. I really do. But I can't."

"I understand," Philip said, and then an idea dawned. "Perhaps you could send someone to build up the fire. It's a bit chilly in here."

"Ar. I can send the girl, mebbe."

"Thank you," Philip said, keeping the triumph from his voice.

He remained seated, pretending to read the Bible, as Jas exited the room, locking the door behind him. It seemed a long wait until the door unlocked again and she crept into the room, the door closing with a snap behind her. Philip pretended not to watch as Junia crossed to the grate and began to sweep out the coal dust, casting glances at him as he ignored her. The fact that a run-down house like this would have coal grates rather than wood fireplaces was intriguing. They were not so far from London as he had feared if the fires in this house were made with coal rather than wood.

She kept her back to him, but he knew it was Junia. He could never mistake her for anyone else. The hem of her threadbare gown was filthy and her arms were streaked with flour and coal dust. He felt a moment of anger that she would end up as a servant in this hovel after her daring escape from slavery, though at least the villains here were likely paying her a few pence per week.

"Is he still outside the door?" he said as softly as he could. She froze, and then nodded without looking at him.

He continued to page through the Bible with one hand, the turning of the paper sounding unusually loud in the silence of the room. With the other, he searched through his pockets as quietly as he could manage. They had taken his purse, of course, and his penknife, and his watch and fob were probably fetching a pretty penny with a crooked jeweler at this very moment.

But he found something more precious the ruffians had over-looked, something far more useful than money in his present predica-ment—a tiny stub of a pencil with a bit of lead still exposed.

He flipped through the pages of the pocket Bible, trying to decide what to do. Writing on the pages might be too dangerous if the villains decided to search her once she left the room. A code of some kind was needed, to pass a message that would not endanger her. After a long moment, he chose a psalm and began to mark it.

She finished sweeping out the grate and piling the new fuel on the fire. She looked over her shoulder at him, and he gestured for her to come closer. She stepped carefully, but one of the boards groaned beneath her feet, and the door began to open.

In a flash, she dropped to her knees before Philip, and he placed his hand on her head, slightly dislodging her cap as the door opened and the other villain—not the one who had given him the Bible—scowled at them both. Dickie, that was the man's name.

"Amen," Philip said, and pressed the tiny square of paper into the palm of her hand as she rose to her feet, head still bowed.

"Amen," she said, so softly he could barely hear her, and scuttled from the room under the furious eye of his captor.

"Givin' out blessings, are we, parson?" the man drawled as he sauntered into the room. Philip kept a wary eye on him. Dickie was more volatile than his partner, and Philip did not want to have to defend himself when Junia and the other prisoner were at risk.

"Do you feel in need of one?" Philip said genially. "I am always willing to accept sinners back into the fold."

"None o' that churchin' for me," Dickie said, and spat on the floor, dangerously close to the toe of Philip's boot. Philip kept his expression placid, though he marked the action down for future retribution. "God never did me no good."

"The door to St. Luke's is open to anyone who wants to be forgiven."

"Is that what you was doing with the girl? Forgivin' her sins?"

"She asked for a blessing and I gave it."

The man gave him a moody glare. "Wenches is all the same. Sweet on the outside, whores at the core."

Rage and fear choked Philip's throat for a long moment. After his years at war, he had an acute understanding of how much danger Junia could be in for as long as she stayed in this house. "She asked me to pray for her ailing mother, and we did."

"That better be all it was, 'cause maids are a penny to the dozen. I could slit her throat, throw her in a ditch, and have another tweeny here afore the sun set."

"Understood," Philip said. Had the girl been a stranger to him, he might have taken the warning and left well enough alone so as not to endanger her further, but he had no choice. Either Junia helped him escape or they might all be murdered.

Back in the kitchen, Junia carefully unfolded the tiny piece of paper Major Avondale had pressed into her hand. It was a page torn from Psalms, and she stared at it for a long moment before she realized small pencil marks were under some of the letters in the passage.

It was a coded message.

The door opened behind her and she shoved the paper into the pocket of her apron to look at when she had more privacy. She turned to see Dickie standing in the doorway glaring at her.

"You'd best not be playing a game," he said, and his quiet tone was more menacing than any bluster she had heard from him. Knowing she was trembling, she kept her gaze locked with his.

"I don't know what you mean."

"That man is here a'purpose, and you ain't. It's easy to make one woman disappear." Dickie drew one dirty finger across his throat, and her hand went to her own involuntarily.

"I... I won't do anything."

"You know what's in store for you if you do," he said, then spun on his heel and strode away.

Junia sank down onto a kitchen bench. She had been able to create a discreet plan to free her father, had had it just within her grasp, and within less than a day of Major Avondale arriving in the house, it was all in ruins.

He was an army officer. He could take care of himself. There was no need to put her father's life in peril just because Major Avondale was endangered as well.

Even though the thought of abandoning Avondale to his fate made her want to weep.

She pushed the note further into her apron pocket, took a deep breath, and began her preparations for the evening meal. Robby had wrung the neck of a chicken and bashfully presented it to her that morning, so she began the loathsome process of plucking it to prepare for roasting. She spent the rest of the day busying herself with domestic tasks, trying not to wonder what was happening to either of the prisoners upstairs.

In her room that night, Junia pulled Avondale's sheet of paper close to the candle, trying to see the tiny pencil marks under some of the letters. She spelled and re-spelled the letters in her head multiple times, trying to make sense of them, sometimes mistaking a speck of dirt for a pencil mark or dismissing one as a mere speck of dirt.

But at last, she formed a sentence that made sense to her, and a wave of relief washed over her.

I am not the man they think.

She had been right, which meant Dickie and Jasper had abducted the wrong man.

The knowledge only made Major Avondale's position more dangerous, though. Even as a duke's brother, it would be easy enough for the men to kill him and dump his body on Hampstead Heath where highwaymen still roamed and make it look as though he had been robbed and murdered. No one would be able to connect them to the crime.

No one but her.

CHAPTER THREE

The tension in the house slowly receded over the next several days. Junia was careful to stay out of Dickie's path except when absolutely necessary, and to keep her head down and her eyes to herself when she did encounter him. He seemed to feel he had sufficiently cowed her, because he returned to his carelessly arrogant way of ignoring her as much as possible.

He was still suspicious enough to ensure Jem or Robby or Jasper hovered in the open doorway whenever she delivered food to the two prisoners or cleaned their rooms. There were no further opportunities for her to have a quiet conversation with either her father or Major Avondale under those bored gazes. Not even a chance for another note to be slipped.

Patience was one of Junia's virtues, and it paid off the day Dickie and Jasper came thundering down the stairs carrying a trunkload of ledgers gathered from her father's room. They supervised Jem and Robby in loading them onto the wagon they would drive to London. She was careful to show no interest in the commotion, staying away from more than a casual peek or two out of the windows as the four men conferred.

When she was back in the kitchen, she looked up as someone strolled in, and her heart sank a little when she saw it was Jasper. He crossed to the pantry, rummaging around in it until she finally said, "What is it you need?"

"Apple."

"I put them in yesterday's pie."

He grunted and took himself off, likely to get an early start on the day's drinking and read some sporting news. Junia picked up her dusting cloth and wandered the house until she was able to determine Jem must have gone to town with Dickie.

Between herself, her father, and Major Avondale, they now outnumbered their captors.

Ruthlessly, she pushed down the surge of hope and returned to the kitchen, trying to act as normally as possible as she prepared the trays for the midday meal. She took Major Avondale's to him first, letting Robby lead the way up the stairs and to the door. Just as she stepped inside, she stopped and stamped her foot.

"Oh, drat!"

"What's that, Miss Josephine?"

"I left the teapot in the kitchen." She gave Robby a pleading look. "Would you be a dear and run down to get it for me?"

Robby shuffled his feet, clearly torn. "Dickie said I wasn't to leave you with none of the prisoners."

"You can lock me in," she said brightly. "I'll be safe here until you get back."

Major Avondale caught on quickly and smiled sunnily at Robby. "Miss Josephine had a question for me about, er, Psalm 45. I can answer it for her while she waits."

"You see?" Junia said. "We will be fine."

"All right, Miss Josephine." Robby shuffled out the door as Major Avondale ostentatiously paged through the shabby Bible in his hand and Junia made a show of setting the tray onto the floor next to his pallet.

They both waited until Robby's footsteps faded down the hall, and then turned to each other.

"They're gone," Junia said, her voice a little breathless in her haste. "It's our best chance."

"I saw them through the window. How many are in the house?"

"Just the two."

Avondale paced over to the window and peered out. "It's a long drop. Good chance we break a leg going that way."

"My father has been making a rope in his room," Junia whispered, and Avondale's head snapped to look at her.

"Your father?"

Footsteps echoed down the hallway, and Avondale crossed to where Junia stood with his Bible held open to Psalm 45. She glanced at the first few lines and suppressed a giggle.

"Why did you pick a wedding psalm?" she whispered.

"It was that or the valley of death," he said, and the door opened, Robby carrying the teapot, but a bit shamefaced as Jasper peered around him.

"What's going on?" Jasper said, his words a little slurred. Clearly, he had started the day's drinking as soon as Dickie and Jem were out of sight.

"Nothing at all," Avondale said in a soothing voice. "I was answering a question about psalms."

Jasper continued to scowl as Junia poured the tea into Avondale's empty cup and stepped away. "This ain't a Sunday school, girl. Get out."

Junia slipped past Robby and Jasper as they re-locked the door and hurried back to the kitchen to fetch her father's tray. She filled his teacup with the pot she still carried and set it down, her hand trembling.

After a deep breath, she hoisted the tray and carried it upstairs to where Jasper and Robby were impatiently waiting next to her father's door.

"I ain't got all day," Jasper grumbled. "Hurry up."

Junia swept her eyes around the room as her father moved the account books from his desk to make room for the tray. With her back still to the door, she formed one word with her lips, not daring to make a sound with the two men watching her.

"Tonight," she said silently, and her father nodded his understanding as she set the tray down on the desk.

Junia took a deep breath and did one last inventory. She wore the heaviest of her worn dresses, with both clean chemises beneath it. She wore both pairs of her clean stockings, one over the other. Her sturdiest shoes were on her feet. Beneath her dress, the small purse that held her few pennies and her comb was tied around her waist, uncomfortable but necessary.

She was as prepared as she could be for their escape without alerting Robby or Jasper.

Now she only had to succeed.

One more deep breath, and she removed the wedge from beneath her door and made her way down the short corridor to the kitchen. Robby was already waiting at the table, and she gave him a brief smile.

"I'll fetch your supper, and then you can help me take it upstairs to the others after you've eaten."

He nodded, and watched Junia as she moved around the kitchen, slicing bread and dishing out the stew left bubbling over the banked fire.

With only a little hesitation, she turned her back and added a spoonful of dried valerian root to his portion, stirring it in well before handing the bowl to Robby. She then added the same to Jasper's bowl. It would not work as well or as quickly as laudanum, but it might slow the men's reactions enough to give them an advantage.

As Robby worked his way through the stew with his usual methodical greed, Junia loaded up a tray to bring to the dining room.

"He ain't there, Miss Josephine," Robby mumbled through a full mouth.

"Sorry, what?"

"Jasper. He ain't in the dining room. He's outside to guard the pris'ners."

It was the last thing Junia wanted to hear. "Are you supposed to go out there after you eat?"

"That's what Jasper said."

"Oh."

She should have remembered Jasper might not be very bright—after all, he had kidnapped the wrong man—but he was sly, and he knew how to keep someone a prisoner.

"Well, I'll just set this by the stove to keep it warm until you're done and he can come in and eat."

Junia ate her own portion quickly before busying herself with kitchen tasks, trying not to let her agitation show as she reframed her plan. She needed to get her father and Major Avondale out of their rooms and out of the house, while keeping Robby and Jasper inside. And she needed to do it before Dickie and Jem returned at sunset.

She looked over at Robby, who was scraping the bottom of the bowl with his spoon. Sweet, trusting Robby.

He would be far easier to fool than Jasper.

With a decisive gesture, she quickly loaded up the tray with bowls of stew for both of the prisoners and turned to the surprised Robby. "We may as well take the food upstairs now, and then Jasper can eat once we're done."

Obediently, Robby rose to his feet and led the way up the stairs, keys jangling in his hand as they walked, the sound grating Junia's nerves until she wanted to scream.

He unlocked her father's door first, which only raised her tension, but she thanked him with a smile as he stepped aside to let her in. She set the bowl on the desk, meeting her father's questioning look with a bland smile, and then went back out the door, meekly standing by as Robby re-locked it and then walked the few paces to Major Avondale's door.

It would be her only chance.

As she passed Robby, she deliberately stumbled over the doorjamb, the tray tilting dangerously, and he plucked it out of her hands.

"Oh, thank you," she said. "I don't know how I could be so clumsy. Would you mind setting it down by the hearth for me?"

Robby obeyed, and Junia locked eyes with Major Avondale.

Now.

Almost faster than she could see, Major Avondale leapt at Robby's back while the bigger man was still half-bent over the hearth. Avondale wrapped one arm around Robby's neck and pressed at the other side with his hand, and Robby collapsed almost before he knew what was happening.

Junia stood at the doorway, a hand pressed to her mouth, the sudden violence bringing a wash of nausea to the back of her throat as she pressed away dark memories from her earlier life. "Is he... is he..."

Avondale stepped back, the keys in his hand. "He'll be fine in a few moments, which is why we need to move quickly."

He scooped his cloak from the mattress where it had been serving double duty as a blanket and they pelted from the room, Avondale locking the door to trap Robby inside before letting them into her father's room and slamming it behind them. Her father rose to his feet, rolling down his shirtsleeves and putting his coat on.

"Where's Jasper?" Avondale said, and Junia wordlessly pointed to the window. Avondale opened his mouth to say something sharp, glanced at her father, and shook his head instead.

"You should have told me," he hissed.

"There wasn't time. And there's no time now."

Avondale crossed to the window and peered out. Jasper's head was just visible from where he sat on the front steps, smoking a pipe at his leisure, but only a few feet from where they would drop. There was no way to get past him without Jasper seeing.

This time Avondale did curse, casting her an apologetic look afterwards.

"Does the window open?" he asked her father.

"I think so. It was painted shut, but I was able to scrape it out."

"If it won't open, we'll break it." Avondale wrapped his hand in the cloak and waited long enough for Junia to begin to fidget.

"What are you waiting—"

A bellow from the next room echoed through the house, bringing Jasper to his feet and darting through the front door. Even as he moved, Avondale first wrenched on the window and then, when it did not budge, punched through it with his fabric-wrapped hand, clearing as much of the glass as possible before laying the doubled cloak across the sill.

In the hallway, they heard Jasper's howl of rage and banging at first their door and then the other, as Jasper worked to free Robby.

"I'll go first, then Junia, then you, sir," Avondale said.

"My father should go first," Junia protested, but quieted when her father held up his hand.

"He's right. Go, young man."

Avondale vaulted over the windowsill, lowering himself by his hands from the edge of the wall. A crashing sound from the other room sent him dropping to the ground, and Junia leaned out to see he had landed safely. He grinned up at her.

Her father appeared at her elbow and threw his blanket down for Avondale to catch. The sounds from the hallway were louder and angrier as Jasper and Robby threw themselves against the door.

"Go, Junia!"

Swallowing hard, Junia hauled up her skirts and swung her leg over the windowsill. The door burst open just as she did and, with a shriek, she slipped and slid, her father lunging forward to grab her arms and swing her within reach of Avondale's outstretched arms.

Even as Junia watched, her father was dragged back into the room by the furious Jasper and Robby. With a last push, her father tipped Avondale's cloak out the window to fall to the ground. Avondale grabbed the cloak and blanket with one hand and Junia with the other, yanking her into a run.

"My father!"

Avondale didn't bother to reply, only dragged her along behind him as Jasper emerged from the house with a howl of rage.

It's only Jasper, she thought. *We can outrun—*

And then she saw the dust of the returning wagon rising only a few hundred yards from them. Dickie squinted from his slouching place beside the driver and then sat up straight with a shout. To Junia's horror, she saw two more rough men in the wagon with Dickie and Jem.

They had brought additional guards.

With no hesitation, Avondale changed direction, pulling Junia through her stumble as they ran into the gathering dusk towards the forest further out. It would be their only chance to lose their pursuers in the dark and the trees. Junia shook off Avondale's hand, yanked her skirts up past her knees, and ran for her life.

They plunged into the underbrush, and Avondale pulled her down to the ground. He gestured for her to crouch and crawl through, and she nodded her understanding. It would be slower, but leave less of a trail for their pursuers to follow. He handed the blanket to her and gestured for her to tie it around her waist before he began to crawl through the brush.

Ears straining for the muffled sounds of pursuit, Junia followed in Avondale's wake, ducking branches that snapped back as he passed so they would not break and leave evidence of their passage. The trailing ends of the blanket continually caught on the branches, frustrating her, but she dared not leave such an obvious trace of their direction behind.

It felt like days, but she knew it could not have been more than an hour before full dark fell and the shouts of pursuit faded away. Avondale kept moving, continuing with a dogged determination Junia had to match, until he stopped abruptly and she realized they had come to a small clearing.

Well, not even really a clearing. A spot where the bushes were slightly lighter, with space beneath the branches to form a shelter.

"Stay here," Avondale said in a low voice, and Junia nodded, seating herself on the cold ground while he dropped the cloak next to her and moved into the darkness. Only a few snapping twigs told her he had not abandoned her alone in this strange and chilly country. She sat hunched, draping the cloak around herself and pulling her legs to her chest to stay warm. Every muscle in her body trembled in continuous shivers of shock and fear and cold, and it seemed forever before she felt him move close to her again.

His arm wrapped around her, and she stiffened even though she needed the warmth.

CHAPTER FOUR

Philip cursed himself as Junia stiffened at the unexpected touch, and he loosened his grip without letting her go entirely. Whether she admitted it or not, they both needed the extra warmth in the damp chill of the forest.

"You should have let me stay with Pappa," she murmured after a long moment, and he barked a short laugh of disbelief before he could stop himself.

"Leave you behind for them to rape and murder? No. Not ever."

She went silent, which he took as an acknowledgement she knew he was right even if she didn't want to admit it.

A twig snapped nearby and Junia flinched. Reflexively, his arm tightened again to protect and reassure her. It took a conscious effort for him to loosen it.

"What was that?"

"A squirrel. Or a fox. Not heavy enough to be a deer. This is England, not America. We haven't had wolves in three hundred years."

As his eyes adjusted to the dark, he released her to scan the surrounding foliage, carefully pushing at branches and testing the thick fall of dead leaves beneath them. With the addition of a few leafy boughs, it should be sufficient for them to get a little rest.

"We can't risk a fire," he murmured. "They would find us in a heartbeat. I'll break off some extra branches to arrange into a pallet." He paused for a moment, knowing she would dislike his next words. "We'll need to share warmth tonight."

"Is that what men are calling it these days?" she said, her voice a little bitter, and he squeezed her shoulder in gentle reproach.

"My word of honor as a gentleman," he said. "Warmth only. Nothing more." The thought of *something more* made heat surge up his spine, but he loosened his hold and dropped his arm.

She turned her head to look at him for a long time as if judging his honesty, her gaze penetrating the gloom under the shrubbery. At last, she nodded. "All right, then. Your word of honor."

He crept out from under their cover to locate a few leafy branches that seemed resilient enough to cushion them from the ground. Breaking them off without the aid of his penknife was more difficult than he thought, but eventually he crawled back into their hideaway in triumph. Junia shifted aside to allow him to lay the branches down.

He arranged the threadbare blanket on top of the branches, testing for any sharp edges that poked through, and then extended his hand to her. After a slight hesitation, she took it and allowed him to adjust the cloak around them both before wrapping his arm around her shoulders to snug her against his side. She sat stiffly for a long time, until finally, with a sigh, she allowed herself to relax a little.

It had been a long while since he had sat so innocently with a woman, but he knew better than to betray her trust. They only had each other to rely on while they made their way to London, and he would never forgive himself if she were put into further danger because of his inability to control himself.

"You're really Major Avondale, right?"

"Correct."

"Why did they kidnap you?"

"They thought I was my brother, Peter. It's an honest mistake, of a sort. We are twins, after all."

"Twins? Identical?"

"Yes. The despair of our mother, and of every schoolmaster we encountered."

"And he's really a minister?"

"At the moment, he's on trial as a curate at St. Luke's in Islington. He was, er, asked to leave his last parish when he disagreed with the vicar about how to best minister to their poor, so he's a bit at loose ends right now."

"Tell me about him," she said, and her head dropped onto his shoulder. His arm tightened around her, holding her closer.

For warmth. Of course.

Junia listened with half an ear as Avondale spoke, drained from their escape. She had to admit it was nice to sit like this in the dark and the chill, almost like their own private little world. Moonlight filtered through the leaves, and she could hear night birds and insects begin to call around them.

She started from her half-drowse when he shook her shoulder. "What?"

He covered her mouth. "Sound carries at night," he said, his lips only a breath away from her ear, and she shivered. "We should both try to sleep."

He made her move so he could straighten the blanket on the ground, and then lay on his side, gesturing for her to lay in front of him as he arranged the cloak over them.

Junia frowned. "Word of honor?"

She could see his smile flash out even in the dark. "Word of honor."

Cautiously, she lay down on her side and his arm went around her waist, pulling her back against his front. She stiffened, a flash of remembered panic going through her, but she slowly relaxed as he made no other move, merely pillowing his head on his arm with a sigh.

When she followed suit by pillowing her head on her own arm, he murmured in her ear, "Then there was the time Peter decided fox hunting was cruel—which it is—but his method of keeping the hunters from the foxes was to hide leftover bits of chicken all around the hunting ground, only some of them were well past their prime... "

With his warmth surrounding her and his voice rumbling his chest behind her back, Junia soon found herself drifting off into a light doze.

Philip let his voice trail off as he felt her relax against him and her breathing fall into a regular pattern. The tension of knowing they were being hunted would be enough to keep him alert during the night, though the danger was reduced with every hour that passed.

A vision rose in his mind's eye of the first time he had seen her, a frightened, half-starved waif clinging to her younger sister's waist as sailors hauled them aboard the British warship.

"There!" She had grabbed Philip's sleeve, her grip surprisingly strong for someone who appeared so frail, and pointed. "My parents. You must help them!"

Philip raised his spyglass and spotted the tiny craft being roiled by the ocean. An older man and woman were aboard it, boxes piled around them as the man rowed and the woman steered towards the warship. Another boat rowed in pursuit, closing the distance until a warning shot from one of the British riflemen pierced the water in front of them and caused them to veer away, American curses ringing out across the water as they abandoned the hunt.

He had barked out orders for a craft to be launched for the rescue as a sailor's wife rushed up from the bottom of the ship to take the girls in hand. Junia had refused to let herself be led away with her sister and stood shivering at the railing until, at last, her parents were safely on board, first her mother and then her father.

Her father had looked around the deck and finally settled on Philip as the officer in charge. Caius Reynolds was a man of middle height, soaked to the skin, dressed in threadbare clothes, but his inherent dignity demanded respect. He walked to Philip and bowed.

"We's claiming asylum from slavery."

Philip had bowed in return. "Welcome aboard, sir."

Junia had watched it all from her place by the railing with her mother's protective arm around her. When he looked at her, a shy but radiant smile had blossomed across her face before she buried her face in her mother's shoulder and finally allowed herself to be led belowdecks.

The ship had returned to England with ninety-seven individuals who had escaped slavery. That war had brought many frustrations and an eventual loss to British prestige, but escorting those people to freedom in England was a wartime action Philip could look back on and be proud.

He looked down at Junia through the darkness and tightened his own arm around her. He had never quite been able to forget her, though his code as a gentleman and an officer had prevented him from anything more than an occasional turn around the deck to catch a glimpse of her.

Over the past four years, she had blossomed into a full-grown woman, but his word of honor kept him from her. Only a scoundrel would take advantage of a woman in her position, no matter how strongly his unruly body urged him to.

Junia woke slowly, staying in a comfortable drowse as she tried to remember where she was. The mattress beneath her was warm and firm, much better than the thin pallet she had been sleeping on for weeks, though it had a few peculiar lumps.

She began to realize the pillow behind her back must be an arm.

Major Avondale's arm.

The thought should have been alarming, but his touch was protective, comforting, not lustful. She peered through her eyelashes and the first light of dawn showed they had shifted in the night so she lay with her head pillowed on his shoulder, her front pressed against his side as he cradled her with one arm, the other pillowing his own head. His face was a little turned away from her, and she took a moment to admire his firm profile in the gathering light. Stubble had formed on his clean-shaven cheeks overnight, blurring the precise lines of his sidewhiskers.

Damp cold seeped up from the ground and through the blanket they lay on, but Junia did not want to move. She had never woken up next to a man before. She didn't want to move and spoil the moment.

Inevitably, a loud cheep from a bird in the trees overhead woke him. His arm tightened around her for a moment and she melted into him, still relaxed with sleep. He turned his head and smiled at her.

"Are you ready to start heading to London?"

Junia pulled away and sat up. "London? What about my father?"

Avondale sighed and sat up as well, running a hand through his wildly disordered hair. "What do you think you and I can do against six armed men, Junia? We must go to London and get reinforcements."

She wanted to argue but reluctantly nodded her agreement, knowing he was right. He got to his feet, stretching against the aches of sleeping on the ground all night, and Junia was suddenly aware of her own aches. She stumbled to her feet and stretched as well, watching him as he turned around the tiny clearing.

"Are we north or south of London?"

"North," she said. "It might be northeast."

He nodded, and looked at her curiously. "How did you find him?"

Junia turned away, shaking out the skirts of her dress. "I saw them take him. They grabbed him off the street." She remembered the terror of seeing her father dragged away and pushed into a carriage that abruptly drove away. In a matter of moments, she had been abandoned on the pavement, standing helpless with her weeping sister clinging to her as their father vanished around a corner.

"But *how* did you find them?"

"I recognized the horse and carriage," she said. "It was one we had hired ourselves, from time to time. I was able to ask at the livery stable and then make my plan for when they returned it."

"Quick thinking on your part," he said.

Junia tossed her head. "I can think on occasion."

"I meant no insult, Miss Reynolds. You are a very clever woman."

"And yet my father is still held prisoner."

"We will remedy that as soon as possible. You have my word on it."

"You give me your word often, my lord. How do I know you don't give it out whenever you please?"

He looked at her steadily, and the anger in her ebbed a little, knowing it was not him she was angry with.

"You will need to trust me," he said, "as I will trust you to help us get back to London so we can save your father."

She had no other choice, really.

He raked her with a critical glance. "Would you be able to untie your headwrap and wear it more like a kerchief?"

Her hand flew to the tucked-in ends. "Yes, I think so. Why?"

"They'll be looking for us, and your complexion is unusual enough in the countryside that people might notice you more than they would in London. If you can conceal your face from casual passers-by, it might confuse our pursuers a little longer."

"All right." Reluctantly, she unwound the patterned cloth and folded it into a triangle that she draped over her head and tied beneath her chin, shading her face with the edges. He nodded in approval. She held her breath as he raised his hand to her face and carefully tucked a wayward cluster of curls under the cloth, his fingertips lingering on her skin for a moment before he withdrew his hand and stepped back.

"If we head straight to the main road, they'll spot us immediately," he said. "I'm afraid we'll have to go across the fields and come to it roundabout. I don't suppose you brought any food."

"I'm sorry, no," she said, thinking of the freshly made loaf of bread she had had to abandon yesterday. "I couldn't figure out how to carry it without alerting Jasper and Robby. I have a few pence with me, though."

"All right. Let's get started. Leave the blanket, but bring the cloak."

The sun was only just barely over the horizon, mist rising from the ground as the air began to warm. Avondale led her cross-country, helping her over stiles and low stone walls when they came to them. The cloak swirled around her ankles and caught at brambles until she took it off in exasperation and folded it over her arm instead.

"Did you walk from London?" he asked.

"Not all the way. I was able to take a hansom to the edge of the city, and then found rides along the way."

"It seemed to take several hours when they kidnapped me."

"It was at least four hours by cart, and that was starting from a market on the north end of the city."

Avondale frowned, and she could see him calculating the distance in his head. "We're further out than I realized."

"Do you... do you think they'll find us?"

"My dear Miss Reynolds," he said, "if I was able to avoid being captured by Napoleon's troops while I was on the Peninsula, I feel confident I can evade a few thugs in my own country."

Junia was less confident, but she nodded and fell into step beside him. As they walked, he scanned and rescanned the area, sometimes turning and walking backwards a few steps to check for pursuit from behind.

After about an hour, he paused and pointed to a tiny speck nestled among some trees on the horizon. "You see that cottage?"

She squinted. If she looked hard, she thought she could see a tiny curl of smoke rising from the speck. "Yes, I think so."

"I think we need to go beg some bread, get under cover for a short while. We're too exposed out here."

"We don't have to beg. I have my wages. I think it's twelve pence—that makes a shilling?"

"Let's save that until we have need of it. For the time being, we can trade chores for some food."

Junia still did not like the sound of it, but he spoke so casually that it must be a common thing to do in the countryside. They turned their steps towards the cottage, which slowly came into focus as a tiny stone house with a thin plume of smoke coming from the chimney. An old woman sat in the front yard with a pipe and watched them approach.

Avondale stopped a good distance away and bowed to her. "Good morning, madam."

"Morning," she said warily.

"My...wife and I are traveling but find ourselves short on coin. Would there be a few chores around the cottage we could do in exchange for some food?"

Junia saw the woman glance at her, so she untied her kerchief to show her face better and smiled at her. "We would be very grateful if you could."

The old woman puffed meditatively on her pipe. "I'll make a bargain with ye. Nancy's gone off to visit her ailing ma, and I twisted my ankle last night. Snowdrop's been agitatin' to be milked for an hour now, and I can't get to the shed to let her out or bend to milk her. Take care of her, and I'll have some cheese and bread for you after."

"It's a bargain, madam," Avondale said before Junia could stop him, and she widened her eyes to try and signal him. She had no idea how to milk a cow, and she was fairly certain he didn't either. He gestured for Junia to precede him into the shed, where she looked down at the animal inside the stall.

"I don't think that's a cow."

"No," Avondale said. "That's a goat. Do you know how to milk a goat?"

Junia shook her head, horrified. "I grew up at the city house. We bought our milk at the market."

Avondale sighed and ran a hand through his hair. "I milked a cow once, when I was a lad. Father thought we ought to understand at least some of the workings of the tenant farmers."

"Then you should do it," she said firmly. "I don't have any idea how."

Junia did not like the look of the animal at all, with its strangely slitted eyes and rough coat, but its bleats *were* rather piteous. She sighed and opened the door to its stall.

The goat bolted past both of them and out into the yard. He cursed and they ran to chase it, only to discover it already standing on a peculiar low platform, its nose stuck into an attached box. It raised its head and bleated at them again, this time sounding annoyed.

"You need to put some clean hay in there," the old woman shouted over from her seat in the yard, seemingly enjoying their confusion. "Keeps her calm while you work."

Muttering, Avondale went back into the shed and came out with an armload of hay he dumped into the box. The goat immediately stuck its head in and began chomping away.

Junia placed the bucket the woman had given them onto the platform and peered under the goat's body. The poor thing's udder did appear quite swollen.

Avondale heaved a heavy sigh. "Are you really going to make me do this?"

"Yes," Junia said, trying to prevent her lips from twitching into a grin.

He stepped forward and bent to take one teat into his hand. He gave it a tentative tug, and the goat bleated and stepped aside.

"You'll have to hold her back legs, missy," the old woman shouted. "Don't be afraid to be firm with her."

Avondale grinned at her, and for a moment Junia considered changing her mind about the milking. She took another look at the bulging udder and shuddered. She couldn't. She just couldn't.

With a sigh of resignation, she moved into position and put her hands around the goat's lower legs to hold her steady. The goat shifted and protested a bit, but soon returned to her breakfast.

Avondale squatted down to examine the goat's teats.

"Don't be shy, young man. Squeeze from the top of the udder and give her teat a little tug. You'll know the motion in a moment."

To her surprise, Junia saw a dark flush—of embarrassment?—climb up Avondale's cheeks. Then he started the motion as directed, and Junia could feel her own embarrassed flush begin. It was... suggestive, that stroking motion, but it seemed effective because milk began spurting out into the pail.

Avondale's blush only deepened, but he continued doggedly as Junia held the goat steady, switching from one teat to the other according to the shouted instructions until he found the rhythm. Junia found herself mesmerized by the motions, watching his strong hands working on the animal, his movements seeming somehow familiar in a primal way. She found herself holding her breath until at last the flow of milk slowed and stopped, and Avondale stood up from his crouch.

He looked at her, and she knew he had been feeling the same primal connection to his rhythmic motions.

Oh. This *is what it feels like to desire someone.*

"You can let go of her now, missy. She's all done."

Startled, Junia let go of the goat, who continued eating, and stepped away from the platform. Avondale picked up the bucket and they walked to where their hostess sat.

"Thankee kindly, and Snowdrop thanks ye, too. Let me lean on your arm a bit, missy, while your man brings the milk."

Once inside, the woman instructed Avondale on how to strain the milk while Junia quietly moved around the small kitchen, rinsing her hands under the kitchen pump and scrubbing the dishes she found there.

"Bread and cheese is in the pantry. May as well cut us all a slice of pie while you're in there, too."

The pie proved to be gooseberry, and Junia brought it out with the rest of the food and some small beer. Avondale had washed his own hands and settled their hostess into a chair next to the banked fire. Junia brought a plate to her, along with a mug of beer, and set it on a small table next to her chair. She arranged a small footstool to prop her sore ankle onto, and the older woman sighed with relief before she started to eat.

Junia joined Avondale at the battered kitchen table, where he had served each of them a portion of the meal. The cheese was goat cheese, of course, tangy and earthy, more delicious than Junia expected and soft enough to spread. The bread was only a day old, a hearty brown loaf of a type Junia guessed Avondale had not seen since his army days, given the way he frowned skeptically at it before taking a bite, and then another, with evident enjoyment.

Having Avondale sitting across from her in his rolled-up shirt-sleeves, dark curls tousled, was more intimate than Junia could have believed. She could almost dream they were married, working together on their farm before retiring for the evening...

She caught Avondale's gaze across the table and immediately redirected her eyes to her plate. Fortunately, he would not be able to see her flush of confusion in the dark room.

Their hostess gave out a loud sigh and a small belch as she set down the empty plate that had held her slice of pie. "Where are ye off to after this?"

"London," Avondale said, turning his gaze away from Junia.

"Never been there. It's a full twenty miles away, at the least."

"Which way to the main road from here?"

"Eh, if you cut across going southwest, you'll reach it. I'll point you when you're ready."

"Is there anything more we can do for you before we go?" Junia asked. "I'll clean the dishes, of course, but anything else?"

"That's right kind of you, missy. There's a thing or two, if you don't mind."

Junia followed her instructions to bring food from the pantry to make it more accessible until Nancy returned the next day, safely covered from mice and other pests. Avondale was sent up to the attic to locate a crutch left there by the woman's late husband while Junia tidied and swept after their meal. At their hostess's insistence, Junia wrapped some bread and firm cheese in a clean rag to take with them. After a short discussion with Avondale, Junia shyly offered her the cloak as partial payment for her assistance, which she accepted.

"I must say, I've enjoyed the comp'ny, too," she said. "Stop on by next time you're around."

Avondale laughed and took the old woman's hand to bow over it. "Thank you for your hospitality, madam."

She cast a shrewd look up at him. "And don't tell none I've seen you, eh?"

"No," he said. "But I promise you we're not thieves."

She waved an airy hand. "You'd've been able to murder me a dozen times over by now if that was your aim. But you're not that kind." She pointed across the fields to a small hill. "Head that way. Village is behind that hill, then go south to the main road."

Impulsively, Junia leaned down and kissed the old woman's cheek. "Thank you."

The woman pulled her close and whispered in her ear, "Hang onto that man of yours, missy. He's a game one."

Junia pulled back, choked on her denial, and just smiled.

CHAPTER FIVE

As they walked in the direction of the village, Junia saw Avondale frown at the sky.

"What is it?"

"Rain clouds," he said. "They're heading straight towards us." He pointed to where dark clouds were gathering on the horizon, and she feared he was right about their direction.

"What should we do?"

"Keep heading towards the village. I don't want to get caught out in the rain if we can avoid it."

After a long stretch, Avondale spoke again. "Why did they abduct your father?"

"We don't know."

"You don't know?"

Junia puffed out a breath. "He's making changes to the accounting books they bring him, but the changes have to add up on each page, and be done in a way that ends with a correct total, which they provide to him on a sheet of paper. He could work through them more quickly, but he's unwilling to do it until he knows what they're planning to do with him once he's done."

Philip frowned. "We need to get him out of there as soon as we can find reinforcements. We don't know what they'll do when he finishes whatever task it is they've set for him."

She stumbled, and he put his arm around her to prevent her from falling. "It's all right. Don't fret, angel. We'll get him out."

Junia let herself lean against him just a little, and his arm tightened. She felt safe with him, safer than she had felt in weeks. Months. Years.

Dangerously safe.

She straightened her posture and his arm fell away.

The road sank down into a small lane lined by hedges and trees. Avondale looked around it, a slight frown on his face.

"What is it?"

"I don't like it. Feels like an ambush point."

His unease put her on edge as well, and their steps slowed as he scanned the hedges until he found a break just large enough for them to squeeze through. She looked into the small space with distaste.

"Really?"

"Humor me," he said, and gave her arm a small, encouraging push. She sighed and followed his direction, squeezing through the small space until they passed through to a thick stand of birch trees just behind the hedge. He helped her squeeze between them until they were standing on a small ridge above the lane that had been invisible from the ground.

Silently, he pointed to a spot just past where the lane rose again. She could see dust settling, as though horses or a cart had passed through.

He leaned down to say quietly, "Come this way."

As they edged their way through the trees, a cart emerged into view, and they both froze, half-concealed by the branches. Jasper and Robby sat together on the driver's seat, Jasper guiding the horse as Robby kept watch.

"That shepherd said he saw them coming this way," Jasper grumbled. "Should have known not to trust him."

Robby's head stopped scanning, and for a moment, he met Junia's eyes. He saw her. She knew he did.

Then he turned his head to the other side of the road and the cart continued on in the opposite direction.

As the sound of its wheels faded away, Junia sagged against Avondale, and he pulled her against his side.

"He saw you."

"I know."

Avondale was silent for a long moment. "He must have liked your cooking."

Junia snorted, and then giggled, and then laughed out loud while he grinned down at her. "That's a terrible joke."

"It's not terrible if it makes you laugh."

The sudden seriousness in his eyes made her cast hers down in confusion. Of its own volition, her hand crept up the lapel of his coat, curling under until she could feel the heat of his body seeping through the fabric. His arm tightened around her, and she yielded, pressing herself against him and resting her head on his shoulder for a long moment before she tilted her face up to his.

He was going to kiss her. And she wanted him to.

He hesitated for a long moment, his eyes searching hers, until she gave his lapel a little tug to bring him closer. With a groan, he tipped his head and brushed her lips with his once, then again, and again, staying a little longer each time until their mouths met and melded for a long moment.

He raised his head, and she smiled at him, knowing she was starry-eyed.

"Avondale."

He dipped his head again. "Call me Philip," he said, his lips only a breath away from hers.

"Philip," she said, and he rewarded her with another kiss, one that sent warmth rushing all the way from her head to her toes and back again until she was clinging to him.

A sudden blast of damp wind buffeted them, and with a laugh and a shake of his head, he stepped back.

"We need to get on to the village before the rain comes."

Junia's head was still spinning from the kiss, so she only nodded and followed his lead as they threaded their way through the trees parallel to the road.

CHAPTER SIX

The sky grew darker and grimmer as they walked, mist mixing with raindrops which became more and more frequent. At last, the foggy shapes of the village came into view.

"I think the inn is that building on the end," Philip said.

"Oh." Junia stopped walking and frowned at the lights glimmering through the gathering fog. "Should we keep going?"

"By no means," Philip said. "We'll stop there for the night."

"What?"

He resumed walking with the determined steps of a man who had spotted a refuge, and she hurried after him.

"We can't stop at an inn."

"Why not?" he said.

"They almost just found us. It's the first place they'll look."

"They'll be looking for us in hedgerows and barns. They assume we don't have any money."

"We don't have any money, at least not enough for an inn. Do we?"

He turned his head to grin at her, and continued walking. She followed behind, not sure if she should be angry or hopeful.

As they came to a small bridge across a creek—no, they called it a brook here—Philip paused to sit on the edge and turn up the bottom of his boot.

To Junia's astonishment, he twisted the heel to reveal a short stack of four or five gold sovereigns that jingled in his hand. He replaced the heel and put the coins into his waistcoat pocket before returning to his feet. The rain was beginning in earnest now, streaming down around them, and she adjusted the scarf that had shielded her face to better cover her hair.

"We need to play our parts well," he said, "to avoid any awkward questions."

"And what is my part, may I ask?"

He shrugged off his coat and put it around her shoulders. "My wife, of course, who is shaken up by our carriage accident and needs a safe place to rest for the night."

Junia couldn't help her little shiver as the warmth from his body surrounded her, carried by the wool of his coat. She inhaled as discreetly as she could, enjoying his scent as it rose around her.

"Lean on me," he said, and she was not reluctant to obey him. He put his arm around her, and she allowed herself to dream a little. To dream she really was his beloved wife, that he was concerned for her safety after their accident, that his head bent over hers and his arm circled her waist because he cared for her.

He pushed open the door of the inn and Junia blinked at the noise and light inside, her eyes taking a moment to adjust after their walk in the fog. Instinctively, she moved closer to him, as timid as the part she was playing, and he took a moment to give her a reassuring squeeze before he shouted for the innkeeper.

A rotund little man hurried over, rubbing his hands on his apron as he took in Philip's fine linen shirt and the quality of the superfine wool of his coat. "Yes, milord? How can we help you?"

"My wife and I suffered a carriage accident," Philip said, and Junia shrank against him under the innkeeper's sharp gaze. "We require a room for the night."

"Certainly, milord. Right this way."

Junia squeaked as Philip scooped her up into his arms and put her arms around his neck to keep her balance. "It's all right, my dove," he said, a wicked gleam in his eye. "Only a few more minutes and we'll be alone again."

She longed to give his neck a sharp pinch, but feared he would drop her in retaliation, so she only glared at him before dropping her head onto his shoulder. The landlord opened a door at the top of the stairs and Philip stepped through. Over his shoulder, Junia could see a curious maidservant follow them in, her eyes widening as she registered the color of Junia's skin before Junia ducked her head back onto Philip's shoulder.

"Build up the fire," Philip commanded. "My wife is lately arrived from Jamaica and is not accustomed to our damp climate."

"Yes, milord!" the maidservant said, her prompt actions filled with a new respect. Junia could see news of the fabulously wealthy mixed-race Jamaican heiresses arriving in London and Edinburgh had reached even in this small village, and the maid was now more interested in a possible tip than in the color of Junia's skin.

He crossed to the bed and set Junia down on it, and she lay back with a sigh. It was certainly more comfortable than sleeping in the woods again.

Philip flashed a golden guinea from his waistcoat pocket, and suddenly the room was filled with a flurry of activity as servants scurried back and forth, bringing food and hot water for washing as Philip directed them all.

Then he closed the door behind the last curtseying maidservant, and they were alone together.

Junia lay out the meal, dividing the meat pie between the two of them and pouring ale from the pitcher. Without further conversation, she dived in, hoping her greed would not disgust him but unable to be more ladylike after more than a day with nothing but bread and cheese. She glanced up to see he was equally absorbed in his food, eventually putting his fork down with a satisfied sigh. She took one last sip from her tankard and sighed herself, replete. They both drowsed in their chairs by the fire, their most urgent bodily needs satisfied.

Which made Junia aware of a new tension in the room. Now that they had food and safety and warmth, the knowledge they were alone —and would be alone all night—was making her wonder what she would do if he kissed her again.

She was not sure of the answer anymore.

He cleared his throat and gestured to the screen in the corner. "I'll go down for a pint while you wash."

"Thank you," Junia said, knowing her voice shook a little.

He crossed to her chair and bent to brush a chaste kiss on her lips before grinning at her. "It's a respectable inn, and I'll be right downstairs. But I'll lock the door when I go, just in case."

She looked up at him, her lips tingling from just that casual touch. "All right."

As soon as the key turned in the lock, Junia leapt from the bed to the washbasin behind a screen in the corner. She made use of the chamber pot before stripping down to wash from the basin. A full bath would need to wait until she was home in London, but having soap and hot wash water was heavenly. She shook out the cleaner of her two shifts, pulled it on, and dove under the covers of the bed, her heart pounding. While she waited, she did her best to untangle some of the mats from her hair. That, too, might have to wait until she could have her mother's or Zillah's help in London.

The key turned in the lock, and she pulled the quilt up to her neck as the door opened and Philip entered. He retrieved the kettle that had been set next to the hearth and went behind the screen to pour fresh water into the basin, but came back looking a little grim.

He sat on the edge of the bed and she stared at him, frozen.

"Junia."

"Yes?"

"If it would make you more comfortable..." He trailed off and then took a deep breath. "If it would make you more comfortable, I could sleep on the floor."

"Oh."

Look into your heart, she knew her mother would say.

She took a deep breath and looked.

Her mother would likely not approve, but her mother was not here.

She looked at Philip, who was watching her, his face still solemn.

"You don't have to sleep on the floor," she said.

He blinked, as if surprised, and then a grin broke across his face. "Really?"

"Really." Daring greatly, she put a hand up to his cheek and leaned towards him. He leaned in the rest of the distance, kissing her softly until she demanded more, and he pulled away with a chuckle.

"Let me wash first."

"All right," she said, unable to stop smiling. She was standing on the edge of a precipice, but she didn't care.

She would worry about the consequences tomorrow.

Philip washed as quickly as he could, trying to leash his eagerness. He could scarcely believe he had found her again, much less that she was waiting for him in a warm, cozy bed. The swiftness of events was still dizzying him, but he had no intention of losing this chance.

He frowned at his shirt, which had become more than a little over-ripe during his weeklong captivity. Serving on the Peninsula had taught him a quick soak in soapy water followed by a rinse would at least reduce the worst of the smell, especially if he could spread it on the hearth to dry. After a small hesitation, he pulled his breeches back on and walked around the edge of the screen, shirt in hand.

Junia was sitting up in bed, the covers clutched to her shoulders, and her eyes widened as she saw him shirtless, a blush giving her cheeks a rosy glow. He chuckled.

"Give me a moment, angel, and you can look your fill."

He spread the shirt on the flagstones of the hearth, far enough away to avoid any sparks but close enough to get a little heat to dry it. He turned to see Junia was still watching him, her lips a little parted as though she was having trouble catching her breath. Unable to resist, he sauntered towards her, enjoying how much she seemed to enjoy looking at him. Leaving his breeches on, he turned up the side of the covers and slid underneath as she slid over. He rolled to his side and propped himself up on his elbow, grinning at her. She followed suit, though she kept her eyes downcast.

He put a finger under her chin and tilted her face up to his. "Hello."

"Hello," she said, her voice breathless, and he kissed her, dampening her lips with his, grazing her bottom lip with his teeth before teasing it with his tongue. To his delight, she responded in kind, following his lead until he rolled over on top of her, luxuriating in the feeling of her soft body beneath his.

He bent to kiss her again... but she didn't respond.

Frowning, he opened his eyes to see hers were squeezed closed, her expression tense. "Junia?"

She opened her eyes, but they were no longer filled with passion. It was something closer to panic. "I... I'm all right."

Philip frowned and rolled to the side, removing his weight from her. "What's wrong?"

"Nothing. I'm fine." The smile on her face was clearly false, and she tensed a little more when he reached out to stroke down her arm.

He sighed and rolled onto his back, tugging her to lie against his bare chest, her head pillowed on his shoulder. She resisted for a moment before cuddling against him with a sigh.

Philip had been to war, and he knew much of slavery. He had a good idea why Junia had reacted the way she had, but he did not want to push her into any confidences she was not comfortable making. So they lay together for long minutes as he gently stroked her back and arms, soothing her into relaxation.

At last, she looked up at him. "I'm sorry."

"Don't be." He hesitated, not sure he wanted to know the truth, but also unwilling to ignore what had happened. "Do you want to tell me about it?"

She ducked her head back down and burrowed her face against his naked chest. "No."

"All right," he said. He continued with his undemanding caresses, willing to be as patient as he needed to be. When she began to speak, her voice was so low he had to bend his head to hear her, and the English accents she had adopted dropped away to her original, American one.

"The young master, he come home for Miss Patsy's debut. We all knew to avoid him, but he caught me in her dressing room while the mistress and her daughters was out paying calls and I was doing the pressing."

Junia drew in a long, shuddering breath, and Philip was careful to keep his touch gentle. "He pushed a pillow over my face, and he put all his weight on me so I couldn't scream, I couldn't get a breath, I thought he was going to smother me..."

She stopped on a shuddering breath. Her hand curved around his shoulder to press herself against him with a sigh.

"When he finished, he said a bag of bones like me wasn't even worth the ride. I ate as little as I could after that, to keep him away."

"Then what happened?"

"Miss Patsy beat me," Junia said matter-of-factly. "For corrupting her brother. And the mistress was angry, too. There wasn't no one else she could train up to be the lady's maid for her girls, and if I got pregnant, it would ruin Miss Ellen's debut, too. But Mama gave me cotton bark tea to bring on my flow so it wouldn't happen."

One more racking breath. "That was when Pappa decided we should escape instead of saving up to buy our freedom. He knew it would only get worse when Zillah started working above stairs like me."

Philip pressed his face into the puff of her hair, pushing down the rage that threatened to claw free. He could vent it later, at Gentleman Jackson's or on the hunting field. He could not, *would* not burden her with his own feelings at this moment.

She tilted her head back to look into his eyes, her face solemn. "Do you think differently about me now?"

"I think," he said, "you are the most courageous woman I have ever met, to come through all that and not be broken by it."

A shy smile crossed her face. "You only say that because you don't know my mama."

He tilted his head down to kiss her, and the sweet fire of her response now that her burden had been shared nearly made him weep.

"I still want to... to be with you," she said, and the trepidation in her beautiful eyes made his heart wrench even as his body tightened at her willingness.

And then an idea sparked, and he let a rakish smile spread across his face as he turned onto his side again and propped his head up on his hand.

"Tell me, angel," he said. "Do you ever touch yourself?"

Her jaw dropped open. "Really, Philip!"

His grin grew wider. He could feel the blush radiating from her skin as she ducked her face into his shoulder. It wasn't a no.

He dipped his head to brush his lips against her ear, and then the little hollow beneath it.

"Show me."

Junia shook her head, keeping her face hidden. "I can't."

He let his lips drift down to the exposed curve of her neck and felt her shiver. "I want to know how to please you, and you know that better than anyone can. Show me."

He felt her take in a deep breath and release it.

And then she rolled to her back and parted her legs, her face turned away from him.

"I can't look at you while I do it," she whispered, and he brushed another kiss across her bare shoulder.

"Don't worry about it, angel."

He leaned back to watch her, memorizing the contrast between the rich brown of her limbs and the stark white of the sheets, the way the neckline of her chemise dipped towards her half-bared breasts as her hand tentatively began to move, her breath quickening as she pleasured herself.

He watched for as long as he could stand it, almost relishing how his hands itched to smooth over her skin and feel the slight sheen of sweat that was beginning to form. Then he leaned forward to kiss his way from her shoulder back to her ear, feeling her breath catch.

"May I kiss you, Junia?"

Her head nodded and turned toward him. He brushed his lips against hers, gently at first, deepening the kiss by degrees until she arched up to him, tongue meeting and playing with his.

Careful to keep his weight off her, he leaned a little away. "May I kiss you other places?"

A puzzled frown formed between her brows. "Where?"

He let his mouth slide down her neck to the top slopes of her breasts. "I could start here."

She nodded, her eyes wide, and he nudged the chemise lower to bare her breasts to his view. She closed her eyes as his mouth moved lower, her breath coming fast, and he licked across one deep brown nipple, feeling it harden under his tongue as her back arched.

"How does that feel, Junia?" he purred.

"I... good. It feels... good."

"Do you want me to do it again?"

"Yes. Yes."

He swirled his tongue, bringing her nipple up hard and tight.

Lightly, he skimmed his hand along her side, down to her hip, and hovered just above her belly. Her eyes fluttered open.

"May I touch you, Junia?" His hand drifted closer to where she used hers to pleasure herself. He could feel the moisture and the heat, and he swallowed hard as she slowly nodded.

She tensed a little as his fingers stroked down the length of her thigh before caressing their way up, gently urging her legs further apart. He leaned down and kissed the small frown between her eyebrows before he kissed her lips.

"Trust me," he said. She nodded hesitantly, and he let his finger brush against the moist opening of her body, gently at first, then more purposefully as he found the entrance and slid his fingertip inside.

She gasped, and he looked up at her sharply. "Does it hurt?"

"No."

He slid it in further, feeling her inner muscles yield to the gentle pressure, watching her face as she closed her eyes.

This was how she would feel around his cock, tight and slick and hot, and he moved his finger the way he hoped to move inside her, stroking deep and retreating, imitating her rhythm until her hips arched upward to follow his motion even as her own hand continued to move, faster and faster.

He slid a second finger in, gently stretching her, feeling her inner muscles clench around him until she cried out and he felt her orgasm surrounding him, drawing him in until she shuddered one last time and relaxed.

He slid his hand away and watched her for a long moment, flushed and beautiful, until at last she turned her head towards him and opened her eyes. He bent to kiss her.

"Still embarrassed?"

"Yes. But–"

Her hand slid behind his head and pulled his mouth down to hers in a kiss so luscious he feared he would lose control right there.

She loosened her grip just enough to let him pull back a few inches. "I still want more."

He stripped off his breeches under the covers and rolled atop her again. Without her conscious volition, her body froze immediately. He slid back to the side, and tears of frustration rose in her eyes.

"I'm sorry."

"It's not your fault." He kissed her lightly. "Besides, there's more than one way to do this."

Puzzled, she watched as he sat up with his back against the headboard before guiding her to sit up as well. She took a moment to admire him, broad shoulders seeming to take up the whole space. She extended a hand to comb through the hair on his chest, stroking across and then down to where it narrowed as if to point to his...

"Oh, my," she said, and glanced up to see he was watching her.

"Do whatever feels right for you, angel," he said. "I can take it."

She swallowed and let her hand stray down the hard line of his stomach hovering just above... it.

"I don't know what to call it," she said, knowing her voice was a little plaintive, and he laughed a rough laugh.

"It doesn't have a proper name, unless you want to give it one. I just call it my cock."

Her hand reached as of its own accord, and she glanced up at him. He nodded, his eyes burning into hers, and she took a deep breath and let her fingers curl around it.

It was a surprise how naturally it fit into her hand, silky-smooth skin with ridged veins underneath. She moved her hand experimentally, and his deep groan made her look up at him. His head was thrown back against the headboard, but he opened his eyes and grinned at her.

"You've already got the right idea, angel. Try that again. Squeeze a little harder, you won't break it."

She stroked her hand down again, then up, rubbing her palm against the head, and his hips bucked upward. To her surprise, he grabbed her wrist to stop her from moving her hand. He grinned at her, but she could feel the tension all through him.

"I think," he said, "that's all I can take for now. If you really want to try everything."

Before she could protest, he enclosed her upper arms in his hands and guided her to straddle him, knees on either side of his hips, bodies pressed together from shoulder to hip with his cock trapped between them.

Her body had a will of its own, arching and rubbing against him, feeling his skin and hair and muscle against her whole front as his arms wrapped around her back to hold her close. She felt a tiny twinge of the panic that would freeze her body at the strength of his arms, but he had been right. Sitting upright made her feel more free, more able to pull away if needed.

He grinned up at her. "You like this?"

"Yes," she said, and ducked her head to kiss him. His hands slid down to tilt her hips, and she gasped as his erection rubbed against her most sensitive flesh. It was delicious.

"I'll show you what to do," he murmured against her ear, "but you're in control. You can stop any time, and I swear I won't be angry."

"Word of a gentleman?"

"Yes. Word of a gentleman."

She swallowed hard, for courage, and then let him help her position herself over the broad head of his cock.

The head slipped inside first, and they both groaned, and then laughed. Experimentally, she wiggled a little lower, feeling her body expand to accommodate him. It carried a little sting, but it felt good, too, like stretching your legs over rough ground to reach the top of a hill.

She braced her hands on his shoulders as she lowered herself, inch by careful inch, until suddenly it seemed her inner muscles yielded all at once and she sank all the way down. The fullness was almost too much and she shivered for a long moment, wrapping her arms around his neck as he held her close.

"Are you all right?" he murmured.

"I…" Experimentally, she moved upward, letting his shaft slide inside her, and they both groaned.

His hands slid back down to rest lightly on her hips. "Don't worry about me, angel. Do whatever feels good to you."

She began to move, slowly and then faster, shifting her hips until she found an angle that slid them together in a perfect rhythm, his hips arching upward as hers descended, going on and on until she whimpered in frustration.

He chuckled, though the sound was strained. "Here, angel, let me help you." And his hand went between their bodies to find the place where her pleasure gathered, stroking in time until fire rippled up her spine and she dissolved, her mouth finding his as she shuddered all around him, her knees clutching at his hips as she sagged against him.

With a groan, he pulled her off and took his cock in his hand. She watched in astonishment as he stroked himself, faster and harder, until he threw his head back with a final shout and a white liquid burst from the head of his cock.

He opened his eyes, and put an arm out to pull her closer as he kissed her. "Sorry."

"What was that?" She put out a careful finger to dab at the remnants of the liquid on his thigh, and he laughed.

"That, my curious angel, is what they call semen. If I had done that while I was still inside you, I could have left you with a baby."

"Oh," she said. "Mama explained that to me, but it's… different to actually see it."

He rolled from the bed and she slid further under the covers, yawning. She watched through half-lidded eyes as he washed himself and then brought a fresh cloth over to her, helping her wipe away the sweat and fluids. Then he blew out the candle and slid back into the bed, bringing her back against his front again, and she sighed in contentment as she fell asleep, more relaxed than she could ever remember being.

CHAPTER SEVEN

The next morning, Junia woke slowly, only to find Philip had already slipped from the bed and was dressing next to the fireplace. When she stirred, he looked over at her and smiled. "Good morning."

"Good morning," she said shyly. She burrowed into the covers, but never took her eyes off him.

"I'm going to go talk to the innkeeper to see if there's a carriage we can rent. If there is, we could be back in London by this afternoon. I'll see if there's breakfast as well."

"Thank you."

He finished arranging his limp cravat as best he could and shrugged on his coat before crossing to the bed and bending down to kiss her. "You'd best get washed and dressed so we can leave as soon as we've eaten."

"All right."

He kissed her again as though he was already regretting leaving her, and then pulled away. She waited for him to lock the door behind himself before she leapt from the bed and began to wash and dress as quickly as she could. She tried to comb her hair, but had to give up doing any more of it than the top layers. She re-wrapped her hair with her scarf and tucked the edges in as best she could.

She crossed to the window and lifted a corner of the curtain to see there was a watery sun out, so the worst of the rain must be over. It would take them a good five or six hours to drive to London through the rutted and muddy roads, but they would be home again and ready to go rescue Pappa.

When Philip returned with the maid carrying a breakfast tray complete with a steaming coffee pot, Junia had prepared what few belongings they had so they could leave as soon as possible. Philip, too, seemed eager to leave, so they ate quickly.

"Were you able to get a carriage?"

He grimaced. "A gig. Pulled by a donkey. At least I will be returning you to your mother in style."

She giggled, and then sighed. He reached his hand across the table to cover hers, and she turned her hand to hold his.

"Don't worry, Junia. I'll bring him home safe."

She nodded, unwilling to trust her voice. Being able to share her worries with a man outside her family was a new sensation.

Philip left a sovereign on the tray for the housemaid, and they departed in the promised style in an ancient, creaking two-person gig behind a ragged donkey.

The morning was chilly, so Philip insisted Junia wear his coat again. She only made a token protest, snuggling down into the body-warmed folds. As they drove, Junia heaved a sigh as a forgotten instruction finally came back to her.

"Pappa will scold me after we rescue him."

"And why is that?"

"Pappa always said if we had any trouble and he wasn't around to help, we should talk to Mr. Force about it. Pappa will say I should have sent Mr. Force a note instead of going off on my own." She had not even thought of it until this moment, now that she had someone else to talk to.

Philip frowned. "Mr. Force... wait a minute. Does your father want you to contact *Taddeo Sforza*?"

"Who?"

"Is Mr. Force a tall, mixed-race Italian man?"

Junia's jaw dropped. "Why, yes. Do you know him?"

He grinned at her. "Signore Sforza—Mr. Force—was my sister-in-law's man of business when she lived in Italy. He and his wife traveled here with her four years ago, before she married my brother."

"That's an incredible coincidence."

"Not really. The community of blacks in London is fairly small, so the odds we would both know someone as prominent as Taddeo Sforza were high."

"Does he know your brother, the Duke?"

"Of course."

Junia marveled at that while he drove. When her family had escaped from America, she had never imagined they would meet anyone who knew a duke. Now she sat next to a duke's brother on their way to see another man who knew him.

The closer they came to London, the more anxious Junia became, until she was all but vibrating next to him as they turned onto the street where her parents lived.

Philip took one hand from the reins to cover hers. "Junia. It will be fine."

She smiled at him, but didn't seem to relax much as she directed him to pull up in front of a small but tidy house on a quiet Islington street. A young man bustled up to hold the donkey's reins and Philip tossed him one of his remaining coins before descending from the cart and handing Junia down from it.

As soon as her feet touched the ground, the front door of the house burst open and a young woman raced down the steps, shrieking with joy as she reached Junia. With a shock, Philip realized this must be Junia's younger sister Zillah. When he had last seen her, she had been a child of thirteen, scrawny and frightened. Now she was a young lady of seventeen who had clearly adapted to her new life, the same age Junia had been when the family escaped.

He stepped back to allow the sisters to have their reunion, and looked to the doorway where Junia's mother, Jerusha Reynolds, waited for her daughters. Even in a fashionably high-waisted dress, he could see she was heavily pregnant, which must have added to Junia's anxiety about rescuing her father as quickly as possible.

Rather than making the older woman descend the steps, Philip walked to her, followed by Junia and Zillah, their arms still wrapped around each other. He bowed to her. "Mrs. Reynolds."

"Why, it's Major Avondale!" Her voice still carried the soft accents of Maryland, strange but warm on this English street. "Come in, come in. There's no need for all of us to make a spectacle of ourselves on the street."

Her daughters did not seem much abashed and each kissed their mother's cheek as they entered the house. Junia removed Philip's coat and handed it to him. Mrs. Reynolds gasped aloud.

"What on earth are you wearing, Junia?"

"I was a house servant, Mama, at the place where Pappa is being held prisoner." Philip noticed that, when speaking to her mother, Junia slipped back to her American accents. "It's a disguise."

"It's terrible," her mother said, and Zillah nodded in agreement, pulling a face. "We need to get you washed and dressed in your own clothes."

Mrs. Reynolds turned back to Philip. "I apologize I can't offer you hospitality at the moment, Major, but will you return tomorrow afternoon? I would like to thank you for bringing my daughter home safely."

"I would be honored, Mrs. Reynolds," Philip said. He shrugged into his coat and bowed over the hand she extended to him. "I need to check on my brother. Miss Junia will be able to tell you of our adventures."

Junia stepped forward. "But you can't just leave. What about my father?"

Before he could respond, her mother frowned at her. "What do you mean? Your Pappa came home last night."

CHAPTER EIGHT

Junia pulled away from Zillah, hiked up her skirts, and flew up the stairs, with Philip on her heels. She flung open the door to her parents' bedroom to see her father lying propped up against a multitude of pillows, frowning at a letter in his hand.

"Pappa!"

She ran to the bed and threw herself into his outstretched arms. He hugged her close, and she finally let the tears she had been suppressing for weeks flow as sobs of relief that he was safely home. Pappa rocked her as she cried, and she was certain she felt a few of his own tears on her forehead.

As she calmed, she straightened and looked around. Philip handed her a clean handkerchief from the table next to the bed, and she took a moment to wipe her eyes and blow her nose. He grinned at her, and she briefly stuck her tongue out at him behind the cover of the handkerchief.

Her father's arm still around her, she leaned against his shoulder. "How did you get free?"

Caius Reynolds shook his head. "It was the strangest thing. They came up to my room last night, loaded me into the cart, and brought me back. They barely stopped when they pushed me out in front of the house."

"Are you well? Why are you still in bed?"

"Your mother insisted." Her father rolled his eyes a bit, but was clearly pleased with this demonstration of wifely concern. "She did bring me the correspondence that stacked up while I was away, so I can get caught up on business."

Junia looked over at Philip, who was frowning in confusion. "Did they say anything about why they had taken you, or why they were returning you?"

"Not a thing."

"That's enough now, Junia," her mother said from the doorway. "Let your father rest." She came into the room and fussed with her husband's pillows until he seized her hand and kissed it. She bent to kiss him and then rest her forehead on his for a long moment.

Junia sighed and got up from the bed, Philip's hand under her elbow briefly steadying her until she got her footing. Zillah watched from the doorway with a little smirk, and Junia scowled at her.

"I need to go see what my brother is up to, and get some fresh clothes," Philip said. "I will see you tomorrow, J... Miss Junia."

He bowed over her hand, bowed to her parents, and even bowed to the giggling Zillah before heading to the front door. Zillah steered Junia out of the room towards the one they shared.

"We'll get you a bath, and wash your hair, and see if those mats will come out," Zillah said. "And then you're going to tell me *everything*."

Junia laughed, because she knew she was never going to tell her baby sister *everything*.

Lacking the key he had dropped when he had been abducted, Philip knocked at the door of the flat he shared with Peter. Their manservant opened the door and his jaw dropped. "Major Avondale!"

"Hello, Nelson. Is Peter here?"

"He returned home yesterday. He was quite upset to hear you had disappeared."

"I'm sure he was."

As Philip walked down the short hallway towards their drawing room, the door was jerked open and Peter stood in the entrance, scowling at him.

"Where in the *hell* have you been?" Peter said. "I've been worried sick!"

"Isn't a curate supposed to watch his language and set an example for his flock?" Philip grinned at his brother as he passed him and continued on into the drawing room. He sank into one of the armchairs in front of the fire with a sigh of relief. Now that he was finally home, he was almost too tired to move.

"They're all sailors. They think I don't swear nearly enough." Peter closed the door and followed Philip, standing behind the chair set on the other side. He frowned at his brother as Philip sprawled more comfortably, propping his boots on the edge of the grate. "What happened?"

"I was abducted by villains."

"You're joking."

"Not in the least." Philip tilted his head up to look Peter in the eye. "I was abducted because they thought I was you."

Peter's jaw dropped. "I don't believe it!"

"Neither did I," Philip said dryly, "but the fact they kept calling me 'parson' made me realize they'd got the wrong man."

Peter fell heavily into his chair.

"I was only trying to help," he said, and Philip groaned.

"That's always where you go wrong. Stop helping people!"

"I have to. I'm a minister." Peter looked pious, and Philip sighed. It was demmed awkward having an idealist as your a brother.

Peter sighed and scrubbed his hands through his hair, tousling his already disarrayed curls even more. "As I said, most of my parishioners are sailors. One of them came to me after morning services, hat in hand, and he asked me what the Lord thought of smuggling."

"And what did you say?"

"I admitted that the Lord frowned upon it. And the man said it was even worse, because they were bringing the contraband through the graveyard at St. Luke's."

Philip sat up abruptly. "The devil you say!"

"You may be sure I investigated and searched all around, but I could find no evidence it was happening. Still, men did seem to be lurking about at strange hours, so it seemed there must be something to it. And then my informant disappeared."

A sudden dread hit Philip. "He wasn't a black man, was he? A middle-aged man in his forties or so?"

"No, no, nothing like," Peter said, and Philip huffed a small sigh of relief. "He was a young man, and an Englishman. Kentish, so I went there to look for him."

"If he got involved with Kentish smugglers, he's likely dead at the bottom of the Channel by now. They don't appreciate any competition."

"That's what I feared, but I had to look for him anyway. I had no luck at all, so I came back to London after a few days, only to find *you* mysteriously disappeared as well."

"There must have been something to it, assuming the men who kidnapped me were of the same gang," Philip said. "But it seems as though that lead came to a dead end."

"But where have *you* been? I was getting ready to send a message to Paul if you hadn't turned up by today."

Philip snorted. "What did you think Paul was going to be able to do?" Their elder brother might be a duke, but he was certainly not acquainted with the criminal class.

"I don't know. Hire a Bow Street runner, most likely. You know I haven't the funds for one."

Philip shook his head. "Are you acquainted with a man named Caius Reynolds? He's as I described him earlier—a middle-aged black man, originally from America. About middle height, with some weight around the middle and close-cropped hair."

Peter shook his head in turn. "I've never heard of him, and the description is not familiar."

"Damn." Philip rubbed his face, feeling the scratchiness of the extra growth of beard that was starting to overtake his carefully groomed sidewhiskers. "I need a bath. And some sleep. And then we can puzzle it out some more."

"You're not going to tell me where you've been?"

"I hardly know myself. Northeast of London. Near a forest. The route we took back was so circuitous that I'm not sure I could say where the house was that we were held."

"'We'? Who did you travel with?"

Philip flushed. "None of your business."

"Oh ho! Like that, is it?"

"Not at all," Philip said stiffly. "She is a respectable lady who required my assistance."

"I look forward to hearing all about her over supper," Peter said with a grin that made Philip want to plant him a facer.

He had more information, but very little knowledge from it. The situation became more confusing by the moment.

He would discuss it with Junia tomorrow, and perhaps try to get more details from her father.

After supper and a long, luxurious bath, Junia sat between Zillah's feet as her sister patiently wielded a wide-toothed comb to coax the mats out of Junia's hair that her days of sleeping rough had left behind. Their mother sat in the armchair in the corner of their room, clearly reluctant to allow her older daughter out of her sight again, and Junia smiled at her.

"You see, Mama? It all came right in the end."

Her mother frowned at her. "It was thanks to the Lord you returned home safely."

"And Major Avondale," Zillah said slyly, and their mother glared at her. She looked at Junia, clearly on the verge of asking a question Junia did not want to answer, but Zillah rescued her with a sharp tug of the comb.

"Ouch!"

"Sorry, sorry," Zillah said, and Junia bit back her smile.

When her hair was combed and wrapped for the night, their mother said, "Zillah."

"Yes, Mama?"

"Go down to the kitchen and ask Mrs. Higgins to make your sister a cotton bark posset."

"Can't Sally do it?"

"Sally's been run off her feet all day helping us. Besides, I want you to do it."

Zillah looked from one to the other of them before sighing deeply and getting to her feet. "Yes, Mama."

Mama waited for the door to close before patting her lap. "Come here, honey."

With a sigh, Junia scooted over and lay her head in her mother's lap like she had done since she was a small girl, her mother gently stroking her shoulders and back to soothe her. The circumstances were different—better—but the comfort was the same even though Junia was grown now.

"Junia?"

"Yes, Mama?"

Her mother hesitated for a long moment, and then said, "You know that man can't never marry you, don't you?"

"I know he can't, Mama." There were too many differences between them. Even the richest merchant's daughter couldn't dream of marrying a duke's brother, and that was even before she considered her race, or her nationality, or the fact most Englishmen expected to marry a virgin, or the smallness of the dowry her father could provide compared to what a duke's brother would expect. She was, in every way, the opposite of what his family would want when it came to choosing his bride.

"I'm sorry, honey."

Junia lifted her hand, and her mother took it in a strong, familiar grip. "Just let me dream a little longer. Please?"

"All right."

They sat together by the fire, Junia taking comfort in her mother's steadfast love, until Zillah returned with the posset. After only a moment's hesitation, Junia drank it down.

Taking the precaution was for the best. For both of them.

CHAPTER NINE

The next day, Junia regarded herself in the mirror with satisfaction, finally feeling confident in her appearance again. The bright jonquil yellow of her fashionable muslin gown made her skin glow as if from within. Zillah had helped arrange her hair into puffs and topped them with a frivolous little lace cap adorned with coordinating ribbons. Her hands were still a little rough from her masquerade, but a good dose of her mother's hand cream and wearing cotton gloves overnight had smoothed them fairly well.

Finally, Philip would see her wearing something other than ill-fitting hand-me-downs or threadbare, dirty servant's clothing.

He's seen you in much less, a sly voice inside her said, and she cast her eyes down to hide the little smile of remembrance.

"What is it?" Zillah asked.

"Nothing," Junia said, and slid a set of thin gold bangles onto her wrist. "Are you ready to go downstairs?"

"Who are you?" a voice piped from somewhere behind him.

Philip turned, hat still in hand, to see a small boy who appeared to be about two years old standing in the hallway. He was dressed in a rumpled blue playsuit, staring up at Philip curiously. His curly hair was twisted into small knots all over his head, presumably to keep it neat and tidy.

Philip got down on one knee. "I am Major Avondale. And who might you be?"

"I'm George. Nya come home last night."

"That she did," Philip said, deducing that "Nya" must be Junia. "And your Pappa as well?"

George nodded. His thumb rose to his mouth as he continued to stare at Philip.

"George Caius Reynolds, what are you—oh!"

Philip rose swiftly to his feet and bowed to Junia's mother. "Good afternoon, Mrs. Reynolds."

She clucked her tongue. "Did that girl wander off before she could come tell me you were here? I don't know what I'm going to do with her. It's hard enough to find servants in the city as it is." Mrs. Reynolds stopped, took a breath to gather herself, and smiled warmly at him, a small glint of irony in her eye. "Please, come in and sit down."

She took George by the hand to lead him up the stairs and through the open door of the drawing room, with Philip following close behind. The same servant who had answered the door and then gone upstairs appeared in the doorway, breathless and cap askew.

"Master George! I've been looking everywhere for you. I'm that sorry, Mrs. Reynolds—he got away from Kitty when she was trying to get him fed and she asked me to help her look."

"Never mind now, Sally," Mrs. Reynolds said. "Please take George back to the nursery and then bring up the tea tray."

"Yes, ma'am," Sally said, taking George by the hand and leading him towards the stairs to the second floor. She scolded him under her breath as they walked, but George looked back at Philip instead, who winked at him. George ducked his head bashfully until the pair disappeared from view.

Philip helped Mrs. Reynolds into a chair by the unlit fireplace and seated himself on the small settee nearby. The furniture was clearly not new—it had likely come with the house when they purchased it—but it had been re-covered in fresh, bright fabrics that made the room a cozy space to gather.

He rose as Junia entered the room arm-in-arm with Zillah, glowing and confident, the very picture of a fashionable young lady about town. He barely recognized her as his Junia, but admired her even more.

She extended her free hand to him and he bowed over it, his lips brushing against the back in a kiss that was only perceptible to the two of them. He could feel her repressed shiver as she smiled at him, sending only the smallest glances towards her mother.

"Good afternoon, Miss Reynolds. I'm glad to see you seem to be no worse for the wear after your adventure."

Her mother cleared her throat, and Junia dropped his hand as though she had been burned. Philip turned to Zillah and bowed to her as well. "Miss Zillah, so lovely to see you again."

Like any seventeen-year-old in adult company, Zillah giggled and ducked her head. "Thank you, Major."

He settled Junia onto the settee with Zillah next to her and took one of the chairs across from the three women. A flashing look from Junia told him she, too, regretted they could not sit together under her mother's stern eye. Sally returned with the tea tray, her cap and dignity back in place, and set it on the small table in front of Junia.

"Shall I pour, Mama?" Junia asked, and her mother nodded.

Philip accepted his cup with a smile and said, "Will Mr. Reynolds be joining us?"

"Not today," Mrs. Reynolds said. "I want him to rest one day longer before he goes back to his office."

Philip cleared his throat. "I'm embarrassed to realize I did not ask what business Mr. Reynolds has established himself in."

"We own a counting house," Zillah said proudly, and Philip nodded, impressed. Given Caius Reynolds' facility with numbers, it was a natural choice.

"We used to live above it," Junia said, "but Pappa has been successful enough to buy this house."

"Enough, girls," Mrs. Reynolds said, looking embarrassed but a little pleased. "Major Avondale doesn't need to know every detail."

"But I *am* interested, ma'am," he said. "I'm impressed at how well your family has prospered since I last saw you four years ago."

"Thank you, Major. Are you on leave from the army?"

Philip took another sip from the cup in his hand. "No, I sold out a few weeks ago. One of my mother's aunts left me a small property in Gloucestershire in her will, and I was tired of army life."

"I'm glad you made it safely through the wars, Major," Junia said, her voice warm.

He looked at her and smiled. "So am I."

Philip pulled his gaze away from hers as multiple footsteps sounded up the stairs and the drawing room door opened.

"My dear Miss Reynolds! How glad I am to see you recovered from your illness."

Philip examined the two young men who stood in the doorway of the Reynolds's drawing room. They could not have made a stronger contrast to one another if they had planned for a week. One was tall and cadaverously thin, with white-blond hair and pale blue eyes to match, dressed in clothes that hung off him like a scarecrow.

The other was short and a little rotund even at his young age, with hair and eyes as dark as his friend's were light. Philip judged him to be not older than three-and-twenty, but he dressed like a much older man in clothes that were at least ten years out of fashion. He carried a nosegay of violets in one hand and presented them to Junia with a flourish as he bowed low to her. The other man followed in his wake to make his bow as well, first to Junia and Zillah, and then to their mother. As his friend worked his charm on Junia and her mother, the pale man glanced around the room. When his gaze landed on Philip, Philip saw the younger man's eyes widen in surprise before he quickly concealed his reaction.

Interesting. Very *interesting.*

The other man finished his speech to Junia and watched in satisfaction as she gave a token sniff to his floral offering before setting it aside with a smile. He, too, looked around the room, and made a quickly concealed start when he saw Philip rise from his seat. Philip was almost certain he, too, recognized him, but Philip was equally certain he had never seen either of them before in his life.

"I see your parents have made a new friend, Miss Reynolds. Will you introduce us?"

"Of course. Major Lord Philip Avondale, this is Mr. Williams and Mr. Hughes."

Mr. Williams was the pale one; Mr. Hughes, the darker. The three men bowed to each other, Philip deliberately keeping his face neutral and pleasant.

"How do you know the family, Major?" Williams said.

"I met them on their voyage from America, four years ago," Philip said. "When I came to London, I decided to look them up to pay my respects."

"So you have only recently returned to London?" Hughes said.

"Yes," Philip said, with perfect truth.

"I feel perhaps we have met before, Major Avondale," Hughes said, proving Philip's suspicion he was the bolder of the two.

Philip kept his expression bland. "I do not believe so, Mr. Hughes. Your face is not at all familiar to me."

"Hm. I don't suppose you have a twin," Hughes said, and laughed heartily. Philip only smiled, and glanced over at Junia. She looked a little puzzled, but was clearly willing to follow his lead and not reveal any information.

Mrs. Reynolds said, "Won't you sit down, gentlemen?"

Williams and Hughes each took a chair across from the ladies, while Philip propped his shoulder against the fireplace mantel in a spot that allowed him to watch everyone. The women were cordial, but did not seem to show any particular favor to either man as they exchanged commonplaces about the weather and the dreadful price of necessities. Sally bustled in with more teacups and hot water, and bustled out again.

"And how is Mr. Reynolds?" Hughes asked at last. "Was he felled by the same malady as Miss Reynolds?"

"I'm afraid so," Mrs. Reynolds said. "But he is recovering now and should be back in the office in another day or two."

Junia looked over at Philip. "I forgot to mention Mr. Hughes and Mr. Williams work in my father's counting house, as junior clerks."

"I am a full clerk now, Miss Reynolds," Hughes said in what he surely meant to be a jesting tone, but came out with an edge of annoyance. "Surely your father mentioned that to you."

"I'm afraid I haven't much of a head for business," Junia said sadly. "So much of what my father says goes in one ear and out the other."

Philip coughed to hide his chuckle. To his eyes, Junia was not very convincing as a feather-witted young lady, but Hughes relaxed a little and smiled a condescending little smile at her. "Of course not. Ladies have so many other things to think about."

When an interminable twenty minutes had passed and a cup of tea had been drunk by each of them, Hughes looked over at his friend and both men rose to their feet. "I suppose we ought to be going, Mrs. Reynolds," Hughes said. "We only wanted to call to see how Mr. Reynolds was getting on."

Hughes looked over at Philip, who smiled and remained planted in his spot. Philip knew the other man was trying to think of a discreet way to ask why Philip showed no sign of leaving well past the polite length of time for an afternoon call.

"Miss Reynolds has agreed to stroll in the park with me," Philip said. "She was just about to fetch her bonnet when you gentlemen called."

Junia immediately rose to her feet and smiled at each man in turn. "I certainly was. If you will excuse me?"

Hughes and Williams had no choice but to bow to all of the women, and then to Philip, and take their leave. Philip strained to hear if they were muttering to each other as they left, but could not hear anything. That seemed perhaps more ominous than if they had talked.

"I'll get my bonnet now," Junia said, and he smiled and bowed to her from his spot at the fireplace.

Junia's mother regarded him thoughtfully. "Zillah, why don't you go help Junia get ready?"

Zillah pouted, but got to her feet. "I always have to miss the *interesting* conversations." With a toss of her head, she left the room, closing the door firmly behind herself.

"Please, sit down, Major."

Philip could feel himself flush and hoped it wasn't too noticeable. If he wasn't mistaken, he was about to be asked his intentions by Junia's mother, and he wasn't certain what his answer would be. Not yet, anyway.

"We do appreciate your help, Major Avondale, very much," Mrs. Reynolds said, "but it's best you don't call on us again after today."

Philip blinked. "I see."

"We both know there's nothing that can come of your friendship with Junia. She's a respectable young woman who can expect to marry well within our little society here, where the gentlemen understand what we came from and make allowances, unlike in your world. She doesn't have to settle as an aristocrat's mistress."

Philip winced. "I appreciate your plain speaking, Mrs. Reynolds."

The older woman sighed. "I wish the world was different. I like you very much, I always have. I think you and Junia would do well together. But we both know your family would never allow it."

"I'm nearly thirty, Mrs. Reynolds," he said stiffly. "I don't allow my family to dictate who I can marry."

She smiled sadly at him. "It's not just your family. It's the whole world. I don't want to see my Junia get hurt."

"I understand."

The door opened, and Junia floated in with a cerulean blue spencer over her yellow gown and a frivolous wide-brimmed bonnet perched on her head. She was a little breathless and still pulling on her short gloves as she looked from one to the other of them.

"Is anything wrong?" Junia said.

"Nothing, honey," Mrs. Reynolds said. "Go have your walk now."

Frowning, Junia bent and kissed her mother's proffered cheek before turning to Philip. "Shall we go, Major?"

Philip bowed low. "Good afternoon, Mrs. Reynolds."

"Goodbye, Major."

CHAPTER TEN

As they walked out the front door, Philip led Junia down the stairs and then tucked her hand into the crook of his arm as they walked.

"Where shall we go first?" she asked.

"Towards St. Luke's," he said. "We can see if anything looks peculiar or different from when you last saw it."

"We don't attend that church very often," she said, a little apologetically. "We usually go to the dissenting church. But George was baptized at St. Luke's since Pappa said it's best to be church members if you want to enter a profession."

"That's likely why you haven't met Peter," Philip said. "He only became a curate there about a year ago."

"I don't entirely understand the system, but you and your brother are lords, the younger sons of a duke. Shouldn't he have a... a..."

"A better posting? More elegant, or more lucrative?"

"Well, yes."

"It's what he prefers. He would rather serve in a parish where he feels he can do some good than the prosperous sort our brother holds the livings of." Philip sighed. "But sometimes Peter is a little *too* eager to do good. I can't tell you how many times I've had to pull him out of scrapes, and it looks like this is yet another one where he got in over his head because he wanted to help someone."

Junia laughed. "Zillah is an idealist, too. I can't tell you how many mangy dogs she's tried to rescue or beggars she's emptied her purse for. We must make sure they never meet."

"Yes," Philip said, and something dimmed in him.

Junia looked at him curiously. "Is anything wrong?"

He shook himself a little and smiled down at her. "No, no. Everything's fine. Tell me more about Zillah. I've always wondered how she had adapted to living in England."

Junia began relating a few light, amusing stories about her sister, but Philip's mood had definitely shifted.

She wondered again what he and her mother had been talking about to make them both look so grim when she had entered the room earlier.

St. Luke's had been built less than a hundred years before, which seemed quite old to Junia until she thought about the many even older buildings that surrounded them in London. There was nothing very remarkable about it, but Philip frowned thoughtfully as they wandered through the grounds and into the graveyard.

"How far is it from here to your father's counting house?"

Junia looked around with a frown. "Not far. Two streets over. Do you think that has something to do with it?"

"I don't know. But it seems significant." He sighed. "I think I would need Peter to come with me to look inside the church itself since it's usually locked during the day. Let's walk over to the counting house."

As they walked, Philip said, "Where did your father get the money to start his counting house? Such a venture usually requires a fairly large amount of capital to start."

Junia tossed her head, but looked away, bracing herself for his reaction. "He had been saving money to buy our freedom, but most of it came from Mr. Reynolds. Our old master. It was our back wages for the four of us, Pappa said. He even left a receipt for the exact amount, minus room and board."

Philip paused and looked down at her for a long moment. Then a smile crept across his face, and she couldn't help but smile back. "How very clever," he said, and they began walking again.

As they drew closer to her father's counting house, Philip's steps slowed almost to a stop. Junia looked up to see his face had become distant and abstracted.

"Philip? Is something wrong?"

A passerby bumped into Philip from the opposite direction and, after checking his pockets, he began walking again.

"What if," he said slowly, "what if the reason the work they had your father doing seems nonsensical because it *was* nonsensical? What if they were holding him prisoner because they needed him to be away from the counting house or another place he does business?"

She shook her head. "But that makes no more sense."

"It does, though. You have no brother to check up on the business. Your mother could not have been there to oversee it, not in her condition. You and Zillah don't know how to run the business, and you were away yourself."

Junia gasped as she understood what he was saying. "So you think maybe they kidnapped Pappa to keep him away from whatever it was they were trying to do, not because they wanted him to do something."

"Exactly." Philip frowned. "We need to ask your father what properties he controls or owns other than your house and the counting house. It could be a warehouse or similar building that's being used for nefarious purposes."

Philip looked around as they walked, his instincts telling him someone was watching them, though he could not see anyone. He pulled Junia a little closer and she smiled up at him. He couldn't help smiling back.

He knew he was being foolish. They had only been barely acquainted while aboard ship, though he had admired her courage even then. Now, with barely a week's acquaintance, he admired her even more. It had taken strength of will and character for her to decide to rescue her father, even at great risk to herself. He admired her whole family, in fact. It was not easy to flee to a strange country and not only survive, but thrive once they arrived. The desperate refugees of four years ago were now a prosperous middle-class merchant family.

And as the younger brother of a duke, he was as out of reach for their daughter as one of the stars in the sky as far as her family was concerned.

He could at least do her this service of finding out why her father had been kidnapped and held prisoner, even if it would be the only service he could provide before he respected her mother's wishes and walked away.

"Here it is," Junia said.

They stopped in front of a medium-sized building with small, high windows on either side of a solid front door. A counting house needed to be a secure place so clients would be comfortable having their money and accounts kept there. There was a second row of larger windows above that Junia pointed to.

"That's the flat where we lived until Pappa bought the house a year ago."

"Is it empty now?"

Junia frowned. "I would need to ask. I can't remember if my parents decided to rent it out or leave it vacant to make the building more secure."

Philip examined the windows thoughtfully. The curtains were drawn, and the rooms beyond seemed to be dark. If anyone lived there, there was no sign.

Philip opened the door of the office for Junia and followed her into the main room. Rows of clerks sat at rows of desks, heads bent over their account books as they scribbled away. He looked around to see if he could spot Hughes or Williams, but neither man seemed to be in the room.

Instead, a young lad of about fifteen approached them. Like many of the other apprentices in the room, he was clearly of African descent. Junia's father seemed to have a policy of hiring apprentices with a similar background to his own.

Junia smiled at the apprentice as he bowed to her. "Good afternoon, Michael."

"Good afternoon, miss."

"Michael, this is Major Avondale."

After they exchanged bows as well, Philip said, "Are Mr. Hughes and Mr. Williams here?"

"No, sir. They took the afternoon off." Michael frowned, as if disapproving of this sloth on a working day.

"I see," Philip said. "As we were walking up, Miss Reynolds and I were wondering if there is a tenant in the upstairs apartment."

Michael shook his head. "It's not rented out. I wouldn't stay there if you gave me a million pounds. There's a ghost lives up there."

Philip and Junia exchanged looks, and Philip said, "Really? How do you know?"

"We can hear it walking at night, but when anyone goes up to look, there's no one there."

"No one there?"

Michael shook his head. "Just the furniture all covered up with sheets."

Junia started, and Philip put a calming hand on her arm. "Thank you, Michael."

The boy nodded and threaded his way through the desks back to his own.

Philip drew back towards the entrance, gently guiding Junia with a hand at her elbow.

"Something about what he said surprised you. What was it?"

"There shouldn't be any furniture up there," Junia said quietly. "We brought everything to the townhouse with us when we moved."

CHAPTER ELEVEN

As they walked back to the townhouse, both Philip and Junia were gloomy.

"It must be one of your father's employees," Philip said. "Or a business associate. Someone close to all of you."

Junia shivered. "That almost makes it worse. I worried less when I thought he had been taken by total strangers. But for it to have been someone we know…"

"Traitors always cause chaos in their wake," Philip said grimly. "The breach of trust is almost worse than any action they might take."

"What are we going to do?"

"*We* are not going to do anything," Philip said. "*I* will go there tonight after it gets dark and see if there's any activity at the building."

"You can't go alone. It will be dangerous."

"I'll take Peter with me. Or your father. Probably both of them." He fixed her with a stern glare. "But *you*, angel, will wait at home. I can't be worrying about you while I'm trying to investigate what's going on."

Junia frowned, but before she could argue, they arrived in front of her family's house. Philip took her by the shoulders and turned her to him. "Promise me, angel."

She looked up at him, a little breathless at the intensity of his expression, and she saw his eyes darken as his gaze focused on her lips. Without conscious thought, she swayed toward him, wanting him to kiss her, not caring they were on a public street in view of anyone passing by.

A sharp rap on the front window carried to them and Philip stepped back, his hands dropping away but his eyes still intense on her. "Promise me, Junia."

The rap came again, and Junia sped up the stairs to the front door. You didn't wait when Mama knocked twice. Sally opened it promptly and glared at Philip before announcing to the whole street, "Your mama wants to see you in the drawing room, Miss Reynolds."

Junia gave a helpless little wave to Philip, still standing on the walkway, and began unbuttoning her pelisse.

She might be in for a scolding from Mama, but the interruption had prevented her from making a promise she had no intention of keeping.

To Philip's surprise, Peter balked at the idea of breaking into someone else's property to look for smugglers.

"I'm a curate now," Peter said. "I can't go around breaking into flats and catching criminals. Besides, Paul said if I got into one more scrape, he would give me that living in Yorkshire, and I would have to take it. I would hate living in Yorkshire."

Under normal circumstances, Philip would have been all in favor of Peter moving to Yorkshire to keep him out of mischief, but of course the one time he needed his twin to act like his usual reckless self was the time Peter had decided to try to do better.

"You can't leave me to do this alone. It's your fault I'm involved in this in the first place."

"I didn't do it on purpose."

"That's always your excuse."

Peter narrowed his eyes. "I can't believe you're the one who wants to do this. I thought you hated lost causes."

"It's not a lost cause. I think we can win."

"And what will you win?" Peter said with unexpected shrewdness, and Philip felt himself flush.

"Oh ho!" Peter crowed. "Like that, is it?"

"Like what?"

"Like you playing knight in shining armor to a damsel in distress."

Philip remembered Junia's absolute determination to free her father and her uncomplaining trek with him to safety when he knew she must be exhausted and frightened. "There is a damsel, but she's stronger than you give her credit for."

Peter eyed him shrewdly. "Are you planning to marry the chit?"

Philip thought for a long moment. He knew it was impossible. Her family would oppose it. His mother would dissolve into hysterics. All of high society would be shocked and appalled that Lord Philip Avondale, the son and brother of a duke, had married a woman who was not only of another race, but a former slave, and American, *and* a merchant's daughter to boot.

And he couldn't bring himself to care what their opinions were, as long as Junia would have him.

"Yes," Philip said. "It's like that."

"Well, then," Peter said. "I suppose we had better form our plan. If you're hoping to woo a wife into the bargain, we'll need to make sure you don't break your neck."

Junia listened to her mother's scolding with half an ear, frowning, smiling, and agreeing in the right places even as she allowed herself to dream about Philip instead, and worry about his plans for that night. After several minutes, her mother sighed.

"I suppose I can't tell you anything about being careful with your feelings, even if it is for your own good."

"Oh, Mama." Junia stood up and crossed to her mother's chair to kiss her cheek. "I do listen to you."

"You're a woman grown now, and most of the other girls around here your age are already married," Mama said. "Your Pappa and I, we just want you to be settled and happy."

"How is Pappa today? I wanted to go up and see him, but I don't want to bother him."

Her mother relaxed a little. "He's much better. Go up and see him. Maybe he can talk some sense into you."

Junia laughed and ran up the stairs, feeling more lighthearted than she had in ages. Perhaps ever.

In her parents' room, she found her father sitting at his desk, fully dressed and with his spectacles on as he read through some correspondence. He smiled at her as she came in, and she eyed him critically. The bruises on his face were fading, and the scrapes were nearly healed.

"How are you, Pappa?"

"Much better, honey, much better. All I really needed was some food and rest."

Junia crossed to sit in a chair near her father's. "Major Avondale and I have been investigating to try and find out who did this to you."

Her father frowned. "You shouldn't be doing that. It could be dangerous."

"We're worried there may be some action happening in the next few days. And that the criminals could be someone we already know."

Junia spelled out all of their information and guesses to her father, from the reason why he had been kidnapped to the possible traitors in their midst. He listened thoughtfully, asking a few pointed questions but mostly allowing Junia to speak.

"If you had to guess, who do you think might have done this?"

Pappa leaned back in his chair, lost in thought. "At the bottom, it's not very clever. A lot has counted on being able to hold onto people who were able to get away. He's likely right that it's smugglers."

"Phi—Major Avondale thinks it could be one of your clerks, or even an associate."

Pappa's brows raised at her slip, but said, "It could be. I think he's right—I think it's someone we know."

"Mr. Hughes and Mr. Williams called this afternoon."

"Your mama told me. What did they have to say?"

"Not much." Junia frowned. "They barely even asked about you. He didn't say it, but I think that's who Major Avondale suspects."

"What do you suspect?"

"It could be. I never thought they were very bright."

"Considering how the scheme has gone so far, that might not be a point against them." He frowned and rubbed his forehead. "Let me think and see if there's anyone else who might make sense."

Junia felt instantly guilty—her father was still recovering, and here she was pressing him to answer questions. "Of course, Pappa. I only brought it up since Major Avondale will be investigating tonight."

"You care for him, don't you?" Pappa said, and Junia gaped at him.

"I... don't worry, Pappa. Mama already talked to me. I know he can never... we can't ever..."

"It depends what a man really wants," her father said. "If he's found the right woman, a man will move heaven and earth to keep her. Your mama and I were kept apart, threatened with separation, didn't see each other for months at a time even after we were married. But I knew she was the right woman, so I did everything I could to stick by her."

"Even escaping and coming to a whole new country."

"No, Junia." He covered her hand with his. "We did that for you and your sister. And now George and the new baby don't have to grow up the way you did, or the way we did. Life will still be hard, but they'll be free in a way we never were."

Junia leaned down to embrace him and his arms closed strong around her as she clung to him like the child she no longer was. When she finally straightened, he smiled at her.

"I don't know if it'll work out. None of us do. But it might be worth giving him a chance."

CHAPTER TWELVE

A s he and Peter prepared to leave, there was a soft knock on the door of their flat. Nelson opened it to reveal a young boy who seemed familiar to Philip. After a moment, he realized it was the one who had held the mule outside Junia's house.

"Package for Major Reynolds," the boy said, and held his hand out for a tip. Philip dropped a shilling on his palm, and the boy's fingers closed over it greedily before he darted away as though fearing Philip would change his mind.

He opened the package to find a key inside, but no note or writing on the envelope. He frowned at it, puzzled.

"What do you suppose it's a key for?" Peter asked.

"It's got to be the key to the flat. But why would Junia send it over without a note?"

"Women," Peter said, and turned away to shrug on his overcoat. Philip continued to frown at the key. There was something off here.

With a sigh, Philip put the key in his pocket. There now seemed to be a good chance they were about to walk into a trap, but if the alternative was letting the kidnappers get away with their crimes, Philip was willing to stick his hand out and see what happened. This was like the tension before a battle, strung taut because of the unknown ahead, but knowing the confrontation was inevitable.

"Are you ready?" Philip asked.

"As ready as I can be," Peter said. "You're not really going to use that pistol, are you?"

"Only if I have to. I hope I won't."

"Lord preserve us if the bishop finds out." His face drawn into lines of gloom, Peter followed Philip down to the street, where they hailed a hackney coach and climbed in. The ride was tense, and Peter seemed disinclined to conversation.

"You're not letting a little danger worry you, are you?" Philip said with a smirk, and Peter glared at him through the darkness.

"When you get in this knight-errant mood, I worry a lot," his brother replied. "But I know there's no dissuading you at this point."

When they were within a few blocks of the Reynolds house, Philip rapped on the roof of the carriage to have the driver let them out and paid the man off. Peter frowned as he saw the residential street.

"I thought we were going to the counting house."

"We need to talk to Caius Reynolds first. I don't trust this mystery key that appeared so conveniently. But since the house is likely being watched, we'd better go in through the mews."

"At least I didn't wear my new boots," Peter grumbled, but followed along through the alley behind the homes until they stood at the back door of the Reynolds house. A light burned inside and Philip could hear a chatter of voices, so he rapped at the door.

A dark-skinned woman, her hair wrapped in an intricate head-cloth, opened the door and glared at them. "What do you want, then?"

"We must see Mr. Reynolds at once," Philip said. "Kindly take us to him."

She peered uncertainly from one to the other of them, clearly taken aback both by Philip's accent and the fact they were twins. Peter smiled at her reassuringly, and she shook her head.

"I'll have Sally take you up, I suppose."

Philip nodded and stepped into the neatly kept kitchen. In the corner, a young kitchenmaid goggled at the fine gentlemen entering their house through the back.

"Go fetch Sally, that's a good girl," the cook said, and the kitchenmaid darted away. The cook went back to work as Philip and Peter waited a respectful distance away.

In his study, Reynolds looked from one to the other of them. "You think they're using the flat above my offices to hide their smuggled goods?"

"Yes, sir."

The older man removed his spectacles and rubbed his forehead. "Junia said you thought the culprits might be some of my own employees."

"It would make the most sense. It would explain why they needed you out of the way, and gave you work to keep you occupied. Those may have been books kept by the smugglers to keep track of their activities that needed to be altered for some reason."

"What's your plan, then?"

"If you'll give us the keys, Peter and I will go investigate at the flat and see if we can find any evidence. We may even surprise the smugglers at their work." He drew the mystery key from his pocket and handed it to Reynolds. "This key arrived tonight, and I think it may be to the flat. We may be walking into a trap."

"That sounds dangerous."

"I was in the army. I'm not concerned."

Reynolds slapped his hands on the surface of the desk and rose to his feet. "It's my property, and I don't want it damaged. I'll come with you."

Philip nodded. "We need to leave as soon as possible. I think they let you go because they're nearly done with whatever it is they're doing."

Reynolds left the room to fetch his overcoat while Philip paced, eager for action now that he had made up his mind. Peter watched him from his seat, an unusually thoughtful expression on his face.

"You know Mother will have a fit if you marry that man's daughter."

"I don't care," Philip said. "We've never agreed on anything. Besides, Mother has terrible matchmaking taste. Did you ever meet that schoolroom miss she was trying to get Paul to marry before the chit ran away? It would have been a worse mismatch than Prinny and Princess Caroline."

"She won't be the only one who shuns you."

Philip turned to face his brother full on. "Will you be one of the ones who shun us?"

"No," Peter said after a long moment. "I may not approve, but I could never abandon you."

Philip took three strides forward and clapped his brother on the shoulder. "That's all the support I'll need, then."

Junia peeked through the curtains of her bedroom as the men exited the house, once again using the kitchen door. Poor Mrs. Higgins would be angry to have her routine interrupted twice in one night. Even Mama was reluctant to risk their cook and housekeeper's wrath when Mrs. Higgins felt her domain was being interfered with.

Dusk was gathering quickly, and the three men were soon out of sight. Her eavesdropping had been incomplete, but it seemed they planned to search the flat and then hide in place to see if they could confirm who the smugglers were.

She knew she ought to stay safely home and wait for the men to return. It was what Philip would want, and what her parents would expect.

But the same cold knot that had formed in her stomach when she witnessed her father's abduction was forming again. She needed to listen to that instinct more than she needed to be obedient.

"What are you doing?"

Junia started and spun around as Zillah came into the room. "Shh! Close the door."

Puzzled but willing, Zillah obeyed before crossing to the window and peering over Junia's shoulder. "Are they leaving?"

"Yes," Junia said, "and I don't like it."

She went to their wardrobe and pulled out a dark cloak.

"You're not going to follow them, are you?"

"I don't need to follow them," Junia said, with a bravado she did not entirely feel. "I know where they're going. I just need to... arrive a little later than they do."

"I'm going with you."

"You can't. You need to stay with Mama."

"Mama will be fine with Mrs. Higgins in the house. I'm coming with you. You know it's dangerous for a woman to be alone on the streets at night."

"It's dangerous for two women, too."

"But not *as* dangerous." Zillah pulled her own cloak from the wardrobe. "Come on. Let's go save Pappa."

Philip scanned the street both as they walked up to the building and as Reynolds unlocked the door that led to the staircase up to the flat. He did not see anything, but the itch at the back of his neck warned him danger was nearby.

"Would someone else be able to get the key to the flat?"

"Easily, if they were dishonest," Reynolds said, his voice equally as quiet. "It's kept hanging next to the chief clerk's desk."

Inside the darkened flat, there was just enough light for Philip to see shrouded shapes which could be mistaken for furniture with holland covers on top. He lifted the edge of one sheet to see what was underneath was not a settee, as the shape might indicate, but a series of crates stacked in such a way as to pass muster once they were covered.

Reynolds whistled softly as he surveyed the room. "We took every stick of furniture with us when we moved to the house."

"That was what Junia said." Philip walked to each grouping of boxes, peering under the cover of each to confirm they were all crates, not furniture.

"What do they have in there?" Reynolds asked.

"Likely tea," Peter said. "It's one of the most profitable things to smuggle. Could be some fabrics and laces as well."

Philip did another circuit of the room, walking slowly. "From what I understand, smugglers do most of their business at the markets at the edge of town rather than risk bringing their goods directly into the city. So what are they doing here?"

"Looks like you're about to find out, parson."

Philip froze at the familiar, sneering voice behind him and then turned slowly, cursing his rusty skills. He should have remembered to check the kitchen to prevent Dickie from ambushing them. The big man who had a soft spot for Junia—Robby, his name was—stood at Dickie's shoulder pointing his own pistol at Philip.

Reynolds turned as well, glancing at Philip as he raised his hands. Philip prevented himself from looking around. He was fairly sure he had heard a soft thud as Peter dropped to the ground, especially since the two villains seemed focused on himself and Reynolds.

"You've been a lot of trouble to us, parson," Dickie said, "but that ends tonight."

"Are you planning to kill us?"

"No need for us to do it. We'll leave you here after we take the goods and let Smythe's men deal with you. They'll be in a temper for sure, missing us and losing their goods."

A clatter of more footsteps on the stairs made Dickie glance away, but not long enough for Philip to make a move. It was no surprise when Hughes and Williams came into the room, herded at gunpoint by Jasper and Jem. Hughes in particular looked far less self-assured than he had in the Reynolds drawing room, and he immediately turned a pleading glance on Dickie.

"Please, uncle," Hughes said. "I don't understand why you need us here. We gave you everything!"

Dickie rolled his eyes and spat at Hughes' feet. "'Uncle,' ye call me now that you're in trouble. You and yer pap wouldn't give me the time of day until you needed me."

Hughes subsided, and Williams kept his head down, clearly miserable. The other two men started to spread around the room, poking at the covered crates.

Out of the corner of his eye, Philip could see Peter rise half-crouched from his hiding spot and began edging his way towards the group, but he half-stumbled on an uneven floorboard and Jasper whirled to confront him. He stared in disbelief, looking between Philip and Peter until understanding dawned in his eyes.

"Bloody hell," Jasper said. "They're twins!"

Dickie cuffed him on the side of the head without looking away from Philip, who he clearly judged to be the more dangerous of the two brothers. "Of course they're twins! And you went and nabbed the wrong one."

"You was there too, Dickie," Jasper said with surprising dignity. "I didn't hear you saying not to do it."

"It's no matter now," Dickie said. "But we can't be the ones to kill them. The excise would never stop looking for us if we killed one dook's son, much less two of 'em."

Jasper and Dickie both looked to where Hughes and Williams hovered at the edge of the room, clearly deciding whether or not to try and make a run for it despite Robby's bulk between them and the stairs.

Philip thought he heard the scrape of a foot near the half-open door to the stairs and coughed loudly to try and drown it out. Robby glared at him, but looked uncertainly in the direction of the noise, clearly torn between guarding them and going to look for the source.

Junia ran down the stairs as quickly and quietly as she could and met a nervous Zillah outside. "They've taken Philip and Pappa prisoner. We need to go fetch Mr. Force. He'll know what to do."

The Force home was nearly a mile away, but Junia and Zillah lifted their skirts to their knees and ran, ignoring the passers-by who stared at them. They ran up the front stairs where Junia pounded on the front door until a footman opened it.

"What are you making that noise for? Go away!"

Junia stuck her boot-clad foot in the door. "We must speak to Mr. Force immediately. Caius Reynolds—my father—is in danger and needs his help."

The footman hesitated at the familiar name, and then reluctantly opened the door to let them into the foyer to wait. Junia stood as patiently as she could while Zillah looked around the grand house with wide eyes.

"Miss Reynolds?" a voice said, and Junia turned in relief to see Thaddeus Force descending the stairs. He was in his early thirties, mixed race, his voice still carrying a trace of his birthplace in Italy. Within only a few years of his arrival in England, and with the help of aristocratic connections that included the new Duchess of Livesay, he was one of the most successful importers of fabrics and laces in London.

Junia curtsied to him, and elbowed Zillah to do the same. "May we speak in private, Mr. Force? It's an urgent matter."

"Of course." He ushered them up the stairs and into his study, where he settled them into the chairs in front of his desk.

"If you will, Miss Reynolds."

Junia took a deep breath. "It all started when my father was abducted..."

Mr. Force listened intently as Junia related her story as quickly as possible, raising his eyebrows when she mentioned Philip and Peter Avondale.

"Sometimes," he said, "I forget how small London can be."

"Philip—Major Avondale—thought the culprit could be one of my father's clerks, and he was right."

Mr. Force rose to his feet. "There's no time to lose. We must go at once."

"We're not murderers, Jack," Williams hissed.

"We're not, but *they* are," Hughes muttered back, gesturing to the men gathered around the shrouded crates. "It'll be them or us that gets killed, and I don't want it to be us."

"Why did I listen to you in the first place?"

"Because you got greedy, just like me," Hughes said. "We're not going to make as much as we hoped, but if we can take care of this... little problem, we'll still walk away with a profit."

Philip was fairly certain the two younger men didn't realize he could hear them. This had never been a clever scheme, but idiotic schemes were just as likely to get one killed as clever ones. Maybe even more so.

The rope they had been tied with scraped his wrists as he pulled and stretched his bonds as discreetly as he could. Glancing over at Reynolds, he could see the older man doing the same with grim determination. He was concerned about Peter, but even the most hardened smuggler should be reluctant to harm an honest clergyman. At least, Philip hoped so.

Just as his wrist slipped free of his bonds, he saw Williams and Hughes finish their dispute and look over to where he and Reynolds sat. He glared back at them, discreetly shifting so he blocked Reynolds from their view as the man continued to struggle with the rope that bound his hands.

Hughes took a deep breath and stepped forward with the pistol Dickie had pressed into his shaking hand. Even as he began to raise it, Philip sprang at him and seized his wrist, twisting hard until the smaller man cried out and dropped the gun. Williams took a swing at him and Philip ducked, pulling Hughes's arm behind him as Philip used the other man as a shield.

"That's enough!" Dickie barked, and Philip turned to see the smuggler with his arm around Peter's neck, half-bending his brother to the ground. "Leggo or I blow the parson's brains out."

Slowly, Philip loosened his grip and Hughes staggered away. Dickie raised his gun even as Robby, standing at the window, frowned at what he saw outside.

"There's men outside," Robby said.

"What do you mean, there's men outside? Which men?"

Robby shrugged. "Dunno. Just men."

Dickie shoved Peter away and gestured to Philip. "C'mere." When he hesitated, Dickie gestured more urgently. "C'mere, or I'll shoot ye where you stand."

Reluctantly, Philip came within arm's reach, and Dickie pushed him toward the stairs. "You go first. I'm right behind you with the gun. If they shoot, they'll get you first."

Dickie formed the rest into a rough line, with Reynolds, Peter, Williams, and Hughes in the middle guarded by Jasper and Jem, and Robby bringing up the rear. "If it's the Kentish gang come to claim their goods, they'll shoot him and we'll have time to run. If it's the excise men, we can say we'll shoot the hostages and they'll have to let us go. Move it, now."

His hands raised, Philip led the way down the stairs, Dickie's pistol cold at his ear as the other man reached past him to open the door.

As the door opened, Philip was momentarily blinded by lights outside and tensed for another confrontation. Instead, he felt the pressure of the gun slide away as Dickie dropped it to the ground with a clatter and raised his hands. Philip took two quick steps to place himself between Caius Reynolds and whoever was outside that door before stepping across the threshold.

To his relief, he immediately recognized Thaddeus Force, who led a group of torch-carrying excise men and local merchants that surrounded the escape route for the would-be smugglers. From the back of the crowd, Junia rushed forward, and Philip caught her up in his arms as she leapt towards him, her face glowing.

"You're all right! And Pappa!"

"And my brother, too," Philip said. Conscious of the men surrounding them, he kissed her forehead and put her a little away from him, his left arm still around her waist.

Force stepped forward and nodded. "Major Avondale."

Philip grinned at him. "Glad to see you again, Force. Relieved, I have to admit. Thank you for your help."

Force bowed, but Philip extended his right hand. After a moment's hesitation, the other man shook it firmly, as an equal.

Aware of the watching crowd, Philip looked around and saw Zillah had made her way to her father's side and was fussing over him as he soothed her. Philip knew standing in a public street like this with his arm around Junia, surrounded by her community, was a declaration of intent on his part.

He raised his voice a little and said, "Thank you, gentlemen. Your assistance was very timely."

Philip turned to see Robby had herded the rest of the smugglers to the excise men and was shaking hands all around. Robby looked over at Philip and nodded, his eyes grazing wistfully over Junia before he turned back to the rest of the excise men.

Junia seemed to suddenly realize they had an audience and stepped away so hastily that he needed to steady her with a hand on her elbow. He took her hand and tucked it into the crook of his arm as they led the procession back to the Reynolds house to relieve her mother's mind while the smugglers were led away by the excise men, including Robby. Philip wondered if he would ever find out what the tale was there.

CHAPTER THIRTEEN

The group was in a celebratory mood as they returned to the house, with Mrs. Higgins and an excited Sally passing around glasses of punch and mugs of ale to the group for a toast or two before Caius Reynolds and Force began to edge everyone towards the door. He was clearly as eager to return to his own snug home as Mrs. Reynolds was to return order to her household.

He and Philip shook hands one more time, and Force and Peter exchanged bows.

"Thank you, Mr. Force," Mrs. Reynolds said, and he bowed to her as well. She led her two daughters upstairs, Junia glancing back only once before she followed in her mother's wake.

"Happy to be of assistance. Good night."

Peter shifted from foot to foot, and Philip clapped him on the shoulder. "Why don't you head back to the flat? I'll meet you there in a bit."

Peter looked from Philip to Reynolds and back again, and then sighed deeply. "You've made up your mind?"

"After tonight, you still have to ask that? Yes, I've made up my mind."

Peter bowed his good night to both of them, and Reynolds closed the front door behind him.

"Let's go up to my office, Major Avondale. I've got whiskey up there."

"I could use some," Philip said ruefully, and let Junia's father lead the way.

Once in his office, Philip accepted his glass and took a seat on the visitor side of the desk. Caius Reynolds set his untouched glass down on the surface of the desk and regarded Philip without expression for a long moment.

"She's a good girl, our Junia," her father said at last, "sweet and dutiful. But once she makes up her mind, she's as stubborn as an old mule."

"I know," Philip said, and the two men exchanged an exasperated smile.

"Well, in this case, she's made her mind up to have you, and nothing on heaven or earth will be able to change her mind, no matter how her mother and I feel about it."

"I can't say I haven't had any hesitations," Philip admitted. "Some people we know will likely shun us, or be cruel to us. But I have every intention of sheltering and cherishing your daughter for the rest of our lives, and as long as the people closest to us accept our marriage, I think we can defy the rest of the world. Together."

Reynolds looked at Philip for a long moment and then, at last, he smiled. "You know," he said, "I think you two just might be able to do that."

Junia accepted her mother's scolding in the parlor with good grace and only half her attention, the other half still standing in the street with Philip's protective arm around her, knowing he was safe, and Pappa was safe, and the smugglers had been arrested.

And he had stayed behind to speak to Pappa.

"Are you listening to anything I say, Junia?" her mother asked in exasperation.

Junia started. "I... um..."

They all looked up at a tap on the door to see Pappa standing there. He smiled at Junia.

"He's waiting for you in my study."

Mama looked from one to the other of them and sighed in resignation even as a wide-eyed Zillah began to giggle with glee, stifling the sound with her hand.

Pappa extended his hand to help his wife up from the settee and plant a kiss on her cheek. "Don't worry so much, honey. They'll be fine."

"I hope so," Mama said in a dire tone, but allowed him to lead her off towards their room.

As Junia started towards the study, her mother's words halted her. "I know the horses have already gone, but leave the door open. I want to at least pretend you all did this properly."

With an irresistible surge of glee, Junia rushed to both her parents and embraced them, kissing each of them on the cheek in turn. "It will be fine, Mama. We'll be fine."

Mama pulled her close for a moment and then gave her a little push back towards the study. "Don't leave that man waiting."

Junia made sure to make her steps as measured and dignified as she could manage when she wanted to run into the room and jump into Philip's arms. She opened the study door and he turned from the fireplace to smile at her, extending his hands to her.

Then she did run, and he caught her against him, crushing her in his arms until she giggled a protest.

"If you ever—and I mean *ever*—put yourself in danger like that again," he vowed, "I will spank you like the hoyden you are."

"Yes, Philip." She pulled back a little and looked up at him, knowing she was starry-eyed, and he smiled down at her, his fierce expression softening.

"I spoke to your father," he said, and her heart expanded even more.

"I know."

"It won't be easy."

"I know that, too."

He let go of her, only to frame her face in his hands.

"I love you, Junia Reynolds. Marry me?"

"Yes," she said, or tried to, because he kissed her almost before she could get the word out, passion flaring between them immediately.

Until someone cleared their throat from the doorway, and they turned to see a wide-eyed Zillah standing there.

"Mama sent me down to make sure you behave yourselves before the wedding," Zillah said. "So *behave yourselves.*"

EPILOGUE
ONE YEAR LATER

A high-pitched screech was Philip's only warning before his brother-in-law, George, flung himself headlong into his arms. With a roar, he lifted George into the air and tossed him skyward as the child giggled uncontrollably. Tucking the wiggling boy under his arm, Philip looked for Junia, who was walking towards them with her youngest sister Sophia, who had progressed to toddling around while safely holding another's hands.

"Mama asked me to bring them outside," Junia explained. "And as soon as Sophie saw the garden, she wanted to walk."

As if on cue, George began protesting and struggling to get down, so Philip set him on his feet so he could join his sisters. Sophia pulled her hands away from Junia's and toddled a few steps on her own before falling onto her cushioned bottom in front of a clump of daisies. George joined her on the grass, accepting the flowers she plucked and handed to him with a comically grave air.

Junia moved close, and Philip slipped his arm around her waist, letting his hand rest on the gentle swell of her stomach. It had not been an easy year for either of them. He had been rejected by some of his old friends and comrades, who could not understand why he would marry a woman so far beneath him. As he had expected, his mother had refused her blessing and ignored their marriage, though his siblings had rallied around. Some of Junia's London friends had turned their backs as well, though they kept their opinions quiet when Mr. Force and his wife Maria showed their support.

Once Philip and Junia had settled into their country house after their marriage, the visits began. The servants had been thrown into a tizzy by the arrival of the Duke and Duchess of Livesey, Philip's oldest brother and his wife. Peter and his new wife had stopped to visit a few months ago during their honeymoon tour and the brothers had reconnected while Junia and Peter's wife became fast friends who now corresponded regularly.

His in-laws had arrived yesterday for a long visit to escape the smoke and crowds of London and filled the house with warmth and laughter. If Caius and Jerusha Reynolds still held any reservations about the marriage, those seemed to be gone now. Zillah had made her debut in their small society of black merchants and declared she needed an escape from her many suitors, none of whom seemed to interest her in the least so far.

"Shall we tell them tonight?" Philip said, giving Junia's belly another gentle caress, and she turned to smile up at him.

"Yes," she said. "Let's tell them tonight." She lay her hand on his, on top of where their child was growing, and they watched George and Sophia play in their garden.

AUTHOR'S NOTE

It's not often I get an idea directly from something I find while doing research, but in this case, Peter Snow's 2014 nonfiction book about the War of 1812, *When Britain Burned the White House*, gave me the seed of this story.

The book contained several passages describing how, when British troops traveled up the Chesapeake Bay to attack Washington D.C. and Baltimore, hundreds of enslaved people took refuge with them and were brought back to England on British troopships to begin their new lives as free people. As in the American Revolution, the American government tried to demand the return of this "property" during the negotiations to settle the War of 1812 but, as in the earlier war, Britain steadfastly refused to return people to slavery and all who wished to remained in Great Britain.

According to records kept by the British Navy, it was not only individuals who escaped, but whole families as well. Most indications are these newly free people settled into the existing Black British communities in London, Bristol, and other port cities. In the Regency Era, it is estimated there were between 5,000 to 10,000 people of African descent living in London alone, with more scattered around the country. For the most part, people in the Georgian and Regency Eras lived according to social class rather than along racial lines, so there were small enclaves within similar social classes rather than large neighborhoods segregated by race as in the United States. Interracial marriage outside the upper classes was not uncommon and was never banned.

Because written records are sketchy, I have imagined this small community of formerly enslaved Londoners acting much like other immigrant communities have throughout history, banding together to help each other in times of trouble and stand against outside forces, and further imagined one of them might be able to have a Cinderella story in her new country with the handsome British officer who helped transport her family to safety in England.

ACKNOWLEDGMENTS

I need to thank my developmental editor at A Book A Day, Regina Lofton McKinney, who read the manuscript twice to make sure I didn't mess up the Black characters I wanted to include. I also want to thank my beta readers, Lisa Cody, Shanti Mercer, and Caro Kincaid, the latter of whom allowed me to pay her in the yarn I was de-stashing from our apartment.

This was a pretty scary book to write, and I thank every person who encouraged me to go for it and didn't immediately think having a heroine who had grown up enslaved was an absolutely terrible idea.

And, as always, I thank my husband, who tells me both when my ideas are terrible and when they're great.

ABOUT ALEXA SANTI

Alexa Santi loves storytelling of all kinds, so it's no wonder it took some time for her to settle on romance fiction after several detours that included an MFA in Screenwriting from Loyola Marymount University. She lives near Los Angeles with her sexy archivist husband and their pesky cats, who insist she take frequent breaks from her writing to pay attention to them. You can find her on Facebook, Instagram, Tumblr, or on her website at https://www.alexasanti.com/

Want to hear what I'm doing next? Sign up for my newsletter either on my website or at https://www.subscribepage.com/alexasanti

THE HIGHWAYMAN'S SURPRISE BRIDE

RENÉE DAHLIA

When Linda Dexington is kidnapped by Sir Bartleby de Muis, a man who has refused to take no for an answer, only one solution is possible: she must rescue herself. Escaping the carriage is not a problem, especially when they are held up by a highwayman. Escaping the unwanted attentions of Sir Bartleby may be a bit more problematic.

Marti Babbitt got more than he bargained for with his attempted highway robbery. Instead of finding an easy mark, he discovered his long-lost childhood friend, Linda. Linda claims she can rescue herself, thank you very much, but when the kidnapper continues to pursue her, maybe Marti can rescue her after all...

Dedicated to the memory of Marti Babbitt, whose wife Linda won the right to name the main characters in a charity auction.

FOREWORD

Welcome to THE HIGHWAYMAN'S SURPRISE BRIDE, featuring Linda Dexington and her childhood friend, turned highwayman.

This novella is part of the Desiring the Dexingtons regency series.

If you love forced proximity, childhood friends to lovers, and marriage of convenience, this is the novella for you.

Please note this book contains kidnapping, murder, threats of rape, and the deadnaming of trans character. Please read it with care.

This book is written in Australian English and some spelling and phrases may be unfamiliar to American readers.

If you are keen to keep up to date on new releases and, more importantly, sales, I recommend you sign up to my newsletter, or follow me on social media.

Social Media Links

Patreon

Twitter

Facebook

romance.com.au

Instagram

BookBub
I hope you enjoy reading this book!
Renée

CHAPTER ONE

"It's bad luck for the groom to see the dress before the wedding day." Linda had already made it clear she had no intention of ever marrying Sir Bartleby de Muis—a man twenty years her senior—and her father agreed that Sir Bartleby was a fortune hunter of the worst order. Unfortunately, Father's agreement meant nothing now that Sir Bartleby had kidnapped her. There was nothing worse than a man who wouldn't listen when she said no, and so she resorted to the only weapon a nineteen-year-old wealthy girl had. Sarcasm. And hatpins, according to her sister Elspeth. She swallowed a sigh. Sir Bartleby would never know that this dress was a simple everyday dress, and nothing like what she might have worn to her wedding if she ever had one. No self-respecting daughter of a fabric manufacturer would wear something so simple as a cotton day gown with a muslin overlay and the tiniest touch of French lace to her wedding. Heaven forbid. Her dream wedding gown would be designed by her sister Jacinda and would feature in all the fashion plates across society.

"Today is our wedding day."

"We can't make it to Gretna Green in one day." She might be the coddled second youngest Dexington sister but even she knew it was 130 miles from Manchester and therefore twenty hours journey by coach if they didn't stop. They would have to stop, because travelling at night would be foolish, and Sir Bartleby de Muis was many things, but he was not foolish enough to risk her safety. She was—quite literally—his future fortune. Her safety was assured ... and would be until he had her money. After that, all bets were off, and she certainly didn't intend to let things get to that point.

"Details. We will stay the night along the way, and in the morning, you will be my wife in every way that counts. I'll only need to sign the paperwork, and it'll be done." Sir Bartleby's words churned in her stomach and an astringent gasp burned her throat. Holy mother of goodness. She was going to have to revise her schedule for escape to a lot sooner, perhaps at the first change of horses in an hour's time. Linda had been hoping to have enough time to work out Sir Bartleby's patterns to ensure her plan was achievable. There was no point in leaping too soon and botching it up.

She stared out the window at the passing scenery. The boring green paddocks and typical English countryside could be anywhere; the trip north was one she'd done several times as a child heading to their country estate or to finishing school. As the daughter of an industrialist, she had more options than the society belles of the ton whose only task in life was to marry well. She could work in the family businesses like her sisters Prudence and Elspeth, or she could marry like Imogen and Hyacinth. The problem was that she didn't know what she wanted. Only that she didn't want to be kidnapped by a fortune hunter.

"I cannot wait to take your innocence." A disgusting fortune hunter. She tried not to shudder, swallowing down the distaste that made her mouth furry. Linda suddenly understood why Elspeth always insisted she have extra long hatpins, because right now, she could shove one up Sir Bartleby's nostril.

The coach jerked to a halt, and she had to grab one of the handles to keep her posture on the seat.

"Stand and deliver." A highwayman. Could this day get any worse? Now she had two terrible men to deal with.

Sir Bartleby tapped his cane on the roof. "Coachman. Deal with this."

"I told you it was bad luck," Linda muttered.

"Silly girl. Sit still and keep your mouth shut. I'll deal with this." He stood up and opened the door on the right side of the coach.

"I said Drive On." He shook his fist at someone outside the coach, and Linda realised this was her chance. Perhaps she'd finally had some good luck. She scrambled to her feet and quickly unlatched the door on the opposite side of the coach and pushed it open as hard as she could. The momentum of the door pulled her forwards and she landed on her knees at the side of the road. Pain speared through her knees, jarring her body. All the air was shoved out of her lungs.

A shot rang out. She ducked, instinctively, rolling sideways into the damp drain beside the road. There was an ungodly scream. The horses bolted. Someone else yelled. The coachman, maybe. It all happened rather quickly. Mud flicked up from the wheels, splattering her dress. It was the least important thing in this moment, and yet it annoyed her most of all. The beautiful muslin overlay would be ruined now. If she were less stubborn, she would've simply lain down in the ditch and stared at the sky, but she was a Dexington. Irish determination from her mother's side combined with her English father's business acumen and success to give her what her governesses often referred to as 'character'.

Damned Sir Bartleby. Now she would have to walk back to Manchester and her shoes were not designed for the task. She stood up slowly and shook out her skirts. The muslin overlay and French lace was ruined, no amount of soaking would get the mud out, nor the blood stains from her scraped knees. Her hands trembled as she stared at the smears on her dress. Slowly, reality started to sink in; she'd leaped from a coach and was all alone, injured—slightly—in the middle of nowhere. She'd saved herself from Sir Bartleby's clutches but now what?

"Isn't this a bit of a scrape?"

Linda glanced up to see a lone highwayman, a slender man not much taller than her, with his face covered by a mask, and four duelling pistols tucked into his belt.

"That is a lot of weaponry." Linda's curiosity would be her downfall—that's what her father always said—and he was probably correct since she wanted to know how a highwayman came to possess such fine examples of gentleman's pistols. As if that was the most important thing right now. *Good one, Linda.*

"I am but one person, and each pistol carries only one shot." Therefore, the highwayman still had three shots remaining. Her unconventional education had included bookkeeping, so simple arithmetic was easy for her. A low bar but she'd heard rumours that some families liked to keep their daughters so ignorant that they couldn't manage their own pin money. Not her family; her father might have been cursed with seven daughters but each of them represented a chance to bring a man into the business through marriage as well as potential labour in their own right, which meant they had a greater education than many of her peers and with that, greater expectations from life.

Linda huffed out a breath and squared her shoulders. She'd earned her independence from Sir Bartleby, at the small cost of injured knees, and now she needed to make her way home before the highwayman did something dastardly, like they did in the books she adored.

"Good day. I have a long walk ahead of me." She nodded once to the highwayman, then began her long walk, hoping that he would leave her alone.

"Wait. Miss Dexington?"

Linda cursed Sir Bartleby under her breath. She didn't recall him mentioning her name in front of the highwayman, but how else would the highwayman know who she was? Although if the highwayman was local, he might know her, which meant he would know that father owned several factories in Manchester and had industrial wealth. For nineteen years, she'd been reduced to how her father's money could serve other people. Case in point, her dowry and Sir Bartleby's kidnapping attempt. No more. She ignored the highwayman and continued walking.

CHAPTER TWO

Marti would have known Linda Dexington anywhere. She still had the same shockingly bright red hair—the only one of her siblings with red hair—and the same cute button nose set on her distinctive Dexington heart shaped face. As she marched down the road back towards Manchester, not letting a highwayman stop her, her straight spine demonstrated that she still had the same determination she'd had as a child.

Marti made the only decision he could—to stay with her and keep her safe—but first, he had to get his horse. A necessity which meant taking his eye off Miss Dexington while he jogged into the copse beside the road and untied Turpin. His fingers shook a little as he pulled the slipknot free. They shouldn't; it wasn't the first time he'd shot someone, and he knew he hadn't killed the man since he'd winged him in the shoulder only. It was a shame the horses had bolted at the sound, as now he had nothing for his troubles. The man had been dressed like a wealthy man, and Miss Dexington's family owned a large portion of Manchester. He sighed. There would be other coaches and now he had a much bigger problem. Why had Miss Dexington leaped from the coach?

He vaulted onto Turpin, and together they picked their way back through the trees to the road. Miss Dexington hadn't made it far, walking elegantly in the middle of the road. He trotted up beside her.

"If you plan to walk, it's five miles to the next town. You can hire a coach from there." He was about to offer Turpin for her to ride to spare her feet on the rough gravel surface of the road.

She folded her arms, glaring up at him. "You shot him."

"I didn't kill him."

"How do you know?"

He didn't. "I hit in him in the shoulder. It's a survivable wound." If it gets treated quickly and he doesn't get an infection. "Is he someone you care for?"

"No." Her tone brokered no uncertainty and now he was thoroughly confused.

"It seems I'm missing some crucial information. Why were you heading north in a coach with someone you don't care for?" It wasn't his business, but this was his former childhood friend—not that she knew that—and if she'd ended up in a difficult situation, perhaps he could help. He breathed in deep to calm the odd flutter in his chest. Miss Dexington had grown into a beautiful woman, but she was far above him in class; the best he could offer her was safe passage to where she wanted to go.

"Sir Bartleby kidnapped me. And now you've shot him. He's bound to arrive in the next town raising merry hell."

"It's good that we are going in the opposite direction then." Marti covered his shock with the simplest of facts. If he asked if the man was a fortune hunter, Miss Dexington would know that he knew her family and that would open him up for questions about himself; ones he wasn't prepared to answer yet. She made a small huffing noise and kept walking and his shoulders relaxed; grateful to avoid an awkward conversation, except what type of man did it make him if he rode while she walked. Without the money to be considered a gentleman, Marti still believed that he could act in a gentlemanly fashion. He dismounted and led Turpin as he walked beside Miss Dexington.

"Perhaps you could ride."

Miss Dexington tilted her head to the side, and the change of angle made the afternoon sun shine on her skin, highlighting the freckles generously sprinkled across her face. Marti stopped breathing.

"You are the oddest highwayman I've ever met."

"You've met other highwaymen?" Marti bit back a grin at being assumed to be a man. It felt right and good. What had started as necessity—to survive in a man's world—had become a uniform that he wore, and it fit him well. He felt like himself now.

"No. But I have read books."

Marti dismounted. "Get on the horse. A gently bred girl shouldn't be left to walk five miles."

"For goodness sake." She fluffed her skirts, which did nothing to disprove his point.

"I know the innkeeper at the Public Arms. If we go there, you can get a room and send a message to your family. They will send a coach for you, I'm sure."

Miss Dexington raised one eyebrow. "I'm afraid you have me at a disadvantage. You appear to know a lot about me, and I know nothing of you."

"There is not much to know." Marti wasn't ready to unveil that he'd grown up next door to the Dexington family, that he had gone to live with Aunt Doris and Uncle Edwin at the Public Arms when his parents had died in a carriage accident when he was fifteen and Miss Dexington only ten. Nor that he shared his profits with Doris, and she supported his highway activities because they helped keep the Public Arms afloat.

"You've just mentioned that we have five miles to cover. Tell me something. Your name, perhaps, or is that against the code of highwaymen?"

Marti smiled. "I'm not sure what books you have been reading, but the only code a highwayman has is … Don't get caught."

"Ahh, the infamous eleventh commandment."

"Miss Dexington. How daring and sacrilegious of you."

Miss Dexington fiddled with her skirts, and it took Marti a moment to realise that she had started to walk with a slight limp.

"Please get on the horse."

Turpin wasn't a big horse, only fifteen hands, and yet, he was tall enough that most riders would need a mounting block. Marti held out his hand to give Miss Dexington a leg up, and she stepped onto his hand and swung onto Turpin easily, with the grace of someone who was an accomplished rider. As she settled her skirts around her legs while seated astride, Marti shook out the odd tingle in his hand left behind from her touch. No amount of fluffing of the fabric could prevent her ankles and shapely calves from being exposed, or the trickle of dried blood down her shin. Marti nearly tripped over his feet and grabbed the reins for something to do. If he led Turpin, walking beside the horse's head, he wouldn't see Linda or her legs.

"Aren't you a pretty chestnut? What's your name?" Linda crooned to his horse, whose ears flicked back and forth, listening to her.

"Turpin."

"You named your horse after the most famous of highwaymen?"

Marti swallowed. "Yes."

"How quaint." Linda's hand appeared in the corner of his eye as she leaned forward and rubbed Turpin between the ears. "Won't that tell everyone of your aspirations?"

"Excuse me?" He felt her roll her eyes, or maybe it was her sarcastic glare on the back of his neck that gave him a chill shiver.

"It's rather obvious, isn't it? To name a highwayman's horse after a famous highwayman."

"Perhaps I'm not a highwayman. Maybe I merely admire someone who could outride everyone else." Dick Turpin was famous for riding two hundred miles in one day, a feat that was surely impossible. Even half that distance would be stretching it for a single horse.

Linda chuckled, the sound whispering over his skin and leaving gooseflesh behind. "I'm sure that will reassure the magistrate."

Marti choked on a laugh. "Lord Flexingham is a drunkard."

"Clever."

"He is?"

"No. You. It's clever to pick a patch of ground where the magistrate is unlikely to be a bother." Linda's compliment sent a flush of warmth over his skin. Turpin flicked his head up. Horses always could feel a change in emotions, and it would appear that there was no hiding from his horse.

CHAPTER THREE

Linda sank into the bath at the inn, closing her eyes as the warm water surrounded her body. It'd been a long day; what with being kidnapped and then Sir Bartleby being shot, and the highwayman escorting her to safety. If she had a nervous complaint, she'd be a wreck, and even with all the resilience of youth, she still needed this. The innkeeper had added some Epsom salts and lavender to the water, and it was luxurious against her chaffed skin, although the salts stung her scraped knees. She'd been given some salve to put on them after her bath. Riding astride in a day gown had left her legs tender and sore, while the rest of her body ached from her wild leap from the carriage, or rather, from landing splayed out on the road. She was tempted to rub at her raw skin to ease the stinging of the bathwater, and she heard her sister Prudence's voice telling her not to, just to let the salts soak in and begin to heal her. She hadn't suffered like this since the hunting season, when she'd fallen from her horse, Belle Du Jour, during a particularly vigorous chase. She loved riding with the hunt, mostly for the social aspects, spending the day talking to friends while they waited for the hounds to find a scent.

She closed her eyes; grateful to be safe from Sir Bartleby de Muis and thankful that the highwayman had been ... oddly pleasant. Having the Dexington name had been a curse at the beginning of the day, but now she was glad that it had helped her end up here, soaking off all the nasty parts of the day in a lovely bath. She was just starting to relax, with all the prickles from the salt on her legs starting to ease, when there was a rude loud knock at the door.

"One minute." Linda pulled herself out of the bath and towelled herself dry before pulling on a robe that one of the inn's staff had left for her after they'd taken her gown to attempt to clean it. Perhaps it would be her gown. She opened the door.

"Miss Dexington." The highwayman pushed past her and pulled the door shut. The highwayman had taken off his mask and Linda had a vague sense that she knew him from somewhere but couldn't place him in this context. He had a sharp nose and was clean-shaven—unlike the fashion of the day—with short brown hair.

"You can't just barge in here." The tip of her tongue rubbed against her teeth as she stared at him.

"There is a messenger downstairs looking for someone with your description. A Mr Clark. He says he works for your father."

She exhaled. Mr Clark was one of their stable boys, and she was glad that her father had sent messengers to find her and save her from Sir Bartleby's clutches, even if she'd had to save herself. "I cannot meet with them."

"Why not?"

"I have nothing appropriate to wear. Get me a gown and then I will meet with the messenger."

The highwayman nodded once and left the room. As soon as the door closed, she flopped onto a chair and sighed. Today's drama wasn't at an end and her bath had only been a hiatus. Now she needed to discover what the messenger would say. Surely her father had enough good sense not to connect her name to that of Sir Bartleby so that she would have some options for her future. Father knew Sir Bartleby was a fortune hunter. He wouldn't want the man to get his hands on her dowry. She closed her eyes and waited. There wasn't much she could do until she was dressed. Father always said the only risk in life and business is ignorance, and so she wouldn't waste her time with planning the next step until she had the messenger's information.

Half an hour later, she was adorned in a servant's dress. It was a functional older style made from dark brown wool that had softened over time with multiple washes until it was felted in places and stretched in others. She'd never worn anything so ancient but she was grateful that she didn't have to be seen in public in her bloodied and mud splattered day dress. She'd already donated that to the servant who'd given her this gown; a more than fair trade if the servant was handy with a needle and could remove all the stains as her day dress could be remade into a few different garments.

The highwayman—with his overly familiar face—sat in a corner booth with young Mr Clark. She slid into the seat next to them.

"Miss Dexington. It's so good to see you. When the inn keeper mentioned that a red-haired lady was here, I was so hopeful it was you."

"How much is the reward my father offered?"

"Ten guineas." Mr Clark's eyes were incredibly wide. It was a huge sum for a stable boy; a year's wages.

"Technically I found Miss Dexington." The highwayman showed his true colours; like all men, wanting to claim her work as his own.

"If we are going to be precise, I saved myself, but I'm not so lacking in manners that I can't offer you a reward too." She paused, biting the inside of her cheek as something occurred to her. "On one condition."

"I'm not going to give up my ten guineas." Mr Clark showed some of the backbone that demonstrated why her father had employed him.

"No one is asking you to do that."

Mr Clark relaxed. "Miss Dexington. Shall I check if there is a horse available for you?"

"Yes." She appreciated his subtle understanding that she might want to negotiate with some level of privacy.

The highwayman waited until they were alone. "What is the reward?"

"I will match the offer that my father will give to Mr Clark, given your kindness to me, on one condition." Her curiosity was worth a lot more than twenty guineas.

"What condition is that?"

"Tell me your name." Linda knew it wasn't a big question and it was an expensive way to satisfy her curiosity. Her father would pay; he was one of the few men she knew that supported her, and even listened to her on occasion.

"Marti Babbitt."

With a thrilling rush of blood to the head, she suddenly knew why she recognised his face. "Related to the Babbitt's who used to be our neighbours?"

"Yes."

"I knew I recognised you. You have the look of their daughter, Martha." When Linda was little, she'd idolised Martha who was five or six years older and seemed so mature. The highwayman shuffled in his chair, saying nothing for a long time, before he sat up straighter and stared deep into her eyes. A deliberate considered look.

"I was Martha, but I prefer Marti now."

Linda's brother-in-law, Mr Chan, used an English name while he was here and his Chinese name when he travelled back to his homeland to purchase silks for the Dexington businesses. It made sense for people to pick the name they preferred, since it was a little illogical to be stuck with the name a parent had chosen if it didn't fit any more.

"Marti Babbitt. It suits you." Linda felt like she'd been trusted with something special; someone's name of choice; and she wanted to honour that gift. "I would be honoured if you accompany me back to Manchester to collect your reward."

The way he stared at her made her feel like he was content to simply be with her, that it was reward enough, and damned if she didn't find him incredibly compelling.

"Excuse me, Miss Dexington." Mr Clark arrived back at their table.

"Yes?"

"There is no spare horse until the morning when the mail coach arrives."

She had enough pin money hidden in her underpinnings to pay for lodgings for tonight, and yes, she was swayed by spending a little more time with her intriguing highwayman. "Then we will leave in the morning."

CHAPTER FOUR

It was not to be. Linda had been stuck in her room, spending the evening alone, for the sake of her reputation. At least the weather was nice with mid-summer putting on golden sunshine and a light breeze to ensure it wasn't too hot for their ride back to Manchester.

"What a glorious day for a ride." As they walked into town, she found herself keen to see her sisters, and even more curious to hear her Father's opinions on Sir Bartleby and how to deal with the repercussions from her kidnapping. The main roads turned into narrower streets before they ended up on the wide boulevard near the canal and her family's mansion.

"It is. How was your dinner last night?" Marti asked. She'd eaten in her room alone as Marti had rushed off to do some task for the inn keeper, and Mr Clark had eaten with the other servants. It wouldn't be the done thing to eat alone in public as an unmarried woman, so she'd had only herself for company in her clean, functional room.

"The fare was excellent. My compliments to the cook."

"I will tell Aunt Doris that you approve." Marti had been very formal with her today and she couldn't work out if he was nervous about getting his reward, or if the presence of Mr Clark meant he was sticking to propriety. Boring. She asked her borrowed horse, a rather nice hunter, to trot because she wanted to get home and get back to her life before she'd met Sir Bartleby.

Soon enough they walked down the mews beside the house and handed the horses over to the stable staff. She walked towards the house, then realised Marti wasn't following her.

"Come along."

"I'll just stay here with the horses."

"Is there a problem? You'll need to come with me to claim your reward." Her father was the one who had the ability to hand over the coins. Linda found this aloof nonsense frustrating. First men made all the decisions about her life and then they did illogical things without explaining their decisions. And, more importantly, she didn't want to do this—face her father—alone and Marti had been so kind so far. She thought they had an understanding, but perhaps she'd latched onto him too quickly and was just annoyed that he was abandoning her now.

"I don't want your father to recognise me."

Oh. It wasn't about her at all. He didn't want her father to know him as the person who used to be their neighbour. "Tell him you are related to the Babbitts who lived next door, but not the details."

"You guessed."

She shook her head quickly. "I didn't. You volunteered the information; presumably because you trust me?"

"I do trust you."

"Then trust me on this. Father will see you as you are now. A man who saved his precious daughter from a fortune hunter. Talk about your duelling pistols or some other manly topic of conversation, and all will be well."

Marti fidgeted, not a lot, just small nervous movements, picking at his jacket and shifting from foot to foot.

"Or if ten guineas means nothing to you, then stay here." She called his bluff and his chest puffed out in a most interesting way as he breathed in.

"Lead away."

She hid her satisfied smile as she walked into the house, through the back door and along the main hallway to the drawing room. The kitchens were detached in this old house, so the ovens and chimneys weren't a risk to the main house, and the servant's quarters were in the attic. The entire ground floor was dedicated to family living. Their butler, Ushnish, stood in the hallway outside the drawing room.

"Ushnish, where is Father?"

"In his office. He has a visitor."

"We will wait in the drawing room." She started to walk past him to the doorway, when Ushnish leaned in close.

"Miss Dexington, the visitor concerns you."

She didn't know what that meant. "Stop prevaricating, Ushnish. Who is it? And what does Father want me to do?"

"Sir Bartleby de Muis." Ushnish's usual impervious expression held some contrition.

"Excuse me?" Rage filled her veins and roared in her ears. He must've travelled in the night to beat her home; to her home. How dare he...

"I don't have instructions on what to do, however, I suppose you could follow me." Ushnish strode down the eastern hallway to her father's office. Frustration surged, like kerosene thrown on a fire, and she supposed she could follow him. What other option did she have but to confront whatever nonsense Sir Bartleby was bound to be saying about her?

"Will you be well?"

"What?" She whipped around and glared at Marti.

"Seeing Sir Bartleby again. It's been less than a day since he kidnapped you."

She snorted. "You were the one who shot him."

"I was wearing a mask. He won't recognise me."

She sent him a pointed look. "And that makes it all better?"

He had the decency to appear uncertain and that moment helped her believe in him; perhaps he wouldn't be like all the other men in her life, running rough shod over her opinions because his thoughts were obviously more sophisticated and important than any of her own. Perhaps ... She breathed in. Just perhaps she might have an ally in this ridiculous situation.

"Let's discover if that is true." She waited while Ushnish knocked on the door and was granted entry. She waited while she was intro-duced. And she waited until she was asked to sit. Then she sat. Marti—Mr Babbitt—stood beside her chair.

Sir Bartleby preened himself, as he sat there with his arm heavily bandaged, and Father casting an assessing glance between herself, Marti, and Sir Bartleby.

"This is quite the situation." Father eventually said.

"No one needs to know anything about Miss Dexington's situation. If she marries me, it will all be hushed up." Sir Bartleby's eyes flashed as if he'd had a win, while her father's eyes narrowed.

What situation? "I'm not going to marry you."

Smugness spread across Sir Bartleby's face and Linda saw her future flash before her eyes. If she did nothing, she would end up married to this selfish ass of a fortune hunter. She sighed. Ass was hardly a word that any gently bred woman should know, even one who'd grown up listening to factory workers argue with machinery.

"As I was saying, I've compromised Miss Dexington and we need to marry for the sake of her reputation."

Oh for goodness sake. "Sir Bartleby lies. He did not touch me during the short time we were in a carriage together." He threatened to, but that wasn't quite the same thing.

"But we were alone in a carriage and therefore whether I touched you or not is irrelevant. All it would take is a quiet word to a few of society's leaders..."

She wasn't going to take Sir Bartleby's threats easily. "I would rather marry Mr Babbitt." Her head spun as all the blood dropped to her feet. Oops, she didn't mean for it to sound like a consolation prize. Trying to untangle what she ought to have said felt impossible and she stared at the carpeted floor.

"I would be honoured." Marti's words sent a flush across her skin. He made it sound like her choice—like he forgave her for sounding petulant—and she adored him for it.

"Even if she's carrying my child?" Sir Bartleby sneered. Linda knew it wasn't possible, but neither her father nor Mr Babbitt knew that. For her father's knowledge, it was more than the time she'd spent in the carriage with Sir Bartleby, she'd been gone a whole day and night without an approved chaperone.

"If there were to be a child, I would raise it as my own. I would love any child as my own and try my best to give them the best life possible."

She wanted to hug Marti for such a considerate response—one she wasn't sure she'd earned—and she dared not glance at Father to see what he thought.

"Everyone can leave now. I will think about the options." Father's declaration was one she'd heard plenty of times before and she glanced up at him, suddenly feeling at home.

"You can't possibly believe a girl and a stable boy over me. I'm a Baron." Sir Bartleby's huffing did little, thankfully. Linda was gratified to see her father's response, a subtle shift in his mouth that showed his disapproval of Sir Bartleby's poor attempt to ingratiate himself. Father was an industrialist; a self-made man; he had a high degree of contempt for people who relied on inherited titles for status. Being born to the right parents was simply good fortune. Luck. What someone did with their opportunity of birth was what mattered a lot more to him.

"Out."

Linda didn't wait to see what Sir Bartleby would do. If he disobeyed or argued with Father, he would further undermine his case, and she wasn't going to lose any strategic advantage that she might gain by being obedient. She followed Ushnish to the drawing room, where her sister Jacinda sat quietly sewing, while two of the servants stood at the side of the room, providing companionship.

"You can sit over there. I'm sure we can get some tea if you need." She indicated to a chair for Marti, then sat beside Jacinda to ask her about her latest creation. But before she could speak, Sir Bartleby came rushing in, shouting commands at the servants.

"We will not be serving Sir Bartleby," Ushnish said. The servants went back to their positions, and everyone sat stiffly while Sir Bartleby strode about making some huffing noises, but thankfully kept his distance from her. Eventually, Sir Bartleby decided to lean against the mantlepiece, placing his good arm on the marble, and making a fuss of his sling while he glared at everyone.

"Oh goodness. People." Jacinda glanced up from her work.

"It's only temporary. We will leave you in peace soon." Linda reassured her sister with a gentle pat on her elbow and was pleased to see Jacinda nod once and return to her sewing. Linda kept her gaze low, half-focused on the fabric in her attempt to ignore Sir Bartleby's domineering presence in the room. It was comforting to know Mr Babbitt could sit in a room without needing everyone to notice him; and the contrast between the two men and their approach to the world was as stark as coal dust on bleached cotton. She lost track of time as she waited, trying not to think too hard about her lack of options. The threat from Sir Bartleby about him taking her innocence had become tangible. He hadn't had access to her body, but even if she married Marti, Sir Bartleby could suggest such a thing, spilling in the right ears as a secret at any time in the future which suited him. Maybe he would get tired of her once he couldn't have her and switch his attentions to some other poor girl's dowry, but immediately, a cool wind crawled over the back of her neck, and she hated that her brain was willing to sacrifice some other woman—even a hypothetical woman—to save herself from misery. If the world had any justice, Sir Bartleby wouldn't marry anyone and wouldn't gain his fortune through such a dastardly method.

"Miss Linda Dexington. You father will see you now." Ushnish had his usual impassive expression and she started to stand when Sir Bartleby pushed past them both.

"I should speak first."

"I wouldn't recommend that course of action," Ushnish said. Linda glanced at Jacinda who was smirking; she might get lost in her sewing at times but she never missed anything important.

"What would you know?"

"I have worked for Mr Dexington for many years. Once he has made his decision, nothing will sway him, and in my experience if you attempt to intercede now, he will be more inclined to decide against you."

Sir Bartleby hesitated, obviously counting the money, because he clenched his jaw and returned to his position leaning against the mantlepiece. In winter, he might have burnt himself ... Linda's wishful thinking grew petty as she walked away from her kidnapper. How on earth he was still standing here making demands was yet another unfathomable way that men allowed each other to get away with nonsense.

She tapped on Father's office door.

"Come."

She pushed open the door and walked inside.

"Oh, Linda. Are you alone?"

"Yes. Ushnish ensured it."

"Excellent. Of all my daughters, you have a certain charm about you that I wouldn't like to see squashed by someone like Sir Bartleby. He's nothing but a fortune hunter who has already run through his first wife's income. Why he thought he could con me into letting him have one of my daughters is an indication of his lack of forethought."

"You do have a lot of daughters."

Father almost smiled. "Having a plentiful collection of daughters isn't going to make me a soft touch."

"No." It was foolish of Sir Bartleby to underestimate her father.

"However..." He dragged the word out. "You've created quite the dilemma."

She wanted to protest; the words sticking in her throat because her father wasn't someone who appreciated being argued with. Technically, Sir Bartleby created this problem, she was just the person unfortunate enough to have been targeted by him.

"The key problems are that Sir Bartleby—"

"Yes. He is the..." Cause of all this mess. Her heart skipped a beat. She wanted to make sure the blame was put squarely in Sir Bartleby's court, where it belonged.

Father interrupted. "Unfortunately, when he kidnapped you, we sent messengers in all directions trying to find you, which means a lot of people are aware that you spent time alone with Sir Bartleby."

She growled under her breath; couldn't her family have attempted some discretion? They didn't have to have told the world he took her. She'd rather be blamed for being a naïve silly nineteen-year-old than have all of Manchester know that Sir Bartleby had kidnapped her. The world never blamed the man for these things; she could easily be cast as a Jezebel and ruined over it.

"He's a terrible fortune hunter, so I'm uninclined to agree to his demands of marriage, and I certainly don't want to saddle another of my daughters with a man who cares more for status and money than his wife." With three of her older sisters married, she couldn't help but wonder whether he referred to Prudence, Hyacinth, or Imogen. It was unlikely to be Prudence, whose Mr Chan was very dedicated to her and her children.

"Mr Babbitt has offered to marry me." If marriage would allow her —and her three unmarried sisters—to retain some respectability, then she'd much rather marry her former childhood friend who'd been so kind when she'd escaped from Sir Bartleby's coach. She held her breath, awaiting her father's decision.

"He is more of an appropriate age than Sir Bartleby, but I am concerned the timing of this current farce means I have not had the time to determine if he is a fortune hunter or not."

"Perhaps you could put some conditions into the marriage contract?" She knew enough about the law, if not the details, to know that a contract could be written to suit any outcome. "Mayhap we could stay here for the first month of our marriage, while you assess him, and then—"

"Clever girl. Yes, let me think about a payment schedule that allows to you to live comfortably while also allowing me to assess his character." He stood up and pulled the bell to summon Ushnish. "Are you certain you want to stay in this house?"

"Yes. I would like some time to get to know him before moving into a property of our own. And this way we can get the banns read and keep it all above board." It would protect her reputation and make a mockery of Sir Bartleby's claims as it would show society that she knew she had the time to wait. She assumed her father would buy Mr Babbitt a house, like he had for her sister's husbands on their marriages. The unfortunate law that meant her sisters were now the property of their husbands with no ability to manage or control their own dowries, and housing was a good way to ensure their safety and health. It was an unjust law, like many laws of the land, although she did benefit in some ways given that her father was a wealthy business-man. Her sister, Elspeth, understood it all better than her, writing to the Gentlewoman's Press about labour laws and the luddite movement and how they didn't like loom technology because women were taking men's job. Linda didn't like the way women and children worked in their factories in often tricky conditions either; the whole issue was terribly complex, and she knew she was very privileged in not having to think too hard about it.

"Very sensible." Her father's approval warmed her, a habit borne of the years.

Ushnish arrived quickly at her father's bellpull. "Please set up the blue room in the western wing for Mr Babbitt. Miss Linda has agreed to marry Mr Babbitt, and he will live here while the banns are read until I am satisfied that he is not a fortune hunter."

Once the banns were read, she would have more freedom to spend time alone with Marti, and she couldn't wait. He was so fascinating in the way he'd chosen to live his life and she needed—with a yearning in her chest—to know everything about him.

CHAPTER FIVE

Three days later, Marti pulled on his new suit for today's Sunday service where the first reading of the banns would occur. He'd kept the servants away for his own privacy, although he did appreciate the assistance with tying his cravat, which was a rather complicated process. He'd barely seen Linda since the announcement at the family dinner table that they were engaged; she'd been busy keeping him busy by ensuring that he had what she'd deemed an appropriate wardrobe. The process of being measured was a stressful one; the tailor's touch had been more intimate than he'd been comfortable with but apparently his binding and packing had passed muster so his identity as a man was safe.

He straightened his collar, reaching up to fuss with his collar but stopping himself from fiddling with it and making a mess of the folded material. With his hands loosely held in fists at his side, he walked down the hall to the drawing room.

"Mr Babbitt. The cut of that wool and that navy blue looks fabulous on you." Miss Dexington, Linda, stroked her hand over the fabric on his bicep and he felt the touch all the way into his soul. All her hair was tucked away under a straw bonnet, hiding its vibrancy, and her ensemble was paired with a light blue ribbon tied under her chin. Had she chosen her dress to match his suit?

He wanted to say something clever about how stunning she looked. He wanted to hold her and kiss her and show the world how lucky he was to be the one who would stand beside her in a church and say those words about commitment; words that he would have to learn so he didn't stand there like a dead fish with blank eyes and gaping mouth.

"Mr Babbitt?"

"Yes?"

"Are you well?"

He cleared his throat. "Yes. You are beautiful."

A light pink flush spread over her cheeks, making her freckles stand out, and he had the urge to kiss every single one of them. She deserved someone who would take their time with her and show her how adored she was.

"Truly." His voice crackled.

"Thank you." A slow smile spread on her lips; he really was the luckiest man in the world to stand beside her as she shone so brightly. From the age of fifteen, he'd worked in Aunt Doris' inn and had seen every way that humans interacted with each other. He'd seen spinster best friends book rooms together, and once—on a memorable evening—he'd accidently walked in on three men engaged in sexual intercourse in the hay loft above the stables. He seen everything, or so he'd thought, until today when he stood in awe of the most beautiful woman in the world and made himself ready to stand beside her in a church as the banns were read. He wanted to kiss her and explore her and make her sigh and scream his name, like those two spinsters had done. They hadn't even bothered to try and keep their relationship a secret, not in a small country inn like the Public Arms. The inn was close enough to Manchester to earn enough to keep the inn afloat—mostly—and far enough that people felt safe enough to be themselves. His occasional work as a highwayman supplemented the inn's income during slow times.

"Mr Babbitt." Her fingers squeezed his forearm. "Marti."

He blinked. "Yes?"

"We need to go now."

He nodded and let her lead him away; still stunned by her presence, as if the sun itself had come down from heaven and punched him in the face, leaving him reeling.

Two boring hours of sermon and formalities later, Marti stepped out of the church to the well-wishers of many people. A swarm of voices thronged around until the buzz had no meaning. He smiled and nodded and hoped no one wondered why Linda had picked him. He knew he looked good in his suit, and he wasn't the only slender medium-heighted man in the crowd, but he kept his distance from habit and necessity. She flitted through the crowd, smiling and laughing with everyone, and every time she reached out and lightly touched someone on the arm or elbow or hand, his stomach twisted, even though she was only being friendly.

"Mr Babbitt. Shall we go?" She hooked her hand around his arm, leaning lightly against him, and it was so much more intimate than she'd been with everyone else.

"Yes." His husky response led him to clear his throat.

"Come along. Before we go, we need to thank the Vicar Green."

He swallowed and led her towards the Vicar; finally, belatedly, remembering all the manners he'd had drilled into him as a child. Performing it from the other side created a small challenge, especially as it was against his nature to be outgoing. He liked being a highwayman, working alone and not having to talk to people, but it wouldn't do to let Linda cart him around the place. It wouldn't be good for her reputation as much as for his, to be seen as someone who would run roughshod over her future husband, especially not with Sir Bartleby still on the scene.

"At least Sir Bartleby has not attended church."

Linda turned to him with a smile that almost knocked him over. "It has been exceedingly pleasant to spend the morning without his disturbing presence." Her giggle was as refreshing as a splash of cool water on a hot day.

"People are looking at you."

She bestowed another smile on him; he was going to collect these smiles for as long as he could. "They are looking at us. We are the most exciting thing that has happened today."

"Why?"

"Our banns were read today. And it's all the more intriguing for the gossip-mongers because Sir Bartleby came to church with our family a few times before ... you know. Some people will have decided that there's a deeper story but they don't know any details so have to be vague. It's that potential for gossip that has everyone desperate for details."

"You don't seem bothered by that."

"People love to talk. It means nothing unless we let it mean something." She kept that smile on her face, but it lost a little piece of the shine.

"You are good at this." He realised that he couldn't ask her to live quietly in a cottage, like he'd prefer, because she thrived on being in a crowd. She loved talking to people and he didn't want to take any pleasure away from her. He'd just have to learn to cope. Somehow. He would have to figure that out later as their walk had led them to their destination.

"Vicar Green. Thank you for the first reading of the banns today." He managed to remember the politeness he'd been taught as a child, while his mind spun on the possibilities of a future surrounded by people. The risks for him weren't insignificant.

"I must say I was surprised when Mr Dexington asked me to do this. I was under the impression that Miss Dexington was being courted by Sir Bartleby de Muis."

Linda's light smile was a sight to behold. "There is a vast difference between being courted and consenting to an engagement."

"But to now be engaged to this Mr Babbitt?"

"Mr Babbitt is more than twice the gentleman Sir Bartleby will ever be. His consideration of my needs and well-being far exceeds any of the ... well, let's just say Sir Bartleby's behaviour hasn't been all above board in this manner."

Vicar Green gasped. "Goodness, that is very blunt of you."

Marti sucked in a breath between his teeth; how dare Vicar Green criticise Linda. "Miss Dexington has made her decision and Mr Dexington approves."

"Far be it for me to cast doubt on any decision made by Mr Dexington," Vicar Green said.

Linda smirked. "I believe my father has recently fixed the roof on your cottage. Remind me exactly how much Sir Bartleby has donated to the church?"

Marti adored this woman and her unsubtle ways of reminded people where their allegiances should lie.

Vicar Green made an uncomfortable coughing noise. "That's all well and good, however, Mr Babbitt here is a nobody."

"I'd much rather spend my life with a kind nobody than a fortune hunting charmer, Vicar Green." Linda squared her shoulders. "Take care. My father is always interested to know if his support is valued."

"Is that a threat, Miss Dexington?"

She giggled. "Of course not. I wouldn't be so crass. We will see you next Sunday for the second reading of the banns."

"Vicar Green." Marti nodded to the man, then left with Linda. They made it all the way to their carriage before she breathed out heavily. She sat on the rear facing seat with two of her sisters opposite, leaving him only one space; beside her.

"Oh that frustrating man. I can't believe he thinks I should've married Sir Bartleby."

"He is a baron. People are swayed by titles," said Linda's sister, Jacinda.

"They ought not to be. Sir Bartleby is a man with no character, a weasel who only wanted my father's money. I'm glad Father saw through that, and I'm thankful that Mr Babbitt was there to help me escape him."

He smiled. "I thought you escaped all on your own."

"I did." She twisted, leaning towards him, and his lips parted, hopeful for a kiss, but she didn't. Of course she didn't, she was a well-raised wealthy young woman in the company of her sisters. "I had a little help from a wonderful man and his horse, though."

"Stop it, you two. At least wait until the banns are read." Jacinda rolled her eyes and Linda, sadly, sat up straight and stared at her sister.

"Mrs Marchant asked me a curious question." Elspeth joined the conversation.

"Oh?"

"She remembered the Babbitt family who lived next to us when we were children."

Marti's heart sunk, his worse fear hung in the air, and he grabbed the seat to anchor himself to the world.

Linda waved her hand in the air. "Isn't it such a coincidence! Mr Babbitt is a distance cousin of them. Don't you think he has the look of Martha?" She touched a finger to his chin and it seared him in a way that he couldn't understand; wanting more and not being able to quite figure out what she meant. Why would she draw attention to that?

"He does. I wonder what happened to Martha after her parent's sad death." Elspeth was a year older than him and she had an astute look about her that worried him.

"Marti?"

Dear holy goodness, he was supposed to come up with something that his distant cousin had done. His head swayed and he wondered if he might topple off the seat.

"There are a lot of Babbitt's, I haven't quite figured out all of them yet." Linda saved the day with a vague explanation, and he swallowed, finally remembering the excuse Doris and Edwin had concocted years ago.

"Yes. My Aunt Doris took her in for a while with me, and then she had an opportunity to be a governess with a family moving to the Americas. It's been a long time since I had a letter from her."

"It's so hard to keep in contact over the seas. One never knows if a letter has been lost on a ship, or if it were never sent at all," Elspeth said.

He nodded. There was nothing much else to say, except to stew over the fact that he'd been stressed about everyone finding out his secret to the point where he'd forgotten that he had a perfectly good excuse. It'd been years since 'Martha' had gone to the Americas and years since he'd had to mention it. Thankfully the conversation moved on to someone's dress and speculation over the source of the fabric, and he slowly let himself breathe again. Once they were married, they'd have to move away from anyone who ever knew a Babbitt. Perhaps to the Americas where it wouldn't be a lie anymore...

CHAPTER SIX

Linda owed Marti an apology. Before lunch with her whole family was even finished, he escaped from the table with barely an excuse, and by the time she'd managed to extract herself to follow him, he was gone. It took her no time to find him, as she headed directly to the most obvious place ... the stables, where she found him brushing Turpin.

"Marti."

He didn't look up.

"I'm really sorry. I should never have done this without discussing it with you first. I didn't think." She should've realised that all society went to church to hear all the latest gossip and the reading of the banns would bring out everyone's curiosity, which meant people would connect Marti to the Babbitt family who'd lived next door to her when she'd been a child. It made their sudden reconnection easier to explain; people had taken that at face value, but she worried about the implications for Marti and who he used to be.

He leaned against Turpin's shoulder and glanced at her. "Neither did I."

"Can I come in?" She didn't want to have this discussion over a stable door.

"Of course. It's your father's stable."

"You are part of the family now too." She slipped inside the door, making sure it was latched behind her. Marti didn't answer, just kept brushing Turpin's already gleaming coat. She rubbed Turpin on the nose. He breathed his fluttery horse breath on her hand, and she leaned against Turpin's head for a moment, collecting her breath. This apology mattered and she had to get it right before they faced the church crowd again.

With a deep breath, she stood up straight and stared at Marti. "To me you'll always be Marti."

He paused mid-brush stroke across Turpin's coat for a moment, then continued working as if she hadn't spoken.

"I'm sorry. I'm sorry that I forgot that everyone is a gossip. I didn't think about how they'd hear your surname and want to know which Babbitt you are connected to and how that might potentially be awkward for you. I'm so sorry that we didn't discuss this before we had the banns read. I was so focussed on being free from Sir Bartleby that I didn't think about the potential harm for you."

"Stop saying sorry." Marti turned to look at her. "I forgot too. I didn't expect to see old Mrs Marchant and have her look at me as if she remembered."

"You do have the Babbitt look about you, but the story about being a distant cousin was inspired."

"Doris thought of it, I just forgot because..."

She wasn't sure how he could forget about something so crucially connected to his identity. "How?"

"I find crowds a bit overwhelming, and it makes it hard to remember things." Marti returned to brushing Turpin for a while and she waited. It wasn't natural for her to wait, but this felt important. It mattered to listen and let Marti explain this to her.

"I've always struggled in crowds, even before, but now it is worse because there's a risk that someone like Mrs Marchant will look at me and see through who I am now to who I was."

"But you are Marti. It's your name of choice and—" She paused, realising she didn't need to convince him.

"People don't like it when someone isn't who they seem."

She could see how that might cause issues, except this was different. "Do they not understand?"

"No. People would prefer that I fit into the identity that they understand. To wear pants and dress as a man, to be a man... It makes me into someone unnatural."

"Maybe they are jealous. At first, I was jealous that you got to have all the advantages in society that men have." She wasn't anymore. "I quickly realised that was silly. Being a man doesn't fit who I am, and any jealousy I had at your advantages disappeared." She paused, staring at him, but he kept his gaze on his horse.

"Listening to you talk makes me understand how brave you are to be the man that you are. Any advantages—" She wanted to hug up and hold him, but she didn't think he would appreciate the fuss.

Marti snorted. "Only exist if no one works it out. It's conditional."

"I'm..." Sorry. She was sorry that she was only beginning to understand him and the challenges he faced. With a deep breath in, she tried to focus on this moment where it was just the two of them, learning about each other.

"If you apologise again—" Marti interrupted. "I'm going to..."

"What? Kiss me?" She stared at the straw on the stable floor because she would never be so forward with anyone else, but this was Marti and he'd been so open about himself with her that she trusted him. He shuffled his feet and she lifted her head to look at him. A bright flush was painted across his cheeks and she smiled.

"I'm so very sorry." She walked towards him with a half-smile—hopeful—as she took the couple of steps from Turpin's head to where Marti stood at Turpin's flank, brushing him. She reached up to touch his bright cheeks. "We are almost married now."

His eyes widened. "They've read the banns once." He swallowed, his throat shifting. "Aren't you supposed to be innocent?"

"No." She loved the way his skin was smooth under her palm. "I'm supposed to appear innocent to counter Sir Bartleby's claims. I don't wish to be innocent, not with you. Please kiss me or I'll be sorry again." Her breath was ragged, shallow, and hopeful.

"We can't have that, can we?" A bright light shone from his eyes, and he placed his hands lightly on her waist and pulled her closer. The gentle pressure of his hands sent a flush of heat over her skin, centring at the point of contact.

"Please." She didn't quite know what she was asking for. Her older sisters talked about the marriage bed but they always changed the subject when she'd entered the room, and she'd only overheard enough to know that it was sometimes beautiful and sometimes awkward or awful. The entire matter seemed terribly confusing. Marti leaned in and brushed his lips over hers, and all confusion disappeared as his gentle whimsical touch on her mouth was nothing like the way she'd ever been touched before. Instinctually she reached up and cupped his cheek, pulling him closer. The press of his lips connected them and her body pulsed with energy; desire, as if she were suddenly much warmer and she wanted to fan her face. It was sensual and incredible, and she suddenly knew why kissing was frowned upon before marriage because if she'd known it would feel like this, she might've wanted to be kissed before now. A little flicker in her head felt like a warning that it wouldn't be this good with anyone else, that this kiss was wonderful because Marti was her person.

"Linda." His voice rasped as he pulled back an inch. Too far, even though the tips of their noses were still touching.

"More, please." She was caught between not knowing and wanting to know and wondering if it was just him or if this was how kisses always were. Marti slid his hand up her back and she leaned against his touch. He kissed her again, a glorious heady feeling surrounding her as she copied the way he moved his lips against hers. He slipped his hand under her bonnet threading his fingers into her hair, and a bolt of energy cursed through her veins, culminating in her core, in that place between her legs that she touched sometimes at night when no one was around. This was better though, and she suddenly knew she wanted his hand there. Until now the idea that someone else might touch her there had repulsed her, and suddenly, she understood that it would never be this good with anyone else, that this was special because it was Marti, and she let herself fall into that knowledge.

"Linda? Can I?"

"Yes." She didn't know what he was asking but she wanted everything. With him and him only. He pushed his tongue between her lips, stroking her mouth with care and attention and she melted in his arms. She wanted to lie on the straw and have him push her body down.

Turpin shifted in the stall and they both stumbled a bit.

"We shouldn't do this here."

Her breath was heavy and rapid and all she could do was nod as he removed his hands from her body with one last caress.

"Marti."

"Linda. We can't."

She glanced around. "We can. Just not here. I'll come to your room tonight."

He stared at her unblinking. "In your family's house?"

"Yes. We are to be married. You can teach me how to be a good wife to you."

He just shook his head and the wave of bravado disappeared.

"I like kissing you and I want to know more."

"And you always get what you want?"

A cool wind made her shiver. "You think I'm a spoiled daughter of an industrialist?"

"I think it's a good idea to wait, given all the attention that is on us with the rumours around Sir Bartleby."

She wanted to stomp her foot and prove him right; that she was spoiled and she should get what she wanted. "Fine. Let's talk about it tonight."

"Linda. There is more to consider than just a few kisses." He reached out and touched her fingers, a gentle connection that made her yearn for more. She nodded, turned away, and gave Turpin a good pat as she walked away, trying not to feel young and naïve and humiliated and rejected. Was she being too demanding?

CHAPTER SEVEN

Marti didn't have a chance to spend the next day settling into life in the Dexington house. After breakfast, he'd been summoned to Mr Dexington's office, and now as he walked along the hallway to the drawing room, he wasn't sure what to make of the conversation with Mr Dexington. He might have just been offered him a job, although it was unclear what the parameters were. It was almost as if Mr Dexington was testing him but he didn't know what the test was meant to prove. Having him state that he'd always provide work for his family members was both reassuring and worrying; Marti wasn't certain he wanted his entire life to be tied to the whole Dexington clan. Just himself to Linda.

"Mr Babbitt. Let's go for a walk." Linda bounced down the hallway with her usual sunny enthusiasm, and he wasn't sure he was ready for more Dexington chatter. Not that her father was chatty, he was much more intimidating than that. He held back a sigh with the air catching in his throat and nodded because she looked incredible in a bright gown of pale yellow and blue vertical wide stripes and a straw bonnet with matching ribbons. Only hints of her red hair were visible, like little secrets just for him. When they were married, he'd get the full glory of it and be able to thread his fingers through the silky tresses.

"Excellent. My maid will chaperone us." She hooked her hand through his elbow and guided him along the hall. Apparently she'd never learned the art of making it look like the man was leading and he adored the way she believed in her own independence despite all the evidence. She obviously grappled with complicated thoughts around her place in the world and yet still managed to be joyful. That she'd admitted her initial jealousy to him was touching, surprising him with her honesty, and then how she'd approached her thoughts about him with empathy, changing her views as she dealt with her own feelings while putting plenty of effort into understanding him, made his chest warm and tender.

Once they were outside, they walked along the wide boulevard bordering the canal with the largest houses in town situated alongside.

"Ushnish informed me that Father invited you into his office for a discussion." Linda didn't disguise her curiosity.

"Yes." He teased her by giving her nothing.

"What did he want? Was he kind?"

The second question bothered him. "Is your father often unkind?"

"No. Why would you ask that?"

"You asked me if he'd been kind."

Linda blinked a couple of times. "Oh, so I did. I suppose I meant that he's very abrupt at times. He's an impatient businessman. I'm accustomed to it."

He nodded. It aligned with his discussion with Mr Dexington who'd quizzed him intensely.

"What did he want?"

"He offered me a job."

Linda twisted her head and gave him a surprised job. "In the factory? No, surely not."

"No." He'd been given a lot more consideration with Mr Dexington interrogating his different skillsets.

"I don't understand why he would need to offer you a job." The stunning innocence in that statement nearly made him choke on a bubble of surprised laughter. He reached up to touch his mouth and sure enough, he hadn't been able to hide his smile.

"Not all of us have the privilege of being born into wealth." Marti was gratified that Mr Dexington had understood his precarious position as the informal assistant to his aunt at the Public Arms.

"Are you teasing me?"

"Yes."

She made a very unfeminine noise, a growl under her breath, which went against all the etiquette training she must've had had. It endeared him further. He'd been forced to do that same process, at least until his parents had died and his aunt had arrived on his doorstep announcing that she would take him. Until then, he hadn't known he had an aunt. It quickly became obvious that his parents wouldn't have approved of Aunt Doris' life with Uncle Edwin as an unmarried inn owner and all the rest.

"You don't like being teased?"

"Not particularly." She sighed. "Even when it's fairly deserved. I am the spoiled daughter of an indulgent wealthy father."

"And yet your kindness shines through." He would rather discuss her virtues than the conversation with her father.

"Thank you. Now tell me everything. What type of job?"

He wasn't to get his wish, but since they were to be married, he supposed he should be honest. "It wasn't one single job. He simply wanted to know what my prospects were—not much—and what skills I had, and what I wanted to do with myself."

"And?"

"I had a typical education for my childhood—" He alluded to the lack of education given to girls without saying it, "And for the last decade, I've worked in my aunt's inn doing odd jobs."

"So you have practical skills?"

"Yes. And please don't interrogate me as well. I have already had plenty of that today."

Linda nudged him gently. "If I'm not to talk to you, how are we to get to know each other?"

"Fine. Ask me anything." He might regret this.

Linda walked quietly for several strides, as if giving a lot of consideration to which question she might ask. With each step and as time stretched, his chest tightened. Not knowing what she might ask became a buzzing anxiety like two cats fighting in his stomach.

"Why were you so quick to agree to marry me? You hardly know me?"

"Are you accusing me of being a fortune hunter?" He swallowed.

She sighed, fiddling with one of the ribbons on her bonnet. "I met you as a highwayman. It's logical to worry that you are interested in stealing money."

It was a sensible question and one he should've expected, but in the interests of honesty, he needed to address an issue that was potentially much more of a problem to both of their futures.

"There's another more pressing reason."

"Which is?"

"Being married lends me a certain legitimacy in the law." He would truly be Mister Babbitt if he had a wife, someone who was legally seen as intimate and knowing of his true self—whatever that might entail —and therefore her presence as his wife would reinforce his existence as a man. And if he knew one thing about people it was that they saw what was presented to them; a man and his wife. It was a simple way to prevent any further doubts or questions.

Linda's fingers tightened on his forearm. "Marti, my childhood friend and saviour from the wiles of Sir Bartleby, I would be honoured to be your wife and help the world see you as you are."

"So you see, agreeing to marry you wasn't a completely selfless act." Marti's breath was ragged and heavy until Linda's statement slowly seeped in, like the damp dew on an autumn night. For her to understand without him having to explain the intimate details was a blessing and the tension in his torso started to unravel. "Oh. You are?"

"Honoured? Yes." She looked at him with such sincerity that he could barely believe his good fortune.

"Even though?"

"Marti. Yes. I never found the idea of a traditional marriage very enthralling. My sister, Elspeth, lives with her spinster best friend, Florencia, and I'm curious about that but I'm not certain that is what I want either."

He nodded. "I didn't have the words to describe myself for a long time too. Uncertainty about things that society is incredibly certain about does leave one in a rather confusing space."

Linda's fingers relaxed. "Confusing is a great word for it. I'm a social creature. I adore people, all types of people, and the idea of being forced into a traditional marriage seems so restrictive."

His stomach dropped and his skin went cold. "You want to have relations with many people?"

"No. That does seem overly complicated with all the issues that might arise. But I do find many people attractive? I mean, it's not... there's nothing wrong with me, is there?" Her little gasp punctured his heart and he wanted to hold her tight and reassure her that she was perfect as she was.

"No. There is absolutely nothing wrong with you." He'd seen a lot of things working in an inn. "There are many things that society says men shouldn't discuss with women—"

"Dash that. Society likes to keep young women ignorant so they don't realise they have more options."

"Linda. That attitude might get you into trouble in good society." He teased her, smiling, because she was right.

"Marti. I'm the daughter of a nouveau riche industrialist upstart. I'm already not good society, not really. My participation is conditional on my father staying wealthy and my manners being up to snuff. At first glance, the marriage proposal from Sir Bartleby would be a good political alliance for the family ... get some more aristocratic blood at the dinner table." Linda huffed. "If he'd been halfway decent, I might have agreed for the sake of my sisters and the charitable work I might be able to do as a Baroness."

"But he wasn't half-way decent."

"No. Father worked it out quickly, and from there it wasn't hard to confirm his debts and his other issues, so the proposal was swiftly refused."

"By you or your father?"

Linda glared at a tree growing happily beside the path. Better the tree than him, he supposed. "Firstly by me and backed up by my father. It's the way of the world."

"Yes." Marti suddenly wanted to make one thing clear. "I promise not to make your decisions for you. We can collaborate."

"Thank you."

He eased out a long breath as her fingers relaxed on his forearm.

"It's nice walking with you. Is it odd for me to feel like I know you from when I was a child, but that I don't really know you at all?"

"A little. I'm much more myself than I was then."

She nodded rapidly. "I was very young. I barely recall you, only that you seemed very nice and you were happy to play picnics with me even though I was a lot younger. I must've been rather boring for you."

He shrugged. "No. Sometimes I think about my childhood and it doesn't seem real."

"What do you mean?"

"My parents died when I was fifteen, and everything before that seems to have turned into soft whimsical memories, as if it was more a dream than reality. Obviously, it's complicated by the sense of unbelonging I had while also being fortunate to have loving parents who provided for my care."

"You didn't argue about who you were?" Linda clapped her hand over her mouth. "I'm sorry. I shouldn't have asked such a nosy question."

Marti waited for the gut punch sensation but it didn't come, and he realised that Linda's kindness allowed him space to talk about some of his more complicated emotions.

"As a child, it is easy to be guided by your parents and to push away anything that didn't fit. The certainty I have now as a man wasn't as strong, not like my Uncle Edwin."

"I didn't know you had an uncle."

Marti sighed. "I didn't either. My Aunt Doris is my mother's sister, but I wasn't aware she existed until my parent's accident. She turned up and announced that she was my mother's sister and I would come and live with her."

"Goodness." Linda's exclamation included a wide range of emotions and he laughed, unable to stop himself.

"It was certainly quite the surprise." To say the least. He'd been in shock, grieving for his parents, and not knowing what a gift it would be to live with his aunt.

"How on earth did you become a highwayman? It seems like a lot of steps between those two things."

"Uncle Edwin, my aunt's lover, taught me."

Linda spun around on the path to face him. "Hold up."

"That's my line."

"Oh hush. I meant, hold up a moment. How can you openly discuss your aunt having a lover? Were they not married?"

Marti cursed under his breath. He should've been more careful. "They were not. Edwin was … like me. It's because of him that I was able to understand how to be myself."

"Was?"

"He died from a fever three years ago." Marti knew the same fate lay before him as there was no way Edwin could get a doctor to visit. The risks to his person were too great, so Marti and Doris had nursed him as best they could.

"How terribly sad. My condolences." Linda turned around again and they continued on with their walk. There was a heaviness to the way Linda walked now, a sombre weight in the air between them, and he was surprised by how natural it felt to discuss these unusual situations with her. She absorbed his grief for his uncle naturally, and he could easily imagine a life where they shared each other's burdens. Was he being too sentimental to think so when they'd only just met?

CHAPTER EIGHT

Linda blinked rapidly as she walked, trying her best to stem the tears that wanted so desperately to fall. Her heart ached for Marti, who'd lost not only his parents but also a dear uncle, and she knew exactly how that felt as she'd been only six years old when her own mother had died from childbed fever. When she'd told Marti that she wanted a non-traditional marriage, that was really what she meant. No children. No child should have to feel how she had. No child should have that awful knowledge of being abandoned by a beloved parent.

With Marti it was achievable to be married and have no children. Maybe. She knew enough about the breeding of animals to know that it should be impossible for her and Marti to create children, or at least, she assumed so. Being kept ignorant of such matters was a frustrating consequence of her life, and the heat behind her eyes became sharper until she wanted to scream.

"Linda?" The concern dripping from Marti's voice nagged at her, then centred her back into a world where many people still cared for her—including Marti—and she breathed in deeply.

"Shall we head back to the house?"

"Yes."

They turned around, walking past Jane, the maid, who turned to follow them home. Lucky Jane to escape her job for a walk along the laneway, although the servants in the Dexington household were well paid and tended to stay for a long time as their working conditions were better than most other households. It was a point of pride to her father that they retained their staff.

"Mr Babbitt." She used his formal address to help calm the unsteadiness inside her. "Did you say that Father offered you a job?"

"Not precisely."

The vague answer tweaked at her curiosity and the heat behind her ears started to dissipate. "What exactly do you mean?"

"He said he'd find me a position and inferred that I could decide what type of work suited me and to make him a proposal."

"What type of proposal?" A fleeting confusion had Linda wondering about their marriage—too many jests over lunch about collecting proposals—but a short breath later she realised that her father probably meant a business proposal.

"We went over this, and the answer remains that I am uncertain."

She recalled the initial conversation where Marti had said he hadn't wanted to replay the whole discussion, but seriously, how typical was it of Father to leave it to Marti. She sniffed. "He would probably buy you a business to run if you were so inclined."

"Oh, I don't think he meant that."

"What questions did he ask?" Linda had a lot more certainty than Marti. Her father—who liked to test people's ambitions—would help Marti achieve something beyond his most wild dreams if he could only imagine it because her father understood that helping Linda's husband succeed would give Linda the best chance of a good future. Her father didn't see seven daughters as an expense—especially after the disappointment of his only son refusing to join the business—but as an opportunity to bring seven men into his empire. It hadn't quite worked out to plan, which amused Linda. Powerful men ought not to get everything they wanted.

"He asked about my skills."

Given Marti's doubt, she aimed for teasing his skills from him, rather than badgering him about her father's aims. She took a few breaths. "I presume you didn't tell him about your highwayman years or how good a shot you are."

"No." He shot her a strange glance, and she grinned back at him.

"It was rather a good shot, hitting Sir Bartleby in the shoulder. I mean, that is, if you didn't intend to him elsewhere?"

"No, I meant to hit him in the shoulder. I only wanted to wing him so he would understand that the situation was real and then he would hand over his money and jewels."

"Shame that the horses bolted, then."

Marti smiled. Gosh she liked his face when he grinned, and she wished she could kiss him again. She sighed because she couldn't, not here, not while promenading along the canal with several of the town gossips also out walking. This light teasing was lovely, much nicer than their conversation before which had touched on her own grief. She gave herself a good shake. No more of that line of thought right now.

"A shame."

"At least you got something useful from it. My father—"

"Promised something vague without any guidance." *Oh Marti, that was rather the point.* She understood the irritation in his voice as she was often frustrated by her father.

"He said he would help you in your endeavours and he shall. Father understands that providing a future for you also provides a future for your wife."

"My wife?"

She wanted to roll her eyes. "Me. In this transaction, you gained a wife from Sir Bartleby."

Marti's eyebrows knitted together. "No. Please don't make it sound like you are being traded between us."

"Oh, but I am. I am mere property to be given by my father to whoever he deems worthy of me." And she was fortunate to have a father who'd listened to her concerns about Sir Bartleby and agreed with her; not all women were so lucky as not to be traded for status. Many of the girls from her finishing school had already been married off in an exchange of money for titles without regard for the type of man they were being saddled with.

"How depressing."

"And yet, I've been lucky enough to have two proposals and can select the man most likely to make a good husband for me." She hated the restrictions of society but without access to politics, it was hardly going to change before she entered the institution of marriage ... Especially not in the three weeks until the banns were finished being read.

Marti blushed a little. "And you think that I am that man?"

"Definitely. It is every girl's dream to be married to a handsome rogue that can outride others, shoot well, and bring down the villain."

"Are you teasing me?"

She grinned. "Of course." It was much easier than focusing on the painful parts of this process.

"And now you have a fiancé who has the skills of a rogue and high-wayman, what advice would you give him?"

"About?" She wasn't sure she could advise Marti on anything. He was several years older and had seen a lot more of life than her.

"About this situation with your father, what should I do?"

Oh, yes, that made sense and was something she had some ideas about. She'd drifted off again, thinking about kissing Marti and wondering what his skin felt like against her fingers, wondering what his experience might teach her about herself. "What is your greatest dream? Your wildest ambition? Father admires people with big plans."

Marti's eyes widened and he made a strange coughing noise. "I dare say I shouldn't tell him I wish to retire quietly to the country and live without the danger of being discovered by anyone."

"No." Her head spun. She would hate that life, leaving behind her family and friends.

"Linda." He touched her hand in a gentle caress, one that seared her very soul with the connection to him and she held her breath, hoping the touch meant something.

"Retreat isn't always safe. You'd be away from everyone who cares about you."

His throat shifted. "I don't have many of those."

Linda blinked back those pesky hot tears again.

"I used to think a quiet life was the safest life for me, but now I've met you, I couldn't do that to you."

"What do you mean?"

"I've only known you a few days—"

"You knew me as a child." Linda protested because the intimacy of this discussion prickled over her skin with an awkwardness that she wasn't sure how to deal with. She knew she was a frivolous silly person who flitted about society, so perhaps it was merely that she wasn't accustomed to Marti's persistent openness.

"As an adult. And you are the bravest, most determined person I've met, and I've met a few tenacious individuals."

"What has that to do with not wanting to move to the country?"

"I saw you at church yesterday. You smiled and talked to everyone—"

She was correct, she was a silly socialite. Even Marti thought so.

"And you made people happy. You talked to them all as if they mattered and it's such a skill to listen to people's complaints and stories and joys and make them feel important. I couldn't take that away from you."

The tears that had threatened to spill over for this entire walk finally fell. No one had ever made her happy chatter sound so useful and important. She dabbed her eyes with her handkerchief, a very fine piece of linen.

"Linda. Please don't be upset."

She sniffed. "I'm not upset. I'm…" She didn't actually know. She felt seen; as if for the first time someone understood how much she enjoyed people and their wonderful uniqueness. "I think I'm happy."

Marti brushed his fingers across her chin, almost on her bottom lip but not quite and she wanted… Oh, she wanted so much more. Behind her, Jane coughed loudly.

"We'd better keep walking."

"Yes."

"Later?" She shouldn't ask. It was far too forward, but they would soon be married and she didn't want to wait. Impatience and an urgency flowed in her veins like a bird soaring on the breeze. She kept glancing between Marti and the pathway, until she finally saw Marti nod, and her body came alight. Soon, she would discover more about kissing with her fiancé who noticed her. He didn't see her as a silly social butterfly like everyone else, he saw her as someone who cared about people and their thoughts and goals and wishes. He cared for her. But who was caring for him? She could do that too.

"What about you? You've said you want a quiet life to protect yourself, but you don't want to do that to me. How are we going to find a compromise?"

CHAPTER NINE

M arti was floored by the astuteness of her question, and he hated that he had no answer. He wished he had the words to describe this stuttering inside him, something like the way Turpin stared at a puddle with nostrils flared, uncertain about whether it was safe to step into the murky water or not.

"If you didn't have to worry, what would you do?" Linda asked.

"But I do have to worry." He shot her a glance but she only stared back at him softly.

"Indulge me."

Always. He would always indulge her; it didn't matter that they'd only just met—or met again—one kiss, one touch, and he was gone. Completely and utterly intrigued by her in a way that he knew would only grow with time. It was a good thing they were going to be married, or he might make a fool of himself chasing after her. He might anyway.

"The only thing I know how to do is run an inn. I've helped Aunt Doris for a decade in her pub, but it's not a good business. Her inn struggles in the winter, when less people travel, and the good times are too infrequent. For years, I thought I would take over the Public Arms one day, when Doris became too old to manage. I didn't have any other options."

"I'm not asking for your excuses about what you do now." Her phrasing was odd, and he squinted at her. It wasn't an excuse.

"No. It's a reason. Doris is healthy as an oxen, and she works so hard for little profit and no holidays. One day, she won't be able to anymore, and it makes sense for me to step in since there she has no one else."

"An interesting dilemma and one that we should consider as an option." Linda demonstrated that she'd been listening, even if she'd fumbled a bit on the way. He nodded, not sure what to say next.

"However..." She drummed her fingers on his forearm, and he realised he'd become so accustomed to her touch there that the change in pressure sent a new tingle up his arm. "...The question isn't what options you have now, but what would you do if you had a choice."

"If I had a choice ... well—" He shook his head. There was one problem. "It's the only life I know. I don't have any other skills, and to be honest I don't even have all the skills needed to do it without Doris."

"What do you mean?"

"I'm no good at dealing with the customers. Doris is better than me but without Uncle Edwin, we try our grudging best. It's just—"

"Missing someone who adores meeting new people."

"Yes."

"Like me." She grinned, bouncing on her toes and he stiffened beside her, thoroughly confused about what had excited her so much. "I could help you run the inn. You said before that I'm good at making people smile, at making them feel relaxed."

He gasped as he pictured it. He could do all the organising in the back of the inn, never seen by the public, and she would welcome them and make them feel at home. She'd be fantastic at it; except she was the daughter of a wealthy man.

"Would you?" Work?

"Help you run an inn and spend my day talking to people? Yes." She laughed. "I'm sure there's more to it than that, but I can learn. I have basic business skills. Father made sure we all learned in case we wanted to work in the family business."

"That's incredibly forward thinking of him."

She rolled her eyes. "It shouldn't be. Why waste all the intellect of half the people, just because they are supposedly the weaker sex."

"Even so."

"We aren't the haut ton with their leisurely view on the world. My father is an industrialist, a businessman. To be a Dexington is to work to earn money."

"But to teach his daughters is incredibly unusual?" Marti couldn't quite get his head around it. As a child, he'd been trained to manage a household—ironically it made him good at managing an inn, which was essentially a house on a slightly bigger scale—not to get involved in the family business.

"I have a brother who refused to be part of the family business. I don't know all the details since I'm a lot younger, however, since then, Father was apparently more open to thinking about his daughters as part of his future plans."

"It's very unusual." He knew he was being repetitive but it truly was unique in this world.

"My father is an unusual man. He's always taken risks and seen the world with a different lens to most others. It's why he's a success; he's not afraid to try things that no one else would dare to do."

Marti hummed under his breath, encouraging her to continue, since he wasn't sure how or what to say.

"Father is usually a terrible listener. He knows what is the right thing to do and he expects everyone to agree, but one thing is interesting in hindsight. He listened to me when I mentioned my concerns about Sir Bartleby. I wonder if he already knew and he was waiting for me to notice anything wrong with Sir Bartleby."

"Sir Bartleby is a lot older than you. That ought to be enough on its own." Marti's skin had crawled that day they'd all been in the Dexington drawing room together. He'd known Sir Bartleby as a kidnapper who he'd shot, but to spend time with him in the same room had solidified his negative opinion of Sir Bartleby as a self-absorbed peacock.

"Bosh. No one cares about that. Society marries off young innocent women to older men all the time."

Marti growled. "They shouldn't. I've overheard enough rich men talking at the inn to realise that these men don't respect their young wives. They only want them young because they are easier to train at that age, easier to make into compliant beings who don't question their apparent authority. They like their power over their young wives, and I've even heard men boast that they've gotten rid of their wives when they've become too old and knowing and replaced them with younger fresher versions."

She shuddered, the vibrations travelling through her hand onto his arm. "I'd guessed this about Sir Bartleby, although not in such brutal terms. It makes me want to bathe in a freezing cold lake or a boiling bath to get rid of the disgust that clings after being in the same room as him." Her breath was ragged and uneven and he wanted to hold her close and rub soothing circles on her spine.

"Yes." He had the same response; a need to clean himself after being in Sir Bartleby's presence.

"It's dreadful to know that there are more men like him out there. Goodness." She shook out her hands. "I was so fortunate that Father believed me when I said I didn't want to marry him. So fortunate."

"Yes." Marti rested his other hand on top of hers, as it lay on his forearm.

"Let's focus on our future instead. I'm done with wasting time on Sir Bartleby. He's already taken up too much of it."

"I think we should make a proper plan before we talk to Mr Dexington again." Mr Dexington was rather intimidating and he'd prefer to have all his options covered and his plans in good shape before talking to Linda's father again.

"Maybe we should go to your Aunt's inn for a few days to get some advice?"

It wasn't the worst idea; and Linda would be chaperoned for the whole time thanks to Aunt Doris' presence.

Marti didn't see Linda again until dinner. After their walk, she'd gone to visit one of her sisters, and he'd taken Turpin out for some exercise. The gelding didn't like standing around in his box. He'd been fidgety at first, then they'd found a decent bridle path and gone for a good long canter, before heading back to the Dexington house. Getting fresh air in his lungs had helped both Marti and his horse.

"The lighting in this house is amazing." He'd never had dinner in such a bright room.

"I installed coal gas lights as soon as the technology was proven. We use it in our factories too. Much safer than candles and as you can see, the lamps provide a lot more light too," Mr Dexington said.

"Just don't ask him how it works, Mr Babbitt. You'll get an incredibly detailed explanation." Linda smiled at her father.

"Technological change is the future and it would do you all well to understand it. It's progress."

"And our empire is built on progress." Several of the people at the table spoke in unison.

"You all jest, but it's true. I wouldn't say it so often if I didn't want all of you to understand it on a visceral level."

Marti listened carefully. He could imagine the astonishment of guests if he had an inn with these lights in it. Oh, some guests preferred the dark shadowy spaces provided by candlelight, and he... A rush of blood to his head made him gasp.

"Mr Dexington, could I ask a technical question?" he asked.

"Yes, you may."

"Is the light level in the coal gas lamps variable? Could you dim them?" He wanted to know if he could have a dimmer space for those guests who preferred it, and a bright space for other guests to be wowed by.

"I presume you could achieve that with a smaller wick, less reflectors, and a lower rate of gas. I'm not sure why you would want to dim the brilliance of technology, however."

Marti nodded, not quite ready to respond to Mr Dexington's point since it would lead to more questions that he didn't have the answers to. Not yet, anyway. "I was just curious as to how they could be adapted to different spaces and uses." He glanced over at Linda, whose eyes had widened, and he tried to send her a quick look that meant for her to wait and not spill their idea just yet. She lowered her chin just enough that he hoped she understood.

"Curiosity is a wonderful trait in this ever-changing world. I believe we are on the verge of great technological breakthroughs. The use of steam power in industry is only the beginning. My children. You are the luckiest generation as you will live through important changes in the world. The old guard will lose their power and a new wave will rise up."

Marti couldn't believe what he was hearing. To speak in such terms, hinting at over-throwing the House of Lords, was seditious.

"Father, you don't need to convince us. We've heard this all before and I think you are being a little too shocking for our guest." One of Linda's sisters, Prudence, the oldest one, glanced his way.

"Mr Babbitt. Are you shocked?"

"I've worked in a small inn for the past decade. Not much can surprise me." He avoided the question because he was a little surprised that they'd all talk about the ruling classes with such presumption.

"And do you intend to keep working in this inn?" Mr Dexington asked.

He swallowed, glancing around the table at everyone, who stared back at him.

"Father. Don't interrogate my fiancé. You know full well that he understands your proposal to him and will respond in due course." Linda had squared her shoulders as she stared at her father. The bravery on his behalf made his chest tighten, as if he'd bound his breasts too tight.

"My dear Linda. Let the man speak for himself. After all, once you are married, he will be the one wearing the pants."

A slight flush painted her cheeks before she lowered her head, and he leapt to her defence.

"My ego is not so fragile that I would care that my soon-to-be wife spoke on my behalf. We are to be a partnership, a team, and she is much better at talking than I am."

Linda lifted her head, her cheeks fully ablaze with colour and her eyes sparkling. Damn he wanted to drag her off and kiss her; his veins pulsing with need. The room exploded with conversation, with several of the sisters debating the fragility of various egos. He took it as an opportunity.

"Shall we take our leave?" he asked—his voice rough—and Linda nodded. They both stood.

"Until tomorrow, Father." Linda curtsied in his direction and she walked out of the dining room with her head held high.

"Thank you for a lovely meal." He wanted to jog after her, but was uncertain about how that would look to his rather domineering soon to be father-in-law. "My compliments to your staff." He walked slowly from the room, ensuring the door was closed before he raced after Linda. She grabbed his sleeve and pulled him through a door.

"This is a cupboard?" It was dark with only the bright coal gas lights shining through the gaps around the door. Linda didn't answer, not with words. Instead, she pressed him against the wall and kissed him and his heart soared.

CHAPTER TEN

In this moment, Linda stopped caring about decorum or societal expectations. As soon as Marti had defended her and said such lovely things about her, all she'd wanted was to kiss him and so she'd pulled him into a cupboard. The close dim space was filled with brooms and shelves of linen, with barely enough space for the two of them, and yet, she'd surprised herself by shoving him against the wall. It was spontaneous. Instinctual. She had to. She kissed him with desperation, with a deliberate need that coursed in her veins like the energy of a summer storm. All lightning and thunder, and his taste in her mouth. He placed his hands on her shoulders and gently pushed her backwards, away from him, until her spine hit the wall on the other side of the cupboard. It felt like forever, a slow waltz together, even though it'd been only a single stride in the small space.

"Linda."

"Please."

He cupped her cheeks. "If ..." His breath was as ragged as hers. "If we are to do this here, you need to be quiet."

Heat rushed down her spine and she ached in that spot between her legs. She bit her bottom lip and nodded.

"Very, very quiet." He placed his finger over her lips and she moaned softly. His finger tasted clean, with a hint of salt, as if he had a sheen of sweat on his skin. She'd believe it; she was so hot everywhere that she probably had the same. The air in the cupboard had the same humid charge as before a storm, as if the air was filled with the weight of the incoming rain, but the only wetness was between her legs. Suddenly she breathed in sharply, needing Marti to touch her there. She wriggled against him, wanting to beg, but not wanting to make a noise. He slid his thigh between her legs, lean muscles from horse riding pressing hard against her mons with too many layers of fabric between them. She licked his finger and he growled.

"I thought we needed to be quiet." Her whisper was hoarse and rough.

"We do, or everyone will know what we are doing in here." He leaned in closer, whispering directly into her ear with hot breath. She shuddered, gripping his elbows tighter. He nipped at her ear lobe. Her gasp was blocked as he moved his hand to cover her mouth with his palm.

"Yes. Moan for me. Moan into my hand and I'll keep you quiet."

Goodness. She was going to melt. He nipped at her again, this time harder and she couldn't stop the moan slipping out onto his hand. Her heart was beating so fast, and her breath even faster. She sucked in air through her nose, the aromas of clean linen and Marti's skin combined with the taste of salt on her lips. Marti nibbled at her neck, and she slid her head backwards, wanting to expose more of her skin to his mouth. With every kiss and every lick, her legs softened until her knees were blancmange. He removed his hand from her mouth with another shoosh and traced his fingers across her decolletage. Before she could react to the way her skin came alight with his touch, he kissed her again. A wild, unfettered kiss that left Linda without breath and without an anchor to the real world. If it wasn't for the wall and Marti's body, she'd be a puddle on the ground, held up only by the way he pressed her into the wall. Every piece of her skin, her veins, all the sensitive places, were alive in a way she'd never felt before. If this was what her sisters whispered about when they hinted that the marriage bed could be a marvellous place, she wanted all of it. All of Marti.

"I want you in me." She didn't know what that meant—not really —although she'd explored her own body at night, so she had some idea. But the desperation to have him inside her was a new fresh idea that she absolutely needed right now.

He hummed, then went right back to kissing her, but this time with a difference. He caressed his hands down over her dress, down past her waist to her hips, then slowly pulled the fabric up, bunching it around her waist until he had her drawers exposed. Perhaps doing this in a cupboard wasn't a great idea because now she wanted to see. It was too dark in here, all shadows, and she missed the way his cheeks might be flushed, like they sometimes did. She brushed her fingers along them, as if she could feel the heat on them, and she was about to protest that they move to his room when he cupped her mons.

She groaned, a deep guttural noise that he captured with his mouth. Her drawers were typical with no seam, and Marti took advantage, sliding his fingers along her wetness, just where she'd dreamed of his touch. He did something with his thumb and her whole body sang, making it impossible to keep any noise inside, so she pressed her mouth against his neck. A rolling pleasure tolled inside her and she wanted to make the same noise as the bells at church, calling out, but Marti's reminder that she needed to stay quiet rang in her head. She sucked on his skin, breathing heavily through her nose, as he played with her nubbin. Goodness, he was better at that than she was, each touch sending vibrations deeper inside her, and when he used his other hand to slid a finger or two inside her and pressed against her, she shook and shuddered, whimpering as the full force of her pleasure ripped through her. Waves of hot and cold washed over her skin like nothing she'd felt before. Oh, she'd done this to herself on many occasions, but having Marti touch her there and having Marti create this sensation duplicated the feelings to an overwhelming level. She buried her face against his neck as the waves faded into a heavy softness.

"Let me take you to your bed." Marti's whisper echoed around the cupboard. She didn't want to go out there, suddenly aware that people might know what they'd been doing. She swallowed, unable to do more than nod in the dark, where he probably couldn't see.

"Let me take care of you."

"What about you?" She didn't sound like herself, not with that raspy whimper.

"I'm great." He smoothed down her dress and opened the cupboard door a crack. "Come."

She let him hold her hand and pull her out into the hallway. The coal gas lights were bright and she blinked hard a few times, but there was no one around. Dazed, she followed him to his room, and when he closed the door, she smiled.

"Can we do that again?"

"Yes."

By rights, Marti should be nervous. He didn't like being naked in front of other people for good reason, but he knew—deep in his heart—that Linda wanted him just as he was.

"Can I be loud this time?"

Be still his beating heart. "Yes."

"And can I see you?" She reached out and brushed her finger across his cheekbone; the same way she had in the cupboard.

He held his breath for a moment. "Yes." And was glad he sounded more confident than he felt because he'd never done this in the light where someone could see all of him.

"Can I undress you?" That she would ask melted his anxiety a little, and he relaxed his shoulders. She'd known him as a child and she'd grown up in a strangely forward thinking pragmatic household. He swallowed, realising that he was justifying this to himself, but wasn't that what trust meant? Did he trust her to be kind and understanding. Yes. She had been so far.

"Yes." He stood still as she took off his jacket with more care than a valet would use. He scoffed. As if he would know what a valet might do.

"What's funny?"

"You'd make an excellent valet."

"No I wouldn't. Anyway, what do you know about valet duties?"

He grinned. "That's why I laughed." He helped her by taking the jacket and hanging it over the back of a chair. She untied a ribbon on her gown, shimmied her shoulders, and the whole thing fell to her feet, leaving her standing there in her stays and drawers.

"You are so beautiful." He couldn't look away, and reached up to take the pins out of her hair. She helped him, and their fingers tangled, brushing against each other, blending with the silky weight of her tresses, soft and smooth over his hands. Her red hair spilled around her face and he wished he could capture this moment forever. If only he could paint.

"I've left a mark on your neck." She kissed it softly.

"I don't mind. It'll remind me of this."

From there, they worked frantically together to remove clothing and fell together onto the bed. She didn't mention his binding, only helping him unwrap it to expose his small breasts. The brush of her fingers over his nipples had him crying out.

"You like that?"

"Yes." He hadn't let anyone else do this for him, but with her, it made sense. He cupped her much bigger breasts in his hands and bent his head to kiss them, loving the way she moaned and cried out his name. Her curiosity was his gain, as she did the same for him, and then stroked her hand down his stomach.

"Can I?"

"Please." Sensation overruled good sense, and when she slipped her fingers inside him—just like he'd done for her in the cupboard—his hips bucked up against her of their own accord. He grabbed her hand, guiding her to where he needed her touch, and soon he was riding her hand, crying out her name, and so very glad that she was here with him.

"Marti. Touch me too." She pulled one of his hands towards her and rolled them so they lay on their sides. Her slickness coated his fingers, filling the air with a combination of their musky aromas. He cried out—echoing her moans—not caring how loud he was, and he let pleasure consume him until he came with a shaky shout of her name, followed by a sigh from deep down in his lungs; an outlet in the aftermath.

He kissed her, conveying his thanks with his mouth because he wasn't able to form words.

"I think I'm going to like being married. Can we do this every day?"

The smile came unbidden. "Whenever you want."

"Tomorrow. Or will you make me wait until the wedding."

He shook his head. "There is no risk of children, so there is no reason to wait." Everything went cold, chilly and frigid, as if he'd jumped naked into a flurry of snow. If she wanted children, this marriage wasn't going to work.

"Good. I had hoped so but I wasn't completely certain."

"Good? You don't want children?" He held his breath.

"No. Definitely not." Her breath shuddered against his skin.

"You don't like children?"

She bit her lip. "I like children. I just don't want any of my own."

"Do you mind if I ask why not?" The shock of his initial worry wore off quickly with her certainty.

She raised one eyebrow. "I would think you just did. Ask me why not."

"You do mind?"

"I'm not sure." She covered her eyes with her hand. "If we are to marry, I suppose you should know." Another shuddery breath had his insides twisting around.

"I can wait until you are ready."

"It's fine." From the way she shook her head, he didn't think that was true. "Do you remember when my mother died? I was six, so you would've been still living next door."

He'd forgotten about that, having suppressed so many of his childhood memories. They weren't awful, they just didn't fit with who he was now, but since she mentioned it, the memory came rushing back. "I remember her funeral and everyone being in mourning. What happened?"

"She died in her childbed. I—" She sighed and he felt the breath all the way to his soul. "I don't want children because I don't want to chance leaving them motherless. I don't want to put a child of mine through that same pain."

He hugged her tight, stroking her hair. "If you stick with me, there's zero chance that you will become a mother by physical means."

"By physical means?" She pushed out of his hug and frowned at him. "What do you mean?"

"Doris and Edwin took me in when my parents died and they became my second parents, not the same but in some ways better as they accepted me. I love them like parents. I always assumed that one day I might return the favour to a child who needs a family."

"A child like us; someone who doesn't fit what society thinks we should do."

"Yes. Someone with unnatural desires." He voiced the commonly heard phrase for people like him, and perhaps like her, since she seemed very enthusiastic about his body.

She giggled. "Am I unnatural because I find all different types of people attractive? I thought everyone was like this and people just partnered up how society told them to because ..." She paused and rubbed her temple. "Oh dear. It's not very logical to assume that everyone is like me, when the evidence isn't there."

"Perhaps we can just enjoy each other without proclaiming it to the world." He lived in hope, never ending hope, when it came to her.

"Goodness. You are safe with me. Marry me and be my husband, hiding in plain sight."

He kissed her enthusiastically, then smiled. "Uncle Edwin used to say that too. If people are expecting to see a man, that's what they'll see."

"Perfect." She kissed him back, and soon enough, their hands explored each other's bodies again.

CHAPTER ELEVEN

They were married. Mr and Mrs Babbitt. Marti walked down the aisle of the church in a daze, stunned that this would be his life. He was married to Linda; the most beautiful accepting kind woman he'd ever met. She wore the most incredible gown—designed by Jacinda—and he couldn't wait to get it off her.

"Can you believe this?" Linda's smile glowed.

"Not really."

Her giggle washed over his skin, hugging him deep inside, and he wanted to keep this precious creature close to him forever. Oh gosh. He'd fallen in love with his wife.

"What is the matter?" Her grip on his forearm tightened.

"Nothing. How could anything be wrong on such a beautiful occasion?" They walked outside together and posed on the steps as one of the artists Mr Dexington had hired sketched their likeness. The entire day had more pomp and ceremony than he'd expected and for the Dexington family to pull this together in only three short weeks spoke volumes to their level of wealth. People spilled out the side doors of the church and rushed around to the front to cheer for them as they waited on the steps until the artist was ready for them to walk down to the waiting carriage.

"You are so handsome in this suit. The dark blue suits you immensely." Linda held out her hand and let him help her into the carriage. It wasn't until they were safely ensconced inside with the doors closed that she leaned forward and whispered in his ear.

"I wish to rip the whole thing off you and kiss you all over."

"You are insatiable, dear wife."

Her blush made her freckles stand out but it was her slow grin that made everything amazing. "Only for you, darling husband."

Taking chances with her had worked out well so far, so he swallowed and took another. "Is it gauche to have fallen in love with my wife?"

She pressed her hand to her decolletage, fingers splayed where he wanted to touch her, and gasped. "If it is, then we will have to be completely unfashionable together." She made it sound like they were ungovernable and he really wanted to see what Linda would achieve when she decided to change society.

"How so?"

"I believe myself to be in love with you also."

He waved his hand. "Wives are supposed to love their husbands. It's part of how the expectation."

"Oh, now you pull out the arrogant husband nonsense. After the legalities are done." But she winked, so he knew she was jesting him.

"Now you are stuck with me. A husband who adores you, loves you, and will support you in all your unfashionable endeavours."

She swallowed, the colour on her cheeks deepening to a dark blush. "You love me? How can you be so certain?"

"I've never been more certain of anything in my life. From the moment I saw your spine stiffen as you walked down the road away from me, I knew that I had to know everything about you. And the more time I spend with you, the more I adore you." The more he wanted to worship her and see her thrive.

"Oh, do tell me more. After all, I am the spoiled daughter of a wealthy man. I do so like to hear about all my good qualities." That she used sarcasm at this moment was perfect because he'd come to learn that it was her way of grappling with too many feelings. Sometimes those feelings were anger at how society expected her to withhold her opinions, and sometimes—he hoped now was one of them—she brushed away feelings that overwhelmed her in a good way.

"I adore the way you cope with the unfairness of the world, how you acknowledge being jealous of men and the way they rule everything, and how you do that without blaming all men for your woes, only the ones who deserve it. I adore the way you hide your insecurities with a smile, always finding kindness for others, and I know how much you worry about being abandoned by the people you love. I—" He didn't get a chance to finish as she jumped into his lap and kissed him. It was several minutes until he breathed again, and then the carriage lurched as the horses leaned into their harness and pulled them away from the church back towards the Dexington house.

"And I love the way you see all my faults and still seem to like me anyway," Linda said.

"What is love but an understanding that someone isn't perfect, and loving all their imperfections regardless?" Marti was the luckiest man in the world.

She cupped his cheeks and grinned. "Are you admitting to imperfections?"

"You know I have many."

"Yes, you are a tyrant of a man. Demanding my attention and adoration while giving nothing in return."

"Excuse me?" He didn't think that was true, but then she winked again.

"Oh, you jest. Linda. One day your sarcasm will come back and bite you, and I will be here for you, to patch up the teeth marks and make sure your joy is never dimmed."

She kissed him again. "Is that the meaning of true love?"

"I think so."

"Then I will be your wife and protect you for the harshness of the world, and people will only ever see you as a man. I will take the blame for our unfortunate infertility. I will be the best wife to my loving husband and the world will see you as you are. Truly you because I love you exactly as you are and I want everyone to know."

"Even when there are too many people and I need some time away."

"Yes. Go and brush your horse and leave the hoards to me." For her to understand that his need for peace and quiet wasn't all about needing to protect his identity was beautiful. He found crowds over-whelming, always had, even as a child.

"I will just tell them; Oh Mr Babbitt is the practical one around here. I'm just here to smile and look pretty while he does the actual work. He's the one you need to thank."

He kissed her on the forehead, a soft loving kiss that demonstrated his feelings more than anything else could. "I can't believe your father is going to buy us a coaching inn for our wedding present."

"I told you that he wanted you to dream big. He respects lofty goals."

"I wouldn't be able to do it without you."

She shoved him on the shoulder and laughed, tipping her head back and exposing her throat for him to kiss. "That's the entire point, my darling. Now let's go to bed before we prepare for our tour."

They planned to spend the next couple of months staying in every coaching inn within the region, and then Mr Dexington would purchase the one they wanted.

1814

. . .

Tomorrow would mark one year since they'd owned The Delicate Owl in London on the main coaching road to Manchester and Marti had become accustomed to hiding in plain sight, as Linda had said once. Being married to Linda and owning an inn worked. Everyone knew him as Mr Babbitt and never questioned it. It was incredible how people saw what was shown to them and that was it. The gift Linda had given him was more than just love; it was acceptance of himself and a place where he could be himself without worry. She would always protect him, and their love continued to grow every day that they worked and lived and loved together. They'd been married for sixteen months now—she'd worn the most incredible gown which she still put on for him every now and then—and every day was better than the one before.

"Oh there you are, Marti. Would you be so good as to help Mike hang the bunting along the front windows." Linda had worked so hard on their big one year celebration that would take place tomorrow.

"Soon." Marti pulled her into the linen cupboard. "Remember..."

"Our first time together."

"There's only one problem."

"What's that?"

"We've never done it in our linen cupboard." He kissed her, pushing her up against the wall of the cupboard. "Remember. You can't make a noise, or everyone will know what we've been doing."

"Goodness, we can't have the entire inn thinking that you are in love with your wife, Mr Babbitt."

He smiled, then kissed her because it was often the only way he could stop her from teasing him. He loved being teased by her, but he loved kissing her more. He was the luckiest man in the world and he used his tongue to show his wife just how much he adored and worshipped her.

A knock on the door. "Mr and Mrs Babbitt. Mr Dexington has arrived."

"Damn. I told you to be quiet!" Linda laughed, and the sound echoed around the cupboard and all the way into Marti's soul.

If you enjoyed this book, you'll love the rest of the DESIRING THE DEXINGTONS series, beginning with LOVE WASN'T BUILT IN A DAY.
A friends to lovers gay Regency romance with a delicious slow burn.

Humphrey Dexington wants his best friend, and colleague, to be happy in love. With him, preferably. After accidentally reading a letter written by David to a former lover, Humphrey realises his own love for David would forever remain unrequited. It's time to finally move on and let David find someone to love who would stick by him. If he couldn't have David, at least David could have the man who he sent such poignant letters to.

Humphrey invites David and his lover to the Soho Club for an evening together, but when David's lover doesn't show, it might just give Humphrey the chance he's always wanted.

Engineer David Mattson doesn't have time for love. Grand engineering projects dominate his life, and he spends most of the year travelling to supervise the works. When his last affair ended, he decided that was it. Love wasn't for him. He'd never find someone who wanted to share the life he adored, who would travel with him, and care as deeply for every detail of every bridge and drain and lock.

. . .

Slowly, David realises that person has been beside him, loyal to him and his beloved engineering, for the past decade. All he needs is to be brave enough to say yes to Humphrey's love.

Sign up to my newsletter for freebies and more updates on the Dexingtons, as well as the rest of Renee's books.

ACKNOWLEDGMENTS

I pay my respects to the Wangal people of the Eora Nation, who are the traditional owners of the land on which this book was written.

Thank you to Lina, the Word Makers, the Carina discord, and Ebony's anthology groups. You've all championed this series and your support has kept me writing during a difficult year in my personal life.

AUTHOR NOTES

I sold the names for this book in a charity auction. They were purchased by Linda Parks who wanted the main character to be named in honour of her wife, Marti Babbitt.

"The reason I bid was not for my name, but for my wife, Marti Babbitt, who passed in March 2021 from metastatic non-smoker's lung cancer. In recent years, she was a beta reader for Jaycie Morrison. She was an audio proofer and cover proofer for Bold Strokes. Marti was one of the women honored last year at the GCLS zoom conference in the group of people that had passed.

We were together 37 years. Marti was a wonderful person, full of wit and humor and could entertain and draw people to her. She was a loyal friend and did everything she could for people and animals in need. We had a love that many people said they envied, and some said they'd never witnessed. She had an infectious and warm smile and that is one of the many things people say they miss. She was warm and genuine and kind. At Marti's memorial service, Jaycie commented, "Marti would give you the shirt off her back, but if you tried to take it, she'd shoot you." She was fiercely protective of me, our animals and friends and those that needed her." Linda Parks

What an absolute honour to use Marti's name for this character. The real life Marti wasn't a trans man, however, this is fiction, and I let the story go where it took me.

It wasn't until I started writing this novella that I researched the origins of the surname Babbitt, and it refers to the region in Suffolk, UK, known as the Hundred of Babegh, which means Babb's enclosure. Babba is an old personal name meaning protector, which was a lovely coincidence to discover for this character.

The name Linda comes from the German Linde, relating to the Linden tree, and became popular in 1803 when it was the main character in Jean Paul's Titan. It has a modern feel but definitely would've been fashionable during the Regency.

The Gas Lighting and Coke Company was established in 1792 and gas lighting in homes slowly became used by rich people after that.

Owl or owling as slang to mean carrying out illegal activities at night dates from 1540. The inn's name was chosen to be a mix of the two characters – a naïve socialite beauty (seen by society as delicate) and a highwayman or owl.

ABOUT RENÉE DAHLIA

An avid reader, Renée Dahlia writes contemporary and historical queer romance. Renée is a bisexual cis woman who is fascinated by people and loves to explore human relationships, with a side of humour, through her writing. Renée has a degree in physics and mathematics, using this to write data-based magazine articles for the horse racing industry. Her love of horses often shines through in her fiction, and she loves a good intrigue and to escape the real world in the pages of a book. When she isn't reading or writing, Renée spends her time with her four children, usually watching them play cricket.

ALL BOOKS BY RENÉE DAHLIA

Thanks for reading THE HIGHWAYMAN'S SURPRISE BRIDE. I hope you enjoyed it. Reviews can help readers find books, and I am grateful for all honest reviews. Thank you for taking the time to let others know what you've read, and what you thought. If you write a review for (title) and email me (renee at reneedahlia dot com) with the link, I will send you a free copy of one of my books of your choice.

If you'd like to know more about me, my books, or to connect with me online, you can visit my webpage www.reneedahlia.com and if you sign up to my newsletter, you can grab a free book.

Twitter https://twitter.com/dekabat
Facebook https://www.facebook.com/reneedahliawriter/
Instagram https://www.instagram.com/reneedahlia_author/
Patreon https://www.patreon.com/reneedahlia
BookBub https://www.bookbub.com/authors/renee-dahlia

PRETTY FIGURES

HEIDI WESSMAN KNEALE

Lady Christina's hoping to escape her past. Lord Anthony's yearning for inspiration. Could they become each other's salvation, or will their dark secrets tear them apart?

When Lady Christina Harrington steals a carriage in an attempt to escape the evil Mr Fawdon, she didn't expect it to come with bonus baggage. When she discovers she's absconded with Lord Anthony Southerland, she had no idea he came with a deep secret.

Lord Anthony's secret life as the sculptor of the famously collectable Southern Figurines was about to come to a whimpering end. He'd feared inspiration had abandoned him, until his life was shaken up by Lady Christina, stirring him once more.

Yet a sinister force threatens to tear them apart when a powerful man threatens to spill Christina's own dark secrets.

I've opted with Australian spelling, which imitates UK spelling, somewhat.

. . .

•Content/ trigger warnings

Threats of physical/sexual violence from Fawdon (unrealised) and some emotional manipulative situations from the Marquess of Lindsey.

CHAPTER ONE

Viscountess Brackley tut-tutted over the state of her youngest son. In spite of the bouncing of the carriage, she reached over with a thumb to wipe away at an imaginary smudge on his cheek. Lord Anthony Southerland's hand itched to bat away his mother's hand. Really. He was no longer a boy. He could keep his own face clean. "I look presentable enough," he muttered. Combed his hair and everything. He tugged at the cuffs of his coat. In his clothing he looked fine.

Clothing was like art, in its colour and shape. At least in that, his mother could not complain. He'd always dressed well.

His fingernails, on the other hand, would have sent his mother into hysterics. No matter how hard he tried, he could never get the clay out of his cuticles. Thank providence for gloves.

You know who didn't care what his hands looked like? The daughter of the Earl of Strathaven. In fact, she cared nothing at all for him. Not in a bad way, of course. There was not a single character flaw in Anthony that could possibly give offence. If anything, the best it could be said about him was he was a quiet lad, er, man. The worst that could be said about him, in any given social situation, was dull.

Those were young Lady Jane Strathaven's words. "You are such a dull person." Said it straight to his face. At least she had the honour to be forthright with him.

Even if it had stung a little.

Wasn't his fault. Well, not entirely. He'd gone out with his brothers earlier in the Season, tried the gambling hells, tried drinking, racing, all the usual vices expected of a lord, and found little interest in it. Except for a few small wins (for he was good at cards), at the end of the evening he'd had nothing to show for it.

How empty he'd felt. None of it had given him any satisfaction.

Now, art. That kept him alive. Not so much the appreciation, but the creation. Painting, not so much, for he couldn't seem to master the finer points of rendering colours in their true forms. But sculpture, that he loved. Let him dig his strong hands into the clay. Let him pound it hard, smooth it, form it, and create something truly beautiful. At least when he was finished, he had something to show for it.

Lady Jane didn't care. Art was not her thing. Oh, she could sing passably, tinkle at the piano, loved dancing, and claimed to have an adequate portfolio of pastoral watercolours. But that was it. She didn't do it because she loved it. She did it because it was expected of her. For her, art was one of those things one got out of the way. There were far better delights for this debutante than the solitary pursuits.

Anthony took a risk. "She does not love me," he stated to his mother.

Viscountess Brackley paused in her rustling through her reticule. "What?"

"Lady Jane. She does not love me. I certainly don't interest her."

His mother drew a breath. "The Earl of Strathaven is an important political figure, one your grandfather has been courting for years."

"I do not see how my courting his daughter will sweeten his attitude towards Grandfather."

"And this is why you are not in politics. If you were, you'd understand." She waved her hand dismissively. "No matter. It's not you on the bench. You don't have to understand in order to offer for the chit."

Anthony drew in a breath and held his counsel. He'd love nothing better than to tell his mother he didn't want to offer for the chit. Familial obligation was not the best way to persuade someone to vote a certain way in Parliament. Besides, didn't politics change from year to year, anyway? What if the Duke of Southerland and the Earl of Strathaven both decided they wanted nothing to do with each other? Then what? Where would be value be in Anthony's marriage then?

It was not as if Lady Jane was some sort of prize. Rather, she was some sort of alliance. If the Duke and the Earl did line up, it would have little to do with the young couple. And if they didn't, then he and Lady Jane were stuck with each other until death parted them. Either way, they would be shoved together, then abandoned.

That was not a reason for marriage.

The carriage came to a stop. They'd arrived and Anthony groaned. This would not work the way his mother hoped. His making an offer would not convince an Earl to capitulate on his political beliefs.

His mother shoved a handkerchief into his hands. "Here. Clean yourself up. You have dirt on your cheek."

Did he? He reached up and scrubbed a gloved hand over his right cheek.

"No, the other cheek." The footman opened the carriage door and helped the Viscountess to descend. Anthony remained behind to make himself presentable, not that it mattered.

The coach bounced again, as the coachman descended.

If only Anthony had a looking glass, he could see to what dirt his mother referred. He wouldn't put it past himself to have a dab of clay on his cheek.

The coach bounced again as someone mounted the box.

"H-yah!" cried out a feminine voice. A whip cracked and the horses bolted. "Yah!" she cried again, before the carriage bolted, driving Anthony back into the seat.

What on earth? As the carriage bounded forward, the door

slammed shut, blocking out the shouts of surprise from those who were outside the carriage.

As for himself, what just happened?

Lady Christina Harrington ducked into an alleyway and paused, catching her breath. Fawdon was an arse! He deserved every bad thing that had come his way.

Nevertheless, he was coming her way, and fast. Who knew such a fat, lazy son of a whore could run so fast?

At least it was only him. Had it not been for her maid Abigail, no doubt his servant or friend, or whoever was with him, would have caught her for sure.

Lady Christina knew one thing: if Fawdon caught her, things would not go well.

Not well at all.

Once he learned that she refused to relinquish the game's winnings, she had no doubt he would carry out the awful threats he'd whispered in her ear the other night at the party. A woman did not need to be a willing participant for the acts of a man to ruin her reputation. Even the description alone made her shudder. He shared, in very exquisite detail, how he would spoil her, how he would beat her, and what he planned to do between her thighs.

He'd muttered them again today, just outside the solicitor's office, before he'd met with her and the Marquess of Lindsey. Legally and morally, Fawdon had lost the right to his final property in that card game. To threaten her, to attempt to frighten her, to giving it back before it could be legally transferred to her was beyond the pale. At least her brother had been there at the time to warn him off. A shame about after. (Assuming she survived this, her now-absent brother and she were going to have Words.)

Perspiration formed on her brow and darkened the seams of her gown. How dare he make her run? Granted, the alternative was much worse.

Her thoughts went out to Abigail. The poor thing didn't deserve what happened. Christina prayed that Abigail was not now being subjected to the terrible acts Fawdon had threatened her. If anything, she hoped he'd see her as nothing more than a servant, to be forgotten and discarded.

His target was her.

Once the stitch in her side had eased up somewhat, she hastened down the mews, turned a corner and emerged into a fine square.

Where was she? Not that she had time to get her bearings. Smoothing her hair, for her bonnet had disappeared during the chase, she tried not to run down the street. Such an action would surely draw attention and possibly delay.

A few carriages rumbled along the cobblestones, for it was the time more genteel folk went calling. How easy their lives must be, to have no other worries than what gown one was to wear and who to call on first?

Christina always chose to visit those who offered the best refreshments first, lest prior visitors take the best cakes and leave her with tepid cucumber sandwiches. If a hostess couldn't manage a decent spread to save her life, then it didn't matter if Christina arrived early or late. The pickings would be the same--sad.

If she survived the day.

She would not have put it past Fawdon to kill her after he'd taken his violent revenge. He'd been made a bloody fool. It wasn't her fault. She was just as much a victim as he.

Unlike her, though, he deserved it. Imagine, refusing to honour his debt! What had Lindsey said that forced Fawdon to actually show up to the solicitor's? She would not have put it past Fawdon to not show up. She would have waved away the *faux pas* and hoped she never saw him again.

But he had, thought it seemed against his will. All the properties he'd lost in that game had been transferred to their new owners: Lindsey claimed the lion's share and she got her one.

She owned a property now! Not her father, or her brothers, but her. In her name. An actual, rent-collecting property, somewhere out in the country.

Wealth of her own, apparently.

But now, Christina needed to get home and she needed to fire off some urgent letters to her brothers. Fawdon had gone too far in today's earlier attack. Something had to be done by those who could solve the solution permanently.

Drat. She'd lost her reticule in their initial struggle. So much for coin to pay for a hack. So much for her small knife with which she could have defended herself.

Oh, for a sabre! If she had been a man, she could have challenged the fool the moment he insulted her in public. She would have run him through and rid the world of the vermin.

But Christina had to survive today.

A shout from the alleyway chilled her bones. "CHRISTINA HARRINGON!" Fawdon roared.

He'd found her.

Damn. Could she not lose the man?

Not too far from where she'd emerged, stood a small private carriage with some sort of family crest on the door. The footman had just handed some fat lady out and helped her up the steps of a residence. The coachman had climbed down from the box to attend to one of the horses.

It was the best chance she had.

Christina dashed to the carriage, hauled herself up to the box, and, in spite of the coachman's surprised cursing, freed the reigns and cried out, "H-yah!" She grabbed the whip and cracked it over the back of the horses, startling them.

The coachman fell back, away from the flying hooves, as the coach lurched forward. "Yah!" Fly, horses. Fly!

Thank providence her brothers had taught her to drive.

The horses leapt under her command and the carriage flew down the square, leaving a very angry Fawdon shaking both fists at her. If her hands weren't needed to drive this coach, she would have spared him at least one finger in reply.

Off she drove, leaving her angry pursuer behind.

She may have escaped for now, but the business was not over. Not by a long shot.

A carriage. What choice did she have? If there had been a single horse, that would have been preferred. With a horse, she could have gotten away much quicker, maybe even ridden Fawdon down, but one did not always have a choice when pursued by an angry, vengeful man.

First priority: get away.

Second priority: find a brother, raise a small army, and deal with the problem permanently.

Only once she'd driven far enough that Fawdon couldn't pursue her on foot did Christina slow down. Carriage horses weren't meant for racing along the streets of London. Even now, the right horse laboured in its breathing. Poor thing. She slowed until they came to another square. Only then, did she bother to stop, driving them to a fountain in the middle. She applied the brake. Both horses hung their heads and caught their breath. She hoped they were all right.

Maybe they weren't. Coachmen rarely left the box, unless there was a good reason.

This coachman had left his box. He'd been tending to the horses. Granted, she'd not looked too closely at what he was doing-- inspecting a hoof, or checking his mouth, or whatever it was coachmen did when a horse had a problem.

Now what? Christina didn't recognise the square in which she'd arrived. Not good to be lost. If she hadn't damaged the horses, maybe she could drive the carriage around until she recognised a street. Then she could set off for the nearest brother and get this whole mess cleared up. At the very least, she needed to find Abigail and pray she was safe.

A sharp rapping came from the carriage, startling her.

In surprise, she threw open the top hatch to peer into the carriage.

There, she found a rather fashionable young man sprawled against the back seat of the carriage. As soon as the light from top hatch fell upon him, he looked up. "Who are you?" he asked.

Christina blinked. No once had it occurred to her the carriage was occupied.

Had she just absconded with someone?

CHAPTER TWO

To Anthony's surprise, when the top hatch opened, a young lady peered in. Her curls bounced and she blinked.

"Oh, hello!" She seemed just as surprised as Anthony.

A woman drove his coach? Where was John Coachman? He repeated his question. "Who are you?"

"Me?" Had his question confused her? She mused it over. "I suppose you should ask," more to herself, than him.

She closed the hatch. The carriage bounced as she descended. Soon, his coach door opened, and she invited him out.

Was that safe?

"Come on," she said. "I promise I won't bite." She amended, "Well, not unless you ask me to."

What kind of creature had stolen his carriage? She had to be a thief, for what else could explain her actions?

Wait. Thieves never worked alone. What if she had accomplices? What if they laid in wait to rob him of his worldly possessions? "No, thank you. I don't think I shall." He was better off inside the carriage. If they were to attack him, they'd have to come in one at a time. Those were better odds.

Instead of trying to cajole him out, she climbed into the carriage with him.

This was a thief? This young lady wore the latest in daytime fashion, albeit sans bonnet. Her curly blonde hair looked as if it had had an argument with the bonnet and came off second best, before the bonnet fled in disgust.

At least she wore gloves. The young lady let out a breath of relief. "I thank you for the loan of your carriage. You have rescued me from a fate worse than death. Or possibly death itself."

Anthony had no idea of what she was talking about. What rescue? If anyone needed rescuing, it was him.

"Ah, I know you now," she said. "You're one of Southerland's get. How many of you are there?"

He stiffened. Just because he had five other brothers didn't mean that he had to be lumped in as a set. "I have a name."

She sat back and regarded him. "And if you are out in Society, I have probably heard it." She leaned forward to study him. "Don't tell me, let me see if I remember."

The scrutiny to which she subjected him made him self-conscious. He scrubbed at his cheek. Was the clay mark still there?

"Not Jacob, not Jonathan... You must be Anthony." She sat back in triumph. "You have to be, for all the others are too old for me to bother remembering."

Interesting. This had to be the first time he was remembered while his other brothers were forgotten.

If only he could return the favour. "I fear you have the advantage of me."

She gave this some thought. "If we have met before, I should feel insulted you don't remember. If we haven't met before, then how awkward, for it is not the thing to introduce oneself. Terribly gauche." She sank back into more thought.

Anthony was at a loss. What did one say to a strange young lady?

The carriage gave a lurch as the horses moved forward. The young lady cursed under her breath and climbed out of the carriage.

Anthony followed, for what else was there to do?

Outside, the horses had simply moved forward to reach the fountain.

It seemed they had come to a stop in a central square of fine town-houses and other buildings, having come through the gate of the park in the middle, all the way up to the fountain.

It wasn't that big a fountain, topped by what looked to be a statue of King George I. The horses didn't care; after their run, they were more interested in the water that flowed beneath His late Majesty.

His abductor looked about the square, then spread her arms and twirled about, head thrown back. "I'm free," she exulted, laughing at the sky. The hem of her skirt flared out, showing quite a bit of stockinged ankle. "I can't believe that worked."

Anthony did not share her enthusiasm. "What worked? Absconding with my carriage?"

Only then did she come to the realisation that she was not alone. Her eyes sparkled and her fair cheeks took on a rosy hue. "Escaping from a madman." The thought of said madman sobered her somewhat. "I do apologise for the liberties I've taken. There was a bit of an urgency."

Urgency indeed! What else could persuade a young lady to take off with a carriage? That said, that was exhilarating. Since when had his heart beat so hard? Was this the adventure his brothers kept trying to pull him into? Or was debauchery a poor excuse for true fulfilment?

"Why were you escaping from a madman?" He had to ask the question. Even if the insane carriage ride, however brief, was the only bit of adventure he was to have, at least there should be a good story attached.

The young woman went over to the horses and inspected them. "Because he's a misogynistic coward who is taking his anger out on me, and not on the true author of his woe."

Anthony leaned against the carriage. "And who is that?"

"Himself, mainly. But really, the Marquess of Lindsey, who's a bit of an ass, though not as much as Fawdon."

Such candour! Did all young ladies speak like this, or only those prone to adventure? Lady Jane had never let such language cross her lips. Then again, she'd never spoken with such passion about anything. Certainly, never against any peer of the realm.

"I must ask again, who are you, to be able to express such opinions without fear--that is, may I have your name?" Oh, that sounded stupid.

"Lady Christina Harrington. I am reminding you of my name, for of course, we've met before." Her pointed gaze lent much gravity to her possibly incorrect statement. No gentleman of good manners would dare contradict her, and therefore, any awkwardness over having never actually meeting before was to be swept under the rug.

"Ah yes. I remember," even though he didn't.

Or did he? Harrington. That name was familiar. Drat him for not bothering to have an interest in *ton* gossip.

Maybe that was for the best, for any gossip could not bode her reputation well, and if her reputation was stellar, he would have heard nothing.

Besides, why would he not want to further his acquaintance with her?

Lady Christina was quite a striking figure, when not madly barrelling a coach down London roads. She was quite tall, far too tall for fashion, and while she properly sported gloves, her bonnet was quite missing. Maybe she'd lost it in her frantic dash from a madman? Her clothing spoke of wealth and her face was more than fair to look at. Indeed, her bosom heaved quite attractively. Her blue eyes sparkled and those lips...

No, they could not have met before, for he should have remembered such a beauty. Especially one who almost matched his own lanky height.

Dainty girls were the fashion. Lady Christina was anything but dainty. Goodness, she handled those horses as if born to an equestrian house.

She sighed and gave up looking over the horses. "I confess I know little about horses. I do hope they were not damaged."

Maybe not. How could someone drive a carriage like that and not know about horses? "Where did you learn to drive?"

"My brothers." She bit her lip. "I... was quite the adventuress when I was younger. Instead of trying to quash my spirit, my older brothers saw fit to harness my, um... adventuresome spirit, and taught me all manner of things, in hopes that it would burn off my penchant for trouble."

"Did it work?" Again with the stupid questions!

"Perhaps." She looked about the square, a frown marring her features. "Or maybe I had outgrown my coltishness, but not before it got me into trouble."

Anthony caught a whiff of regret. "Did you do something wrong?"

Her gaze flickered to his. "Me? No. If it wasn't for the tutelage of my brothers, however, things could have gone terribly, terribly wrong."

She looked back to the horses. "I suppose we ought to get you home."

For some reason, that depressed him. Why? He didn't mind going home, usually.

But until today he'd not met anyone that made him want to not go home. "Do we have to?"

She shrugged. "I was thinking more of the horses."

He came forward, not that he was any better a judge of horses either. "Is something wrong with them?"

"Possibly," she admitted. "Your coachman didn't get down for no reason."

He sighed. She was right, as far as he could tell. Best they got the horses home. Only one problem. He didn't know how to drive a coach. "I guess I couldn't prevail upon you to drive us home?"

She lifted a shoulder and turned away. "I... I don't know where we are."

Anthony perked up. "Oh, that's easy. We're in Leicester Square."

That didn't buoy her up.

"What's wrong?" he asked.

"I can't navigate. I couldn't find my way home even if it was just around the corner."

That surprised him. He thought everyone knew their way home, unless, "Are you not from London?"

She confessed, "I've lived here my whole life."

"So how do you not know where you are, or where to go?" He didn't mean it to sound so cruel.

Lady Christina didn't take offense. "Why would I? It's not like a lady of my class walks anywhere. We're always bundled into carriages and taken wherever. We know where we're going. It's not like we've ever needed to know how to get there. We simply say, 'Piccadilly,' or 'Mayfair', and the coachman takes us there." She fiddled with her gloves. "I never expected to be the coachman."

Her confession sobered him. "How did you learn to drive, then? Where did you learn?"

She offered him a shy smile. "Hyde Park, round and round. But my brothers were never game to let me drive on the streets."

The rushing of blood from Anthony's head made him feel faint. "You mean... that was the first time driving through the streets of London?" Oh my, they could have been in an accident, or worse.

She only gave him a self-conscious smile.

Now what?

"I can drive, if you can navigate. I trust you know how to get home?"

He did.

But was that such a good idea?

When one wasn't being pursued by a madman, driving a coach could be a rather sedate activity. Practically enjoyable.

Why had Christina never learned how to get around London? Aside of it not being a necessary skill for a lady. Granted, moving through London's narrow streets was nothing like racing around Hyde Park in a curricle. At least she could handle a pair of horses.

She had the fascinating Lord Anthony Southerland to direct her. "Turn right at the next intersections. Through past this crossroads. Left after this shop." Kept her wits about her, and she wasn't doing too poorly.

He had an honest curiosity about her, which she found refreshing. It was as if he was interested in her, for her sake, and not because he was trying to woo her over, or thinking she was a prize to be won.

A brief shudder at the thought of the Marquess of Lindsey. While not quite as bad as Fawdon, he wasn't exactly a prize himself.

Nor was she.

If anything, Lord Anthony could be a little too direct. "So, why were you running away from a madman? What did you do to raise his ire so?"

She sighed. "I won the last of his property from him during a card game. I did not intend to, but to not win that hand would have been most disastrous for me."

"If he put up property, what had you put up?"

She inhaled. Should she tell him the whole story? She'd not even told her brothers the whole tale. They'd certainly call out the Marquess for sure. And he, was he a good shot, or would he have found some other devious way of getting around the challenge?

For that was how she had been caught.

In for a penny, in for a pound. "Several weeks ago, I was at a party thrown by the Cumberlands. As the night wore on, I found the company had become less, ah, shall we say, enlightened? But my brothers were not yet ready to leave, something about a deal they wanted to make. I don't know. They could have been arranging a picnic for all I knew.

"So I spent the next few hours avoiding the punch and wandering around bored. Anyone who was considered good company had long quit the party and only the harder society remained. Demimonde, second sons, anyone who had more reasons to remain, than to simply be seen for five minutes.

"Eventually I gave up finding something to engage in and took to watching others fleece each other in cards."

He guided her for the next turn. "Down this street, and we'll be home," he said.

So soon? But she'd only begun her story. "Now, I don't mind the occasional friendly wager--penny points and all that--but now the stakes were getting high. No way was I going to join a table." At least her brothers had taught her that much. As soon as the stakes went beyond pin money, you abandoned the tables, no matter how lucky you were feeling.

"One particularly heavy game featured the Marquess of Lindsey against a greasy piece of work named Mister Fawdon."

Lord Anthony wrinkled his nose. "I know of him. Can't say I've had the bad luck to meet him."

"Keep it that way," Christina replied. At least she didn't have to explain who he was. "Anyhow, he'd been going up against Lindsey and not doing too well. Kept wanting to "recoup his losses", fool's errand that it was.

"Then Lindsey saw me."

She hesitated. This part she'd never told anyone. Even Fawdon had never mentioned it during their business dealings. Had he even seen what had happened before Christina took the seat, or had he been so wrapped up in his revenge he missed it?

She'd not realised she'd drifted off until Lord Anthony nudged her. "And? What happened next?"

Christina shuddered. She'd been there, a veritable wallflower, watching the game until Lindsey saw her.

It was not the first time he'd noticed her in Society. She wished he'd never seen her. Lindsey had a wife. Any attention he'd paid to Christina was not honourable.

Lindsey had made a show of rising from the table, threating to quit while he was ahead. Fawdon begged him for one more chance to earn his winnings back. Lindsey mocked him--openly mocked him--telling him he'd been a fish in a barrel, and it would be cruel to deprive him of all his wealth.

That was the wrong thing to say to Fawdon. In anger he rose up, nearly knocking the table over, and demanded one more hand.

But Lindsey wasn't done mocking him. "You are so pathetic, even a woman could beat you." That's when Lindsey's gaze fell on Christina. He smiled at her, coldly, lustfully.

Before she could slip away, he reached out and snagged her by the arm, pulling her close. "I'll make you a wager, my dear," he purred in her ear. "Play this last hand. If you win, I keep everything I've wagered. You may claim the rest."

Coldness ran up her spine. "And if I lose?"

"You accept my *carte blanche*."

If she had been any other innocent debutante, she would have slapped him there and then, before dashing away from such a wicked offer. But she was not an innocent debutante. How much did the Marquess of Lindsey know? Surely nothing. But maybe he suspected, or he would not have offered as he did.

Christina found herself seated at the table, the chair still warm from Lindsey's bottom. No escaping now. If he knew something that could be used against her, to flee now would all but give him permission to call her out. Ruin her.

She had been such a fool in her younger days. Even just learning unladylike skills could be enough to get her banned from Society. She'd done worse.

Time to play.

Christina looked across the table to the fop of a man who had part-nered Lindsey. Lindsey had been the one making the contracts and the fop had done little else but play the dummy. Fawdon's partner, to her left, had been a portly man Christina had never met. While he had no cup nearby, the ruddy bloom across his nose did not speak well regarding his sobriety. No wonder Fawdon had lost, if this was his partner for whist.

Christina consulted her cards, counted up the value of her hand. Sixteen points. Strong hand. She opened her bid: Two points. Best to let her fop partner know what she had.

This stirred the crowd. To bid Two was rather bold. But what good did it do her to suggest a weak hand?

Fawdon's partner bid Three.

The fop bid Four. Christina stared at him, but the fop wasn't looking at her, but over her head; Lindsey stood behind her, his hand on the back of her chair, his fingers toying lightly against her back. Bold man, to assume he'd win either way.

Christine also realised that Lindsey could see her hand. She drew a breath. He and the fop were cheating. Lindsey was using her to lure Fawdon and his portly partner into a false sense of hubris.

Fawdon, likewise, didn't have his gaze on Christina, but on Lind-sey. "Four," he bid.

Rumbles of opinion rolled through the observers. Lindsey's finger slid ever so delicately up her back, to linger on her neck. She shook off the distraction. "Six," she bid, hoping that the fop had bid a true hand of at least twelve points.

The drunk to her left passed. After a moment, the fop dropped his gaze and also passed.

But Fawdon... Fawdon didn't bid. He scowled at his cards. A bid of Six was a Small Slam. Only a bid of Seven was left, claiming one could take all the tricks of the game. No way Fawdon could do that, even if he was a madman. Her opening bid of Two told everyone that she felt confident to win several hands.

Fawdon passed, which was the only logical choice.

But that put her in a quandary. In order to win, she'd have to take all but one trick. For Fawdon to win, he'd have to take but two tricks, not a difficult task, if one had sufficient strength in one's hand to bid in the first place.

The fop laid out his dummy hand. To Christina's delight, he held at least two Kings, two Queens and one Ace, complimenting the other Kings and Aces she had in her hand. If she played this right, it would be a bloodbath.

Now that the cards were down, all the wagers went into the middle. Lindsey leaned over her to deposit several folded pieces of paper into the centre of the table. Fawdon scrawled something on a scrap of paper and threw it into the middle. But these weren't pennies. They weren't even crowns. It was all paper. Paper points?! She turned around to scowl at Lindsey. The Marquess returned her scowl with a smug look.

Had she been swindled for mere paper points? She had half a mind to tip the entire table and huff off.

Then a metallic sound reached her ears.

The fop had dropped a jewelled stickpin onto the stack of paper. The drunk dropped what looked like bank notes.

What on earth was going on?

Only way to find out: win the hand.

Between the cards the fop had dummied out, and Christina's careful balancing of her low cards against his high, it was the blood-bath she'd predicted. As she laid out the last trick--Seven to them--the crowd erupted in a cheer.

A loud rush filled her ears, and spots appeared before her eyes. "Well done," someone greasy murmured in her ear. "I'm almost sorry you didn't lose." The Marquess.

Her vision cleared as Lindsey scooped all the winnings her direction. He selected out the bits of paper he'd contributed. "These are mine. The rest is yours, my dear," he said. "I hope we can play again sometime."

Not if she could help it.

The conviviality of the crowd was brought short when Fawdon slammed his hands on the table. "You bitch!" he shouted.

Everyone fell silent.

The fop rose. The drunk looked up, bemused.

Lindsey ushered her up and away from the table. "Now, now," he tossed to Fawdon. "You lost fair and square." His voice grew cold. "Take your losses like a man."

"I'm not losing to a woman," Fawdon spat. He reached for the winnings in front of Christina, but the Marquess' walking stick came down hard on his hand. "You didn't lose to a woman. You lost to a lady. And you. will. honour. your. wager." To Christina, he said, "Gather your winnings, my dear. I think it is time we left the party."

We? Who was this we? Christina looked about. Surely the Marquess wasn't going to demand Fawdon honour his wager, and then renege on his deal with Christina?

She spotted her brother Michael, who had just entered the room. As soon as he saw Lindsey, he strode over, fire in his eyes. "I say--" he started, but Lindsey let go of Christina's shoulder.

"Harrington! There you are! Have we a tale to tell you."

And in about two breaths, Lindsey told him all about Christina's win.

Michael said nothing, so stunned he was. His gaze turned to Christina. "You were gambling? With what? These are high-stakes games."

Lindsey interrupted him before he could drag Christina away. "Now, now, I was more than happy to front her wagers, and she earned every cent."

Michael drew himself up tall, just a few inches taller than Lindsey. "My sister is not for sale," he said, low and dangerous.

The Marquess fanned himself. "Goodness, I wouldn't dream of it. I dare say with her skill at cards, I could not afford such a lady."

Her brother refused to rise to the bait. "You keep telling yourself that." Never had Christina been so happy to have her brother usher her away.

Only after they had left the party, did the fop who had partnered her follow, calling, "Lady Christina!"

Her brother wanted to hurry on, but she stopped.

The fop paused to catch his breath. "May--" he gasped, "May I have my pin back?"

"Your pin?" she asked, not sure what he meant.

"The wager," he explained. "See, it's the arrangement I have with Lindsey. If I partner him, letting him play the hand, any winnings I've wagered come back to me."

Michael's gaze narrowed. "Oh really?"

The fop shrugged. "What can I say? Lindsey only plays against those who he knows he can fleece."

Michael looked to Christina. "And my sister? Did he seek to fleece her?"

The fop looked askance. "I think he had other things in mind," he confessed. He gripped Christina's hands, still clutched around the paper winnings. "He will help you honour your winnings."

Christina sighed. She gave him back the pin. Shame, for she would have been happy to keep it.

Later that night, Christina took stock of what she'd come away with. Minus the fop's pin, she'd claimed at least seven thousand pounds in bank notes. Seven thousand!! Even her brother looked fit to faint. Only later would she learn that the wager had been a thousand pounds a point.

The only other scrap of paper in her winnings was to a country property out west, or so her brother said. Fawdon had scrawled the details on the page, along with his signature. Property! Could one simply give away property just like that?

It wasn't until the next day when Lindsey's Man of Business came calling that she and her brother learned the truth.

Yes, one could wager property just like that.

In fact, Lindsey had an appointment in a week's time for the official transference of said property. He insisted Lady Christina come along.

So, turns out Fawdon had wagered nearly every scrap of land he owned, barring some unwanted place up north. Most had been won by Lindsey, all but that last wager, which, as far as the Marquess was concerned, belonged to Christina.

Property. Actual, income-earning real estate. Her father was unable to attend, due to his gout, but Michael was able to come, albeit only briefly. They, along with Lindsey and his men of business, met with an attorney and Fawdon for the official transfer of property. Christina's property was transferred first, for Michael couldn't stay long, and only remained long enough to ensure he signed for Christina on behalf of their father.

When Lindsey offered to see Christina home, along with her maid Abigail, Michael chillily refused his offer.

Christina had no objection to her brother's choice. No way would she spend any more time with Lindsey, especially alone.

Alas, she couldn't go with her brother, for he had pressing business on the other side of town. Not that she would have minded travelling with him, even staying in the carriage, but he refused.

Someday she'd have to ask him what was so important she couldn't come along.

Instead, he bundled her and Abigail into a hackney, with instructions to take her straight home.

Off he drove, before he could see the hackney catch its wheel on the cobblestone and lurch sideways, a loud crack coming from the axle.

Oh dear. Their transport broken, Christina and Abigail hopped out. They'd have to find another hackney.

Christina drew a deep breath. She gave an apologetic look to Lord

Anthony before continuing her story. "And that's when Fawdon came out. He saw me and gave chase. Poor Abigail told me to flee. I wasn't going to leave her behind, but she knew we were no match for that madman. So, I ran." Christina drew a shuddery breath. "I hope she is all right. She stayed behind to protect me." That was but a half-hour ago, if that much. She had only hoped that Fawdon would dismiss Abigail for the servant she was, and pursue Christina instead. Which he did, until she came across Lord Anthony's carriage, and absconded with it.

Lord Anthony stared at her, agape. "Did that really happen?"

Christina froze, her hands tightening on the reins. Wait. Did she just tell him the whole story? Out loud?

She drew a deep sigh. "The story is not yet over."

"We're here," Lord Anthony replied, pointing to the front of a rather elegant townhouse. After some discussion, they decided it would be best to pull around to the back of the mews, for the sake of the horses.

"Also," Christina added, "What would your family say if they saw me unchaperoned?"

Anthony conceded her point. He'd have enough issues explaining the disappearance of the carriage to his mother, whom he'd left behind at the Strathavens'. "But I can't turn you out to make your way home either."

She certainly couldn't walk home, even if she did know the way. Alas, her reticule had disappeared in the flight, along with any pin money she had to pay for a hackney. "I must write to my brother. He'll know what to do."

As she guided the carriage around the block and into the mews in the back, she pondered on what she could possibly say to Michael that wouldn't paint her in a bad light.

She came up with nothing.

CHAPTER THREE

Anthony studied the bright young lady lingering along the edge of the mews. How on earth did such a splendid creature fall into his life? She had told him quite the story, and he had no reason not to believe her. No fellow thieves had sprung out of nowhere, and her consideration in taking the horses home could only be seen as thoughtful. A true thief would have taken him someplace else, surely.

She looked lost, standing there, arms wrapped about her, head uncovered. His first thought was to scoop her up and carry her away from the awfulness of the afternoon.

At least, with the rest of the family gone, he could offer her some sort of shelter. She could dash off a note to her brother to come collect her, and one for home to see if her maid had made it safe. And then...

Good question. They'd figure it out later. Letters first.

"Please," he said to her, "Come inside. I would not have you waiting outside."

She accepted his offer.

They went in through the kitchen, slipping past uncurious kitchen staff and up a narrow staircase.

"Servants' entrance?" she commented as he made sure she did not slip on the steep stairs.

"Quickest way up," he said, without guile. When he got to the next floor, he peeked out as if in fear of being caught.

Lady Christina let out a little chuckle. "My, my. Am I your dirty little secret?" Her eyes twinkled.

He blushed. "What? You? No..." he moved to the nearest bedroom door. "This," he said, laying his hand on the dark-panelled door. "This is my dirty little secret."

He opened the door and ushered her in, to a place that few others had been, and as far as the world was concerned, never knew existed.

It was not a bedroom. Not anymore.

As Lady Christina entered, she paused, drawing in a breath. The curtains had been pulled back from all the windows, letting natural light fall onto his central wooden table, strewn with clay. Shelves along the walls held boxes and bags, and so many, many figures of pots and projects and who knew what else. He'd forgotten half of what he'd worked on. And everything was grey, as if a layer of clay had settled on everything, which it had. One could never keep a potter's workroom truly clean. It was a fool's errant to bother.

In the middle of the table lay several small lumps of clay, covered with dampened cloth. He tried not to think of those failures, as much as they irked his heart. He'd been struggling for weeks, struggling and failing to capture whatever it was he needed to make.

"What is this place?" she asked, somewhat breathless.

"My workshop," he answered. "Pay it no mind." He opened a door on the other side of the room. "Come through here and you can use my writing desk."

But she didn't follow, not immediately. She lingered. Why? There was nothing interesting about unfinished art.

He urged her along. "The sooner you pen your letters, the sooner..." what? The sooner she could leave? Did he want that?

Something inside him wanted her to stay. His first image of her had imprinted itself on the back of his eyelids, not when she lifted the hatch of the carriage, but when he'd climbed out, watching her twirl in blessed freedom. She had been so carefree, so joyous. Now that he'd heard her story, it made her joy all the more real.

He led her through the small antechamber, originally for servants to cater to the two bedrooms, into his bedroom.

This room was far nicer than his workroom. While the dust of clay did seep its way into the cracks and crannies, he'd done his best to keep work there and life here. Warm mahogany wood dominated this space, from the display cabinet to the writing desk, and even the bed.

"Here." He pulled out the chair at his writing desk. "You can use my stationery. I'll dispatch a servant as soon as you're done."

But she wasn't looking at the writing desk. Her gaze rested on his bed, a large four-poster of deep pillows and luxurious bedclothes.

His cheeks flushed. Surely, she didn't think he'd bring her here for... Oh, good heavens! He turned away. "I-- please. Come write your letters." Her earlier teasing about being his 'dirty little secret' pricked at him. He would never take advantage of a lady thus! Especially one who had had such an adventurous day.

He was simply helping her out, even though she'd taken off with him in a carriage.

Only now did he realise he should have taken her to the front parlour, or even the library. Nobody else was home; nobody would know. She would never have seen his workroom, or known anything about it.

As she sat at the desk, the pen scritching on letter paper, she hummed gently to herself. Such a nice sound.

To give her privacy, he turned to study his figurines in the display cabinet. There were more than thirty, and each one a figure of a young lady of society. Earlier models had copied the Attitudes so many young ladies liked to strike. They were not based off the Greek statues the ladies like to imitate, but the figures of the young ladies themselves. One claimed to be Daphne fleeing from Apollo, or some such thing, her arms raised up melodramatically. But with the progress of the figurines, they left such dramatic poses behind and settled into more contemporary scenes. A young lady with her fan, a young lady strolling. A young lady sitting. Each one becoming more tepid and dull.

He hated the lot. He especially hated the thirty-sixth figurine, the umpteenth draft sitting smashed in squishy raw clay on his worktable in the other room.

A soft voice broke his reverie. "You collect the Southern Figurines?"

He turned to Lady Christine, who held two completed letters in her hands. She offered them, along with a gentle smile. The addresses had been penned on the front.

He left her to study his figurines while he rang for a servant to take the letters.

When he returned, he watched her gaze longingly at the figurines. "You're familiar with them?"

"All of London is familiar with them! Anyone who aspires to fashion will fight each other to get a figurine." She looked longingly on them. "My mother has managed to get five of them. They're rare, you know, with only a certain number made." She pressed her nose to the glass. "And you have..." she counted them up, "...all of them." She paused as the penny dropped. "Southern Figurines... Southerland." Her hands flew to her mouth as she turned to him.

What could he do? He offered her a shy shrug.

"No way!" she exclaimed. "You're the man behind Southern figurines?" She looked back to the door through which they'd come. "That is where you make them?" She looked back to the cabinet. "But they are so..."

Without a second though, she fled back to his workroom.

Anthony had to follow, lest she touch something she shouldn't and break something, not that there was anything in there he'd suffer if it broke.

Truth be told, he had felt as dry as the clay he worked.

Lady Christina roamed the shelves where he'd kept his supplies and his mistakes. She studied everything on the tables and floor. "I've never stopped to think of how they were made."

What was there to tell? He pulled out a wire frame stuffed with paper. "I start with a skeleton, then I layer clay. I sculpt the primary figurine. When it's complete and dry, I send it to my craftsmen who make a mould. They do the porcelain slip, as many as I want, then ship them back here. I trim them up before sending them back to be fired. Then they come back here where I paint them before their second firing and glazing. Only then, when I am satisfied they are complete, are they released to the world."

She looked about as if this were an inner sanctum of magic. It wasn't. It was just his dirty, clay-streaked workroom, where he shed his coat, donned his apron, and got clay stuck under his fingernails.

It was also where his inspiration wasn't. A full month had passed, and nothing had left his workroom. He was ashamed to have shown it to her. What had possessed him to let her in on this secret?

She came to rest before his worktable, with the lumps of clay covered in damp cloth. "When is your next figurine coming out? I would dearly love to have it, if I could."

Anthony wanted to crawl even deeper inside himself. What could he say? To throw out any old sculpture just because someone demanded it made him feel tawdry. "I don't know if I..." he hung his head.

Lady Christina came up to him. "What's wrong?" She laid a hand on his cheek, tilting his gaze back to her.

He drew a shuddery breath. It would not do to break down in front of her. "I think I'm done," he confessed.

"No!" Her reply was more vehement than he expected. "How can you be done?"

He turned from her. "I've been trying. For weeks, God help me, I've been trying. I can't do it anymore." How to explain? "It's like my passion is gone."

"Gone?" she echoed.

He gave in. "It's like I've forgotten how to live life." He wandered to the window. Outside the overcast English weather reflected the dullness of his soul. "My brothers tried to help. They'd take me out to sample everything London had to offer. They even took me to places that--" he paused, "--that I won't mention in front of a lady's delicate ears."

Did she give a snort?

Not that it mattered. "All the pursuits that other men say keep them alive, it all did nothing for me."

She ventured, "The opera?"

He shrugged. "Plays, musicals, racing, dancing, the club, fights... you name it. My brothers took me everywhere."

"Gaming hells?" she suggested. "Molly houses?"

At this, he startled. "What? Good lord, no!" How could she suggest such a thing?

Then again, there was that one time at that house of low repute. Even that did nothing for him. It was like there had been no connection.

He'd always felt connected to his art, pouring his soul into it, until his soul ran dry. A painted lady-of-the-night had finally given up that one time, failing to stir him.

Briefly, he considered the molly house idea.

Nah. His tastes had never run in that direction.

How did his tastes run?

He had no idea. He looked to Lady Christina. Her standing here, studying him. Her earlier, trying to melt into the walls of the mews. No. That wasn't her.

Lady Christina, giving herself over to her new-found freedom in Leicester Square. Lady Christina popping open the hatch of the carriage, looking upon him from above. Lady Christina stealing a coach, and him beside.

His heart beat.

Now he knew why he'd brought her here. Her act of desperation had shaken him. For the first time, he felt like he was not in control, that his life was in the hands of someone else.

Her hands. They had controlled the reins of the carriage with such surety. It didn't matter that she didn't know where she was going. She didn't care.

"I lack inspiration," he confessed. "Tell me what to do?"

Anthony pulled at his cravat. Was it getting too tight? He pulled at it until it came off, to trail to the floor. He turned back to the window. "My brothers thought I needed fire in my blood." Isn't that what they said drove a man? The heat of a fight. The burn of lust. The triumph of beating one's fellow man in a sport, a game, a wager, proving one to be the superior male. That raw, animal passion.

"Fire in your blood," she echoed. "Interesting." She said it more to herself. "My brothers say I have too much fire in my blood." She drew closer. "Said they had to bleed it out of me." She let out a small chuckle. "Interesting," she repeated, "that many of the things they introduced me to was supposed to temper that fire. And here your brothers were dragging you into the same mess in hopes of igniting it."

A thrill ran up his stomach. "Surely your brothers didn't take you to a fight?"

"No. But they did teach me to box." She tilted her head, sending her curls bouncing.

He swallowed. "Is there," his breath caught. "Is there anything they didn't teach you?"

Her gaze bore into his. How could blue eyes look so heated? "They certainly didn't teach me this."

Without further warning, she pinned him up against the wall and thoroughly kissed him. Her lips suckled onto his, and her tongue encouraged them to part. Her hand tangled into his hair, to hold him while she savoured him.

Anthony could barely breathe, so unaware he'd been. Her knee nudged between his, encouraging them to part. Not that they were strong to begin with. His body threatened to slide down the wall. Only his hands firm on the panelling kept him from succumbing to weakness entirely.

She paused, but for a moment, her tongue tracing a line along his lower lip before she punished him again with a deep kiss. Where did he end and she begin? His heart beat so hard he feared it would escape his chest, not that it had anywhere to go. She'd truly pinned him against the wall.

Not all of him remained limp. Oh dear. Did she sense his growing arousal? She'd practically straddled his leg, preventing him from moving away. With her holding him by the hair and by one shoulder, he could go nowhere until she saw fit to release him.

Instead, she feasted on him like a hungry beast, consuming every last dead leaf, and setting his world on fire once more.

He didn't want her to stop. Let her take him completely! He was ready.

It was like waking up when one didn't realise one had been asleep.

He had been asleep, lulled into an ennui so gradual, he hadn't realised he'd given in. No wonder his art had left him. He'd had no muse, no fire.

She had plenty, and it looked she was more than willing to share.

He wanted it all.

His hands had sought her waist, to pull her closer. They roamed up her back, to the buttons that held her in.

A knock on the door startled them both. "M'lord?" came the muffled voice of a servant. "A visitor has come calling."

Immediately, Lady Christina broke away, ethereal like the dream she was, to flow away through the open door to his bedroom.

Anthony could do nothing but lean against the wall, afraid his legs would not support him. "Yes?" his voice came out weak, thready.

The servant eased open the door.

A whirlwind of a man pushed the servant aside and thrust himself through the doorway. Lord Michael Harrington, Lady Christina's brother. The resemblance left no doubt, from the colour of his hair to the fire in his gaze and the letter on familiar stationery clutched in his angry hand.

Lord Harrington gave Anthony a brief glance up and down. "Where is my sister?!" he thundered.

Anthony looked himself over. No cravat, hair quite mussed, cheeks flushed. Oh dear. His heart sank.

"I'm in here," came Lady Christina's light voice, all carefree and without worry. She sailed in from the other room, not a hair out of place. "I'm so glad you got my letter. To be honest, I was not expecting you to arrive for another hour or more."

Anthony ran his hands through his own hair, hoping to restore it to some semblance of order before Lord Harrington cleaned the floor with him. It would not matter that she'd been the one doing the ravishing. He'd bear the brunt of it.

But Lord Harrington ignored him. Immediately, he dashed to Christina's side. "Are you all right?!" he cried, suddenly the doting brother instead of the vengeful relation.

"Is Abigail all right?" Lady Christina clutched at her brother's hands.

Her question baffled him. "How would I know? I only just got your letter. But are you all right?"

"I am fine now," she replied breezily, "thanks to Lord Anthony Southerland. You remember him?" How could she sound so casual, especially given the events this morning?

Lord Harrington collapsed on his sister's shoulder. "I should never have left you. What happened? You never said."

The story of the broken hackney spilled out of her, and the discovery of her and her maid by Fawdon, his mad pursuit, and then her story deviated. "It was by sheer luck that Lord Anthony came by in his carriage." And that was all she said. Nothing of the mad dash through London, of getting lost in Leicester Square, or anything. "Where were you?" she begged.

His countenance darkened. "I... never you mind. I should have never left you. I will never leave you, not as long as Fawdon is free in London."

Without relinquishing his sister, Lord Harrington addressed Anthony. "I thank you for the rescue of my sister. Why did you not bring her home?" It wasn't an accusation.

At this, Lady Christina intervened. "What if Fawdon was waiting? Surely, it's not that difficult to figure out where we live. What if he forced Abigail to tell him?" Her voice caught on her maid's name.

Her deferral did nothing to still Anthony's beating heart.

She continued. "I thought it safe we wait here, where Fawdon couldn't possibly find me, and I immediately sent word to you."

Lord Harrington embraced his sister once more, enveloping her with promises never to leave her unchaperoned ever again. For some reason, this irked Anthony. He wanted to see her again, to speak with her again, to have her push him up against the wall and take such liberties with him again. His face warmed and he turned away.

A gentle hand fell to his shoulder. Lady Christina said, "Again, I thank you for your assistance today." He turned, to meet her amused blue eyes. His breath caught again. "I am in your debt. I would be honoured if you would come dine with us one evening. You are welcome to call at any time."

Hope lifted his heart. "I would like that very much." So very, very much.

With that, the Harrington siblings took their departure. As much as he would have loved to have her stay, something else in him was glad to see them go, for it meant he could do something about this burning urge that had risen within him.

For the first time in over a month, he felt alive again. Tossing aside his jacket and rolling up his sleeves, Anthony turned to his worktable, dipping his fingers in water and slapping the covered clay.

With furious fingers, he began to sculpt.

CHAPTER FOUR

Once Christina was safe in Michael's carriage, he turned to her. "All right. Full story. What really happened?"

She sighed. No way was she getting out of this. "The hackney wheel--"

Michael waved that away. "I meant with Southerland. Don't think I didn't notice his disarray."

She blushed. "I don't know what you mean..." The rumbling of the carriage over the cobblestones lost to the thumping of her heart.

"I think you do."

Christina bit her lip. What to tell him? What to say? Lord Anthony's role in this whole fiasco was one of bad luck and good timing.

Michael continued. "I know Southerland. While one could never say a bad thing about the man, he's not exactly the one to suddenly rescue a damsel in distress."

"He, ah, didn't rescue me." Here it came, "I abducted him." She held up her hands. "Completely by accident. I didn't know the carriage I stole was occupied!"

"The carriage you stole?!"

"It was the only way to escape Fawdon!" Christina laid out the whole pursuit, leaving out no details. As she shared the awful things Fawdon had shouted at her, the terrible, terrible things he vowed he'd do to her once he caught her, Michael's face grew paler and paler, his hand clamped firmly over his mouth. "So you see, to take that carriage was the only way to escape. No way would I have been able to outrun him forever."

A shudder ran through Michael's body. Tears glistened in his eyes. "I am furious," he admitted. "I am furious at that ass Fawdon. I am furious at Lindsey for putting you in that position. I am furious at myself for thinking I could leave you alone."

"How do you think I feel, that I am unable to protect myself?" She flung herself to the far side of the carriage. "No matter how much I learn, I'll never be faster than a man, stronger than a man, or do anything to protect myself. If it wasn't for Abigail sacrificing herself to slow him down, he could have easily caught me!"

Suddenly, she felt very vulnerable. It didn't matter that her brothers had taught her how to punch, how to wield a sabre, or even how to drive a carriage. There was still so much more she couldn't do. "I am furious that I need protecting, but I have no choice." She wilted. "You are right. Until Fawdon is no longer a threat, I'm not safe. Not here, not anywhere."

Michael scooted over and gathered up his suddenly-weak sister. "I vow I will not leave your side until this threat is gone."

A sob ran through Christina, but she didn't dare cry. "But what about Margaret?" While Michael was her brother, she was not the only lady beholden to his protection. If anything, his wife, Margaret, came before her.

"Margaret is going nowhere for the next few months." Her confinement was rather imminent, and Margaret had expressed no desire to leave the house. "She'll understand."

"I wish I could challenge Fawdon to a duel and shoot him in hot blood!"

He stroked her hair. "Bad idea. While I find the thought of you challenging Fawdon to a duel fascinating, he is not a man of honour. He would cheat."

"Couldn't we cheat back and shoot him before he shot me?"

"Don't tempt me." He mused on this thought. "Until we can ensure he won't keep coming after you, I vow I'll not leave your side."

She shoved her brother back. "You shouldn't have left me in the first place!"

Michael spread his arms. "How was I to know Fawdon was going to try something so blatantly ugly?"

"Where did you go?" Christina accused him. "You all but threw me into a hackney and took off? What was so important that you had to dash off so suddenly?"

Michael templed his fingers before his lips as he weighed his answer. "I was dealing with what I thought was a different threat." He inhaled. Was he debating what to tell her? Why didn't he just tell her everything? What was he trying to protect her from?

"Am I under another threat? Is there another unknown danger?"

"I..." he hesitated, then gave in. "Maybe."

"Maybe?" she shrieked. He attempted to mollify her. It didn't work. "Why did I not know of this danger?" No way was she letting go of this until she got some answers.

"Because until Fawdon decided to--" He shook that thought out of his head. Christina had held nothing back in relaying every terrible thing Fawdon had shouted at her. She wasn't sure of half of what he was saying, but Michael seemed to know. "Until today, you weren't actually in any real danger." He looked at her, baring his soul. "If anything, I would have said the Marquess of Lindsey was the biggest danger, especially after what he said to you at the card game."

Christina had not held anything back from her brother when she had explained how she'd come into possession of a piece of paper granting her the ownership of a property out country somewhere. She had no idea what conversations her brother had had with Lindsey, but Lindsey was willing to support the fact Christina had won it legitimately. He even insisted it be transferred to her name. Said it should become her property, and hers alone, else he wouldn't support the claim. He'd even arranged the official signing of the paperwork today, with Christina, Michael (representing her father in legal matters), Fawdon, being the former owner, and himself, for there was more than just the one property transferring ownership.

It wasn't until this morning that Christina learned that Fawdon had all but gambled away every bit of property he owned. No wonder he was bitter! It was his own folly, naturally, but if he was so angry, why take it out on Christina, instead of on the true author of his misery, Lindsey?

"Because Lindsey is a powerful man. There is no way Fawdon would ever be able to win against a man like Lindsey. But you, you are a woman. You are a target he can lord it over." Michael spat. "Fawdon is a coward and wholly lacks honour." He fell into dark brooding. "I will have to do something about him. While he's only a bit player in this game, he's still a dangerous splinter."

Before Christina could ask what his plans were, they arrived home at her parents' residence, where only Christina and a younger sister remained at home, all other siblings grown, married and gone.

Christina jumped down from the carriage and dashed into the house, calling, "Abigail! Oh, did Abigail make it home?"

She failed to shake an answer out of the footman in the hallway, and only another servant pointed her to the kitchens.

Christina pushed her way through the green baize door and hurried down the servants' stairs.

There she found her maid Abigail, sitting at the table. "Abigail!" she cried. "You're safe!"

Against all sense of propriety, Christina flung herself at her maid, enveloping her in a giant hug.

Abigail squeaked and extricated herself. "Easy there, miss." She seemed rather embarrassed. "I should ask if you are all right. You got away, right?"

Tears flowed from Christina's eyes. "I did, thanks to you."

When Fawdon had followed them out of that solicitor's office and gave chase, it was Abigail who had shouted for Christina to run. She said she'd stay behind and stop him, not that a maid could ever stop an angry man. But she had delayed him enough to give Christina a head start.

Christina sat in the nearest chair and reached out for Abigail's hands... or rather, hand, for one of her arms was bound up in a sling. "Oh no! What happened?"

Abigail looked away. "'Tis nothing. I'm glad you got away."

"No, 'tis not nothing! You got hurt!"

Abigail met her gaze, not as servant to mistress, but woman to woman. "But you got away, right, miss?"

Christina could only nod.

"Then it was worth it." She offered nothing more.

Guilt blossomed in Christina. "Did... Fawdon do that to you?"

Abigail shrugged and looked away.

But Christina wasn't leaving until she had answers. "Why did you do it? Why did you try to stop Fawdon?"

Abigail met her gaze again. "Because I know what sort o' man he is. I done seen his kind before. He was going to hurt you in ways no lady should ever see." A shudder ran through her.

"But he hurt you instead!" Why did she not insist Abigail run with her?

Abigail lifted her slung arm as much as she could. "What? This? It was nothing compared to what he would ha' done you."

"But he could have done worse to you."

Abigail shook her head. "I'm nobody. He was hell-bent for you. I knew he wouldn't do nothing to me. I done slowed him down." She lifted her arm. "I done got this when he threw me to the ground to chase you."

Christina drew a shuddery breath. "I'm so sorry."

"Not yer fault, miss. Just glad you're safe."

Mrs Galloway, the Harringtons' chief cook, came over to shoo Christina away. "She'll be fine, miss. We'll look after her. Our Abigail done us proud today. Let her rest and heal."

Before she knew it, Christina had been ushered up the steps and back through the green baize door, with promises that Abigail would be carefully looked after.

Abigail was home and safe.

So why did Christina get the feeling there was something Abigail wasn't telling her?

One week later Lord Anthony came calling during the At Home, a box in his hand. As the footman brought him into the parlour, it was all Christina could do not to throw herself at him.

He washed up quite handsome in the latest of fashion, though not too macaroni. His manners were impeccable as he greeted Baron Harrington and Lady Harrington. That boded well. At least her brothers didn't see the need to be present, as surely she should be safe at home? Granted, it took some convincing to entice Michael to go home to Margaret. Honestly, did he think this single guest would drag her off, to deliver her into Fawdon's hands?

Lord Anthony handed her the box. "A gift for you."

She was not expecting that. Her mother didn't seem so surprised. Then again, her mother had not seemed surprised when Christina had first suggested they invite the grandson of the Duke of Southerland over for dinner. All Lady Harrington knew is that Lord Anthony had rescued her daughter from a random madman on the street. She had been spared the other details. Had she hopes of a potential courtship?

When Christina opened the box, she found an exquisite porcelain figurine of a young woman, vibrant with life. Her skirts whirled about her, her arms outstretched, her head hatless, as she rejoiced.

It was Christina, down to the specific blue-sprigged muslin she'd worn that awful morning.

Lady Harrington leaned in closer to see what Lord Anthony had brought her daughter. A breath caught in her mother's throat. "Is that..." she uttered, unable to say more.

Baron Harrington leaned over, curious more over his wife's reaction, rather than what was in the box. "I say, is that one of those little trinkets everyone likes to collect?"

Lady Harrington gasped, hand to her bosom. "My dear man, this is no mere trinket!" With reverent hands, she lifted it from the box. "This is the latest Southern figurine!" She studied it. "Where did you get one? As soon as I heard they were released, I hastened to Piccadilly this very morning but was too late."

Lord Anthony turned his face in apparent modesty, but only so only Christina could see his subtle wink. "It was worth getting up early," he replied, offering nothing more.

Christina gave the box over to her mother to gush over such an extravagant gift and moved to Lord Anthony's side. "It's me, isn't it?" Surreptitiously, she linked her pinky with his.

Now he had the need to blush. "Thank you for waking up a part of my soul I thought was dead."

"Thank you for rescuing me."

"Thank *you* for rescuing me."

That seemed to surprise her. "Whatever do you mean?"

He twined her hand in his. "Until you made off with me that day, I had been pondering on what had happened to me to make my life so dull. It came upon me so slowly, I'd not realised it. Only, I think I did, for my art had all but died within me." He gazed into her blue eyes. "Thank you. You are a ray of sunshine."

Her eyes glistened and her words deserted her.

He chuckled and ducked his head, suddenly abashed.

Christina's heart skipped about. He was so different from the other men in her life. He was soft--not in a weak way, but, how would she describe it? Approachable. Touchable. Unlike the other men in her life who blustered or insisted or stood firm with their sharp edges and refusal to give a thought to anyone else, here was a man who took his time. He observed. He was thoughtful. It was as if he took a look at the world around him and figured out how to fit in. Even now, how his hand fit so perfectly in hers lifted her soul. He hadn't claimed it, or even demanded it, but moulded his to hers.

She welcomed it.

They had unfinished business. "Mother, I'm going to show Lord Anthony the rest of your figurines." She reclaimed the gift box from her mother. She had not relinquished his hand but dragged him out of the parlour, into the hallway and up the stairs to the next floor.

"Honestly," her mother called out from the parlour. "You know I hate the stairs."

She knew.

The upstairs salon occupied the room above the parlour. Whereas the downstairs was where they usually entertained guests, upstairs was for family. It was more private, more personal.

It was just right for what Christina had in mind.

No sooner had she pulled Lord Anthony in through the door, than she shut it and pushed him up against it, to ravish him with a deep, yearning kiss, the box still in her hand.

At first, he didn't respond, so surprised he was, but then he cradled her face with his firm hands and returned her kiss.

When she finally let him come up for breath, he uttered, "I've been wanting you to do that to me ever since that first day..."

But before she could reclaim his lips, the sound of her aging mother and her awkward clunking up the staircase gave her sufficient warning to pull Lord Anthony away from the door, lest they be discovered compromising each other.

By the time her mother opened the door, she'd dragged him over to a small case on the far side of the room. Inside were various curios and ornaments, each as elegant as the next. There was no particular theme or arrangement, but rather, they all had been clustered inside like the valued treasures they were, not so much to be displayed to their best ability, but each holding a precious memory.

The Harringtons were not one much for showing off their collection to others, but to enjoy on their own. Each piece had not been locked away to be looked at, nothing more, but lived here, to be taken out, handled, explored, enjoyed.

Christina sorted through the items, placed in the cabinet in no particular order, until she found all five Southern figurines. These she brought out to the centre table, setting each one up reverently.

"This is our collection."

Lady Harrington, who had huffed her way to an overstuffed chair, sat back with a sigh of relief. "I collect what I can, unless others buy them out first." She caught her breath. "Honestly, I'd wish they'd make more. This limited number is most frustrating. I tend to miss out more often than not." Baron Harrington had not accompanied her into the room, but had gone off to find something more interesting than his wife's collections.

Lord Anthony studied them as if he'd never seen them before. Christina's heart faltered. They were Southerns, weren't they? She hadn't mistaken someone else's work. Had she insulted him, unwittingly? "I have been told that if they were produced as common as china plates, then everyone could have one. Then no one would want one and nobody would buy them."

"I will always buy them, no matter how many there are," Lady Harrington replied. "I've loved them before anyone else."

"I believe you," he replied, his gaze still on her collection. The figurines started out with a young woman striking an Attitude. Christina couldn't remember the name of the pose, nor which Greek Myth it represented. She hadn't really cared. She liked it because the young woman had a hand raised as if searching for something, her little foot kicking out as if for balance. It felt like she was going somewhere, this little figurine.

Until Lord Anthony had given her the box this morning, this one had been her favourite.

The next figurine also sported a similar Attitude, though not quite as dramatic. This one had a hand lifted as if trying to remember something. Her head tilted into her other hand, brown curls falling against her shoulder. Pensive, she'd describe this one.

The other three were rather dull in comparison, seemingly a handful of young ladies standing about as if waiting for someone to ask them to dance, nothing more.

Lord Anthony arranged them in a line, with Christina's original favourite at the lead, and swapping the order of the last two. He held out his hand for the gift box. "May I?"

She gave it to him.

He removed the last figurine and place it at the end, next to the dullest of the figurines, a young woman standing there, staring vacantly at nothing. At least the previous figurine had the young woman looking over her shoulder as if hoping something better could be found other than what was before her.

Christine drew a breath. Could two figurines have been so different? Her hand itched to move the figure of her to the beginning of the line where it belonged.

Lord Anthony's hand moved before hers. He picked up the first, holding it reverently. "You have the first," he breathed.

Lady Harrington puffed up. "Of course I do. I saw it, fell in love, and got it. I'd never give it up for anything." Early Southern figurines were in great demand, with people offering vast sums of money for them.

Christina added, "Please don't tell anyone we've got it. We have no intention of selling it."

Gently, he replaced it. He ran a finger over the second. "And you've got number four." The rest he also named, but did not touch.

Only then did Christina realise he'd placed them in chronological order. They went from interesting to dull. Indeed, if these later figurines weren't Southerns, she doubted they would have bought them at all.

So that's what he meant when he said he'd thought his soul had died. Whatever magic had gone into the earlier, obscure pieces had been lost by the time they'd become popular. It wasn't for their beauty the later ones had become high-demand, but their name.

And now, the latest figurine, so vibrant and full of life, had restored the magic that had been lost.

Over in her chair, Lady Harrington had been nattering on about something. Christina had not been paying attention. It seemed, neither had Lord Anthony.

"What is your next figurine?" Christina asked low, so her mother couldn't hear.

"I don't know," he confessed. "I was hoping you could inspire me further."

Christina's heart swelled.

"Would you like to come walking sometime, or maybe a drive about the park?"

"Oh yes, please!" She rose in eager anticipation. "Mother, Lord Anthony has proposed a walk in the park."

"What?" her mother replied, alarmed. It was as if a cold bucket of water had been poured over them. "Not without your brother."

She deflated. "But he's not here." And fair enough, for he did have a life of his own. "Surely we can take one of the footmen..."

But her mother refused. "Please do not see this as a slight on you, Lord Anthony. I am sure you are as noble and honourable as any other gentleman, but there are those..." she hesitated. "No. The world is too dangerous."

So much for getting Lord Anthony alone again. Before she could sink into utter melancholy, Lord Anthony took her hands. "I guess I'll be staying here for the next hour or so, though a promenade up and down the corridor may not be quite as invigorating as a stroll through Hyde Park."

It was Lady Harrington who perked up at this. "Then you shall stay for morning tea?"

Christina perked up. Morning tea, usually served down in the parlour. "What a brilliant idea!" She leaned forward to whisper into Lord Anthony's ear, "I so wanted another opportunity to kiss you again."

He whispered back, "I wanted an opportunity to watch you move."

She needed no further convincing. Just as her mother suggested they ring the bell here in the sitting room, Christina said, "We'll see you downstairs!"

Before her mother could protest, she had dragged Lord Anthony out of the sitting room.

She'd gotten him half-way to the stairs when he resisted.

When she stopped, instead of concern, she found mischief in his eyes. He pulled her back to him and fulfilled her greatest wish.

His kiss, unlike hers, was gentle and loving, the kind that made her want to melt into her shoes.

The door to the sitting room opened and she pulled away lest her mother catch them in such an intimate act. She turned to the staircase, but he still held her hand. She looked back. A smile couldn't help but cross her face. Why did he bring her such joy?

She did not relinquish his hand until they were down the stairs, into the parlour, and he needed it to hold a cup of tea.

CHAPTER FIVE

Two weeks later, when Anthony was half-way through painting his next figurine in the Southern series, an invitation arrived for him.

His mother, of all people, brought it in. She held it up, unwilling to lay it out on his dusty worktable. "The Harringtons wish the pleasure of your company at dinner." She sniffed. "Not us, you."

The paintbrush in Anthony's hand paused. His heart thumped. Lady Christina had promised to ask him around. "Oh?" he replied, as nonchalantly as he could. Viscountess Brackley never learned the identity of the person who had stolen the carriage. She'd even bought the story of Anthony having brought it back after the thieves (for he had told her it was more than one thief) realised that the carriage only contained him. He pushed back the chagrin that his mother accepted this tale, for he knew she considered him the least of her sons.

"I hope this doesn't mean your dirty little secret has gotten out and Adelia Harrington is plying you for your latest little offering."

Anthony pretended to return to work, although his hand shook. "I have not besmirched the family honour by letting anyone know what I do, least of all Lady Harrington. I barely know the family."

His mother tapped the invitation against her ample chin. "I know. So why their sudden interest in you?"

"Maybe because I'm the grandson of a duke?"

"A younger son."

"Still nobility. And unmarried." He swirled the paintbrush in the rinsing cup. "Say, do the Harringtons have any eligible young daughters?"

Viscountess Brackley sniffed. "They do, but you don't want to get involved with her."

"Oh?"

"She's..." his mother leaned forward to whisper, even though they were the only two in the workroom. "...wild in her ways."

"Sounds exhilarating."

She drew in a breath through her nose. "If it wasn't for the fact that I think you should get out of the house, I'd say to turn it down."

Anthony sighed. His mother despaired when he got lost in his work like this. One should not be absorbed so by one's hobbies, she believed. That she tolerated his "little playtime", as she put it, was a miracle in and of itself. He looked at the hundred or so half-painted porcelain figurines on his workbench and sighed again. As much as he wanted to complete the work, he had to maintain his mother's good graces. "When is the invitation for?"

"A week hence."

He perked up. His pieces were already bisqued. There was sufficient time to finish this painting and the glazing, assuming he finished the batch tonight so it had sufficient time to dry before kilning. "I suppose I should go along, if only to meet this daughter of theirs." He returned his attention to the figurine in front of him. He'd sprigged the gown in blue, to match the figurine's eyes. It contrasted nicely with the blonde of the figurine's bouncy curls. "She couldn't possibly be any worse than Lady Jane."

"Lady Jane is a paragon of virtue!" His mother was still insulted he'd turned down the tepid Lady Jane. The thought of the limp daughter of the Earl of Strathaven pushing him up against a wall to melt his innards with a single kiss made him laugh.

"I'm serious," his mother huffed. "Why would you turn down the daughter of an Earl for the daughter of a Baron, I don't know."

"Perhaps I need to find a young lady who will forgive me my strange quirks and odd hobbies. I've told you, Mother. Lady Jane deserves someone who shares her same qualities." Someone boring.

He held out his hand for the invitation. "I shall reply in the affirmative." To further mollify his mother, he said, "And I promise I'll attend you and Father for the next social event to which you receive an invitation."

She accepted his offer. "And if there is dancing, you will stand up with no less than three young ladies."

Must he? "Very well." Anything, to get her to go away and let him finish his work. He was on a tight deadline, if he was to present his muse with the next of the works she'd inspired.

Anthony's mother called up her favour to him sooner than he realised. They were to go to the theatre that night, and Anthony was to come along.

And why not? His figurines were all dry and done and had been shipped off for their final kilning. He'd not had any ideas yet for his next figurine, but that would come to him soon enough, especially after he'd seen Lady Christina again.

Just the thought of her made his blood sing and his heart to dance. And it had happened because he'd gone out.

Here he was, out again, bouncing along in the family carriage, the same one Lady Christina had absconded with that day. Granted, going out that fateful day had been against his wishes, but after having called upon her and her family and seeing their small collection of his figurines, he realised why he'd died inside. He had failed to nourish himself. Of course he'd honour his parent's wishes and be seen out in public. Probably was a very good thing.

Soon the carriage pulled up in front of the theatre. The footman handed them out. As both his parents stood on the pavement in front of the theatre, they called out to acquaintances and lost themselves in a wave of friends.

Nobody went to the theatre for the performances. They were there to perform for each other and to gossip about the true drama of the *ton*, rather than what some playwright had forced onto the stage. Anthony had never been into gossip; he never saw the point. Yet his being there would most likely stir a few people to say something. Not that such gossip about him would last long. He simply wasn't interesting enough to remain on people's tongues.

A delightfully intrusive thought of being on the end of Lady Christina's tongue flitted through his head. His face flushed. Where had that come from? He looked about in case anyone had noticed; they hadn't. He stood on the fringe of his parents' social group, not really belonging but not really able to slip away.

Anthony looked about. Surely there was someone he knew, perhaps from a party? An event? He'd even take one of the match-making mamas that insisted on thrusting their daughters at him during dances, not because Anthony himself was a Desirable, but only because he had a title.

A glimpse of a curly blonde head adorned with flowers caught his eye, as the young lady in question lowered the hood of her cloak. Her back was to him, but he could have sworn it was Lady Christina. He drew closer, looking for Lord Harrington, her brother, to ascertain it was her. A few more steps, and he'd be at her side.

Before he reached her, another man approached her. He grabbed her by the arm and spun her around. "I found you!" he shouted.

The young lady in question cried out. It was not Lady Christina. This one was a bit shorter, a bit plumper, and quite startled.

"I beg your pardon," the older man next to her cried out. Her father, perhaps?

The assaulter did not apologise. He cursed, spat at the ground, and thrust her arm away. Such rudeness.

Wait. Anthony recognised the man. Cold dread pooled in his gut. The blighter had done the exact same thing Anthony had done; he'd mistaken this young lady for Lady Christina.

Anthony could not stand around and say nothing. "I say. You're that ass Fawdon, the one who likes assaulting respectable young ladies," he said, before he could check himself. "Don't think we don't know how you went after La--" He corrected himself "...another such young lady. Such a cowardly act."

Everyone in society turned, their gossip forgotten. Oh dear. He had nearly invoked Lady Christina's name, nearly exposing her to further gossip.

Fawdon backed off a couple of steps. "That bitch cost me my fortune!"

At this, the young lady cried out, as if she were the wrongly accused. She turned into the chest of the older man, who cradled her and glared at Fawdon.

A strange feeling--rage--blossomed in Anthony's chest. "I will thank you not to address any young lady by that vulgar term." He drew himself up. He might not have been as broad as other men, but he had his height. He'd make the most of it.

He'd had the story from Lady Christina when they first met, of how she'd been tricked into playing that last hand. "Besides, it wasn't her to whom you lost, but to the Marquess of Lindsey. Everyone knows it. If you can't recognise your true foe and you take your wrath out on inno-cents who don't deserve being victimised by you, then you best not show your face in public ever again."

Fawdon sneered at him. "Or what?" he spat. Such bravado, for a man with no allies.

Anthony's fists balled.

No, no. He would not be the one to clean Fawdon's clock, no matter how much he deserved it. That would be justifying the insult as worthy. Instead, he delivered a truly awful blow, the Cut Direct, by staring at him for a moment longer, then, without a further word, turned his back and walked away.

Keep walking, he told himself. That said, he did keep his senses up, in case Fawdon had the cowardice to attack him while his back was turned.

"What?" cried Fawdon as Anthony continued to walk away. "You're all cutting me?!"

At this, he smiled. Seemed he wasn't the only one to turn his back on the mongrel. The rumble of the crowd picked up as various people turned away, commenting on the sheer audacity of Fawdon, who, by a simple act of mistaken identity, had sealed his fate socially.

Never had a group of people flocked into a theatre so quickly.

For any other gentleman of his acquaintance, such a cut would have been enough to destroy him. But Fawdon was another breed entirely. Anthony dreaded they'd not seen the last of him.

When the Harringtons showed up to the theatre, few people lingered outside. As her other brother Stephen peered out the carriage door, he berated Michael. "Now you've gone and made us late. Everyone's already inside."

Michael consulted his pocket watch. "No, we're not late." It had been Michael's potentially last night out in Society before his wife Margaret gave birth. Once that happened, he would not be available to chaperone his sister, so they were making the most of what tethered freedom she had. Then it would be Stephen's job to ensure she remained safe.

Christina worried her lip. "Perhaps we have the wrong night?"

Only one way to find out. They hastened from the carriage into the theatre.

Inside, the lobby teemed with people. Over in one corner a most distraught young lady cried in her father's arms. Quite a few of the *ton* had gathered about, most curious over her distress. Had something *momentous* happened? Is this why everyone was crowded inside, to witness whatever drama unfolded?

Christina recognised Miss Wright. They did not move much in each other's social circles, but Miss Wright had come out at the same time as Christina. The creature had even managed to score a voucher to Almack's. Such a respectable young lady.

"What happened?" Christina wondered aloud. Nothing created more drama than to see the crumbling of a pillar.

"Such a spectacle," came a smooth male voice over her shoulder.

Christina turned to see Sir Jonathan Coates, an acquaintance of her brothers. At the sound of his voice, both Michael and Stephen turned, recognised and greeted him. He returned their bows with a bit more flourish, for Sir Jonathan fancied himself a dandy. Lace and colours were his thing, as was a cloud of scent that enveloped Christina. While he did his best to ensure the most anyone could hold against him was his fashion sense, that didn't put him above sharing the foibles of others.

The delicate handkerchief in his hand quivered as he yearned to share the latest *on-dit*. "A most interesting to-do occurred before you arrived. A low-class cur assaulted yon lady, mistaking her for someone else." At this, Sir Jonathan looked at Christina, noting the colour of her hair. "She is very much blonde like you, my dear Lady Christina."

Her insides chilled. "He didn't go by the name of Fawdon, did he?"

"I see you are acquainted with the gentleman."

"I assure you he is no gentleman."

"I concur," purred Sir Jonathan, who sniffed. "Anyhow, said fellow laid hands on her and accused her of terrible misdeeds."

A hand flew to Christina's mouth. Had they arrived earlier, it could have been her he approached, not poor Miss Wright.

Sir Jonathan tugged at the lace on his sleeves. "To be honest, I was hoping there would be some fisticuffs. Mr Wright was perfectly in his right to plant one on Fawdon's kisser after he so crudely handled his daughter so." He tapped eagerly on Christina's gloved hand. "But instead, they went one better."

"Oh?" What could be better than punching Fawdon out?

"As soon as Fawdon realised his mistake, he got called out."

"Mister Wright called him out? Like, as a duel?"

"Someone even better." Sir Jonathan put on a voice as he imitated her champion, "'I say. You're that Fawdon ass, aren't you? The one who enjoys assaulting respectable young ladies?'" He put a fist on his cocked hip. That did not strike her as Mister Wright. He was more of a huffy, rumbly bear of a man, one who'd front up to Fawdon and attempt to push him out into the street by broad girth alone.

Sir Jonathan's imitation was someone much lighter, more graceful, (or was that Sir Jonathan being a dandy?)

Christina racked her brains to think of what kind of man would have the courage to openly say something like that in public. Sir Jonathan continued, "You'd think that would have been enough to make Fawdon turn tail and run, but our champion wasn't done with the blighter." He struck a ridiculous attitude and put on the voice again. "'You're the sore loser who thought he could win a card game against Lindsey, and didn't know when to quit.'"

At this, Sir Jonathan drew in a breath, as if shocked by the scandal. "Imagine calling up a man's past folly like that in front of everyone. Granted, that Fawdon ass deserved it, after what he did to poor Miss Wright." Again, Sir Jonathan looked at Christina's hair. She raised a hand to her curls and wished she'd worn something, a turban, even a bonnet, to cover it up.

"'I don't know why you bother to show your face in public.' And then he gave him a once-over, and walked away." Sir Jonathan minced off a few steps, most ridiculous.

Christina put a hand over her mouth to stifle a giggle. "Who on earth said that?"

"Not sure." Sir Jonathan had to think about it. "One of Souther-land's get, I believe. One of his younger sons?"

No! It couldn't be. "Surely not Lord Anthony?"

At this, Sir Jonathan shrugged. "Never did bother to learn their names. Not really ones for the fashionable set, the Southerlands. But after what I watched I want to make the acquaintance of that good gentleman."

Sir Jonathan finished his tale of how Fawdon had been shamed into retreating from the scene, not just by (presumably) Lord Anthony, but several others, who had joined in on the pile-up. "The whole of the *bon ton* cut him! I believe that will be the last we see of Fawdon, the rotter."

While Christina would like to think him correct, something in her gut said otherwise. Men like him didn't know when they were down. Strategic withdrawal wasn't in their vocabulary. They kept on and on until they lost every single thing or they were imprisoned, or even killed.

That card game.

Christina and her brothers thanked him for the news and let Sir Jonathan hurry off to find fresh new ears.

Michael departed the lobby for the boxes, apparently lost in thought. Christina and Stephen hurried after him, up one floor. Along here, lamps lid the corridor with its red carpet and gilded walls. Instead of climbing the staircase that would take them up to the second floor to their box, he passed it by, moving several doors along. He ignored Stephen's reminder that they were on the wrong floor.

Michael looked up at the door numbers, stopping in front of a particular one. "No, I'm exactly where I want to be."

His siblings waited, hoping for an explanation, but all Michael offered was, "This thing has gone on long enough." He looked to his sister. "Tina, we need to sort something out with a certain Marquess."

All the joy fled her evening. Lindsey? "And what are we going to say to him?"

He asked her a rather pointed question: "Do you love him?"

"Gads, no!"

"Do you even like him?"

"Not even. That stunt he pulled has put me in clear danger. I've lost any respect I may have had."

Michael drew in a sharp breath. "Good. Tell him that. Tell him everything in your heart. He seems to have forgotten you're a human being with feelings. You need to let him know you're not a pawn in his little chess game."

Absolutely. She would just march right in and...

...lose her courage. "I can't do this."

"You're not going in there alone. I'm going with you. Believe me, I have plenty to say to Lindsey. But he's got to hear your story from your lips. Me, he'll dismiss lightly. But you," he took her hands. "You have more power than you realise."

Christina doubted his words. However, he had a point. Until they confronted Lindsey, he might continue to think his actions above consequence. The longer they put this off, the worse things could potentially get.

Think of that poor lass who had been mistaken for her.

Michael did not bother with knocking. He opened the door to Lindsey's box and strode in, followed closely by his sister. Stephen had agreed to stand outside, should they need assistance.

The play had started, not that anyone cared. Half the boxes were still empty, as most were still congregated in the lobby, presumably to learn more of what had happened.

They found Lindsey paying flirtatious attention to a woman not his wife. Christina didn't recognise her, nor did she care.

Lindsey's smarmy attention broke away from her as soon as he noted the intruders in his box.

Michael sat down uninvited. Christina remained standing. She had no intention of staying long. She remained back in the shadows, near the curtains that cut off the back of the box from the front. Perhaps they hid her enough?

Michael began without preamble. "Tonight, not yet a half-hour past, a young lady was assaulted quite rudely outside this theatre by a mutual acquaintance of ours. I'm laying the blame at your feet."

The faintest of frowns furrowed Lindsey's brow before his gaze settled on Christina. He brushed aside her brother's words. "Ah, my dear. So good of you to join us. Please, have a seat."

Her reply was cold. "No, thank you. We are not staying long."

At least Lindsey's manners hadn't deserted him completely. He rose and retreated to the back of the box, tugging the curtain a bit closer. His lady companion opened her mouth, then shut it, turning petulantly away from them and toward the stage.

Michael followed, pushing into the semi-darkness. "As I said, someone assaulted a young lady in front of the theatre tonight, thinking it was my sister. That assaulter was Fawdon."

At this, Lindsey drew a breath. "I assure you I did not put him up to it." He reached for Christina's hand, but she pulled it away.

Michael continued. "Not tonight, no. Not directly, no. But his actions stem from that initial humiliation at the card game where you practically divested him of all his personal wealth."

Before Lindsey could retort, Christina stepped in. "He wasn't your only target that night, was he? I remember what you said to me, that so-called wager you made with me.

"You used me," she growled at him. "You didn't offer for me because you liked me. I was nothing more than a tool, and you saw an opportunity to get what you wanted, no matter which way things went. You offered me that Hobson's choice of playing a hand of whist. I was nothing more than a way to further humiliate Fawdon."

Lindsey didn't even have the sense to look abashed.

"Congratulations, that succeeded. And while I would not be one to deny that Fawdon needed the humiliation, by that very act, he's taking out his frustration on me. Not you, but me, because he is a coward and doesn't dare go up against you. But me, that's another matter entirely."

Lindsey inspected his fingernails. "But you won. I don't see what you're so upset about?"

Christina wanted to slap him. "You and I were not playing cards! You know that. I can't think of why you would have made the offer you did. I don't like you. I never have. I can't see why you would wish to form an attachment to me, even a demi-mondaine attachment. And even then, you had to try to trick me into it. Had I been favourably disposed to you, all you had to do was ask and I might have said yes."

Lindsey opened his mouth, but Christina carried on. There was nothing he could say that she wanted to hear. "But you knew I would say no, thus the trickery.

"So, either I win the hand and Fawdon suffers great humiliation at having been beaten by a lady, or I lose the hand and instead of several properties adding to your wealth, you get to claim me."

Michael loomed a bit closer, challenging Lindsey with his seething gaze. "Bad idea," he growled.

Christina took strength from her brother. "Oh, I can see how that would go. Every time I did something you disapproved of, you'd hold those lost properties over my head, trying to guilt me into submissive behaviour.

"That would not work." She shook a finger at him. "If you knew anything about me, you would know such a thing would never work. Why would you ever think I'd settle for a carte blanche offer?"

Lindsey gave a cold chuckle. "Oh, I doubt you have the standing to hold out for an honourable offer."

"What do you mean?" Ice clenched about her heart.

He flicked at invisible lint on his lapel. "Let us say I have heard certain rumours, and I have no reason to doubt them. See, certain footmen are liable to boast."

The bottom of her world dropped out. "Surely you don't put credence into the rumours of servants?" It came out weaker than she meant.

Lindsey's mouth spread in a satisfied grin. She'd seen that before, at the game, as soon as she'd picked up her hand. "When a servant suddenly has to find a new job, there is always a reason. One listens to the rumours, then attempts to verify them. Many a servant has been let go for, ah, shall we say 'fraternising' with the family? No servant is ever let go without a cause." He ran his tongue over his teeth. "But is their cause what they say, or something else?"

Christina backed up, seeking the strength of her brother.

"When a young lady has been compromised, the servant is let go at best, punished at worst. But the young lady in question? Her behaviour changes, at least, her outward behaviour. Absolutely no hair is out of place, no wrong word uttered, no misbehaviour at all. So much effort is poured in to the act so her reputation appears to be beyond the pale, and no misstep can be attributed to her at all. How could anyone possibly think such a paragon of virtue has stepped beyond the bounds of propriety?" He let out a chuckle that chilled her very bones. "Can I say, this is NOT you?"

Spots appeared before Tina's eyes. Why was her brother not saying anything? She reached for his hand and found it.

Lindsey continued. "But when a young lady has been accused of taking advantage of a servant... and then goes on to learn how to fence, learn how to box, learn how to play cards and drive carriages? One can only presume such licentious behaviour permeates her entire life..."

Michael, who had been quiet this whole time, let out a small snort, just a tiny one. Quickly he hushed it up, drew a Very Serious Face, and murmured, "Apologies. Go on."

But that one snort had been enough to derail Lindsey's pointed jab. His momentum gone, he stared at Michael.

Tina let out a small hiccup and turned away. Inside, she wanted to cry. She wanted to slap her brother for letting Lindsey's accusation go on for far too long. How dare Michael leave her there, hung out to dry, blasted by the painful and true accusations of Lindsey?

"Really, old bean," Michael said. "My sister is the last lady you'd wish to offer carte blanche to. If you were were not already shackled, I'd even dissuade the thought of marriage. Your title is high and bears much weight, but you, as a man, are sorely lacking. How can you not see that someone like my sister would chew you up and spit you out?"

Lindsey took a step back. He'd not been expecting this.

Michael leaned against the wall, nonchalantly. "But of course you do. Otherwise, you would not have pitted her against Fawdon, knowing full well that she'd dish out to him the kind of humiliation you could never achieve, even if you did reft him of all his worldly wealth. That one property you allowed her... I'm not sure if it was more to buy her, or to humiliate him?" His humour took on an edge. "I presume it was the latter."

He pushed himself off the wall, his backbone suddenly the strongest steel. "But then, here is where you lose my respect: you placed my sister in clear and present danger. You made her a target for a man like Fawdon. So much so, he even attacked a young lady who looked like her tonight. Even if you were her protector--which you are not--would you have stepped up to defend her, even if she were demi-mondaine? Would you defend her, even if she was not present?" He left this question hanging.

Christina glanced to the other lady in the box. That unknown woman (for Christina doubted she was a lady) did not hide her face, or pretend she wasn't listening.

The property transfer. That had to have been the moment Fawdon broke. True, he had no choice but to sign over his property legitimately lost in a game of cards. That final property, lost in the hand to Christina, had been signed over to her. Not her brother, not her father, but in her name.

It was hers, never to be taken away. That must have been the final straw to paint the target on her back.

Had she stayed, how would have things gone? Fawdon surely had some unsavoury things to say about her. Would Lindsey have stood up for her in her presence? Did he stand up for her in her absence?

Probably not. After all, she was a mere tool, being used by two unsavoury men, to strike at each other.

Only now did she see the wisdom of her brother's hasty exit.

But then even he had abandoned her. Why? If Michael knew so much about Lindsey, about what he knew, about everything, why did he shove her in that hackney and run off in his carriage? What was so pressing that he had to dash off?

The more she thought of it, the more she realised he held more secrets than he gave up.

Michael wasn't finished. "But you didn't defend her honour, did you? After she left, you never defended her honour. Instead, Fawdon, thinking her championless, sought to target her, to take out his anger against you on her, someone weaker than he.

"But he failed. He tried again tonight and failed again. But he could have succeeded. Then what?" Michael drew close to Lindsey, to drop his accusations directly in his face. "You failed her. You failed her in so many, many ways. To put a lady in such danger is a low blow indeed.

"Leave my sister alone. No more insulting offers. No more drawing her into awkward situations. No more leaving her undefended, not just her, but any young lady Fawdon seeks to target."

But instead of backing off, as Christina had expected, Lindsey sneered. "Do you think I am put off by such tepid threats, Harrington?"

"I do."

At this, Lindsey laughed openly in her brother's face. "Don't think I don't know how much you value your sister. Unless you give up your stupid little attempts to ruin me, I will never give up my stupid little attempts to ruin your sister."

Ruin him? What did Lindsey mean?

Michael ground his teeth together. "It is too late for Diana," he growled.

Lindsey's mocking humour faded. He even took a step back.

Michael advanced. "Everything I do now is for Diana. Everything I've ever done was in her honour. Consider yourself lucky my wrath is not greater.

"However. Now you bring my sister into this? No." He jabbed a finger at Lindsey's brocaded chest. "You will leave her alone. You will have nothing more to do with her. You will solve the problem of Fawdon without further incident to my sister or anyone else. I don't care how you do it, but I do care when you do it. Do not delay. Until this is done, any ill thing befalls my sister, even if I have no proof it was because of you, I will solve the problem of *you*. Permanently."

Lindsey's mockery had devolved into a cold rage. "Don't threaten me, Harrington. Despite your little," he waved his hand, "one-ups, I'm still a far more powerful man than you."

"Power's only good while you're still breathing."

Lindsey froze. For a moment, it was as if his own life had paused. "You wouldn't dare."

"Don't cross me, and you'll never find out."

Michael spun on his heel, dragging Christina away. He even slammed the door to the box.

Outside, Stephen had had his ear pressed to the door. "All done then?"

Michael only had words for Christina. "Never speak to the man again. If he approaches you, walk away. No clever words, no witty insults. Cut him and walk off. The world will understand."

"I don't understand," Christina said, her feet hurrying to keep up.

Michael did not look at her, did not slow down. "May you never."

She tried a different tack, "Who is Diana?"

Stephen's footsteps faltered.

Michael did not turn. "Someone I knew before Margaret." And nothing more was offered. She glanced towards Stephen, but her other brother offered nothing. His averted gaze told her he knew about Diana, but would not share.

It was not until they had climbed the stairs and entered their own theatre box that Michael offered an apology and somewhat of an explanation. "Lindsey's interest in you is my fault. I'm sorry. He saw you as a way to get back at me for ruining him."

Christina rubbed at her arm. Her brother had not let her go until they were well and truly away from Lindsey. "He doesn't look terribly ruined."

Her brother drew a sharp breath. "He will be. I have a plan. It is taking a long time, but it is working."

"What is working?" For something she appeared to be deeply involved in, she was very much in the dark.

He didn't answer her question. "I owe you an apology for the original incident with Fawdon. I'm afraid I'm just as guilty as Lindsey."

Him? Guilty? "What did you do?"

"I used you to distract Lindsey."

"You used me?" Her image of her brother as her ultimate protector splintered. Was he no better than the men he said from whom he'd protect her?

He held up his hands. "Hear me out. When Lindsey named the time and date for the property transfer, I knew he was doing it to get back at me." He sank against the back wall of the box, his face hidden in darkness. "See, we were going up against each other later that day in an auction for some property. He thought if he could distract me with your property transfer, knowing I wouldn't dare leave you alone, but didn't dare take you along with me to the auction, he'd waylay me, and he'd make it to the auction and win.

"But I'd done him one up. I'd convinced the auctioneer to move up the auction to the time of the property settlement."

Things began to fall into place for Christina. "So that's why you insisted we transfer my property first, and that's why you dashed off!"

Her brother nodded. "I knew Lindsey would be taken up with the transfer of the other properties, and wouldn't be able to make it to the auction."

She looked to Stephen. "And you knew about this?"

He nodded. "I was his backup, should you both fail to distract Lindsey."

"But if you were already at the auction, why didn't you make the purchase?"

Michael gripped her arm. "Because it has to be me who ruins Lindsey."

Christina's head spun with the deviousness of her brother. "All of this because of something to do with this Diana?"

Michael raised a sorrowful gaze to her. "You don't know what he did to her. May you never learn."

"What?" she insisted. "Please tell me."

He only shook his head. "Never."

"Michael..."

He did not relent. "Only thing you need to know is that you're safe, and I'll never let anything like that happen to you."

She fronted him with a stark truth. "You can't protect me forever."

"I know. But I will protect you for as long as I can." He sank forward, head in his hands. "I'd like to say this isn't my fault, but I never realised how low Lindsey would stoop to strike a blow at me." He fell silent.

"One thing I can promise you--I will never let him use you, or anyone else against me ever again."

CHAPTER SIX

As much as Christina wanted to lose herself in the play, she couldn't. All she could think about was how the men of her life used her for their own ends. How could Michael do that? At the very least he could have told her the plan. She was already complicit. At least armed with the knowledge of what was truly going down, she could have played her part effectively.

Maybe she could have stood up to Fawdon better. Maybe she could have come armed and defended herself properly. Instead, she had to improvise by stealing a carriage and abducting Lord Anthony.

Lord Anthony. Was what Sir Jonathan said true? Christina scanned the theatre boxes. If he was right, then Lord Anthony was here.

She spotted him and his parents on the third level, nearly across from the Harringtons' box. He looked as bored as she did, chin in hand, idly watching the play. He'd been shoved to the side, his parents on the edge of the box closest to the stage, peering at the players with opera glasses.

Christina rose from her seat and quickly exited their box. "Tina?" her brother called after her, but she'd shut the door on his inquiry. A mad dash to the staircase carried her up one more floor. She sped along the corridor ringing the back of the theatre, counting the doors, hoping she'd gotten the number correct.

Her brother calling her name echoed back, but faint.

Here was the door. She eased it open and slipped in quietly, not wanting to disturb anyone further.

She laid a gentle hand on Lord Anthony's back briefly before withdrawing to the shadows. He started and turned.

Christina laid a finger in front of her lips, then beckoned.

Lord Anthony rose and joined her in the darkness. "You're here at the theatre?" he whispered.

"Is it true you defended me, even when I wasn't there, even if Fawdon had mistaken Miss Wright for me?"

"Of course. What Fawdon was doing wasn't right."

"Oh, you beautiful man!" She pulled him even deeper into the darkness and kissed him thoroughly.

He drew a deep breath when she gave him the chance. "Do you want to stay here?" she asked him. "Watch the play?"

He shuddered. It had been some tepid re-telling of a farce he'd no interest in at all. "Not at all."

She opened the door and pulled him out into the corridor. "Then let's leave."

Lord Anthony opened his mouth, but nothing came out. He did follow without resistance as she tugged on his hand.

Soon, they'd hurried down the staircase, through the lobby and out the front door of the theatre, to hail a small, single-horse two-wheeled hackney. "Where are you taking me?" he asked as she herded him into the hackney.

"Home." She quickly followed, shutting the door behind her.

"Your home?"

Christina shook her head. "My parents are home. Yours are not." She gave the address--his address--to the hackney driver sitting behind. "Round back to the mews," she added.

The driver pulled away.

The hackney was not a terribly large vehicle, having room only for the two of them. Curtains on the side windows gave only a half-privacy, for the front of the hackney was quite open to the weather.

Christina didn't care. She lifted her skirts to better enable her to straddle Lord Anthony's lap. "Of all the men in my life, you have proven yourself the most noble of them all. You've kept no secrets from me and defended my honour at every opportunity."

With that, she drew him into a kiss, plundering his lips and urging him to open to her.

He gave in, letting her have her wicked way with him. His hands tightened on her hips, pulling her in closer.

He froze, turning his face from hers, gasping for air. "I can't."

She paused, hands still tangled in his hair, his cravat half-undone. "You.... what?"

"I will not treat you thusly. I cannot be the one to take your virtue, not like this, not here."

Realisation settled across her shoulders. She'll have to tell him. "You have been honest with me. I can only be honest with you." She did not leave his lap, but did settle back somewhat to be able to look him in the eye. "I was rather, ah, reckless in my youth, one could say. A little too much so." How to put this? "Let us say I got one of the footmen into trouble."

He drew in a breath. "Did he... compromise you?"

Full honesty. "Rather, I compromised him. His sin, other than being a target for a hot-blooded young lady, was boasting of his supposed 'conquest'. My brothers found out, gave him a good thrash-ing, and dismissed him on the spot. To give them credit, they did not inform my parents, for they had already confined me to the dull 'lady-like' pursuits. Boredom had been my downfall. They, meaning my brothers, thought it best I burn off the heat of my blood in other, more respectable outlets. Thus, they taught me more athletic activities, such as fencing, boxing and driving horses. All the things generally reserved for sons, in an effort to keep them out of trouble." She grinned at him. "After all, we know what boys are like."

She kissed him again and he did not resist at first. It was she who paused. "I can hear that thought tumbling in your head."

He swallowed. "These..." he hesitated, "*manly* pursuits. Aren't they supposed to do the opposite? Aren't they supposed to stir the blood, make a man of you?"

She thought upon it. "I don't know. For me, they sufficed in their purpose. Since that day, I've not needed to bother the footmen, or anyone else, really." She paused. "Then I met you."

Instead of kissing him once more, she pressed her forehead to his. "Can I keep you?"

His breath caught in his throat. "Are you proposing marriage to me?"

"Only the most noble of offers for you."

His hands trembled on her hips. They tightened, bringing her closer. "I don't know what to say."

"Then find something else to do with your tongue until it remembers its other purpose."

He obliged. Thus, they kept each other occupied until the hackney delivered them to the Southerland Mews. Lord Anthony tossed a coin to the driver, and together they snuck in through the servants' entrance.

Anthony's head spun. If it wasn't for Lady Christina leading him up the dark, narrow staircase, he would have left himself in the kitchens, unable to move, unable to think. Goodness, he may have left himself in the hackney.

Was this really happening?

In his workshop, a low-banked fire supplied enough heat to light a taper, to light the lamp. This he kept low, just enough light to follow her into his bedroom.

But instead of conquering his bed, he found her at his writing desk, scrawling a note. "I may have lost my heart, but I have not lost my head." The note, folded only once, simply said, "I'm safe. --Tina". On the outside was her brother Harrington's address.

Anthony did not recall ringing for a servant, only the handing over the note for delivery and carefully closing the door.

His heart thumped hard and spots appeared before his gaze. The scent of her assailed his nostrils. Lavender. That's what it was, and something else, almost masculine.

How quickly she had eased him out of his coat, handing it over to the care of his desk chair. His cravat was a hopeless cause, having been undone completely in the hackney. "Are you sure you want to do this?" he breathed. Last chance for her to say no, for he feared if she did not step away, he would divest himself of everything and let her have her way.

"I am sure for the rest of my life." One by one, she undid the top buttons of his shirt, removing his collar and exposing his throat. Against his throbbing pulse, she placed her lips, to nuzzle and suck on his skin, sending his head into another spin. His loins quivered. For the first time in his life, he did not fight it, but gave in to the sensation.

She wore too much. Already she'd lost her cloak. His hands gripped at the back of her gown, unsure of where to begin.

"A little higher," she prompted. "You'll find the buttons."

Fiddly little things they were! He resisted the urge to tear them loose. At his growl of frustration, she paused in her exploration of him, to aid him.

One by one she released the buttons as far as she could reach, then turned about to let him finish the job. As soon as the last one was free, he eased her gown off her shoulders, sampling the skin with his tongue. She tasted so good!

But what was this? Laces? Was women's clothing always this challenging? Her back still to him, she reached up and untucked the lace ends at the bottom of the stays, loosening the bow he had not noticed.

He couldn't wait. Urgently, he tugged out all the strings, pulling them from their eyelets, until the whole thing came free.

Only her shift remained. This he pulled off her shoulders, letting it fall to the floor.

Her skin was so exquisite! He'd not felt anything this soft since he couldn't recall when. His hands roamed her back, his lips to follow.

Lady Christina groaned and pulled at his hands, to wrap them about her waist. Next, she guided them up to her bare breasts, showing him how to stroke them, to play with her nipples.

His own body protested at his clothing. Even his phallus strained against the falls of his trousers. But when he tried to wrest his hands away from hers, she refused to surrender them.

How was he to free himself? "You have me at a disadvantage," he whispered in her ear.

"Good," she murmured back, before turning to him. With nimble fingers, she freed up his waistcoat, divested him of his shirt, and undid his falls, letting the fine fabric of his trousers slide down his thighs. His smallclothes soon followed, to bunch about his knees.

"Wait. Shoes." He'd forgotten about his evening shoes. A good thing he'd not worn boots; they were for day wear.

She shuffled him to the bed and thrust him upon it. Before he realised it, she'd slipped off each shoe, each stocking, his trousers, everything, leaving him quite bare and standing to attention.

Only she had her stocking on, tied above the knee with garters. A ripple of delight ran through him at the wan lamplight glinting off her skin.

With fire in her gaze, she joined him on the bed, prowling over him, her hands running up his thighs before gripping his manhood.

He inhaled. No one had ever taken him apart before, not like this. Then again, no one had ever stirred his blood enough for him to let them take him apart. A previous attempt on the part of his brothers to drag him to a brothel had ended in disappointment. He shoved that memory aside, for no matter how much the prostitute had tried to stir him, he'd not reacted. Not even a limp niggle.

This was... this was nothing like that. The liminal glow of the lamp defined her luscious body as she straddled his hips. "I know what to do," she assured him, her hands still on his member. Ever so carefully, she lifted her body up, to settle it about his, her hands guiding him inside her.

His breath shuddered as she slid her tight way onto his member. He gripped the bedclothes. How could anything feel so soft, yet so secure?

Gently, she rose up again, sending another ripple of pleasure along his shaft. Little by little, she established a pleasant rhythm, ever so gentle, though he ached for her to go faster.

More. He wanted more. His hands moved to her hips in hopes of encouraging a faster speed, but she caught them up with hers. "Now, now, I want to enjoy this."

Which she did. Ecstasy crossed her face as she lifted it heavenward. He gave in to her pace, letting it increase naturally as she approached her climax.

The glory of her naked body towering over his stole his senses. He encouraged her to a faster rhythm, for if she didn't, he felt he'd leave her behind.

Her hands gripped his shoulders as she arrived. Just in time, for he couldn't last any longer.

Together they spilled over into the height of pleasure. Warmth flowed from his limbs to his central core, to rush forward into her. His orgasm rolled over and over until it had spent itself entirely.

Anthony dropped his head back to the pillow. Such clarity! It was as if the entire universe had opened up to him.

Lady Christina settled back, her body still gripped about him, gasping in fresh breaths of air. Her wits returned. She smiled down at him, running a hand over his chest. "You are so beautiful," she murmured. "I want to explore you further."

With that, she leaned down and kissed him once more.

To his delight, she proved she was nowhere near done with him.

Christina stood at the window, wrapped in Anthony's shirt. Clouds scudded across the night sky, opening to show a waning gibbous moon. For the first time since that awful card game, Christina's heart felt at peace. Soon the Season would end and summer would come, changing their world again.

Behind her, Anthony stirred. She heard him slide off the bed to come join her.

She had ravished him twice, plying his body with pleasure after the first time until he was ready to go again. If it wasn't for her thoughts for the future, she would have collapsed in his arms after that, to let Somnus claim her into his inky depths.

He pulled on a dressing gown, the sleeves of which enveloped about her as he embraced her. "Regrets?" he asked.

She shook her head. "I will only regret if we never do this again."

He bent his head and pressed his lips to her neck, the shadow on his chin sandpapery against her skin. They stood like this, saying nothing, watching the dark clouds against a navy-blue sky pass by the moon. The sounds of a night-time city sounded so far away, maybe a carriage in the distance, or a dog barking. Who cared?

Even the distant pounding on a door on the other side of the house only made her sigh. Anthony's arms tightened about her and he sank his head deeper into her shoulder. "It was too good to last," he murmured. "I look forward to a time when you are here when the sun rises."

Raised voices reached their ears. She would claim these last few moments. Who knew when such quietude came again?

Angry feet on the staircase. Michael and Stephen shouting her name. Honestly. Was there no subtlety about them? She turned and inhaled the masculine scent of Anthony's luxurious hair. She'd miss that.

Her brothers pounded on the door, then tried the doorknob. It opened. Perhaps it was a good thing she hadn't locked the door, though she'd considered it. Knowing them, they would have kicked it down.

"Tina!" Stephen shouted.

Neither Christina nor Anthony flinched. They didn't even turn around, even when the lamplight fell upon them.

Michael strode forward, but stopped just short of the quiet couple. "Are you," he began, "all right?" He held back Stephen, who muttered choice words.

"I was," came Christina's chilly reply.

Another voice joined them. "Oh, Anthony," his mother bewailed. "How could you?"

At this, Anthony stiffened. But he did not pull away from Christina.

His father huffed in the background and muttered something about banns.

"How could I not?" he answered her. "You have no idea the treasure I've found." He lifted a lock of Christina's hair and inhaled deeply.

Michael cleared his throat a few times. "Uh, perhaps after you've, um, gotten yourself together, we will be going?"

Christina stared at the moon. It had long passed the zenith. Soon dawn would be touching the horizon. "Must we?" Given her druthers, she'd stay here forever.

"You cannot be seen leaving here by the light of day."

"Sneaking off under cover of darkness, then?" She sighed. He was right. She'd been reckless. They all had been. Christina turned her gaze to meet Anthony's. His reflected her own resignation. "Come calling tomorrow? Or rather, today?" Yes, dawn approached far too quickly.

"Of course," he replied. "After all, I have an answer for that question you asked."

She perked up. "Oh?" What had she asked him? Faster? Slower? Kiss me here, do that again?

Before she could inquire, Stephen had located as much of her clothing as he could. He tossed her her shift.

All too soon, she found herself back in her own clothing, having reluctantly handed Anthony back his shirt. At least his scent still lingered on her skin. It would be too long before she could refresh that again.

Deliberately, she left one stocking behind.

So that was that. Michael took Christina straight home to her parents. This was a secret even he could not keep. Even made her wait while he told them. Instead of anger, her parents had expressed disappointment, which had to be worse. They insisted she be confined to home. It wasn't so much a punishment, as a way of dealing with her while they figured out what this meant.

And what about poor Lord Anthony? She'd all but stolen him away from under his parents' noses. It had been no secret. For all she knew, they'd fretted and worked things out together before showing up at the Southerland home.

But what did it all mean for Christine?

Isolation.

First day wasn't so bad. Second day bothered her. Third day had her going quite spare, but nobody would listen to her pleas for clemency.

Instead, she spent her time in the upstairs parlour, cradling the Southern Figurine of the carefree young woman who'd just escaped a terrible fate. The joy of her sudden freedom made Christina's heart ache. Would she ever have that again?

Downstairs a knock rang out on the front door. Postman? Lady Harrington had already declared to the servants that they were not At Home to anyone today. Even her brothers hadn't visited. She hoped they hadn't been visiting Anthony. It would break her heart if they broke his legs.

So many, many times she'd considered penning him letters, but what to say? Sorry I abducted you again, sorry I let my brothers know where we were, sorry I made everyone worry about us?

Of all the things she was sorry for, taking him that night was not one of them.

Voice arose in the hallway downstairs. The footman argued with someone, whose voice insisted on carrying up the stairs.

A cold shudder ran across her shoulders. She knew that voice.

Christina stomped her way down the steps. "I thought he told you we are At Home to nobody!" she shouted.

The Marquess of Lindsey stood in the hallway, his morning suit quite resplendent, his hat tucked under his arm. "Am I Nobody now?" he quipped. "For when you hear what I have to say, you will be very much At Home to me."

Without an invitation, he strode into their front parlour, much to the consternation of the footman.

Christina followed. "I have taken the very sensible advice not to speak to you. No good will ever come from me speaking to you. Now that you understand that, you have no reason to remain. I bid you good day."

The footman had run off, presumably to find her parents, leaving them very much alone. Christina drew in a deep breath as she realised this. Surely Lindsey wouldn't attempt anything foolish, would he?

He twirled about before sitting down. If he was expecting tea, he would be sadly disappointed.

Christina remained standing. "What do you have to say?" The moment his words offended her, she would bellow the roof down.

His demeanour grew serious. "I present to you an offer, which I hope you will present to your brother." He paused. Was he waiting for her consent?

"Go on."

"The matter that exists between him and me is just that--between him and me. It was not... wise... for me to bring you into it. In that he may have gained some justification in--" he broke off. "Lady Christina. You are a powerful and, some might say, admirable lady. If you were a man, you could very well terrify me."

She huffed at this half-compliment and folded her arms. What could one say to that? She let her silence stand.

He continued. "I hope you would consider our business together complete, and hope that you are willing to accept my offering of the removal of Fawdon."

Removal? "What do you mean?"

He rotated his cane as he pondered his next words. "Let's just say that Fawdon will not be bothering you, or any other lady.

"In saying that, I ask one last boon of you."

Her arms remained folded. No reason to call for help yet. "What do you ask?"

"I know what your brother is doing and why. I do not blame him for such ire, but the past is in the past. We've done each other enough harm. It is time for this to stop."

"Why are you telling me this?"

"Like I said, you are a powerful woman. He would not believe me, but he might, if it came from you."

"You're using me again."

He held up a hand. "It is not my intention. But please. He will not listen to me. This is over. It needs to be. Only you can convince him."

She could only stare at him. "What makes you think I have such power over him?"

Lindsey returned her stare. "You truly have no idea of what you are capable, do you?"

She waited for him to go on.

"Random strangers defended you the other night at the theatre. Granted, they may not know your reputation, yet they were willing to stand up for you. No doubt as you grow older and come to realise the power you have, you would be a formidable force within whatever circles you move. A woman like you would do very well in the demi-mondaine."

Somewhere, someone knocked on a door. Christina gave a small smile. "That may be my brother now. Do you want to explain your presence here?"

At this, Lindsey rose quickly, gathering his hat and cane. "Remember what I said. You get your brother to back off, and I shall leave you alone. Consider Fawdon a gift."

The door opened, but it was not Michael. Instead, the footman bore a note on the silver salver. "Addressed for you, m'lady." Was he out of breath? Upstairs she heard the heavy footsteps of her father, rousted from his library. Would he arrive in time to defend her?

She took the note, thinking it might be from Michael.

It was not. She studied the single word written on there. Her heart swelled, but other business first.

To the Marquess of Lindsey she said, "I will need that in writing. Only way Michael will be convinced.

"As for that other matter, I thank you for the compliment that you think I would do well in the demimondaine. I appreciate that you recognise a skilled and competent lady." She pressed the note harder between her fingers. "However, I intend to move within the respectable world."

He drew in a sharp breath. "If you do succeed in that endeavour, then you are truly a powerful woman. I wouldn't dare stand in your way."

Lindsey gave her a brief nod and departed, before her father made it down the stairs.

Only once he'd quit the house completely did she let out a sigh of relief. Lindsey may be devious but he did have a strange sense of honour. Fawdon was done. He'd never bother them again. Did that mean they were free?

As for the business between Lindsey and her brother, she'd present it to Michael. Unless there was more to the Diana business, surely Michael would see reason if it meant protection for his sister.

That was for Michael to sort out.

Christina turned her attention to the note in her hand. She opened it once more. All it said was, "Yes." Lord Anthony didn't need to sign it.

She cradled the note to her bosom. She'd enjoy this moment for herself, for once she shared the news with her parents, there would be no peace in this house until after the peal of her wedding bells had faded away.

EPILOGUE

Nearly a year after their wedding, Lady Christina Southerland woke one morning in a petulant mood. Her belly had grown sufficiently large that it was no longer prudent to appear out in public. She was not looking forward to confinement, and it irked her.

Lord Anthony, her husband, said he understood, but really, what man truly understood what it was like to grow frigate-sized and just as clumsy? Lying down felt uncomfortable. Even sitting felt uncomfortable. Walking was the only thing that really let her move, but the extra bulk made that intolerable after long.

Anthony had promised not to go socialising, but to stay at home, keeping her company. Not that she counted him spending hours in his workshop as "staying at home", even if it was upstairs. He wasn't here in the sitting room with her.

She looked to the window, to his latest Southern figurine. This one, the marketing had claimed, was not designed to sit on a shelf, or get locked away in a cabinet. It was designed to stand on a window sill. London had been all a-stir at this proclamation, but once the Fashionable Set had fought over the purchase of their figurines and got them home, once they'd displayed them as recommended, they saw why.

Here was a figurine of a young woman, hands raised up and pressed against the glass. Her head tilted as if peering out the window, lips parted in anticipation, possibly waiting for someone. Her knee pressed forward to steady herself against the window, almost as if hoping to push through it and rush outside. Anthony had said it had been modelled after her, as most his figurines were, but Christina could not recall herself pining at a window, unless it had been these past few weeks, yearning to escape the house and her imminent confinement.

Anthony had slipped out earlier that day, claiming an errand. Christina had no idea. He'd not finished his initial sculpting of his next figurine. There was no casting scheduled, no bisque firing and certainly no glaze firing upcoming that she knew of. These things were weeks away.

So, what was Anthony up to?

Before she had to wonder too long, he arrived home, an unadorned box in his hands. "A gift for you," he explained. But he did not hand over the box. "Is the figurine still at the window?"

Of course she was. Unless the figurine was pressed up against glass, she never did look right, standing on her own, hands upraised for no reason.

Anthony fetched it for her, saving her the trek. "Hold this."

He opened the box. Whatever was inside was obscured by tissue paper. "I've made a one-of-a-kind figurine, just for you. There's only one in the world and will never be more."

A unique figurine? Just for her?

From the box he lifted the figure of a young man. He wore no hat nor jacket, only a waistcoat over his white shirt. His hands were splayed back as if trying to keep his balance, and his legs were parted as if weak at the knees.

What on earth? Christina was left speechless.

Anthony held out his hand for the other figurine. "They're a matched set."

This Christina had to see.

With some gentleness, he slid the young man into the arms of the young lady, them matching perfectly, her hands just above his shoulders, her knee between his, and their faces all but touching in a kiss. Together, he propped them up not at the window sill, but on the mantlepiece, bracing them up against the wall.

Then she knew. "Our first meeting."

"Our first kiss," he answered her.

Suddenly, the figurine wasn't just some young woman pining at a window for who-knew-what. She'd become a lady who knew what she wanted, who would let nothing stand in her way. "It's beautiful. Thank you."

She sighed, wistfully, for it would be another couple of months before she could pin him against the wall again. Didn't stop her from hauling him down by the lapels for a kiss.

The End

ABOUT HEIDI WESSMAN KNEALE

Heidi Wessman Kneale is an Australian author of moderate repute. By day she suffers through the day job, dreaming of escaping to something better. The rest of the time she writes novels and stares at the stars. Discover more of her books (including audiobooks) at https://www.heidikneale.com.au/Regency Romance:
Just a Glimpse (a Soho Club novella)
Currently Unchaperoned
Her Endearing Young Charms
Historical Romance:
The White Feather
Marry Me (A Candy Hearts Romance)
As Good as Gold
Fantasy Romance:
God of the Dark
Bride of the Dark
House of the Dark

OPERATION SCOUNDREL

SONIA BELLHOUSE

Feisty Sophia Davenport longs for independence and not just an approved marriage. Impulsively kidnapping her sister's intended is just the beginning of her adventures. The man she captures aggravates her, but he also makes her heart race. When her plan goes disastrously wrong, Sophia's shot at, taken by ruffians and needs rescuing herself. After a daring escape, Sophia is alone with a man whose kisses provoke her deepest longings and passions.

CHAPTER ONE
LONDON, 1813

"Five girls and not a fortune between them, they'll be lucky to find husbands." Sophia lifted her chin and stared defiantly at two matrons who were supervising the ball. She was afraid they were right. If at least one of the sisters didn't make a good match, Sophia and her sisters would have to rely on distant relations to find them posts as governesses or companions. Felicity was the eldest, she should marry first. Conventional Felicity wouldn't chafe at the lack of freedom or feel rebellious, which meant Sophia could enjoy her relative freedom a bit longer. She was grateful the younger girls didn't know how precarious their situation was. Sophia guessed Father's investments hadn't been doing well. The crumpled sheets of the financial pages bore witness to that. She tried to smooth the frown from between her eyebrows, so unbecoming. All they had was their genteel breeding and their looks.

Often Sophia gave in to her wilder instincts and messaged the stables to ready her horse. She was relieved to get away from the house, filled as it was with unspoken expectations. Once far away she would allow her horse the freedom to gallop. Shoving her bonnet off her head, she let it dangle by its strings, as she whooped with delight at the caress of the breeze, the soft scent of the grass and her senses coming alive.

Sophia stretched those stolen moments, reluctant to return to her sedate and dull life. There, she had finally admitted it, life was dull. Ladylike behaviour made it almost impossible to do anything interesting.

Her parents had longed for a boy, while Sophia wickedly wished she was one. Boys had so much more freedom. They smoked, they drank, they swore and could go wherever they liked, unaccompanied: to gaming halls, the races, and boxing matches, even to the theatre and the music halls. Places no refined lady could go.

Sighing, Sophia reluctantly turned her horse's head toward home. She piled her hair back into a semblance of order and jammed her bonnet back on top. How ridiculous that she must be properly dressed in a bonnet and gloves before she left the house. Even sneaking off for a ride she had been compelled to obey. Sophia allowed her horse to crop at the grass for a few moments before encouraging it to walk on. Leaving the fields and open countryside behind her to return to the confines of the manicured garden of her home.

Luckily Bess was walking sedately when they arrived back at the house. Hearing raised voices Sophia thought her absence might have been the cause. She was helped dismount and made her way across to the house. here she was able to hear more through the open window.

"He didn't suggest calling here?" Her mother's tone was shrill.

"No Mamma." Felicity's answer was difficult to hear.

From Felicity's tone, Sophia sensed that not just her sister's hopes, but her heart was involved. Flick had confided how much she liked and admired Lord Hetherington.

"Charles," Felicity whispered, her voice almost a caress, "when we were alone, he asked me to call him by his name. He said that so very few people do."

Now Felicity was back home and there was no sign of Lord Hetherington. Sophia squared her shoulders and went inside.

"And where have you been?" Her mother rounded on her as soon as she entered the room. "Don't we have enough to worry about without you going missing?"

"I wasn't missing, Mamma. Robert knew I had taken Bess for a gallop."

"A gallop! Felicity is home and without the hint of an offer."

The sisters glanced at each other. Mamma wasn't liable to calm down for hours yet.

"Let me get you a drink, Mamma." Felicity soothed "Please sit and don't distress yourself, I am sure all will be well." They sat in silence while Felicity went to the kitchen. Returning moments later, Felicity said, "Mary will bring it through."

"How will all be well? You have let him slip through your fingers!" Mamma wailed.

"He was called away unexpectedly," Felicity began.

Her mother snorted. "Conveniently, more like. He's had his fun and now you are discarded." The words hung in the air, both explanation and condemnation.

"No, indeed Mamma, nothing improper happened and I believed him. He was shocked when word came, and he had to leave."

Their mother sniffed into her handkerchief, shaking her head.

"You girls know nothing of life. Men can be tricky creatures, especially when it comes to their freedom."

And why do we know nothing of life? Sophia tried to banish the rebellious thought but couldn't. They had been shielded, patted on the head, and told that being agreeable was enough. A little conversation, the ability to dance, perhaps painting or embroidery. How was this supposed to equip them for marriage? No wonder so many husbands and wives lived separate lives.

"So, marriage is a trap that we set for men? One they do their best to avoid." Sophia was shocked to realise she had spoken her thoughts out loud. Her words hung in the air as Felicity gasped and their mother sat straighter and glared at her.

"You wicked girl. It is the way of the world, *and you won't change it.* Marriage is respectable, you get to be mistress of your own house. The mother of his children, you get status and respect."

"But what about love?" Felicity said, her voice a little shaky.

"Love?" Her mother sniffed. "Well, you can't have everything. You should be satisfied with a good man who supports you."

"But what if it's not enough?" Sophia couldn't keep silent although she should.

"You make it enough. You adjust. You have your position, your children, and the respect of your community." There was finality in their mother's words.

Sophia felt a sense of sadness. Could it be enough? It wouldn't be enough for her.

Then an idea came to her A daring plan to settle the matter for Felicity. She would have to ask her some probing questions and risk disapproval if she were to be found out. She wouldn't allow her plan to be found out. A smile curved on her lips; she was going to have an adventure. Better than that, she was going to create an adventure.

"And you, miss, what have you to smile about?' Her mother's sharp tone brought her back to reality.

She bobbed her head and said as meekly as she could, "Nothing Mamma, I have nothing to smile about."

"You have exhausted me, all of you, leave me now. Before you go, tell Cook I will have some cakes and tea now."

"Yes, Mamma." The sisters bobbed their curtsies and left the room.

Sophia linked her arm through Felicity's. "Come into the garden."

Then crossed the manicured lawn before reaching the door to the walled garden, it was quieter in the walled garden. Strolling to the shady arbour arm in arm they sat on a stone bench.

"Now, we are far enough from the house. Tell me everything about Lord Hetherington."

Felicity didn't need coaxing. "He's wonderful, I felt extraordinary when I was with him. The way he looked at me, the way he talked with me. He's got lovely brown eyes," She sighed dreamily.

"Brown eyes be damned." Sophia said.

Felicity gasped. "That's unladylike language."

"Why isn't he here? Speaking with Papa and asking for your hand?"

Felicity faltered. "I was sure he *would* be here." She bit her lip as her eyes filled with tears and her shoulders drooped.

"All right, what did he say to you last evening?" Sophia coaxed. She had to get the whole story out of her reserved sister if there was any chance of helping. So, she clasped Felicity's hand in hers and gave it a quick squeeze. "Believe me, I am trying to help you."

"We danced," Felicity's voice lowered. "I could see the admiration in his eyes and felt a tremor when he touched my hand. It was all very proper and correct, of course, but I know how I felt."

But what did *he* feel? He could have been thinking of another easy conquest, or perhaps he had honest regard for Felicity. Their upbringing had left them woefully unprepared to deal with men.

"And Mamma was there, supervising?"

"Of course. Although she was enjoying a gossip with some of the other mammas."

So, her mamma had been supervising and doubtless was feeling herself at fault for becoming distracted. Felicity added, "He did ask her permission to take me into supper." And doubtless mamma was delighted.

"What did you talk about?" Sophia queried.

"His career and managing the estate."

"Sounds exciting." Sophia's flat tone contrasted with her words.

"It *was* exciting. He has plans for change, to modernise the estate and make it more profitable. His father has recently come into the title and the estate management has been left in a mess."

"And where is this estate?"

Felicity waved her hands and said, "Up north somewhere."

"Scotland?"

"No, the north of England, somewhere near Manchester. There are staffing problems and land disputes."

'So, a bit distracted then. Did he give you any sign he would call on Papa?'

A slow blush spread across Felicity's fair features as she glanced sideways at Sophia. "I expected him today, indeed I would not have been so forward if I did not. I can only assume some crisis has caused a delay." She fidgeted with her fingers, not quite meeting Sophia's eyes.

Sophia squeezed her hand in sympathy "Where is he lodging? Did he say?"

"He's staying at King's Coaching Inn, as he intends to travel north with various supplies and equipment."

"Well, that's a start. Let's despatch the stable lad to ask if he still resides there."

Felicity gasped. "We shouldn't." She pleated her skirt between her fingers.

"Of course, we should." Sophia was already planning what to do when the information came back. "Let me deal with it."

Despite her misgivings, Felicity didn't say not to do it.

Before they went back into the house Sophia making sure she wasn't seen, had a quick word with the stable lad.

"I'm going to explore the attics, if you'd like to come," Sophia said, encouraging Felicity.

"No, I think I will sit with Mamma in the parlour, you know I have a calming effect on her, and I have some embroidery to finish."

Sophia crept quietly upstairs; she didn't want to be observed. She'd tell Isabella her plans later but wouldn't mention them to Felicity. Now, he needed to be alone to think it all through. She moved beyond the broad carpeted staircase and the uncarpeted wooden stairs of the servant's quarters, to the pull-down ladder to the attics. The pole to hook the ladder down was there and she mastered it after a couple of tries.

Anything that was no longer needed found its way up to the attic.

Sophia stood at the doorway and looked around. As she stepped forward, her skirts brushed the floor raising a thin layer of dust. She sneezed and listened ears alert for any sound. The attics were a repository for all sorts of discarded items and Sophia hoped she could find what she needed.

Trunks stacked in the middle of the floor were a good place to start. The leather bindings were stiff, and she struggled to undo the hasp of the buckled strap. A short while later Sophia grunted triumphantly, as she fell back on her heels. The lid creaked open.

On top was a pair of old curtains, which she put hastily to one side. They were of no use. Beneath them though was a man's greatcoat, which she inspected. Promising. It was of an older style, its dark grey woollen fabric showing no signs of wear, or holes. Sophia set it to one side. Then she found a pair of breeches, a shirt, waistcoat, and tricorne hat. Perfect. A dark bandana would complete the outfit. These must have been her Pa's when he was younger and slimmer.

A flare of excitement bubbled inside her. It was a daring plan. Would she have the nerve to carry it out? She straightened her shoulders. She could, she must.

The next trunk also yielded useful clothing. A smaller greatcoat, breeches, and shirt. Sophia held them out to inspect them, they might well fit Isabella. Persuading her sister to wear them and go with her might be more difficult. Boots? They would have to wear their own riding boots. That was not ideal, but it was unlikely any male boots would fit them. One problem at a time.

Pistols, she needed a believable pair of pistols or better yet, two sets and shot. She wasn't going to shoot but they wouldn't know that, and waving a pistol around should convince anyone.

Again, luck was on her side, and she found a fine pair of pistols with silver chasing on the handle. They might be duelling pistols, owned by some old ancestors perhaps. She looked around but didn't find much else of interest. She shrugged. If necessary, she would sneak Papa's pistols out of the gun cabinet.

Poking her head down the hatch she listened. There was only the buzz of a busy household as the staff dealt with their chores. It was now or never. She threw the greatcoats and clothing down to the floor below. Jamming the tricorne hat firmly on her head, Sophia tucked the duelling pistol case under her arm and made a shaky descent.

At the bottom of the ladder, she sagged with relief. She'd made it. All she needed now was to fold the ladder back up and hide the stack of clothing hidden in her room. She wasn't sure how much time had passed, but with any luck the stable boy would be back. Sophia made a heap of the clothing and, clutching it carefully, made her way back down to her room.

Once there, she let out a shaky breath. Part one of her plan was complete. She laid the duelling pistol box in a drawer and tried on the grey greatcoat. It came to her ankles but fitted surprisingly well. Sophia pulled back her hair into a tight knot and placed the tricorne hat on her head. Then tied the bandana across her nose and mouth until only her eyes showed. She scowled menacingly at her reflection in the mirror. *Is it believable? At least it will be night, the night hides a thousand secrets.*

She stored the greatcoat and hat away in her clothes press. Trying on the breeches, gave her a few moments of anxiety when it seemed they might not fit, but once she was accustomed to them, she liked the way they fit. They gave her a great deal more freedom of movement than her skirt did.

She still had to convince Izzy, but she didn't anticipate any problems there. Isabella would be up for an adventure; however, hare brained the scheme was. It was Felicity and their parents who had to be kept in the dark. because they would be horrified at what she was proposing. *She* should be horrified by what she was proposing. Instead, she felt a tingle of excitement as she exited the side door to head to the stables.

CHAPTER TWO

It wasn't far to the stables and Sophia relaxed there. The soft snuffles and snickers of the horses, the smells of polish and straw, made her feel at home.

One of her earliest memories was of crowing with delight when she was placed on a placid pony. Horses responded to Sophia, and she relished the freedom of being out on horseback. It took her away from the daily rules and restrictions of home.

She'd snaffled an apple from the fruit display and went to talk to her horse Bess, a graceful chestnut mare. Bess nickered softly at Sophia's approach. She fed Bess the apple as soon as her head appeared over the stable gate and patted her. They spent a few minutes together, Sophia chattering softly to the horse.

Young Rob returned as Sophia was preparing to leave. "Tis as you thought Mistress. Mr. Hetherington's coach leaves tonight and he is going with it."

Oh, so he wasn't using his title. Interesting.

"Thank you, Rob, you've done well." She slipped a few coins into his palm. "What time do they depart?"

"Seven o'clock, they hope to make good time to the next inn."

So, he probably had plans to change horses there and continue onward. The spring weather was mild, and the roads should be passable, although travelling at night was unusual.

It remained to be seen if it was a move made from urgency, or stealth. Whatever the reason, it didn't give her much time to set her plan into action. Her thoughts were in turmoil, with much to do. The easiest of the tasks would probably be to convince Isabella to help, so she gave Bess's soft muzzle one last pat and left the stables.

Sophia found that the French doors to the garden were open and slipped into the house that way. Isabella was seated and doing some embroidery.

"Mooning about with the horses again?" Isabella teased good naturedly, Isabella much preferred to be indoors. Sophia beckoned her closer whispering, "I have a plan and I could use your help."

Isabella's eyes brightened at once as she said loudly, "A plan for what?"

Sophia shooshed her. "A plan I want to keep quiet about."

She gestured to Isabella to move closer and then explained her plan.

"It should not be too difficult; Mamma and Papa dine early. After the meal we can plead tiredness and retire. It's unlikely they will disturb us."

Isabella's eyes widened. "And you think it will help, Felicity?"

Sophia answered honestly, "I don't know, but at least Felicity will know the truth. So, will you help me?"

"Count me in." Isabella nodded; her eyes sparkling with excitement. "Can I see the pistols?"

Sophia grinned and led the way to her room, where she wedged a chair under the doorknob. "We don't want to be disturbed."

Satisfied they had some privacy; she pulled the smaller of the greatcoats from her closet and urged Isabella to try it on. It was slightly large, but it would have to do. Next, Sophia produced the breeches and

Isabella strutted about in them. Neither of them was able to control they giggles.

Sophia gnawed at her lip. "We need to find you a hat. Your hair is too distinctive."

"Red. You mean, my hair is red." Isabella tossed her head, and her luxuriant auburn curls cascaded around her face.

"Your hair is gorgeous, why ever would you think otherwise?"

Isabella shuffled her feet and looked downcast. Eventually, she said, "I heard Prissy Singleton's mamma commenting that red hair was such a common colour."

"You mean mousy Prissy Singleton?" Sophia smiled. "I think her Mamma is jealous of how pretty your hair is."

"Thanks." Isabella smiled. "I know its noticeable, I will have to find a hat"

"Bundle your hair up tightly. You may have to borrow Papa's hat and pray that you don't lose it."

Sophia sighed, each step of the way more complications faced her, but she was determined to find out the truth for Felicity. She pulled out the drawer where the pistols were stashed and opened the case.

Isabella's eyes widened. "You intend us to be armed?"

"Yes, who would listen to us otherwise?" She lifted one of the heavy guns from its case and gazed down the sight. "This is a fine pair of Flintlock pistols. Each has two shots." She gestured towards the case. "Try one for size. See how it feels in your hand."

Isabella nervously approached the gun case. "You really think it's necessary?"

Sophia inclined her head. "I do."

Izzy's caution reminded her that this was a dangerous action she was planning and involving her sister in. She searched her brain for another way but failed to come up with anything. They could wait and let Felicity hope and then despair. No, it was better to find out the truth now.

Isabella picked the gun up delicately with two fingers, then steadied herself leaning the pistol arm against her other forearm as if to fire. Her lips clenched and her eyes half closed, until she looked quite different from Sophia's easy going younger sister. It was encouraging

"We will do well if we keep our nerve." Sophia reassured. "Go and take some rest. We must be abroad later.

Time went so slowly when you were watching it, Sophia had made all the preparations and waited with nervous expectation. The saddle bag retrieved from the stable was packed and ready. It had a narrow length of cloth, and a length of rope. If all went to plan, she would need them both. She sat and then immediately stood again, unable to settle. Her thoughts too were all over the place. Was she doing the right thing? Was there another way?

The long-case clock in the hallway ticked on the hour and the half hour. Finally, it was time to dine. Thank goodness their parents kept country hours and dined early. There was little conversation at the table. Felicity was downcast and scarcely spoke. The younger girls took their food in the nursery, so their antics did not enliven the scene. Papa was talking about some invention. Sophia who often showed an interest and asked him questions, didn't enquire further. Without her encouragement, he gradually came to a halt. Mamma spoke only of the food to praise or disparage it as she felt it needed.

It seemed like the meal might go on for ever. Finally, Papa pushed back his chair and threw his table napkin onto his plate.

"I believe I will retire to the study, my dears." He said as he did every night. There, he would drink his port and doze by the fire.

"Will you girls join me in the parlour?" Mamma said, as she did every night. They would sit and chat desultorily and maybe work on embroidery if the candlelight allowed. Mamma might indulge in a small glass of sherry and Felicity had recently been allowed to join her. Sophia had a novel she was reading aloud to entertain them. changing her voices for different characters. After about half an hour she laid the book aside, being careful not to end on an exciting moment.

"I'm sorry, Mamma, I am feeling quite fatigued. If you will excuse me, I will go to my bed." Sophia forced a yawn, which Isabella quickly copied. "I am afraid I must beg leave too, Mamma." Isabella said in her meekest tone.

"Well, off to bed with you both. Felicity and I are made of sterner stuff and will stay here a while."

They made their curtsies and kissed her cheek before leaving the room. It was difficult to contain their excitement, now the time to act was approaching.

"I have eased my window catch and the back door bolt," Sophia whispered. She had almost been caught in the kitchen but had begged a small sweetmeat saying she was hungry.

If Felicity came into their rooms and found bolsters set into their beds, she was not likely to raise an alarm.

"It's now or never," Sophia said with a slight quiver in her voice. It was one thing to think of a daring plan, but another to act on it. They changed into the breeches, shirts, and greatcoats. Isabella had one of their father's slightly battered hats, but it would do. Her hair was bound tightly, and she jammed the hat on her head. The transformation was remarkable. Sophia faced Isabella towards the looking glass.

"Hello brother," she said, grinning. Isabella scowled menacingly, before dissolving into peals of laughter. Sophia rammed the tricorne hat onto her head and took a deep breath. They were going through with it.

Sophia eased the bedroom window open and delicately lowered the wrapped bundle holding the guns. One jolt could be disastrous, but it landed safely with the gentlest of thuds. Next, she lowered the saddle bag, and then it was their turn. Hopefully the old trellis for the ivy would be strong enough to support their weight.

"I'll go first, just to make sure it's safe." Sophia said lowering her leg over the windowsill. It looked higher from that vantage point. For a moment she wavered, but forced herself to climb over the sill, setting her feet into gaps in the trellis. After muttering a hasty prayer, to whom she wasn't quite sure she placed her hand on the trellis. It swayed and she drew in a quick breath and waited. The trellis held firm and she was able to climb down. It took less than a minute but felt much longer.

Looking up to where Isabella was, she waved her down.

Isabella didn't move. She shook her head, eyes wide with fear. Sophia dared not shout, so she held her breath and willed her sister to go. Without Isabella her plan fell apart. Felicity would be left not knowing what had happened to Charles and Mamma would start nagging Sophia to find a suitable match. Encouraging Isabella with a wave, she was relieved when her sister swung one leg over the windowsill.

Once they were both safely on the ground, she handed Isabella the saddle bag. Gathering the bundle with the pistols, she pointed toward the stable. The outdoor lanterns were almost burnt down as pale moonlight illuminated the scene. They made their way across the damp grass, and then their feet crunched on the gravel, surely twice as loudly in the stillness of the night. Horses nickered as he women crept forward.

"How do we get in?" Isabella whispered.

"The door shouldn't be bolted, I asked young Rob to see to it earlier."

There was little moonlight, just enough to see by as Sophia fumbled with the small side door. After a few moments she gave a hum of triumph as the door swung open. The horses whinnied and fidgeted at the intrusion. Sophia calmed them with gentle murmurs and soothing sounds. She coaxed Bess out of her stall, cheered by the horse's soft greeting. Isabella chose her favourite horse and, speaking softly, let the mare out too. Saddling the horses took more time than Sophia would have liked as they weren't used to doing it. Finally, they were ready, and pulled the stable door all the way back. Sophia handed Isabella one of the pistols. "Put it in your pocket. You can wave it about, but *don't* fire it."

Isabella raised an eyebrow, but said nothing.

Once outside, Sophia pulled the stable door closed. She helped Isabella to mount and used the mounting block to boost herself up onto Bess's back.

"Follow me," she whispered as she dug her heels into her horse's side.

Darkness enveloped them, the moonlight giving little light to navigate by. Luckily, there was only one route for a coach to take, which was heavily wooded. This would be to their advantage. After a swift ride they reached a spot where the road curved, and the coach would have to slow. It was a perfect spot for an ambush.

Sitting on Bess, Sophia listened for the sound of the oncoming coach. Isabella was on the other side of the road. The plan, although risky, was to straddle the road and stop the coach where it had no chance of turning round. Of course, their horses could be run off the road, but Sophia was determined to try. Felicity's happiness was at stake.

She strained to hear any sound. Finally, the dull thud of hooves resounded through the forest. Her heartbeat echoed a similar rhythm.

Sophia stage-whispered to Isabella. "Pull you coat up higher and cover your face with the bandana." She did the same, as they manoeuvred their horses into the centre of the road. They drew their pistols and waited. The hoof beats sounded louder, and the coach pulled around the bend. If the coachman didn't stop, they were on a collision course. Sophia waved the pistol in the air menacingly and held her breath waiting for the inevitable impact of the moving horses. The coachman pulled at the reins, calling, "Whoa."

The horses skidded to a stop, stomping, and shaking their heads in protest.

Sophia deepened her tone, shouting, "Stand and deliver." Isabella also waved her pistol about, and moonlight glinted off the barrels of their guns.

"All right, All right. It's those toffs in there you want not me. I'm just a poor working man."

"Cover him," Sophia snapped to Isabella. "If he makes a move, don't hesitate to shoot him."

Once she was sure Isabella had things under control, Sophia wrenched open the carriage door. Startled figures stared back at her. A woman cowered in a corner beside an older man.

A young man glared at her. "Do you have to wave that damn pistol around? Can't you see you're scaring her?"

That was the general idea. Sophia pointed her pistol directly at him. "And just who are you?"

Dark eyes glowered at her. "And why is that any of your damn business?"

She prodded at his chest with the pistol. "Indulge me." For a moment she thought he wasn't going to answer and held her breath. She hadn't planned on having to shoot anyone.

Finally, he spoke. "C. Hetherington, on my way to the family estate."

"Oblige me by getting down from the carriage."

"What, get off this coach? I regret to say I am disinclined."

Of course, nothing was easy. She prodded him in the chest with the pistol again. "Indulge me, or do you need encouraging? I could shoot you in the kneecap." *That was good, who knew where it came from? Maybe I have a talent for abduction.*

He gave her an assessing look and side-stepped the pistol. Too much time had been wasted so she cocked the pistol and stared at him challengingly.

"Time to go." Sophia said, tired of his delaying.

He made as if to come towards her and she fired off a shot. It ricocheted and instead of grazing his kneecap it hit his thigh.

He yelped in shock, "Damn it! You've made your point."

He limped toward the door as she backed off enough to allow him to dismount. He jumped down, winced and glared at her, before attempting to take off. Isabella was fast and nudged her horse in front of him He came to a stop, cursing.

"Coachman, hand me down his bags," Sophia demanded.

The burly coachman did as he was bidden throwing two bags down from the luggage rack. Their captive made to protest and then thought better of it and shrugged his shoulders.

Sophia waved her pistol again. "You can be on your way."

The coachman needed no encouragement. "Right, you are, sir." He said, raising his whip and urging the horses onward.

Hetherington stood quietly, assessing them. Sophia hadn't thought much beyond capturing him and that had gone spectacularly well.

"We need to tie him up," she muttered to Isabella. "Give me the rope and keep your pistol trained on him."

She tied his hands behind his back, before realising if he was to ride with them, he would need his hands in front, so she untied and retied them, Up close she caught his masculine scent, mixed with the coppery tang of blood and was that sandalwood soap?

"I'm sorry about your leg."

"An inept villain, but one with a conscience." He scoffed.

"We could treat you a lot worse," Sophia reminded him, only now thinking seriously about the consequences of her plan. She had an injured man on her hands, and they needed to get away from the road urgently. He had to be able to mount the horse, but his hands were tied. There was nothing for it, she made her tone gruffer.

"You need to mount my horse, if you are boosted you up, do you think you can manage that?"

He stared at her, his eyes lazily assessing as her cheeks flamed.

"Why me, what do you want? Why should I go with you?"

Typically male behaviour, being arrogant and annoying. "I'll ask the questions; I could just as easily shoot you here." She waved the pistol, but he appeared unimpressed.

"Oh, what choice do I have? Have it your way, I will try and mount the damn horse."

Sophia swung herself up awkwardly onto the horse's back, a feat she could not have accomplished but for a handy tree stump and wearing breeches. She breathed a sigh of relief that she had managed so well, Sophia then manoeuvred Bess into position and waved to him to come forward. As Isabella's pistol was trained on him.

"My companion is an excellent shot, don't give him an excuse."

Then he was close to her as he put his foot on the tree stump and swung his leg across the horse. Bess, snorted with the unfamiliar scent and weight of him on her back. Instinctively, he spoke gently to the horse and Bess calmed. His voice was luxuriant and intimate, making Sophia acutely aware of their proximity. There was something appealing about a man who could gentle a huge beast.

What would it be like if he spoke to her like that? Gently, caressingly? She shook her head. He was Felicity's intended, so she had no business thinking about him like this. Sophia settled herself in front of him aware of his scent, his body heat, everything about him.

"You need to hold onto me," she said. "My partner will ride behind us with a gun trained on you, so don't try to escape." He grasped the sides of her coat. Isabella waved the gun to reinforce the point, as they set off.

Sophia's plan had been hastily put together. Her heartbeat raced and her palms felt clammy. They'd pulled it off. Well, so far anyway. At first, she'd thought they could hide him in the icehouse. seeing as it was out of the way, and no one was likely to visit it, but it had a terrible chill, so she reconsidered. He was Felicity's intended and he couldn't be harmed. Well, any more than she already had. It was just a flesh wound any way.

The next choice was the disused dairy. It was still a solid building, set far away from the house and no one was likely to visit it. Yes, this would do nicely.

They made good time, considering her horse was burdened with an extra rider. She was aware of their captive seated behind her. It was as well he couldn't feel her feminine shape through the bulky coat. The arrogance he'd already displayed would be even worse should he realise she was female.

Almost reaching the dairy she slowed Bess to a walk and let her meander a bit. The horse had earned her gratitude tonight. She expected a protest from her prisoner, but none came. Once Bess had stopped munching on a tasty bit of grass, Sophia urged her forward once more. They came to a halt beside the rounded honeypot shaped dairy, and she slid from the saddle.

"Can you dismount?"

He swung his leg over the horse and dropped to the ground, wincing. He almost buckled but quickly righted himself. Sophia's natural urge was to comfort him, she cleared her throat instead. "You can rest inside."

Isabella opened the dairy door, and they went in. The pitched roof, stone floor and tiled walls ensuring the interior stayed cool, but it wasn't as cold as the icehouse. There were two rooms, one previously used for cheese and butter preparation and the other to clean all the utensils.

Two of the dairy maid's stools were still there. Too bad she hadn't thought far enough ahead to supply a chair. Well, for now, this would have to do. She motioned for him to sit down. He did hesitating and wincing stretching the injured leg out in front of him.

Even in the moonlight the wound looked nasty, although the blood had congealed. It needed tending. She bit her lip, that was a complication she hadn't anticipated,

"I need to look at your leg," she blurted out. "You will have to remove your buckskins."

He waved his still-bound hands in front of her. "Better untie me then, unless you want to do it?"

"That won't be necessary." She deepened her tone.

Isabella drew in a startled gasp, at the idea of their captive being untied. While Sophia debated what was best to do. Sophia wondered if it would be safe to untie him. Was inviting him to remove his pants unseemly? It probably was. What if he had followed the latest male fashion for no underwear? She realised she would have to untie him.

"Keep your pistol on him, while I untie him," she instructed. Isabella moved close, as Sophia bent down to untie his hands.

He struggled to hit out at her, knocking her hat off. She felt the bandana around her face slipping and hastily tugged it upwards before slapping his face.

"Do not mistake me for a fool," she snapped, as her heartbeat pounded, and her forehead was clammy with sweat.

He shrugged his shoulders nonchalantly. "I had to try."

"I could leave your leg untreated if you prefer."

He sobered then, saying contritely, "Thank you, I will behave."

She loosened the ties from around his wrists and motioned for him to take off his pants, while she disappeared to the back room to fill a pail with water and find a cloth.

When she returned, he was sprawled on the stool. long, bare legs stretched out in front of him. She gulped. He must have had under-things to cover his manhood, but he was essentially half naked.

She wasn't going to blush. It was probably commonplace with males, they sport and wrestled and swam naked together. Sophia cleared her throat and knelt to take a closer look at his leg. It wasn't as bad as she had feared.

"This will hurt." She warned.

He shrugged, "God dammit man, get on with it." He closed his eyes and leant back on the stool.

She gulped, she'd never been so close to a naked man and sneaked a quick look. His body was hard where hers was soft and dark hairs formed a line down his chest thinning as they reached his navel. Sophia lowered her gaze away from him and dipped the cloth into the bucket, trailing chilly water over his thigh. He flinched and she backed off, but then rallied and did it again. The wound needed binding and then he wouldn't be able to get those skin-tight buckskins on.

I wish I had never tried this hare-brained scheme; I'm giving myself one problem after another. He is Felicty's intended and shouldn't be harmed. If she doesn't get an offer soon Mamma will start trying to marry me off.

She cleared her throat. "Have you a flask upon you, sir?"

His eyes flew open, and he scowled. "What, do you now fancy a drink at my expense?"

"Well, have you, or haven't you? I thought to cleanse the wound properly, as I've heard they do after fighting."

He reached into his long coat pocket and pulled out a monogrammed silver flask. He took a quick swig and offered the flask to her. "It's brandy, feel free to take a swig."

She put the flask to her mouth and let the liquid flow down her throat. Then the warmth and fire of it hit her and she coughed. To hide her confusion, she leant forward and poured a generous amount over his leg.

"God's teeth, that stings!" He jolted backwards and then shivered.

It was cool in the dairy, so he couldn't be left there virtually naked. No matter what kind of heartbreaking villain he was. She grabbed the rope, rebound his hands and fastened him to the stool.

Isabella shuffled her feet and had the gun pointed at their captive, but her face was turned away, her younger sister. Isabella wasn't out in Society and knew few males. Sophia gave her sister an encouraging glance.

"Keep your pistol trained on him and I will be right back."

Isabella raised frightened eyes, muttering, "Hurry up". Then mouthed almost silently, "I'm scared".

CHAPTER THREE

Sophia ran to the back of the house, which was still in darkness, and eased open the side door praying it would not squeak. Half-light came in through the window as she crept silently to her bedroom. The door creaked open, and she held her breath.

Seconds ticked by but nothing else in the house stirred, so she grabbed the spare pair of men's pants she'd taken from the attic, which had been too long for the sisters.

Next, she made for the linen press. Opening the blanket chest, with its scent of cedar wood, she grabbed a woollen blanket. At the bottom of the cupboard was a bag of fabric scraps and she rifled through it for a pillowcase so thin it could no longer be mended. She tucked it in her greatcoat pocket, closed the doors and crept downstairs again.

The side door creaked as she pulled it to. Her heartbeat thudding as she glanced around the dark grounds. Burdened with the cumbersome blanket, she struggled to open the dairy door.

Their captive was slumped on the stool, Isabella standing well back from him.

"I don't like this. You shouldn't have shot him. I think he's passed out."

Privately, Sophia agreed. "Too late now, I did."

At the sound of her voice, he stirred and mumbled, "You tie a damn tight knot."

Startled, she snapped back. "Your comfort isn't my concern." Which reminded her of what was her concern. To bandage his leg and then to question him.

"Give me your flask again." She said, waving her fingers as if to summon it to her grasp.

"I can't."

"Just do it," she said losing patience with him.

"I can't unless you untie me, you will need to get it, it's in the great-coat pocket." He squirmed on the stool.

A slow flush spread over her body. How stupid of her to demand it. She approached him cautiously; He could still kick out or struggle. He looked dishevelled; his hair was too long to be fashionable, and a stray lock fell across his brow. Meanwhile, his dark eyes assessed her, making her feel uncomfortable.

She stopped beside him, "Which pocket is it in?"

"You will need to come closer, it's in the inside pocket."

Of course, it was! Another clever ploy to gain advantage perhaps? Sophia shook her head; this was no time for weakness. She must do what they came here to do.

"The left side, or right?"

"The left."

Which meant she would have to lean across him, which brought them perilously close. Leaning across him, she was acutely aware of his glance, his shallow breath, the sandalwood scent on his skin. He drew in a sharp breath, as she fumbled in the greatcoat pocket, finding nothing.

"It's not there." She huffed.

"Well, it must be in the right side, pardon my confusion." His smile said that nothing was further from the truth, and he had deliberately misled her. As she leant across him again and slipped her hand into his inside pocket, he inhaled and let out a breath on a sigh.

"You smell ..." His brow furrowed, but he didn't finish the thought.

Sophia moved back the flask in her hand undid it and knelt before him to better tend his leg. Her head was bent as she poured more brandy over his thigh "You are the first fellow I've met who smelt of jasmine," he said conversationally. "Are you of that persuasion?"

Sophia rocked back on her heels "What?"

Isabella gasped at the scandalous comment.

"Do not be so weak as to not admit it. Some men, well they engage with other men. I do not despise them for it. It leaves more women for those of us who do appreciate them."

No wonder poor Felicity was bereft. He was a rogue of the first order. Probably he had many women, all distraught and waiting for him to commit. What a loathsome creature he was!

She straightened and the bandana slipped from her face. Her hand flew up to grab it, but too late. He stared, eyes exploring her every feature, eyes lingering around her mouth. Sophia flushed.

"How could I have ever thought you were a man? Undoubtedly a woman and a lovely one." He shook his head. "This does not explain your abduction of me though, however delightful you are. I am sure it must be a case of mistaken identity, lovely lady. So, untie me and release me. There's a good girl."

The arrogance of the man. He thought so little of women that he expected to wriggle his way out of this. She straightened to her full height and glared at him. "You are C Hetherington are you not?"

"Yes, I am."

"In that case, sir, there is no mistaken identity.' She shot him a look of contempt "I will bandage your leg as Christian charity bids me to do and *then* we will leave you to reflect on your sins."

"I have no more sins than any man." He protested as he tried to squirm himself free of the bindings.

She smiled as she knelt to the task of bandaging his thigh.

slathering salve on it, which she'd taken from the kitchen where it was used to treat burns and minor injuries. It really worked. It also stung. When she applied a liberal dressing to his knee. he sucked in his breath and blew it out again, tears springing to his eyes.

"God's teeth, have a care. That hurts."

"Oh dear," Sophia said in pretend confusion. "Does it hurt as much as dancing with a lady for two dances, taking her into supper, making promises to her and then leaving her alone. Is it that sort of hurt?"

Isabella stifled a laugh.

He stared at Sophia head tilted and brow furrowed. "You are very pretty." He acknowledged. "But you are undoubtedly mad, I did not act as you describe. I would not do such a thing."

He sounded sincere and for a moment Sophia wavered, had they got the wrong man?

"But you are C. Hetherington?"

"I am."

"Then sir, you lie, and we will leave you to reflect on it."

She threw the blanket across his knees, so he was covered and before he could protest, she stepped behind him. and tied the fallen bandana across his mouth. He wriggled but she got it tied securely.

Sophia faced him again, ignoring the imploring look in his dark eyes. "Have a pleasant night and we will talk again tomorrow. Perhaps then your recollections will be better."

She had no qualms about leaving him in the dairy, with the sturdy door locked. and the windows barred. Even if he should work the bandana free from his mouth, the dairy was far enough from the house that no one would hear his calls.

Sophia slept well, with no bad dreams to trouble her sleep, or any concern for their captive. She stretched, relishing the coziness of the bed and the comfortable bedroom she shared with her sister. She smiled; Mr. C Hetherington was sure to have spent an uncomfortable night. Being gagged and tied to a stool was no less than he deserved.

Sophia ran her fingers through her hair and got out of bed. Isabella was slow to awaken, so she shook her sister's arm.

"Wake up, sleepyhead."

All she got was a low moan, followed by, "leave me alone, I'm tired."

"Mamma will have something to say if you miss breakfast."

Isabella opened her eyes "I think Mamma would have more to say if she knew you had a man in the dairy and that you shot him."

"I plan to interrogate him today and find out exactly what is going on."

"Not me. I plan to stay well away from you and your hare-brained schemes. I shouldn't have gotten involved." Isabella yawned.

"It was exciting though." Sophia's eyes sparkled.

"He was flirting with you, wasn't he?" Isabella said.

Sophia raised her eyebrows in disbelief. "Was he?"

Isabella sat up. "Yes, and you were flirting with him too."

Sophia flushed. "I wasn't. At least I don't think I was."

"Unconscious flirting then." Isabella stretched and got out of bed.

Once washed and dressed and breakfasted the household went its several ways. Mamma into her parlour to discuss the rest of the day's meals with cook. The little girls to the schoolroom with their governess. Papa riding out to who knows where, no one dared questioned him. Which left Felicity, Sophia, and Isabella in the cheerful and sunny front parlour. Felicity was red eyed and bent over her embroidery. Isabella had her sketch pad and pencils out and was drawing Felicity.

Sophia sat on the arm of a chair and said in her most coaxing tone, "Flick, tell us about Lord Hetherington, what he looks like, for I have only seen him at a distance as he was monopolising you."

Felicity put down her embroidery and stared into space.

"He is good looking, with dark hair and green eyes, and I believed him to be a good person. He spoke with such sincerity. I didn't doubt for a minute that he would be here speaking to Papa."

Sophia looked down at her lap, she could clearly picture the dark eyes of their captive.

"He has green eyes?"

"Oh yes, a lovely shade of green, darker than grass, bottle green."

"And that is C. Hetherington?"

"Yes" Felicity looked puzzled "Although he asked me to call him Charles, when we were alone." She smiled at the memory, before becoming downcast again.

Sophia's pulse raced, if Charles Hetherington had green eyes, who was that in the dairy? She fought down a sense of panic and tried for a casual tone. "I think I may go for a walk; would you care to come with me Isabella?". She locked gazes with her sister, and tilted her chin in the door's direction, her lips more a grimace than a smile.

"Thank you, you go. I'm perfectly comfortable here."

It was too maddening, but Sophia could do no more than shrug. The fluttering in her stomach would not be quelled, they had the wrong man.

She had got the wrong man. Could there be two men named C. Hetherington? What could she do now? How to make it right? How to apologise for abducting and shooting the wrong man?

Sophia groaned biting her lip as her mind ran this way and that. There was nothing for it, she would have to face him, make apologies, humble apologies she hastily amended. She ran her hands through her hair, pacing back and forth as different scenarios flashed through her mind. No, she shook her head. It was no use, she had to face him. Maybe it was lucky she had chosen an appealing dress. The blue flow-ered print on the white background with the blue trim on neckline and sleeves was one of her favourites.

Sighing, she squared her shoulders. Unpleasantness was best faced head-on. Walking to the dairy took less time than she would have liked, and her thoughts were not helping. All she'd thought of and discarded were feeble excuses. There honestly was no excuse.

Sophia unlocked the dairy door and stepped inside. Their captive had not fared well during the night. He, and the stool were lying on the floor, There was a large bruise on his forehead and dirt across his face.

She gasped, all thoughts of apologies forgotten, and raced to his side. She pulled the stool upright. Once righted, she untied his hands, and then tugged the bandana from his mouth. Before he could speak, she had dampened a cloth and pressed it to the bruise on his forehead.

"I am so sorry that you are injured."

For a moment, he stilled as she attended to the bruise.

"You have some explaining to do." He glared at her and suddenly all thoughts of contrition left her.

"If it comes to that, so do you."

He raised an eyebrow, "Are you telling me that I am responsible in some way for my abduction?"

She swallowed nervously. "Not exactly, but why did you tell me your name was C. Hetherington?"

"Because it is."

"Charles Hetherington?" She sounded sceptical.

"*Of course not,* I'm Christopher, my brother is Charlie. My friends call me Kit, but I won't be numbering you among them."

Sophia shut her eyes momentarily appalled at what she had done. He rubbed his arms and flexed his wrists.

Oh no. The rope had cut into the flesh of his wrists. She grasped his wrist and began soothing and stroking them. Sophia felt her eyes filling with tears. She tried to choke them back, ending with a sob.

"Come on, it's not that bad." He coaxed, "I hate to see a woman cry."

She raised her tear-stained face to his. Her blue eyes were swimming with unshed tears.

His gaze swept across her face landing on her mouth. Before she knew it, he had placed one arm around her and drawn her to him. She could have resisted. She should have resisted, but curiosity got the better of her.

His soft lips found hers, and she responded eagerly. She pulled back a little, laughing in his arms. Then, he was kissing her properly. His lips brushing across hers, soft yet insistent. He gave the slightest of nips to her bottom lip, stunned she paused for a moment, before she nibbled back. She could hardly think, as experimentally, she worked her hands into his dark hair, coaxing his mouth back down onto hers. He murmured, "Minx" His grip tightening about her waist as he pulled her closer. She knew she should have been appalled, but it was glorious, and she revelled in it. Sophia kissed him again, enjoying the feeling of control as he responded eagerly to her. When he finally released her, his eyes glittered, and he gave her a lopsided half smile.

"There, crazy lady. I hope I've kissed it better."

She ran her fingers over her lips, as if she had never felt them before. They felt softer, fuller, more alive. She felt more alive. When she spoke, her voice was husky, and she gave him a half smile, shocked at her own boldness.

"I'm not quite sure." She paused to give him a teasing smile. "Do you think we should do it again, just to check?"

He needed no further invitation. This time she thought she was ready, but when his tongue pressed between her lips she stepped back with a gasp. The sensation had been strange but exciting. A bit invasive even

"I have scared you," he said, "and I did not mean to. You are so lovely that I forgot myself." He turned aside from her.

Had she offended him?

"You surprised me. It felt strange. I'm not sure if I liked it." Her fingers brushed across her slightly swollen lips.

"That's fine, we don't have to do that at all." He became brisk and business like "We have other things to concern us. I will need help to get home." He gestured to the ill-fitting trousers she had supplied him as well as his own damaged buckskins. "And we need an explanation for why I am in this state. A convincing one."

She bit her lip, in the cool light of day her capture of him seemed foolish in the extreme. But then, she still needed to know where his brother was and why he had let Felicity believe he cared. "Where is your brother Charles? Do you know?"

"He could be anywhere; I don't pay attention to what he does." He shrugged then held her hand and smoothed his fingers over her knuckles. "Why does it matter to you?"

"Not me. My sister Flick, Felicity, he gave her to understand he would be calling on Papa."

"Did he indeed?" He sounded surprised, "When I get home, I can ask him."

"Is he a man of his word?" She held her breath, hoping against all hope that Charles wouldn't shame Felicity.

Christopher spent some time considering before he answered "Yes, if he gave his word, then he will keep it."

"So where is he? My sister is beside herself, that's why we abducted you. To get answers."

"From me?"

"No, of course not you. Answers from Charles. Who would have thought there would be two C. Hetherington's?"

"Actually, there are three, I have a younger brother whose name is Colin."

"Do your parents lack imagination?" Sophia gasped, then looked down at her shoes, horrified by her lack of tact.

"No. Charles was the heir, then they lost interest with my brothers and me. My mother has always wanted a girl, but it was not to be."

"You have more brothers?"

"There are six of us, each one more of a disappointment than the previous one. I'm surprised they gave my youngest brother a name at all." He sighed "For a long time, he was simply known as Six."

"How sad," Sophia said.

"Yes, and he's wild and gets up to mischief, just to claim attention. But we have rambled. How am I to get home?"

"Does your family have a coach they could send?" She thought for a minute "Or simpler still, I will introduce you to my family, explain you had been set upon by ruffians and asked for my help."

"And would they believe you?"

"Why shouldn't they?" She raised an eyebrow and gave him a mischievous grin. "It is, after all, the truth".

He raised an eyebrow and cocked his head to look at her.

She lowered her eyes. "Well almost the truth.

He grinned back, "As long as I don't have to describe the 'ruffians', then your secret is safe."

"It was for a worthy cause. My sister's happiness." Sophia looked pleadingly at him. "You wouldn't tell?"

"Indeed, your secret is safe, I know you acted with good intentions." Christopher said.

Sophia looked anxious. "Are you fit to walk to the house? Are you sure you won't tell?"

"Yes," he groaned "Let's get it over with. I will leave you to tell the tale."

CHAPTER FOUR

Sophia led the way, taking it slowly as Christopher hobbled alongside her.

He refused to take her arm. "Give me some dignity," He protested.

They entered the house through the front door and Sophia escorted him through to the parlour. It was a comfy room with big windows, allowing the spring sunlight to enter. A well-tended fire and some comfortable chairs meant the family gathered there. Mamma leapt to her feet in surprise.

"My goodness what has happened?" She rang the bell for a servant to attend them. "Bring brandy and ask Mr Davenport to join us."

Moments later, when all was settled, Christopher was offered a chair by the fire where he could stretch his leg. Papa stood with his back to the fire, hands clasped behind his back.

Sophia told the tale so convincingly that Christopher himself almost believed it. There were gasps of consternation and exclamations of horror that a gentleman should be subjected to such an attack, and so close to their home.

Sophia, wide-eyed, told how Christopher had escaped the villains after being shot, and stumbled into the garden and into her arms.

"What was I to do Papa, but to help a gentleman in such distress?" Her every word quivered with emotion.

Her Papa raised a quizzical eyebrow. "Now tell me again how you came across him?"

"You know I do not sleep well. I was at my window, when I saw him stagger into the garden. I could tell at once he was in trouble and went down to help him."

Her father eyed her shrewdly. "Did it not occur to you to wake your mamma and me?"

"It did, but I didn't want to disturb you." Sophia sounded most sincere.

"You did not awaken your sister?"

She shook her head. "I let her sleep."

"Hmm, the servants then?"

Sophia clasped her hands "Oh, you know how they gossip; I didn't want to cause a scandal."

"But you going to his aid wasn't going to cause a scandal?"

Sophia lowered her eyes. "To be honest, I did not think, I just acted."

The most honest remark she has made, Christopher thought.

Her father offered the use of his carriage to take Christopher home, which he accepted. He was loaned some more respectable trousers and crammed his boots back on. He thanked everyone at least twice, before he was finally allowed to depart. He wasn't sorry to leave. He needed time to recover and to talk to his brother.

Sophia clasped his hand, whispering, "You will talk to Charles?"

"I give you my word. I will let you know what I find out." Christopher squeezed her hand as he bade her and her family farewell. It was a shame there was no prospect of kissing her again. She was a tempting mixture of passion and innocence; one it would be a pleasure to teach the ways of love.

Two days passed slowly with both the older girls unable to settle to anything. Sophia took Bess out for a gallop but even that left her restless. Sophia and Felicity fretted, expecting to hear from Charles, or Christopher. They speculated endlessly as to what had happened, until Isabella was ready to scream.

"Who cares about those stupid men? They are not wasting any time on you." She stamped her foot, causing both sisters to stop and look at her in surprise. "Well, they are not. They are getting on with their lives, and you should do the same."

It was good advice, but their hearts were engaged. Sophia was now more sympathetic to Felicity, having met Christopher, or Kit as she called him mentally. He'd said only his friends called him Kit, Surely after their kiss, she could count herself among them. If she felt like that, then Felicity, who had been wooed, must feel it more acutely?

"Your turn will come Isabella, and you will find someone worthy of your regard." Felicity said.

"If it makes me as silly as you two, I don't think I'll bother." Isabella snapped. Sophia bit back an angry remark. There was no need for Isabella to be curt just because she was feeling left out.

Two long days later, Christopher returned. Once his horse was attended to at the stables, he strolled over to the house and was greeted with enthusiasm by the family.

After the greetings had been dealt with, their father spoke, "What news?"

"Charles has disappeared, and the family are frantic." Christopher said. "Papa is furious not knowing what has happened to him. The Hetherington Heir, Viscount Rufford. Whether he has been set upon, press ganged, even murdered." The grim set of his features showed that he shared those fears.

"Has a reward been posted for information?" Pappa asked.

"Yes, it has, and we have had no news. Someone must know something. I had to tell you, and let Felicity know that my brother is missing. I knew she would be concerned."

Felicity raised her chin. "I sensed something must have happened to him. I hope he is safe and soon found."

"It's what we all hope for," Christopher said. "I know Charles would never stress our parents like this."

"Is there anything we can do?" Pappa asked. "Perhaps those ruffians who set upon you, have also set upon him?"

Sophia gulped; would Christopher reveal her deception now? She cast an anxious glance at him.

"I can't believe so, that would be too much of a coincidence." He replied straight faced. Only his eyes betrayed him, with a glimmer of mischief when he caught her glance. Sophia gulped, knowing she was at his mercy.

"Stay, tell us what you have been doing," Pappa invited.

"I can't stay long," Christopher replied with regret in his voice. "My mother is beside herself with worry. We boys don't seem to be much comfort to her."

Their mother answered him. "Ah, of course not. A mother's tender heart is so easily bruised by loss. I would go to her myself. Alas, I cannot leave my dear husband and younger children alone." She sighed, "I would, of course, invite her here, but I know she will not wish to be away from your home."

"You are most kind, Madam." Christopher replied. He was ready to take his leave but still lingered.

"Ah, I have the answer," Mamma said. "I will send my dear girls to keep your mother company and to cheer her."

"Ma'am I'm not sure..."

She brushed his protest aside, already bustling to gather supplies. "It's the very thing. Felicity is such a comfort and is also anxious about your brother. She will be a great solace to your mother. But of course, I cannot send her alone into a household full of men. Sophia, you will need to accompany her."

It was a masterful piece of work; Sophia could only stand back and admire her Mamma. How could Christopher protest?

He gulped. "Indeed, madam it is a most generous offer, but can you really spare them?"

"Oh yes, I insist." Mamma smiled and said, "I see it as my Christian duty."

Christopher sighed. He was beaten, the young ladies would be going with him.

Their mother clapped her hands. "Hurry girls, go and pack a bag each and be quick about it. We must not delay the search."

Sophia felt her face flame. Did Christopher think this was as blatant a piece of work as she did? She could not meet his eye as she passed him to go and pack a few things. Isabella sat on her bed and watched as Sophia dithered about, unsure what to pack.

Soon, the coach was brought around and their bags were loaded. Then the girls were saying their goodbyes. Father gave them each a swift kiss on the cheek, but Mamma pulled the girls close. "I've given you each a chance," she whispered, "make sure that you make good use of it."

"Yes, Mamma," they chorused, as they each kissed her cheek.

CHAPTER FIVE

L uckily, Christopher had arrived home before them and informed his mother of their impending arrival. She came out to the front portico to greet them with a welcome Sophia scarcely felt she deserved. If only his mother knew what she'd done to her son.

Christopher introduced them to his mother. "Mamma, allow me to present Miss Felicity Davenport and Miss Sophia Davenport."

They dropped the expected curtsies.

"My mother, the Countess of Scarisbrick, but she prefers to be called Lady Margaret."

She motioned them to rise. "How generous," Lady Margaret their hostess said, as she presented her cheek to be kissed by the girls. "And you must call me Margaret. I am most grateful to your mamma for having sent you to me." She shuddered a touch theatrically. "Men cannot understand how we women suffer." Scarcely pausing for breath, she tucked each of the girl's arms through hers and walked them into the house. "Kit," she called, "see to their bags."

Sophia stifled a laugh at his expense as she glanced around the grandeur of the hallway. It had a chequerboard black and white tiled floor and an imposing dual stairway. A glittering crystal chandelier was suspended high above them. Their hostess gave them little time to look around as she escorted them into a charming room.

"My little sanctuary," she explained. "In a house full of men. I need somewhere that is mine alone."

The walls were painted the palest yellow, reminding Sophia of sunlight. Large double French doors opened onto a garden terrace, with a small table and chairs.

Their hostess sank elegantly onto a chaise longue and waved to the girls to sit. There were several comfortable looking chairs scattered around. And Sophia chose an upholstered yellow chair beside a stylish side table that supported a vase filled with roses that scented the air.

"How lovely to meet you," their hostess said, giving them a bright smile. "Although I wish it was under better circumstances."

Felicity murmured, "We hope our unexpected arrival won't inconvenience you."

"Not at all, I am glad of the company." .

Biting her lip, Felicity asked, "Has there been any news of Charles?"

Lady Margaret shook her head. "No, nothing," she said with a catch in her throat. Then she visibly pulled herself together and rang a small bell. Smiling brightly, she said, "We will take tea and you can tell me all about yourselves."

A short time later, a loaded tea tray was wheeled in by a plainly dressed but cheerful older woman. She bobbed a swift curtsey while stealing a curious glance at the girls.

"Thank you, Abigail, that will be all," Lady Margaret said.

"If you need anything else just ring," Abigail insisted.

Their hostess raised her eyebrows and Abigail departed.

Margaret warmed the teapot with some hot water, then took the key for the tea caddy and unlocked it. After pouring the warming water into a dish, she measured some tea into the silver tea pot. and poured hot water into the pot. "While we wait for the tea to brew, tell me a little about yourselves."

The sisters glanced at each other, uncertain what to say. Did his mother know of Charles's advances to Felicity?

Sophia swallowed nervously before replying. "We are a family of five girls. Our parents needed a boy, but it was not to be."

Margaret sighed in sympathy "Your poor mother, I myself am similarly afflicted, for I have nothing but boys." She shook her head before adding, "Of course, I love them dearly, but it is hard being a lone woman in a household of men."

"I suppose it must be," Felicity replied, closing her eyes and taking a calming breath before continuing. "I have met Charles and he speaks of you with much affection."

Margaret brightened momentarily. "He is a dear boy and speaks well of you."

Felicity gave a tremulous smile. "Then he has spoken of me?" She held her breath.

"Oh, my dear, yes. He confided in us his wish to court and marry you."

Tears began to pool in Felicity's eyes. Impulsively, Sophia got up and hugged her sister. The girls clung together as Margaret joined them putting her arms around them both.

"My dear, you've shown me that you care for Charles. We must hope that he is found soon."

The hug seemed to have calmed them all, and soon they were engaged in chit chat.

Margaret sat back, holding her teacup and smiling. "I am so grateful to your mother for sparing you to me, at this difficult time." She squeezed Felicity's hand. "You and I can worry together, and we can talk about our dear Charles." Looking across at Sophia she said simply, "The boys think I am very silly for worrying, but what else is a mother to do?"

The afternoon passed pleasantly and when they had exhausted their gossip Margaret rang for a servant to show them to their rooms.

The sisters had a room each, instead of sharing as they did at home. Luckily, the rooms had an inter-connecting door, which they left open so they could talk to one another. The rooms painted in the palest greens and blues. A warm fire burned in each fireplace.

Sophia was given the blue room, while Felicity had the green.

"It's to match your eyes," teased Felicity, although she then whispered, "isn't this luxurious?"

It was, and Sophia revelled in it, except for the reason they were there.

There was a knock on Sophia's door. When she opened it, a young maid bobbed a curtsey and said, "The mistress said to tell you that they keep country hours and dine early."

"About what time?"

"They will be in the drawing room before five of the clocks."

"Thank you." Sophia nodded.

The sisters gazed at each other in dismay, time was already ticking away, they hadn't got long to get dressed for dinner.

"We will just have to do our best with what we've brought with us," Sophia said, voicing her fears.

Each stared with dismay at the clothes hanging in the closet. Dresses that had seemed suitable at home looked drab and boring in these grander surroundings.

Felicity pulled on a light petticoat. Next, she added her pale pink dress, it had a low neckline and puffed sleeves. The skirt fell from a braid-trimmed high waistline. Her throat and arms were bare.

"Should I wear gloves?" Felicity fretted.

"It's a family dinner, I don't think so," said Sophia, adding practically, "You can't anyway, we didn't pack them."

Felicity squinted at herself in the mirror. "My neckline looks awfully bare."

Sophia guessed her sister was having a crisis of confidence meeting Charles's family without Charles being there. "Do you have your cameo brooch?"

Felicity nodded. "Let's thread it on a ribbon so you can wear it around your neck, it will look very pretty.

Next, Sophia began to dress Felicity's hair. Without the benefit of the curling tongs they used at home, this was an awkward task. Sophia used tons of hairpins, pinning little curls into place and then looped another ribbon through the carefully styled hair.

Finally, it was done.

Felicity squinted at herself in the mirror and nodded. "I don't look bad"

Their primping hadn't left Sophia as much time to dress herself, but she was unconcerned. This visit was about Felicity. She selected a turquoise dress that brought out the colour of her eyes and added a small silver locket around her neck. She quickly pinned her hair in loose curls and wound a silver ribbon through them. A glance at her reflection showed her pink-cheeked and bright-eyed. She linked her arm through Felicity's. "We're ready!"

The dinner gong sounded, and the girls stared at each other. "Come on, we must face them," Sophia urged. After a quick squeeze of their hands, they descended the stairs.

Christopher was waiting for them at the foot of the stairs. "You both look lovely." He smiled and bowed. "Permit me to escort you to the dining room."

Each took his arm, and he walked them through to the dining room. Sophia guessed his leg was troubling him as he walked stiffly.

The room was well lit, with candles reflecting from several mirrors hung on the walls. The room was filled with young men sitting at the table. They rose to their feet as the girls entered.

Margaret patted the seat beside her. "Felicity, I insist that you sit with me."

Felicity did as she was bidden, sinking into the seat gratefully.

"And you, Sophia. There is a place for you, between my husband and Kit."

Christopher gestured to the spot and Sophia took it. Then the men sat. They all took after their father, equally as tall and handsome.

Lord Edwin, spoke, "Welcome to our home. I wish it were in better circumstances."

Felicity flushed, answered for both of them, "Thank you, my lord, I hope that Charles may soon be found."

He inclined his head, "As do we all." He swallowed hard and cleared his throat.

Margaret, beamed down the table saying proudly, "Let me introduce my boys." She indicated the young man on her left "Colin".

He inclined his head and muttered, "Charmed to meet you."

Next to him was Simon. He too inclined his head. Opposite Sophia was Stephen, and the youngest Sextus.

"Ah you must be Six," Sophia said, blushing as she realised she had spoken out loud. She raised her hand to her mouth as if to cover it.

Sextus grinned, "Yes, Six, will do very well, I'm used to it."

Margaret raised her voice, "That's enough, boys, you will overwhelm our visitors."

She rang a bell and two servants appeared with the soup, which they ladled out at each place from a silver tureen. Sophia was conscious of Christopher, sitting close beside her. His leg was slightly stretched out, no doubt because of his wounded thigh.

If I move my knee I could touch him, not that I would of course, but I could. And why him anyway? Six is nearer my age and looks like fun. She watched, fascinated, as Kit's capable fingers held his soup spoon. Sophia imagined Christopher's fingers curling around hers, his lips pressing down on hers. Heat rose to her cheeks.

Across the table, Colin relayed a recent exploit, and his brothers teased him. Sophia gradually relaxed. The meal passed pleasantly and the conversation flowed more generally. The boys lost their formality and the girls their shyness. Margaret was adroit at making small talk and including both Felicity and Sophia. They were laughing at some silly nonsense when a footman entered and approached the Earl of Scarisbrick.

There was whispered conversation until he threw his damask napkin on the table, rose to his feet, and said, "Pray excuse me a moment, my love."

Margaret too got to her feet "No," she said, "that won't do at all, Charles is my son, and I *will* be involved."

"I am merely trying to spare you, my love." The Earl gazed at her with a tender expression.

She smiled "Edwin, I know. However, not knowing is worse than facing whatever this is."

He inclined his head, "You know I can deny you nothing."

There was a pause after they left the dining room, and then the boys all spoke at once.

"Wonder what's up?"

"Let's hope its good news."

"There was no way Mamma was going to be left out," Six said grinning.

"Charles will be okay, he always is," Kit tried to reassure them.

"Mamma is seriously worried, so is Pa," Colin said.

Then they heard a scream from the hall followed by a thump.

CHAPTER SIX

Sophia followed everyone from the Hetherington dining room and rushed into the hall, from where the scream had come. Margaret was collapsed on the floor. The Earl was by her side. He snapped at the boys, "Help me carry her and someone fetch brandy."

Sophia picked up a sheet of paper from the floor. It was impossible to ignore the crudely printed message. IF YOU WANT TO SEE YOUR SON ALIVE, GO TO THE THREE BELLS TAVERN. TELL NO-ONE OR HE DIES. She gulped and showed the message to Christopher.

His expression was grave. "I was afraid of that."

"But why?" Sophia whispered.

"He's been involved in some serious endeavours."

She gasped in horror.

He answered her, "Nothing illegal, but potentially dangerous."

She shot back, "And you know this how?"

"Well ... I also may be involved." He shuffled his feet and would not meet her eyes

"Do your parents know?"

He shook his head, "Let's just say its preferable they don't know."

He gave her an easy smile. "We'd better join them in the drawing room."

Margaret was reclining on a chase lounge, while Felicity waved a bottle of smelling salts under her nose. The Earl knelt by her side holding her hand.

"Come on my darling, we will face it together." He murmured.

The boys stood back, looking anxious and helpless.

Sophia took charge. "Open a window and give her some air." She shooed them back and they retreated, looking relieved. "You boys can't do anything; your mamma is being looked after and will recover. Go and wait somewhere else."

They dispersed. The Earl nodded gratefully. Felicity had roused the countess enough to sip the brandy and her colour returned.

"So silly of me, to worry you all" She sat straighter and gazed tenderly at the Earl.

"It was the shock my dear," he said squeezing her hand, "but we will deal with it."

Christopher spoke then. "Papa, I've seen the note and I think I should go. Mamma needs you with her. I know that place a little, and that could be to our advantage."

Before she had considered fully, Sophia said, "I think I should go too, they won't be expecting a couple and that could give us more of an advantage."

Christopher shook his head before she had even finished speaking. "That's absurd. Ridiculous." He folded his arms across his chest as though the discussion was over.

"Is it, though? Why shouldn't it work?" Sophia argued, annoyed at his patronising attitude. "They won't be expecting it."

"She has a point," the Earl agreed, surprising her.

Felicity clutched her cameo, and twisted it absently "Sophia why do you want to put yourself in danger?"

Sophia smiled at her sister, "Why, to see you happy again and to see Charles safe. Besides, Christopher knows I am resourceful." She gave him a playful look. He sighed.

"We couldn't expect that of you, to go to our dear Charles's aid." the countess said.

"I offered. I didn't think Kit would be so churlish about it." She gave him a sideways glance to see if her words were having any effect.

"All right, you can come, but I expect you to do as I say," he said flatly, obviously feeling out numbered.

Sophia flashed a brilliant smile. "Thank you."

"If you will excuse us." Kit bowed to his parents, grasped Sophia by the upper arm and marched her out of the room. Once out of their earshot, his dark eyes turned stormy. His mouth was a hard line. "What the hell do you think you are playing at? This is a serious business."

"Yes, spying generally is." She agreed.

"How do you know that?"

"You just confirmed it."

He shook his head. "You are willingly putting yourself in danger? Danger I can't guarantee to protect you from, although I will do my best."

"I know. Now tell me about the Three Bells Tavern," Sophia said eagerly.

"This is not an adventure."

He gazed at her and groaned. "The Three Bells is a known meeting place, where gossip is exchanged, and deals are done. It's not a very genteel place, and you may see or hear things which could distress you." He gazed at her ruefully. "Believe it or not, I was trying to protect you."

"I know that you were, but I long for an adventure" She gazed at him her eyes sparkling and her cheeks pink "My life is so dull and prescribed, I can go nowhere and see nothing."

He raised an eyebrow. "So abducting me was simply a break from boredom?"

498

She flushed. "Of course not. Mind you, we managed well, didn't we?"

"By getting the wrong man."

She waved her hands airily. "Well, that could have happened to anyone. You said you were C. Hetherington."

"I am C. Hetherington, it was up to you to be sure you got the right one."

"Who knew there would be three? All right, I should have checked. You can't deny it was exciting."

"And there we are. *We* are professionals, we don't do this for excitement or fun. It's a task for discretion and secrecy."

"You need to change your dress."

"Why, do you not like it?" Sophia twirled to give him the benefit of a better view.

He sighed, "You need something plainer. We don't want to stand out."

Sophia rushed upstairs. A quick look through her clothes, and she picked the drabbest, most boring dress she could find. She unwound the silver ribbon from her hair and took off her silver locket. Sighing, she picked up her plainest bonnet and put it on. Then stared unhappily at the figure she saw in the looking glass. Ordinary, forgettable, drab.

Downstairs, Christopher had undergone a similar transformation. He wore a plain dark coat, which looked a little worse for wear, a faded waistcoat with a rumpled cravat and a pair of looser breeches. His boots were scuffed and unpolished. He'd rumpled his hair, so it fell over his face.

When Sophia looked more closely, he appeared in need of a shave, which he hadn't needed when she left him. He looked even more masculine and dangerous with that hint of stubble. Her fingers itched to run along his jawline and feel it for herself.

"How has your beard suddenly grown?" Sophia couldn't resist asking.

He grinned. "Trick of the trade. It's coal dust, just a quick dab with a cloth and some of the dust creates the effect. Luckily, that works with my dark hair."

And it emphasized his eyes and mouth too. She drew her gaze away from him with a conscious effort. "So, what are we going to do, how shall I act?"

He lifted an eyebrow. "You intend to follow my instructions and behave?"

"As long as your instructions are not too outrageous, I will certainly try."

Her mind drifted to a place where he was instructing her how to kiss him and caress him. Then, he'd decided she needed more instruction and showed her how a kiss should feel. She closed her eyes and swayed on her feet with the power of her imaginings. He coughed, and she opened her eyes with a start.

"Very well, we want to be inconspicuous," he said, "but have our eyes and ears open."

"Eyes and ears open," she repeated dutifully, her mind still assessing their kiss.

He opened the front door, took her hand, and tucked it over his arm. "Let's go."

The carriage drew up by the kerb. The coachman touched his hat with his whip and muttered, "Sir."

Christopher nodded, "Good evening, James, the Three Bells if you please." He held his hand out to Sophia and helped her inside, then climbed on board himself. Inside was compact and they were drawn closely together. Sophia clutched Christopher's arm as the carriage turned a sharp corner, then left her hand there. She again smelt the faintest scents of soap and sandalwood. He leant back against the upholstery and closed his eyes.

Could he really be that relaxed when she was almost quivering with excitement, or it was it tension? The journey took less than five minutes, before the carriage slowed. When it stopped James, came round and lowered the step. Christopher got out first and held his hand out to Sophia to help her down. His grip was warm and reassuring as he squeezed her fingers.

"Careful in there, Master Kit, this ain't be the best of places," James warned.

"Thanks, we will. Wait for us out of sight if you can. I will whistle when we need you."

"Right, you are, sir" James touched his hat with the whip, climbed back on the coach. and set it in motion.

Sophia shivered, the adventure becoming far too real.

"Courage," Christopher whispered, "It's time to learn what we can."

The smell of stale ale and raucous voices greeted them at the door. Sophia faltered. "I have never been anywhere like this."

"I know, but they are still people. Stay close and listen."

Pushing the door open, the fug of pipe smoke and ale greeted them. Christopher stepped inside; Sophia followed, scarcely daring to gaze around. She was suddenly glad of her plain dress.

A girl with paint on her face jostled Sophia, clutching Kit's elbow. "Lookin' for a good time dearie?" Her eyes were on his face, but her hand was already searching for his pocket. He caught her wrist and turned her to face him. Beneath the face paint there was a bruise.

"Not tonight," he said, "but I can pay for a few minutes of your time to chat."

"You wanna pay me just to talk?" Her eyes skimmed across the room.

He followed her gaze and saw a heavy-set young man observing them. He nodded to him and drew her to one side, motioning for Sophia to follow.

Attempting to follow them, Sophia was pushed and jostled.

The young woman gave Sophia a hostile glare. "She ain't goin' be no good- I ain't teachin' her nothink." She pushed past them as if to merge back into the crowd.

"That wasn't my intention at all." Christopher held out a silver coin. She grabbed it and bit it before tucking it into her bosom. "Stay a while longer, I simply want to ask you something."

"And her?" She glanced with ill-disguised hostility towards Sophia.

"She's here to hear what you have to say too, it's that important." Christopher tried a little flattery, which seemed to work.

"She's not on the game and lookin' for a new patch?"

"Good heavens, no. She is a church goer and most devout." There was a gleam of mischief in his eyes as he glanced at Sophia. She cast her eyes down as if in submission, while plotting how she would get back at him.

The girl accosted her directly, facing her with a hard stare. "I don't need savin' and I don't like God botherers."

Sophia gulped, never having been spoken to in such a manner. "All right, understood."

"Come, sit." Christopher found a free table and chairs and waved his hand for the server.

The heavy-set man, came over, "Yus?" He scowled.

"An ale for me, and ladies?"

"A gin for me," the girl said.

Sophia looked miserably at Christopher wondering what she should order in a place like this He must have sensed her confusion.

"Brandy?" He suggested, and she nodded gratefully.

Moments later their drinks were slapped down on the table, and, after another scowl, the heavy-set man left them. The girl knocked back her gin, while Sophia sipped her brandy and gave a hasty cough as the heat hit the back of her throat.

"What do you want, I ain't talkin' dirty with her 'ere," the girl said.

"Nothing like that," Christopher said hastily. "Just a little informa-tion, we are looking for a man who has recently disappeared."

The girl shrugged. "People disappear all the time, why ask me?" While her tone wasn't exactly hostile, it wasn't friendly, either.

Christopher gave her his most charming smile, "In your profession, you are used to sizing people up. You notice things."

She gave him a hard stare before whispering, "Sometimes it's best not to notice."

"I see. Can you tell me what you *didn't* see?" He let the coins in his pocket jingle. A not-too-subtle hint that he would pay for information. She glanced around.

"I didn't see a fella who looked a bit like you being bundled into a coach."

"Of course not." Christopher tipped some coins into her hand bending closer to her ear. "Do you happen not to know where he was being taken?"

The heavy-set man wandered closer, so Christopher ordered another round of drinks, which arrived quickly, accompanied by another scowl. "You be keeping' Jen from her proper job," the barman accused.

"I am paying her for her time, while educating my ward so she doesn't fall into temptation."

The man looked Sophia up and down and scoffed. "Her? A drab scrawny little thing like her. Nah, she ain't the type."

Sophia flushed to the roots of her hair as her hands curled into fists. How humiliating to be dismissed like that, and by a ruffian such as him.

"You and I are men of the world," Christopher said. "We know that even the saintliest can be tempted."

The man guffawed and winked, before moving away.

Sophia moved closer to Chris and stamped hard on his foot. He winced and issued a string of expletives that Sophia had never heard before.

"How dare you," she said. "How dare you talk about me like that."

The girl snickered, "Ha, I might take to her after all."

"I might, as well," Christopher said grimly.

Sophia trembled, until common sense reasserted itself and she realised he was playing a part, just as she was.

"She's had a very sheltered upbringing," he explained. "Now, what weren't you going to tell me?"

The girl lowered her voice. "The coach came back empty and there was blood on the seat."

"Ah that is worth something." He handed her another coin. "Do you happen to know where it went?"

She shook her head. "No, could be several places. The Crossed Keys has a cellar. The Blue Anchor on the harbour has a boat. The Windmill is so full of nooks and crannies you could hide a dozen people there."

"Thank you." He made a show of handing her the shilling, as he unobtrusively slipped her half a crown.

"You are a proper toff, just like he was," She smiled and looked almost pretty for a moment. "The word was, he was a spy."

Sophia gasped, but Christopher nodded easily. "Well, could be, but for which side?"

"Word was, it was the French." Jen spat on the floor at the name. Then, with a wink and toss of her head, she was off.

Sophia's mind whirled. Could it be true? Christopher grabbed her arm saying loudly, "Come along, just let that be a lesson to you." He busied himself ushering her out of the tavern, inclining his head to the heavy-set man as they left.

Once outside, he pulled her into the shadows of a nearby bush and waited. She was about to speak but he put his hand across her mouth whispering, "Wait."

Moments later two men left the tavern, big hulking brutes. One went to the right and one to the left. Their footsteps echoed as they retreated. Once they were gone, Christopher whistled for the coach. It was a few moments before it came into view. Christopher let down the step and then handed Sophia up into the carriage. She sank back into the cushioned upholstery with a sigh of relief. Shortly afterwards he joined her, and also sank back into the upholstery, knocking on the roof so the driver could take off.

"You didn't have to stamp on my foot." He complained, massaging the limb.

She tossed her bonnet to one side, ran her fingers through her hair and glared at him.

"I had plenty of reason to do so" She flicked open the top two buttons of her dress, and gulped in a breath. "What role were you playing? Obviously a rogue, and you *were* insulting."

He swallowed and looked away, distracted by the slim column of her neck and throat. He pulled his thoughts back with an effort to concentrate on his throbbing foot.

"Maybe you did" he conceded, "but you didn't have to stamp so hard."

She dipped her head and gave a secret smile. He'd deserved it, taking her into a place like that, letting her hear and see things no gently born young lady should see. Then her conscience kicked in. He'd treated her like an equal, as someone who deserved to know the truth. Wasn't that what she had wanted? A true partnership with a man who valued her and listened to her.

Sophia bit her lip, deciding she needed to speak. "Thank you for taking me with you. I was uncomfortable and felt out of place, but I know a little more about life now. I shouldn't complain."

"No, you should be grateful every day that you are housed, clothed, fed, and loved. Now I must tell my parents the shocking news, that Charles has been taken and we don't know where.

"Couldn't we look in the places the girl suggested?" Sophia raised an eyebrow. Why were they wasting time?

"It's better to let the family know what is going on and what we suspect. Charles has already disappeared, suppose we did too?"

Sophia considered before replying, "You mother would be even more frantic."

Chris nodded agreement, "I suppose next they will get a ransom demand."

Sophia gasped. "Would your parents pay a ransom?"

"Yes, I am sure they would, whether it would do any good." He shrugged, "I couldn't tell, but of course, Charles is the heir. He's been groomed for it all his life. It's his role, although there are plenty of brothers."

Sophia sighed. "Are you really so cold, so analytical?" He could have been talking about anyone, not his brother. His lips on hers had felt warm and tender but if his heart was cold, she wanted no part of him.

"It's my job," he said, "to assess odds and decide whether to take risks. It's what I do. It's how I stay alive and how Charles stays alive too. He's usually pretty good at it, so maybe someone has talked."

Sophia studied him in the half-light of the carriage. The planes and angles of his face showed more deeply in the dim light and the dark fake stubble on his chin let her study his mouth in more detail. Now he was serious, those were not the eager lips that had kissed her, or the laughing ones that had teased her. He was a man facing a problem, one to which he had no solution. His lips were compressed tightly together. He raised one hand to pinch the spot between his eyebrows.

The poor man must have a headache. "If you are serving our country, then there must be someone to whom you can appeal."

He looked startled at her remark. "Hmm?"

"Who knows about this? Who can you ask?"

He shrugged. "We work alone."

"So not even official spies then? Not able to call on the government for help?"

Christopher's posture stiffened. "Have you made a study of spying?"

"It is mentioned in a few novels, not very flatteringly. Against the gentlemen's code of honour, that sort of thing."

"So, we should sleepwalk into being overtaken by the French? Napoleon could be planning to land in Britain right now."

She gasped, "Is he?'

Christopher shook his head. "I don't know, and even if I did, I wouldn't tell you. A secret shared is no longer a secret." He closed his eyes and leant back against the upholstery.

"Will you continue to spy?"

"I'm an investigator, that's what I do. Winkle out secrets and lies. It's usually dull." He yawned, shut his eyes again and wasn't inclined to speak any further until they arrived back at the house.

Sophia didn't mind, as it gave her plenty of time to study him with his arms folded, as if he hadn't a care in the world. She knew now that his indolence was a pose, that he was always listening and seeing.

Should she take him at his word-that there was no spymaster, no official channels? She considered. If there were no official channels, no one to send the information to, there was no use to what he was doing. If he thought she would swallow that lie, then he had seriously misjudged her. But then, most men misjudged women, which could be to her advantage.

They arrived back at his parent's house and Christopher jolted awake as the coach stopped. He glanced around, raised his hand to stop her moving and said quietly, "Wait."

He gazed out through the coach window, sliding it down so he could swivel his body and look in both directions. The chill night air entered the carriage, and her breath misted before her. It was an agonising wait. She scuffed her feet together with impatience. Finally, he came back into the carriage. "We can go in now."

He stepped down before her and held out his hand as she stepped down. Her foot had just touched the pavement when a shot rang out. Sophia ducked instinctively as a bullet whizzed past her head. Christopher pushed Sophia behind him, pulled a pistol from his coat and fired back. Nothing happened, just an eerie silence. Sophia gazed wide-eyed as a splinter of wood flew off the carriage near to her.

He took command. "Let's get you inside." He practically dragged her to the front door.

The door opened as they reached it and Sir Edwin stood white-faced. "We heard shots." He didn't waste any time closing the door behind them.

Chris nodded coolly. "Yes, there were a couple."

Sophia's knees buckled. "They were firing at me."

CHAPTER SEVEN

When Sophia came to, she was seated in a comfortable chair and Margaret was waving a bottle of smelling salts beneath her nose. Felicity clutched her hand. A few anxious glances came from his brothers, who were looking at them with varying degrees of alarm and curiosity.

She sat straighter, "Well, that was an experience. I've never been shot at before." Her voice quivered on the last words, and she had to bite down on her lip to stop it trembling. It was almost worth it to see the admiration in Christopher's eyes.

"Kit get her a brandy, she's still in shock." Margaret's tone was crisp. "No young lady can relish being shot at."

She was right, Sophia would relive that moment, wondering if she had moved her head to the left or to the right would she still be here? "It makes no sense to shoot me, it's not like I am important or anything." Her voice quivered as she spoke.

Felicity said, "I've been so worried about you as well as Charles."

Kit's tone was bleak. "It's a warning for me, that they can strike at any time." He gazed at her sombrely, "Hurt the people I care about."

He'd confessed it in front of everyone. Could they have a future together once this whole sorry mess was sorted out.

He bent over her tenderly and pressed a brandy glass into her shaking hand. "Try and drink, it's good for shock."

She grasped the glass but the liquid swayed dangerously as her hand shook. Kit knelt beside the chair and covered her hand with his, she felt his warmth and strength as he guided the glass to her mouth. It was like swallowing liquid fire as it spread through her veins.

Lord Edwin paced the room, muttering about lawlessness and no good rogues. "Hanging's too good for them."

The brothers stood silently by. Sophia roused sufficiently to feel more like herself.

Margaret turned to Kit. "Do not keep us in suspense a moment longer, what have you found out?"

He shook his head. "Far less than I would have liked, and I am not even sure if what I was told is true." He relayed all the information he'd gleaned. "So there are at least three places he could be, and he's probably injured."

Felicity groaned and Margaret gasped, saying, "What do we do now? What can we do?" She turned to her husband and reached blindly for his hand.

He put his arm around her. "Come, my dear, be strong. We will face it together." She squeezed his hand, almost crying, but managing somehow to keep her composure.

There was a discreet cough as the butler entered, carrying a silver tray. He bowed and addressed the Earl.

"A note has been delivered, My Lord." He lowered the tray so he could take the note. It was on rough paper and crudely written, but its message was clear.

IF YOU WANT TO SEE YOUR BOY AGAIN PAY UP INSTRUCTIONS TO FOLLOW.

The paper fell from his hand as he turned to his wife with such a look of despair on his face. Margaret gasped, then rushed to his side and hugged him. "Come my dear, we will think of something," she said.

He shook his head. "This is all my fault, my own damnable fault. My pride and stupidity have led to this."

Christopher spoke up. "We made our own choices, Pappa, no one forced us. We knew what we were getting into."

The Earl sighed. "I encouraged you, now look what has happened."

"What's done is done. We must think what to do next." Margaret patted Lord Edwin's hand consolingly. "Christopher, what do you advise? Do we pay a ransom?"

He frowned. "I don't know what to tell you, it's never clear cut. You pay and they still might not release him, instead demanding more money. Or they do release him, and all is well. Or perhaps he escapes."

He began to pace as he thought things through. The other brothers dispersed, hastily leaving their parents to sort things out.

"Do you think he will escape?" Sophia said.

Christopher frowned. "Normally I'd say yes, but I don't know how badly injured he is."

Felicity paled at his words. "Poor Charles." She sank down onto a sofa. While Christopher continued to pace, hands behind his back.

"What about a rescue?" Sophia said, "Could you attempt one?"

He raised an eyebrow. "They would be alert to that possibility."

"What if it didn't go how they expected?" Sophia gave him an enquiring look.

He looked puzzled. "What did you have in mind?"

"They will be on the lookout for you. But what if it's not you, what if it's me?"

He stared at her. "You?"

She flushed at the surprise in his voice "Yes, me. Have you forgotten that I managed to get the better of you?" She heard him hiss in a breath. Sophia had almost said capture, but she doubted he'd want his brothers to hear about that. She gave him a melting smile and ducked her head when she saw the look of alarm and annoyance that crossed his face.

"That is impossible. A terrible idea." Christopher said.

Margaret cocked her head and looked enquiringly at Sophia. "Have you a plan?"

"I've not worked out all the details yet, but even ruffians can be foiled, I am sure of it. Besides, I have a score to settle, someone fired a shot at me."

Christopher sighed exaggeratedly. "Well, if that isn't a good enough reason to stop, I don't know what is."

Sophia gave him a pitying look before she continued. "When they demand a ransom, we must try and follow the messenger. That should lead us to where Charles is being held."

"Do you think we won't be recognised?" Christopher said with a look that implied she was clearly out of her depth.

"Of course not, but if the coachman were to wait outside, he might be able to follow them. And if they are on foot, maybe one of the other servants could go?" She glanced at Margaret, seeking reassurance.

Margaret appeared to think about it for a moment. "I think it's a splendid plan."

The Earl nodded approvingly. "We need to be prepared, so when they come, we are ready." He smiled at his wife, "Can I leave that to you, my dear?"

She kissed him on the cheek and patted it. Turning, she frowned at Christopher. "I don't know where you get such outdated views of female competence from. I thought I had supplied a good example."

He looked down, shuffling his feet. "Of course, Mamma, but you are the exception."

She shook her head and said, "There are more capable females about than you know. I am sure Sophia is one and Felicity is another." She linked her arms through the girls' arms. "Come sit with me and we can discuss it."

When Christopher made to follow, his mother shut the door firmly in his face, saying, "Go and think of something useful to do."

Sophia *almost* felt sorry for him. Almost, but his jibe about her capabilities rankled.

They were in limbo, waiting for more instructions. The countess, Felicity and Sophia drank endless cups of tea and spent time plotting.

Meanwhile, Lord Edwin sent a message to his bank about making a large withdrawal, if he needed it, instead of the usual promissory note.

Sophia had just seated herself on a rustic bench beneath the rose arbour when Kit strolled into the garden. He scowled at her, she smiled back and patted the bench beside her.

"Come and sit with me."

"I prefer to stand."

"How can we discuss confidential matters with you towering over me?" She patted the seat again. "We need a plan."

"I thought you had a plan?" He said, taking the space beside her.

"I have an idea. What if I go to the rendezvous, pretending to be Felicity. A worried fiancée, I am sure I can create enough of a distraction to enable someone else to sneak inside and rescue Charles?"

"That's a terrible plan," Kit said flatly, folding his arms and glaring at her.

"Is it though, or is it just because you didn't think of it?" Sophia glanced sideways at him. She ticked off the advantages of her plans one by one on her fingers. "One; they won't be expecting a woman. Two; that should cause some confusion. Three; they will have to rethink their plans, and while I'm wailing and crying in distress, their attention will be on me." She nodded "Giving you the chance to sneak in and get Charles out."

She waited as the silence lengthened, until she couldn't stand it any longer and tapped a foot.

"Well?"

He cleared his throat, "It's not entirely terrible."

She gazed at him "It's a good plan, go on admit it."

He scowled, "I've never liked working with amateurs."

Sophia sighed; Christopher was being difficult. "What choices do we have? They know you and your brothers, while no one knows me."

He scuffed his feet, "I suppose it might work."

Sophia restrained herself from smiling, saying simply, "Thank you."

The waiting was the worst part. Everyone grew short-tempered until finally a note was delivered. Lord Edwin showed them as Margaret sank slowly into a chair with tears in her eyes.

THE WINDMILL BRING £250 AT 8 PM COME ALONE

He patted her hand, "Lucky I got the money, and in bank notes not gold. My dear, it could be much worse."

"Worse, how could it be worse?"

"They are willing to trade."

She shook her head, "Edwin, we have six sons, what if they kidnap all of them?" Her bottom lip trembled, she was close to tears.

He squeezed her hand, "It's highly unlikely, my dear."

"But possible. I know I moan about the boys, but they are dear to me, every one of them."

They all exchanged worried glances. Margaret getting hysterical wasn't going to help anyone. She was Lord Edwin's rock, and they couldn't bear to see her crumble now.

"We have a plan," Sophia spoke up. "Kit and I have worked out a way forward."

Christopher shuffled his feet. "It's more of an idea, Mamma, don't get your hopes up."

Sophia glared at him, "It's a good plan." She insisted.

Margaret waved her hand in front of her face, "I don't want to know, I wish you luck, but I can't take anymore. I am going to lie down." Sir Edwin followed her out of the room.

Sophia turned to Felicity. "I need to borrow one of your dresses."

"Of course, anything that will help get Charles back."

"I don't know if it will, but we are going to try." Sophia patted Felicity's arm and gave her a swift hug. Sophia didn't mention how her stomach was churning or that her heartbeat was racing. She'd made the offer, she would have to carry it through.

CHAPTER EIGHT

The fluttering in Sophia's stomach increased with each moment that passed. She'd been full of bravado suggesting the idea. Now, her hands were clammy and her lips trembled. She bit her lip and concentrated on adjusting Felicity's dress to fit her. The pink wasn't her best colour, but that didn't matter, she planned on looking as little like herself as possible. A large-brimmed bonnet would hide much of her face, she hoped that would be enough.

When she descended the stairs, Christopher was waiting and handed her a small pistol.

Ignoring her gasp of surprise he squeezed her hand, saying, "If you need to use it, don't hesitate."

Sophia gulped, as she murmured, "Thanks." It reinforced what Kit had said; she wasn't a professional, just a bungling amateur. She wished she could take her stupid words back, because now she had to go through with it. The servant sent to follow the messenger who had delivered the ransom note had come back shamefacedly saying he'd lost him. It wouldn't pay to underestimate the kidnappers.

The clock moved on slowly until it was time for her to leave.

Christopher touched her arm for reassurance, and she almost screamed with suppressed tension. "You don't have to do this." He said softly once they were inside the coach and James was taking them to their destination.

Relief flooded through her. She didn't have to do it, but then, she would never know if she could have succeeded.

"I do, I gave my word." She was proud her voice didn't tremble and thankful that the coach was dim so he couldn't see her bleak expression.

The coach stopped far too soon for Sophia's liking, and she gave an exclamation of surprise. Christopher squeezed her hand and bent his head to press a kiss on her lips.

"For luck," he whispered. "Go well."

James opened the carriage door, let down the steps, and held his hand out to help her.

"Good luck Miss," he said.

Her stomach lurched but she smiled. "Thank you, James. "

Squaring her shoulders, she pushed open the door to *The Windmill.* The talk was stilled by her entrance. Buxom young women wearing low cut tops, pushed their way through the crowd carrying brimming mugs of ale. It was much as she had expected, a squalid dive where ale flowed freely, filled with tough looking men. Sophia gazed around and met the gaze of a dozen leering men. A fug of pipe smoke and chatter filled the air. Her stomach lurched as she felt bile rise in her throat, how had she thought she could do this?

"Taken a wrong turn, Darlin?" One of the men leered at her, she shrank back for a moment, before gathering her nerve.

"I was invited here," she said, "I have business to discuss."

An older man pushed through the crowd, his eyes skimming over her body in an unpleasantly familiar manner.

"We've got all the girls we need," He snapped and turned on his heel. Sophia grabbed his arm and turned him to face her.

"It's the other business I'm here to discuss."

"Other business? You?" He scoffed looking her up and down again.

She drew herself up to her full height and raised her chin. "Yes, you are holding a man hostage. That man is my fiancée, and I need to see him before I agree to pay the ransom."

Something flickered in his eyes. Sophia couldn't sense what it was, maybe amusement?

He nodded. "Right, your ladyship, I'll just get him fetched for you."

The ruffian motioned to one of the men and whispered something and they waited.

Seconds ticked by as she fidgeted with her reticule, while cursing her tendency to leap before she looked. The lout came closer to her, and she backed away from his smell.

"You came alone? That's not very clever of you, my dear." He sneered.

She backed further away from him and screamed, loud and long. He covered the distance between them his arm grasping her across the shoulders while his hand covered her mouth. She kicked back with all her might, and felt her foot connect with flesh. She also tried to bite him. He was a big brute. Still struggling, she managed to get the gun out of her reticule.

She fired wildly, aiming toward the ceiling. Dust and plaster fell but her captor was unmoved. There were sounds of running feet as the man he had sent upstairs earlier came back.

"He's gone! Scarpered." He shook his head "He ain't there."

"Not to worry, we've got this plump little pigeon now." Her captor smiled, showing a few missing teeth. Among her panicked thoughts Sophia knew Kit had been right. She had blundered in, but at least Charles would get back to Felicity.

Her captor leaned closer. She recoiled from his stale breath. "Better be nice to me then, Darlin' I can make your stay extremely comfortable. A little kiss and a cuddle could see things improve for you." He swooped down as if to kiss her, his hands fondling her breasts.

For a moment Sophia was paralysed with shock, never having been treated in that way. She shuddered and, recovering herself, spat in his face. There were jeers and laughter from the crowd. The last thing she remembered before it went black was a huge hand slapping her across the head.

CHAPTER NINE

The minute he heard the shot, Christopher knew there was trouble. Why had he ever allowed Sophia to persuade him? He abandoned his search of the outbuildings and raced to the front of the tavern.

As he entered the taproom, the buzz of conversation ceased. He looked about. No sign of Sophia. A serving girl offered him a brimming mug of ale. He shook his head instead saying, "The woman who was here earlier, where is she?"

She didn't look at him as she mumbled, "Didn't see no-one, sir."

He knew she was lying. He raised his voice, "A guinea to anyone who can tell me where the young woman who came in earlier is."

There was a general hubbub of chatter, but no one came forward. He waited, knowing that it was a long shot. A big, roughly dressed fellow approached. Seeing his bald head and cauliflower ear, Christopher guessed he was an old bare-knuckle fighter. His tone, when he spoke, was respectful. But the look he sent Christopher's way wasn't.

"You be looking in the wrong place sir, we've wenches aplenty, but none likely to tempt you. Best you be on your way." It wasn't exactly a threat, but neither was it an invitation to stay.

Christopher felt a familiar sense of frustration, knowing there was nothing further to be done. Thieves and rogues stuck together. His offer of a guinea, although generous, wasn't worth getting a knife in the ribs for.

He gave an ironic bow, "Then I will bid good day to you sir."

Christopher strode over to the door, expecting at any second to be stopped, but was allowed to leave unhindered. If they ran true to form, he would be followed. Maybe roughed up, he didn't even care about that, he was spoiling for a fight. *It was all his fault; he'd allowed himself to be persuaded.* Sophia was in danger, and he'd put her there. That was bad enough, but there had been no sign of Charles. The whole damn day was a dismal failure.

The sound of footsteps behind him, didn't unnerve him at all. He swung around fists at the ready, to see a ragged urchin following him.

What the hell? "What do you want?"

"It ain't what I want, it's what you want, and I reckon it's worth a shilling."

"All right, tell me and I'll decide if it's worth a shilling."

The boy turned to walk way.

Kit quickly said, "Fine, a shilling it is."

The urchin extended his grubby hand up. Only when the coin was placed on his palm did he speak. "They've got her up in the attic, he clobbered her one and she passed out."

Christopher drew in a quick breath. "God's teeth she's hurt?"

"Couldn't say, but reckon she'll have a headache." The boy replied.

"Will you see her?"

The boy shook his head. "Nah, I'm just the pot boy."

Christopher scrabbled a few more coins from his pocket and gave them to the boy.

"Good lad, if you do see her, tell her Kit knows. Can you remember that?"

"Yes, sir."

A subdued Christopher went home. The walk gave him time to

think, or rather to condemn himself for his stupidity. Why had he allowed Sophia to go through with it? Now they had to rescue her, it had all just become more complicated. He'd scarcely walked up the path when the front door swung open.

Hewson, the butler greeted him. "Welcome home sir, they are all in the library."

Christopher thought that was odd, so went towards the library, he hastened his steps when he heard a familiar voice. He flung the door open, "Charlie!"

His older brother gave him a quick grin. Charles was encircled by family, Margaret had her arm around his waist, while Felicity held his hand. Lord Edwin beamed from ear to ear, as the rest of the brothers crowded around them.

Charles was a disreputable sight, with a tattered shirt, torn breeches, unmentionable boots and what looked like a black eye.

"Been havin' fun?" Christopher queried.

A knowing look passed between the brothers, there would be a full debrief of events later.

Charles smiled lazily "You should see the other guy." He deadpanned, making light of the event. His brothers roared with laughter.

"You escaped?"

A quick nod, "Luckily, they didn't think to look on the roof. That commotion downstairs helped."

Christopher shuffled his feet, then winced as Felicity glanced at him.

"Where is Sophia?"

He groaned, "Captured. All my fault, I should never have listened to her hare-brained scheme."

Felicity rounded on him, "I knew it. What have you done?"

He looked at his feet mumbling, "We went to rescue Charlie."

"And?"

"Sophia was to create a commotion, while I searched for him." He said unhappily.

Felicity glared at him "He's here, so why isn't she?"

Christopher shook his head, saying slowly. "They took her. She's locked in one of the attics." He paused. "I was outnumbered, I couldn't do anything."

"How do you know where she is?" His mother linked her arm through his.

"The pot boy told me." He flushed; knowing this was the most ridiculous conversation he'd ever had with his mother.

"Do you think the pot boy is reliable and if he is, what are you going to do about it?"

He straightened his shoulders, standing taller. "I'm going to rescue her."

Margaret nodded approvingly. "Good boy, then, don't let her go."

He answered, "I won't."

That infuriating minx had wormed her way into his heart. He couldn't imagine life without her, and he'd put her into danger. If he rescued her. No, *when* he rescued her, she would have to promise never to do anything like that again.

He turned to Charles. "When we've both cleaned up, I need to talk to you."

Charles nodded. "Of course."

There was a general hubbub of muttering and conversation, as the brothers discussed what happened and what to do.

Sextus said, "Can we do anything?"

Christopher shook his head "Thanks, I got her into this, I will get her out!"

They jostled him a little, "If you need us, you only have to ask."

"Thank you." It was a kind offer, but he didn't need any more amateurs running around. "Charles and I can handle it."

Sir Edwin said" I suppose you two have things to discuss? "He poured them each a whisky, downed one himself, and escorted the ladies and the rest of the boys out of the library.

Christopher waited until they were sure the group had gone.

Charles spoke first. "Well, this is a fine mess, why didn't you trust me to escape?"

Christopher glared at his brother, "You could have been a bit quicker about it. Ma was going frantic."

"They first put me in the cellar and I'd no hope of escape." He shrugged, "One way in, one way out and guarded."

Christopher nodded. "So, what happened?"

"Don't know why, but they moved me to an attic." Charles's voice was tinged with amusement, his climbing and acrobatic skills were well known within the family.

"I popped open the gable hatch and stepped out onto the roof." He grinned modestly, "then I slid down the corner of the building. All that commotion helped, and I was away."

"You got here quickly."

"James, the coachman saw me and drove me home."

"Hmm he could have checked on us. All the time, we were trying to rescue you!"

"Sorry." Charles looked downcast for a moment before suggesting "I could pop back and rescue your girl."

"That's my job," Christopher snapped, "You've got your own girl to impress. Go and court Felicity."

Charles gave an ironic bow, "Well, tell me if you need me."

Christopher sighed. He could have done with Charles' help, but no way was he letting anyone rescue Sophia but him. *He wanted to impress her. Damn it, he'd fallen for her, as maddening as she was and there was nothing for it, but to rescue her.*

An idea began to form. He wouldn't call on Charles, but maybe he would include his other brothers in Operation Scoundrel, as he called it. He'd have to work out the details, muscle and but backup could be helpful.

Sophia looked round the attic. There was a guard on the other side of the door, that was certain. She huddled in the corner, crouching on the floor. There wasn't even a bed or chair. Sophia gulped as tears threatened. *She wasn't going to cry.* She bit the inside of her cheek hard as she felt her arms for bruises. Her head was pounding, that brute had hit her hard.

Adventure was all very well but what she wouldn't give to be safe at home right now. She whimpered. *Stop That! You wanted adventure, now you've got it. What can you do? Smash the window and scream?* If she did, would anyone care? From what she had seen outside *The Windmill* she thought not. Could Christopher rescue her and was Charles here?

Wearily, she wrapped her arms around herself, in an attempt at warmth and comfort.

Listening intently to the noises from the tavern. The sky had darkened, so it would soon be full night. Sniffling softly, Sophia laid her head on her arms and tried to sleep. Her body ached all over and she had no one to blame but herself. A single tear rolled down her cheek as she swiped at it with her hand.

Later, the door opened. Sophia shrank back further into the corner. and the brute who had shut her there came in. He laid a plate on the floor. "Food," he said, "eat it or not." He left the room, and she heard a bolt scrape in the lock. Her stomach rumbled as she edged toward the plate. It was some kind of stew and didn't smell too bad. Beside it was a hunk of coarse bread. No knife or fork, just the bread. *Of course, you could attack someone with a knife or fork!*

After a moment, Sophia tore a hunk off the bread and scooped up some stew. She ate hungrily. At least they wanted to keep her alive. She scraped the last of the stew from the dish and licked her fingers. She settled down to sleep.

Her dreams were troubled and confused, a mixture of all the things that had happened between her and Christopher. Loud noises woke her, the sounds of shouting and fighting. She was still half asleep when the door opened, and Christopher stood there. Sophia had automatically cowered back into the corner.

He put his finger to his lips as he whispered, "Time to go."

She stumbled to her feet. "You're here!" She swayed, and he caught her in his arms. "We need to be quiet," he whispered guiding her to the door. Once out of that attic he led her into the next room where Charles had broken the window. "We have to leave."

"What if someone comes?" Sophia glanced around nervously.

"They won't." he said confidently. "My brothers are keeping them busy."

Dressed in their oldest clothes, the brothers were downstairs in the tavern. As agreed, they were brawling and fighting, cursing and keeping the staff occupied.

Occasional yells could be heard.

"I must go through there?" Sophia pointed to the smashed window her voice wavering.

"Yes, I'm afraid so, it's not bad, I've got a rope ladder."

"I'm not good with heights." She shuddered remembering her climb down the ivy. "And there's this," She gestured to her dress, a slim column of fabric which allowed limited movement.

"That's soon fixed, step out of it." Chris said impatiently. Sophia hesitated, after all it was Felicity's dress.

Christopher acted before she could. He pulled out a knife cutting into the fabric of both dress and petticoat and ripped it. As the material fell away. Sophia gasped at her unaccustomed freedom and exposure. Part of her whispered that he knew about women's clothing. Her face flamed as she looked down seeing that her skirts were hardly covering her thighs, and her stockings and garters were displayed. At least she still wore the dress bodice and her stays.

Christopher drew in a sudden breath longing to stare at her and caress her. Reluctantly, he recalled his thoughts, this was a pleasure for later.

"Do you want me to go first, or will you try? The ladder is strong, it took my weight." He reassured her.

Sophia shuddered. "I will go first, or I may not go at all."

Christopher wrapped his hand in her discarded skirt fabric and smashed out the rest of the glass. Then he spread the fabric over the bottom of the window frame. He took her hand and steadied her as she lowered one leg over the opening.

She was halfway across the opening when he said, "James our coachman is below holding the ladder".

He felt her grip tighten on his hand. "He will see me like this!"

"He's the soul of discretion. There is a rug in the coach to keep you warm."

Was he really that stupid? Didn't he realise how scandalous her attire was? If anyone of note saw her, she would be ruined.

Sighing, knowing there was no other choice. Sophia swung her other leg across the sill and grasped the rope ladder. It swayed, but she took a step downwards and then another. They were the worst few seconds of her life. Her mortification was so strong that Sophia felt her whole body was one big blush.

James had the tact not to look at her, muttering, "Step inside the coach, Miss."

She was glad to do so and a few moments later Christopher joined her.

"Well done," he said picking up the rug and wrapping it around her, while trying not to stare at her shapely legs. He could feel the hardness in his breeches growing. Her jasmine perfume filled the coach Chris thrust his hand through his hair exasperated. The rescue had gone better than he'd expected; but where could they go now? He couldn't take her home in this state of undress.

It would have to be an inn and that would be difficult enough. He could pay to ensure silence, but if word got out, Sophia would be horribly compromised. Christopher stepped out of the carriage to regain his composure. The cool night air helped. He drew in a deep breath, feeling the throb of his heartbeat pounding and the film of sweat on his forehead. He was pleased to hear that when he spoke, his voice sounded normal.

"James, can you recommend a decent and discreet inn? Miss Sophia cannot return in this state."

A look of understanding passed between them; they were both men of the world. A coachman saw and heard plenty, and James had proved to be discreet. Christopher regretted every dalliance he'd had and knew that James had kept silent about them. That kind of loyalty was to be prized and they needed it now.

"The Mermaid, Sir. Mrs Hobbs as runs it, knows a thing or two, but never have I heard her blab."

"Would the kidnappers know it?" Christopher had no wish to encounter them again.

"Couldn't say for sure sir, but I doubt it."

"Right, The Mermaid it is, thank you, James."

CHAPTER TEN

Christopher thought briefly of sitting on the box with James, but Sophia needed his support, and he should re-join her. He must keep his imaginings to himself. Now was neither the time or the place. He swung himself up and into the carriage. Sophia was white faced, with the coarse rug wrapped around her. She was shivering, whether from cold or shock he couldn't tell. He joined her on the seat and wrapped his arms around her, gentling her as though she was a spooked horse.

"You have done so well." He said, "Its nearly over, we will get you cleaned up and then we can go home."

Her eyes pooled with tears, but she sniffed them angrily away, scrubbing at them with her closed fists. "I never cry."

"Of course not. Understood." He squeezed her hand, "But if you were to cry, it would be totally understandable, given what you've been through."

"Do you think so?" Sophia almost hiccupped.

"Yes." He placed his arms around her, drawing her close, kissing the top of her head, as she snuggled closer to him.

It was torture to feel her so near soft and yielding in his arms.

Knowing how little she was wearing. If he were another kind of man, he might have coaxed her and taken her virtue. Christopher wouldn't want that. He wanted her to have a choice and for her to want him, happily and freely.

Their journey didn't take long and soon the coach pulled up outside the Mermaid Inn.

An ostler came forward to take the horses through to the stables. James leapt from the box and engaged him in conversation, supplying a distraction for them to enter the inn.

Christopher urged Sophia, still wrapped in the rug, down the coach steps and into a side lobby. It had a warm and welcoming feel. Soft candlelight glowed and there was a brass jug of flowers on the counter. Chris put his arm around her shaking shoulders.

"It will be all right." He whispered.

A pleasant looking woman stepped forward, "Sir. How can I be of help?" She was neatly dressed in a simple dark green dress and white apron. There was a motherly air about her.

Chris cleared his throat. "We need a room. Or better yet, two rooms, the young lady has been attacked and needs to recover."

The woman gasped and moved closer to Sophia. She clasped her hand. "My dear," she said, "are you all right?"

Sophia looked into her kind eyes, "Yes, I am, now. Thank you."

Mrs Hobbs addressed Christopher, "I only have the one room left, sir, but it's quiet and private. If that will do?"

"That will do very well, thank you."

"This way," she said, taking one of the candlesticks Mrs Hobbs showed them up staircase and they followed her. She opened the door to a charming room, with oak beams and a polished wooden floor. A patterned rug was set before a small settee and a fire was laid in the grate. Thick curtains hung at the windows and there was a large bed. A jug and bowl were set on a washstand further back in the room.

Mrs Hobbs closed the curtains. "I can send a maid to light the fire, sir."

Christopher shook his head. "The fewer people who know we are here the better, I can do it."

"Will the young lady require to wash?"

Before he could answer, Sophia did, "I would like that very much."

"Get the maid to bring the water up and leave it, if you will ma'am." Christopher said and indicated by an incline of his head that he would prefer to speak to her outside the room.

Once outside, Mrs Hobbs tilted her head in enquiry and waited to hear what Christopher had to say. He cleared his throat, *could anything be more awkward?*

"Can you provide the young lady with a dress?" Adding hastily, "any kind, it does not matter, the young lady's clothes have been, erm, damaged."

She eyed him carefully, "You do know sir, we are not that kind of house?"

He flushed, "Indeed, ma'am. I was told you were respectable and kind. Should a young lady's good name be soiled because of misfortune?"

She nodded "As long as we understand each other, sir." She gave him a severe look. "I will send the maid up with hot water and see what can be done about a dress."

"Thank you."

She left and he went into the room and checked the fireplace. The fire was well laid. All he needed to do was strike the flint on the flint stone, ignite the char cloth and set it to the paper and kindling. The brief roar of the flames was followed by a steadier blaze.

"Come by the fire, you must be freezing."

Sophia shivered, "I am a little, it is strange to feel the air around... me."

Had she been about to say legs? What he had seen of them were long and shapely. Christopher drew in a breath and tried to control his wandering thoughts.

"What about James?" Her question drew him out of his reverie. "Will he be allright?"

He nodded "I expect he's settled with a pie and a pint of ale in the inn below."

"Will he talk?" she flushed and gestured to her state of undress "about this?"

"No." Chris was happy to reassure her. "He's the soul of discretion, he's seen me through a scrape or two."

She gave him a mischievous grin as she warmed herself by the fire, the rug slipping a little, so he saw her pert bosom and her pretty legs. She gave him a clear-eyed gaze, whispering.

"Have you been a naughty boy, Christopher? Have you a wicked past?"

He had been a bit wild. Finding and giving pleasure. He regretted it now, but then it meant he wasn't going to rush her or hurt her. He knew what women liked and how to please them. He would woo her and take it slowly. He would learn what pleased her and delight her so thoroughly that she could not speak or stand,

Thinking about turning her on he'd aroused himself. He half turned from her, before she could see his arousal.

Christopher raised his eyes to meet hers, speaking before he lost his nerve. "I have, but I would give it up in an instant, for the right woman."

"Do you think you will know her when you meet her?" She teased.

The look he gave her, was so thoroughly assessing as if he wanted to know and examine every part of her, that it brought a flush to her cheeks.

"Yes." His gazed fastened on her lips, soft kissable lips that he was intending to explore. A knock at the door startled them both. and he cursed under his breath.

"Yes?"

"The hot water, sir."

"All right," he snapped.

They heard the footsteps retreating, sighing he opened the door and brought in a steaming ewer of hot water. The glance Sophia gave him was part amused and part bravado as she moved to the basin.

"I may need your help." She warned him.

He carried the ewer to the basin and poured it in and added some cold water from the jug. There was a disc of fine milled soap close by and a linen towel.

Sophia let the rug drop completely as she stood there, Felicity's lovely dress was hacked off above the knee, but the bodice and stays still held Sophia's breasts up high. Her hair was tumbling round her shoulders, her cheeks flushed and her eyes bright. He'd never seen a lovelier sight.

She locked gazes with him. "I need you to help me out of what remains of this dress."

Both her arms were bruised where that brute had held her. He growled low in his throat, "I'll kill him, that bastard, he hurt you."

She shrugged and winced, "that's not important, come and help me."

He wanted to crush her to him, he wanted to treat her like spun glass. In two strides he was beside her.

She turned away from him saying, "Can you please unbutton me?"

The fastening of her dress was a row of tiny buttons, which normally a maid would deal with. Christopher's larger hands struggled with the task, keeping him far too close to her for his comfort. It was agonisingly slow work as he saw the swell of her breasts, the curve of her backside, all the while the hint of jasmine perfume wafted from her skin.

Sophia glanced over her shoulder, saying teasingly, "Are you always so slow in undressing your ladies?"

His hands stilled as he turned her to face him. His voice was husky and his eyes darkened as he gazed at her. "I regret every one of them, because they were not you." His tone was sincere, so she could not doubt that he meant it.

"Oh!" Her lips opened as she gazed up at him, eyes shining.

He drew her to him, lifted one finger under her chin and tilted it upwards, as his mouth covered hers. Gentle, tender, exploring, softly questioning. Sophia uttered little murmurs of joy, her body arching upward so she could kiss him back.

The faintest hint of stubble brushed her cheeks. Harsh, masculine, exciting. *He's holding back, he thinks I'm some ninny to be frightened of him!*

Mischief sparked in her eyes as she pressed her body against his, her breasts thrust against his chest. Sophia deepened the kiss, allowing herself to nibble his lower lip and feeling his immediate response as he pressed against her. His grip tightened on her. Chris groaned, it was all he could do to keep self-control.

She clasped one of his hands and put it on her breast. He let it lie there, his heartbeat pounding, while he fought the urge to caress her breast and take her.

Sophia pouted, "Are my breasts unpleasing to you?" As if to emphasize her point she moved herself closer, pressing her breast further into his hand. Christopher sighed, *never had temptation been so delightful, or so difficult to resist.*

He cleared his throat, "Men have different needs, if we start this, I may not be able to stop." Adding honestly, "I won't want to stop."

"And I wouldn't want you to stop, either." Sophia said huskily. "Can you swear to me your womanising days are over? I need to know, if I can trust you." She eyed him steadily, her lips moist and desirable from kissing him, her palm placed on the flat of his chest. She could feel the pounding of his heartbeat, surely hers beat to the same rhythm.

"Yes, you temptress, those days are over. I can think of nothing but you." His hands shook as he eased the remains of the dress off her shoulders, down past her waist. He knelt before her. Through the thin fabric of her petticoat, he could see the sweet spot between her thighs.

He imagined his hands on her there, his lips there, pleasuring her. His cock sprang to attention at the thought.

Each stockinged leg had a pink ribbon garter to hold the hose up. She rested her hand on his shoulder waving her foot "Help me out of these."

Chris drew in a breath as he inhaled her natural womanly scent; he was so close to where he wanted to be. His fingers fumbled with the tie of the garter. Once it was undone, he gently rolled her stocking down. Holding her instep in the palm of his hand, and kissing it, before taking the other leg and performing the same ritual.

He gazed up at her, clad only in her stays and the torn petticoat, she had never looked more beautiful or desirable.

"You may as well know now that I have decided to marry you," Sophia said, "I think you will make a good husband."

Kit started to speak, but she gently shushed him, pressing her palm across his lips.

"I don't mind about those other women. I don't care to know about them. I do want your solemn promise there will be no more." Sophia assessed his reaction, *was he shocked, how would he respond?*

He stood and drew her closer for him, it was an easy promise to make. "Yes, I swear Sophia, no more women."

"Thank you." She kissed him. Smilingly she said, "As you know I have no experience, but I am ready and eager to learn."

His heart leapt. "That's good, because ou are in a very compromising position." He conceded.

"And totally ready to be compromised, by my own scoundrel." She teased and settled herself on the bed, resting her arms behind her head and gazing up at him; her breasts rising and falling as her breath quickened.

He gently covered her body with his own, and showered kisses on her lips. His bigger hands pushing the thin fabric of her shift down so he could see and caress her breasts. Pink tipped and rosy, they invited his hands and then his lips. His tongue gently describing circles around each nipple.

It felt wonderful, Sophia sighed softly and pressed closer, while her back arched in ecstasy. She wound her fingers through his dark hair drawing him closer. Lying back, thrilling new sensations engulfed her. *I want to feel him inside me, possessing me, making me his and him mine.*

Sophia moaned, and Kit let his hand stray downwards gently easing her legs apart. She allowed it, then gasped, unsure what to expect, as his fingers traced slow circles up her thighs and higher to her sweet core. *So dangerous, so daring, so right.*

His fingers played as if she were a fine-tuned violin and he a maestro. Sophia gasped as she felt the dampness on her thighs while her body reacted to him. She delighted in him so close to her as she inhaled his male scent. *Love is intoxicating.*

He moved away from her momentarily and she almost screamed with frustration.

Christopher quickly shed his clothes and was back with her. His warm masculine scent enveloping her as his muscular body pressed closely against hers.

She was still partly clothed in her stays and petticoat and excited by his nakedness.

He took her hand and guided it to his enlarged cock.

He sighed, whispering, "Touch me too, darling. Hold me." He demonstrated, as he placed his hand over hers, guiding her into a rhythm.

She felt his manhood grow as she caressed him. For a moment Sophia faltered, *will this huge thing fit inside me?*

He must have sensed her anxiety because he drew back from her, "we can stop now, if you wish."

"Will it hurt?" *Oh, to be so woefully ignorant of what happened between a man and a woman,* Sophia bit her lip, worried that her question had spoiled things.

Apologetically, he replied. "Yes, it will a little, but only the first time." He wanted her so badly, but he had to be truthful too. "I'll be gentle. If you ask me to stop, I will."

Sophia snuggled deep into his arms looking up at him, "I want you to make love to me." *Was that too forward, too bold?*

She became lost in sensations, as his hands found her soft places that needed caressing, his lips sought hers, and he whispered in her ear, "Sophia, Sophia."

Her every sense was awakened. He led, she followed. This was a master class as her whole body shivered with anticipation and delight.

She was soaked when he stopped teasing her, and positioned his pulsing cock towards her feminine centre. He caressed her for a moment as he placed his cock a fraction of the way inside her. She felt him and raised herself higher, and he thrust a little further. He stopped. Sophia bit her lip, her body taut with anticipation.

"Shall I?" Chris's voice was husky with desire.

Her fingers dug into his shoulders as she lifted her hips higher and higher. "Yes, yes! Make love to me." She moaned.

He started to thrust into her, slowing as he felt resistance until her virginal membrane tore and she let him in

Sophia squealed and he stopped momentarily, but she arched upwards and grabbed his buttocks, so he could slide deeper inside her.

She was everything he had imagined and more. Pleasuring a woman, he cared for felt different, more connected. Chris struggled for control, to stay with her longer. They moved together, in union, in ecstasy until he could no longer contain himself.

"I'm sorry," Christopher whispered raggedly as he withdrew from her, spilling his seed onto the sheet. It had taken all his determination to leave her.

They clung together, tousled, breathless, happy. His arms locked around her,

"I'm sorry if I hurt you." He gently kissed her cheek, then claimed her mouth. "I promise next time it will be easier."

She smiled at him, teasingly, "I'll be a willing student," she gave him a shy smile, "I suppose I'll need lots of practise."

He nodded gravely, "Of course, I expect nothing less." Christopher roused himself from the bed, dipped his hand in the water to cleanse his cock and then dressed. "You wash; I'll ask the landlady for clothes for you."

Sophia lay back languidly, it pleased her to watch him, to contrast his male body with hers. To remember where his hands had been, where his mouth had been, how his cock had felt in her hand and then inside her. She sighed and patted the bed beside her.

He laughed and shook his head, "We will have plenty of time to explore each other. Now I need to get you home and see that my brothers are safe too."

He left the room and Sophia reluctantly got out of the bed. The water had cooled. She washed her face, arms and hands, before she sponged her thighs. Felicity's beautiful dress was beyond repair. Sophia tore a strip from it and wiped her thighs. She adjusted herself, so that her bosom was now suitably covered, wrapped the rug around her again and sat in the chair set by the fire. Watched the flames crackle as she replayed their lovemaking. His nakedness, and hardness, contrasting with her softness. Who knew that his desire and hers, and the pleasure of their loving, would be so thrilling, exciting and energising?

Bliss!

CHAPTER ELEVEN

Maybe she'd dozed, but the sound of the door opening startled Sophia. For a moment she wondered where she was. Christopher reached down and kissed her forehead.

"You must have slept," he said.

"Well, it's been an exciting day and a most *stimulating* evening." She teased, loving the look he gave her, which promised more. Lowering her voice she added, "who knew being kidnapped could be quite so thrilling?"

He shook his head, "no more adventures, please, it's far too dangerous." He leaned over her, staring into her eyes he said, "I can't risk anything happening to you."

I feel the same way about him and he's not going to stop. Well, I'll fight this battle later.

"Of course, I don't want to worry you," Sophia said, seemingly agreeing with him.

A brisk knock on the door startled them both, Cristopher opened it. Mrs Hobbs bobbed a quick curtsey.

"I've found a dress sir; I hope it will do." She handed over a cloth bundle. "Would you be wanting supper sir?"

He shook his head "Thank you, no, I need to get this young lady home."

"As you think best sir, your coachman said to tell you he's ready when you are sir."

Christopher nodded his thanks. "I will be down to settle up with you shortly."

He closed the door and took the dress over to Sophia. She unfolded it and held it against her. It had been made for someone far shorter than she was and would display her ankles.

"I'd better try it on," she said running her hands over the rougher cloth. It was a serviceable dress, in a plain style. She let the rug fall off her shoulders. Christopher felt another pull of desire as Sophia stood there in her stays and torn petticoat.

I'm reacting like an untrained boy, will I ever tire of her, ever stop wanting her?

He watched as she pulled the dress over her head, there were no fancy buttons needing his help. No excuses to go closer. He went anyway and placed a kiss on the tender nape of her neck.

She rolled her neck and gazed up at him, as she gathered the excess fabric and pinned it to her waist with her hands.

"How do I look?"

Like a child playing dress ups. "It's far too wide, you need a belt."

"I don't have one, do you?"

He shook his head, but then his eyes fell on the twisted cord curtain tie backs. He unhooked one, "Try this."

It was better than nothing, Sophia could at least leave the premises decently covered in spite of showing a fine pair of ankles.

"I'll add that to the bill too," Christopher said as he left to settle the account with Mrs Hobbs. *I need to get moving, to reassure my parents that all is well. and see how my brothers are and to stop me from making love to Sophia.* That was the real temptation.

He'd tipped Mrs Hobbs a generous amount and she was effusive in her thanks. Chris and Sophia made a discreet exit and the coach headed for home.

They gazed at one another across the dimly lit coach interior.

Sophia pouted. "Why won't you sit beside me? I know you want to."

His voice was husky as he answered ,"Yes, I do want to, but then I will want to kiss you and..." his voice deepened, "do other things."

Delicious, daring, intimate things Sophia imagined.

"My parents will be worried, my brothers may not have returned home, they don't know if you and I are safe." He sighed, "I must reassure them. And what about Felicity? She will be concerned about you."

Sophia knew he was right "We will do all that you suggest, but afterwards, I will expect a hundred kisses."

"I would happily give you a thousand kisses, but I must see your father and ask him for your hand in marriage. Unless you have changed your mind about marrying me?" He teased.

"You know I haven't." She smiled. "Let's be married with all speed and then we can truly be together. I doubt we will be allowed a moment to ourselves once we get back."

As Sophia had predicted, the coach had scarcely stopped before they were surrounded by his parents, his brothers and Felicity, all talking at once.

Margaret hugged them both before shrieking at the state of Sophia's costume.

Lord Edwin beamed that everyone was safely back.

Christopher glared at his brothers for giving Sophia appreciative glances.

Felicity was standing close to Charles, her arm linked through his. She left his side briefly to hug Sophia too, while Sophia stammered apologies for losing her dress.

"So, have you had enough of adventures?" Felicity gave Sophia a shrewd glance.

Sophia nodded, "For now, at least. My next adventure will be marrying Christopher, but after that," she raised a delicate eyebrow, "Who knows?"

HISTORICAL NOTES.

Why couldn't Lord Edwin just call the police?

Before 1829 when Sir Robert Peel organised it, there wasn't a professional police force in England, although there was a successful police force in Dublin. Instead, there were various watchmen and constables appointed by merchants and wealthy people.

https://en.wikipedia.org/wiki/
History_of_law_enforcement_in_the_United_Kingdom

Coinage and Notes.__https://www.oldbaileyonline.org/static/Coinage.jsp

The Bank of England introduced £10 and £15 notes from 1759. During the Napoleonic wars £1 and £2 notes were issued. Notes weighed far less and were more convenient than heavy coins. Lord Edwin used notes for the ransom.

Ladies' underwear or lack of it!

Women at the time of this story (1813) wore chemises, petticoats and stays BUT they didn't wear panties or knickers. Sophia was far more exposed that we might imagine with her petticoat torn and her garters showing.

https://www.bustle.com/p/the-underwear-of-jane-austens-time-will-make-you-seriously-grateful-for-modern-conveniences-2350928

ABOUT SONIA BELLHOUSE

Sonia Bellhouse writes steamy Regency or Viking romances, for believers in happily ever after, in a way that leaves readers wanting more. Passion and warmth combined with storytelling and real history. As an ex-pat Brit, Sonia happily calls Australia home. She will always ignore the housework in favour of playing with her cats. Previously published in local and international magazines. Her book *Fire & Ice* featured an ice-skating couple in present day Norway who connect with the Viking past. Sonia contributed to the anthologies, *The Revolution Won't be Downloaded. Writing the Dream, Passages, and Sexy Secret of Swain Cove.*

You can find her on Facebook https://www.facebook.com/soniabell house.author/

Or her Chatting with Authors page https://www.facebook.com/ groups/1031642857187598

Or visit her blog https://soniabellhouse.blog.

ABDUCTING HIS DUCHESS

VIVIAN MURDOCH

Warning!!!

Kinks, Fetishes, Triggers:
Including but not limited to...

COCK WORSHIP, ROLE PLAY, KIDNAPPING, SHIBARI, MILD KNIFE PLAY, MILD EXHIBITIONISM, PRIMAL PLAY, PRAISE, EDGING, SUBDROP.

For anyone who's ever had a kidnapping fantasy and wanted to make it come true.

Acknowledgements

Husdom
One of these days, you're going to kidnap me. But I don't want to know until it happens! I love how much you love and care for me.

My Awesome Alphas
You guys are my rock. Thank you for allowing me to keep throwing these books at you at rapid speed. You guys are incredible.
Shout out to Ashley, Alexis, Bianca, Rita!

Delightful Editor
Thank you sooooo much Jessica for working with my tight deadlines. You never bat an eye when I send something your way. Thank you for EVERYTHING.

Map of AR Regency England

LIST OF DUKES

House Barrington
— Lewis Barrington, Duke of Whiteport
— Charles Barrington, Duke of Norhaven - Previously Earl of Glendale

House Harding
— Joseph Harding, Duke of Foxford

House Dowding
— Robert Dowding, Duke of Blackport
— William Dowding, Duke of Birchleigh - Adopted Son - Previously Earl of Hazelwick

House Fitzwilliam
— Edward Fitzwilliam, Duke of Redleigh

House Fortescue
— Benedict Fortescue, Duke of Portswell

CHAPTER ONE

CATHERINE

Nausea rolls through me as the landau pitches from side to side. It's not through any fault of the driver, of that, I'm sure. However, it doesn't help the stab of fear rolling through me as I glance outside to watch the trees go past.

After the forced ride from Hades with Mister Beaumont, every step into a carriage of any sort is cause for alarm. My heart pounds so hard in my chest I fear it will leap from me and onto the other passengers sharing this mode of transportation. Glancing about at the myriad of faces, I force the dread back down where it belongs.

Besides, it wouldn't be good to upend the contents of my stomach all over the dowager duchess to my side or my new siblings in front. The girls blink up at me, their wide eyes growing even larger as they stare at my face. No doubt I must look a fright. Sliding my hand over my stomach, I clench my fingers inward, willing breakfast to stay down.

Next to me, the older woman reaches over to pat my knee, a glimmer of pity shining in her expression. I don't want or need anyone's compassion; however, having a warm, comforting hand certainly doesn't go amiss. I take her wizened fingers in my grasp and hold on, allowing her strength to pour into me.

Guilt slams into me hard, nearly edging out the panic threatening to bubble up to the surface. The only reason we're making this trip is because of her poor health. I should be attending to her and not the other way around. Glancing back, I notice a hint of a smile tilting up her lips.

In truth, these last few days, she's seemed in much brighter spirits than when I was first introduced to her at my marriage breakfast. She looked so pale, so frail. Now, it seems as if she glows from the inside out with some strange mirth she keeps to herself.

Perhaps it's relief at going back home to the country? Honestly, it causes the guilt to ease just a touch. Perhaps everyone worried for nothing. With the way she looks right now, I surmise she might have many years left in her.

It's my prayer, seeing as I've had far more brushes with death than I care to think about. A shudder wracks my body as the phantom pain from the broken bond twists my insides. It's far better now that both William and I have claimed each other, but some days the agony threatens to steal my breath.

Turning my attention away from such morose thoughts, I look at the scenery as it goes by, repeating to myself that it's not the same. These aren't the same trees, these aren't the same roads, and my travel companions certainly aren't the same.

I watch as my new brother, the Duke of Blackport, rides alongside us, his stance rigid in the saddle. I can't see his face, but his body speaks of an alert and watchful eye. Truthfully, since William cannot escort us, I'm happy to have his brother instead.

With him traveling with us, no harm will come to his mother or sisters, and by proxy, that means I am safe as well. I should be able to allow ghosts to lie, knowing he will fight to the death if need be to keep us safe. Still though, I cannot keep the tingle of awareness away for any longer than the span of a few minutes.

Hopefully, once we're out of this dreaded landau, I can finally breathe again. In front of me, the sisters hold their heads together, tittering laughs drifting from their side. Next to them, the new governess grips her skirt, her fingers digging in as if holding on for dear life. Strange, but she seems just as ill at ease as I do.

"Do you not travel often?" I inquire, desperate to put my mind on other things.

She looks over at me, her light brown eyes darkening for a second as a waft of fear drifts through the carriage. Both sisters stop whatever it is they are doing and look over at her, curiosity evident in their eyes. Again, that sense of unease drips from the governess as she looks at their questioning gazes.

"Forgive me," I murmur, sliding back further into the seat. "It was not my intent to put you on the spot."

"Nonsense," the dowager duchess cries, her smile growing wider. "'Tis far too long of a trip not to be regaled with some tale of mystery and woe. Tell us then, child, what has you so uncomfortable?"

Red tinges her cheeks as she glances out the window, only to train her gaze swiftly back onto her hands. "Forgive me, Your Grace," she whispers. "I have never been in the presence of someone as great as you before. I- I find myself a little unprepared."

"My child," the older woman chuckles. "You will find me to be far more affable than most. I did not garner my title by being one of high esteem. In fact, I started out much like you, a governess to someone in a very high position."

At those words, the younger woman glances up, something akin to hope shining in her eyes. Again, she lets her gaze dart out the window, and for a moment, I wonder if this has anything to do with Blackport. To my knowledge, they haven't even met properly. Could she already have designs on a stranger?

Then again, I knew nothing of my William, and yet my heart knew in an instant he was the Alpha for me. I will, however, keep my lips sealed in case I'm incorrect in my line of thinking. It could very well easily be that she looks to him as a guardian of sorts and doesn't wish to alarm him with her troubles?

Leaning forward, I give her a soft smile and a conspiratorial wink. "Do not fret. I am sure no one outside this carriage can hear your tale. The pounding of the horses' hooves should drown out any scandalous stories you might have."

"A scandal?" the older sister, Lady Margaret, pipes up, her blue eyes shining. "Oh, I do love a good intrigue!"

The dowager duchess gives a loud harrumph as she leans back in her seat. "Not at your age, you should not."

"It's not fair," she pouts, crossing her arms. "You never allow me any fun."

"Fun is for when you're married off to a respectable man, and not before."

The governess and I exchange glances, the ghost of a smile tilting our lips as the mother and daughter go at it. Thankfully, Lady Margaret knows nothing of my fall from grace, or else she'd be absolutely besotted with the scandal which I found myself embroiled in. As it is, it will remain my dirty little secret, never even leaving me on my deathbed.

"Fine. If you do not wish to allow me any fun, I shall turn the conversation to something far more sinister. I have heard tales that highwaymen are in abundance, traversing these roads in search of gold and trinkets." There's a smug look of satisfaction on Lady Margaret's lips as she leans back and crosses her arms.

If my face is anything like the governess's, we both look pale and shaky with fright.

"Hush, child," the dowager duchess chides, shaking her head. "We are perfectly safe. Why do you think your brother rides next to us? And the men controlling the landau, do you think they're merely for show?

Every man accompanying us has our safety at heart. Nothing will happen."

With another huff, Lady Margaret slumps just a touch. "Of course nothing will happen. Nothing ever happens."

Sighing, I glance back out the window, my heart thumping in time with the wheels carrying us away. "Take it from someone who knows. Nothing happening is usually a good thing."

"I knew it!" she cries out, sitting at attention once more. "Something did happen to you! I knew the rumors had to be true."

Once more, fear's icy grip wraps around my heart and squeezes. "There are rumors?" My fingers shake as I lay my hand across my chest.

An odd haze impedes my vision as it crosses over my eyes, making everything fuzzy for a moment. My insides flip, as if my body is rolling about, turning feet over head. However, the instant my terror becomes too much, a familiar warmth spreads through my body.

My love. Are you well? William's deep tenor rolls through my brain, driving away the madness with his overwhelming heat.

F- forgive me, I answer back, my vision clearing enough to see four pairs of eyes staring at me, concern wavering in their depths. *Your sister has heard rumors about me, and I panicked.*

Has she said what these rumors are? Perhaps you can dispel them? If not, I will be on my way shortly and can address them when we meet up.

No, I admit, shame twisting my insides. *I didn't even get the chance. I felt faint before she could say more.*

His fingers brush along the inside of my mind, bringing a soft sigh to my lips. They wrap around me in a tight hug, firm enough to bring all the jagged splinters of my soul back together as one. The love he feels for me pours in, reminding me I'm not alone.

"What do you suppose she's doing?" Lady Elizabeth whispers to her older sister.

"I'm not sure, but it looks odd. As if she's staring right through us.

Perhaps we are now ghosts? Specters only to be talked of but never seen?"

Their voices sound muddled and thick, as if I'm hearing it underwater. Shaking my head, I do my best to bring myself back to the present, just in time for Lady Elizabeth to shriek.

"I do not wish to be a specter. I am a flesh and blood girl. Please, Mama, I do not want to be a ghost."

"Enough," the dowager duchess grinds out, her gaze flitting over to the governess. "Are you sure you still wish to be in our employ? Seeing as the girls are prone to theatrics and hysterics?"

"I bet she's talking to William," Lady Margaret bursts in, her lips tilting up into a smug smile.

Lady Elizabeth looks about the landau, her gaze looking at every nook and cranny. "But he is not here, and I did not hear her speak?"

"You're too young to understand." This time, Lady Margaret's voice matches her haughty demeanor.

"As are you," the dowager duchess counters. "Where do you even get such ideas?"

"Mama, it's not as if I'm blind. When Father was still with us, I saw how you both would stare off into the distance, and then smile as if some lark passed between you. Since Catherine is now married as well, I can only assume she's doing the same. In fact, I would surmise that it's the act of marriage which opens up this strange portal between husband and wife."

The older woman and I exchange a glance. If only it were that simple. Resisting the urge to touch the mark over my heart, I mourn the idea that all it takes is a simple act of nuptials. If that were the case, I still wouldn't feel as if a piece of me was missing, ripped out when William had the bastard who kidnapped and marked me executed.

Never once did I say any sort of thing that would constitute binding myself to that loathsome man in marriage, and yet, here I am, still mourning the part of me he stole. Wrapping my arms about my waist, I continue to listen as Lady Margaret pours out her theories on marriage and the boons it brings with it.

Thankfully, most of them are incorrect, laughable musings proving she's still very much an innocent. It's what I would want for her. I revel in the idea that she knows nothing of the depravity which can take a woman and strip her of everything she holds dear.

Turning my gaze out the window, I watch as more trees go by. If only I had stayed behind and come up with William, but he insisted I go. Not only would I have had my mate alongside me, keeping me safe and in his care, but we could start our honeymoon early. With everything that's happened, we've been in a whirlwind since coming back to London.

Though I know William in the most carnal sense, I still feel as if I could learn more about the man himself—his likes, his dislikes, his passions... Well, the passions which don't include ravaging me every moment he can.

A different warmth runs through me as arousal threatens to make me squirm. I cannot allow these thoughts to continue. Not when four other ladies can no doubt smell it. Even now, as I glance over at the dowager duchess, she smiles at me with that knowing grin of hers.

Oh, the humiliation. It's enough to drive all thoughts of William from my mind. "Pray tell, Lady Margaret. Which rumors have you heard?"

She turns away, unease flitting from her. "I do not wish for you to be wroth with me."

"I doubt you can ever do anything to cause my anger to burn toward you. Besides, I have a younger sister of my own, and I know they can be prone to teasing."

"I-" she pauses and looks over at the dowager duchess. "I heard you were kidnapped. That William had to save you from the clutches of a madman."

Grief strikes at my heart as I take in her unsure expression. "And what else," I manage to croak out, needing to know the worst of it.

"And that you and he are a rare love match. Is that why you can talk to him in your mind? Mama? You too?"

With a sigh, I sit back, relief flooding through my veins. If this is all the rumors are saying, then I can live with that. "And that's all?" I question.

She nods, her eyes holding no trace of guile in those bright blue depths. "That's all."

"Then let me reassure you. Unfortunately, the rumors are true. I was stolen away by a terrible man, but rest assured that he can no longer hurt me or anyone else. Your brother saw to that."

Next to her, Lady Elizabeth beams. "William is so strong and brave. I'm happy he saved you."

Smiling down at the younger girl, I nod. "As am I. I truly don't know what I would do without him."

Next to me, the dowager duchess sniffs and dabs at her eyes. "A true love match is rare, my darling girls. What your father and I had, what Catherine now shares with William, is what I want for you both. But do not let that cloud your judgment when it comes to suitors. Do not allow your minds to run away with thoughts of love. It will come in time."

Again, she pats my knee, giving me a watery smile. I grab her hand in my own, drawing on her strength. Since my mother and sister are no doubt back at Overton, she's stepped in as a surrogate for me. I couldn't ask for a better mother, a proxy in my own Mama's stead. She has treated me with nothing but kindness, causing my heart to ache as she turns from me and coughs.

The landau is quiet, save for the rattling sound as the dowager duchess continues to wheeze. We all look at her, our souls hurting. It will only be a matter of time, but hopefully, it will not be so soon. Closing my eyes, I send up two small prayers.

May the dowager duchess find peace and healing back at Whitmore Manor, and may William close the distance fast and get to us.

Already, I ache, desperation flooding my veins like lead. It's not just because I worry about his mother, though that is a large part.

The distance eats at me, sends shafts of pain into my heart. With us being parted, it allows the festering wound of that illicit bond to open, driving pain into my heart until I can barely breathe. It helps to feel William within my soul, but soon, I'll need to touch him, to remind myself he's here with me physically.

Soon, my love, he whispers into my mind, driving out the agony threatening to overwhelm me. *I'll be by your side by this evening. Just hold on a bit longer.*

CHAPTER TWO

WILLIAM

Fire races across my brain, halting me in my tracks. With a firm hand, I jerk on the reins, sending Storm rearing back, his massive hooves pawing at the air. His indignant snort and squeal ring out into the chilly air, pounding through my body.

"Yes, I know you're mad at me," I soothe, bending down to stroke his neck.

Ever the rambunctious stallion, he doesn't accept my apology straight away. Instead, he throws his head back, tossing his mane as he slams his hooves into the ground. A soft smile lifts my lips as I let him throw his tantrum. Honestly, after everything he did for me in my quest to bring Catherine back to my side, I'd allow him almost anything.

With a sigh, I close my eyes, feeling out my mate through the bond. She's distressed, of that I have no doubt. Even now, I feel my own breathing catch in my throat, mirroring the agony piercing her heart. I know not what else I can do. Ever since that bastard marked her, she's been jumping at shadows, unable to properly eat or sleep.

Perhaps my rouse, my plan to capture her and do delicious things to her body, is an insane idea. With how distraught she's feeling, I should just ride on ahead and join them as normal. It would be the charitable thing to do.

But then, the pieces are already set in place. With no way of communicating with either my brother or my mother, they will carry on as planned. Damnation. If only I'd gotten to her before she was marked. If only I kept her safe. Then, this would be a fun time of kidnapping and frolicking, a good start to a honeymoon she so desperately deserves.

As it is, I could just kick myself for concocting this hare-brained scheme. Even Robert thought it was idiotic when I mentioned it to him. Honestly, it's for the sake of my ailing adoptive mother that I'm still even considering going through with it. Since she was to be in the landau along with my wife, I needed to make her aware so it did not strain her heart.

The way her face lit up as she clapped her hands together. It would be the best lark of all, and she couldn't wait to play her part. Besides, if her stories were to be believed, she had plans for the opera, if not for falling into employment as a governess. This would allow her to act out her fantasy of being on stage.

Only... this will be a rather small audience. Besides, my brother could lighten up a bit. With a firm nod of my head, I grip the hilt of my rapier and continue to follow after them. I want them far enough away that my "misdoings" would not cause a fuss or ruckus among others not privy to the information of my plan.

The very last thing I need is to be cast in prison for crimes I'm not planning to commit. Though true, I look every inch a rapscallion highwayman, the only prize I plan on carrying off is my wife. That is, if her nerves can last long enough for me to whisk her away and do delicious things with her body.

My cock lengthens, pressing against the pommel as I hurry forward. She will be frightened at first, of that I have no doubt, but I fully anticipate that fear morphing into unabashed need. If not, once I get through with tormenting her body and mind, she'll have no choice but to spread her legs for me, showing just how much I drive her wild.

Clenching my jaw, I shift in the saddle, irritated at the smooth leather pressing into me. Unfortunately, I'm unable to aid in the situation, and so I must press on and relieve myself before too much longer. Thankfully, they aren't much further ahead, and so my conquest shall be swift.

I keep Storm at a slow walk, my brain churning as I go over the plan in exhausting detail. Since she will no doubt be frightened, I have to make sure I don't create any extra undue anxiety. Knowing my mother and my brother, they'll make sure it doesn't go too far.

Still though... Am I making the wrong decision? We've spoken at length about how much she wants to fight past her fears, to live her life unburdened by the ghosts which haunt her. As her husband, I am duty bound to help in that endeavor. It doesn't hurt that I'll enjoy the lesson far more than she will.

Even now, my thoughts stray to her lying in the grass, her limbs spread wide as I take in the vision of her naked beauty. My cock pulses again, bringing that delicious image to an abrupt halt. Time slips by in agonizing slowness. Yet, for her, I will suffer a far greater multitude of agonies.

CHAPTER THREE

CATHERINE

The chill is the only thing keeping the nausea at bay. The incessant prattle of my new sisters helps with the panic. They verbally spar with each other, reminding me of my sister back at Overton. Tears prick my eyes, but this time it's happiness.

Seeing her those short weeks ago reassured me she was well. Despite Mr. Beaumont's lies, my sister grows stronger each day. In truth, her health has always been on my mind. She still looks so frail, so delicate despite the hearty timber in her voice. Deep in the recesses of my mind, I wonder if it's all for show.

Could she be putting on a brave front for Mother and me? I sincerely hope not. However, it is quite possible being so secluded in the countryside has made it possible for her to recover. It is, after all, the reason the dowager duchess is making her way toward home.

"You have a sister, do you not?" the matronly woman asks, her eyes kind. "I saw her briefly before leaving your wedding breakfast."

"Yes. She is a few years younger than me."

"She has your mother's eyes and your sense of spirit. I can tell these things about people you know. One might say I'm near clairvoyant."

"Oh, Mama," Lady Margaret chides. "You are not. No one says you're clairvoyant. Meddling, perhaps."

The older woman narrows her eyes. "It will be my meddling ways that secure you a good match. Come now, how can you doubt my abilities? Did I not say William would succumb this season?"

"You did," the younger sister pipes up. "But you also said Robert would take an arrow to the knee. And yet, there he sits astride with nary a projectile to be seen."

"Silly child. That's what you get for listening at keyholes. To take an arrow to the knee simply means-"

"Halt!" Blackport's voice rings out. "Who goes there?"

My heart thumps painfully in my chest as my vision wavers. It's happening again. That same sense of dread which clung to me like a shroud when Mr. Beaumont had me in his grasp now covers me, suffocating me. I reach out into the bond to alert William that something is amiss. However, there's nothing but silence.

In all honesty, that worries me far greater than whatever threat is coming. He never shields from me unless he himself is in danger or needs to concentrate. What could be happening to him to cause this disruption, and does it have anything to do with the peril at hand?

"Oh," my brother-in-law continues, his voice taking on an oddly stilted quality. "It is but a highwayman bent on causing harm. However shall we defend ourselves from such a farce- I mean force." Blackport bends low and looks into the landau. "Steel yourselves, women, for we are about to be beset. But worry not. For I shall defend you."

There's something peculiar in the way he speaks to us. It's as if he's bored by the whole affair and putting on some act. In truth, I've seen many plays with far better acting, even at a discounted price.

It's reminiscent, in fact, of how some of the women at The Rose and Thorne used to talk about their conquests. They played them out with the same aplomb and gravitas, only to dissolve into a pile of giggles. The Duke of Blackport, however, does not seem so inclined to fall into a fit of laughter.

In fact, I've only seen him smile a handful of times. There must be something else at work. Perhaps he's putting on a front to lull the ruffian into a sense of ease before striking? None of this makes sense.

All it does is twist my insides as thoughts and counter-thoughts collide, leaving me breathless and nauseated. Running my hand over my stomach, I command the small breakfast I had mere hours ago to stay put. Casting up my accounts will not aid this situation in the slightest.

Across from us, the sisters sit huddled together, the acrid stench of fear rolling off of them. The governess, though clearly frightened herself, holds herself in front, acting as a shield for whomever is set to attack. Her limbs tremble as she holds her arms out, making herself appear larger than she is.

Next to me, however, the dowager duchess seems almost amused. Her eyes glimmer as she cranes her neck to look outside. How can she be so calm at a time like this?

Sliding my fingers up and over my corset, I dip them inside to where the small knife lies sheathed against my breastbone. If need be, I'll be the one to keep a clear head. Ever since William got me out of the clutches of that madman, he's been instructing me on basic self-defense.

Right now, touching that metal hilt is the only thing keeping me from spiraling out of control. My breaths still come in ragged gasps, but at least I'm still coherent, cognizant of what's going on around me. In fact, if William could see me now, I'm sure he'd be proud.

Turning my way, the dowager duchess gives me an affected frown, the mirth in her eyes not matching the seriousness of her expression.

"Whatever shall we do? What if poor Robert cannot defend us? Why, the highwayman might strip us of our jewels or worse, our-" she pauses, glancing over at her daughters as they hang on every word. "Or our... dignity. Yes. Dignity is an appropriate word."

Dignity, such a small word compared to the enormity of what she's implying. I'm no longer naïve or innocent like they are. I am quite capable of comprehending what she's not saying. If this highwayman finds us lacking in the treasures department, then our flesh might suffice.

I can't do this again. I cannot go through with another man taking a part of me he has no claim to. When Mr. Beaumont marked me, I longed for death. Could this blackguard do the same or worse?

Gripping my fingers into fists, I allow a small bit of madness to take over. Just for a moment, enough to give me a modicum of relief from the present situation. As my vision hazes over, I rest in the soft hum of the bond.

Whatever may happen, William will find me. He always does. Besides, if I can handle the agony of a shattered bond, I'm sure I can live through another. Shaking my head, I pull myself out of my stupor. I cannot allow myself the freedom to drift away from the situation. Not when there are other, far more innocent women who can be taken advantage of.

Glancing over at the dowager duchess, I note her expression. I'm not sure if it's my imagination or delirium threatening to take hold of me again, but it seems as if the older woman is nearly glowing, bursting with anticipation. It's as if she knows something but isn't revealing it. Granted, with the way the younger girls huddle in on themselves, perhaps she's attempting to be optimistic for their sakes?

If only it would work on me. Instead, it does the complete opposite. Now, instead of just worrying about some rogue highwayman, I'm concerned for her health. Could she be descending into depths of delirium? I long to cry out to Blackport, to warn him of his mother's potential condition, but I dare not drag his attention away from the foe about to beset us.

"It will be quite all right, Elizabeth," the older woman nods. "Robert is an expert at dispatching with unpleasantries. He will protect us."

"Yes, but...your vision."

Her face crinkles for a moment, as if unsure of what the younger sister is talking about. "What do you mean, child? What vision?"

"About Robert," she wails, burying her head in her hands. "Is this where he takes an arrow to the knee? Will he even still be able to defend us while crippled in such a way?"

For a moment, silence descends on the interior of the landau. The dowager duchess blinks at Lady Elizabeth before dissolving into a peal of laughter. "Oh child, how I envy that imagination of yours."

Before I can interrupt, to explain what this phrase means, the door opens, revealing Blackport's face. I search his eyes, looking for some reassurance, but finding none. His lips thin as he peers in at us. "We are beset," he grumbles, his tone still devoid of any actual inflection. "We will not make it out of here with our lives."

Next to me, the dowager duchess throws her hand over her eyes and flops backward, as if in a faint. "Oh my. Whatever shall we do? This cannot be the end."

Suspicion niggles at my brain as I watch the theatrics before me. Neither she nor Blackport have even a whiff of fear coming off of them. It's as if they knew this was going to happen and are merely playing their part. While the older woman moans and rocks back and forth, Blackport looks off down the road, his expression more bored and annoyed than actually concerned.

"Oh. Oh my," he cries out, rolling his eyes. "You have cornered us. Whatever shall we do?"

"Your sword," Lady Margaret shrieks out. "Use your bloody sword!"

"Language," the governess, Blackport, and the dowager duchess cry out at the same time.

For a moment, Blackport's gaze drifts over to the governess, where he locks eyes on her. "If you are to be their guardian, then I expect her mouth to remain pristine. I never want to hear another oath fall from her lips. Are we of an accord?"

"Yes, Your Grace," she whispers, her face turning crimson.

"I take no issue with filling your mouth with a cake of soap if I catch her saying something like that again."

I blink as I watch the interaction between the two. Blackport seems to cast aside all notions of a highwayman so he can be a demanding oaf. Unfortunately, it's made all the worse as a slight tendril of arousal drifts off of her. From there, her blush becomes even redder, as if she's fully aware we know the effect his words have on her.

"Oh, Robert. Be kind to the poor girl. After all, are we not beset with a madman descending upon us?"

"Oh. Yes. Yes, you are quite right." Clearing his throat, he pulls away from the door and draws his sword. "Behold. It is he. Come forth and fight me like a man or slither off like the coward you are."

The man draws into view as the dowager duchess alternates between gripping her hands and pressing them against her heart. "Oh, shall we yet be saved? Shall Robert keep this ruffian at bay?"

Before I can remark, a familiar scent teases my nose. *William!* Though he's cloaked in a garment I've never seen before, I know the breadth of his shoulders and the width of his hips anywhere. He moves with a fluid grace, brandishing his sword high in the air.

"I have come for your bounty," he roars, my heart flipping at the decadent sound.

"There is no bounty to be found," Robert intones, his voice flat and despondent.

It confirms what I was hoping for all along. They *did* know about it. Now that I'm certain it's my husband and not some stranger set to defile me, I can breathe easier. More importantly, I can now play along.

"Stand aside. I shall judge for myself whether or not there is a prize to be found in this landau."

"No. You will have to get through me first." At this point, Blackport seems so bored with it all, unable to even muster the strength to put in a good fight.

However, to the sisters, this is all too real. They stare out of the windows and watch, their mouths agape. There's no way this will not affect them. I'm not sure how they will feel after the farce is revealed, but for now, it's as if they see their lives flashing before their eyes.

Unfortunately, I'm unable to comfort them as the sound of metal upon metal rings out. I watch, transfixed, as my husband and his brother spar. With William's mouth covered like it is, I can't see the smile on his face, but the crinkle around his green eyes tells me everything I need to know.

More than that, the bond hums between us, nearly sizzling with sexual tension as he glances my way. Lust pours over me, hot and heady as he steps in for the attack. Though I'm not sure how long this interlude between the two was supposed to play out, Blackport seems to just want it over with.

Raising his arm, he allows William to slide the sword home, pretending as if he has been struck down. "Oh, life. Oh, horror. Shall I now die while my family is ravaged? I shall haunt you from beyond the grave."

His speech is without flourish, delivered as dryly as the cook reading off her list of needed ingredients. Still though, the sisters buy into the act as tears stream down their cheeks. Next to them, the governess simply watches on, her brows furrowing as she watches Blackport twitch in a far more dramatic flair than his words.

William storms over, sending his mother into a flurry of false hysterics. She rocks back and forth, clutching at her fichu as she mumbles a prayer to the heavens. Unable to contain myself, I throw my body over hers and look up at my husband.

"Oh please, Sir. Spare us. You may have whatever you like. Just spare us."

He pokes his head into the landau and looks at each of us before spearing me with a heated glance. "I am after only the finest of treasure. What baubles do you carry?"

"Sir, we are without decoration, as you can plainly see. Just some women heading off to the country to take in the good air."

I look over at the sisters who still sob and quake. Can they not smell their brother? Are they so far gone they can't even recognize his voice? I would laugh, but it would ruin the scene he set up.

"If you have nothing for me, then I shall have to take one of you instead. What about that younger one? She seems strong enough to cook and clean for me."

At the very mention of doing chores, Lady Elizabeth howls a heart-rending cry to the heavens. This has certainly gone on long enough.

"Pray, good sir. Take me in her stead. I will work hard for you. If, indeed, hard work is what you require."

"I'm sure I can find other ways to make you useful. Come. I shall look at you in the light of the golden sun, unmarred by the trappings of this landau."

His mother reaches out for me, her fingers digging into my arm. "Do not sacrifice yourself. What about William? Whatever will he do without you?"

"Oh, I think he can manage. I've spent far too many days in his presence and long for a change of scenery."

"Clearly, Madam," he growls out. "You do not know a good thing when you have it."

"In truth, my good sir, he was beginning to bore me. I'd much rather give up my life in sacrifice than live cloistered away." Looking over at Lady Elizabeth, I gather her hand in mine. "I do this for you. Do not let my sacrifice be in vain."

Stepping over the dowager duchess, I give her a conspiratorial wink and open the door. Before I can step out, William's warm hands wrap around my waist, dragging me against the hard planes of his body.

"Please," I cry out as he carries me away. "Do not forget me. Allow my memory to stay poignant on your lips."

CHAPTER FOUR

WILLIAM

"Allow my memory to stay poignant on your lips?" I laugh, swatting her arse as I carry her to my stallion. "Who knew this lass I found would be such a poet and so very accommodating?"

She beats at my shoulders, her blows light and playful. "Please, you fiend, be gentle with me. I am a married woman and not accustomed to such rough treatment."

Pausing, I throw my head back and laugh, the dark chuckle reverberating through the trees. My little wife has such a penchant for the theatre. "I shall do as I like. You gave yourself to me, remember? And if that means ruining you for your husband, then so be it."

Her scent of arousal drifts about my head, making my vision swim. All I want to do is bury my cock inside her, to knot her as I slam her wrists down into the dirt. It's agony playing this farce, but it's a game we will both enjoy if I can only muster the patience to see it through.

"Please, my husband is but a humble man. One with very little to his name. I am his prized jewel. If I were to be returned tarnished...

Well, I'm afraid he'll have nothing to live for. I would so hate for him to sully the floor with his untimely demise."

"You went a bit dark with that one, my love," I chuckle, running my fingers up the back of her thighs. "Fictional or not, I do not wish for you to picture your husband as deceased."

Her soft laugh caresses my skin just like a cool breeze in the hot desert. It runs across me like phantom fingers, touching, teasing. "I do apologize. I guess I was caught up in the moment. Shall I make amends?"

I lower her to the ground next to Storm, pressing her back up against the solid wall of horseflesh. "Do you think you can?"

Her lashes flutter as she glances down at my erection straining against my buckskin breeches. "My husband has kept me in the dark about how a woman can please her man, but if you promise to teach me your dark secrets, I'll strive to be the perfect pupil."

Damnation. Though I've fucked her in nearly every way imaginable, she still manages to wear her innocence like a cloak. It's tantalizing, tempting, and far too difficult to resist. When she runs her fingers up my shaft, her eyes wide with feigned innocence, I'm nearly done for.

"Please, good sir. Teach me. I so long to learn what it's like to shatter under a man's touch."

"And your husband?" My voice is gruff, hoarse with need.

"So what if his jewel comes back a bit tarnished? I was far too hasty with my words. Here I'm given a golden opportunity, a chance to be completely wanton. My travel companions think me kidnapped or worse. It would not be my fault if you had your wicked way with me."

Though we both know this is a game, there's something almost taboo about the idea of fucking her as someone else and not as her rightful husband. Precum pearls at my tip as my balls clench in need. Oh, we shall definitely be playing this game more often.

"You have but one chance to flee with your sensibilities intact. Run into the forest. If I catch you, I will make you mine, unfit for any other man. Do you understand me?"

"Clearly, my dastardly highwayman. But what if I do not wish to flee?"

"Would you rather I take you here on this public road where anyone could see?" My heart thumps in my chest as she weighs my words.

How I wish she would say yes, but even in my lustful haze, I know it's unwise for a duke to cavort with his duchess in this manner. Hellfire and damnation, but we already dodged a bullet with our nuptials. It would be imprudent to press our luck in this way. Besides, we're still on tenterhooks with the Ton as it is.

Still, as I watch her glancing up and down the road, I can't resist a bit of fun. No one is around to watch as I yank her leg up and around my hip, opening her wide so I can slide my hand up her inner thigh. I pause just shy of her quim, waiting impatiently as she rocks her body close to me in a needful entreaty.

"Do you wish for me to pleasure you?" I groan into the crook of her neck. "Do you wish for me to show you the secrets I can bestow on you?"

"Yes," she cries out, her hips jutting against me. "Please. I'm desperate for your touch."

"Then run."

She blinks up at me, her gaze a touch hazy and unfocused. "Pardon?"

"If you wish for me to pleasure you, then run. The longer it takes for me to catch you, the more your pleasure shall be." Lowering her leg, I run my thumb across her bottom lip, noting the concern in her eyes.

"Don't worry, love," I croon, switching back to my normal timber. "I chose this spot on purpose. You will suffer no harm. Not too far back is a shelter. I will meet you there." Straightening back up, I put on my affected voice. "But do try to make it a bit of sport for me? If I am to hang for kidnapping one so delectable, I'd like to at least have some fun first."

Breathless, she straightens her clothes, her fingers fidgeting a touch. But I know it's no longer fear that makes her quake. Arousal pours from her as she glances back into the tree line. Straightening her shoulders, she gives me a haughty look.

"Try as you might, but I've run through forests before. You will never catch me."

Quick as lightning, she takes off, far quicker than I expect. My cock aches as I watch her dress flit about as she maneuvers through the trees. Keeping my thoughts calm and collected, I take Storm's reins and lead him toward the small cottage I mentioned earlier.

I've inspected the location many times and found it to be abandoned, yet clean. It's the perfect spot to defile my wife before taking her back to London to start our honeymoon. Taking a small trail, I make record time, ducking around some overgrowth to side up next to the rocky exterior.

Looking into the bond, I monitor Catherine, making sure she still hums with arousal and not fear. This should be safe, but it is England, after all. A small bit of anxiety pricks my heart, causing me to tie up Storm even faster. With a quick glance around the cottage, I make sure all is still set and ready to go before taking off after my wife.

I pull the covering concealing my face lower so I can tip my nose into the air. So far, the only scents I can detect are the vegetation, the animals native to this area, and the alluring dusky rose that belongs only to my wife.

It calls to me, pulling me forward as I work my way through branches and grasses. There should be another path up ahead where my wife will be traipsing along, waiting for me to capture her yet again. However, when I turn onto the beaten earth, she's nowhere to be found.

The minx is taking her role far too seriously. I never thought I'd have to actually hunt her down. No matter. All it does is make me far more ravenous to taste her pussy, to drink her into me before I make her choke on my cock.

Turning off the path, I hunch down and study the broken twigs and bent grass, smiling as her steps are laid bare for me. Hunting for both food and sport is in my blood, something both Robert and I share. However, hunting for my wife is far superior in my opinion. Ear to the ground, I listen for anything that might alert me to her location.

There. It's a touch further away than I'd like, but I hear her. Rising from the ground, a snarl rumbles through my chest as I take off. Oh yes. We will need to play this game far more often, but perhaps once we're at Birchleigh, where I'll have complete control.

I race through the woods, ducking under low-hanging branches and sidestepping thorns. Pausing, I listen as curse words fill the air. She's not frightened, just angry. And so, I take my time, leisurely strolling over to her until I see just what has her so wroth.

She twists and turns, her skirts caught in a mass of thorns. Every time she yanks herself free, she manages to catch a different part, rendering her almost immobile. It's as if the gods smile down upon us, serving her up to me on such a delectable platter.

Smirking, I slip the covering back over my face and make my way to her. "My, aren't we in a high dudgeon. Does your husband allow such vulgar language to slip past your lips?"

A startled shriek flies up from her throat, but soon her eyes narrow in indignation. However, the longer I stare at her, my arms crossed and my fingers tapping, she slumps a bit, her gaze shifting to and fro. At least she has sense enough to look ashamed as red tinges her cheeks.

"I suppose he would be quite put out to hear me speaking as such."

"Indeed. A lady should never utter any of the words I've just heard. Tsk, tsk, tsk. So unfortunate I happened upon you in a fit of pique. Shall I allow you to do penance for your actions, then?"

Arousal blossoms into the air as she nods, her fingers still prying at the briars. "I feel it will be for the best."

"In that case, allow me to assist you, so I may commence with teaching you the errors of your ways." Walking behind her, I study the situation before wrapping my arms around her waist. "I fear this dress will not make it. I must part you both if you are to be free."

"Truly?" she cries out, slumping forward. "I quite liked this dress."

"Well, I'm sure your husband can get you another. Still though, such a mess you've managed to get yourself into. Have you scraped your delicate skin?" Before she can answer, I interject. "No matter. I'll just have to inspect you myself. No sense in allowing you to go back to your husband anything less than pristine. Well...physically, that is. You will return to him tarnished in other ways."

Inching my way up, I feel her breath catch in her throat. If she thinks I'll indulge her, give her any sort of relief, then she is mistaken. Dipping my fingers into her corset, I feel for the knife I gave her.

Today, it will serve a far greater purpose, one of arousal and titillation. With a quick draw, I unsheathe the small dagger and contemplate holding it at her throat, becoming a true highwayman indeed. But I stay my hand, not wishing to bring back any ghosts of her past.

Instead, I drag the tip through the fabric, ridding her of the tangled mess, until she stands there in her shoes, stockings, shift, and corset. My, but what an erotic picture she makes. Already I can see the proof of her desire as it coats the shift, causing it to stick to her skin.

It perfumes the air, dragging a ragged groan from my lips. "I swear, you'll be the death of me," I groan as I pluck her out of the briars and stand her in front of me. With a quick jerk of my shoulders, I remove my coat and put it on her, keeping the cold at bay. Once she's wrapped up in it, I haul her over my shoulder. "But what an alluring death it would be."

She squirms, as if halfheartedly wanting to fight, but I know my little kitten. All she wants is to lap at my cream. Thankfully, our desires are one and the same. Glancing about, I ensure we're still alone as I take my somewhat exposed wanton to the cottage to dress her up in my ropes.

As beautiful as she is, there's just something so decadent about seeing her trussed up, waiting for me. Though I wished to defile her amongst the grasses and flowers, I find I'm far too possessive. No one seems to be about, but I refuse to chance anyone taking an opportunity to gaze upon her naked flesh. That view is mine and mine alone.

My cock lurches forward as I lengthen my stride, desperate to feel my wife clenching around me. Soon. Oh, so achingly soon.

CHAPTER FIVE

CATHERINE

My breaths come in quick gasps as I cling to William's shoulders, burrowing my face into his coat. His scent calms me, soothes me, and yet I cannot keep my thoughts from straying. In fact, it's his very scent that drives me to distraction.

Though I know he's my husband, there's still this tremor of a thrill, an unknowing. It's not frightening, exactly, but it feels so wrong. Unfortunately, it's what also makes it feel so right.

Somehow, my amazing mate finds a way to switch things up, to keep me guessing. Granted, we're still within a few weeks of our marriage, and I shouldn't even worry about things cooling down between us. However, it's the fact he loves me so much he planned all of this out as an illicit surprise for me.

It makes my heart swell to know my husband not only cares about keeping me satisfied but also continues to show me how fun marriage can be. He's considerate that way. Or, more likely, I haven't even begun to scratch at the surface of his depravity. That thought alone makes my insides quiver with anticipation.

Resting my head against his shoulder, I revel in the heat of his skin as it burns against my cheek. The bond hums between us, surrounding me in a cloud of contentment. In all honesty, the only thing difficult about all of this is keeping to the role I'm supposed to play. Part of me wants to eschew all these pretenses and love my husband as man and wife.

And yet, it's this farce which has slick gathering between my thighs and my body aching for this illicit touch. Am I wrong for this? Does this bode ill for our marriage?

My love, he whispers into my mind as his hand skims up the back of my thigh. *I hear your thoughts, and they do not serve you. This is a game between us, one we both willingly play. It's not as if you're seeking out some other company other than my own. Because know this, my little kitten, I will never share you with anyone. The moment you decide to try some other man will be the day I start digging graves in our backyard.*

I melt against him, my heart pounding. Though I have no thoughts of other men, it still warms my heart to hear how possessive he is. And I do take him at his word. After seeing what he did to Mr. Beaumont, I don't doubt him capable of dispatching anyone who would dare approach me in a sexual manner.

Digging my fingers into the sides of his shoulders, I close my eyes and listen to the sounds around us. There will never be anyone for me but him. And though we play this game, it's still my husband who brings me pleasure.

That's right, my little minx. And don't you forget it.

The moment he steps inside the small enclosure, a warmth envelops us, driving away the chill from the outside. He sets me down, allowing me to look about, noting the cheery fireplace blazing in the room. It's as if we're wrapped up in our own little cocoon, far away from London, people, and even my horrific memories that threaten to buckle me on a daily basis.

"I thank you for the fire, good sir. Never thought a highwayman would be that considerate."

"You believe the fire to be for you? How naïve," he teases, removing the coat from my body and laying it on the worn floor. "Unless you feel as if I should freeze as punishment for my crimes against lovely ladies such as yourself?"

At his praise, my cheeks heat, no doubt flushing as I turn my gaze away. "Forgive me. I do not wish for you to be cold."

Though I'm not looking at him, I can feel the heat of his gaze as it roves over my body. Suddenly, I feel oddly naked. He's seen me in less, and yet, this all feels so new. It's as if I'm back at The Rose and Thorne, waiting for him to do his worst.

"Look at me."

Those three little words force me to drag my gaze over to him. He doesn't use an Alpha command. He doesn't have to. I will forever obey him in a heartbeat.

"My, what a lovely lass I procured from the landau. Seems as if I have the best treasure after all. Turn so I may remove your corset. That is," he pauses to pull out my small dagger from his pocket, "unless you'd rather I cut it from you."

My breath comes in haggard gasps as I watch the blade glint in the firelight. "I am your prisoner," I murmur, sinking down into a curtsy. "My body is yours to do with as you will."

The air grows heavy and even warmer as his arousal floods my senses. My thighs tremble as desire and need grow into an inferno that rivals the blazing fire.

I want him.

I need him.

I crave him with every fiber of my being.

"Yes," he murmurs, walking around me. "You are certainly mine. Now, if I remember correctly, I was going to inspect you for any cuts the briars caused, but first, your atonement for your ghastly language. On your knees."

I sink down onto his coat, my mind fuzzing about the edges. It is my submission to his wants and desires which make my body burn.

Knees splayed as best as they can within the shift, I rest my hands on the tops of my thighs and look up at him. Desire flares in his eyes, turning them nearly black. I can feel the lust through the bond, and it only makes me crave him even more.

"Such a pretty little kitten. Shall I fetch you some cream?" With slow, methodical movements, he works at the front of his breeches, taunting me with the erection I know is caged behind the buckskin.

Finally, he releases it, allowing the scent of his need to flood the room. My core aches as I watch the bit of precum pearl up at the top. I want to taste him. I *need* to taste him. But I'm supposed to be innocent, unable to pleasure a man such as him.

"My, you are far bigger than my husband. However shall you punish me with that instrument of torture?"

"Careful, love," he grinds out, his voice taking on a dangerous edge. "Men don't like to be compared. Even if this is a work of fiction."

"My apologies, my good sir," I simper with a wink before placing the back of my hand against my forehead. "Oh my. And here I thought you'd be quite large, when, in fact, it is my husband's phallus which holds the record for girth and length."

With a playfully, ferocious growl, he leaps forward, taking me backward, splaying me out underneath him. "I'll show you how large I am," he teases, wrenching my legs open.

I resist the urge to groan as his large head prods at my entrance. This is what I've needed since the moment he appeared next to the landau. Instead of thrusting in, he hovers there, so achingly close.

"On second thought, I will still punish that wayward mouth of yours." Reaching down to curl his hand around the back of my neck, he urges me back into a kneeling position. "You will worship my cock with your lips and tongue. You will show me just how repentant you are in your cruel words about my size."

"And the penance for the awful language I used?" I blink up at him, the picture of innocence.

His eyes narrow, and though I cannot see his mouth, I can imagine the wicked grin that slashes across his face. "I have something far more potent in mind."

At that, my insides quiver. Not from fear. Never from fear. But from an arousal so intense, it steals my breath. As he comes closer, I open my mouth wide, prepared to take him inside. However, he doesn't move.

He just stands there, cock jutting out, tempting me. Normally, he grabs my head and uses me to find his pleasure, but this time, he doesn't. He keeps his arms crossed as he looks down at me.

"Well? Are you going to worship me? Or should I cast you out into the chilly air in naught but your rail and corset to conceal you? Though, to be honest, it doesn't hide much."

I know they're idle words, but they cause slick to gather and the incessant ache to resume. Until meeting William, I never knew I was such a wanton. Leaning forward, I run the tip of my nose up and down his length, taking in his musky, masculine scent.

God, but it makes everything in me clench with need. I long to reach down between my thighs and touch myself, but William, or rather, this highwayman, hasn't given me permission. Groaning, I reach forward and cup his balls, giving my hands something else to do.

They're weighty and full, drawing up as I caress them. With a sigh, I run my nail over the wrinkled skin, smiling as his cock jerks. Though he means to punish me by forcing me to indulge in my love for his cock, it will truly be he that suffers.

I plan to take my time, touching, kissing, and licking every inch. It's something I've never been able to do before now. Our coupling is always so frantic, so fierce. For once, I can enjoy myself and learn my husband. Cupping both balls in one hand, I squeeze, watching his face to see if it's causing him any discomfort.

Though I was his courtesan first and his wife second, there's still so much I do not know about how a man works. And so I explore, squeezing even tighter until he gives a small grunt and pulls back. But now, I know what pressure he likes.

"Do you prefer my fingers elsewhere? Or are they fine cupping you like this?"

"God," he moans through clenched teeth. "Your hands feel like heaven on my body. But now, I wish to feel your tongue and lips."

"All in good time, my good sir. It was your command for me to worship, and true, heartfelt worship takes time."

Bringing up my other hand, I explore his length, running my fingers over his large member. I'm unable to even circle all the way around with one hand. I know my husband is large, but actually taking the time to gather his length and width reminds me of just how well he stretches me out.

A soft moan slips from my lips and whispers over his delicate skin. He's so warm, vibrant, and soft...like velvet wrapped around the hardest metal. Rigid yet yielding as I explore him.

Taking my finger, I run it down the thick veins that surround him, following them down to his knot, which already begins to swell. "Damnation, Kitty," he groans, jutting his hips up. "You're enjoying this, aren't you?"

"How can you tell, my good sir?" My voice is breathy and soft as I look up at him.

"Because," he growls, "I can smell your arousal. With each pass of your fingertips, it grows stronger. I'm sure you're soaking by now, aren't you?"

"That I am, my good sir. But please, allow me to continue my penance. I must atone for my words."

He stands there, rigid as precum continues to well up and bead at his slit. Once there's enough, it drips down his length. Unable to resist, I lap at him, dragging my tongue from his balls to his tip, savoring him as if he's a sweet treat. Like melted chocolate, his bitter, earthy flavor explodes on my tongue, driving up my lust.

Now, his arms are no longer crossed. They dangle at his side as he clenches and releases his fingers. He wants to grab me to force his cock down my throat. I can tell by the rigid lines of his body as he holds himself still.

Taking my time, I drag the tip of my tongue around his head, coming close to the slit, which is now sticky with his essence. Coming around underneath, I tease that bit of skin that connects down with the shaft, growing wetter as oaths fly from his lips. Unable to tease him any longer, I swallow his fat head into my mouth, groaning at the feel of it on my tongue.

William finally runs his fingers through my hair, gripping the strands as he leads me down his shaft. He's not rough this time, but urgent, insistent. Widening my lips as far as I can, I continue down his shaft, running my tongue along the underside as he feeds me his cock inch by maddening inch.

Once his head hits the back of my throat, I place my palms against his muscular thighs, grounding myself as I force my mind to calm. I know I can breathe, and yet, when I'm so stuffed with him, it's sometimes hard to imagine. Giving in, I allow him to take over.

Gently, he pulls out and rocks back in, easing his tip down into my throat one stroke at a time. We stay like this for what feels like an eternity until his knot finally grazes against my lips. He holds me there, his cock pulsing in my mouth as sinful groans fill the air.

I no longer care if I can breathe or not because every inch of me is consumed with my husband and the pleasure his body brings me. My eyes flutter closed as he pulls out once more, allowing me precious air. Each time he eases inside, he holds me close, almost as if he's caressing me, before reluctantly pulling away.

CHAPTER SIX

WILLIAM

I stare down at my wife, lust swirling through me. God, but I want to come down her pretty throat. Perhaps if I allow myself, I'll be able to drive this madness from my brain and finally be able to think. There's so much I want to do to her, with her, but I can't when my cock controls my actions.

Gripping the back of her head, I hold her still as I glide in and out. My balls clench, drawing up until they're so tight stars spark behind my eyes. Grunts and oaths fly from my lips as her lips massage me and her tongue caresses me.

When I first met her, I wasn't able to fuck her face with such wild abandon. Now, after a few weeks of teaching and training her, she kneels there before me, her throat softening as I force myself down, choking her. Tears stream from her eyes as her lips thin, accommodating my massive girth.

Those tears are precious to me. They speak of her willing submission. Whereas the scent of arousal that drifts up from her pussy speaks of the pleasure she derives from being my vessel.

My knot swells, tingling as I slide into her one final time. Holding her still, I jerk my hips as cum spurts out from me and shoots down the back of her throat. Her fingers frantically clench at my thighs as I fill her stomach with my essence.

Like the good little omega she is, she swallows me down as best as she can. She sucks me hard, drinking every drop. Groaning, I fist her hair in my hands and pull her away.

With practiced ease, she drops her hands back down to her thighs and proceeds to clean me with her tongue. "My good little omega," I murmur, brushing her mass of ebony curls from her face so I can watch her pretty pink tongue lap at my slit.

Already I grow hard again, needing her with a passion which will never die. And it will always be like this between us. I just know it. It's not because of these little games we play with each other, but because our souls recognize each other as our other half.

Forcing myself away from the warm haven of her mouth, I painfully tuck my cock into my breeches. I need my strong-willed anatomy away for what I plan to do next.

"You are far more skilled than you let on. Perhaps your husband is a luckier man than you admit?"

With a feigned coquettish sigh, she lowers her lashes, simpering as well as any practiced courtesan. "My good sir, it is you who are my inspiration. I've never been able to handle even the mere idea of such an activity from my husband."

"Indeed," I murmured, motioning for her to stand up. "I wonder how well you'll fare with my next task. You will not move until I give you permission." Again, I pull out the dagger and watch as her pupils dilate.

It's been far too long since she's felt the kiss of a knife on her skin. As I stalk forward, her chest heaves, forcing her breasts to rise above the top of her corset. It's such an alluring visual, one that has my knot throbbing with need.

I make quick work of the strings, making a mental note to stock her wardrobe with clothes far less expensive. This way, I can destroy them at will and not cause her mental anguish. Somehow, she still doesn't understand that I would buy her the moon if it only hung low enough for someone to put a bill of sale on it.

She carries these unnecessary sensibilities around her like a shroud. Someday, I'll be able to cut through the mental barriers, to prove to her she's safe with me. I will provide every need and then some.

Still though, I don't miss the pang that shoots through her heart as the corset falls to the floor. Dropping character for a moment, I lean forward. "Love, we can easily replace the strings. Your corset is not destroyed."

Catherine's fingers twitch at her sides, and through the bond, I feel the overwhelming warmth and happiness my words bring her. "Thank you. I was rather fond of this one."

Coming around the front, I tip her chin up to look her in the eyes. "When we get settled, I will have you separate your favorites from the garments you wouldn't mind having roughed up. Believe me when I say this. Today is not an exception but the rule. I will find any moment to cut these fabrics away from your flesh. Understand?"

"Yes, my love," she breathes, relief causing her to sag against me.

"Oh dash it all," I cry out, ripping the cover from my face.

I wish to kiss those pretty pouty lips, and nothing will stand in my way. Gathering her into my arms, I slant my mouth over hers, easing her into a tender kiss. Soon, however, it becomes wild and desperate.

Our teeth clash together as our tongues duel with each other. Moans flit into the air as I bury my free hand into her hair, fisting for a moment as I pull her back. "Such a pretty mouth. But there are other lips I wish to taste. Now then, stand still as I remove this shift from you. No objections, I take it?"

"None, Sir."

At her honorific, my cock pulses. More precum wells to the surface as need tightens my muscles. "Good fucking girl."

The knife slides through the flimsy fabric with barely any resistance. Just like that night when I first saw her, it slips down to the floor, exposing her body to my hungry gaze. And, just like that night, I plan to keep her socks and garters on.

There's something so inherently arousing, seeing her so unclothed and yet not quite. All it does is make me want to dishevel her even more. Placing the knife between my teeth, I bend low and pull her calf up to me, as if she's a prized steed, which I'm about to shoe.

This image shouldn't be erotic in the slightest, and yet, for a moment, all I want to do is put a bridle in her mouth and waltz her about for all to see. The delicious humiliation of turning her into my horse to truss up and breed at will... It must be the haze of lust which has me thinking in this manner. Still though, it's something I might bring up to my friends. Perhaps they have experience in this area?

Shaking those thoughts from my mind, I make quick work of her shoe, tossing it to the floor before I grab her other leg. Now, I can begin. Walking over to the side of the room, I gather the bits of rope I stashed here earlier. They're soft as silk in my hands, a far cry from the horrendous bite of rope Hugh Beaumont trussed her up with.

Since that fateful day, I've only ever used the softest of ropes with her, never once allowing her mind to drift back to his unforgivable actions. The pain I cause her will never mimic anything he ever did. I'll die before I hurt her like that.

With the knife still firmly in between my teeth, I'm unable to speak out loud to her, but my motions are swiftly obeyed. Her pupils dilate as I slip the rope around the back of her neck and drag the length down her front. For a bit of fun, I rub the silken strands against her nipples, my cock swelling as her soft moans fill the air.

God, but she's a vision. Removing the knife, I sheath it once more and slide it into my pocket. Right now, my lips want to wrap around those tight buds that beg for my caress. Bending low, I lap at her nipple while my fingers pinch the other.

She writhes under my touch, her body coming alive with every lick and nip. Pulling away, I follow the rope down until I reach her apex. God, but she's soaked. I drag my fingers through her lower lips, my balls clenching as her slick coats my fingers.

At this rate, I'm going to fuck her before too much else happens, and I so want to truss her up first. Making a small knot in the ropes, I line it up with her clit before I drag the tails up and in between her arse cheeks. Once I slip the ends under the portion around her neck, I pull tight, waiting until I hear her gasp of pleasure as the knot grinds into her clit.

She squirms, no doubt attempting to dislodge the irritant, but the ropes hold firm. "Please," she whimpers, her body shuddering as each minute movement forces the rope to pleasure her. "I- I can't take much more of this."

"Oh, I'm sure you can. You're such a good little omega. I know you can hold off on your release until I give you permission."

Again, her soft whimpers meet my ears as her arousal blossoms around us. She can never resist being my good girl. And I love her all the more for it.

Taking the ends, I weave them around the front, caging her breasts in a tight caress. Catherine gasps as I pull them even tighter, making them distend from her body just a touch. From there, I pull here and tuck there until pretty diamond shapes go down her body.

Once I get to her mound, I take the ends and slip them through, extending out the rope resting against her clit. It drives that little knot even further, drawing a cry from her pretty lips. Through the bond, I monitor her, prepared to cut through these ropes in an instant if it causes her undue distress.

But there's only physical discomfort and an intense need to come. I can live with such emotions. Easing her down onto the floor, I draw my knife back out and drag the tip along her delicate skin.

"If I were an actual highwayman, I could do so many nefarious things with this knife. For instance..." I bring the blade up to her throat, resting it against the thin skin of her neck.

Her lashes flutter as she slips into that hazy space between heaven and earth. God, but I love getting her to this point. Taking care to keep the pressure even, I lean down and kiss her pouty lips before pulling away.

"You're so beautiful, my love," I whisper, looking down at her with all the tenderness within me. "I will never be able to think of a day when you will not be by my side. But know this: when I fuck you, it will be hard and raw, full of passion and need. You bring this side out of me. Your soft sighs, your elegant submission...I want all of you, and I shall have it."

"Always, my love."

Pulling away, I toss the knife to the side and go to retrieve a different item altogether. I keep my back turned so she cannot see the dilator I pull from a sack hidden in the corner of the room. Truthfully, it doesn't quite matter, seeing as her mind is in a haze.

I use her arousal to coat the blunt head before pulling the ropes to the side so I can wedge it deep into her ass. "Did I not say I'd find a way to punish you for your language? Though, knowing you, this is more of a reward."

Keening moans claw at her throat as I stretch her wide, impaling her with the rigid phallus. Her tight ring fights me, threatening to push it out. Growling softly, I wait until her body relaxes before gliding it the rest of the way in.

I watch, transfixed, as her body swallows it up, pulling it deep inside her. We still haven't explored me taking that bottom hole, and as much as I want to indulge, I'd rather her first time be somewhere other than a dirty old cottage. Soon, though.

Fully seating the dilator, I bring the ropes back around and cover the base, keeping it snug within her. My cock jerks as I stare down at her, watching her rock from side to side, arousing herself with the bit of rope between her thighs. As much as I want to drag this out, to keep her on the edge, for both of our sanities, I need to take her now.

Glancing outside, I watch as the sunlight begins to wane. I don't want us out here after dark. Not out of concern for me, but for her safety. With me so consumed with lust, I might miss hearing movement outside. We've already pushed our luck, and I don't want to endanger either of us.

CHAPTER SEVEN

CATHERINE

The stretch is immense, nearly stealing my breath. The only respite I have at the moment is the lack of internal burning. At least this time, he didn't apply that infernal ginger onto the dilator.

Still though, I don't need any extra stimulation. Not when my bottom hole aches and that knot continues to grind at my clit. My body clenches as I toss about, desperate to find relief.

William kneels above me, his hands gliding over his massive erection. Hopefully, he'll actually finish inside me this time and not splatter his seed upon my body, or worse, this wretched floor. I've come to crave the feeling of his essence filling me, the heat adding yet another layer to the arousal that seems to never fizzle out.

With his free hand, he traces the bond mark on my inner thigh—the first place he bit me. Even now, I shudder as memories of our first heat race through my mind. Whether it's from my own consciousness or he's feeding it to me from his mind, I cannot tell. And truthfully, it doesn't really matter.

We both look upon that moment with an erotic fondness that

surpasses many other memories. Groaning, I shift my legs, giving him better access to my quim. I'd much rather he pull the rope aside and stroke me there instead. But he doesn't oblige. Not surprising, seeing as he seems to live to torment me.

Pulling his hand away, he brings it up to my heart, covering the mark that resides there. Such an ugly, twisted thing forced upon me by Mr. Beaumont. And yet, somehow, William managed to make it beautiful. One more tether to bind us together. Tears prick my eyes as I lay my hand on top of his, flooding the bond with my undying love for him.

He keeps his hand there as his other hand spreads me wide. The blunt tip of his cock prods at my entrance, inhibited by the rope. Mournful whines pour from my throat as I buck up against him, desperate for the release he has so far denied me.

With a cocky grin, he pulls back, sliding his hand away. "Aww. Poor little kitten. Is it truly agonizing? How badly do you want my cock sliding deep inside this greedy cunt of yours?"

The harshness of his words only seems to amplify my need. Groaning, I glide my fingers over my breasts, hoping to force him to relent if I pleasure myself. His breaths come in harsh gasps as he watches me pluck at my nipples, mewling as I writhe in his ropes.

"Damnation, Catherine, you're perfection. But I will have your words. How badly do you want me?"

"Please, my love," I moan out, arching my hips up as best as I can. "I am so desperate for you to fill me. Please. Please, Master." The word rings out in the small cottage, bouncing around, echoing as if several of us cry out at once.

"Then you shall have me." His thick fingers graze my lower lips as he maneuvers the rope, spreading it open.

The infernal knot grinds harder into my clit, forcing a wail from my lips. "Shhh, pretty omega. Soon, my cock shall soothe your discomfort. Endure for me just a little while longer." Working his head between the splayed rope, he slides his tip into me, grunting as he takes his time.

I toss my head back and forth, the need building into a raging fire. With each little rock of his hips, he impales me, stretching me open until I'm about to bust. With the dilator still lodged in my backside, William feels twice as large.

Biting down on my lower lip, I revel in the feel of him opening me up, filling me as only he can. However, the moment he looks down, my husband cocks his eyebrow and reaches for my mouth.

"Oh no, my little wanton. I want to hear every sound as it flees your delicate lips. I want everyone in all of England to hear how well I can fuck my wife."

"I thought you were merely a simple highwayman. Would you really like England to know how well you ravage someone else's wife?"

"Minx," he growls out, sliding his hand down to grip my throat. "Now that I'm fucking you, I want only thoughts of me to flit through your mind. No one else, even fictional." At that last word, he snaps his hips, surging forward to slide the rest of the way in.

"There will only be you," I cry out, my inner walls fluttering around his girth. "Always and forever."

"Damn right." Bringing his hands lower, he grips my hips, holding me steady as he pumps in and out. With the rope stretched impossibly tight, every minute movement causes the knot to rock against me, tormenting me in a way that steals my very breath.

"P- please, Master!" The tearful wail floods my ears, sounding so foreign, so far away. "I- I need-"

"Yes, wife. What do you need?"

"Please!"

"I hear you, love. Come for me. Let yourself go. Shatter, break apart, and trust me to pick up the pieces."

At his words, my body explodes as the long-denied orgasm comes crashing through. I shudder in his grasp as he continues to slide in and out, riding me through one release and straight into another. The rope continues to torment me, forcing my body to continue quaking and shuddering.

William stares down at me, his eyes locking with mine. Sweat beads on his brow as he strains against me. His cock pulses deep inside, jerking every time he seats himself fully. The dilator in my bottom hole rocks against the ropes, continually stretching me out until the burn sizzles across my synapses.

I hold on to him, needing his solid strength. As his muscles bunch under my hands, my inner walls flutter again, gripping him tightly as another release causes me to bow up against him. A soft growl drifts from his lips as he shoves his desire for me through the bond.

It's overwhelming, a cacophony of sounds, feelings, and emotions as they run through me. Bright light flashes in front of my eyes as my lips part in a silent cry. Every muscle in my body screams at me, tightening up as my body explodes again.

Thrashing about, I grip his biceps, unable to even say a word. But I don't have to. He hears me. He always hears me. Bringing his hand down, he wedges his finger in between us, pulling the knot away so I have a small modicum of relief.

It's short-lived, however, because soon, his knot begins to swell. Grunting, he snaps his hips once, twice, three times before letting out a shameful groan. His knot engorges, pressing against my poor abused inner walls and the dilator in my bottom.

Black encroaches my vision as yet one final release slithers through my body, spurred on by the heat of his seed as it bathes my insides. The moans that leave my lips drift up into the air, barely audible over the loud growl of satisfaction that pours from his body. Letting go of the rope, he skims his hands along my back, making quick work of unbinding me.

Though the rope between my thighs remains, imprisoned by our bodies, the relief at no longer having that blasted knot grinding into me has me floating on the ether. With a tender grasp, he gathers me into his arms and turns us so I can lie on top of him.

In truth, the moment he does this while we're conjoined by his knot makes my heart sing. Even though I adore the stifling heat of his body as he envelops me, there's something so considerate, so loving in this action. Letting my thighs part even more, I straddle him and nuzzle deep into his chest.

Just as he did mine, I run my fingers over the mark I gave him. Though not nearly as ragged or deep, it signifies something which will never be taken from us. He's as much mine as I am his. With a soft sigh, I allow myself to drift, lulled by his throaty purr and the gentle skimming of his hands down my back.

Darkness surrounds me as I open my eyes. The only light visible is from the dying fireplace. No longer is my husband underneath me. Instead, I lie wrapped up in his coat on the floor.

Panic threatens to eat at me, but I hold it at bay, reminding myself of his love for me. He wouldn't just abandon me.

"That's correct, my incorrigible kitten. I merely prepared for our departure while you slept. Between the nightmares and...well...the broken bond, you've not been able to sleep all that well. Any chance I can give you to rest, I ensure you remain undisturbed."

Rising, I groan as my muscles cry out in protest. "Honestly, I feel as if I could fall back asleep if only I were submerged in a hot tub."

His throaty chuckles bring another wave of arousal thrumming through my body, but instinctually, I know we cannot act on it. Not while nighttime looms over us. Running my hands over my body, I feel for the rope in between my thighs and find it absent. Same as the dilator. Somehow, I feel so empty, but it's a ridiculous emotion.

With a heavy tread, William walks over to me and gathers me into his arms. "Not ridiculous, my love. You always feel depleted and morose after an intense session with me. It's normal and to be expected. Come, let me take you home and bathe you. I'm sure Cook has some sweet treats for you which I know will set your spirit to rights."

I give him a watery smile, still unsure as to how I managed to snag someone like him. "I just don't understand. It makes no sense. I should be happy, beaming, and yet, I feel as though I wish to crawl into a hole and sob my heart out."

"Ahhh. But it doesn't have to make sense. I know you, my love. I know when I push you hard, when I break you open, you are prone to fits of melancholy. If I wasn't already accustomed to such actions within The Rose and Thorne, I'd call for a doctor and some leeches. But it seems good food, a hot bath, and me holding you in my arms puts your humors to rights."

A small smile creeps across my face. "And here I thought you'd use it as an excuse to use your knife on me."

"Ahhh, my love, you give me far too much credit. I am not versed in bloodletting and would rather not cause you more harm than good. Come now, let's get you dressed and fed."

We remain silent as he helps me into my clothes and positions me near the door. Most everything else is gone, no doubt packed away while I was sleeping. He really does think of everything. With one final sweep, he extinguishes the fire and gathers me into his arms.

A full moon lights our way as he carries me over to his stallion, Storm. Pausing near his muzzle, the massive beast knickers softly as I caress his warm, velvety nose.

"Enough of that. You'll spoil the horse." But even in his gruff words, I hear the smile.

Setting me down, William grips me by the waist and lifts me up, placing me on his saddle. The pommel digs into my hip, but I don't feel it. Honestly, the moment my love hoists himself up and pulls me into his lap, I feel nothing but his warmth surrounding me.

I snuggle into him, running my fingers over his chest. Since that day I was taken from his side, I still reassure myself that he's real and this isn't just some dream I'll eventually awaken from. Purring, William wraps his arm around me and holds me close.

"We will never catch up with your family at this rate," I murmured.

"Never you mind. We are, in fact, heading back to London. There is still much to do to prepare for our honeymoon. Soon, we will go to Whitmore Manor and join our family. It's not too far from the coast, and I'd so love to see you looking out over the ocean."

At the very thought of seeing waves crashing against the shore, my spirits lift a touch. "And Blackport won't mind?"

William throws his head back and laughs. "Call the poor bastard Robert. He's your brother now."

"But he has not given me permission."

"No, but I am. And if he has an issue, he can bring it up with me. Besides, Robert headed back to London as well to finish up his business. He only accompanied you ladies, so he could ensure no harm came to you all or me in this little farce."

A soft smile tilts up my lips as I look into William's face. "Your mother seemed quite pleased."

"Yes, the meddlesome woman had a bit of sport, I'll bet."

"I do worry about your sisters, though. The governess seems to have caught on, but I fear they're still worried about me."

"I'm sure Robert explained everything before he left them. If not, the governess seems to have a good enough head on her shoulders. She could have found a delicate way in which to explain to my sisters. I wouldn't worry too much."

His eyes narrow a touch as his features tighten. Through the bond, I feel the worry he has about his adoptive mother. It eats at him, keeps him up at night. Though his ghosts are different from mine, we still share a load of grief that seems to never lessen.

Running my hand over his chest, I push feelings of love into the bond, sighing as his rigid stance melts just a touch. "No matter what happens, I will never stop loving you."

He pulls back on the reins, stopping Storm for a moment. Tipping my face up, he smiles down at me, the love and adoration nearly blinding. "Even in death, I will always find you. You will never be alone. You are my mate, the half of my soul who can never be replaced. I love you, Catherine Dowding, now and forever."

I hope you enjoyed this hot, spicy story. If you want to know more about Robert and the little governess that accompanies his family on their journey, preorder In Service to the Duke. If you're new to my series and want to start from the beginning, The Duke's Christmas Rejection introduces you to all the Alphas getting paired up this season. To read how William and Catherine meet and fall in love, check out A Tale of Two Dukes.

If you enjoyed this story, make sure to sign up for my newsletter so you can receive updates on all things bookish!! For those who devour my books and want even MORE, check out my memberships with all different levels and perks to satisfy your thirsty soul! And if you're *extra* knotty, join my group! I don't bite... hard.

The End

ABOUT THE AUTHOR

Vivian is a sassy romance writer that likes to brat just as much as she writes. As a fly-by-the-seat-of-her-pants author, she's usually working furiously into the night when her creative juices hit her the hardest. Her books like to take you to the dark side and force you to dip your toes in, but don't drown you. She loves writing alphaholes, anti-heroes, and heroes you just love to hate. She likes to try out everything she's putting her heroines through, so the phrase "for science" is used in her house a lot! When she's not writing, you can probably find her playing Animal Crossing or tormenting her cats and Husdom.

𝕏 x.com/murdochvivian

⬡ instagram.com/authorvmurdoch

BB bookbub.com/profile/vivian-murdoch

g goodreads.com/vivianmurdoch

ALSO BY VIVIAN MURDOCH

Marked Omegas

Prelude to a Revolution

Dark Revolution

Dark Company

Dark Goodbye

Dark Hunger

Seven Omegas for Seven Alphas

The Duke's Christmas Rejection

The Duke's Unwilling Bride

A Tale of Two Dukes

Abducting his Duchess - Regency Abduction Club Anthology

In Service to the Duke

To Ensnare a Duke

The Annual Game Night World

Sold: Limited Edition Darkverse Anthology

The Wolf

Knotted For Life

Bound to the CEO

Bound to the DA - Dirty Daddies Anthology

Bound to the Chef - All Hallows' Eve Anthology

Darkly Ever After

Ruining Red - Shifter - Twisted Beasts Anthology

CONTEMPORARY ROMANCE

Loftry University Playthings Series

Teacher's Toy

Bratva's Brat

Psychiatrist's Puppet

Bastard's Bride

Holiday Wishes

Dark Holiday

Black Light World

Black Light Cured

Masters of the Forbidden

Paid in Full

PNR ROMANCE

Midnight Doms

One Night With a Vampire (All Souls' Night anthology):

The Vampire's Prey

Bratva Vampires

From Russia With Blood

You Only Die Twice

ROMANCING THE STONE COLD ROGUE

EBONY OATEN

Pertaining to events a the B- House Ball: Every lady and their maid saw Lady A- T- step out of Mister L-'s carriage. It might have been during the darkest eve, yet people saw her face, plain as day.

If that wasn't scandalous enough, L- himself made an appearance from the carriage, only moments later.

What a sensation!

Considering the circumstances, the only good and right thing is for a marriage to take place. He will be delighted, of course, while she will probably want to keep a very low profile in society until the next scandal comes along.

Will love grow from this inauspicious beginning, or will these hare-brained nincompoops need to be shut in a room together before they can see sense?

CHAPTER ONE

Hot, angry tears streamed down Lady Adelaide Thornton's cold cheeks as she dashed from the crowded ballroom. "Blast it!" she muttered under her panting breath, steam pouring from her lips in the night air. Blast was the ugliest curse word in her retinue. Checking to make sure nobody was within earshot, she said a little louder, "Blast you all!"

What a timid creature she was, unable to swear with any great conviction, even in the aftermath of public humiliation. Which she had just suffered. Being overheard swearing would hardly make things worse, but her ingrained manners would not allow her to say anything stronger or louder. Would she ever be able to show her face in society again after the humiliation she'd suffered this night?

The braziers that lit the estate in a beautiful glow against the moonless, black night lost their glow as she ran away into the gardens. Shame filled her soul. And cold. Silly chit, she hadn't even grabbed a shawl as she'd run out. Her whole body shivered.

It didn't matter the direction she took, as long as it was away from that blasted ballroom. On she trampled, not sure of the way, increasing the distance between herself and the scene of the very worst moment of her three and twenty years.

A neat row of fir trees came into view. She stopped to catch her breath. Blast again, muddy water seeped into her slippers. Physical discomfort piled on top of emotional catastrophe. It was winter, the grounds of Bevington House were soaking wet, and she'd been a silly fool who'd given her heart and reputation away far too easily.

Shame upon shame. It was bad enough that people pitied her for the misunderstanding and subsequent tragedy with Learmonth scant months ago. She'd gladly have that pity back if it could replace the outright derision she'd experienced tonight.

Mister Sandhurst had played her for a simpering kitten, and Adelaide had played right into his hands. Beautiful, elegant hands that she'd allowed to hold hers. The way Sandhurst had rubbed his thumb against her wrist when he was sure nobody else could see. The sort of intimate encounter that had Adelaide sure they were a true love match. Especially after her disappointment with Learmonth.

But no. Apparently, Sandhurst 'barely knew her at all'. His face had filled with confusion when she'd spied him twirling a lock of Miss Elizabeth Barnwell's hair by the refreshment table at the ball tonight. Fie! What an addlepated goose she'd been to believe Sandhurst's overtures. It wasn't merely what she'd seen, but what she'd heard.

"Her dowry will do us to a nicety, have no fear."

Sandhurst had uttered this while gazing upon Miss Barnwell and making love to her with his charming words. There was no doubt in Adelaide's mind whose dowry Sandhurst had been talking about.

If Adelaide had been the only witness, she could have removed to another room and stayed warm and dry - albeit heartbroken - at the Bevington Ball. But no, there were so many others present, so many witnesses to her personal, private disaster.

Shivers brought Adelaide to her immediate predicament. Her slippers ruined, she would not be able to return to the ballroom even if she'd wanted to. There had been a garden path at some point, but in her haste to get away, she'd lost sight of it. In the darkness, she walked on from the fir trees and stumbled toward the orange glow of the lanterns, hanging from the sides of waiting carriages.

From bad to worse, it began raining. Her slippers already ruined, now her dress hem became soaked. Her pretty ringlets were turning to rats' tails. She'd be such a miserable, cold mess when she got home. The thought of being home, warm and tucked up in her room away from everyone, was the one glimmer of hope that kept her momentum heading towards the row of carriages.

At last she sighted a familiar carriage. Without waiting for the footman, she reached for the door handle and scrambled on board. The second she pulled the door shut, she thudded the side of her fist on the ceiling. "Coachman, take me home, immediately!"

Feet scuffled outside as the Thornton family's coachman and footman rallied from whatever conversations they'd been having with their social set, and raced to take their positions. Not fast enough for Adelaide's liking. "Now! Coachman!" She would apologize to them when they were home, and give over some of her pin money to make up for her rudeness. Right now, she needed a blanket. Mother always had one folded on the forward-facing seat. If only she could find it.

The horses lurched the carriage into motion. Adelaide fell onto her bottom, shivering with cold from the elements and her emotions. She pulled the curtains closed to hide her misery from the outside world. In the dim light, the cream-colored curtains appeared heavy grey. Everything looked a little bit wrong in this carriage; hardly surprising because her eyes were filled with tears. With the curtains drawn, she was safe from anyone else's sight. More than that, she was on her way home.

Now to get warm. Where was that blanket?

The clip clopping of the horses created a satisfying rhythm to her thoughts as she fumbled around for the knitted rug she knew had to be around somewhere. *This too will pass, this too will pass.*

It was at this moment she heard someone stir in the seat across from her. Shock dried her tears smartly. Her eyes adjusted to the soft glow of the exterior lanterns. Adelaide realized with sudden cold clarity that she was, in fact, not alone. Trembles of fear took hold, shaking her more than the chills shivering her body. There was a man in here with her.

Her voice wobbled as she said, "What are you doing in my family's carriage?"

The man sat upright from his prone position, rubbed his head and blinked in the dim glow. "The what?"

Ice swooped through Adelaide's body. It wasn't her tears making everything appear slightly wrong. She'd climbed into the wrong carriage entirely!

They were moving at a steady clip, thanks to her demand that they leave immediately. She thumped the roof again and screamed, "Stop at once, there's been a mistake!"

The man in the carriage with her slowly shook his head. He was moving cautiously, as if woken from a deep slumber. Or perhaps a sore head. He rapped the top of his cane against the divider between passengers and driver. "Be a sport and pull over, good man."

His voice sent quivers of familiar longing through her. Painfully familiar. It couldn't be …

She slumped in her seat. Adelaide's words rushed forth. "As I live and breathe. It's you!"

The man made a gentle cough to clear his throat as the carriage came to a stop. "Lady Adelaide Thornton. To what do I owe the pleasure of your company?"

CHAPTER TWO

The man rose in his seat, then dunked his head slowly to bow in her direction. Learmonth. Shivers spread over her body. He was the last man she ever wanted to see in her life. Well, the second last man after Sandhurst. All the same, a frisson spread over her. The feelings were not completely unwelcome, which had her more confused by the second.

Learmonth had wooed her several months ago, until things *went badly. Very badly indeed!* No, she would not entertain warm feelings for him. Not one bit!

"Why are you even here?' Adelaide asked. "I thought you'd fled to the continent after you killed my brother.'

His face fell. His sigh epitomized remorse. Sympathy peeked into her heart, but she banished it. Learmonth had fooled her once before. She was not going to be made a fool of twice. At least not by the same gentleman. Well! He was no gentleman, at any rate.

'Believe me, Lady Thornton, I never meant to harm your brother. I am deeply sorry for the turn of events that transpired after our ... dalliance." At this his hand reached for hers. His warm fingers touched the side of palm, searing her skin. "You're chilled to the bone," he said, his tone warming her in places it shouldn't.

She withdrew her hand out of self-preservation. Holding hands with Learmonth would lead to other things, and she'd lose her mind. Again. And possibly another family member into the bargain. She said accusingly, "It's going to take more than a mere apology to make up for what you did."

"I deserved that," he said. "I deserve all of it." His head slumped in self-pity. "Did I really break your hear-?" He cut himself off with a delicate burp.

Adelaide demanded, "Are you drunk?"

"Very. And you are cold and … goodness, look at the state of you. You must be frozen." He took his jacket off and moved to her side, where he placed the clothing over her shoulders. "Your shoes are ruined as well. What happened?"

"You broke my heart and tore my family apart."

Talk of broken hearts only sidetracked Adelaide from her genuine problems. She had to get out of the carriage, quickly. His jacket, warm from his body, played havoc with her senses.

Learmonth gently placed an arm around her. "You need to get warm. Have a sip from my flask, it's good whisky."

With one arm rubbing hers, heat began to spread through her. She did not want to welcome it, lest she fall under his spell again. When he held the flask up to her lips, she nevertheless took a sip. Fire burned in her mouth and throat and began to travel south. For a moment she couldn't breathe, then a coughing fit took hold. He put his hands over hers to take the flask back; his touch sending fresh bolts of heat through her.

After everything that had happened, she still could not control herself around him. *Adelaide, you goose. Get away from him, he's no good for you. There are too many painful memories associated with him.*

"I must leave," she said. They couldn't have gone far, she could walk back to the row of waiting staff and find her family's rightful conveyance, then start the journey home. Again. Properly this time. She took another sip of fire water and welcomed the rush of heat into her chilled body. She'd need it for the rest of her journey home, in her family's carriage.

Learmonth screwed the lid back on and set the flask down. "Did I really break your heart?"

She would not answer that. "Please ask your driver to turn us around."

He nodded at the request and moved to the other seat, where he opened the slide between driver and passengers. "I say chap, could you turn us back, there's been a misunderstanding."

The coachman replied, "There's no room to turn here, we'll have to go a ways farther."

They must be on a narrow part of the track, and could not turn the horses. Of all the addlepated things she'd done tonight, alighting into the wrong carriage, and Learmonth's carriage at that, had to be the worst. Adelaide called out, "Then let me out here, please."

The carriage lurched as the footman leapt down from his position. A moment later he had the door open and the steps down.

Learmonth said, "Smith, please escort Lady Adelaide to the Thornton's carriage."

"Yessir," Smith said.

It wasn't so dark anymore either. Such a relief. The strong glow of nearby lanterns guided the way. Adelaide would not be heading back in darkness at least. Perhaps her luck was changing. Her feet were so cold they were on fire, but she would walk barefoot if she had to, simply to get into her own conveyance.

If she'd stopped for even a heartbeat to look at her surroundings, she would have realized the lanterns were a sign of people in the area. A great many people. She stepped out of the carriage anyway, because she'd accepted Smith's hand and gravity compelled her to complete her downward trajectory.

Once on the ground, she took in the size of her audience. They were not on a narrow path. John Coachman had reached the circular drive at the front of Bevington House. It was populated with everyone milling about as they waited for their own coaches to arrive. When the coachman had said there was no room to turn around, Adelaide hadn't for one moment thought it was because they were completely boxed in. Surrounded on all sides by people and other carriages and seemingly every pair of eyes in society looking her way.

Dozens of dozens of witnesses saw Lady Adelaide Thornton alight from Mister Learmonth's carriage. Her friends Jane, Eleanor, Mary and Mariah, with mouths shaped like little o's as she stood before them in muddy slippers and drenched hems. Dear heavens, she was utterly ruined!

Terrified, Adelaide spun around and climbed straight back into the carriage. Once inside, she buried her face in her hands. Whimpers of impotent fury swept over her. Tears flowed hot and fast.

"Fine then, I'll leave," Learmonth said. "Coachman, come back and collect me later, there's a good man."

What? "No!" Adelaide screamed. Too late, Learmonth had already leaned out the door, in full view of everyone in the immediate vicinity.

"Oh dear," he said, and pulled himself back into the carriage. "I believe we are both exposed."

White hot fury stole the very last of Adelaide's manners. "You did that deliberately!"

"They'd already seen you, why does it matter?" He took his seat opposite, then reached for her sodden, muddy feet. He took her slippers off and rubbed her bare skin.

Unrecognizable needs roared up her legs, sending confusing signals through her body. The cad. He should not be touching her. She should not be letting him.

So why did she not withdraw her limbs?

Learmonth said, "My reputation will suffer more than yours. The ton tabbies will claim I've abducted you."

"That's on your silly head, for sticking it out the door so that everyone could see you," Adelaide said. It was safer to be angry with him. He knew precisely why alighting from the carriage after her mattered. He was an expert in ruining a young woman's reputation. "It's one thing for me to be seen alighting from someone else's carriage, someone I'm not married to. I could have been in here alone and nobody would have been any wiser. You had to stick your head out and remove all doubt."

Learmonth sighed in resignation. "I did not fully appreciate our location." He untucked and removed his cravat.

What was he doing, undressing before her?

"I have been in my cups this eve. What is your excuse?"

"My excuse? My excuse is my state of distress, which you have either been incapable of appreciating, or have willfully ignored. Perhaps you won't be happy until you see me *completely* destroyed."

"I am not aware of your distress. I gave you my jacket for warmth. And now this." He wrapped his cravat around her feet, tucking them together in the cloth. His hands continued chafing, helping to restore the blood flow. "Can't have you getting frostbitten toes on top of your woes, can we? That rhymed. I'm a poet and -"

"- Please get me out of here." Adelaide wanted to keep crying, but no more tears were available. Possibly because his warm touch robbed her body of angry emotions. Drat the man, she wanted to be furious with him, but he was being ridiculously kind.

Learmonth opened the slide between passenger and driver and spoke softly to John Coachman. "It appears there has been a great deal of misunderstanding tonight. Could you please drive us to the Thornton town house first, so we may take Lady Adelaide home?"

"Of course," he replied.

"This is a disaster," Adelaide said, wiping a hand over her warming face. Of all the carriages to get into, how on earth had she climbed aboard his? Why had she not stopped for one moment to make sure she was getting into the correct one?

Now she was stuck in here with the man who had destroyed her family over ... what had begun as another messy misunderstanding. Oh dear. She was rather making a habit of this. Tomorrow, mother would most likely send her away. But where? She couldn't go to Brighton because her brother the duke and his new duchess were not yet returned from their honeymoon.

Her present situation would spread like grassfire through the tabbies of the ton. Nobody would let her remain friends with their daughters, as she would be considered a bad influence. Worse, they wouldn't let her within ten yards of eligible sons, even with her generous dowry. A dowry they'd nearly lost to Learmonth's schemes. Yet now she'd been seen with him, in public, again. She both yearned and feared what people must be saying about her at this very moment.

He was carefully massaging her feet to restore circulation. Every now and then his warm hand travelled up to her ankles.

And she wasn't stopping him.

She hoped and prayed he would remain silent for the rest of the journey home. No sooner had this thought travelled from one side of her head to the other than Learmonth spoke.

"I am so deeply sorry for the turn of events; both tonight, and those that took place soon after we first met."

Adelaide huffed. Would *anything* happen in her favor tonight? "You can be truthful now. Was any of it real?"

She had thought herself in love, once. But then, her heart and her family had fallen to pieces. Instead of being in love, she'd learned he was not honorable at all. He had no family name to speak of. Some declared he was an orphan, yet some gossiped that his mother made buttons from seashells.

"All of it was real." He said. "Despite giving me a worse welcome than a stray cat; all spitfire and claws. But believe me, it was real. It still is."

Blast his charm. Blast his warm hands sending her heart soaring.

"This isn't some devious scheme to rob me of my dowry. Again?"

"There is that," he grinned wolfishly, "I cannot pretend the dowry won't keep us comfortable. Who wouldn't want comfort? But I also am deeply, catastrophically in love with you, and I will spend the rest of my life making that up to you."

The rubbing of her feet slowed to more deliberate strokes over her ankles. Why was she not withdrawing to her side of the seat?

She really should.

In a moment, I will, she promised herself. It was hard to form coherent thoughts with his hands warming her ankles and now her calves. She would stop him when he reached her knee.

She really would.

Onwards the carriage trundled through the streets. With the curtains closed, there was no way to see where she was. Learmonth had instructed the coachman to take them to her family's house. If they stopped out the front, in the middle of the night, someone was bound to see her alighting from his carriage. It didn't matter if people could see whose carriage it was; all they need do was see the state of her getting out of it.

Was there a way to make the horses walk more quietly on the streets?

Learmonth's hands kept gently massaging warmth into her, restoring life into her feet and toes. Each time his hands roved toward her calves, flames of heat flickered through her body. Tormenting her.

"I appreciate your ministrations," she managed. "Alas, we cannot resume where we left off," she said.

"Why is that?" he asked, rolling his thumb through the arch of her right foot.

"Because," she had to breathe through the deliciousness and appear unaffected. Otherwise he'd know she was lying. "Because there is the very real matter of killing my brother."

All massaging stopped. "That was an accident, you must believe me. He's the one who challenged me to a duel after he discovered I wished to marry you, not the other way around."

"He was defending my honor."

"Your honor was intact, although after tonight I'm not so sure your reputation will be."

Adelaide chose to ignore that. "You could have explained to him. You could have refused the duel and left."

Learmonth resumed massaging her feet. "And never see you again? I'd rather have died."

He sounded so sincere, she couldn't help believing him.

Delicious sparks danced along her nerves as he continued caressing her toes, gently pinching warmth into each one. "Nobody will tell me what happened. You must be a marksman or something to best my brother."

Learmonth sighed heavily. He had to unburden himself. Adelaide deserved to know what really happened that foggy December morning.

"The truth is, I was shaking so much I could barely hold the pistol." He pressed his thumbs into the arch of her delicate foot. What had begun as a simple measure to restore circulation was developing into something he couldn't name. It created a convenient distraction from his miserable dishonor. Each time he gently pressed into the muscles of her feet and ankles, her eyelids fell shut. It made his confession easier if she wasn't looking at him with those keen brown eyes that could somehow see right through to his soul.

"I had every intention of raising my arm and firing into the heavens, so that I would not injure anyone. A heavy mist was swirling around us, which gave me some reassurance nobody would make a good shot anyway. After the counting, I turned and raised my pistol; made ready to fire upwards. His shot rang out. It was so loud and terrifying my whole body shook. Your brother's men were shouting. I walked closer to see what was going on and ... that's when I saw him on the ground."

Her deep brown eyes that set his heart racing opened slowly. Every time he closed his own, he saw hers; the depths of her soul that made his heart sing. In the carriage, they were even darker and deeper, a mystery to unravel. He paused to swap feet and began massaging the other.

"You didn't fire?"

God she was beautiful. Her usually shining brown hair was a sodden wet mess, and she'd never been so enchanting.

"I did not." He shook his head at the memory. The rapid escalation of events. He'd been wooing Lady Adelaide, with mostly good intentions. Everything had been going so well. One thing lead to another and a duke of the realm was dead. He was to blame. In a duel of honor, if the pistol explodes in your hand, is that not a sign that the holder was in the wrong?

It was catastrophic. The duke's hand was a misbegotten shape, which he had no intention of describing to Adelaide. In hindsight, it would have been less painful for the Duke if Learmonth had been able to shoot the man directly. Not that he was any great aim.

"How did he die then?" Adelaide pulled her feet back and tucked them under herself. Learmonth felt the loss keenly. "Nobody in the family will tell me what happened."

"I will tell you the truth, but a modified version to spare your nightmares. Duels are not the romantic, clean, test of honor some would have you believe. They are messy, stupidly dangerous and an unreliable arbiter of who is in the wrong."

"You're saying my brother was right?"

"In a way, yes." He had to come clean. Purge his conscience. He couldn't continue on this trajectory, lest he end up like the late duke. "I took this as a sign that I must mend my ways, and be truthful in all things. When I told you tonight I loved you, I meant it. It is the truth. I do so love you. Perhaps it wasn't pure love at the beginning. I will freely admit your dowry beguiled me in the first place, but it grew to love on my part so quickly I cannot tell you the exact moment. Only that it was real. Being away from you these past weeks has been torture. Which I fully deserve for not realizing you truly are a diamond of the first water."

It was the truth, he was madly in love with her, but admitting to his raging passions would scare her away. He had to woo her carefully. Alas, he'd used all his methods when they'd first met. Here in the carriage, alone again, he was in uncharted territory. If he used the same techniques, she'd notice the pattern and never believe him.

This time he had to mean *everything* he said.

"Meeting you was the best and worst thing that ever happened to me. I will spend the rest of my days making sure you never suffer further heartbreak or torment as you have this past month."

The carriage slowed and the coachman tapped on the divider. "The house is a little farther on, is there a secluded place to take the miss home?"

He'd run out of time. Words would not make any difference now. He had to show her how much he cared for her, and her reputation. He'd been the one to damage it, he had to mend it. He replied to John Coachman, "Into the mews, good man, and fetch a cloak to disguise our passenger."

Her frame was not large. A coachman's cloak should cover her from bedraggled head to chilled feet.

He slid his boots off and held them out to her. "Wear these. If the neighbors did hear us arrive, they will hear a man's steps to the door, not a woman's."

Sparks burned behind his eyes when her fingers brushed his as she accepted the boots. In a heartbeat, she was wearing them. Then the coachman's cloak enveloped her and she was gone.

CHAPTER THREE

After her public exposure with Learmonth, Adelaide had few options. Perhaps she could take up a position as a lady's companion, provided that lady never moved in London society. Unlikely.

Or she'd be sent to live with Wolster in Brighton. He and the Duchess would keep a keen eye on her. Keener than her mother was capable of at any rate. Perhaps she would be required to care for the children they had?

There would be no gentleman callers for Adelaide in either situation. How unfair that Thomasina, who was a lowly governess to her cousin's children, was allowed a caller. But that caller had been a duke. Dukes had carte blanche. As the mere sister of a duke, Adelaide had no such *cartes* to play.

Mamma Thornton chose a third option that Adelaide had not considered. "You will marry Learmonth," she commanded. "If you'd done that in the first place…" leaving the rest of it unsaid.

Adelaide didn't blame her. Things had gone very, very badly the last time she and Learmonth had been courting. If it could be called that. Possibly closer to sneaking about, when all was said and done.

"What if Learmonth won't have me," she countered. He'd made declarations of his love, but that was a play for her dowry.

"Your brother will see to it that he does."

"Mamma, not a day goes by where I don't regret believing the lies Learmonth said to me. But you cannot blame the rest of the events on me. I did not call him ou-"

A howl of rage and grief from Mamma Thornton cut off her sentence. "I'm only glad your father is not here to see you bring our family so low!"

Adelaide removed herself from Mamma's eyesight. A few days secluded in her bedchamber held tremendous appeal. After a break from seeing each other, the family matriarch would be calm, she'd be reasonable.

Several days more or less locked in her chambers only served to make Adelaide lonely. No letters or messages arrived during these times. No gentlemen callers either. She wasn't at all surprised by the latter, but she was brought low that none of her friends had enquired into her health or disposition. Jane and the rest of them had seen her heartbreak as she fled Sandhurst, then they'd seen her in the wrong carriage. Had any of them inquired to her health? Not a one. Not even Sandhurst had bothered to maintain the farce of his wooing.

The timing was hideous. Her family were technically still in mourning for her late father, and on top of that, fresh mourning for her eldest brother, Matthew, who had died protecting Adelaide's reputation. Her next eldest brother, Gerard, had inherited the title. He'd bucked convention and married during the family's deep mourning period. Despite this, the wedding had been a merry affair. Adelaide hummed to herself at the memory of catching Thomasina's bouquet.

Alas, the chance of making a love match, like Gerard and Thomasina, had never seemed so distant.

The maid knocked at the door and waited for Adelaide to allow her in. "Your mother has asked me to get you ready for a visitor."

Relief washed through her. A new face to look upon, even if it was only Gwen, the maid. "Who is it?"

"I did not think it pertinent to ask. The dowager duchess has been so grief stricken of late, none of us wants to be caught up in it."

Taking slow, steady breaths, Adelaide allowed Gwen to fuss over her and make her presentable for an audience. It would not do to be flighty and excitable at this time. She needed to show Mamma she could be reliable and dependable. If she were honest, she needed to prove that to herself as well. The time alone in her room had given her ample opportunity for personal reflection.

She'd come to a blinding observation about herself. Whilst some events of the recent past had been beyond her control, her reactions to them were within hers.

It was time to prove to her mother that she was a mature young woman who did not fly into hysterics when faced with discomfiting events. Her behavior in the next few minutes would demonstrate that.

A smile fixed in place, Adelaide walked into the receiving room to find her mother and Learmonth in conversation.

Don't scream, don't scream, don't scream. She chastised herself. *No matter what transpires, you will not bring the family into disrepute.*

Further disrepute.

"Mamma," she said as she curtseyed to her mother. Then she turned to their guest and fought the tremors rattling through her body to deliver the same decorum his way. "Mister Learmonth."

How her mother coped with being in the same room as Learmonth came as a huge shock. Adelaide hoped she succeeded to keep this from showing on her face.

Learmonth stood and bowed formally to her, but said nothing. Adelaide moved to a nearby seat and lowered herself into it, emotions were in tumult.

Mamma spoke. "Adelaide, Mister Learmonth has agreed to marry you. For that I am grateful. In time, you will be too. As your brother his grace is not yet returned from his honeymoon, I took it upon myself to arrange the banns."

The scream inside Adelaide remained unreleased. Nobody appeared more surprised than she. How was she not howling the walls down? A meek, "The banns?" came out in reply.

"The only other option is to send you off to Gretna Green." Mamma said.

Adelaide stammered, "'ret-na?" Her mind whirled with the impossibilities of the situation. "At this time of year?"

Travelling there by carriage in the depths of winter would take days and days in sleet and possibly snow. They would be stuck together. Perhaps she could talk Learmonth around in that time? Make him come to his senses. Help him see that he really should run off to the continent. Just as he should have after the duel. It was horrible enough being in a carriage with him for a few minutes after the Bevington Ball. A week would be her utter undoing.

The other option was three weeks away after the banns. Her friend Mariah, who attended the same church, would know about it after the next service. Perhaps Mariah might protest the match on her behalf?

Mamma continued. "I have petitioned the Archbishop of Canterbury for a special license, but parliament is an exceptionally busy time for him. I doubt he'll be able to reply in time. What's it to be, our parish church or Gretna?

It was hard to swallow past the lump in her throat. Then an idea struck. She turned to Learmonth and asked, "What do you propose? Parson's noose or the anvil?"

He appeared to give this serious thought, then turned to Dowager Thornton. "You know your daughter's disposition. Which is she more likely to endure. Three weeks of house arrest or a week or more of travel?"

They were being impossibly polite to each other. Then something snagged in her mind. "House arrest?" Adelaide cried out. "What do you mean?"

"It's for your own protection, dear," Mamma said. "Three weeks is a great deal of time, after all, and who knows what ideas you might have between now and your wedding day?"

There had to be something else. Some other option. "Boats?" she offered. "We could sail instead of take horses through the inclement weather?" It would be kinder to them both, and the horses. The poor Coachman and footman on the outside would thank them, too. "We could have separate berths to maintain propriety."

Mamma scoffed. "It's a little late for that, don't you think? Anyway, as angry as I am with you, I would mourn your loss, should your boat be smashed against a rocky cliff on the way north."

Adelaide's options evaporated. "We could not possibly travel so far at this time of year. It's perishing cold. Think of the poor horses."

"The house it is," Mamma agreed. "Learmonth will take up residence until the time comes for you to marry. I shall retire to the dower house." Mamma stood up and bid a polite but curt farewell to her soon-to-be son-in-law.

"Mamma, wait," Adelaide said. "You mean Learmonth and I are to live under the same roof, before we are even wed? That would be quite impossible."

"You may say so, but the banns are posted, there is a great deal of supervision here, and your reputation could hardly be any more besmirched." With that, her mother kissed her softly on each cheek and said, "Make the best of it."

CHAPTER FOUR

Taunton House was large enough that Adelaide and Learmonth could have whole wings to themselves and not see each other. Yet somehow, every time Adelaide ventured from her room, there he was. In the library, reading books by the fire. In the sitting room, checking the post. He left the pile there; nothing with her name on it. Had her friends been warned off from contacting her, or were they cutting her of their own volition?

Maybe she should have chosen Gretna Green after all. At least that way she'd be seeing a little of the countryside instead of stuck inside the family townhouse. She could have planned some kind of daring escape ... in the winter, with no transport. Foolish chit, there would be no chance of that, and she'd most likely freeze to death.

Mealtimes created further forced intimacy. She had to look at his handsome face. His delightfully curly dark hair and light brown eyes. This was a huge mistake, as it reminded her of the time they'd been secretly courting, when she'd stolen sweet biscuits from the kitchen and gifted them to him. His eyes had closed with bliss as he tasted the buttery goodness. Now he was tormenting her with saucy expressions at the breakfast table. The way he dabbed butter on a roll, then tore a chunk away and consumed the morsel. The way his lips moved in appreciation. The way his eyes closed ...

Mouth turning dry, Adelaide had no appetite.

Not for food at any rate.

Sixteen more days of this. She was marking them off in her head. Then he'd be her husband. Husband! How was she to bear it? Surely everyone's tongues in society were wagging like lamb's tails at their predicament?

A messenger arrived at the door. Adelaide leapt to her feet in the hopes it would be from one of her friends. Even better, it might be the local vicar with word of a protest against the banns.

"Your mother left strict instructions that you're not to leave the house," Learmonth said.

Kidnapped in her own home. How infuriating. "I'm allowed to read correspondence if it comes."

Learmonth put down his cutlery and pushed his chair back. "I'll come with you."

Did he have to be so overbearing?

They reached the front door at the same time, she pushing to get a few inches ahead just so she could be first.

It was from the Archbishop of Canterbury! Dear heavens, the special license had arrived!

Worries filled her empty belly, an invisible swarm of wasps filled her head, making rational thought impossible.

Did he have to stand so close to her, radiating heat from his body?

Perhaps that was her own?

Adelaide was grateful she had not eaten anything that morning, as she reached for the wall to stop herself fainting. Despite sour acid in the back of her throat, she steadied her breathing and found a chair in which to sit.

This paper meant there were no further impediments or delays to their marriage, no more time to plan a way out of it. This was really happening. She was going to have to marry Learmonth.

"Is marriage to me so bad?" Learmonth asked.

Did his eyes have to be so kind?

She sobbed, "My life is over."

"Always ready with the compliments, my darling," he said.

Desperate to avoid her fate, Adelaide grabbed for the license. Learmonth held it out of reach, a smile crossing his face.

She wailed, "Don't laugh at me!"

"I would never." He replied with a winning smile. "But there's also no chance I'm letting this out of my hands either. This is my ticket to freedom."

Throwing herself bodily at him, she tried again. Her hands gripped his sleeve. She almost had it. He switched it to his other hand.

Adelaide grunted in frustration and cried, "Give it to me!"

Learmonth stood up to his full height and held the license higher. She'd have to climb his body like a tree to get to it.

Despite jumping a few times, the precious paper remained annoyingly out of reach.

Still holding it aloft, Learmonth said, "I will message your mother at the dower house. By this time tomorrow, we will be married."

Adelaide climbed onto a chair and launched herself at him like a wildcat. She caught him by the arm, hanging on to it for dear life as he switched the paper to his other hand once again.

He grabbed her and held her to his body. His warm body that sent shocks through hers. "I had no idea you were so acrobatic!"

Her soul wanted to hold him forever, but her head cried out, "Let me go!"

He loosened his grip and she slid down his front. Dizzy and embarrassed, she ran off to her room to clear her mind. Their bodies pressing together had robbed her of rational thought.

Once safely alone, her mind raced for possible ways out of this.

He couldn't hold that paper forever. At some point he'd have to put it down.

Of course! Once he was asleep, she'd sneak into his room and take it back. She'd throw it in the fire if she had to. Then she'd have more time to come up with a much better plan to not marry this charlatan who messed with her senses.

Learmonth folded the special license under the bed pillow and rested his head. It was strange enough having to sleep in this house - the house of his future in-laws - let alone sleeping on folded paper. It crinkled and crunched each time he moved his head. He changed positions a few times but nothing helped. Sure as the sun would rise in the morning, Lady Adelaide Thornton would do whatever she could to get the paper off him.

He sighed heavily at how little she trusted him, and how much she did not appear to want to marry him. He'd said he loved her. He should say it more often, because he meant it. He'd shown her nothing but kindness since the dowager duchess had made her decision. He'd tried to give her space in this enormous house, and yet wherever he went, she always seemed to find him.

Her feet appeared unaffected from their night in the cold. She had the most perfect feet in the world. How he longed to touch them again. Any excuse would do.

Turning in frustration, the paper crinkled under his head. Should he move it under the mattress? As he mulled over the thought of finding a new hiding place, soft footsteps reached his door.

Closing his eyes, he pretended to sleep.

Whoever it was made a terrible burglar. The doorknob squeaked as they turned it, and made a noisy click from the latch. He squinted one eye open as the person stepped into his room, holding a small lantern in her hand.

Dear heavens, it was Adelaide. Waves of dark hair flowed over her shoulders and down her back. She was in her night attire, with no slippers. Did she have any idea of what the mere sight of her beautiful toes did to him?

The glow from the lamp was not that strong. Useless if she needed to search for anything valuable in here. Some notes in his pocket book perhaps?

As she looked about the room, she happened to hold the lantern in such a way that the glow illuminated her silhouette. Lust jolted through him. She was utter perfection. Lovely firm thighs that curved delightfully. Two beautiful globes of her bottom. The rest he couldn't see as she placed the lantern on a desk.

It didn't stop him from imagining how magnificent her small beasts would taste in his mouth. He hardened at the thought.

Absolutely no chance of getting any sleep tonight. No point even pretending.

"Lady Adelaide, if you don't want to marry me, you shouldn't be in my bedchamber."

Barely two words in, she spun around, her face pure shock. "How long have you been awake?"

"I have yet to fall asleep. It's unlikely to happen with you here. Aren't you cold? Walking around in bare feet?" Would she be scandalized if he offered to warm them again? Only one way to find out. He lifted the bed covers and made room for her. "Get in, then. You're making me cold just looking at you."

"That is a terrible idea." She said, absently rubbing her arm against the evening chill.

The woman was a goddess and had no idea what she was doing to him. A wicked thought came unbidden. "I know why you're here."

She slumped in lost confidence. "You do?"

"Yes," he teased. "You've come to seduce me and ruin yourself, in some last-minute attempt at calling off the marriage."

"Hmm?"

It was obvious that she absolutely was *not* doing that, but Learmonth couldn't help himself. "Yes. You're about to prove how unsuitable you are. Any woman willing to tumble ahead of the ceremony is a slave to her passions, rather than good sense. You're planning to scare me off by making wild, animalistic love to me." He'd over-egged the pudding, but he was having fun. It was delightful watching her confused but beautiful face in the glow of the lamplight.

"I ..." She started.

Learmonth held back peals of laughter threatening to break free. Any moment now, he'd burst.

"Would that work?" She eventually asked.

Lust tore through him, draining the blood from his brain. She was so very innocent, standing there in only a few layers of nightwear. Her beautiful, perfect feet peeking out from below the hem.

Damn her innocence. A confession burst out. "I am making fun at your expense. It is badly done. I am sorry."

"What?" Confusion ruled her face.

Despite yearning for her most perfect feet, he couldn't tease her any longer. "Why don't we start again? I believe you're here for the license."

Her head dropped. "Yes."

"Come on, you're freezing." He removed a blanket from the bed and wrapped it around her. Then he lifted her up and carried her to the other side of the bed. After he set her down, he simply had to take hold of her feet in his hands. It could well be the last time. "They're even colder than the night in the carriage! Am I going to spend the rest of my days warming your toes?"

A little whimper came out. "I thought you might have the fire still on," she said.

"Paper burns in fire. I have a precious paper that needs to remain intact until after we are safely married."

"Why are you so keen to marry me?"

"I told you." He kissed her perfectly perfect big toe. Then he reluctantly tucked the blanket over her feet, wrapping her like a gift. "It's because I love you."

"And my dowry."

"I'd be lying if I said otherwise. I do have debts that must be repaid. Most people do, they're just better at hiding it."

"And when it's spent, what then?"

A chuckle broke free. "Then it will not be our problem, but our grandchildren's."

She did not share his mirth. Her voice was brittle as she said, "You're a stone-cold rogue. How can you assure me you won't take my dowry and run off to the continent with your mistress?"

His heart flipped.

Chills of fear filled his body. "There is no mistress, and there never will be. I promise you that. Believe whatever you like of me, but please know there will only ever be you."

How could he turn this situation around? They were about to wed, and she not only didn't love him (surely, that would come with time?) she didn't even seem to *like* him, much less trust him. "Do you truly think so little of me?" He asked, knowing how plaintive his voice sounded. Pride be damned, he was desperate.

"What else am I to think? You are an adventurer, loving one woman until her family pays you to leave, then moving on to the next. I just happen to be the end of the line, where you'll get your biggest windfall."

Every word darted poison into his soul.

He would keep saying this to his dying day. "Adelaide, I love you."

She sat up in her roll of fabric, looking like a butterfly emerging from a cocoon. "Prove it then."

He sat blankly, his mind spinning with no result. The answer arrived like a thunderbolt. He reached under his pillow and retrieved the special license. With a quick unfurl, she would see what it was. It might be difficult to read the full detail in the low light, but there was no mistaking what it was.

"My life and future is in your hands, Lady Adelaide. What you do next is completely up to you. You may burn it, you may frame it, or you may bring it to church with you tomorrow and we will be married. All I ask is that you do what is right for you."

Heart beating impossibly fast, he swallowed past the dry stone in his throat. He'd said he loved her, so many times, and she hadn't believed him. What a dolt. It wasn't words that mattered, but actions. Why had it taken him so long to reach this point? He only hoped he wasn't too late.

The paper shook in her hands. Adelaide eased herself off the bed.

Hands clenched, Learmonth watched her collect the lantern. To his immediate relief, she did not set the license to the lantern flame there and then. Breathing came only a little easier after that, but not by much. She dropped the blanket as she reached his door to leave. Then she took herself, the lantern and the license with her and shut the door.

In the darkness, Learmonth scooped up her blanket and crawled back to bed. Her scent was still in the fabric, and he drifted off to sleep wondering what the morrow would bring.

CHAPTER FIVE

The church was incredibly cold the next morning. Not a surprise, churches weren't exactly known for their roaring fireplaces. Probably why so few couples married in the depths of winter. Learmonth sat in the first pew, absently tapping his foot against the flagstone floor. The Vicar encouraged him to pray for a healthy and fruitful marriage. Instead, Learmonth directed several prayers to ensuring his bride showed up. If she wanted to. If it was her choice.

A quiet part of his mind told him all was not lost. His name and Lady Adelaide's were on the banns notices alongside others in the parish. If she didn't show today, they could still marry in a little more than two weeks.

If he didn't show for that one, then things would be dire.

Who was he kidding? Things were dire. If she did not show today, she would not show at the next wedding day either. If she was sensible, she would have barricaded herself into Thornton House to keep herself safe and keep him out.

Rather than dwell on the worst-case scenario, Learmonth filled his time flicking through some of his favorite bible verses. This did not help calm his nerves at all.

The minutes ticked by agonizingly slowly. The vicar cast a sympathetic look his way. "Pay no mind to the time, it's a bride's prerogative to be late."

Losing all feeling in his cold buttocks, he rose and walked back and forth a little, then heaved a sigh. She wasn't coming. He'd given Adelaide her freedom and she'd taken it.

He'd told her to do what was right for herself, and she'd made that decision. She didn't love him and most likely never would. A bitter lesson he would carry with him for the rest of his life. Lady Adelaide was doing what was right for her, and he had to be content with that.

No point sitting still, Learmonth took a walk back down the aisle and headed out the front doors.

His heart leapt against his ribs, she was here!

Adelaide and the dowager duchess alighted from a carriage, dressed in warm furs against the cold. She looked incredible, her glossy dark hair in neat ringlets framing her face, the rest curled atop her head in a complicated bundle of curls. Learmonth laughed in relief and delight, steam pluming from his mouth.

It truly was cold, but his body glowed. "You're came!' He said.

"She did," Dowager Thornton said. "I'm possibly more surprised than you are. Let's get this over with."

Hardly a ringing endorsement of his suit. Learmonth sighed, he had a hard road ahead to convince the Thornton family that he would be a good husband to Adelaide.

"Are you ready?" he asked Adelaide.

"I'm here, am I not?"

He took that as the best he'd get, and held his arm out. It wasn't until she put her hand in the crook of his elbow that he began to hope they might make it through this.

Pulse thumping in her ears, Adelaide walked down the church aisle with Learmonth, the special license in her trembling hand. He looked impossibly handsome with his hair neatly brushed off his forehead. His light brown eyes were glistening with promise.

"My feet are cold," she muttered as they closed the distance to the altar.

He lifted her hand and stroked her palm with his thumb, sending pulses of heat through her blood. "I will warm them the moment we are back in the carriage."

He was good at rubbing her feet, she'd give him that. What he'd done last night was remarkable. Not just in restoring heat to her extremities, but in handing over the license. He'd given her such freedom in that small act. The decision was hers, nobody else's.

True to his word, he'd been waiting for her at the church.

As a little girl, she'd often dreamed of a large wedding attended by the very diamonds of society. Growing up the daughter of a duke, it wasn't an unreasonable dream to have. In her dreams she'd worn a dress of such finery every unmarried woman in attendance vowed to copy the pattern for their own betrothal.

Yet now she wore her regular church dress. A good dress, but nothing exemplary. She would wear it at the next service, and for many years afterwards. Nobody was here to gasp at its perfection. In fact, it was just the four of them, herself and Learmonth, Mamma and the vicar.

It felt cozy.

Personal.

The service soon followed, perfunctory and private. The way Learmonth smiled at her sent warmth flooding her system. Almost down to her toes.

Would her feet ever be warm?

She lost her place in one of the hymns as she imagined him gently rubbing her feet back to life. She wanted the service over with so he could get to work on her feet in the carriage.

Possibly not the sort of thing that most marriages began with, but then, they were hardly a good example of how a marriage should begin.

Suddenly the vicar was looking at her expectantly. Oh! She had to say something. "Would you repeat that, please?"

"Lady Adelaide, do you take this man to be your lawfully wedded husband ..." the vicar droned.

"Yes, yes I do." She said, toes prickling with the onset of numbness.

When at last the vicar said they were married, Adelaide tried to stand on tiptoes to kiss Learmonth. There was so little sensation in her feet, she had no idea if she were any closer.

His lips descended onto hers. The contact shot flames of desire down to her knees.

What a magnificent kiss. She should have known it would be. The stolen kisses to her wrists months ago, which had filled her with swooning at the time, were nothing compared to this. Such warmth, such tenderness, with a hint of restrained power behind it. Wondrous new sensations fluttered in her belly. Excitement of what might come later stole rational thought. Her body burned for him. They were in a house of God and her thoughts were only of lust. Could Mamma get a different carriage home, perhaps?

The wet winter air swirled around her feet as they stepped out of the church. A flower seller walked alongside them and tossed petals in congratulations.

It certainly was an 'intimate' celebration, and yet Mamma had organized this unexpectedly sentimental flourish. Not that Adelaide was willing to completely re-appraise her relationship just yet, but it was a lovely touch.

"Thank you, Mamma." She embraced her mother and kissed both her cheeks.

Mamma stiffened, then leaned back. "Do your duty, there's a good gel," she said, patting Adelaide on the shoulder.

In the blink of an eye, she and her husband were in their carriage, a warm stone at their feet, and a large blanket over their laps. Had Mamma organized this as well? Unlikely, as they were in Learmonth's carriage.

"Thank you for the warm stones," Adelaide said.

He canted his head. "Can't have you getting cold feet."

Welcome heat radiated from the stones. "I could get used to this."

"Excellent. I'd like nothing more than to keep my wife warm and happy."

He'd said, 'my wife'. It felt strange and somehow a little silly. "I would like nothing more than for my husband to keep me warm and happy," she countered.

They shared a chuckle. He held her hand and kissed her knuckles. "Please show me how to make and keep you in this manner, I shall be your most ardent student."

Hot flurries robbed Adelaide of sensible thought. "I suppose I should learn your first name at some point? That might be a good start?"

"It is Harold."

Adelaide rolled the name around in her head and repeated, "Harold."

Learmonth closed his eyes. "I've never much cared for it, but from your lips, it warms my heart."

She gently swatted his arm. "You can stop the wooing words, we're married now, you don't have to try so hard."

"But I mean it."

They'd reached Taunton House. Interesting that they were going to live here for the foreseeable future. Perhaps when her brother returned, he'd reclaim his birthright. Then they'd need to find a new residence, which would be paid from her dowry no doubt.

The many staff were lined up to greet Mr and Mrs Harold Learmonth. Each wanted to greet the newly wedded couple and shake Harold's hand. No longer "Lady Adelaide," she was Mrs Learmonth now. Her fall in status would take some adjustment.

Greetings over, she waited for her husband - goodness, her husband! - at the foot of the stairs. They linked arms and they walked together, neither looking back. A show of unity; they were about to begin their new life together. The staff, loyal as they were, would have absolutely nothing to gossip about.

Time to 'do her duty' as mother had said.

But what exactly was that? Mother had been vague about the details. Hardly surprising, the woman was in deep mourning. Adelaide couldn't help thinking a little information could have helped.

She was overthinking. All she need do was keep her arm linked with Learmonth's and he'd lead them into his chambers. He'd know what to do.

Indeed, he did. He opened the doors, walked them inside to his study and sat her on a chair near the fire. It was burning warmly and there was plenty of chopped wood in the iron basket.

Wordlessly, he stalked back to the doors and closed them.

Yes, of course, to give them privacy. Rather thoughtful, she supposed.

Then, still not speaking, he opened the doors to his bedroom. A warm fire burned in the hearth in this room, chasing the damp from the air.

Should she follow him? Adelaide didn't know much, but she knew they had to do something called 'laying together'. Sitting in different rooms certainly wasn't that.

Nervously, she stepped into his room and closed the doors to the study behind her. His bed loomed large before her.

He opened another set of doors that had all the appearances of a wardrobe. Once the doors were open, it was obvious there were no clothes in here. It was a short passageway to another bedroom.

Oh! It was hers!

Shaking her head, she made another mental adjustment. These were the chambers for the lord and lady of the house. They must have belonged to her parents all those years ago. The staff had moved every-thing from her old room to this one.

"I'll leave you to rest," Learmonth said, stepping back into his room.

Adelaide spun around. "What?"

"You must be tired from today's events."

"Not really," she started. Hope crashed in her chest. He was pushing her away? Hadn't he just declared he wanted to make her happy ... and now he was leaving her on her own ... on their wedding day? "That would not make me happy."

His voice cracked on a simple, "No?"

"I am not as worldly as some, but there are certain things that need to be done after people are married. Leaving me alone in my room is not one of them."

"I did not want to rush you."

"It's a little late for that, don't you think?"

"Well, I mean, I ..."

They stood there, at an impasse. Frustration had Adelaide clenching her hands in frustration. He didn't seem willing to suggest anything, and she didn't know the right kinds of things to suggest in the first place.

This could not be how they were to go on.

Inspiration finally struck. Raising her skirts above her ankles, Adelaide kicked her slippers off and stood there in her stockings. "My feet are cold."

"Your feet?"

"Are cold, yes. It would make me happy if you were to warm them. Please."

A slow smile of understanding was her reward. "I shall warm your feet." He lifted her into his arms, holding her steadily and confidently as he walked back to his room. It was warmer here - had the staff not lit the fire for her? She'd investigate that later. Being in his arms had to be the beginning of better things.

Every fiber of Learmonth's body demanded he throw his wife on the bed and make passionate love to her. Alas, he doubted how receptive his bride would be to such a rash act.

Instead, he would warm her feet, as she'd asked.

He'd do more than warm them; he'd worship them. Lady Adelaide Of The Perfect Toes deserved no less.

The chair by the fire would accommodate this. He lowered her carefully into the seat and brought an ottoman over to rest her feet. Then he knelt beside her and placed one palm onto the bridge of her foot. In soft, calm movements, he brushed his palm back and forth, down to her toes, then up again almost to the ankle. He did the same thing with the other foot, loving the smooth feel of her skin beneath the stocking. Would she permit the undressing of the limb? He guided his hand further up her shin. Wordlessly, he looked at Adelaide, the blacks of her eyes growing larger in the yellow firelight. He moved his hands further toward her knee, loving the way the curve of her calf filled his palm.

A slow blink was the result.

"These stockings, however lovely, do need to come off," he said, as he slowly embraced the stocking garter at her knee. It was tied with ribbon, which he slipped between his fingers for a little while, before giving them a tug. To his relief, they had been tied with a simple bow, for ease of removal.

Adelaide's breath shuddered. Sparks of lust flew through his body. He'd not even exposed her feet and he was already stiffening.

Partly why he sat below her eye-line, so he wouldn't scare her when she saw it at full size.

Another steady breath from her was his cue to remove the other garter ribbon, which also came away with a deft pull. Slowing his own breathing, he rolled the stockings down her legs, one after the other, then neatly folded them on the floor.

His reward was her naked, perfect feet, with the skirts arranged haphazardly below the knees. Everything from the shins and calves downwards was his to explore. He gave his palms a fast run down the side of his breeches to warm and dry them, then enveloped one foot in both hands. His thumbs massaged the muscles in her instep and arch. His eyes were on her, and hers fixed on him, her pupils dilating wildly. He kneaded and adored her feet, warming and blessing them, and thanking his lucky stars that she had turned up to the church today.

He raised her foot carefully towards him and kissed her big toe. Checking to see she approved of the action, that she was comfortable with him. She nodded and wriggled a little in the seat. He kissed her other big toe. Soft mewling noises were his reward. His head nearly exploded and he became hard as a rock.

Take your time, he reminded himself. He maintained his ministrations on her feet and slowly advanced to her ankles. He kept checking her face to make sure she was comfortable. A sly smile spread across her face, as her eyelids closed. Her knees, which had been reasonably close together for much of this time, relaxed enough to drift away from each other.

His hands moved to her calves, where he spent a good amount of time worshipping their perfect form. He again kissed her skin, this time the shins, then trailed more kisses all the way to the edge of her hem. Slowly, he moved the ottoman out of the way and angled himself at her feet again. She would have no idea how much restraint he needed not to lift her skirts and bury his face into her thighs.

He hadn't been lying when he'd declared his love. He could die a happy man at this very moment, even without completing the act. Being this close with Adelaide was already beyond his wildest imaginings. Everything else that happened from this moment would be the stuff of legend.

Heat pooled low in Adelaide's belly. Learmonth's hands on her feet, ankles and calves stole her breath, creating the most delicious ache. These sensations were so strange and yet welcome. She had no idea what they were doing, only that it felt wonderful and right. Was she responding in the right way? All she'd done was try to breathe, talking seemed incredibly difficult when he caressed her calves and kissed her legs so tenderly.

Somehow, his head was between her knees. Jolts of need staggered her breath as he kissed the inside of her exposed thigh. If she lifted her skirts would she ... oh heaven's, he kissed her again and her thoughts turned to mush.

A soft, "yes" escaped her lips, shocking her with its audacity.

"Thank you," came the reply.

"Yes," she said again, more forcefully this time.

"I love you," Learmonth said, pushing her skirts up and kissing a trail along the inside of her thigh.

Oh goodness, he was getting closer and closer to something she-
"Yes!"

He traced his fingers between the folds of her core.

A cramp seized her muscles.

"Please!"

"Thank you," he said again. In one move, he grabbed her by the buttocks and pulled her to the edge of the chair. Her skirts ruffled up around her middle, exposing her to him fully. Her thighs were parted, her legs bent at the knees, resting on his shoulders.

Her buried his face in her. She gasped and yelped at the same time in shock and wonderment.

He paused. "Do you want me to sto- ?"

" -Don't you dare!"

He plundered her with abandon. A scream of joy escaped. How could this be called duty when it was so incredibly wonderful?

Ripples and waves of pleasure rolled through her body. The grew more intense and exciting with each lick and suck. Falling and soaring at the same time, her whole body came alive with sensation. She was tumbling and climbing something. She'd find names for them later because right now everything was so incredibly intense. Breaths came short and hard. Through her dress she grabbed at her own breast, squeezing it in time with the pulses of need growing stronger and stronger.

Explosions of ecstasy took hold. She forgot how to breathe. Heart hammering behind her ribs, she smothered her mouth and screamed.

Learmonth stopped the onslaught on her core, changing his momentum to slowly kiss her thighs instead.

"That was intensity itself!" Adelaide said, struggling to get her heartbeat back to normal.

"A mere *amuse-bouche*," he said, changing direction and kissing a trail northwards onto her belly. "There is so much more."

His kisses reached the waist of her dress, and there was no more skin within easy reach. "We will need to divest ourselves of clothes to fully appreciate the next course."

A mouth-watering thought.

"Should I ring for the maid?"

Learmonth balked and then raised one eyebrow. "You want an audience?"

Peals of nervous laughter burst free. "But I cannot undo the buttons myself."

He changed position from between her legs and placed her knees back together. A moment later, he added two more split logs onto the fire. What a thoughtful man, but surely the bed would be warm enough in time?

That was where they were heading?

Another surprise. He took the cover off the bed and folded it onto the floor near the fire, then guided her to it.

She stood, trembling not from cold but nerves, as he worked his way down her back, releasing each button in time. With each button he freed, he kissed the thin layers of beneath, until at last the dress dropped in a messy pile around her feet.

Next came her stays, which he unlaced with a few swift moments. It too fell at her feet. Now she stood in her loose chemise, feeling incredibly exposed.

She stepped to the side, so he could toss her clothing away. When he returned, she reached forward to return the favor and undress him. Her fingers trembled with anticipation, but to her surprise, he didn't take over. He patiently waited until she had all the buttons of his waistcoat undone, then he draped it over a nearby chair. He stood there in his shirt, his eyes dark and knowing.

CHAPTER SIX

W hat divine torture. Her warm fingers branded his skin as she slipped the buttons free from his shirt. He fought hard to remain in control. Impossible with so much blood draining from his head and pooling in his nethers. He wanted to impale her, take her hard and hearty. It would terrify her, no doubt, and begin their marriage with a frightening note. His lust frightened him, he had to admit. The way she bit her lip in concentration nearly caused his undoing. Perhaps he might count slowly from one thousand, to keep his silent partner in check.

She pulled his shirt up and he gladly assisted, dragging the material from the back of his neck. He threw the shirt over the waistcoat. When he turned back the flames highlighted her soft silhouette beneath her shift and he nearly blew it there and then. Had it been so long since he'd lain with a woman that he'd forgotten how to hold it back? Yes and yes. Of course it was yes. But there was something so much more in Adelaide Th... Mrs Adelaide Learmonth. His wife. His rich, incredibly beautiful wife who was the answer to his dreams and prayers.

Her shaking hands reached the buttons at the front of his breaches.

With a steady breath out, he waited and kept right on counting. He needed to sink his cock into her hot wet depths, he needed her to trust him first and not run screaming the moment s-

The placket fell open.

His worse half stood up, proud and strong.

A sharp intake of breath filled his ears.

Adelaide stepped back.

"It won't bite," he said, half joking. "We can take things as slowly as you like." Even though every fiber of his body yearned to join with her as soon as possible.

"I've seen horses with smaller appendages," she said.

He should take it as a compliment, but the damn thing had ruined the moment by jumping out and scaring her.

In time, she'd get used to it. He hoped.

"I will never hurt you, I promise," he said. He meant every word of it. To show her how much, he guided her hand to his engorged penis. "I am in your hands, do what you will."

She let go. Not the result he was after.

She blinked and quietly said, "I don't know what to do."

"The let's work it out together."

Once more he guided her hand, trusting her to explore in her own time and at a pace of her choosing. Her grip firmed, making him jolt involuntarily.

"Sorry," she said.

"Don't be. That's perfect."

Innocence and curiosity made an intoxicating combination. She stroked and touched, caressed and rubbed. There seemed no rhythm or pattern. It messed up his head. His heart crashed and thumped like the battery machines in a mine.

Body jerking like an unbroken colt, he sucked his breath through his teeth.

Knees losing their strength, he fell into the chair he'd been pleasuring Adelaide in.

"Are you all right?" She gasped.

"More than all right." He wasn't. Not in the slightest. "Please keep going. If you're so inclined."

"I have hurt you," she said, waving her hand in the direction of his red flesh.

He checked the raw appendage. It was still attached to his body; that was all that mattered.

"Let's move to the bed, it will be easier there."

He sat up (with difficulty) and removed the rest of his clothing. Then he moved to the bed and pulled the covers back. Would she follow him in or flee to her rooms?

Relief flooded him as she stepped closer to the bed, climbed in and pulled the sheets up to her neck.

With absolutely no idea what to do next, Adelaide hid her furiously blushing body under the bedsheet. Nerves consumed her, when what she should be thinking about was *consummation*. Not that she was all that sure of the ins and outs of what came next. The moment she'd compared him to a horse, she'd had a strong idea of what would be next. He would cover her, like a stallion covered a mare. The mares did not seem to like it all that much, but they did their duty.

Adelaide would do hers.

Then again, stallions did not seem to pleasure the mares as he'd pleasured her. Ripples of loveliness moved through her body from the stimulation. No wonder her friends who had married had suddenly become so busy. Who had time for visits and balls when there were such pleasures to be had at home!

"I want you to be completely comfortable with your body," her husband - husband! - said. "Find what makes you happy, find what makes you glow from within."

Adelaide nodded. Knowing exactly what she wanted, her hand slid down her body, finding that place where his mouth had been so recently.

"May I kiss you while you pleasure yourself?" He asked.

"Of course," blurted out before she knew what she was saying. But then, why did it matter if she were forward at this point? He'd given her permission to touch herself, they were married, they'd begun exploring each other's bodies. She had to turn her mind off, otherwise she would overthink things and ruin the moment.

Her fingers played back and forth between her own folds, slicking quickly as she skated over her opening. There was something else he'd found down there, and it didn't take long before she found it as well. What a magical thing to discover. If only she'd known about this years ago, she might never have bothered attending balls at all!

Stop thinking, just feel.

His lips touched hers robbing all thought. Sensations flooded her, burning her blood, hammering her chest. The feelings were magical. Touching herself, she explored her own body. Her back wanted to arch, so she arched. Her legs parted, she let them fall.

He kept on kissing her, while she played and explored. Her mouth fell open on a gasp and he nudged the inside of her lips with his tongue. Hers darted out and they met, teasing, testing, challenging.

A soft shudder moved through her body as she rolled her fingers over that magical nerve ending that robbed her breath.

Learmonth shifted his body over hers, holding his weight above her.

"Are you going to cover me now?" she asked.

He creased his brow in response, as his hand moved down to where hers already was. She rubbed back and forth over that incredible place, while he slowly dipped one finger, then two, into her core.

She gasped a soft, 'Yes.'

He pressed in harder, then withdrew.

"Get back in."

He wasn't listening that much, as he did not do as she asked.

Instead, he suckled on one breast. It was too hard to pleasure herself any more as his lips and tongue stole her ability to focus.

He shifted himself between her legs. "I want so badly to be inside you."

Hadn't he just done that with his fingers? Coherence was not her strong point at this moment. "Yes."

He held himself steady, and for a moment Adelaide wondered if it was all over.

Oh heavens!

It was not.

He pressed himself in, where his fingers had been. It felt firm and hot, then suddenly he was out again.

That. Would. Not. Do.

When he did it again, tentatively pressing in, Adelaide reached down for his bottom and drew him into her. Then she clasped her legs around him so he couldn't withdraw again.

He kissed her, one breast then another, loving her body.

She had a hand on each buttock now, holding him in to her as he moved and bucked his body against her.

Magical madness.

The rocking unleashed something wild within. Something inside her could not get enough of this ... whatever it was. Panting for breath but keen to keep racing, she matched his rhythm as they pushed themselves on and on to some kind of finish line. He shifted and changed position.

"Yes!" exploded on a scream.

Whatever he'd done, it was incredible. Her body pulsed with need and exhilaration. Her heart thumped hard and her breath stalled.

Her soul expanded and contracted all at once.

"Learmonth, I love you!" came out of nowhere. The truth of it shocked her.

He shuddered and groaned her name. They both grunted and laughed and collapsed together into oblivion.

CHAPTER SEVEN

The weather turned ugly. Hardly surprising considering the time of year. Rain splattered the window panes. Winds howled down the streets. Everything looked sodden and gray on the other side of them. Not that many were out in this weather. Is that why there were no letters from friends on the salver? Adelaide could not blame them for staying indoors. After all, she'd been completely house-bound since her marriage. Mostly to do with the arousing things she and her husband - husband! - had been doing to each other. But also, the weather was so inclement she felt no need to venture out.

It would be nice to promenade together in the near future. They could wear warm coats and a footman each side could carry umbrellas.

Hmmm. That wouldn't exactly be fair on the footmen.

Thank goodness they had not gone to Gretna Green after all. Looking over the latest news sheet, she gulped in shock reading about the wild winds in Edinburgh causing widespread destruction. Gretna was ... near that city, was it not? It was in Scotland in any case, and if the weather in London was miserable, it had to be even worse farther north.

The rain and wind would hold off at some point, she hoped. They simply had to. Then she and Learmonth would go visiting. (He's asked her to call him Harold, but she'd become used to using his family name. Which was now hers.)

As much as she yearned to spend every waking moment in his arms, she did need to see some other faces. Notably, her friends. She was respectably married now; free from scandal. She would host an afternoon gathering and all would be well.

She rang the bell for the footman to get her writing set. The moment the weather cleared, they'd be able to deliver her messages.

The footman took far too long.

She rang the bell again.

Harrumph. No sign of the young man. Odd.

Fine then, she found the necessary items herself and spent a lovely hour writing invitations for a simple afternoon gathering. Once the ink was dry she rang for the footman again to give him instructions.

Taking a seat, Adelaide sat quietly and waited. Quietly.

Goodness it was quiet.

How odd, the house usually bustled with staff going about their duties.

No cooking smells either. Very odd! Had she completely lost track of days and it was Sunday afternoon already?

Aha! There was a noise. Coming from the back of the house. Something scraping on the floor, along with heavy footsteps.

"Learmonth?" She called out.

Half heard words melted into the walls between the sitting room and activity. A strong draft carried through the house.

Pulling her shawl around her shoulders, Adelaide walked towards the sounds of people. There was her husband, helping somebody load dining chairs onto the back of a wagon!

"What are you doing out in this weather?" She asked as a pair of weather-worn men threw a large canvas sheet over the furniture, but it would hardly make a difference in this downpour.

"Hello darling!" Learmonth said, smiling broadly and waving in her direction. "Stay indoors, it's perishing out here."

She took his advice and closed the door to the elements. She'd ask him later, after he'd dried by the fire. Yes, the fire. Best get that built up so that Learmonth didn't catch a chill.

There still wasn't much in the way of familiar household noises happening, which niggled in her back of her mind for a little while. The house should be bustling. She'd get the fires going until she could find where the staff were.

It took longer than she expected, but the fire in Learmonth's room eventually glowed brightly, chasing the damp away. Next, she set the fire in her rooms to dry the air. In fact, the entire house was probably growing damp, especially the rooms they closed off during the winter months.

Grabbing another shawl and adding an extra apron of skirts to keep warm, she ventured into the summer dining room, which had been closed since late autumn.

She'd expected it to be damp. She did not expect it to be empty.

Footsteps sounded on the stairs. Learmonth burst in, panting for breath, his hair wet plastered his handsome face.

"Why are you in here? It's so dank and dreary."

Hands planted on hips, she shot back, "What have you done with the furniture?"

Her voice bounced off the walls. It wasn't just the tables and chairs that were gone, but paintings, the carpet runner and a decorative side table. "Are you here to pawn the drapes too?"

"I'm ... redecorating!" He added a smile that didn't look quite right.

Her eyes narrowed. Body shivered. Staying here arguing would see them both catch a chill.

"Where is everyone?"

"I gave them the afternoon off, as a wedding present."

"Then it's not Sunday?" Because if there was one thing worse than selling off her family possessions, it was trading on the Lord's day of rest!

Cold fear settled into the pit of Harold's stomach. He'd known this day would come, he just hadn't realized how soon. This side of the house was closed up for winter; he hadn't expected anyone to open the doors this early in the year. Let alone his wife, who he'd left sleeping after a searing night of lovemaking.

He'd been hoping that by spring some kind of financial miracle would come his way, and he'd be able to buy everything back. Or buy new furniture to make up for the losses of the old.

His stomach clenched at the look of betrayal his beautiful bride sent him.

"I will make it up to you. I promise. But, my darling, can we go to a warmer room? I'm chilled to my skin here."

"Of course," her voice took on a haughty tone that sent ice into his veins. "Can't have you dying from exposure before I thrash you to within an inch of your life!"

If her words were daggers, he'd be bleeding to death at this very moment. The woman was fearsome when angry, and he'd made her very, very angry.

Which, all things considered, she had every right to be.

She stalked out of this room and left him to close the doors behind them. "Has my dowry not provided enough for you that you sell my mother's furniture?" she said as they made their way back to his rooms.

At least the staff weren't around to overhear this. He'd given them the day off as a gift, but also, to make sure none of them were around to see him dealing with tradesmen directly.

Tradesmen, la! A handy euphemism.

"May I close the doors?" He asked as they reached his rooms. "Not to keep you from leaving, but to keep the heat in. My goodness this fire is wonderful. I'm so grateful you kept it going. Thank you -"

"- Cut the flowery language, dearest husband and get to the truth."

He instantly became transported to that time as a naughty child when the governess had caught him stealing shortbread. This was multitudes worse.

"My darling, I did marry you for your dowry. I have extensive debts as I've explained. I never claimed otherwise."

She fell into one of the chairs near the fire, her chin wobbling. His stomach flipped at the tears that would soon follow.

"I say this because I am a truthful man, and that is the truth of the situation. I also told you I was in love with you, and that is the truth as well. I also informed you I was in debt. I said these things before we married, in order that there would be no secrets between us."

Her face contorted into hopeless shapes. "Which do you love more, the money or me?"

A bolt of lightning couldn't have shaken him harder. "I ... honestly, my darling, I did not realize I had to put them in order."

That was clearly the wrong answer. She stood up, her hands balled into small fists by her side. Her face changed to a blotchy red and tears ran free. Pain lanced his throat at seeing her like this. He'd done this to her. He was lower than a worm.

"How can I make this up to you?" He pleaded.

"That's the p-problem," she wept openly now. "I don't think you can. I don't think you ever can!"

It was Harold's turn to fall grab onto something to stop him falling down.

CHAPTER EIGHT

Several days later, lying in her own bed after yet another restless night, Adelaide concluded her marriage was a sham. Oh, sure, he'd said he loved her, but it was the money he really loved. He hadn't wasted any time selling family heirlooms. For all she knew, the summer wing would be lucky to still have drapes. The truly bizarre complication was that her dowry had not yet come through. Her father would have dealt with that, but he was no longer with them. Then it would have fallen to her eldest brother, but Mathew had blown his hand off and then died. Why hadn't the blasted pistol gone off in Learmonth's hand instead of her brother's? Her only brother was now the Duke, who should have sent the money through by now. He couldn't still be on his honeymoon? Perhaps they'd become trapped in some far-off place, isolated by floods or trees falling over the road. No, the Taunton men couldn't be that unlucky. If he'd died they should have heard something by now ... probably a cousin arriving to assume ownership of the family home.

She chose to believe he was still alive.

Goodness her mind took her to strange places when she was left with her thoughts. Dangerous, upsetting places that she should not think about at all.

She rose and pulled a dressing gown over her nightclothes, found her warmest slippers and headed down to for breakfast. If she stayed in her room and breakfasted alone again, she'd send herself insane.

Her husband - urgh, husband! - had arrived ahead of her. He busily attacked two boiled eggs with thin slices of toast.

"Good morning, my darling," he cheered, letting the staff know how happy he must be.

Blast him!

"Good morning," she replied, but to the room in general. Mrs Bampton had a pot of tea and refilled Learmonth's cup.

Yes, tea. That's what she needed. She retrieved a cup and placed it in front of her seat. "Thank you."

Two slices of toast would do her for now. Thank heavens Learmonth hadn't sold off the marmalade!

"It's good to see you up and about," he said giving a saucy smile as he dipped a wedge of toast into the soft egg.

Heaven help her, the action reminded her of their first week of marriage. Her body throbbed in response. She was furious with him, but all she wanted to do now was rip his clothes off and take him.

His eyes in return were so dilated and dark, it was a wonder he could focus on anything. He missed his mouth completely with the toast and left a splodge of egg next to his lip.

"You goose," automatically she fetched a napkin and touched it to his face to clean him up.

He grabbed her wrist before she made contact. The searing heat of his touch sent common sense plummeting and her blood racing. She wanted to chastise him, but a soft "Blast you," fell from her lips like an endearment.

Footsteps shuffled from the room, leaving them alone.

Blast him indeed. He still held her hand away, so she leaned forward and licked the egg off his lip. Instantly he crushed her to his body and she responded with equal pressure. Animalistic urges took hold. She flicked the buttons free from his breeches. He sprang free like a soldier, ready for duty.

His hand had let go of hers at some point. Both of them lifted her nightclothes to her waist. He caressed the globes of her bottom and squeezed.

"I'm still incredibly cross with you," she said. "I have not forgiven you in the least."

"I will spend the rest of my life earning it back."

Well, of course he'd say that, as she pressed the tip of him against her entrance, teasing and taunting as she slicked back and forth. Her breathing came hot and fast. The need to have him insider her was so strong. "I'm going to make your life miserable," she declared.

He gave a dirty chuckle. "I'm in complete agony right now."

She slid down, slowly at first, making herself comfortable.

His breath hissed. His eyes closed.

She adjusted and slid up a little, then pressed down hard.

Explosions racked her body. He grunted something in another language and pulled her into his body. "Steady on."

"No, I want to punish you for what you've done."

Those words had come from her lips? What had marriage done to her?

Filled with this new power over him, she adjusted again and slammed down hard once more.

Familiar thrumming took hold. The glory was waiting for her with just a few more moves. The rhythm built and she and Learmonth were one being, joined together in delirious joy.

They shuddered their release together. Blast her body needing him so much. Blast him for being so accommodating. The fury remained as delicious ripples of afterglow ran through her.

Blast her blasted husband.

Blast her own body for wanting so much of his.

In the kitchens, the staff noisily stacked pots and pans together to smother the sound they'd been making.

Eventually he said, "We should probably finish breakfast."

Her tea had cooled, but it didn't matter. She drank it quickly and wrapped the toast in a napkin. He too added more items to his plate. Without needing to say anything further, the two of them headed upstairs to his rooms.

A sparkly thought took hold. If she kept him busy with their insatiable lovemaking, he'd have no time to be up and about, selling family belongings.

Her blood thrummed at the thought of it.

From sunup to sundown, they feasted on each other. For energy, they ate from the trays of vittles left outside the door to his rooms. The staff were incredibly accommodating to their requirements, moving silently about the house to keep things running smoothly. For so many people, they were incredibly quiet. Bless them. Adelaide wasn't sure how she was going to face her maid, Gwen, when she next saw her. She had not bathed properly - Learmonth running a sponge over her naked form hardly counted, although it did bring her to ecstasy many times. After a week of athletic lovemaking, she felt sure they would run out of energy and enthusiasm for each other. To her surprise, the more they made love, the more she craved his touch. His fingers, his lips, his tongue, and his magnificent member that rose to the occasion every time.

Gasping for breath after their latest furious coupling, Adelaide splayed across his body. His rooms utterly reeked of their bodies. It should be enough to send her back to her rooms for a decent soak in the bath. Yet all she wanted was more indulgences. More of his kisses and caresses and fabulous fondling. Her body was already pulsing again with fresh need as he reached for her feet and began caressing her toes. He kissed each one like a precious treasure. Her legs opened to invite him home, yet he remained contentedly focused on her extremities. His seemingly inexhaustible penis was alert and ready again as well. She pulled him over and pushed him onto his back, so she could ride him to completion.

How could she be so wet, again? How could he be so hard?

"I know what you're doing," he said, between kissing her toes and massaging the arch of one foot. "You are keeping me as your prisoner of love."

She rocked herself over him and pressed down hard, finding that magnificent fulfilment she required. "How do you know it's not the other way around?"

"We are both captive to each other then," he said, bucking and thrusting in time with her.

A soft but determined tap sounded at the door. "Mister Learmonth, we have guests."

"Just a moment," he groaned out.

It would be impossible for the valet to think anything other than he'd interrupted them in the midst of something important. Adelaide ground her body into his and held in the scream, breathing hard against the eruptions inside her. It was as quiet as she could manage while wanting to scream for joy.

A second later, he breathed hard and followed her into rapture.

No time for luxuriating in the afterglow this time, they apparently had guests.

A half bottle of cologne through his hair and doused over his nethers would have to suffice. Whoever was downstairs had waited long enough. If it was a debt collector, he'd beg forgiveness and hope like hell they only broke his fingers on the left hand. He needed the ones on his write, for his wife's sake.

As he reached the sitting room, he was stunned hear their man-about the house announce that the Duke and Duchess of Wolster were in attendance.

They had a man about the house these days, rather than the full compliment of household staff. Luckily, they hadn't tested his valet or buttering skills, as they'd not received any visitors before, nor had Learmonth needed to dress for visiting anyone else.

When would his wife notice the lack of staff? She'd stopped him selling furniture, keeping him a slave to her passions. A fair trade.

"Your grace," he bowed to the man, whom he knew to be the previous duke's younger brother. Then he bowed to the woman. "Your grace." This would be the -oh shit.

Thomasina Burke.

Learmonth and the former Miss Burke mutely stared at each other for a moment. The duchess turned pale and didn't seem know where to look. For his part, he couldn't talk past the stone in his throat.

"What are you doing here?" The duke stood up and stepped in front of his wife. A delightfully protective gesture of love. It warmed Harold's heart to know she had married so well.

Still, the connections were too close for comfort.

Learmonth cleared his throat. "I married your sister, your grace."

"Adelaide?" He appeared stricken.

A cheeky "You have others" remained unsaid. That kind of messing around was one of the reasons he was in such terrible financial strife. He and his silly mouth. So good at wooing women, excellent at making men furious.

"Gerard?" A woman said from the doorway. "It is you! Hello dear brother."

The Duke took in the sight of his sister and his expression softened. "Addy. How are you?"

"Very well, darling Gerry." They kissed each other on the cheek and embraced. "I couldn't *possibly* have heard raised voices just now, could I?"

"You should probably call me Wolster now, at least when we're in public."

Learmonth's heart grew at how easily Adelaide had cut through the tense situation. With his wife by his side, he could do no wrong.

In fact, he left all the talking to her.

Meanwhile, the duchess looked as if she'd seen a dead puppy on the side of the road. She must have known who Adelaide had married. Surely Adelaide's mother had been in contact?

"I'll ring for tea," Adelaide took charge of the situation. She turned to the remaining man serving them. "Jones, inform the kitchen staff we have esteemed guests."

Moments later, Mrs Bampton from the kitchens arrived with a serving tray. Jones then added extra fuel to the fire. Would the duke notice the same staff performing multiple tasks?

"I hope you had a dry journey, it's miserable out there," Adelaide said, pouring the cups and adding teaspoons of honey.

Harold could only sit back and marvel at how little he had to do. He'd told Adelaide he loved her. Now that feeling had grown to something even greater. Blind adoration and admiration came closer to how he felt, for how easily she'd diffused the tension.

Over tea, it was time to clear the air about his horrible duel with the previous duke. When he'd told Adelaide, in the carriage that night, the darkness had spared him having to see her expression. No chance to hide that during the day now. Wolster's grief-stricken face ate into his soul.

But it had to be done, and again, he was so grateful to have Adelaide by his side to help him explain things and smooth things over.

There was still a long road of explanations ahead, which took up most of their time together. Lady Wolster held her tongue. It was as if there was some unspoken rule that everybody in the room had decided now was not the time for talking about *their* earlier dalliance. Anyway, he'd met Thomasina a year or more before he'd met Adelaide, his one true love.

All things considered, it was jolly generous of Wolster to give them the time of day.

Wolster said, "I had thought about waiting for better weather, but who knows when that will come?"

"I am so glad you have paid us a visit, dear brother." Adelaide said. "Thomasina, may I say how well you look. I trust your journey here was not too arduous?"

"Hot rocks and thick blankets are a godsend at this time of year," Thomasina responded. "And may I also extend my felicitations on your marriage."

They all congratulated each other, as if by mutual agreement things would be light as bubbles from this moment on.

Adelaide asked, "Have you visited mother since your return from honeymoon?"

"We have indeed," Wolster said. "She is the one who informed us of your recent news. Which is why we visited as soon as we could."

Adelaide nodded and said, "The weather has been so ghastly, it's kept all our friends away. We are so glad you have braved the elements to make a call."

Learmonth sat back and sipped his tea, feeling something close to comfort. Possibly even relaxation. It had been so long since he'd been able to truly relax, the experience was alien to him.

The reprieve was short-lived when the duke turned to him and said, "I believe my wife is owed an apology. You may deliver it now."

CHAPTER NINE

Harold Learmonth swallowed hard and took another sip of tea to help. It did not. He spluttered and coughed as if he had a fishbone stuck there.

The duchess sat serenely, awaiting him.

Best get this over with, then. "I, ah, do so very deeply apologize for my previous treatment. You see I ha -"

Jones opened the doors to the sitting room and announced the arrival of more visitors.

Dowager Thornton and Learmonth's mother stood there. He hadn't seen them since their wedding, where his mother had thrown flowers over his new bride.

Would Adelaide recognize her?

Jones took the women's shawls and coats to hang near a fire to warm them.

He bowed to his mother-in-law, then to his mother.

"I said naught," his mother said, as she tucked a thinner shawl about herself. "M'Lady made the connections after you went home from the church."

For the very first time in his life, Harold was not sure if he would faint or cast up his accounts. Or possibly both. The room started spinning and he fell down into his seat.

"Is this about selling the furniture?" Adelaide asked her mother.

"What furniture?" the duke and the dowager duchess asked at the same time.

"You're selling the furniture?" Learmonth's mother interjected. "Fallen backwards into a pot of jam and you're abusing the privilege already? My second husband at least waited a few months before he did that to me."

Adelaide burst out laughing.

Harold wanted to burst into tears.

Keep it together, man!

The Duchess joined in the snickering as well, then pretended she had a cough. She cast one look at Adelaide and could not hold it in any further. The two set each other off, and now his own mother was beginning to giggle.

"Righto lad, which room am I moving in to?" His mother said. "Happy to be upstairs or downstairs, somewhere warm would be lovely."

"She can have my rooms," Adelaide said. "I certainly have no need for them."

The Duchess gasped at the lack of manners. Learmonth pretended not to have heard it and muttered something about the weather.

"I thought you might stay with me at the dower house," Dowager Thornton said. "I had thought we were getting along rather well, and I do so much enjoy sensible company."

"It is cozy, that's for sure," his mother said. The two of them then set off to the kitchens to find more tea, and leave the 'children' as they called them, to 'sort themselves out'.

In case any more people arrived, Harold had to get his groveling in quickly. He turned to Lady Wolster and said, "I am deeply sorry for the way I treated you last season, your grace, and humbly beg your forgiveness. I was in deep financial straits - not an excuse, but an explanation - and required a dowry at short notice. I did not respect your delicate emotions at the time."

She pursed her lips in thought and then nodded. "Very good, we shall speak no more of it."

A long breath fled his lungs. That had been much easier than he expected, even though the duchess still looked pale and somewhat queasy.

"However," the duchess continued. "It appears you are still in financial straits, as you call it, and you have helped yourself to the duke's property."

That dry stone in his throat came back.

Why were they making such a big deal of this? Adelaide had everything well in hand. As long as she kept her husband - *husband!* - trapped in his rooms during daylight hours, the remaining furniture was safe. Sure, she was shocked and horrified when she'd first discovered her husband's trading. With a little time between then and now, and a lot of lovemaking in between, her feelings towards Learmonth had changed.

He hadn't sold anything more, which was a relief. They'd been busy discovering things about themselves. The world barely existed. In fact, now that she had to behave in company again, she realised they had far fewer staff to help.

Had Learmonth sent them away to save money?

They'd have to discuss things, when they had a spare moment that wasn't taken up with them ravishing each other's bodies.

The duke delivered flatly, "There's no dowry."

"What?" she and Learmonth said at once.

"As the duke, you did not seek my permission to marry. I'm within my rights as the head of the family to hold off," he told Adelaide. "He's not even a gentleman."

A small bubble of laughter broke free. Adelaide had the perfect t comeback. "We couldn't contact you, you were on your honeymoon."

"Then you should have waited for our return." Wolster shrugged, as if that was all there was to it.

Blast and double blast.

Footsteps sounded near the front doors. Once again, Jones announced more visitors.

Was there an 'open house' sign on the street?

The faces of her dear friends smiled upon Adelaide.

Oh Blast! She'd completely forgotten about writing those invitations! One of the staff must have delivered them! Although for the moment, the only ones she'd seen were Mrs Bampton and Jones. If there were only two servants remaining, how had either of them had any time to deliver invitations?

"We're going to need more tea," Adelaide told Jones. Then she turned to her friends and fixed on a smile. "Jane, Eleanor, Mary and Mariah, how lovely of you to come!"

Her heart became lighter upon seeing them. It had been too long.

Mariah delivered a welcome embrace. "I wanted to visit much earlier, but the weather has been terrible."

Adelaide mentally swapped out 'the weather' for 'your reputation'. She and her friends were close, they knew how to skirt around an issue without hurting feelings.

Adelaide nodded. "It has been dreadful, but sunny days will return soon."

They exchanged knowing smiles.

Eleanor handed over a jar of conserve. "The last of the quince jam. I know how much you love it."

Gladness spread through Adelaide. How lovely to have her friends together again. She quickly wiped a tear from the corner of her eye. "Quince jam is my favorite, thank you so much for remembering. Now, all of you come in and I shall make introductions. You may remember my brother, who is now the Duke of Wolster ..."

Each friend in turn gave a warm greeting and polite curtsey to their graces, as Adelaide introduced them. Then she turned to her husband - husband! - who stood up to receive the women.

"Delighted to meet you. Know that you will always be welcome here and be met with good cheer and hot tea! Ah, here comes a fresh pot."

Learmonth poured the cups so that Adelaide could continue to embrace and natter with her friends. What a sweetheart!

Niggling in the back of her mind was Learmonth's invitation that friends would be welcome at any time. Fine for him to say, but they'd need to restock the pantry. With no dowry, maybe they would need to sell more furniture.

That thought caught her by surprise. Perhaps selling furniture wasn't such a horrible thing to do, given the alternative was to do without staff.

People visiting the receiving room would not see the rest of the house and any such empty rooms. But they would notice the lack of servants.

Her bother the duke put his cup down and stood. "Thank you, dear sister, for the tea. We should be on our way."

The words, "But you've only just arrived" formed in her head.

The Duchess, still looking a little pale, said, "We shall leave you to speak freely with your friends, I'm sure you have much to catch up on."

"Of course," she replied. Even though her husband had made a generous apology, it must be hard for Thomasina to be in the same room as he. Lady Wolster could not possibly be jealous, that would require her to still have fondness for him. In any case, Thomasina was married to a Duke. Her life from now on would outshine just about anyone's. "Thank you so much for visiting us and welcoming dear Learmonth into the family."

She said that as much for her friends' benefit as her husband's. Her brother had to accept them into the fold, he simply *had to*. It would be a scandal for a duke's sister to be brought low. Given time, Gerry would not have refused the match. They'd stopped the scandal by marrying, everyone could see that.

Even her friends were allowed to visit her, now that she was safely wed.

The Wolsters said nothing further. They kissed her tenderly on the cheek and fare-welled the rest of the guests.

Adelaide would speak to her mother, get Mamma to explain to Gerry the circumstances and speed of their marriage. Then he'd hand over the dowry.

Looking at the tea set, she wondered how many they had in the house, and what they'd be worth.

"Sorry, I missed that," she apologised to Jane.

"I was asking about the ceremony," her friend said, blushing a little, and then delivering a warm smile. "I am so terribly sorry I could not make it. The ... ah ... the weather, you see."

Yes of course, the weather. "It was a charming, *private*, service. We were married by special license."

Jane tilted her head and smiled again, then sipped her tea. "We simply must keep in touch. I'm sure the weather will be so much nicer in Spring."

"How goes the rest of the season?" Adelaide asked innocently.

The friends gushed about dresses and mishaps and charming gentlemen. Mariah was hoping to create an understanding with one in particular. All past misdeeds and missteps forgotten as they fell back into old patterns of gossip and fun.

Delightful stuff, Adelaide thought, wishing she'd been there to witness things. That pesky *weather* preventing invitations from reaching her door.

"Now that I have settled into married life, I would simply adore the chance to chaperone any of you, at whichever ball you may need."

Adelaide suggested. "Just send a note and I shall let you know if I can make it."

The other four nodded and smiled and promised that as soon as *the weather* improved, they would.

Learmonth poured more tea and Adelaide rang the bell again. Jones appeared. Adelaide asked if they could have scones or some tea cake. He nodded and vanished to the kitchen.

As if on cue, her stomach rumbled. Goodness, she hadn't eaten, and her recent activities with her husband had left her rather famished.

Learmonth nodded in her direction and said, "I'll take care of it."

He left the women to chat gaily and laugh heartily. After a good wait, Mrs Bampton appeared with some oat cakes for them to slather with jam, but no butter. It was an otherwise charming afternoon, and they soon stopped making any references to *the weather* at all.

The refilled tea was paler than before. At least if anyone spilt the tea, it wouldn't stain and therefore devalue the furniture. Furniture that Adelaide was starting to look at with an eye for the price she could get for each piece.

Learmonth begged Mrs Bampton, who was also doubling as the cook, to boil the tea leaves longer to get the color up.

"I could wring them in a napkin and not get any darker," she replied.

They were out of tea. How dire!

This was his fault entirely. He should have known the family would be low on the readies with two funerals and then two weddings in such close succession. Maybe the visit and the refusal to hand over the dowry was Wolster's way to save face? Was he pretending he *would not* give over the money, when perhaps he *could* not.

His mother and the dowager reappeared. "Lady Wolster gave me a

lovely tour of the house. Grand to see my son come up in the world."
She pinched his cheek as if he were little more than a school boy.

Oh dear, how much of the house had they seen? Hopefully not the
one empty room denuded of decorations. He'd have a calm discussion
with his wife about how they might go on from this point.

Lady Wolster said nothing about cold rooms or missing items.
Instead she touched him on the shoulder and said, "I trust you are
treating my daughter well?"

It may have looked like a soft touch, but she pressed down hard on
his shoulder. "Absolutely, Mother Wolster." Now was not the time to
raise the hold-up with the blunt he'd been expecting.

"Excellent. We'll be off then. Your mother may have no connections, but she is good company. I expect better quality tea for us both
by our next visit."

"If you send us some of your favorite, I'll be sure to get cook to buy
more next time she restocks the pantry."

"My favorite is hard to obtain," Lady Wolster said. "I'll send a batch
in due course."

With that, the two women - Learmonth was suspicious of how
they had formed such a fast friendship - walked to the door. Jones
dutifully retrieved their coats and shawls, then borrowed an umbrella
one of Adelaide's friends had placed in the stand to help them to their
carriage.

With a heavy sigh, Harold knew they were down to the fewest
staff they could manage a household with. Something his wife had
not apparently noticed. Or at least, hadn't said anything about.
Perhaps she had wanted to and was too fatigued to do much about it?
Why did a wife need a ladies' maid when she barely rose from bed but
to eat, then return and keep him deliriously happy for the rest of
the day?

It had been his sad duty to inform the staff, during the dead of
night, that he could no longer pay them. Adelaide has slept through all
of these occasions. Such a delicate little snore. It worked to wake him

when needed, and showed him she was completely unaware of his goings and comings in the dark.

In the light of day, there was no avoiding the cold reality of their situation.

If Adelaide was to retain any of her friendships, they needed decent tea.

CHAPTER TEN

How had he slept through the entire night? The sun - welcome back dear friend - knifed through the drapes. The bed beside him was empty. Had Adelaide returned to her rooms?

Dressing quickly, he stalked through the connecting doors and found her domain bitterly cold and empty.

No point pulling the bell to ask the staff where she was. He had to let the cook-maid-housekeeper get her rest, and the footman-butler-valet needed his.

He'd become used to the quiet of the big old place, but it was impossible to ignore the growing echoes through the halls.

Noises floated up from the mews behind the house. Had the collectors come early to take more belongings? He'd have to beg them off. Maybe a few silver knives and forks would tide them over?

"What ho!" he said, upon stepping outside and seeing his darling wife dealing with tradesmen. "Enjoying the sunshine, darling?"

"Very much so, darling," his wife replied back with an enormous smile. "I thought I'd let you sleep a little more, you do need your rest." She ended her sentence with a saucy wink.

This was not the wailing banshee he thought she'd become once she learned of his activities. How was she so calm about this?

"The uh, furniture from your old rooms?"

"Yes, dear. I don't need them, and these lovely gentlemen are giving me a very good price for them. What with them belonging to the sister of a duke."

He wanted to hug her with relief. He wanted to shake some sense into her. How had she come around so quickly? As much as he wanted to think he'd played some part in it - their lovemaking had been beyond his wildest dreams - this was clearly her decision and he could take no credit.

The tradesman delivered a scowl his way. "Drives a hard bargain, this one," he said. "What with an invalid mother and sick wife and five children to feed, she's bleeding me dry."

Adelaide's mouth quirked. "You told me four children."

The tradesman scrunched his hat in his hands. "She's expecting again."

"No wonder she's sick," Adelaide shot back.

Befuddled and needing to sit down, Harold looked for somewhere to park himself. The only bench seat that had been out here a few days ago was now missing. It wasn't on the back of the wagon either.

Adelaide looked his way and finished his thought. "It made excellent firewood that day my friends visited." Then she shrugged.

"I thought ... I thought you'd be furious when you ..." Harold couldn't complete his sentence. Adelaide gave him a pocket book with several high-value coins in it and a few notes. "I was. But needs must. I have had some time to think, in between our ... ah ... *sessions*, where I cannot think to save myself. Dear brother of mine is holding out on the dowry. I still want friends to visit and I am keen to have some kind of return to society. I was very angry at first. But now I see we have few options and must adjust."

She was being remarkably responsible and sensible about their perilous situation.

Then she added, "If I have to drink such weak tea ever again, I'll smash every window in the house."

Ahhhh, there was the wife he knew and loved.

"I love you so very much, darling wife."

"I know," she replied. "You've always been forward about that."

The fact she did not say it back to him, niggled his soul. Then again, they had tradespeople to deal with. Sentimentality had to wait.

Adelaide watched the tradesmen, their horses and wagon leave the mews. With a sigh, she said, "I hope they find a good home."

Her husband crinkled his forehead. "Your old clothes?"

"No, silly. The horses. I hope their new owners are kind to them and don't take them out in miserable weather."

The mews were pathetically empty. "When did you do that?"

"Earlier today, when you were sleeping. It not a decision I came to lightly. I fervently hope we can buy them back once we have funds again."

He shook his head, then breathed a few times and made a heavy sigh. "Oh dear, you sold my carriage as well."

"I removed any identifying features," she said. "It is a rather common carriage and easily mistaken for others." This last part she delivered with a giggle behind her hand.

"I have fond memories of that carriage."

Laughter broke free. "As do I. It fetched a good price. I will miss it too. However, we still have our memories which will always belong to us."

"We're not out of the woods yet, though, are we?"

"Not even close. I'm rather cross with you for sinking me with so much debt. Why didn't you tell me before we married how much you owed?"

"But I did? I told you I was in love with the dowry almost as much as I was in love with you."

Blast him, he had. Multiple times. "Well, I'll do the negotiating from now on. I do love you, Harold, but if you sell our belongings too cheaply in the future, so help me I'll sell you as well."

"You love me?" His face burst with joy.

Adelaide sighed, "Yes, I really do. I did say it a while ago but you didn't seem to notice."

"Oh, I noticed," he said, wrapping his arms around her. Leaning close to her ear he said, "You'd just had an explosive release. I heard it loud and clear, but wasn't sure if you meant it or were merely dumb-struck with lust at the time."

His cheek was so close, she gave it a little nibble. So help her, her belly responded with ripples of need.

"Are you expecting guests today?" His hand slipped down the front of her blouse and he pressed himself into her.

Her body responded with equal fire and she cupped his bottom. "I have invited nobody since the day my brother and his wife visited."

"Good. Let's go upstairs and get lusty."

He carried her into the house, then headed for the stairs to his room.

"I will be ah, that is to say," Adelaide began as they reached his bed. "I think we will have a visitor in Autumn."

"That's far off enough," he pushed her skirts up and then flicked off the buttons on his breeches. "We'll be able to get tea and scones by then."

Adelaide made a disappointed face and grabbed hold of her favorite piece of him. "You goose, I don't mean friends coming over, I mean a *new arrival*."

He plunged into her, hard and hot, starting a familiar rhythm. Then he stopped mid-thrust. "Wait, you mean … you're expecting?"

"Hooray! He finally understands."

He chuckled, nibbling at her neck as he resumed lovemaking. "In which case, we'd best hurry and sell the rest of the furniture."

EPILOGUE

Summer came with a long dry spell. There was no need to stock the fireplaces with wood and no need to cook quite so many hot meals. Lemonade became her daily staple. Adelaide didn't even mind weak tea either.

In Adelaide's enlarged condition, she had the perfect excuse to not visit friends, which saved her hiring cabs and taking small gifts with her. It also meant nobody called in as she was nearing her time of confinement. She'd been in touch with Gwen, her former ladies' maid, with a promise to re-employ her as soon as their fortunes changed.

Learmonth rubbed her feet, the darling man.

Sitting in the cool of the kitchen, the two of them were accompanied by their remaining two staff. Mrs Bampton and Jones.

Adelaide suspected her mother might be paying them to stay on, as she was convinced they'd run out of money by mid spring.

The debt collectors had stopped arriving, so that was a good sign. Perhaps their furniture sales had paid down Learmonth's debts at last?

As much as she should be worried about money, Adelaide held onto hope that if her brother didn't come good with the blunt, her mother at least would make sure they didn't starve. Plus, she was carrying the family's first grandchild. That should count for something.

A rap came at the front door.

The four of them looked at each other, wondering who it could be.

Jones stood up and headed to the sound, as whoever was at the door rapped again.

"I didn't think debt collectors came to the front door," Adelaide said. There was so little left to sell, did they need to part with the very bed they slept in?

Her brother soon appeared as Jones brought him to the kitchen. Her brother, the Duke of Wolster, his face filled with remorse like the time he'd been in trouble for teaching her how to climb trees. Jones should have taken him to the sitting room. They still had furniture in there for guests.

Slowly, Adelaide rose to her feet. "Your grace. Is all well with you?" It did not seem right to call him Gerry any more.

He took in the size of her and the color leeched from his face. "My God, what happened?"

Confused, Adelaide said, "What normally happens after people marry. We're expecting a child."

He stood there, gibbering like an idiot. "In which case, congratulations. I ah ... came to visit to see how you were getting on and to ... deliver this."

He gave her husband - ahhhh husband - a small package. Learmonth took it with thanks and opened it. He gasped and closed it just as quickly and handed it to Adelaide. Now it was her turn to see what all the fuss was about.

It was a promissory note, from Wolster's bank, to Learmonth. Her dowry, in full. Relief washed over her at the sight of it. Gwen would be back even sooner than she'd hoped. Then decent tea, then everything else in turn.

Wolster used his older brother voice on her. "I was cross that you married without my permission. Mamma explained how she took matters into hand at the time and so ... well ... what I mean to say is ... I am sorry for not delivering this earlier. It's jolly hard to travel back and forth between London and Brighton when ah ..."

"Is Thomasina unwell?" Adelaide demanded. "What are you doing leaving her when she needs you? You could have sent this by messenger."

"Thomasina is ... oh, we're all family here. Thomasina is also expecting, although not as far along as your good self." His face turned dark with embarrassment. "Alas, she has been dreadfully wretched. You see, I was hoping the two of you, well, the *four* of you, can't leave Jones and Mrs Bampton all alone in this empty house ... that you'd come to Brighton and be able to keep her company as we finalize the town houses."

"In a heartbeat." Adelaide said. "Come on, let's go."

Wolster cast confused looks about the kitchen. "I'll give you time to pack, we don't need to depart immediately."

"What's there to bring?" Adelaide replied as she stood up. "We've sold everything that wasn't nailed down, and possibly a few things that were."

Twenty minutes later, they were ready to leave. Jones stood on the back of the carriage until they cleared London, then he sat up front with the driver for a while. Learmonth, Mrs Bampton, Wolster and Adelaide sat inside. Learmonth removed Adelaide's slippers and rubbed her feet. Wolster didn't know where to look, so cleared his throat and stared out the window. Mrs Bampton pretended to sleep. Her eyes closed firmly, although from time to time she peeked out at them and grinned.

He was wonder with her feet.

By the time they arrived in Brigton, Adelaide swore off carriages forever. "Gerry, you must send for Mamma and Mrs Learmonth. They will need to come here. I cannot make the return to London in my state. I cannot even look at another carriage! Her body ached everywhere. Her back, her hips, her feet!

Inside Wolster's Brighton estate, the sheer number of staff overwhelmed Adelaide. Such noise! So many faces! So many people wanting to help.

"Please take me to my sister, I need to see how Thomasina is faring."

They found her in a north-facing room, away from the sun. It was so lovely and cool in here. Thomasina lay on a chaise, looking weak and wan.

"Oh, darling sister, what has that brute a brother done to you?" Adelaide asked.

Thomasina gave a weak smile. "From the state of *you*, I think you can guess."

Adelaide gave instructions to the maid to fetch their respective husbands. *Yes, it was fine that they see them like this, in fact, it was their duty to at least spend some time being uncomfortable at the sight of them.*

"The very least dear Gerry can do for you is to rub your swollen feet," Adelaide commanded. "Once they're in, I'll ring for some weak tea with lemon."

The gentlemen entered the room and Learmonth moved to Adelaide's side. "How can I be of assistance?" He asked.

"Her grace's feet are bloated and sore. Teach my addlepated brother how to help her."

Learmonth directed his grace to sit on the end of the chaise and take his wife's swollen feet into his hands.

Needing to rest her own feet, Adelaide found a chair to sit in. Travel was no fun at all in her condition.

Learmonth backed away from their graces and retrieved his wife.

"I've only just sat down, now you want me to get up again?" She said with a laugh.

"If I start rubbing your feet in here, I will forget we're in company."

He made a good point. She accepted his assistance in rising. A moment later, a maid arrived with tea and lemon slices. Adelaide and Learmonth left her brother and his wife to their tea and privacy.

A new life awaited Adelaide and her darling husband - husband! - in Brighton. With her dowry secured, their future was also secure. Her entire body felt lighter; miraculous considering the state she was in.

As a maid showed them to their guest quarters, Adelaide couldn't help noticing the vast quantities of furniture and fittings. Not that she was seeing price tags on everything. No, not in the slightest. Well, just a little.

Alone at last, Adelaide stretched out on the bed and gave a hearty sigh. "This bed feels so good, I may never get up."

"I shall wait on you, hand and foot," Learmonth said with a glint in his eyes.

Then he removed her slippers

ABOUT EBONY OATEN

Ebony Oaten loves history, but doesn't like living through it.

She is especially glad she was not around during the Regency era, as she would most likely have died in infancy from asthma, or something hideous like diphtheria. In the unlikely event that she'd made it to adulthood, she would have probably been a scullery maid or a lowly servant, as she 'talked too much and didn't pay attention' because ADHD diagnoses hadn't been invented.

http://ebonyoaten.com/

facebook.com/EbonyOaten

x.com/WriterEbony

ALSO BY EBONY OATEN

Unsuitable Suitors (Sweet Regency)

1. Marquess and Tell
2. Me and Mr Jones
3. Fetch The Earl
4. Miss Remington's Steely Resolve
5. A Swain For Miss Penhurst

Regency Romps (Sexy Regency)

1. There's Something About Miss Mary
2. Weekend At Baron E's
3. Scandalous Charlotte
4. Hot August Night
5. Duke Around and Find Out
6. Romancing The Stone-Cold Rogue

http://ebonyoaten.com/

THE ABDUCTION OF AN EARL

LINDA RAE SANDE

CHAPTER ONE
A LADY SUFFERS A SURPRISE

The last strains of the orchestra's final selection reached Persephone's ears when the dowager countess spotted her town coach and waved at the driver. He had managed to position her equipage in a most convenient location in the queue of other vehicles awaiting their owners in front of Weatherstone Manor, the Mayfair location always hosting the first ball of the Season.

Parker tipped his hat as he opened the coach door. "My lady," he said as he offered his gloved hand in assistance.

"You know me too well if you've timed your arrival for this very moment," Persephone commented as she placed a silk-gloved hand in his and took the step up and into the velvet-lined coach.

"I never left, my lady," he replied. "Nice night to watch the stars." He closed the door before his mistress could reply and then bounded up and onto the driver's seat. A moment later, and the coach pulled away from the pavement.

Persephone settled into the blue velvet squabs and sighed in relief as she extracted her feet from her dance slippers. Wiggling her toes, she had a thought to simply leave her shoes off when it was time to make her way into March House.

In the middle of taking a deep breath, she stopped and sniffed. The air inside the coach bore an unfamiliar scent. A cologne unlike anything her late husband had worn. Walter's usual *parfum* brought to mind leather and musk, a rather manly odor for a gentleman who wasn't.

This cologne was spicy. Citrusy. She sniffed again and then gave a start when the sound of a snore filled the coach.

"Who's there?" she asked in alarm as she straightened on the bench.

A snuffle-snort was followed by a moan and a groan and a "bloody hell."

Stuffing her feet back into her dance slippers, she pressed herself as far into the corner of the coach as she could.

"Where the hell am I?" a male voice asked from the other side of the coach. From the way the prone form suddenly moved—a long lump rising on one side—Persephone realized the man had been sleeping and was now propped up on an elbow. She reached over to the window curtain and drew it back so the light from the coach lantern illuminated the interior.

"Ack!" the man complained as he lifted a hand to shield his face from the sudden glare.

Persephone gasped. "Lord Wilmington? Is that you?" She dropped the curtain, but the panel remained parted enough to allow some light into the coach.

Another moan and groan sounded as he moved to sit up, although his head ended up in his hands as his elbows rested on his knees. "If I am, you have my permission to shoot me. Put me out of my misery," he whispered hoarsely.

"Lord Wilmington?" she repeated.

He lifted his head and regarded her in the dim light. "You have me at a disadvantage, my lady," he said.

"Jack, it's me. Persephone March," she replied. "What are you doing in my coach?"

"Your coach?" he repeated before he groaned again.

"And whatever is wrong with you?"

Jack straightened and allowed his head to fall back onto the top of the squabs. "What day is this? It feels as if I've drunk an entire bottle of brandy." One of his hands went to the side of his head to hold it, as if it required assistance in remaining on his neck.

"It's the first Tuesday after Easter," she replied. "Lord Weatherstone's ball?" she added, sure that would give him enough information to sort his loss of time.

"I don't recall being there," he murmured before he inhaled sharply. "Wait. Yes, I do. I arrived at the same time as the Marquess of Reading," he commented. "I remember being thirsty... went for the punch..." He straightened. "That's it. Someone must have poured a good deal of brandy into the punch," he stated.

Persephone scoffed as she leaned forward in an attempt to get a closer look at her passenger. "Jack, trust me when I tell you the punch was definitely not spiked. A bit too much orgeat, but... there were no spirits in it," she said as she placed a hand beneath his chin and lifted it slightly. "You *look* as if you're drunk," she accused.

"I feel like I was," he replied, grasping her hand to bring it to his lips. He pressed a kiss on the back of it. "Not now, though." He let go of her hand, and Persephone quickly pulled it away.

Jack pushed his hand over his head, his fingers leaving furrows in his dark hair as a wince crossed his handsome features. "If it wasn't alcohol, then how do you explain this splitting headache? And my tongue feels as if it..." He paused, grimacing.

"If you're going to be sick—"

"I'm not," he assured her. "But I do think I've been... poisoned or... or drugged or something," he murmured, his eyes narrowing as he struggled to remember anything from earlier that evening.

Persephone inhaled sharply. "By whom?" she asked in alarm.

"Well, if I knew that..." he murmured, his gaze going to the coach window nearest him. "Good God, what time is it?"

Her blonde brows furrowing in concern, Persephone said, "About two, I think."

"In the morning?" Jack countered, straightening on the bench seat. He hissed as his other hand joined the first in holding his head.

"Yes. Shall I have Parker take you to your apartments? Are you still at the Albany?" She started to reach up to tap on the trap door, but Jack intercepted her hand.

"No need, my lady," he replied, placing his other hand over the top of hers so he could hold onto it. "Might I be allowed to join you this evening? At least until I can sort what happened?"

Persephone inhaled softly, surprised at how he held her hand. He had done so in the past the very same way. A long time ago, when he had proposed marriage. Since she had already been forced by her father to accept the Earl of Castlewait's offer of a marriage of convenience, she'd had to decline Jack's offer.

At least she'd had the benefit of a few months of Jack's attentions. A few months of young love and stolen moments. Despite the intervening twenty years, Jack still sported his handsome good looks, although he appeared a bit rough around the edges. His face, tanned from daily horseback rides, displayed creases on the sides of his eyes, and a scar from a wound he'd suffered due to the tip of a fencing foil marred his right cheek. The hair near his temples was graying, and his usual black hair was peppered with strands of gray.

The thought of him spending the night with her at March House had flutterbies dancing about in Persephone's stomach. They hadn't been together in a bed since the week after he'd taken her virtue all those years ago. "Of course you can stay," she finally replied. "As long as you need."

He nodded and then winced as the slight movement seemed to cause him pain. "I'll be a perfect gentleman," he said. "I promise."

Persephone frowned. "And what if I don't want you to be?" she asked in a whisper, barely loud enough to be heard over the sound of the coach wheels on the cobbles.

His eyes narrowed, and Jack allowed a wan grin. "Is that... is that an invitation?"

Her confidence faltered. "Would you accept it?" she countered. "Or have I grown too old for your tastes these days?"

For a moment, she wished she could have taken back her last words. But Jack Kirkpatrick, Earl of Wilmington, had a reputation of late. One that proclaimed he preferred younger widows and virgins. His name was synonymous with words like *scoundrel* and *rake* and *libertine*. His initials were frequently to be found in the articles printed in *The Tattler*, London's premier gossip news-sheet.

"Don't believe everything you hear, Sephie," he replied, tightening his hold on her hand. "Or read. And you'll never be too old for me."

Persephone grinned at hearing his pet name for her. No one but him had called her 'Sephie', not in her entire life.

"Damn, but I wish I felt better, because I'd really like to prove myself to you right now."

"Perhaps in the morning," she whispered.

"I'd like that," he replied.

The coach came to a stuttering halt, and the countess scoffed. "Well, I do believe we're about to shock Parker. That is, if he didn't know you climbed into my coach."

Jack furrowed a brow, an expression of worry crossing his face. "I don't remember getting into this coach," he said. Then his eyes rounded. "Did you... did *you* arrange this? Did you have me drugged?"

Persephone scoffed. "I rather I wish I did, but no, I assure you, it was not me," she said on a sigh. "I would have hoped you would come of your own accord, if I'd sent you an invitation."

His eyes narrowing briefly, Jack considered her words. "I would have," he whispered.

The coach door opened and Persephone, heartened by his response to her last comment, allowed her driver to help her down the step. He was about to close the door, but she held up a staying hand. "Tell me, Parker. You said you didn't drive away from Weatherstone Manor the entire night."

The driver gave a start. "That's because I didn't, my lady. Just... stargazed all night," he said on a shrug.

"Were you *always* with the coach?"

Parker's eyes darted to the side. "I... I might have stepped away a few times. To get a better view of the sky," he admitted in a halting voice. "There's a rather large tree on the one side of the Weatherstone property. It was in the way."

"So... no one gave you any coins to look the other direction or... or to take on a passenger?" Persephone pressed.

His eyes rounding in confusion, Parker shook his head. "No, my lady. Nor would I have accepted," he claimed.

"All right then—"

"There were a couple whom I thought seemed out of place, though," he added as his gaze turned to his mind's eye. "A few hours ago."

Persephone's gaze darted to the interior of the coach. "What do you mean?" she asked, well aware Jack had moved closer to the door so he could listen in on her conversation with the driver.

"They wasn't dressed right for a ball, is all. I just thought they was there to watch the arrivals like some of the common folk do. But usually the onlookers take their leave after most of the guests have arrived, and they were still there after you went into the house."

"Oh?" she responded. "When did they leave?"

Parker shrugged. "I didn't take note, my lady, but it might have been about the time a gentleman was leading another out of the house. Drunk, like. Dressed all fine, but stumbling about, barely able to walk."

Persephone's eyes rounded. "Would you recognize the gentleman if you saw him again?" she asked, just as Jack emerged from the coach.

Parker gasped, one hand going to his chest before he stepped between his mistress and Jack, as if he intended to provide protection. "It's *you*. The drunkard," he said in shock.

"*Drugged* would be the more appropriate word," Jack remarked. "Any idea who escorted me out of Weatherstone Manor?" he asked. "Was it just one person? Or two?"

Shaking his head, Parker glanced back at Persephone. "Just the one. I haven't seen him 'afore," he said. "But he was about your age, I think. Seemed to know you, given how he was talking to you. Cursin' at you, mostly."

Jack winced but didn't say anything.

"Was he dressed for the ball?" Persephone asked.

Parker furrowed his brows and thought for a moment. "Well, yes. Dressed as fine as you, sir," he said with a nod to Jack. "He didn't have a hat on, though. But you did."

Persephone and Jack exchanged quick glances. "I don't remember that," Jack said. He poked his head back into the coach, and after a moment of rummaging around, he emerged with a top hat in one hand. "Well, it's a hat, but it's not mine," he murmured.

"How can you be sure?" Persephone asked. The black beaver looked like any fashionable men's top hat of late.

Jack turned it over and aimed it so the coach lantern could illumi-nate the label inside the hat band. "I only buy hats from *Fitzsimmons and Smith* in Oxford Street," he said. The label in the hat he held was for a shop in New Bond Street. "Which means my hat is probably still back at Weatherstone Manor."

"Or the man who escorted you out of the house has it," Parker said, obviously intrigued by the unusual events of the evening.

"Perhaps a good night's sleep will have your memory returning, Lord Wilmington," Persephone suggested. She turned to Parker. "If you remember anything else about what you saw this evening, will you please let me know? Or tell Bentley?" she said, referring to the butler of March House. She took Jack's proffered arm.

"Of course, my lady," Parker replied. "Will you be needing the coach again tonight?"

Chuckling, Persephone shook her head. "Of course not."

The driver hesitated, obviously bothered that he was unaware of the earl's presence in the coach. "If you'd like, I can go back to Weatherstone Manor," he offered. "Ask about his lordship's hat. And return this one at the same time," he added, pointing to the hat Jack still held.

Persephone inhaled softly and turned to gauge Jack's response. When he merely shrugged, she said, "That's very kind of you." She was about to fish a few coins from a pocket in her gown, but Jack beat her to it, pulling several from his waistcoat pocket. He gave them to the driver.

"Be sure to give a coin or two to the footman who assists you," he said. "Especially if he shares any news with you."

"I will, my lord," Parker said as he took the hat.

"Should you acquire Lord Wilmington's hat, simply leave it on the hall table if Bentley is no longer up and about," Persephone requested, deciding she didn't wish to be disturbed. Although she sensed Jack's growing unease, she knew he needed to sleep off the effects of the drug.

"Yes, my lady."

"Good night, Parker."

"Good night, my lady," the driver replied as he watched Lord Wilmington lead Lady Castlewait to the front door. He hurried back to the coach and set the horses in motion.

CHAPTER TWO
AN ABDUCTION GONE AWRY

MEANWHILE, IN CHEAPSIDE

W hat the hell do you mean you *lost* him?" Baron Abraham Kravets asked as he paced before the desk in his study. "He drank the punch, didn't he?"

"Yes, sir, he did."

"And?"

Elias Turnbridge winced. "I got him out of there, mostly unseen."

"What do you mean, *mostly*?" Kravets asked, his annoyance evident.

"I think there might have been too much of that sleeping powder in the glass of punch, and he drank it all in a single gulp. It took effect right quick, and, well, I had to get him up the stairs and out of there by way of the front door," Elias explained.

The baron gave a start. "You were supposed to go through the gardens," Kravets said as he continued to pace. "What were you thinking?"

"The ballroom was a crush, sir," Elias replied. "Always is, from what I heard some people say. There was no way to get him past so many guests without drawing notice of his condition."

"What happened then?"

Elias rolled his eyes. "A footman helped me get him out the door. Gave me a hat..." He paused, a grimace forming when he wondered if the hat had indeed been the earl's. "So I put that on him," he explained. A wince crossed his face when he realized his final departure from the manor house by way of the gardens meant his own hat was still at Weatherstone Manor. He would have to make a trip back to Park Lane to retrieve it. "Once we were out of doors, I turned him over to the two you hired to watch for us. They held him in the dark next to some bushes until I got back to the front door. Before I stepped back into the house, I saw 'em put Wilmington into the coach. By then, he was completely out, sir."

Kravets stomped a booted foot on the Turkish carpet, which had Elias jerking in response. "Well, he wasn't *in* the coach that arrived here at eleven o'clock now, was he?"

Sighing, Elias rubbed a hand over one side of his face. He didn't know if Wilmington was or wasn't in the coach. He had still been in the ballroom at Weatherstone Manor at that time. "I don't see how he could have regained consciousness and escaped the coach, sir, which means..." His eyes widened and he swallowed. "They must have put him in the wrong coach," he whispered.

Kravets jerked back as if he'd been punched in the jaw. "What the hell did you say?"

Elias swallowed again. "Well, there were a whole line of carriages pulled up along Park Lane this evening," he said. "Most of them bearing their owners' coat of arms. They must have misread the Kravets family crest and put him into the wrong coach."

Kravets brows had furrowed into one long graying brow, and beneath it, his eyes blazed with fury. "Idiots," he hissed. "Did you see the driver?"

"Sir?"

"The driver of the coach you saw them putting him into... did you see the driver?"

Furrowing his brows, Elias struggled to remember everything he could about the coach. About the horses.

Although it was a fairly dark night—he didn't recall seeing the moon—there had been a string of Japanese lanterns lining the pavement up to the manor. The light they gave off didn't do much to illuminate the space beyond the pavers. The scent of rain had hung in the air due to the low layer of gray clouds that were slowly clearing to reveal a sky full of stars, so everything not lit by the lanterns had appeared in shades of black and gray.

"There was no driver on the bench, sir," Elias murmured. "The four horses were all black... or a very dark gray," he added. "The crest was in gold, but it was too far away for me to make out the details."

"Shite," Kravets cursed. "My driver was specifically told not to leave his post and to be ready to depart no later than half-past-ten."

"I had Wilmington out there at quarter past the hour. I know because I checked my chronometer when I returned to the ballroom, and it wasn't even half-past," Elias explained. He grimaced before asking, "Was *anyone* in the coach, sir?"

Kravets' face once again reddened with rage. "Of course not."

Elias scoffed. "Your driver didn't check to see that he had a passenger before he left?"

"He was told not leave his post. Not even to take a piss," Kravets countered. He inhaled as his gaze went to the coffered ceiling. "Coach-and-four, black horses, no driver," he murmured. "With a crest similar to mine."

Unfamiliar with most of the crests of the aristocratic families, Elias knew he would be of no help in identifying the coach holding Jack Kirkpatrick, Earl of Wilmington. "I rather doubt the earl will regain consciousness before the morning," he said.

"Which means someone will have discovered him in their coach. Surely they raised an alarm," Kravets said, his eyes widening. "The

Weatherstone footmen will be the first to know." He pulled out his chronometer and checked the time. "It's barely two. If you leave now, you can be there before most of the guests have even departed," he said with some excitement. "The orchestra is probably still playing, and the card room will be occupied until the sun comes up."

"Yes, sir," Elias replied. "Should I go in your coach?"

Kravets sighed. "It's parked out front. Renner knew enough not to put it away for the night," he said, referring to his driver. The poor man had looked as if he might die of fright when his master had cursed and kicked the coach wheel upon discovering there was no passenger inside.

"Very good, sir," Elias replied. He gave a slight bow and hurried out of Kravets' office, relieved to be out of the baron's sight.

CHAPTER THREE
AN EXCHANGE OF HATS

MEANWHILE, IN PARK LANE

Determined to do his part to discover what might have happened to Lord Wilmington, Parker had the Castlewait coach-and-four speeding down Park Lane faster than he had ever driven in his life. He thrilled at the sensation of air blowing over his face, and he knew the horses were enjoying the opportunity to run for a few minutes.

Expecting to find the street nearly deserted in front of the Weatherstone Manor, Parker was surprised to discover nearly a dozen coaches still lined up. The first ball of the Season had not only attracted a large number of guests for the ball, but those who enjoyed playing cards.

Parking the equipage at the end of the line of coaches, he retrieved the top hat from inside the coach—he had placed it on a bench in the event of rain—and made his way to the front door.

As a servant, he was used to having to enter houses at a back door. Given his assignment, he felt it necessary to use the front, and was relieved when a couple exited only a moment before he would have used the brass knocker. He stepped in, giving a nod to an ancient butler who was helping another gentleman into a coat.

Noticing several footmen guarding shelves of hats and hooks containing all manner of outerwear, he approached the first one who nodded to him.

"Good evening. It seems his lordship was given the wrong hat when he took his leave earlier." He offered the beaver to the footman. "He wondered if his might still be here. A bit taller, black, and made by *Fitzsimmons and Smith*," he added.

The footman's eyes rounded at the mention of the hat maker in Oxford Street. "Ah, the hat that makes the gentleman," the servant said, quoting the hat maker's motto. He took the errant hat and placed it on a table while he checked under the hats of those that were lined up on a shelf. "Your master is in luck, if this is it," he said as he brought the hat to Parker. "It's the only one with an F and S label," he added.

With no other means of identifying the hat, Parker gave the footman a nod. "I'm sure this must be it. You'll see to it the rightful owner gets the other one?"

"Of course... if he hasn't already left. He's probably in the card parlor. Since the orchestra stopped playing a few minutes ago, most of the guests have taken their leave."

Parker nodded his understanding but paused. He was tempted to mention the issue of Lord Wilmington, but instead said, "Tell me... did you happen to see a man escorting another out the door? He might have appeared... drunk?"

The taller man scoffed. "Had a few of those this evening," he said with a grin. "But it was odd when the first one happened so early."

"Oh?" Parker responded. Interested to learn more, he leaned in closer. "Do you happen to remember when that might have happened?"

"Oh, mayhap ten o'clock? The receiving line had broken up by then, of course," the footman replied. "Can't say I recognized either of the gents, though." His eyes rounded. "But I remember only one of them had a hat when they went out the door." He winced. "I would have gone after them, but I'm not allowed to leave my post."

"I understand," Parker replied, disappointed he couldn't provide more information.

"It's been a night of excitement, I must say," the footman remarked.

Parker furrowed a brow. "Oh? Something besides drunkards having to be escorted out?"

"Aye. Lord JW was caught kissing a young lady behind a hedgerow," the footman whispered. "Ever since he returned from his Grand Tour, the rake's been having 'is way with the chits at every entertainment."

His eyes rounding at hearing this bit of news, Parker was about to ask if the footman knew the identity of Lord JW, but a marquess stepped up to request his hat and coat. Parker handed over the coins Lord Wilmington had given him. "For your trouble," he said.

"Thank you," the footman replied, an appreciative expression appeared on his long face. "G'night."

Noting the butler was no longer near the front door, Parker tucked the top hat under one arm and let himself out. He was deep in thought when he nearly collided with another gentleman. "Pardon, sir," he said as he stepped aside.

He was about to continue on the Japanese lantern-lined path when he realized the man wore no hat. Despite a second glance, he didn't recognize the gentleman and hurried on his way to the Castlewait coach. Disappointment settled over him at not learning the identity of whoever had removed Lord Wilmington from the ball.

At least he had secured the earl's hat.

CHAPTER FOUR
A MYSTERY DEEPENS

MEANWHILE, BACK AT MARCH HOUSE

T he butler, Bentley, had the dark green front door opened before Persephone and Jack stepped up to it.

"There's been an incident this evening, Bentley," Persephone stated as she sailed into the hall and turned to allow the servant to help her with her mantle. "Someone attempted to abduct Lord Wilmington from the ball this evening, but they put him into the wrong coach," she said, her words the first to describe what she had come to realize was the only explanation for what had happened that evening. "Is the master suite ready for a guest? His lordship is in need of quarters for the night."

Bentley's usual bored expression was replaced with one of alarm. "It is, of course, my lady. Should I send Carlisle to fetch a constable? Or... or a Bow Street Runner?"

Jack exchanged a quick glance with Persephone and shook his head. "That won't be necessary, although I may see to it myself in the morning," he murmured.

"Will you require a valet, sir?"

Once again, Jack shook his head and then winced at having made his headache worse. "I can dress myself, but I really could use a glass of water," he said.

"I'll bring up a pitcher and a glass to the bedchamber right away," Bentley replied.

"I can escort you to your room," Persephone offered before she turned her attention back to Bentley. "No one outside of this household can know Lord Wilmington is here," she stated firmly. "Do I make myself clear? And tell Cooper I won't be needing her this evening," she added, referring to her lady's maid.

His brows rising nearly to his hairline, Bentley swallowed. "Of course, my lady. I shan't tell anyone he's here."

Persephone hooked her arm into Jack's and led him to the staircase set off to one side of the hall. She was aware of his attention on her and sensed he wished to speak, but she didn't say anything until they were at the top of the stairs. "What is it?" she asked in a whisper.

"I don't recall seeing *you* at the ball tonight," he said as they moved to climb the flight of stairs to the second floor. "I'm sure I would remember, given your gown," he added. "You always look stunning in blue."

Glancing down at her sapphire blue ballgown, Persephone huffed. "It would have been far more memorable if it had been the only one of its style and color," she groused. "I saw similar gowns on at least three other ladies tonight," she complained. "I was rather late with my arrival, though. Ten o'clock or shortly thereafter."

"Oh?" he replied. "What kept you?"

"I despise having to go through a receiving line, and Lord and Lady Weatherstone must be the last aristocrats who insist on greeting their guests before they're announced at the top of the stairs," she complained. "I had hoped to avoid it—"

"Why?" he asked. They were stopped in front of a door near the end of a corridor.

"I had no one to escort me this evening," she stated before she turned the door handle and pushed the dark wood panel open to reveal the master bedchamber. She moved to an ebony dresser and opened the top drawer. "Once I'm in the ballroom, I'm fine. It's always such a crush... but they were still greeting guests when I arrived. I had the unenviable honor of being the last one in line." She pulled a night-shirt from the drawer and shook it out before her eyes rounded.

"What is it?" Jack asked as he noticed her alarm. He glanced around the room, expecting to find something wrong. The bedchamber seemed in perfect order, though, and the stale odor of disuse wasn't evident in the air.

"Do you remember if the receiving line was still in place when you were taken from the house?" she asked, her attention still on her mind's eye as she absently handed him the nightshirt.

Not expecting the query, Jack scoffed. "I don't think my... my *abductor* would have used that route if they..." He clamped his mouth shut.

"What?" she asked as she reached up to undo the knot in his cravat.

"The receiving line couldn't have been there because I remember seeing Weatherstone in the ballroom. When I went to get a drink," he murmured. "That means the receiving line had broken up before... before I was drugged."

"Do you remember going up the stairs?" she asked as she undid his topcoat buttons.

Bentley appeared at the door, which was still open. He carried a silver salver on which rested a pitcher of water and a crystal glass. "Your water, sir," he said as he set the tray on the dresser and poured a glass. He offered it to the earl. "I've taken the liberty of requesting hot washing water be brought up for you, but delivered to her ladyship's bathing chamber," he explained in a quiet voice, nodding his head in the direction of a door in the corner of the room.

"Thank you, Bentley," Jack replied before he downed the entire glass in a few gulps. He closed his eyes a few moments before taking a deep breath. "That's better," he whispered.

"Will there be anything else, my lady?" the butler asked, his attention on his mistress. He refilled the glass of water.

"I think that should do it," she replied. "I appreciate your discretion, and I rather doubt we'll be in need of your services before noon," she added quietly.

"Very good, my lady." Bentley took his leave, although he didn't shut the door.

Sensing Jack was going to ask about the room arrangements, Persephone said, "The mistress and master suites are connected by way of the bathing chamber..." she waved to the corner door, "...and the dressing room," she added as she pointed to a door adjacent to the main door. "If you have everything you need, I'll go to my room now," she said as she moved to the still-open door.

Jack reached out and gently hooked a hand into her elbow. When she turned, her eyes met his as she furrowed a brow. "I'll have everything you need if you join me," he said in a whisper. "I may not last long..." He let the sentence trail off before he sighed in frustration.

Persephone inhaled softly. "All right," she replied, her pulse accelerating at the thought of spending the night in bed with Jack. Even if they only held one another, it would be a welcome change from sleeping alone. "Lock your door. I'll be about a half-hour," she said. "You'll hear the footman when the water arrives."

"Thank you, Sephie," he replied, pulling her into his arms. He kissed her softly. Slowly. And when he finally pulled away, he left his forehead pressed to hers. "You would never believe how much I have wanted to do that."

A slow smile lifting the corners of her lips, Persephone whispered, "Perhaps you can endeavor to convince me in a half-hour?" Without waiting for a reply, she turned and left the bedchamber, pulling the door shut behind her.

CHAPTER FIVE
A FOOTMAN AND A HAT

E lias cursed under his breath as he rushed up to the Kravets' town coach. "Back to Weatherstone Manor," he called up to Renner. "And hurry."

The startled driver, who looked to be no older than seventeen, nodded. "Yes, sir."

Before Elias had a chance to shut the coach door and be seated, the equipage jerked into motion. He cursed again as he settled into the shabby leather squabs, his nose wrinkling when he smelled the odors of cheroot smoke and unwashed bodies. For at least the tenth time that evening, he regretted having agreed to be part of Abraham Kravets plan to avenge his daughter's honor.

Like most who read the gossip found in the pages of *The Tattler*, Kravets assumed the rake referred to as *Lord JW* was John "Jack" Kirkpatrick, Earl of Wilmington.

After reading the latest issue, which included an article describing a scandalous incident that took place during a *musicale* at Worthington House, Kravets was convinced his daughter, Honoria, had been ruined by one *Lord JW*. He had been sure there could be no other young lady matching the article's description but her.

As a means to see to it the earl was held responsible for his rakish behavior, Kravets set about planning his revenge—drug and abduct the man from an early Season entertainment, haul him to Kravets' townhouse, wake him up with a right cross to his jaw, and inform him he was to marry Honoria by special license the following day.

Kravets still hadn't decided if her dowry would be paid or not.

Honoria had yet to speak to her father. When he confronted her on the matter, she immediately turned into a watering pot and claimed she didn't know the man who ravaged her in an alcove at Worthington House. She didn't even deny the event had occurred.

Her mother and Kravets' baroness, Lady Margaret Kravets, was doing her best to claim that the young lady described in the news-sheet could not be her daughter since Honoria had been with her at the time of the so-called ruination and that they had not been in attendance at the *musicale*. "We weren't even invited," she told her husband.

As for those who had claimed to have seen the baroness at the *musicale*, she would tell them that Honoria wasn't with her that evening but had stayed home complaining of a megrim.

Kravets wasn't convinced.

Sure Honoria was protecting the identity of her lover, he called on new friend and business partner Elias Turnbridge to help with his plan.

Not expecting the baron to concoct such an elaborate scheme involving a drugging and an abduction, Elias had agreed to go along with whatever Kravets planned. He only meant to appease the man because they were business partners. He feared the baron might pull out funding for his latest venture and force him to have to line up another investor.

Now he wished he had left town with the excuse that he had business in the country.

When the Kravets coach stuttered to a halt down the street from

Weatherstone Manor, Elias was relieved to see a number of coaches still lined up along Park Lane. Stepping out of the equipage, he paused to examine the baron's coat of arms on the door.

At first glance, he thought it looked like any other coat of arms. It was painted in gold. There was a shield. There were supporters. There was a crest. And across the bottom was a motto in Latin on an open-scroll banner.

He studied the details more closely before making his way to the next parked coach. He nearly stopped when he saw that the crest on its door had the motto at the top. The supporters were a pair of dragons.

When he passed the next coach, he lingered for a moment, pretending to adjust his cravat in the reflection from the coach window. That coat of arms had dogs as supporters and the motto was at the bottom.

Coming upon the lanterns leading to the front door of Weatherstone Manor, Elias nearly bumped into a man who had just left the residence.

"Pardon, sir," the younger man said, the style of his caped coat and top hat that of a driver. He seemed to stutter-step and do a double-take before continuing on his way to a coach parked farther down Park Lane.

Curious at the driver's odd behavior, Elias lifted a hand to remove his hat and was reminded that he wore no hat.

No wonder the driver had given him such an odd look!

Elias hurried into the house and immediately came to a halt when he recognized his hat among the half-dozen a footman was rearranging on a shelf. When another footman turned from giving a coat to a departing guest, he said, "Yes, sir?"

"I'm here to collect my hat," Elias said.

"Of course, sir. Must have been some game going on in the card parlor this evening."

Relieved the footman hadn't seen him come in by way of the front door, Elias merely shrugged. "No more than usual," he replied. "Tell me... have there been any reports of someone being found in the wrong coach this evening?"

"Sir?"

"Any... guests... making a fuss out front?" he hedged.

Pulling his head back so his chin doubled, the rather tall servant seemed to think on it a moment before he glanced about and then leaned in closer.

"A young lady was caught being kissed by that Lord JW behind a hedgerow in the gardens out back, but I haven't heard about anything amiss out front," he said in a quiet voice.

Elias gave a start. "Lord JW?" he repeated in a whisper. "When... when was this?"

"Oh, it's been hours ago, sir. Probably around midnight, if not before." His eyes suddenly widened. "It was definitely 'afore midnight. Supper hadn't yet been served." The servant grinned, apparently pleased with his powers of deduction.

Elias furrowed his brows. Given the amount of sleeping powder he had dumped into Lord Wilmington's punch, he was sure the man could not have awakened, made his way out of a coach and into the house, descended the stairs to the ballroom, flirted with a young lady, and escorted her to the Weatherstone gardens for a tryst—despite his reputation as a rake.

Besides, Elias had been standing near the open French doors to the garden for nearly an hour after he put Wilmington into the coach. With the number of guests in the ballroom—the Weatherstone ball was always a crush—he needed the fresh air. Surely he would have seen Wilmington if the earl had exited by way of the French doors.

"You mentioned you were here to claim your hat, sir?" the footman prompted.

Pulled from his reverie, Elias nodded. "That one right there on the end," he said as nodded to his beaver.

The footman blinked. "Oy. If you had come any sooner, it wouldn't have been here for you, sir."

Elias frowned. "Whatever do you mean?"

Aware he might be speaking ill of one of his fellow footmen, the servant lowered his voice and said, "It was mistakenly given to another gentleman, sir, but it's been returned and exchanged for the correct one." He lifted the hat between two sets of fingers and held it out to Elias. "It doesn't appear to have suffered, sir. You'll want to check the label just to be sure it is yours."

Turning the hat over, Elias confirmed it was the beaver he had purchased in New Bond Street only the week before. "When was it returned?" he asked. "And by whom?"

The footman had already begun searching for another guest's coat but said, "Only a moment ago, sir. By a driver. Don't know his name, though."

Elias inhaled sharply. "Do you know whose driver?"

Appearing to think on it for a moment, the footman shook his head. "Can't say as I've ever seen 'im 'afore."

Tossing the footman a coin, Elias rushed out of the house in search of the driver he had passed on his way into the house.

CHAPTER SIX
A FORMER SPY CONFESSES MUCH

MEANWHILE, AT THE CASTLEWAIT TOWNHOUSE

J ack regarded the nightshirt Persephone had given him with a wince. He rarely wore one to bed now that he was back in London. These days, he didn't have to spend his nights half-dressed and be ready to move on a moment's notice.

When he was assigned to a small unit of agents in the Kingdom of the Netherlands, he had grown used to settling on an uncomfortable cot or on the ground, rarely able to enjoy a full night of sleep. As an aristocrat and an officer in the military, he would have been provided a private tent and a clerk or two to see to it he wasn't disturbed.

As a spy, he didn't have that luxury.

For the past two decades, he had thrilled at carrying out the clandestine assignments. Excitement at receiving new orders had him looking forward to donning disguises and traveling incognito. Intercepting enemy orders and decoding their messages had provided a daily dose of adrenaline and provided him a sense of purpose his position as Earl of Wilmington couldn't begin to match.

Now... now he was glad to have his days of deception behind him.

Only a month ago, his last assignment in Belgium had resulted in what the Foreign Office was sure would be a turning point in the war against Napoleon and the French.

Although he had suffered a slight wound from a bayonet, he was otherwise undamaged. Despite assurances he could continue his work on the Continent, he received orders claiming his cover was blown and that his services would no longer be required by the Crown.

He had returned to British shores dressed as a commoner. Arrived at his apartment in the Albany finding it much the way he had left it. Resumed life as an aristocrat. Discovered he hadn't been missed.

He hadn't been missed because either someone had taken to pretending to be him, or he was a victim of mistaken identity.

His reputation as a rake, one he hadn't suffered since before he had inherited the earldom nearly twenty years ago, had returned thanks to someone who had his initials.

Lord JW.

Through no fault of his own, he was suddenly back in the gossip pages. Rumors claimed he was deflowering virgins and having his way with young widows despite his absence from Society. Given he hadn't been with a woman since his return to England, he couldn't decide whether he was amused or annoyed by the situation.

Well, after what had happened tonight, he certainly wasn't amused.

Tossing his coats and shirt onto the back of a chair before removing his shoes and stockings, he headed into the bathing chamber. A candle lamp provided more than enough light to see by given the size of the mirror over a dressing table. Another mirror hung over a console on which a ceramic bowl and a pitcher sat. Steam poured forth from the pitcher as he emptied its contents into the bowl. He helped himself to a linen cloth and doused it in the water. Sighing with satisfaction as he washed his face and chest, Jack was about to help himself to a bath linen when he realized he wasn't alone.

He stepped to the side to discover Persephone's reflection in the mirror.

"I apologize. I didn't mean to interrupt," she said in a quiet voice.

Jack couldn't help his body's reaction to seeing her again, especially given her mode of dress. She wore only a thin silk wrapper tied at the waist, the fabric doing nothing to hide the swell of her breasts or hips nor the dark triangle at the apex of her thighs.

"You're not interrupting," he murmured. He rubbed the linen over his face and chest, well aware her gaze had settled on the once-black hair that covered most of his chest. The graying, crisp curls tapered to a thin line of dark hair that disappeared behind the top of his black breeches. "You're a very welcome sight, in fact."

Persephone approached him, one hand landing on his chest as she lifted her face to his. Their kiss was quick but thorough, and when she pulled away to allow her gaze to sweep over the rest of his body, she winced. "What happened here?" she asked in alarm, her finger darting to where the bayonet had glanced off a rib.

"A frog got me," he replied. "Before I could kill him."

From her immediate reaction, Jack knew she had jumped to the wrong conclusion. "I did a stint on the Continent. I've only been back in England a few weeks."

Persephone furrowed a brow. "How... how is that possible?" she asked in a whisper.

He kissed her forehead and led her into the master suite. The bed linens had been turned down, the expanse of white an overt invitation. "Tell me, when is the last time you remember actually *seeing* me here in London?" he asked, his own memory of a night he attended the theatre with his mother while Persephone had been escorted by her husband.

Her brows furrowing, Persephone looked as if she was about to respond and then scoffed. "I suppose it was that night at the theatre. About a week before... before Castlewait died," she stammered. "You were escorting Countess Wilmington, as I recall."

"I had already received orders to go to the Continent," he said as he turned down the flame on the room's only candle lamp. "I left England two days later."

Persephone inhaled softly. "I didn't know you were in the army," she said as she sat on the edge of the bed.

"I wasn't," he stated. He had moved to the darkest corner of the room while he undid the fastenings at the top of his breeches. Pushing them down along with his smalls, he stepped out of the garments, well aware Persephone watched in fascination.

She'd had the very same expression on her face the first time she had watched him undress. One of awe mixed with embarrassment and mayhap a dose of fright.

"Navy?" she guessed as her gaze followed his movements. He bent to lift his breeches from the floor before draping them over a chair and then made his way to the bed. His manhood, only partially erect, jutted out from a nest of dark curls.

"I wasn't in the military," he said as he lifted a hip onto the edge of the bed. He lay down and stretched as he inhaled deeply. A chuckle erupted as he pulled the bed linens up and over his naked body.

"What is it?" she asked as she moved to join him.

"This bed is more comfortable than anything I've slept in for a very long time," he said in a quiet voice. He slipped an arm beneath her shoulders and pulled her so she was half atop him. The wrapper still hid most of her from his view, but at that moment, he was glad she wasn't naked. He needed to think. Needed her to remember.

"I don't think I've ever slept in this bed," she murmured.

He grunted. "Castlewait didn't share this bed with you?" he asked in surprise.

"He always came to mine," she replied.

"Was he good to you?"

Persephone gave a start, surprised by the query. "He wasn't a bad man. Not at all," she said in a whisper. "If he ever took a mistress, I never learned of it. He was a good father, too."

Jack jerked. "Where *are* the boys? You had... you had two, didn't you?"

"They're away at university, and my daughter is spending this Season with her grandmother in Kent," she explained as she waited for his reaction.

"You have a daughter?" he asked with a grin, wondering how he had missed learning about her.

"She'll start finishing school this autumn," Persephone said on a sigh.

"Who's seeing to the earldom?"

Persephone hesitated before saying, "I am, along with a man of business. At least until Robert is finished with university," she said, referring to her oldest son, the new Earl of Castlewait.

"You're probably doing a better job of it than he did," Jack murmured.

Furrowing a brow, Persephone sighed. "It's given me something to keep my mind occupied this past year," she admitted. "And it's really no more difficult than running the household."

Jack scoffed—he had worked in service to the Crown in order to avoid running his own earldom. Between a man of business and his solicitor and regular reports on the matter, he had to trust that the Wilmington earldom was in good stead.

"What about you?" Persephone asked. "I never heard if you married... and if you weren't in the military, what were you doing on the Continent during a war?"

Jack considered her queries and decided to answer them in order.

"Still haven't married," he replied sleepily. "Because you were the one that got away," he added before he kissed the top of her head. "As for war, I worked for Chamberlain," he murmured, referring to the head of the Foreign Office. "For Crown and country and all that rot," he added.

As he expected, Persephone lifted her head from his chest to gasp. "You were a... you were *a spy?*" The last two words were barely audible.

Her eyes suddenly rounded. "Do you suppose that has something to do with how you ended up in my coach this evening?"

His gaze darted to the dark fabric of the canopy above the bed. For some reason, her shock at learning he had worked for the Foreign Office had him amused. "I was." He considered her other comment. "I rather doubt my ending up in your coach has anything to do with my assignments in the Kingdom of the Netherlands, though," he murmured. He paused before he asked, "Who the hell is Lord JW?"

Still holding herself up on one elbow, Persephone ignored the curse as she stared down at Jack. She shook her head. "You mean... you're not?"

He rolled his eyes and winced when it caused his headache to worsen. "I am not. I mean, I am a 'Lord JW,' but I am not *the* Lord JW *The Tattler* has been writing about," he claimed.

Her gaze drifted down the counterpane as Persephone considered his words. "You're right," she murmured. "If you were on the Continent until a few weeks ago..."

"I was. When did these mentions of a 'Lord JW' start?"

"It's been a few months now, I think," she said, her attention still on her mind's eye.

"What was the most damning?"

Persephone blinked. "Well, there was one where he allegedly climbed into a coach whilst it was stopped at an intersection and had his way with a young lady."

"He raped her?" he asked in alarm.

"No. According to the young lady's maid, the dalliance had all been arranged in advance," she replied as she displayed an expression of amusement.

"Well, who was the man?"

"The young lady wouldn't say, and neither would the lady's maid."

Jack scoffed. "What else?"

"The Kravets girl. I don't recall her first name, but she and her mother, the Baroness Kravets, were supposedly attending Lady

Worthington's *musicale*, and the girl and Lord JW were discovered kissing in an alcove."

Although the incident didn't sound too damning, Jack realized kissing a young, unmarried lady could land a man in hot water. "When was this?" he asked.

"About a fortnight ago. I was actually in attendance that evening," Persephone said with some excitement. "It was my first time attending a Society event since coming out of widow's weeds," she added with a grin.

"Did you see anything? Hear anything?"

About to respond, she clamped her mouth shut. "No," she finally admitted. "I don't even recall seeing the baroness there, which has me wondering why *The Tattler* would even make mention of her."

"They printed her name?" he asked in surprise.

"Well, no. Not exactly. They always just use a peer's initials, but in this case, 'Baroness K' had to be Agnes Kravets. There's no other baroness with a last name beginning with a K," she explained.

Jack furrowed a brow. "And the daughter?"

"Lady Kravets only has the one," Persephone replied.

Jack blew out a breath in frustration. "What else?"

"There have been some young widows—"

"You?" he asked, jerking as if he intended to sit up.

"I said *young* widows," Persephone repeated as she pressed a hand against his chest to force him to lie down.

"You're still young," he argued.

She scoffed, but another grin touched her lips. "It's times like this I really wish you had challenged Castlewait for my hand," she whispered.

A grimace crossed his face. "As do I," he admitted.

He liked hearing her slight inhalation of breath. The way her blue eyes rounded whenever he surprised her. His eyes closed as he felt sleep coming on, but he still had things he needed to say to her. "Over the years, I've been very good at my avocation," he said in a fading whisper. "But I've been a terrible aristocrat. Oh, I've attended Parliament when I can, but I don't have a wife, which means I don't have an heir, which means..." His voice trailed off as his body relaxed into the bed.

Persephone watched as he fell asleep. Although she felt the weariness of a long day, her body was well aware a naked man was pressed against her. At some point, he would awaken and he would see to providing satiation for her swollen breasts and throbbing core.

Her racing mind was another matter, though.

If Lord JW wasn't Jack, Earl of Wilmington, then who the hell was he?

CHAPTER SEVEN
A HAT MAKES A MAN

EARLIER, IN FRONT OF WEATHERSTONE MANOR

About to step up to the driver's seat of the Castlewait coach, an idea had Parker pausing. If he waited for a few minutes, he might a learn the identity of the hatless man he had passed.

He placed the Earl of Wilmington's hat into the coach and made his way down the line of carriages, calling out greetings to other drivers as he took note of the gold crests on their coach doors. He recognized several as belonging to aristocrats who apparently preferred to play cards over dancing. It might be dawn before their owners took their leave of Weatherstone Manor.

"You still stargazing?" one of the older drivers chided.

"Always," he replied, giving the driver of the Marquess of Reading's coach a wave before he strolled on.

From the way the horses in front of the last coach were breathing and stomping, he knew the equipage had delivered the hatless man. He glanced up at the driver. "Haven't see you 'afore," he said. "Name's Parker."

"Thomas," the young man replied, his expression sullen.

"Your lordship still in the card parlor?" he asked, glancing back toward the house to be sure the hatless man hadn't yet emerged.

Thomas scoffed. "I wish," he replied on a huff. "Then I'd be in me bed for the night."

"What do you mean?" Parker asked.

"The baron didn't even attend the ball, but his business associate did. Left his hat behind," the young driver remarked with a scoff. "Thought I was going to lose me job."

"Over a hat?" Parker asked as he pretended to study one of the horses.

"Over the coach not having anyone in it," Thomas replied. Younger than most drivers, he displayed cheeks pocked with acne, and his top hat looked to be too large for his head.

Parker gave a start. "Who's your employer?"

"Kravets," the young driver answered, saying the name as if it were a curse. "I left exactly when I was supposed to," he added, holding up a chronometer. "Can't help it if some gent missed his ride to the baron's house."

Confused, Parker said, "If Lord Kravets didn't attend the ball, and your other fare missed his ride..." He paused as it dawned on him exactly what the boy meant. "Then whose hat have you come back for?"

"Mine," another voice said from behind him.

Parker whirled around to discover the hatless man from earlier approaching the coach. The short top hat Parker had returned only a few minutes before was on his head, and an expression of recognition was apparent on his face.

"You," Elias Turnbridge said as he stopped in front of Parker.

"Me, sir?" Parker replied, pretending ignorance.

"Did you... did you just return a hat to the Weatherstone house a few minutes ago?" Elias pointed to the top hat on his head. "This one?"

Parker exchanged a quick glance with Thomas. "And what if I did?"

Momentarily speechless, Elias sighed. "Well, I would wish to thank you and ask who might have ended up with it by accident," he explained, attempting to sound reasonable. "So I could send a note of thanks," he added. "I thought it lost, you see."

Not recognizing the gentleman as someone he had seen attending Society events in the past, Parker furrowed a brow. He didn't want to tell the man he had been sent by his mistress, nor did he want to say anything about Lord Wilmington. "Well, truth be told, sir, I found it out here. On the pavement," he said. "I like to stargaze, you see, and I nearly kicked it given the dark. I hope it's not ruined, sir."

His face falling at hearing Parker's response, Elias merely shook his head. "It's fine," he said. He sighed again. Loudly.

"What is it, sir? What's wrong?" Parker asked.

"I've lost a man," Elias stated, rolling his eyes as he realized he had no news to share with Lord Kravets. The baron would be livid when he told him he didn't know the whereabouts of Lord Wilmington.

"Sir?" Parker said, his eyes rounding in pretend shock.

Elias gave his head a shake. "My friend was terribly drunk, and in my haste to get him out of the house and into the coach, I apparently put him in the wrong coach." He glanced up at Thomas, who just then realized he was supposed to get down and open the coach door for the gentleman. "I'm surprised someone hasn't reported a stowaway," Elias added as his brows furrowed. He glanced down the line of coaches. "Unless..."

The young man jumped to the pavement next to Parker. "Sorry, sir, about all of it." He moved to open the door.

Elias held up a gloved hand to the young driver. "Start checking inside these coaches," he ordered. "My drunk friend may be in one of them." Although his expression conveyed finding the missing gentleman was still possible, Elias had already given up hope. After what the footman had said about Lord JW kissing a young lady behind a hedgerow in the gardens, he was fairly sure Lord JW and Lord Wilmington were two different people.

Parker exchanged a glance with the younger driver, immediately aware that Elias would not find the drunk friend in any of them. "I should get back to her ladyship's coach," Parker said as he gave the gentleman a slight bow. Although he desperately wanted to return to the Castlewait townhouse with the information he had learned, he knew he couldn't leave directly. Both the young driver and his passenger believed he was merely waiting on his mistress. "But I can help your driver look if you'd like."

"Your help would be most welcome," Elias stated.

"We can see to this, sir," Thomas said.

"All right," Elias replied. He climbed into the coach as Thomas and Parker made their way to the next coach in line.

Parker called up to Lord Reading's driver. "Any chance you have a stowaway in your coach?"

The older driver scoffed. "Not a chance. Been sitting here all night," he replied. "But you can look if you must."

Thomas opened the door and peeked in, whistling his appreciation at seeing the interior of the marquess' coach. He closed the door and they moved on to the next in line.

"This gent that was drunk... who was he?" Parker asked as they made their way.

Pausing, Thomas shrugged. "Near as I can tell, some bloke who's friends with Mr. Turnbridge."

"Turnbridge is that gentleman back there?"

Thomas nodded. "What I can't sort is how he knew the man was going to be drunk and exactly when," he remarked as they looked into the next coach. He shut the door. "I was just told to drive to the baron's house no later than half-past-ten. So I did."

"Was Mr. Turnbridge in the coach at the time?"

Stopping to consider the query, Thomas frowned. "No, he wasn't."

"Well, didn't you just bring him here from the baron's house?" Parker asked, now confused.

"I did."

"Well, how did he get to the baron's house if he wasn't in the coach when you left at half-past-ten?"

Thomas waved a gloved hand. "Oh, he didn't get to the baron's house until much later," he replied. "Arrived in a hackney mayhap an hour ago."

Parker gave a start. Turnbridge had apparently been instructed to send his drunk friend in Lord Kravets' coach and then remain at the ball. "So... when you arrived at the baron's house with the empty coach, what happened exactly?"

Thomas threw up his hands in despair. "When Lord Kravets opened the door and discovered the coach was empty, he was fit to be tied. Kept asking me where Lord Waterford...Waddleston..."

"Wilmington?" Parker offered.

"Yeah, Wilmington. He was supposed to be drunk, in the coach."

Parker grimaced. "Any idea why?" he asked before he called up to the next driver. "Can we look inside your coach? Like to see how the rich folk ride."

The driver looked up from a book he was reading by the light of a coach lantern. "Fine by me."

"Accordin' to the servants, his lordship thinks his daughter was ruint by Lord Wilmington, so he's going to make 'im marry her," Thomas said as he opened the coach door. The scent of floral perfume spilled out, which had Thomas coughing and Parker sniffing in delight.

"Well, I can tell you, it wasn't Lord Wilmington doing the ruining of Lord Kravets' daughter," Parker remarked dryly. "He's a right proper gentleman."

Thomas gave a start. "Well, if it weren't 'im, who was it?"

Parker furrowed his brows as he shut the coach door. "Well, now that's the question, isn't it?"

When the last coach—Lady Castlewait's coach—proved empty, Parker gave a shrug. "I guess Lord Kravets won't be getting a drunk Lord Wilmington on this night," he murmured.

Thomas nodded, but his attention was on the gold crest on the Castlewait coach door.

"What is it?" Parker asked, following the younger driver's line of sight.

"Looks a lot like the baron's crest is all," he said with a shrug.

Parker did his best to display a passive expression. "A little, I suppose," he replied, stunned by the similarity. Only the motto was different. "Well, you have a good night."

"Thanks for the help," Thomas replied. "I'll be getting Mr. Turnbridge home now."

"Good to meet you. I'm sure we'll see one another at future entertainments," Parker said.

He watched as the young man hurried back along the line of coaches, losing sight of him when he climbed onto the driver's seat.

As anxious as he was to drive to the Castlewait townhouse to return Lord Wilmington's top hap and tell her ladyship what he had discovered, Parker knew he would have to remain in front of the manor until long after the Kravets coach departed.

CHAPTER EIGHT
A LADY DOES HER RESEARCH

MEANWHILE, BACK AT THE CASTLEWAIT TOWNHOUSE

S ure Jack was sound asleep, Persephone slipped from beneath the covers and made her way back to the mistress suite. The initials 'JW' had already brought to mind images of three aristocrats, but they were all far too old to be engaging young ladies in dark deeds in dark alcoves. Determined to learn who else might be 'Lord JW,' she pulled the counterpane from her bed, wrapped it about her shoulders, and crept out of the mistress suite and down the stairs to the library.

Turning up the flame on a candle lamp, she immediately went to the shelf containing a copy of *Debrett's Peerage and Baronetage*. Although it wasn't the most recent edition of the book of aristocrats and their families, it would do. After all, 'Lord JW' had to be of an age old enough to engage in salacious behavior.

Helping herself to a sheet of parchment, an ink pot, and a quill from her late husband's desk, she settled herself at the library table and began paging through the book. Since the initials JW could refer to a given name or to a first name and a title, she thought to start with the W's. Excitement gripped her when she discovered the first name was a candidate.

John Wainwright, Duke of Chichester.

She was about to write his name but remembered he had died in a fire. His son John had a reputation as a rake, but he, too, had died in the same fire. The younger son, Joshua, was now the duke, but he had suffered severe burns and had sequestered himself in the ducal estate in Sussex.

Persephone moved onto another page.

Wallingham, Weatherstone, Wentworth, Wessex, Whitney, Winthorpe, Wolverhampton... Not even halfway through the book, she was becoming discouraged when she noticed that the listing for the Whites included a John.

Lord John, son of the Duke of White. Too handsome for his own good, he already had a reputation as a flirt and a libertine from his days at university. From his date of birth, he would be two-and-twenty.

In the middle of writing his name on the parchment, Persephone gave a start when she heard the faint sounds of a coach pull into the mews behind the townhouse. *That will be Parker*, she thought. She put the stopper onto the ink pot, pulled the counterpane more tightly around her shoulders, and was about to make her way to the stairs when she collided with a body larger than hers.

She nearly let out a scream until she realized it was Jack who had wrapped his arms around her.

"Apologies, my sweet," he whispered hoarsely. "I didn't mean to frighten you."

Persephone inhaled softly. "I didn't mean to wake you," she said, relieved he had found a velvet robe to wear.

"You didn't. I think Parker has returned."

"He has," she affirmed. "He's been gone long enough that he must have discovered something. Are you feeling better?" she asked, raising a hand to press it against his forehead.

"Much. I think I just had to sleep it off." He gaze darted to the library. "Whatever have you been doing?" he asked. The candle lamp was still burning, so the room was partially illuminated.

"Looking for 'Lord JW's," she replied as she steered them to the stairs.

"And?"

"It's only a possibility, but Lord John—"

"White's spare heir?" he interrupted, nearly stopping on the stairs.

"Indeed. What do you know of him?"

"Handsome, rich, and a rake. He was born the day you gifted your virtue to me."

Persephone gasped. "You remember that?"

"Twenty-two years has not dulled my memory of our week together, Sephie," he whispered hoarsely as they descended the last flight of stairs.

Touched by his words, she was about to respond when Parker appeared and stopped short at the table near the base of the stairs.

"Pardon, my lady. I... I didn't mean to wake you," he said as he held out the top hat he carried to Jack. "Your hat, my lord."

"You found it!" Jack's expression conveyed stunned surprise. "Apologies, but I don't seem to have any coins on me at the moment," he added as he patted the sides of the velvet robe.

"Oh, it was my pleasure, sir. It's been a most interesting evening."

Persephone and Jack exchanged quick glances. "Oh?" she prompted.

"We may have discovered the identity of 'Lord JW'," Jack whispered. "Do you have news?"

"Indeed," Parker said. "And I have names."

About to encourage him to continue, Persephone was prevented from doing so when Jack glanced around and lifted a finger.

"Might we move this discussion to the study?" he suggested in a quiet voice. "It appears your servant has earned a drink. Could I pour a brandy for this young man?" He turned to Parker. "You must be chilled to the bone."

The servant's eyes widened. "I wouldn't turn it down, sir."

Remembering she wore only a silk robe beneath the counterpane wrapped around her shoulders, Persephone encouraged the men to precede her as they made their way to the study. Other than Bentley, no man had been in the study since Castlewait's death. She had certainly spent time in the room, though, for she had been seeing to the earldom's business for the past year.

She turned up a candle lamp but stayed in the shadows when Jack moved to the credenza behind the desk. As he saw to pouring brandy from a crystal decanter into tumblers, he said, "Tell us what you've discovered." He lifted a glass and gave it to Parker.

"Much obliged, sir," the driver said as he took the brandy. He sniffed it, his gaze darting to Persephone. "Is this all right with you, my lady?" he asked as he indicated the brandy, obviously nervous.

"Only if I'm given one as well," she replied, her attention on Jack.

He chuckled as he brought her a glass. He leaned over and dropped a kiss on her head, which had Persephone gasping softly. "Jack," she scolded.

Parker pretended not to notice the earl's overt show of affection. "I spoke with one of the footmen. He was most apologetic about the hat, sir," Parker began. He relayed what had happened with the hatless gentleman. "While he was inside retrieving his hat, I spoke with his driver. He told me the gent's name was Turnbridge. A business associate of Lord Kravets who was sent by the baron to see to it a drunk man was put into the Kravets coach and taken to the baron's town-house no later than half-past-ten."

Persephone straightened in her chair while Jack merely furrowed his brows. "Elias Turnbridge?" he asked after a moment.

"I couldn't say for sure, sir. He never mentioned a Christian name."

Persephone scoffed. "So why did Lord Wilmington end up in *my* coach?"

Parker winced. "The coat of arms on the door of your coach is similar to that of the Kravets crest," he replied. "And Mr. Turnbridge didn't actually put his lordship into the coach. Apparently the two commoners I noticed hanging about the bushes were lackeys of the baron. They were the ones who put you into her ladyship's coach," he explained as he turned to Jack.

The earl's attention was on Persephone, though. "You mentioned Kravets had a daughter who was caught kissing in an alcove at Worthington House," he prompted.

"Honoria," she said as she remembered the young lady's name. "According to *The Tattler*," she added. She took a sip of the brandy and closed her eyes as the warm liquid slid down her throat. "I suppose Kravets expected to kidnap you as a means to force a marriage to her."

"Did Kravets' driver suspect anything?" Jack asked, his attention on Parker.

"No, sir. I pretended her ladyship was still inside the Weatherstone house, and I even waited until they were well on their way before I returned here. To keep up the ruse."

"Good thinking. What about Turnbridge?"

Parker shrugged. "He seemed most concerned about what Baron Kravets would do to him. He fears him, I think. Said the baron would be livid if he returned without you."

"Who *is* this Turnbridge?" Persephone asked, sure she hadn't heard the name mentioned before.

"He's an inventor," Jack stated. "Always looking for someone to back his latest venture." He cursed under his breath. "He was with me at the punchbowl. Speaking to me about some sort of steam-powered invention. He was looking for investors. I pretended interest if only because I've been away from England so long, I wished to learn what I'd missed," he added with a shake of his head.

"He must have put a sleeping powder in your punch, sir," Parker said. "Which is why he has to be wondering how 'Lord JW' was able to ravage another young lady behind a hedgerow in the Weatherstone gardens later in the evening."

Jack and Persephone stared at the driver. "What's this?" Jack asked.

"When I was making conversation with the footman, he mentioned there had been an incident right before the midnight supper was announced. 'Lord JW' was caught kissing a young lady behind a hedgerow," he repeated. "Said he was a rake and that he'd been caught with a number of young ladies since his return from his Grand Tour, which means that 'Lord JW' has to be younger than you, sir." He paused a moment. "No offense, sir."

Throwing his head back, Jack guffawed. "I've a mind to take Lord John with me when I pay a call on Lord Kravets tomorrow," he said before he drained his brandy. "Maybe the duke, too."

"You're going to confront Kravets?" Persephone asked, stunned by his words.

"I am," he affirmed. "Might Mr. Parker be allowed to drive me in the afternoon? I rather imagine I'm going to be abed well past noon," he said as his eyes darted to the clock on the fireplace mantel.

"I'm going with you," Persephone announced.

Jack blinked before he regarded her with an assessing glance. "If you're sure," he said.

"Oh, I'm sure," she replied. "Mr. Parker, I shall see to it there's something extra in your pay this month."

"Why, thank you, my lady. I didn't mind doing it at all."

"Well, don't be getting any ideas about becoming a Bow Street Runner," Jack remarked. "This household can already boast a former spy."

Parker's eyes rounded. "Sir?"

Persephone inhaled softly, but she didn't say anything as Jack raised his empty glass to the driver. "I am retired and ready to resume my duties as an earl," he said before setting the glass on the salver behind the desk. "After I get a good night's sleep."

"Yes, sir," Parker said, doing the same with his glass. "My lady," he said as he bowed and made his way out of the study.

Persephone made no move to rise from her chair, deciding she should wait until Parker had made it down the corridor and up the servants' stairs to his quarters. "A good night's sleep?" she repeated softly.

Jack moved to stand before her and then bent to lift her from the chair. "Eventually," he whispered. He kissed her forehead and then wrapped his ams around her shoulders. "After I've done to you what I've been accused of doing to others these past few weeks."

Persephone glanced up at him, the heat at her core due to more than just the brandy. "I look forward to it," she whispered.

After several minutes of kissing, the two made their way up to the master suite.

CHAPTER NINE
A TRUTH IS UNWELCOME

MEANWHILE, AT THE KRAVETS TOWNHOUSE

Dreading his next conversation with Baron Kravets, Elias stepped down from the coach and gave Thomas a beseeching look. "I hate to keep you, but I should only be a moment," he called up to the driver.

Thomas tipped his hat. "I'll wait, sir."

Elias didn't expect a butler to open the door for him, so he was surprised when it did—he hadn't even crossed over the area when Lord Kravets appeared in the opening. "I see you found your hat," the barrel-chested baron groused.

"It was mistakenly given to another and had been returned only moments before I got there," Elias replied as he stepped into the vestibule.

"And Wilmington?"

"He's not 'Lord JW'."

Kravets, garbed in a thick, dark banyan drew his head back and scoffed. "He tell you that?"

Elias shook his head. "'Lord JW' was found kissing a young lady behind a hedgerow. Before the midnight supper was served," he said as they made their way into the study.

"That's impossible," Kravets replied. "If he drank even half of the sleeping powder you put in his glass of punch, there's no way he could have awakened before midnight," he added.

"Exactly," Elias stated. "He drank all of it." He waited a moment to allow Kravets to do his own reasoning before he said, "'Lord JW' is not Wilmington, sir. In fact, he's a young man. Described as being in his early twenties, at least according to the footman who relayed the information."

"That's... that cannot be," Kravets said as he shook his head.

"Why not? 'Lord JW' only ravishes young ladies and young widows."

Still not convinced, Kravets poured a glass of brandy and nearly downed it in one gulp. Still chilled from his late night foray to Weatherstone Manor, Elias was glad when the baron poured a glass for him, too. "Much obliged, sir." He savored the smoky aroma before he took a drink. His gaze settled on the amber liquid for a moment. "I had your driver check the other coaches that were still parked along Park Lane, just to be sure Lord Wilmington wasn't in any of them."

"Which means he went home with someone," Kravets groused. His eyes suddenly widened. "Will he remember *you* were the one who helped him out of the ballroom?" he asked.

Elias had been fearing the very same. Would the Earl of Wilmington remember their brief conversation as Elias handed him a glass of punch? He had seemed interested in learning more about his latest application for a steam engine—a sort of dog cart that would allow its user to push heavy crates around without the need for horses or muscle-bound laborers.

"He might," Elias hedged, "but if he should see me again, I'll do my best to avoid him, and if I cannot..." He allowed the sentence to trail off. "I'll say I noticed he didn't seem to be feeling well."

"Probably for the best," Kravets murmured. "Well, I don't know about you, but I'm going to bed."

Relieved to hear he was being dismissed, Elias set his empty glass on the edge of the desk. "Thank you for the brandy. I look forward to receiving your bank draft for the investment," he said before giving the baron a bow. He took his leave of the townhouse.

Thomas had stepped down from the driver's bench and stood next to the coach door, his attention on the crest.

"What's wrong?" Elias asked, pausing to follow the driver's gaze.

"Oy, nothing, sir. I was just thinking about how similar this crest is to the one on the coach of that driver we was talking to earlier."

Weary from the long night, Elias merely shrugged and climbed into the coach. When Thomas angled the coach to stop in front of the Albany, Elias was about to get out when the significance of the driver's words hit him.

He would have asked as to the identity of the other driver, but he decided he didn't want to know.

CHAPTER TEN

AN EARL CLAIMS HIS FUTURE COUNTESS

MEANWHILE, BACK AT THE CASTLEWAIT TOWNHOUSE

Anticipation. Excitement. Trepidation. Nervousness.

All of these and more had Persephone trembling when she and Jack were finally back in the master suite. She slid a hand along the collar of his velvet robe to push it from his shoulder, her palm barely touching his heated skin.

He inhaled sharply at her caress and lifted the hand from where it smoothed over the skin above his upper chest. "I apologize for having fallen asleep earlier. We were discussing important matters."

"It's all right," she whispered, using her free hand to push the robe from his other shoulder. She had expected they would already be on the bed. Wished he was atop her and doing to her what he had so masterfully done all those years ago. The pleasure he had imparted had been extraordinary. Intense and all-consuming. Intoxicating. "I'm rather surprised you could sound so coherent after what you suffered."

He kissed her lips and then her jaw. "I had more to say," he whispered. "I have more to say."

When one of his hands smoothed over a silk-covered breast to gently mold it, Persephone nearly jerked from his hold. "Could we maybe talk afterwards?"

Jack chuckled as he pulled back to regard her with an expression of curiosity. "You're trembling," he said, sobering.

"Of course I am. You have me..." Her hand slid down the front of his body until it reached the nest of curls above his turgid manhood. Her fingers slid around the base of his member and gently squeezed. The skin there felt as velvety as the robe that had fallen to his feet.

One of his hands briefly covered hers as he groaned his appreciation. "Aroused?" he guessed. His hand let go of hers, the palm sliding between her thighs to discover the curls were already damp. He used his middle finger to press against her swollen womanhood, jerking when she tightened her hold on him at the same moment she cried out.

If he didn't get her on the bed right now, they would end up on the floor.

"Come, my sweet," he whispered, pulling her hand from his member so he could lift her into his arms. He placed her on the bed and undid the bow that held her silk wrapper closed. Peeling the edges apart, he lowered his head to one breast and kissed its engorged nipple.

"I already have. Now it's your turn," she said, her hand once again reaching for his manhood.

He chuckled at her comment, finally climbing onto the bed so he hovered over her. "You do know that there will be repercussions?" he murmured before his mouth covered the other breast.

Persephone jerked as she moved her hands to the sides of his head, her thumbs at his temples. "Repercussions?" she repeated, giving a start when his teeth gently bit her nipple.

"Yes, my Sephie. You're going to marry me," he said before he moved his kisses down the front of her body and one hand between her thighs.

She inhaled sharply. "Why do make it sound so...? Oh!"

Jack chuckled into her belly, which had her squirming. "You're going to be my countess," he said before he had her knees spread wide and his mouth pressed against one thigh.

"You make it... sound so... so ominous," she responded between gasps for air. When his tongue touched her womanhood and circled it, she hummed as her head arched back into the pillow. Sure he was going to leave her on the precipice of a release she desperately needed unless she gave him an answer, she mewled and said, "It would be my honor."

He shoved his tongue inside her, the rough texture sending her over the edge of the precipice and into an ocean of pleasure waves. Although she didn't know where one began and another ended, Jack certainly seemed to. He was up and over her, burying his cock into her at the very moment another wave of pleasure crashed.

Persephone's knees gripped his thighs as he thrust into her over and over. When his body suddenly stilled and the cords of his neck appeared in relief as he lifted his head, she knew he had finally allowed his own release. Heat filled her lower body.

Knowing what to do to prolong his pleasure, she tightened her inner muscles so she gripped him harder. She slid a hand down the side of his body until her fingertips could reach his stiff sac to lift it. She hummed when he jerked in her hold and grinned when she heard his quiet curse before he finally, slowly, lowered himself to lay half atop her.

His head landed on the pillow between her neck and shoulder. "Damn, but I've missed you," he whispered before his body relaxed.

At first, Persephone was sure he had fallen asleep, so she was surprised when his lips captured her earlobe and gently nibbled it. She gave a start and then purred. "I've missed you as well."

They lay quietly for a few minutes, Persephone well aware when his manhood finally softened. Jack lifted himself from her body and rolled onto the bed, one arm bent and landing above his head while he slid the other behind her shoulders to pull her against his side. She expected he had fallen asleep, so she was startled when he turned and kissed the top of her head.

"I didn't mean for my proposal to sound so... daunting," he murmured.

She grinned. "I was curious about that," she admitted.

He tightened his hold on her. "You've been running the Castlewait earldom until your son is old enough?"

"I have. It's no different from running the household," she replied on a sigh. "Arrange goods and services where needed. Pay the invoices. Keep a ledger."

Chuckling softly, Jack asked, "Will you help me with mine?"

She angled her head in the small of his shoulder so she could better see him. "Of course."

He kissed her on the lips and then settled his head back into the pillow.

Once again, Persephone was sure he had gone to sleep when he said, "Am I mad to think I should give Kravets some sort of gift when I pay a call on him later today?"

Persephone lifted herself onto an elbow and stared down at him. "Whatever for?" she asked in alarm.

Jack shrugged in the pillow. "Well, if it wasn't for him, we wouldn't be here. Like this," he said.

Scoffing, she stared at him as if he were mad. "If it wasn't for him, we would have found one another during the ball tonight," she countered. "We would have danced—twice—and we would have ended up in the gardens, where I would have invited you to join me in my bed before the supper was served." She huffed. "We could have made love two or three times by now."

Jack regarded her for a long moment, a grin spreading over his face as he pondered her words. "All right. So no gift for the baron," he said. He lifted himself onto an elbow and kissed her. "Maybe I'll plant a facer on him instead."

A snort erupted from Persephone. "If you don't, I will."

He let out a guffaw. "I'm so glad I ended up in your coach. And I promise I'll make up for the lost time later," he murmured.

Giving him a prim grin, Persephone lowered herself back onto the bed. "I don't know about you, but I'm looking forward to life with you."

He chuckled as he collapsed back onto the bed and wrapped his arms around her. "I'll remember you said that when you learn the state of my earldom," he murmured.

A few seconds later, and he was sound asleep.

Persephone would have joined him in slumber, but his last remark had her worried. Concerned. Nervous and excited.

Challenge accepted, she thought as she dozed off.

CHAPTER ELEVEN

AN EARL AND HIS LADY PAY A CALL

EARLY AFTERNOON

Jack held a hand for Persephone as she stepped up and into the Castlewait coach. Despite the gloves they both wore, he felt a welcome warmth when their hands touched.

Parker closed the door behind him once he was seated next to her.

"What is it?" Persephone asked as she settled into the velvet squabs. Despite having spent only the past night with one another after so many years apart, she knew something was bothering the earl.

"Nothing. Everything." He sighed as he straightened in the squabs. "Thank you for insisting on coming with me," he added before he reached an arm behind her shoulders.

Since the hat she wore was pinned at a jaunty angle, she was able to rest her head on his shoulder. "I take it the light of day has you reconsidering what you were thinking to do in the middle of the night?"

Jack frowned. "What? If you mean that I'm not as inclined to throttle Kravets—"

"Not that," she interrupted with a bemused expression.

His mind cycled through everything he had said whilst they had discovered the most likely 'Lord JW' candidate. What they had talked about with Parker. What they had talked about in bed.

"Are you having second thoughts about marrying me?" Jack asked in alarm.

Persephone lifted her head from his shoulder and regarded him with surprise. "Aren't you?"

His eyes rounded. "No. I thought... well, that is, if you hadn't changed your mind, I thought that perhaps we might secure a marriage license after I'm finished with the baron."

Leaning away from Jack until her shoulder hit the coach wall, she tittered. "I haven't changed my mind," she said.

He grinned. "Good."

"Have you decided what you're going to say to the baron?"

Jack allowed a shrug. "Well, I thought I would start with admonishing him. Threaten him with bodily harm. And then, after he groveled enough, I would begrudgingly forgive him since his arrangements meant we were reunited, but in a less than optimal manner that would have happened if he hadn't been involved in his nefarious scheme in the first place." He paused as he regarded her with a questioning glance. "Does that sound reasonable?"

Persephone had a gloved hand covering her mouth as she laughed. "Poor Lord Kravets," she murmured. "His wife is never going to forgive him if *The Tattler* learns what he's done."

"Oh..." Jack breathed. "Is that possible?" he asked, his brows furrowed.

"I could mention the circumstances over afternoon tea in someone's parlor," she hinted. "One never knows who's a contributor to that rag."

He gave her a grin. "Remind me never to anger you."

"I will if I must," she teased.

After a few minutes of contemplation, Jack inhaled softly. "I'm still curious as to why Mr. Turnbridge was involved," he said absently.

"Well, you mentioned he was an inventor in need of investors," she reminded him. "Perhaps the baron saw an opportunity to make the poor man work for his money."

"Could be," Jack agreed. "Which means it's rather doubtful Turnbridge would ever speak to me again."

"He wouldn't dare, unless it's to apologize," she agreed.

The coach stuttered to a halt, and they both straightened in the squabs. When Parker opened the door, they stepped down and walked arm in arm to the front door of the Kravets townhouse.

When the butler opened the blue door, he gave a nod and stepped back.

Jack pulled a calling card from his waistcoat pocket. "Lord—"

"Lady Castlewait," Persephone interrupted, her gloved hand held out. A white pasteboard calling card was clutched between her thumb and forefinger. "Could you let Lord Kravets know I wish to speak with him, please?"

His gaze darting between Jack and Persephone, the butler took another step back. "I'll see if he's in residence, my lady."

When the servant had disappeared through a door further into the hall, Jack whispered, "What are you doing?"

"Securing us an audience with the baron," she replied. "Although you are a very handsome man, I think Lord Kravets is more inclined to agree to see me than you."

Jack's head fell back on his neck as he guffawed. "God, she's clever, too," he whispered.

When Abraham Kravets emerged from his study, his pleasant expression faltered when he realized Persephone wasn't alone. "Lady Castlewait," he said by way of greeting, taking her gloved hand to his lips. When he straightened, he furrowed a brow when his attention went to Jack. "Lord Wilmington. Haven't seen you much of late," he said, his nervousness apparent.

"That's because I've been on the Continent, Kravets. Working for King and country and all that rot," he replied, his manner testy. "I've only been back in London for a fortnight." He arched a brow to emphasize the last word.

Kravets rocked back on his heels as his expression held a hint of fear. "A fortnight, you say?"

"Aye. It seems in my absence, Lord White's whelp, John, has been doing dirty deeds in dark places and getting caught by whoever provides the *on-dit* to that damned *Tattler* rag," Jack stated. He turned his head in Persephone's direction and said, "Pardon the curse, my sweet."

"Oh, you're pardoned," she said brightly, her gaze darting beyond the baron to see that his baroness, Patience, had come down the stairs. She was no doubt curious as to the identity of her husband's callers.

Jack continued his scold. "And you had the audacity to think that your daughter would have anything to do with a man old enough to be her father during a *musicale* at Lady Worthington's house?"

Kravets' mouth opened and shut a few times, making him appear much like a fish.

"You do realize that marrying your daughter off to a duke's son would be a far superior choice than to an earl who is old enough to be her father?" Jack went on, well aware Lady Kravets was in the hall beyond her husband, wringing her hands in front of her chest as if she feared for his life.

"Well, I hadn't because... everyone said *you* were 'Lord JW'," Kravets finally blurted.

"Well, I'm not," Jack countered, allowing his anger to show. "Do you know how upsetting this has been for my betrothed?"

"Betrothed?" the baron repeated as he blinked.

"That would be me," Persephone said in a hoarse whisper. "Imagine my shock when my intended was drugged and forcibly removed from the Weatherstone ballroom last night. Why, if your henchmen hadn't mistaken my coach for yours, I would have had to hire a Bow Street Runner to find my 'Lord JW,' and then, when the banns were read for your daughter's wedding, I would have had to put voice to my objection," she claimed, her annoyance apparent. "Imagine the gossip. Imagine the scandal. There isn't a man in this town who would dare ask Honoria for her hand after that."

While Patience let out a quiet cry of fright, Kravets audibly gulped. "I... I didn't know," he said with a shake of his head. "I swear. What must I do to make this right?"

Not expecting an offer of contrition, Persephone glanced up at Jack. He was apparently as surprised as she was.

"You... you can pay for our marriage license," Jack suggested.

Kravets looked momentarily stunned. "I'll see to it. A special license, if you'd like," he said, his eyes still round.

"You won't tell anyone, will you?" Patience asked as she rushed forward to stand next to her husband. "I had no idea what he did," she claimed, punching Kravets in the arm to punctuate her claim. "But my daughter shouldn't have to suffer for his wrongs."

Persephone reached out a gloved hand to take one of the baroness'. "Oh, Lady Kravets, I assure you, Honoria's honor will not suffer further from us," she said. "But I do think Lord Wilmington has the right idea with his suggestion that your daughter be betrothed to Lord John as soon as possible. That is, if you don't mind having a rake for a son-in-law."

Lady Kravets' face screwed up in a grimace before she sighed. "Well, he is a duke's son," she countered, as if his aristocratic relationship was enough to overcome the young man's reputation.

"Well, there is that. And he is rather handsome," Persephone added. She ignored Jack's jerk at hearing the comment, but turned to glance up at him, giving him a wink that she hoped would calm him.

When his brows furrowed, she asked, "What is it?"

"Was Honoria at the Weatherstone ball last night?" Jack asked of the baron.

"Yes," Kravets replied after a pause, his gaze darting to his wife. Patience gave a quick nod.

"Was she with Lord John behind a hedgerow in the gardens before the midnight supper was served?"

The baroness gasped as her eyes rounded. The baron seemed to pale. "Why... what do you know?"

Jack inhaled to answer, but it was Persephone who said, "Since the Weatherstone footmen knew of it, the editor of *The Tattler* is sure to know of it. The next issue comes out tomorrow, so I would suggest that if it was Honoria behind the hedgerow with Lord John—"

"I know what to do," Kravets stated. He lifted his chin. "Let the archbishop's office know I'll pay for your license at the same time I'll be seeing to one for my daughter and Lord John," he stated. "Patience," he turned to his wife, "Have our daughter dressed and down here in a half-hour."

The baroness curtsied and hurried up the stairs.

Persephone and Jack exchanged quick glances. "Very well," Jack murmured. "I'll see you in the next session of Parliament." He nodded as Persephone curtsied, and the two turned to take their leave. Before they were over the threshold, though, Jack paused and said, "Oh, and do be sure to fund Mr. Turnbridge's latest venture."

Kravets frowned. "I don't know what you mean," he responded.

Scowling, Jack said, "Oh, I think you do. Good day." He tipped his hat as he offered his arm to Persephone.

CHAPTER TWELVE
NEWLYWEDS READ THE GOSSIP

THE FOLLOWING MORNING IN THE MASTER SUITE OF THE CASTLEWAIT TOWNHOUSE

As Persephone lounged in the pillows and drank her cup of chocolate, her new husband was paging through the latest issue of *The Tattler*.

"Do people really believe this rot?" Jack asked, scoffing.

His new wife arched a brow. "I would not expect you of all people to ask that," she countered with a grin.

He captured one of her hands in his and raised it to his lips. Kissing the back of it, he squeezed it tighter. "I suppose it merely depends on who you imagine these initials to be," he murmured, already engrossed in another article about the Weatherstone ball.

"Have you found a mention of our marriage in there?" she asked, leaning against his shoulder in an effort to read an advertisement for a New Bond Street modiste.

He gave a start. "They write about weddings in here?"

She tittered. "Of course, darling. Why wouldn't they?"

"I wouldn't expect them to be scandalous enough," he mused.

"Well, ours might appear that way given how quick it was," she countered.

He chuckled. "Who knew you could obtain a special license and be married all in the same day?" he asked rhetorically.

Persephone smirked but didn't respond.

"I do hope you don't regret it," Jack murmured, his gaze lifting from the news-sheet to regard her with worry.

"So far, I'm a very happy bride," she said before kissing him on the cheek. "But then I haven't seen the ledgers for your earldom yet."

He winced. "Let's wait until after our wedding trip before I subject you to the Wilmington earldom," he murmured.

"Oooh. A wedding trip?"

"Hmm. I was thinking of taking you to my country estate."

"Oooh, in what country?" she teased.

He chuckled. "If I tell you that, it won't be a surprise," he said. He suddenly straightened, aiming the news-sheet so she could better see it. "Well, well," he whispered.

"What is it?" She followed his gaze to an article and grinned.

It is with much excitement that we announce the betrothal of Lord John, second son of the Duke of White, to Miss Honoria Kravets, daughter of the Baron and Lady Kravets. We've reported on this couple's exploits in past issues—they've been caught canoodling at a number of Society entertainments—so it comes as no surprise that this Lord JW would finally be brought to task. He was said to be honored to offer for Honoria's hand and hopes for a quick wedding so that they might canoodle whenever they wish.

"Patience will be mortified to read this," Persephone murmured. "Honoria is her only daughter." She waited for Jack to reply, but he was still reading, his grin widening.

Curious, she continued where she had left off.

. . .

As for another, older Lord JW—who hasn't been seen in London for some time (rusticating in the country, perhaps? Or mayhap he's been serving King and country on the Continent?)—it seems a wedding is in his very near future. A special license was issued only yesterday, but we've yet to discover who he plans to wed. About time this earl be married. He's not getting any younger.

"You might not be getting any younger, but your new wife certainly doesn't mind," Persephone whispered as she slipped a hand beneath the covers. She covered his manhood with her palm, not surprised when it twitched and hardened beneath her hold.

"I rather like that you seem to enjoy canoodling," Jack remarked, setting aside the news-sheet. "Imagine the scandal when we're caught in an alcove canoodling during a *musicale*."

"Or making love in the gardens during a ball," she whispered.

"Or in our box at the theatre," he countered.

"We have a box?" she asked in surprise.

He chuckled as he gripped the edge of the bed linens and flipped them off the both of them. Persephone giggled as he lifted his body over hers. "We have a box," he affirmed. "But first..." He thrust himself into her and sighed with pleasure. "I'm going to abduct you..." He pulled out and kissed her throughly before thrusting into her again, groaning when her hips met his. "And take you to my house in the country..." He pulled out, but not all the way. "Where I intend to get a child on you..."

Persephone moved her hands to his buttocks, and she pulled on him hard enough so he was caught by surprise as her hips lifted to meet his. "If you haven't already," she finished for him, her face glowing in the morning light.

She adored how he kissed her then, the same way he had done so all those years ago when they had first fallen in love. When he finally ended the kiss, he stared down at her.

"What is it?" she asked in a whisper.

"Is that even possible?" he asked, breathless.

She blinked. "Well, of course." When he didn't resume what he'd been doing before their kiss, she added, "But please do continue. Just to be sure."

His face split into a grin and he kissed her again. "Gladly."

EPILOGUE

TWO YEARS LATER, AT THE WILMINGTON COUNTRY ESTATE, CHESHIRE

His attention on the ledger spread open on his oak desk, Jack entered numbers matching those on an invoice he held in his other hand. Although he hadn't excelled at simple arithmetic as a student at Eton, he had discovered he was far better at keeping the books for his earldom than he had expected.

He was also coming to the realization that he was interested in farming, at least to the point of learning about planting, crop rotation, farm implements, and irrigation techniques. Since he owned several books on the topic, he had read them all. As for actually doing the farming, he thought it best he leave that to his tenants. Since he was sure he couldn't keep a house plant alive, he doubted he could mange a field of wheat.

Having met all his tenant farmers in person, he had also discovered he rather liked knowing a bit about their lives. Accompanied by his countess, he met their wives and children as they delivered baskets of food and gifts for Christmas. He was invited to their weddings and was sure to be present for their baby's christenings.

The wedding trip he and Persephone had taken to the Wilmington country estate was still ongoing. If it had been up to him, it might never end, but he was prepared to do his duty as an earl and attend Parliament. Squire his countess about the capital to attend the usual Society entertainments.

When the new Earl of Castlewait finished university and took his seat in Parliament, Jack and Persephone would move out of the Castlewait townhouse and into another one Persephone had found only one street away.

Shortly after he had finally taken his bride, Jack had met with his earldom's man of business, J. Arthur Peabody. Expecting the worst, he had learned that all was well. There was income from his farmland, expenses were reasonable, and maintenance had been done on buildings when it was required.

"There is one way you might increase your income," the man of business had remarked upon their last meeting.

"Oh?" Jack had responded.

"There is an inventor, one Elias Turnbridge, who has come up with a rather unique application for a steam engine," Mr. Peabody said. "For a small investment of one-hundred pounds, you could see your money doubled in only a year's time."

Persephone, who had been sitting next to him during the meeting, hid her mouth with a gloved hand but said nothing as Jack merely stared at Mr. Peabody.

"Sir?" his man of business had prompted.

Jack cleared his throat. "I am not interested," he stated.

Apparently surprised by the response, Mr. Peabody had merely shrugged and moved on to other business.

It was after that meeting that Jack decided to see to the business of the earldom himself.

· · ·

The sound of babbling had him glancing up from the invoice to discover his countess standing on the threshold of his study. Dressed in an aquamarine day gown of muslin, she looked as gorgeous as the day they had married. A moment later, and he was thinking of how she had looked that morning, her sleep tousled hair hiding one eye as she kissed him awake.

He always enjoyed what happened a few minutes later, when he slowly made love to her, or when she climbed atop him and rode him to a quick and satisfying release. Mornings as a married man were far better than his days as a bachelor.

"Well, good morning, my sweet. Is it already time for tea?" he asked.

She grinned and seemed to stutter-step into the study. "Probably, but there's something far more important for you to see."

"Oh?" He stood from the desk and realized almost immediately what she meant.

His son and heir, John Junior, dressed in a long gown, was standing rather unsteadily in front of his mother. Chubby fingers were wrapped around Persephone's forefingers as the babe took a tentative step forward. A grin split his face at the sight of his father, and more babbling ensued as he took another unsteady step.

"Is that my son?" Jack asked in surprise.

"Well, I should hope so," Persephone replied with a scoff. "He's most certainly mine."

"Well, every time I see him, he's taller," Jack said in his defense. "And now he has teeth." He returned to his seat so his outstretched arms were more level with the year-old boy. "But he's not bald anymore."

Persephone tittered. "You see him every day," she scolded as the babe let go of his hold on her fingers and lurched forward. Three steps later, and he was in his father's arms, babbling incoherently. Tears of joy pricked the corners of her eyes. "Oh, my darlings," she whispered.

Jack lifted the boy into the air and stood. John giggled and spread his arms wide as his father swooped him through the air. "What shall I teach you first, young man?" Jack asked as he settled back into his chair. "Your mother tells me you're already a consummate flirt."

Enjoying the show her husband was putting on for her, Persephone crossed her arms and leaned against the door frame. "You might warn him about fast girls," she suggested. "Remind him to be wary lest he be abducted and forced into a marriage."

Jack glanced at her in alarm. "You make it sound as if that's what happened to me," he countered.

Her eyes darting sideways, Persephone decided it best she not to remind him that in a somewhat roundabout manner, that's exactly what had happened to him.

ABOUT THE AUTHOR

A self-described nerd and student of history, Linda Rae spent many years as a published technical writer specializing in 3D graphics work-stations, software and 3D animation (her movie credits include SHREK and SHREK 2). Getting lost in the rabbit holes of research has resulted in historical romances set in the Regency-era as well as Ancient Greece.

A fan of action-adventure movies, she can frequently be found at the local cinema. Although she no longer has any tropical fish, she follows the San Jose Sharks and makes her home in Cody, Wyoming.

For more information:
www.lindaraesande.com
Sign up for Linda Rae's newsletter:
Regency Romance with a Twist
Follow Linda Rae's blog:
Regency Romance with a Twist

f facebook.com/LindaRaeSandeAuthor
X x.com/lindaraesa
◎ instagram.com/lindaraesa
a amazon.com/Linda-Rae-Sande/e/B00BUYEIOS
BB bookbub.com/authors/linda-rae-sande

ALSO BY LINDA RAE SANDE

THE DAUGHTERS OF THE ARISTOCRACY

The Kiss of a Viscount

The Grace of a Duke

The Seduction of an Earl

THE SONS OF THE ARISTOCRACY

Tuesday Nights

The Widowed Countess

My Fair Groom

THE SISTERS OF THE ARISTOCRACY

The Tale of Two Barons

The Passion of a Marquess

The Desire of a Lady

THE BROTHERS OF THE ARISTOCRACY

The Love of a Rake

The Caress of a Commander

The Epiphany of an Explorer

The Choice of a Cavalier

The Bargain of a Baroness

The Jewel of an Earl's Heir

The Vixen of a Viscount

The Honor of an Heir

The Rose of a Sultan's Son

THE LADIES OF THE ARISTOCRACY

The Lady of a Grump

The Lady of a Sultan

The Wager of a Wallflower

BEYOND THE ARISTOCRACY

The Pleasure of a Pirate

The Making of a Mistress

The Bride of a Baronet

The Caton of a Captain

THE LYON'S DEN (DRAGONBLADE PUBLISHING)

The Courage of a Lyon

The Lady of a Lyon

Made in the USA
Monee, IL
03 November 2023

45710419R00441